CW00539723

HOMESTEAD

Other books by Kittredge McKee:

PRAIRIE

Copyright © 2023
All rights reserved
First Edition

NEWMAN SPRINGS PUBLISHING
320 Broad Street
Red Bank, NJ 07701

First originally published by Newman Springs Publishing 2023

ISBN 979-8-89061-393-6 (Paperback)
ISBN 979-8-89061-395-0 (Hardcover)
ISBN 979-8-89061-394-3 (Digital)

Printed in the United States of America

SUMMARY

A NEW LAND AND A NEW JOURNEY...

After the deaths of her family during their journey West in the summer of 1863, ten-year-old Frankie Harding continued on the trail, determined to find her family's homestead waiting for her somewhere deep within the Sand Hills of the Nebraska Territory. When she finally pulls her team and wagon to a stop on her family's homestead, she believed her journey was over.

Frankie learns, however, that settling into life on a homestead is its own unique journey—a new and different journey. She learns that living within the land of the Sand Hills is vastly different than the life she knew on the open prairie; this new land, along with its unique and profound beauty, has its own rules and ways, as well as its own mysteries and unknowns. To survive and thrive on her homestead, she must unravel the mysteries and find the answers to the unknowns. With winter approaching—and the harsh weather and storms that will come with it—she has a limited amount of time to learn the truths about her new homeland.

And, there are other challenges to this new journey that Frankie must face. Other homesteaders who have settled in the Sand Hills have their own rules and their own ways of doing things—and they have certain ideas about a ten-year-old girl living alone on a homestead. There are tribes of Indians roaming the Sand Hills with their own customs and their own ways of living—they, too, have their own ways of dealing with a young white girl living alone. And, Cavalry troops from distant forts have their orders to follow—they have their own regulations and dictates regarding ten-year-old girls living alone on the land.

Frankie Harding has been tested by life before and she fought whatever battles were necessary to hold her life and her future together. Now, once again, she has to face all the twists and turns, dangers and complications that arise in her life. But this time, she's forced to find different ways to deal with adversity—because now, disappearing into the prairie is no longer an option. Because she's already home. And now, there's nowhere else to go.

True to herself and to her future, Frankie's not willing to give up what she sees as rightfully hers. Once again, she's chosen her direction—and once again, she's determined to complete a new journey. A very different journey.

HOMESTEAD

KITTREDGE MCKEE

Newman Springs Publishing

To Tara and Erika:
They are always at my side,
They always watch my back,
And somehow, they always manage to be
two steps ahead of me at the same time.

And to Laura Welty Costy:
who somehow always manages to apply
an astonishing level of excellence
to everything she does.

Jacket/Cover Illustration
by the author Kittredge McKee

Historical Map (i) & back cover
inspired by a compilation of maps
from author's private collection

Jacket/Cover Design & Line-Maps
created in collaboration between
the author & Laura Welty Costy

CONTENTS

PART I

SOMETHING PERMANENT

Frankie Harding sat on the wagon-seat, staring at the meadow in front of her. There was a massive long barn and a chicken-house. There was a dugout-soddie in the side of the valley wall to her right and a windmill pond sitting off to her other side. And across the quiet meadow, there was a house—a perfectly square house sitting calm and sure. Comfortable. Tucked into a grove of trees and protected by the hillside behind it. The house looked sturdy and strong, standing firm on its foundation. Immovable. Peaceful.

She studied the house; it was a square house built of square-cut logs, standing straight and solid, looking like it had been built and placed with care, looking as if it was expecting someone. Looking like, just maybe, it had been waiting for its new person.

And to ten-year-old Frankie Harding, still sitting on the seat of the massive wagon—the massive blue-green Conestoga—on the track at the valley's entrance, it looked like home. She felt the driving-lines shift in her hands, and she glanced to the team, looking at the four black Shires that had pulled the Conestoga across the miles and miles of prairie grass. Sunny Jim was tossing his head, tugging on the lines and making the bit-rings rattle. She smiled at him, knowing he was just entertaining himself. *Or maybe, just annoyed that he's being required to stand still.*

She put her attention back on the house, studying it. She could tell that the house itself was square; the roof angled up from each of the four walls to meet at a single chimney standing at the peak. There was a wide veranda that looked as if it wrapped around the entire house. On the front wall of the house, tucked under the veranda roof, she could see two doors and several windows, all of them shuttered, except one at the right front corner.

A long, narrow addition with a peaked roof was attached to the southeast side of the house; it was built of gray river-stone with a peaked roof and its own porch across the front with a door and two windows. The room was as long as the house itself, but only half as wide. And to Frankie's eyes, it looked every bit as solid and strong as the house itself.

Staring at the log house with the long stone-room, she suddenly realized the truth. It was *her* home, on *her* homestead. It was what she had longed for. Yearned for. And it was here now, sitting right in front of her as the rays of the evening sun stretched across the meadow. The square house, with its long stone-room, basked in the last orange-golden light of the day, quiet and safe. Sitting silently in the summer-green grass of the valley's meadow. Looking as if it had been waiting for her—looking as if it had maybe been waiting for this very moment.

Frankie didn't know exactly what she had pictured in her mind; she wasn't sure exactly what she had expected, other than something permanent—since nothing had been permanent for the last several months. But never once had she pictured anything more beautiful and more perfect than this pretty little meadow with this perfectly square house and its sturdy stone-room. Whatever she might have imagined, this, she decided, went far beyond her imagination.

This secluded home—sitting quietly and patiently in its own little meadow—is what had been calling to her. It had been pulling at her heart; drawing her northward. *This* is what her heart had been crying for. *This* was home; *this* was where she belonged. This was her place on the prairie. Deep in the Sand Hills. *My own piece of the Nebraska Territory.*

Frankie Harding stayed on the seat of the big Conestoga, feeling the warm evening air of late July coming off the grasslands beyond the valley; the soft-moving air was sifting down the hillside and drifting across the little meadow. She could feel it lifting the wisps of hair that had worked loose from her braids, tickling at her forehead and cheeks. *My little meadow.*

Behind her, she could hear scratching sounds—scraping and scrambling sounds coming from the tailgate of the wagon. She grinned, knowing exactly what it was. It was the sound of collie-dog toenails—the sounds of a tawny little collie-dog scrambling into the wagon. And she knew what would happen in a moment.

Sure enough, a moment later, a white collie-muzzle poked through the pucker-hole of the canvas top. Then the little collie-dog wriggled through the opening and sat herself on the wagon-seat.

Frankie ruffled her ears. Apparently, Matilda had decided her job of moving the herd was done. Because now she sat looking over the meadow, looking as if she figured her person would be asking her opinion about the valley.

Off to the left of the track she had followed into the meadow, Frankie could see a windmill standing near a cluster of trees, cater-corner across the meadow from the house. The windmill pond was shaped a little like an hourglass, and it stretched along the base of the hillside. It sat quiet and still, its surface dappled with a mix of the last reflections of the evening sky and the leafy shadows of the trees that surrounded it. Frankie studied the trees for a moment. Ash, cotton-wood, and hackberry. A burr-oak. A handful of elderberry trees. And at least a half-dozen that she didn't recognize.

The windmill's wooden tower reached above the treetops, high enough above the branches for its sails to catch the prairie winds that coursed above the valley walls. The wooden wind-sails were stirring, turning slowly, responding to the evening breeze. The tower stood in place, steadfast, looking happy enough to be doing its job of keeping its pond full. Looking as if it knew a young girl and her blue-green wagon would be arriving with an assortment of livestock that would all need its cool water.

She eyed the structure for a moment longer, trying to remember exactly how a person would work the brake to stop the sails when necessary—there was a way to set the sails to spill the wind. She studied the frame of the tower, trying to spot the brake-lever. She pictured the other windmills she knew—the ones back in Indiana. This one looked similar, but studying the tower and the pipes and the sails, she could tell it was different. She figured she'd probably need some education about this particular windmill.

Her mind drifted back to the couple she'd met downriver a couple of hours earlier—the older couple with the seal-brown mare hitched to the light spring-wagon. Everett and Ida Dunbar. Frankie thought back to the conversation, to the friendly smiles and their delight at having new neighbors moving in to the 'Kinison place'. *They seemed nice enough. Everett Dunbar seemed to know plenty about this place. He might be able to teach me something about the windmill. Surely, he'll know about workings of the tower and the gears.*

Frankie watched as the loose herd—*her* animals, *her* livestock—wandered over to the edge of the windmill pond. Slowly, calmly. Taking their time, drinking deeply, and then raising their heads to look around. The water dribbled from their jaws as they stood studying their surroundings, looking at the trees, the pond, and the buildings. Looking at the grasses of the meadow. Looking around the meadow as if, maybe, they felt the same way she was feeling. Maybe feeling like they were in an odd kind of trance too. Feeling both a little mystified and a little content at the same time. Maybe they were aware, in some way, that they were done with their journey.

Somehow, they seemed to understand they were home; they seemed to know they could settle in and settle down. *Maybe they understand this is home. Maybe they know that tonight, after everything gets quiet, they'll be sleeping in their new homeland.*

Surely, she thought, they must be realizing—just like she was—that this was something permanent.

"We're home, Matilda. We're here. This is where we belong."

Frankie wasn't sure exactly why she hadn't already climbed down from the wagon. Thinking about it, she was surprised she hadn't jumped down and gone running across the grass—wildly excited over her arrival. But for the moment, it felt right to stay quiet and still;

it felt right to take her time. Maybe, she decided, it even felt a little safer to stay where she was there in the Conestoga's jockey-box.

And after thinking about it for a moment, she decided 'safer' was a strange word to be using, because actually, there *was* no danger here in this meadow. No danger at all. Nothing but peace and quiet. And a stillness.

Yet she stayed where she was, not quite willing to relinquish her vantage point on the high wagon-seat.

"There's plenty of time," she told herself, realizing she was talking out loud, speaking softly to herself, the same way she'd talk to a horse that needed calming. "Plenty of time."

The song of a meadowlark came to her; it was singing its evening song, its song to the twilight. A mourning dove called out softly; its mate cooed a soft response a moment later. Somewhere in one of the trees growing along the slopes of the hillsides, a woodpecker banged its beak into a trunk, rapping out some sort of message into the deepening gloom of the evening.

Matilda nudged her side and nuzzled her hand with her wet muzzle. Frankie ruffled her ears, spoke softly to her. Acknowledging her. Knowing the tawny little collie-dog was probably wondering why they weren't getting down from the wagon.

Frankie stood up in the jockey-box, scanning the meadow, her eyes pausing for a moment on the massive barn that stood across from the house, the massive barn that stretched along the valley wall beyond the pond. A large barn-lot stood at the front of the barn. Along the side of the barn, she could see a string of stall-doors, each with its own outside pen. Another lot was at the far end of the barn. Beyond that, she could see two smaller buildings.

And beyond those buildings, out where the meadow narrowed, a plank fence stretched between the hillsides of the valley. On the far side of the fence, was another valley with its own meadow that looked to be bigger than the home meadow where she had pulled the Conestoga to a stop. The second meadow had more fences dividing it into four pastures. And there in the midst of the fences, down a center track, another windmill tower stood sturdy and tall.

Not far from the Conestoga, off to her right, was the chicken-house with a wire-fenced chickenyard. Frankie studied it for a moment before letting her eyes move to the hillside behind it. At the base of the hill were two wood-framed doorways—twin doorways, standing some twenty yards apart and each tucked under its own A-framed roof. The doorways cloaked with bricks of sod, making them look as if they had been carved right into the slope. *Sod-dugouts behind the doorways? Maybe. Probably.*

She turned her attention to a log building that stood between the chickencoop and the main house—a building that looked a lot like the main house. It was just as square and straight, just as strong and solid, but smaller. It, too, had a four-sided roof with a chimney poking up in the middle of the peak. A narrow porch stretched across the front wall.

And just beyond that building, the big square house stood solid and silent in front of a tree-covered valley wall, the house still looking as if it knew she'd be arriving this evening in the big blue-green Conestoga with a four-hitch of black Shires. Looking as if it had been keeping an eye out for a young girl who would drive her wagon down the entrance track into the meadow with a Jersey cow and calf, four brindle oxen, a herd of shiny-hided horses, and three skinny mules.

Looking across the meadow from the house, Frankie studied the long barn once again; it was settled in front of its own tree-filled hillside, looking as if it had been waiting, too—maybe, waiting to hear the sound of animals that belonged on a homestead. Maybe, it had been waiting for the sounds of cows lowing in the evening; waiting for the sound of streams of milk hissing against the bottom of a milk-pail. Maybe, just maybe, the barn wanted to hear the sounds of horses snorting and nickering inside its walls once again.

To Frankie, it seemed as if the whole valley—with its pretty little meadow and its quiet, tree-shadowed pond and the silent, sturdy buildings—had been waiting patiently. It all looked safe. Everything felt protected. It all seemed sheltered and secure. And it was all sitting pretty. Her Uncle James and Aunt Sarah, she decided, had chosen well.

Her aunt and uncle and four cousins—her only family after her father and mother died—had made plans to leave Indiana and move out here. Out to the West. Back when her father was alive, the plan had been to settle in the southwest part of the Nebraska Territory, far to the west and south of this place. But when a new opportunity presented itself, months after her father had died, the decision and the direction had changed.

This place, far to the north of the original homestead, was deep in the region of the Nebraska Territory known as the Sand Hills. Her family had heard about this homestead from a woman who had been widowed out in the Nebraska Territory and had returned to her parents' home in Indiana. Frankie's Uncle James and Aunt Sarah had changed their plans; they decided to come here to this homestead. Because as her Aunt Sarah had said, 'it felt right in their hearts'.

Her Uncle James said it felt right in his gut. Frankie's cousins, Isaiah and Thomas, wanted *this* place to be the family home too. Her oldest cousin Samuel, nearly a man himself and someone who usually stayed deep in his own thoughts, had spoken his mind—he said he had strong feelings about this place in the Sand Hills. Like his father, he believed that a future could be made on this homestead. And Frankie's younger cousin, Little Charles, didn't care where they were going, because much like Frankie, he just wanted to go on an adventure.

The widowed-woman's husband, Daniel Kinison, had a dream for his family; and he had spent five years building the homestead. He had been fatally injured out here on the homestead, and when he died, the dream died with him. Because shortly after his death, his widow left everything behind; she gathered her children and returned to Indiana to her parent's home. She was done with the homestead, done with everything about it. She had abandoned her husband's dream.

Once back in Indiana, Lillian Kinison had spoken to James and Sarah Harding about the homestead. And once again, the homestead in the Sand Hills had become someone's dream—this time, it became a dream for James and Sarah Harding and their four sons. And for their niece, Frankie Harding. Because she had become part of their family, and they had become hers.

And the dream of settling into a new home and a new life had settled deep into her heart and mind—just as it had for the rest of her family. The dream had taken shape; the plans had formed; the papers and deeds had been signed. Everything had been finalized.

She had traveled out West with her aunt and uncle and four cousins in two wagons from Indiana. They crossed the Mississippi River and, then, the Missouri River. They traveled along the Independence Road that followed the banks of the Little Blue River. The massive blue-green Conestoga pulled by the four black Shires and the smaller Murphy-wagon pulled by the four brindle oxen, had carried the family's belongings and supplies. They had traveled with the dark-chestnut Morgan mare, Fanny, and the Jersey milk cow, Blossom.

The hearts of everyone in the Harding family had been set on the homestead that waited for them far to the north of the great Platte River—this very homestead sitting deep in the midst of the grass-covered hills of the Nebraska Territory. The dream of a new life and a new community and a new future had bonded the Harding family together with a fresh hope and excitement. A new home; a new direction; a new world.

But then, the fever that haunted the trail along the Little Blue River—the same fever that took the lives of thousands of emigrants traveling in the thousands of wagon parties moving westward—struck her family. Her uncle and aunt and cousins died from fever beside the Little Blue River Road; they died while traveling to this homestead in the Sand Hills of the Nebraska Territory.

Frankie had been left behind, orphaned a second time. And with no home in Indiana to return to and with no other family, she chose to continue on the path—to continue with the dream. She decided that the dream was her inheritance; the direction and the path and the waiting homestead had become hers. It had been her family's future, so she had adopted it, just like they had adopted her. She had hitched the four Shires to the big blue-green Conestoga, and she had continued the family's journey—because she had become the family—she had become the whole family.

Nothing had stopped her from coming home. Some of the people in the wagon party tried; the Army at Fort Kearny down on the Platte River had tried. No one had been able to sway her mind, and no one had been able to beat it out of her. But some had tried.

It had been her family's dream, and the dream had grown bigger as she traveled home. She had begun her journey with the four black Shires; she had reclaimed the four oxen, the Morgan mare and the milk cow, along with her newly-dropped calf. Two dogs—the half-grown collie-dog and the brindle greyhound-wolfhound mix—had joined her on her journey. Three mares, four geldings, a fine-looking stallion, and three sorry-looking mules had joined her too. They had all become her new family, and they had all walked toward a new future right alongside her. *So we're all here now. This is the dream. This meadow.*

As the sky-color changed into the soft spreading pinks and oranges of twilight, Frankie stood in the high jockey-box of the blue-green Conestoga watching her animals watering-up; she watched as they turned and began walking back to the center of the meadow, wading through the tall summer-green grasses of the pretty front-meadow of their new home.

And right now, right here on what was her own homeland, Frankie realized she still didn't want to get down from the wagon-seat. She felt fear rising inside her—a sudden fear that if she took her eyes off what was in front of her, for even a moment, it would all disappear.

She sat down on the wagon-seat, thinking about how many miles she had traveled riding on the seat of the Conestoga, holding the reins to her Shires and sending them forward, sending them toward their new home. Trusting the journey. And now that the journey was done, suddenly, she was afraid. She sat on the wagon-seat in the deepening twilight, afraid to breathe. Afraid to move. She waited. She listened.

The sounds of the twilight breeze in the grasses whispered to her. Reassuring her, reminding her that she was home. Speaking gently, telling her that she belonged here, that she was safe here. The leaves in the treetops murmured. The birds of the prairie sang softly to the coming night. The turtledoves called sweet and low to the colors of the coming twilight.

Benjamin and Bo, Buck and Billy—the four brindle oxen—all lowered themselves to the meadow floor, almost at the same time. All making the same soft, chest-to-the-ground thudding sounds. They lowered their heavy bodies slowly to the prairie soil, giving their contented oxen-grunts and ox-groans that said they were done moving for the day.

Fanny, the Morgan mare, and the three bay mares—Belle and Easy and Silk—left the windmill-pond and moved out into the sweet-scented grass, lowering their heads as they walked, starting the chomp-and-tear rhythm of their grazing. The big chestnut geldings, Solomon and Samson, were already in the middle of the meadow, their noses down in the grass. Rock and Boone, the other geldings, had already worked their way toward the far end of the meadow, down near the plank fence that stretched between the two slopes of the valley, standing in companionable silence, looking as if they were more interested in dozing than grazing.

The three mules—Septimus, Aloysius, and Artemis—snorted and snuffled and rolled; they stood up again and gave themselves a good shake, sending their long ears flopping. From across the meadow, they looked at her, eyeing her on the wagon-seat for a minute or two, studying her calmly with that wise and knowing look that all mules could direct at humans.

Still standing in harness, High Boy tossed his head and pinned his ears back against his head to show his annoyance; he knew his work was done for the day. He was showing his bossy streak, displaying his irritation, as he always did, when things weren't going his way. Frankie grinned. High Boy was letting her know it was time for the harnesses to come off. And as the other three Shires gave airy-soft snorts, she laughed—Little Bub, Sunny Jim, and Black Mack were thinking similar thoughts.

Still tied to the wagon-seat where he had traveled through the day, Trumpeter stomped on the meadow floor—the blood-bay stallion pawed the ground then, echoing the sentiment of the four

Shires. Frankie's grin grew bigger. Seemed like all her animals had made plans for the evening.

Laughing Girl, the long and lean wolfhound-greyhound mix, came toward the wagon in her pretty-stepping, long-reaching trot; she was grinning her sly-eyed grin, apparently content with her evening patrol of this valley that was nestled down into the prairie land.

Frankie took a long, slow breath. The air was starting to cool as the twilight faded to dusk. Night was settling in. She climbed down from the jockey-box, putting her foot on her land. Her homeland. *My first night on my homestead.*

Once on the ground and standing on her own land, Frankie realized she was feeling an urgency, a sudden pressure to hurry and see everything before darkness settled in. And that was a feeling she didn't want. Because she didn't really want to run around, trying to see everything in a hurry; she didn't want to scurry around in half-light, or by lantern-light, trying to see everything and learn everything about her homestead. Because she didn't want that to be her first memory of her home.

Right now, she decided, she wanted to hold onto the memory of driving her team across the little ford on the North Loup River and up the track leading to the valley's entrance. She had liked the way it felt to follow the track up and around and down—down below the level of the prairie—and right into the meadow. She already had the first memory of her homestead. She would always remember her first sight of the quiet little meadow, her first sight of the meadow grasses and the trees and the hillsides. Her first sight of the sturdy buildings and the quiet windmill pool. And she didn't want to let go of those fresh and new memories. She didn't want them pushed out of her mind and heart.

It seemed to Frankie that she was already pretty full-up with new things and new memories; she decided she already had plenty to sleep on. The rest of the new things and the new discoveries could wait until daylight. *Right now, I'll do the normal things. The things*

I've been doing every evening. Unhitching, unharnessing. Watering the stock. Milking the cow.

She decided to take her time on her first evening at her new home. She wanted to settle down slowly because, after all, there was no reason to rush or hurry now. There was plenty of time because no one was hunting for her right now. No one was following her; no one could find her. So she had all the time she wanted. Because she was home.

Tonight, she decided, she would sleep in the Conestoga. And tomorrow, after the morning sun woke her, she would have a day of adventure and exploring, of looking and learning. Tomorrow, she would walk through this dream that her family had dreamed.

Frankie started the process of settling in for the night, the same process that had been part of her life every evening on the trail. She unhitched and unharnessed the four Shires at the tailgate. Same as always. She released them then, letting them go to water-up and then graze in the meadow. *In my meadow.*

She untied Trumpeter and led him to the windmill pond, letting him drink long and slow; she waited while he lifted his head to look around, waited while he lowered his head to drink again. He lifted his head and looked around the meadow again, dripping his sloppy-drops of water on her head and shoulder. Frankie grinned, realizing that it was *her* water that was dripping on her. Trumpeter stood beside her, towering over her, turning his head to the side and back again, surveying his domain. *My domain.*

When the blood-bay stallion finished watering-up, Frankie walked him back to the big Conestoga. Smiling at the feeling of *her* ground beneath her feet as she picketed him close to the wagon. *I'm on my soil. And my grass.*

She haltered Blossom and brought her to the wagon. Lifted the milking stool and the pail from their hooks on the side of the Conestoga and started milking, sending the streams of rich Jersey milk hissing against the sides of the pail. She leaned forward, pressing her forehead against the soft fawn-colored cowhide, listening to the familiar belly-rumbles and gurgles deep inside the milk cow. Just the same as she had done every night on the trail. The buff-colored heifer, Primrose, snuffled around her shoulders, nuzzling her. Wet-muzzling her. Leaving baby-cow slobber on her. Frankie smiled her crooked little smile. Because, she realized, it was actually *her* baby-cow slobber.

By the time Frankie finished with Blossom and released her for the night, the moon was showing above the eastern slope of the valley, just high enough to send its pale light slanting across the meadow. She watched as the early planets and stars were revealing themselves, twinkling. Winking at her as if they knew something wonderful. The North Star stared down, eyeing her—calm and serious—as if it knew something that she didn't. As if it knew about life on this homestead and the life in this pretty meadow within this quiet valley.

Once her work was done and her animals and their needs were seen to, Frankie settled herself on the tailgate, sitting cross-legged and breathing in the cooling air of the prairie, night air that was thick with the scent of sweet grasses and warm soils. She drank a cup of warm Jersey milk and ate some of the cold rabbit meat with a few pieces of bacon and cornbread. She tossed pieces of cold rabbit and bacon to Laughing Girl and Matilda and then opened a can of peaches. She ate the peaches slowly, watching as her animals settled down into the moon-bathed meadow grass. Calm, relaxed. Homing themselves to the meadow.

She finished her supper and stayed where she was for a while longer. Calm and relaxed. Homing herself to her meadow.

Once the full of the night settled down around her, Frankie moved back into the Conestoga, slipping in among the boxes and crates and barrels. Realizing it was the last time she'd do so. Because tonight would be the last night she would live in the Conestoga—it would no longer be her only home.

Because tonight was the end of her journey. Tomorrow, there would be a change; tomorrow, at least some of what was in this big wagon would be in the big square house across the meadow. And tomorrow night, she would sleep in that house. In her new home.

Frankie listened as a mockingbird started up his repertoire of stolen songs while she untied the laces of the canvas top and raised the edges to let the night air flow through. She pulled back the quilt—the quilt that had covered her Lieutenant while he lay on the mattresses, healing from the snake-bite. It was the crazy quilt, with its silk and satin and velvet patches, and all its crazy stitching and embroidery, her Aunt Sarah had made.

She could picture her Aunt Sarah sitting in the house back in Indiana, working in the evenings, always sewing on her quilts. And she could see Isabelle in the little white cottage back at Fort Kearny, sitting on the settee doing the hand-work on a newly made dress. *Her* Aunt Sarah. *Her* Lieutenant. *Her* Isabelle. Gone from her life. The tears rose in her eyes, welling-up, and then spilling down her cheeks.

Frankie curled up on the narrow bed, pulled the crazy quilt to her shoulders and let the tears trail down her cheeks. The pillow dampened with the tears. Tears of sadness. Tears of relief and peace and safety. And finally—after the tears stopped and her heartbeat slowed—she felt herself drifting into sleep.

As her tears slowed and finally stopped, the mockingbird was still working his way through his night-songs; somewhere beyond the meadow, a killdeer sent out its string of sharp staccato-notes. From under the wagon box came sounds of the two dogs making their night-beds in the grass—turning and scratching, and then turning some more. Settling down. And then giving their soft dog-sighs.

Above the meadow, high in the Sand Hills sky, the waxing moon sent its light slanting across the land, bathing the meadow in soft silver-blue light. And Frankie realized she had somehow made a shift in her life. Somehow, she was in her own future.

It was a rooster's crow that woke Frankie in the morning. She stayed where she was under the crazy quilt, lying still, staring at the canvas cover of the Conestoga. Trying to gather her thoughts. Trying to understand why she was hearing a rooster. Because she hadn't heard a rooster since before she and her family had crossed the Missouri on the journey to the Nebraska Territory.

There had been no roosters in the wagon party, and there hadn't been any roosters at Fort Kearny either, because all the milk and eggs had come from Fort Farm Island, more than a mile from the fort. The only things crowing in the mornings at the fort were the bugles.

But the crowing that had awakened her this morning was definitely *not* a bugle. Frankie knew that much for sure. It was *definitely* a rooster. And to her thinking, it seemed a little strange she'd be hearing a rooster crowing way out here at the end of her Cheyenne Trail. She stayed where she was. Thinking. Knowing it couldn't be some neighbor's rooster, because Everett and Ida Dunbar were her closest neighbors, and they were almost ten miles away.

And then she remembered Everett Dunbar talking about seeing some of the chickens Lillian Kinison had left behind. He'd seen some of the chickens that had gone wild wandering around in the trees when he had been here in June, 'checking on the place'. He had told her 'they were far too wild to catch'.

Frankie listened, hearing the crowing once again in the cool morning air. And then, another rooster's call sounded—it was a croaking call, rather than a true crow. A third rooster sounded off with another croaky-call, and then another. One adult rooster, she thought, and at least, two young ones. *Maybe three.*

The croaking-calls told her they were immature birds that hadn't found their true voices yet. And that told her something else; it told her that there *had* to be a hen or two around. At least. Because the young roosters would have to be from a fairly recent hatching. From the sound of things, they probably weren't much more than three or four months old.

While she busied herself pulling on her shirt and trousers, and then her boots, Frankie looked out from under the edges of the wagon-canvas, looking across the meadow as the daylight was coming on. She grinned, confident that somewhere out there, pecking around in the brush and leaves under the trees, there were three or four roosters. And probably, a hen or two. *Hopefully more.*

She felt her grin growing, knowing that no matter how 'wild' the chickens were, she could have them penned in the coop by midnight. And within a couple of days, she would be eating her own chicken eggs for breakfast. *Her* chickens and *her* eggs. Because she knew of a few tricks to handle half-wild chickens. *Even if the Dunbars don't.*

Frankie squeezed out through the front pucker-hole of the wagon-canvas and climbed up onto the wagon-seat. She surveyed her meadow and the buildings scattered around it. Neat, clean, comfortable. Secluded, hidden, safe. Pretty. Frankie felt her crooked little grin becoming a wide, relaxed smile. *My home. My homestead.*

Out there in front of her was her meadow. Out there in front of her were her livestock. Her oxen and her milk cow and calf; her horses and her mules. They were all there in her home meadow. Some were lying in the meadow grass, slumbering and snoring and snoozing in little groups. Others, like the three underweight mules, were already awake and eating, going for weight-gain just as they should be. The mares were still sleeping; High Boy and Little Bub were dozing nearby. Sunny Jim and Black Mack were standing beside the windmill pond, scratching each other's necks and shoulders with their teeth.

Matilda was standing on the ground beside the wagon-tongue, looking up at the wagon-seat, her ears cocked and her head tilted. Watching her person as though she was wondering what was on the to-do list. From the brush and trees on the slope beyond the house came the full crow again, followed by the jumbled croaky-crows of a couple of younger roosters.

Up on the western hillside, Laughing Girl was moving through the trees, trotting along the slope, already busy with her self-appointed task of patrolling the boundaries of the little valley. Frankie whistled her in, and when the big hound came bounding across the meadow, grinning her wolfhound-greyhound grin with her tongue lolling out from the side of her mouth, Frankie tossed a few pieces of jerky to both her and Matilda.

"Home is where the food is, Girls." She watched the two dogs snatch the pieces of jerky out of the air. "Home is where you eat."

Frankie watched them chomping on the beef and gulping it down. She grinned at them when they sat their bottoms down, watching her, expecting more meat to fly through the sky. She tossed a few more pieces of the jerky, wanting to get them 'homed'. The faster they realized this meadow and these buildings were home, the better. She decided to 'home' herself, too, and started gnawing on her own piece of jerky.

She smiled at the thought of homing herself, smiling as she remembered the way the stars had been looking down at her last night, winking. As if they were happy she had made it to the meadow. She climbed off the seat, jumped down from the wheel, and looked toward the wood-framed dugouts over against the hillside.

The adventure, Frankie decided, would start there. She'd begin on the eastern edge of the meadow with the first dugout, then move to the chicken-house, then on to the second dugout.

After that, she'd head to the small square building and find out exactly what it was. Then she'd explore the main house and the long stone-room. She'd cross the meadow after she was done, and go through the barn and the buildings beyond it.

Frankie looked across the meadow. Looking once again to the big house, she felt a shiver run up her spine. The main house; the perfectly square house. The smaller building; perfectly square. An outhouse stood behind them, close to the base of the hillside. *My buildings. My outhouse.*

"In a little while, Matilda, we might just sit and have our first meal in the kitchen of that perfectly square house." She looked down at the little collie-dog standing beside her, watching her, waiting for their morning work to begin. "I'll bet there's a stove we can fire up and get a breakfast going. And maybe, we'll brew up a pot of coffee."

She laughed as Matilda tilted her head, listening. The little collie-dog wasn't particularly interested in hearing about brewing coffee; she was listening for certain words that would explain exactly what work she would be doing. Because Matilda's heart was always happiest when she had work to do.

Frankie took a deep breath, readying herself. There was a lot going on here this morning; a lot to explore and a lot to understand. A lot of treasures here—household furniture and items, farming tools and equipment. The Kinison woman had said she had left everything.

'You won't need to take much,' she had said. 'All the furnishings and such are still there. It all goes with the sale of the place, and you're welcome to all of it. I don't want anything to do with it.'

Looking toward the square house again, Frankie could see lace curtains in the un-shuttered window at the front corner of the house. Lillian Kinison must have been telling the truth; she must have left a lot behind if she hadn't even bothered to pack up the curtains.

Frankie headed toward the eastern hillside, toward the first structure in the little valley—the wood-framed entrance of the nearest dugout. Looking at it as she approached, it looked a bit like the dugout-soddy she had seen back in the hidden valley, way back on the Cheyenne Trail. This one, though, was standing firm; nothing about it looked ready to cave in. This one had a sturdy, well-built wood-frame for an entrance with sod-bricks built up and packed tight against the outside walls of the entryway.

When she pushed the door to the dugout open, she learned a few things right away. First, the wood door was solid and strong. Second, the dugout went deeper into the hillside than she had expected. And third, the dugout wasn't a simple dirt cave that had been carved into the dirt of the hillside—the entire interior was actually wood-framed.

Looking at it, Frankie decided the man named Daniel Kinison must have dug the whole space out of the hillside and built a little wooden house within the space. Then, he had filled in around it, and above it, with dirt and blocks of sod. The peaked wooden roof and walls of the entry still showed from the outside, but the rest of the dugout disappeared into the hillside.

The inside walls were vertical board-and-batten, built straight and clean. A bunk was built into one wall; a table sat against another wall with two wooden boxes for seats. A potbellied stove stood against the back wall of the snug little room, with the stovepipe going straight up through the ceiling, rising up through the sod and the hillside. The wooden structure had been built simple and solid; designed as it was—insulated with the surrounding dirt and sod—it would stay warm in the cold months and cool during the hottest days.

Frankie studied the room and the structure itself. Intrigued and pleased. This, she decided, must have been the first thing Daniel Kinison had built. And probably, he had lived in it while he was building the rest of the homestead. As she looked around her, she decided that *this alone*—this neat and sturdy little sod-dugout—would have been a nice enough place for her to live.

Clearly, Daniel Kinison had known how to build something that would last. Frankie could almost hear her Uncle James's voice; he would have talked about the skills of the man who built it. He would have been pleased with this little dwelling place; he would have remarked on how well it was built. And Frankie could hear him saying that everything that could be seen here in this structure would bode well for the rest of the homestead.

She stepped outside and closed the heavy door behind her. She smiled, deciding it was a perfect little dwelling place, so she christened it as such. It was only the first structure in her meadow she had seen, but she had learned a lot, not just about the dugout, but about Daniel Kinison himself. She stepped back and gazed at the entrance, at the hillside. *My hillside. My Dwelling Place.*

The next structure on her list was the chicken-house and its coop. It was standing empty not more than a dozen yards out from the hillside, placed about halfway between the Dwelling Place and the second dugout.

The chicken-house might have a different purpose than the Dwelling Place, but to Frankie's eyes, they had a lot in common; everything about it was neat and solid—both the henhouse and its coop were built well and built to last. And at the moment, standing out in the grassy meadow all by itself, it looked like it was lonely for its chickens. The henyard gate had been fastened open, and from the look of things, instead of giving the chickens to her neighbors when she left in the middle of winter, Lillian Kinison had simply released them to fend for themselves. To Frankie, it seemed an odd choice to make and an odd way to leave things. But up to this point, she hadn't really understood any of the choices Lillian Kinison had made.

Given the way Daniel Kinison had built it, it must have been in his mind to keep the chickens well protected. The henhouse itself looked to be pretty snug; the posts of the henyard were solid. Heavy timbers had been trenched deep into the ground around the coop's edges. The chicken-wire was fastened firm and tight to the posts and timbers, stretched tightly around the sides and across the top of the yard. It would be difficult for predators to dig underneath; no hawks or owls would be poaching chickens from above.

As pleased as she was with what she saw from the outside, she was every bit as pleased when she explored inside. The roosts were solid and the bars were wide; the nest-boxes were built well, off the ground and fastened to the wall. And there was a window that allowed light and fresh air to fill the space. A separate door led into small room with a row of hog's-head barrels along its back wall.

A feed-room. Frankie smiled at the thought. Daniel Kinison had seen fit to build a separate storage-room for the feed; it was a smart way to raise chickens, clean and easy. The barrels held a variety of grains, and at first, it surprised her to see that most of the barrels were completely full—the winter's supply of feed for the hens had barely been touched. Thinking about it though, it made sense. Because Daniel Kinison had died in mid-January and his wife had left soon after. No one had touched the feed since then.

To Frankie's mind, it was a nice discovery because, depending on how many chickens were actually wandering around in the brush and trees, there might be enough feed left for the coming winter. It was a nice little treasure, Frankie thought, both for herself *and* for the chickens.

Stepping out of the feed-room and into the morning sunshine, Frankie glanced toward the hillside beyond the house. The spurts of crowing had come from that direction earlier, and now, along with the crowing, she could hear different chicken-sounds. Chicken chortles and chicken clucks, and an occasional outburst of squawking—flustered rants, excited bluster, and a few angry tirades. Frankie knew those sounds and what they meant. *Hens! Those are hens squawking! Perhaps tonight then. Tonight the chickens will come home to roost.*

Every bit as happy with the henhouse as she was with the Dwelling Place, Frankie headed to the next building on her tour—the second dugout—sitting in its own little nook along the hillside.

From the outside, it looked to be a twin to the first, with the same wood-frame entrance packed with dirt and blocks of sod. But as she swung the door open, Frankie discovered this dugout was very different than the other one. A long, low stairway led downward into a deeply-situated dugout. Ten steps down, Frankie found herself in a room much larger than the Dwelling Place, a room that went much further into the hill—a good thirty feet, by Frankie's figuring, and looking to be at least half as wide.

The inside walls had the same vertical board-and-batten as the other dugout and the chicken-house, but here, all the walls of the room were lined with wooden shelves and bins. Down the middle of the room were more bins, lined up and stacked as neatly as she had seen in Fort Kearny's commissary. Tucked in among them and beside them was an assortment of hog's-head barrels, the lids all tight and secure. A long worktable stood in front of the row of bins and barrels.

With light from the morning sun filtering down the stairs and into the room, Frankie could see exactly what the room was designed to be—it was a root-cellar, built to be a safe and protected storage space for garden produce. For squashes and pumpkins, beets and carrots. Onions and potatoes. Any and all kinds of crops.

While she waited for her eyes to adjust to the low light, she sniffed the air. Her Aunt Sarah used to say the 'scent of the air is the true test of a good cellar'. This air smelled clean, and Frankie figured her Aunt Sarah would approve. And true to a good cellar, the room itself was cool and dry; winter or summer, it would always remain so. It would never be hot, and it would never freeze. And *that* was one of the wonderful things about root-cellars.

Frankie grinned; this room was another treasure. It was as valuable as any building on the homestead. On a homestead, a root-cellar could make the difference between eating well year-around, or scraping-by through the winter months, perhaps even starving.

Frankie made her way along the rows of bins, knowing she was probably grinning like a fool. She was so busy looking into the bins and barrels that twice she tripped over Matilda, and once she bumped into Laughing Girl. The dogs were both busy snuffling along the floor, carrying out explorations of their own.

She knew her grin was growing wider as she eyed the stored produce, because even now, well into the summer, there was still a lot of food from the previous winter. The bins along the walls held potatoes and yams, turnips, beets, and onions. Parsnips and carrots. Winter squash. A good number of the bins held pumpkins. One hog's head barrel held walnuts; another was full of hazelnuts. Another was full of oats, rolled and ready for cooking.

There was a crate of apples that were past saving, and there was some spoilage in a few other bins. But all told, most of the food was still fine from the winter storage, and *that* spoke of a good cellar. Long-term storage was the glory of a good root-cellar.

Frankie headed up the stairs, back into the sunshine, still smiling at this wonderful find. She closed the heavy root-cellar door and looked to the next building on her route of discovery—the smaller of the two square buildings. And for Frankie, that building was a bit of a mystery, because there was no obvious purpose for it. Not one that she could figure out. Not yet, anyway. She took a breath and walked toward it, wading through the meadow's grass. She headed around the side of the building to the front porch with Laughing Girl and Matilda trotting beside her.

The small square building—just like the big house, the outhouse and the barn—was built from heavy, square-cut logs. Solid and strong. And even though it stood fairly close to the end of the long stone-room on the main house, it still had a quality to it that set it apart; it stood there by itself, looking sturdy and solid, a match for the big house in both shape and roofline. It looked to be only about half the size of the main house, but every bit as solid. And like the main house, its chimney went right up through the center of a roof that sloped up from all four sides.

She was surprised when she stepped onto the front porch and through the door, because four feet inside, straight in front of her, a single wall split the building into two rooms, one to each side. The fireplace sat in the middle of the wall, opening into both rooms. Each room had five beds. Two sets of bunks, upper and lower, were along the side wall with a window between them; a low bunk was along the back wall, below its own window.

It reminded Frankie a little of the soldiers' barracks at Fort Kearny—it wasn't nearly as big and it didn't have rows and rows of bunks—but it was built for the same purpose. Lillian Kinison had spoken about her husband's plans to raise beef for the Army, a plan that meant a lot of cattle and a lot of work. Which would require a number of men. Looking around her, Frankie suddenly understood the reason for this building—it had been built for the future hired-help. Kinison had planned well.

With solid walls of square-cut logs and the fireplace in the middle, there was no doubt it would be warm in the winter; with the windows and door providing a cross-breeze, it would have good ventilation in the summer.

Looking at the windows, Frankie realized they were still shuttered tight for the winter; she grinned and decided it was time to change things up. She made her way around the outside of the building, standing on the rock ledge of the foundation, reaching to release the hooks on the shutters.

At one point, she caught herself wondering if anyone would mind. Then, she laughed at the thought. No one would mind. Because no one was here. No one but her. Because this was, after all, *her* building. *Her* barracks.

Frankie swung the shutters wide and fastened them open, letting the sunlight pour into the barracks. Prairie sunlight. Sand Hills sunlight. When she was done and stepped to the front porch, she looked at the sunlight illuminating the interior and decided that the building seemed to be waking up. Coming alive. Because suddenly, there was a return to life in the meadow. In her meadow. On her homestead.

She had her own little Dwelling Place. And a chicken-house. She had her own root-cellar. And now, she christened the building before her. The Barracks. *My own Barracks.* She grinned and went back inside, unhooked the windows and opened them wide on their hinges, letting the morning air flood inside. Prairie air. Clean and fresh.

Satisfied with her exploration of the Barracks, Frankie stepped out onto the narrow porch and studied the next building to explore. The one that excited her the most. The one that had been waiting for her.

Frankie eyed the big square-house with its long stone-room addition. The end wall of the addition stood a few strides away from the Barracks with its gray-brown, river-rock walls soaking up the heat of the morning sun. The long room looked plenty strong and sturdy, as if it was made to stand alone, even though it was attached to the main house.

She called to Matilda and Laughing Girl still wandering inside the Barracks, doing their sniffing and snuffling among the bunks. She heard their toenails clicking on the wood floor, coming through the front door and onto the porch, ready to follow their person in this new game of discovery.

When they reached her, Frankie headed toward the long porch that ran across the front of the stone-room, walking straight to the door sitting halfway along the length of the rock wall. She eased it open, curious about the room, still wondering about the reason for it. Wondering why it had been built that way—attached to the big house as it was.

The minute she stepped inside, she understood. It was a pantry-room—a very long pantry-room. Its walls were lined with shelves and cabinets and counters, and under the counters were tilt-out bins. Checking them, Frankie discovered that the situation here was much the same as in the root-cellar and the henhouse. The bins and the cupboards in the pantry were nearly full. There were crates and bins of cornmeal and flour, kegs of oats and beans and rice. Bags of dried peas and parched corn, of pepper and salt and sugar. In the cabinets, there were bags of coffee, jars of dried fruits, tins of molasses and vinegar, bottles of spices and herbs. Cans labeled as baking powder and baking soda. Pots and pans, bowls and sifters, pitchers and platters and baskets were stacked on the counters and lined up on the shelves above them.

At the far end of the room that stretched toward the Barracks, there were counters and shelves that held pails and buckets and an assortment of pans. Pans that Frankie recognized as separating pans for milk and cream. And along with the separating pans, there were milk-tins and churns and jars, wooden-molds and butter-crocks. Everything in that part of the room told the story; it had been designated as the dairy-room.

From the look of all the pans and buckets that were stacked and sitting on the counters and shelves in the rest of the room—some arranged neatly where they belonged and some scattered and in disarray—Frankie figured it was exactly as Lillian Kinison had left it the day she walked away from the homestead. At the end of the counter, she spied a large galvanized tub filled with plates and cups and glasses crusted with dried food. *Probably left unwashed after the last meals in the house. Probably, since January.*

Frankie looked at the tub of dishes and then, at a pile of cloth on the floor beside the counter. Dirty tablecloths. Dirty dishtowels. Some shirts and trousers for kids. Socks. A lady's blouse. A couple of aprons.

Apparently, Lillian Kinison had indeed just left everything behind. She just let things lie. Maybe because she was too exhausted to clean and tidy things. Or maybe she was hurrying to leave because she was scared to be alone. Or maybe she was too sad. Or given the hateful way she had talked about the homestead, maybe she had just been mad.

Looking around the room, Frankie figured the rock walls and the rock floor kept the room cool and quiet—and from the look of things, Daniel had done his best to make it tight against rodents. When she opened the window in the end-wall of the dairy-room—the wall that faced the Barracks porch—Frankie felt the prairie air surge into the room, swirling and freshening everything it touched.

Studying what had been built into the room and what had been stored there, she knew that this room contained items that were *far* beyond basic necessities; this room was nicer and bigger than the pantry in the big white house back in Indiana. This room had been built to please a woman, built to make her life easier.

Apparently though, it hadn't pleased Lillian Kinison. Apparently, nothing here on the homestead had pleased her, not from the way she had talked on the night she came to visit the Harding family. On that night, the papers had been signed. On that night, the homestead had passed into the hands of James and Sarah Harding.

Frankie looked toward the room's second door, a door on the short wall that attached to the house. She had entered the pantry-room from the outside door on the long porch wall, but the door in front of her, she figured most likely, would lead into the kitchen. She opened it and found she was right.

The doorway opened right into the kitchen, and when she stepped out of the stone-room into the house itself, Frankie could see the marvelous plan of the house. She felt Matilda and Laughing Girl push past her, eager to explore yet another new space.

Frankie let them go ahead without her. For the moment, she was busy taking it all in. She stayed in the pantry-room doorway, surveying the kitchen, eyeing its furnishings. The table, the chairs, the cupboard. The baking cabinet and the fireplace at the inner corner of the room.

For a moment, Frankie had a hard time taking her eyes off the fireplace—she stared at the rocking chair sitting on a braided rug in front of it. Her mind drifted back to another rocker, in another house—a pretty little white cottage at Fort Kearny where her Lieutenant would sit with her. She shook her head, pushed back the rising tears and brought her mind out of the past.

She moved her eyes away from the chair and looked toward the un-shuttered window by the kitchen's porch door—the window with the lace curtains showing from the outside. She spotted the other doorways leading out of the kitchen, looking at the darkened rooms beyond—the rooms with all the shuttered windows. Through one door, a few steps to her right, she could see a bed against the far wall in the darkened room. Another doorway, cater-corner from where she stood, led into another shutter-darkened room.

Suddenly, she understood how the square shape of the house worked. Four rooms. Probably, a sitting-room through that doorway. Probably a second bedroom in the far corner of the house. And to her right, the bedroom that opened into the kitchen. *So. The kitchen, a sitting-room, a bedroom, and another bedroom.* It was simple and sensible. The center fireplace, a single fireplace, would heat each room from where it stood at the inside corner of each room.

Frankie crossed the kitchen to the doorway that she assumed would lead to a sitting-room. The room was dark, except for a bit of light filtering in from the un-shuttered window in the kitchen. She stared into the room, seeing only darkened silhouettes of furniture. Her heart was thumping; a mixture of emotions was bubbling up— excitement, contentment, confusion. Because it was all new to her. And because, in an odd sort of way, it all felt familiar to her.

She knew what she needed to do—the same thing she had done with the Barracks; she wanted to open the house to the meadow's light. *I need the prairie light and prairie air in here.*

Turning around, she headed out through the kitchen's porch door next to the un-shuttered window. She began her first walk along the veranda—a veranda that did, indeed, wrap around the house— interrupted only where the stone-room was attached. She unlatched all the shutters, swinging them open and letting the outside light flow inside.

Looking through the windows as she opened the shutters, she saw each of the rooms—four big square rooms. And sure enough, just

27

like she had figured, the single fireplace in the center of the house opened into each room. Each mantle was angled across the inner-most corner of each room.

From the outside, she learned the sitting-room had two outside doors, one on each outside wall, and each bedroom had one outside door. Each room in the house had two doorways, leading into the adjoining rooms. So, Frankie realized, a person could circle through the whole house, going from one door to the next, stepping from one room into another. She smiled. And then she laughed, pleased with the clever design.

And that was just the start of finding all the clever things about her new house. After her trip around the outside of the house, she began a slow walk through the inside of the house, exploring each room, opening the outside doors and lifting the window-sashes as she went, letting the morning air wash through the house.

She had expected to find furniture, because Lillian Kinison said she had left everything, except the clothes she and her children needed for the trip back East. But Frankie still found herself aston-ished by what she saw. Every room had all the necessary furnishings. Some of what she saw she knew had been freighted in; some was homemade, probably crafted by Daniel Kinison. But there was more than just furniture.

There were curtains in every window, some of lace and some of linen. There were tables and kerosene lamps. Beds and bedding. There were rugs and chairs. Mirrors and pictures. In each room there were bookshelves—some standing shelves and some hanging on the walls—all made from the side-planks from the square-cut logs. Some shelves held books—some titles she recognized; some were new to her. But there were plenty of books.

She walked through each room, moving from door to door, touching some of the furnishings, running her fingers along the edges. Studying everything. Tripping over the two dogs several times as they traipsed through the house. When her tour brought her back into the kitchen, Frankie stopped to look once again at the first room she had encountered.

Staring around her, Frankie already knew this would be her favorite room; it would be the heart of the whole homestead. The air from the meadow was drifting through the open door, filtering through the screen door. When she leaned to lift the sash on the window beside the door, she stood for a moment, feeling the fresh breeze flowing into her kitchen. She watched the bottom edges of the lace curtains rippling and flowing with the movement of the morning air, realizing suddenly that the breeze would always flow into her kitchen and lift the lace curtains. *Just like it is today. Making the curtains ripple just like this. Making the same patterns of light and shadows flit across the floor. My kitchen. My curtains.*

A long trestle-table stood on an oval rag-rug in the center of the room, looking as if it was ready to be loaded with plates and platters of food. Looking as if it was expecting people to gather around it.

A baking cabinet with a long work-counter stood along one wall. On another wall, plates and cups, pitchers and glasses, platters and serving bowls were lined up on homemade shelves. They showed some dust after their lonely vigil over the past months, but they were all lined up neat and orderly. Bowls and plates were stacked; coffee cups stood side-by-side. It all looked a lot different from the pan of dirty dishes and the disarray in the pantry. *Mostly, Lillian Kinison kept a nice house. In the end, she gave it up. Too tired or too scared, too sad or too mad before she left.*

And then Frankie's eyes went to the stove standing beside the door that led into the pantry. It was a massive kitchen stove, and it stood there against the wall, sturdy and strong. Massive and practically immoveable. It was standing there like it knew its purpose and could get it done. Looking as though it was just waiting to get fired up.

Frankie stared at the monstrosity, grinning at it, because she knew exactly what she had before her. It was a Majestic stove. The best of the best. It was the queen of kitchen cookstoves. It looked exactly like the one her aunt had in her kitchen in the big house in Indiana.

And now, right in front of her in this very kitchen, way out here in the Nebraska Territory, Frankie was looking at her own big and beautiful Majestic stove. It was there in all its glory, with six burners and all its clever ovens and warming shelves. It stood there with all its glistening nickel scrollwork showing bright against the black surfaces, flanked by a wood-box on one side and a kindling-box on the other—both piled high with wood.

She knew her grin was getting bigger. Because *this* was a treasure. There was no doubt in her mind that it must have been a very big deal to freight it out here from the stove factory in Michigan. But somehow, Daniel Kinison had managed it because it was here now.

Looking at this big beautiful monster of a stove, Frankie was feeling deeply pleased. In a funny way, she felt as if she was looking at an old friend; she knew exactly how to use this gigantic stove; she knew exactly how to manage the wood and the heat. She had helped her aunt cook a lot of meals on the big Majestic back in the family house in Indiana. And they had done plenty of baking too.

It took a lot of experience to know how to hold the temperatures for the different ovens and burners, and there were plenty of tricks to manage it. But her Aunt Sarah had known them all. The biggest difference with using this stove out here in the Nebraska Territory would have to do with the kinds of woods she would be burning. *But that's something that's easy enough to learn. It's all about soft woods and hard woods. And practice.*

The two dogs found their way back to the kitchen, nosed around for another minute or two, and then satisfied with what they had learned, they turned and trotted outside. Frankie, though, wanted another go at the house and its four rooms. She wanted to take a second trip, a slower trip to assess things. It was time to get a feel for exactly what she had.

She turned and tripped over Matilda, who had wandered back inside. Apparently, the collie-dog had rethought things, and now, she was heading toward the corner fireplace of the kitchen. Frankie watched her settle herself on the rug beside the oak rocking chair. Having a rocking chair cozied up in front of the kitchen fireplace seemed to be a perfect idea—and having a pretty little farmyard collie-dog curled up on the rug next to it made it seem even better. It was a homey touch. And Matilda was making herself at home.

Frankie took a last look around the kitchen, realizing that Matilda had figured it right. They were home.

She started her second go-around, leaving the kitchen and going through the doorway into the next room—the other room that faced the meadow. It had been used as a sitting-room, and Frankie could see no reason to change it. It was the same size as the kitchen, the same size as the bedrooms, and like the other rooms, it possessed its own share of the house's center fireplace across its inner corner.

Looking around her, Frankie liked the comforts of the room— the bookshelves and wall-shelves, a heavy parlor table, chairs and a long settee. A heavy desk was sitting against the side wall. And here, too, just like in the kitchen, a large wooden rocking-chair sat in front of the fireplace. *Apparently, Daniel Kinison had a true understanding of the glory and comfort of rocking chairs.*

Just as she had supposed, the two rooms at the back of the house were bedrooms; the first room, which joined the sitting-room, had two double-beds, two wardrobes and dressers and a washstand. Like the other rooms, it had its own corner mantle and fireplace at its innermost corner. And its own rocking chair.

The second bedroom—the one leading back to the kitchen—had its own wardrobe and dresser, a double-bed, a washstand, and of course, a rocking chair on a rug in front of the corner fireplace.

In the wardrobes and dressers in each bedroom, Frankie found the shelves and drawers still filled with bed linens and towels and clothes; Lillian Kinison had abandoned all of it in her haste to leave the homestead.

On the night Lillian Kinison had visited the Harding house back in Indiana, she had spoken about the homestead in great detail. She had declared that she had returned East, 'once and for all', and had no interest in retrieving any of the things she left behind; she was including all of it in the sale of the homestead. Frankie remembered listening to the woman's words of bitterness and hatred for this homestead.

'I want nothing to do with any of it,' she declared. 'It has nothing to do with me anymore. It was all Daniel's idea. It was his mess. Not mine.'

Frankie remembered her Uncle James signed the papers two days later—it was after they had all talked. The decision had been made by her uncle and aunt and her four cousins—and by her, because she was family too. On the night of Lillian Kinison's second visit, the papers had been signed. On that night, the homestead had passed into the hands of James and Sarah Harding.

There had been words on those papers that stayed in Frankie's mind; she remembered seeing the words that said Lillian Kinison was selling 'the land and everything on it, all buildings and their contents, all property and plantings, all livestock and equipment'. The Kinison woman wanted to be rid of it; she wanted to be rid of all the memories of it. It had never been *her* dream, she said. It had been her husband's.

Now as Frankie stood in that very house, on that very homestead, her mind went back to the night in Indiana when the papers were signed. She could hear Lillian Kinison's spiteful words. She could picture her face and recall her expressions. She could see the way the corner of Lillian Kinison's lip lifted when she spoke of the homestead and her husband's dream.

And there was more of the story that Frankie recalled—the story of how Daniel Kinison had lived out here in the Sand Hills by himself for several years, working alone to build the homestead. Returning periodically to visit his family and to arrange for more freighters with more furniture and supplies. He had worked to ready the homestead for his family, and once he had everything ready, he had sent for them. And Lillian Kinison moved out here with their boys.

She lived on the homestead for eight months before Daniel died. And, just a matter of days after his death, right in the middle of January, she hired a man—a neighbor, she said—to take her and her children back to the stage station at Fort Cottonwood. She had

taken a stagecoach to return to the East for good, leaving everything
else behind.

Finished with her walk-through of the house, Frankie went
out to the front porch. She sat herself down on a bench built against
the log wall between the sitting-room door and one of the kitchen
windows. She looked out across the front meadow, thinking about
this homestead that had become her whole family's dream just a few
months before. Back in the springtime. And then it had become her
own dream. Hers alone now—because she had become the whole
family. Because her uncle and aunt and cousins were all gone now.

There were odd feelings coursing through her mind and pulling
at her heart. Confusion and discomfort were swirling around inside
her and swirling all around her. Because all this had been someone
else's dream—a man named Daniel Kinison had dreamed it up. And
now she was feeling a mounting unease because it seemed like she
was taking away someone else's dream. She was feeling confusion
about everything in the house and everything on the homestead;
feeling discomfort because this was all a treasure, and it was far more
than she expected—probably more than her family had expected.

And the confusion and discomfort were growing. She had
already seen a lot and she knew she was barely halfway through the
homestead's buildings. There had been a lot to see, a lot to figure out,
and a lot to understand. She knew it was all going to get more confusing and disconcerting if she didn't sort out the jumble of feelings
swirling through her brain. And at the moment, Frankie couldn't
even figure out whether she should be feeling guilt or gratitude.

So for the moment, she decided to bring everything to a halt;
she decided to stay there on the kitchen porch for a while. Just to let
things settle in her mind and her heart. Just to see if maybe the confusion and the discomfort would quiet.

Thinking about it, a whole lot had happened in her life lately—all
in less than a year. A lot had occurred, and as of last night, a whole lot
had been completed. This had all been a long journey on the inside—

in her heart and her mind and her gut. And it had been a long trail on the outside—across the prairie and the rivers and into the Sand Hills. So maybe, it would be wise just to sit for a bit, just to watch everything around her. To listen, to wait. For just a bit. Because there was no hurry.

She stayed where she was, sitting on the bench, hearing the birds of the prairie, listening to the songs in her meadow. She watched Laughing Girl and Matilda roaming around the meadow, heads down, still doing their sniffing and snuffling, still looking and searching. Still learning about this new home of theirs. She watched her livestock strolling through the meadow—some grazing their way through the summer grasses, some standing and snoozing in the warmth of the morning sun.

To Frankie's eyes, they all seemed awfully content; they didn't seem to be worrying about why they were here, or who had been here before them. They seemed happy enough to be where they were, enjoying what was in front of them. They weren't thinking about papers that had been signed. They weren't worried about things that had been left behind. Or *why* things had been left behind. They didn't seem at all concerned about furniture and belongings. Or where all of it had come from. They were just living and relaxing in the meadow. And that seemed to be good enough for them.

She decided to follow their lead. She stood up from the bench and stretched. Yawned. And then she grinned as she felt the warm prairie sunshine on her face. She looked toward the long barn and started walking across the front meadow, heading toward the front entrance. Matilda and Laughing Girl left off their personal investigations and trotted over to join her; they fell into line and followed along.

The barn, as Frankie figured it, was a little wider and at least three times as long as the house. The lower half was of the same square-cut logs, but the top half was a wood-frame with board and batten. She wrestled with the large double-doors at the front of the barn, shoving and grunting until they suddenly gave up the fight and slid open.

She stood staring down the long alleyway as the daylight flooded inside, a little amazed and more than a little pleased at the sight of the barn's interior. Because there was a lot to see.

Far down the length of the barn she saw another set of massive doors. Along one side of the barn, the side facing the meadow, was what her uncle would have called the 'working-side' of the barn—the livestock side. The other side of the barn, she knew would be the 'storage-side'—the wagons and equipment side.

Beside her, just to her right, was a corner room with board-and-batten walls and a closed door. *Probably the tack-room or grain-room.* To her left, taking up that corner of the barn, was an open workshop. Implements and tools hung on the two walls; another wall made up of tall shelves separated the shop from the rest of the barn—shelves filled with boxes and crates and more tools. *Probably every tool needed to build a homestead.*

Frankie stayed where she was for a moment, scanning the work-shop, eyeing the array of tools, deciding to wait to explore it later; the closed room to her right could be explored later too. Because first, she decided, she wanted to understand the scope of the entire barn. There was a lot to see in this barn, a barn that was every bit as big as Bill Wheaton's long barn on Fort Farm Island.

She started a slow tour down the barn's center alleyway. Walking slowly, assessing what she saw, comparing all she saw, to all she had known about the barns in Indiana and the stable at Fort Kearny. Nodding to herself. Pleased with what she was seeing. Making sense of it. Learning about this barn and the reasons for everything it held.

A narrow alley ran beside the wall of the corner-room, leading to a personnel door that faced the meadow and house. Beyond that, all the way down the barn, was a row of stalls—eight stalls inside, opening to eight pens outside. Beyond the stalls, in the far corner of the barn, was a large pen with three stanchions and a door that opened into a cow-lot. Frankie grinned at the sight. *The milking-pen and the cow-lot. All part of Blossom's new domain.*

At the end of the alleyway, Frankie wrestled the double doors open and stood for a moment, eyeing what lay beyond. A back barn-lot to her left; part of the cow-lot to her right. Both lots had gates leading to a fenced track that ran out to the long plank-fence that separated the home meadow from a second meadow in its own valley. Between the cow-lot and the plank fence were the structures she had seen from the wagon-seat the evening before—there was what looked to be a garden surrounded by a low stonewall, a corncrib, and an odd little stone-building.

All of that, Frankie decided, she would explore later. For now, she had a whole barn to learn about. She started back the way she had come, walking along the alleyway once again, this time looking over everything on the storage-side of the barn.

That side of the barn—across from the livestock pens—was wide and open, designed to provide plenty of space for wagons and equipment. The Conestoga, Frankie realized, would sit easily inside this barn, just like it did in the barn on Fort Farm Island. Just like it did in the huge white barn back in Indiana. Her grandfather and her Uncle James had always kept the Conestoga in the barn; they used it plenty for freighting and hauling, and even for training teams, but it had always been protected from the weather in the barn. Built in the Conestoga Valley in Pennsylvania forty years before and protected as it had been, it was still strong and solid.

Here, Frankie decided, it would be the same; here, just like always, the Conestoga would be stored inside, safe and secure. Protected. Because it was, after all, a family heirloom. It had been built for her grandfather when the family lived in Pennsylvania and passed down to her Uncle James and her father; and now, it was in her own hands. It had moved the family from Pennsylvania to Indiana, and then, from Indiana to this homestead. And now it was under *her* watch. Now it would be kept safe under the roof of *this* barn.

Walking along the alleyway, Frankie looked over the assortment of equipment Daniel Kinison had gathered together—everything he believed would be sensible to have here on the homestead.

36

There was a heavy farm-wagon and a sturdy buckboard wagon, with an odd open space in the row of equipment. After thinking about it, Frankie realized the space had likely been for the spring-wagon that Lillian Kinison talked about the night she had visited the house in Indiana. She said she had hired a neighbor to drive her and her children to the stage-stop at Fort Cottonwood after her husband died—she had given him the wagon, along with a team of horses, as payment.

Beyond the wagons, there were two plows, a sickle-bar mower, and a sulky hay-rake. And then, to her surprise, Frankie spotted a long and heavy rock-sled; it was sitting in its own place at the end of the line of equipment, looking as if it was crouching on its low and flat steel-runners, half-hidden there in the midst of the high-wheeled equipment.

It wasn't the first time she had seen one; they had been plentiful back in Pennsylvania, and they weren't rare back in Indiana, but she was surprised to see one out here, because it didn't seem as though a rock-sled belonged in the middle of the sandy-soiled hills. But thinking about all the rock-work on the various buildings—the fireplaces and the rock foundations and the pantry-room walls—Frankie decided it probably had already proven its worth.

Hanging on the long barn wall was an assortment of double-trees and single-trees, a couple of neck-yokes, two ox-yokes, and a light-wagon tongue. There was a collection of extra traces, short tugs, different sizes of hames and horse-collars, and coiled lines, all hanging neat and orderly from pegs on the walls. Leather straps and ropes and chains were hanging from the barn's support posts.

Frankie stared at the array, her grin growing. Understanding the wisdom in having all of it. *Anything and everything for replacing and repairing harnesses and hitches. Because this is a long way from stores and harness shops.*

The sound of farmyard-collie and wolfhound-greyhound toe-nails clicking on the loft floor above her, snapped Frankie out of her musings. She eyed the layout of the loft—it extended over the front half of the barn with a long gallery that extended farther out, running above the stalls; hay was still piled high along the galley. *Plenty of hay. Simple enough to fork down to the livestock.*

She had seen a loft-ladder built into the wall next to the personnel door on her first trip down the alleyway. But now, she spotted another access to the loft—something she hadn't expected. A wide staircase had been built against the long wall of the storage-side of the barn, which explained exactly how the dogs had found their way aloft. She grinned at her own pun and headed for the stairs.

Once aloft herself, and still grinning at the pun, Frankie started wondering if this sort of circumstance actually explained the origin of the term 'aloft'. She left off pondering and started exploring the space. There was a hoard of lumber up there, all sorted and stacked along the sidewalls and across most of the barn's front wall. Planks and studs and posts. Stacks and stacks. Higher than her head. *Apparently, Daniel Kinison had plans to do more building.*

After a few minutes of wandering among the sorted-and-sized stacks, Frankie started questioning the amount of work that had been involved in toting all the wood up the stairs. But at the open end of the loft, she found her answer. She also found herself grinning again, because Daniel Kinison had surprised her once more. He had set up a clever system for himself.

Frankie's eyes were on a hay-trolley. A trolley running on its track under the peak of the roof wasn't an uncommon sight in a barn with a loft, but this hay-trolley was different. This one wasn't limited to lifting hay; this one had been rigged with a wooden platform instead of a hay-hook—Daniel Kinison had used the platform to hoist loads of wood to the loft. The hay-trolley, with a little improvising, had been put to use for lifting lumber. And apparently, it had worked well.

"Look at that Matilda," Frankie squatted beside the tawny little collie-dog, rubbing her ears. "Daniel Kinison had his ways of inventing things. Not all that different from what Uncle James could do."

She headed back down the stairs, thinking there was a lot on the ground-floor that still needed to be explored. And at the moment, her mind was on the closed-off room and the workshop across from it.

The workshop took up the entire front corner on the storage-side of the barn. Two long workbenches separated the space from the alleyway, and tall shelves built into the barn's supporting posts separated the shop from the wagons and equipment. The shelves were filled with tools and boxes and crates. There were kegs filled with different sizes of nails and bolts, along with a number of things that Frankie couldn't name.

The two barn walls of the shop were jam-packed with every kind of hand tool imaginable; tools of all shapes and sizes—wood-planes and corner-squares, clamps and vises, hammers and tongs, and pliers. There was a variety of saws and wedges and chisels. Hatchets and axes of all shapes and sizes.

Most were tools that Frankie recognized, but a good number were mysteries to her. And no matter what their names were and no matter how they were used, it was clear that Daniel Kinison had loved his work and his tools. They were all meticulously arranged on the walls and shelves in what seemed to be a well-planned order and, to Frankie's eyes, almost magical.

When she had her fill of the workshop, she walked across the alleyway to the closed corner-room, eager now to see what was behind the walls. When she opened the door, she found what she expected—the tack-room. On one wall, there were shelves holding brushes and curry-combs, horseshoes and nails, rasps and clinchers. Water pails and grain-buckets were hanging from pegs.

On two of the room's walls, arranged neatly on pegs and racks, was an assortment of tack—bridles, halters, and lead-ropes. Two saddles. Coils of ropes and leather lines. There was a single medium driving-harness and collar, and a pair of matching light-harnesses and collars. *Likely, for the buckboard.* There was a pair of heavy field-collars and work-harnesses. *For the heavy farm-wagon.* Which made her start wondering about Daniel's livestock, wondering where the animals had gone. *Probably, Lillian Kinison sold the animals, or maybe, gave them away to other settlers in the area. But then why did she just* release *the chickens? Why didn't she give them to someone?*

Frankie shook her head, pushing away her musings, and continued her assessment of the room. Filled with everything such as it was, it was clearly a tack-room, but it was intended to be more than that because it was a finished room—a room very different from the rest of the barn. It had a wood floor and two windows—one in each of the outside walls.

This room was both living-quarters and a tack-room. There was a potbellied stove. A bunk stood against one wall with shelves on the wall above it. A table and chair stood in the corner. A rifle and shotgun rested on wall-pegs just inside the door. All in all, it was set up a lot like the Dwelling Place.

Standing in the doorway of the room, Frankie's thoughts drifted back to the big barn in Indiana; that barn had a tack-room where the barn-manager lived. *So that's what Daniel Kinison intended.*

He clearly had *big* plans for the future—big enough that he knew he would need a manager to oversee the whole operation, someone who would oversee the other workers who bunked in the Barracks. This room, along with the Barracks and the Dwelling Place, all told the story—Daniel Kinison had planned for a number of men to work this place with him. Looking around her, Frankie realized she was learning even more about the man who had lived here and built all this.

Stepping out of the tack-room, Frankie looked down the alley-way toward the double doors at the back entrance. This was all about the plans and the dreams for a future. Everything she had seen so far spoke to that. And now, in the hush and the silence of the barn, Frankie could feel a change happening within herself—something was changing and growing inside her. In her mind and in her gut, things were coming together.

There were two dreams here in this valley—two dreams that were starting to converge. Daniel Kinison's dream was somehow blending with her family's dream. It was all starting to come to her; the dreams—both Daniel Kinison's and her family's—were becoming hers. And today, she realized, she was actually standing in the middle of her dream. *In my barn. In my meadow. On my homestead. In my dream.*

Frankie took a deep breath, feeling the cool, sweet air of the barn filling her lungs. She shivered, feeling tears rising from deep inside her, from deep in her heart. This, she realized, this was what had been calling to her, drawing her here, leading her far to the northwest—all the way from the six graves on the trail beside the Little Blue River.

She glanced down at Matilda, the tawny little collie-dog who had been with her most of the way. Matilda was sitting in front of her, showing her toothy-smile, sweeping the dirt of the alleyway floor with her wagging tail. Waiting for her person to decide what was next on their list of things-to-see-and-do.

"Come on then, Matilda. Let's open up this barn to the daylight, and then we'll see what's out back." Frankie bent down to tickle the collie's ears. "After that, we'll see about some breakfast. When we're done with breakfast, we'll start getting some things out of the wagon and into the house."

Frankie started down the barn once more. This time, she stepped into the first stall where she unlatched the stall-door and swung it open to the meadow. She grinned as the horses and the mules grazing in the meadow threw their heads, snorting. Spooked by the sudden motion.

She smiled because Blossom, the Jersey cow, looked only mildly surprised as she turned her head toward the barn; she was lying down in the grass, working her cud, moving her jaw in the slow side-to-side, lazy cow-kind of way. Primrose, her heifer calf, flicked her little tail up over her back and bucked and frisked around in the meadow grass. She had been startled into bucking at first and then apparently decided to keep bucking, amusing herself with her own antics.

Belle, the prettiest and sweetest of the bay mares, gave her pretty little nicker. Septimus, the youngest of the mules, let loose with a stuttering bray. Probably, Frankie decided, just because he wanted to. *Probably. Because he's a mule, and mules don't always need a good reason for doing what they do.*

Frankie continued moving from stall to stall, opening the doors to the pens outside, welcoming the bright light, letting the fresh air pour into the barn. In the milking-pen, she stopped to fiddle with the stanchions, working the latches to release the neck-catcher and braces. Realizing she needed to do the milking soon. *The first milking on my first morning in my own barn. On my own homestead.*

At the back of the barn once again, Frankie stood in the light that flooded in through the back doors, surveying this part of her domain. Studying the rock-walled garden-plot, she figured it to be twenty feet wide and at least twice as long. *A good-sized garden, almost as big as Aunt Sarah's.* It sat in front of the cow-lot, with a corncrib next to it and another building—an odd little stone building—beyond that.

Frankie walked along the chest-high rock wall, peering into the garden. Her Aunt Sarah, she decided, would have liked the garden; she would have considered it 'well situated'. Positioned as it was, it would get sunlight in the morning and early afternoon, and during the hottest part of the day, it would be shaded by trees and the hillside.

It was clear that the garden had been sitting barren this year, but she could see how the rows had been laid out from the previous year. There were smatterings of self-sown plants growing within the garden—some carrot-tops, a patch of dill, and a few hills of squash. Some cluster of what looked to be mint. A few overgrown rhubarb plants along the back wall.

To Frankie, it looked like a nice garden with a lot of potential; there was plenty of size to the plot, with plenty of room to grow food for a whole family—the amount of produce in the bins in the root-cellar seemed to confirm that.

In one corner of the garden, an odd contraption caught Frankie's eye and held her attention. The more she looked at it and the closer she got, the more confused she became. She could see a long, raised V-shaped wooden-trough of some sort that straddled the far corner of the rock-wall and angled down into the garden itself. There was another flue that branched off and continued to the water trough in the cow-lot.

The best she could figure, it was part of a water-flue system of some sort; from what she could see, it had its origins in the back valley—the main wooden flue followed along the fence-line, fastened tight against the railings. Traveling all the way from the pasture-well, as it did, it appeared that it was designed to transfer water all the way into the garden and the barn.

Frankie didn't know whether it was actually what she suspected it was—and even if it was, she didn't know whether it would actually work or not. But to Frankie's eyes, it looked like an awfully clever contraption. And given that Daniel Kinison had thought of it and rigged it up like he did, she was betting it did exactly what he designed it to do.

She studied it for a while, trying to figure exactly how the system of V-shaped flues could actually manage such a task. When she felt as though her mind was getting all jumbled with thoughts of waterways and troughs, flues and fences, she decided to save the final figuring about the entire contraption for another time.

Finally done with her wonderings about the water-flue system, she continued her tour, rounding the corner of the garden and heading for what she already knew was a corncrib. It was solid and well-built, with slanted walls of horizontal planks with gaps allowing for air to circulate. To her surprise and delight, the crib was more than half-full of corn. *No livestock left to eat it.*

To Frankie's mind, it was a stroke of luck for her and her animals. But she found that her thoughts kept drifting back to her questions about Daniel Kinison's livestock. Lillian Kinison had turned the chickens loose to fend for themselves. She had spoken about trading a team of horses and a wagon to pay for her trip down to Fort Cottonwood.

But there had clearly been more livestock than just a team of horses and a flock of chickens. The milking-pen and the stalls and the barn-lots showed signs of use. Plenty of use. The harnesses and equipment meant that there had been wagon-teams. Yet Lillian Kinison had never mentioned any animals other than the single team of horses in the discussions about the sale of the homestead.

Thinking along the same lines as before, Frankie figured it was likely the stock had been sold or, maybe, given away to other settlers in the area. Which meant there were certainly other neighbors somewhere in the region. She had met Ida and Everett Dunbar, her closest neighbors. And their daughter and son-in-law lived on the claim adjoining theirs. When she had crossed the Middle Loup River, she had seen a homestead near the main track. She thought back to her first encounter with the Dunbars—other than their daughter and son-in-law, they had said nothing about other settlers. But surely there were other families in the region.

She shook her head to clear it of the speculation, deciding she had enough to keep her mind occupied for the time being. She still had plenty to figure out right here on her own place. She left the corncrib behind and moved to the next building. The last one in her meadow—the little stone building that had rock walls that looked like the garden and the stone-room addition to the house.

At first sight, Frankie thought it might be an outhouse, even though it was probably three times the size of the one behind the house. She was wrong. When she opened the door, she saw an assortment of hooks hanging from the ceiling and open-slat shelves along three walls. No windows. The stone building had its own little firebox, but oddly enough, it sat along an outside wall with a low-lying stovepipe directed into the building through the stone wall.

She had never seen anything like it, and all she could figure was that it had been designed for a very specific use. She decided to think on it, and if she couldn't figure it out, Everett Dunbar would probably know.

Outside again, with the dogs still following along, she looked beyond the little rock-building. There were several stacks of the square-cut logs, stacked high and wide. Beyond the stacks were two large piles of river stones.

Next to the piles of stones, the plank fence that separated the home meadow from the pastures of the second valley stretched across to the opposite hillside.

Frankie climbed on the fence-rails, gazing out into the second meadow, studying the center track and the fences of the four pastures. It would all serve her and her animals well. There was plenty of room in one pasture for Blossom and her calf and the oxen. One for the Shires and geldings and mules, one for the mares, and one for Trumpeter, unless she decided to turn him in with the mares. It was well beyond spring and a bit late in the year for breeding—at least, it was later than her Uncle James preferred. But only by a month or so. That too, she decided, was something to think about.

Looking to the position of the sun, Frankie figured, it was halfway into the morning. For the time being, she was tired of thinking. Her tour was done; she had given the front valley a thorough going over. She had seen and studied everything. And now, she realized, she was starting to feel overwhelmed again. She decided to stop her search-and-discovery mission and do something normal. Something that would calm and slow her mind down. Because there had been a lot of sights and thoughts that had filled her mind. And because she wasn't at all sure her brain could hold any more.

She walked out through the grass of the meadow, heading toward the Conestoga to gather up the milk-pails and the milking-stool and the lead rope for Blossom. She caught herself smiling at the sight of the fawn-colored Jersey with her pretty dish-face. She was picturing her Aunt Sarah's face—thinking about how pleased she would be at the sight of her favorite milk cow here in her new home. Right where she belonged.

Frankie led Blossom into the deep quiet of the barn, letting Primrose follow along and learn about the new surroundings. Letting the little heifer wander around the first barn she had ever been in.

She put Blossom in the stanchion, then sat down on the three-legged stool and took her time milking. Laughing when the heifer stood, staring wide-eyed at the stanchion, apparently shocked to see her momma entrapped. After eyeing the situation for a moment or two, Primrose began exploring the milking-pen and the fences; she nosed the stanchion and tried tasting it; she turned and trotted around the milking-pen a few times. Then she gave a couple baby-cow snorts and baby-cow huffs and followed up with a few baby-cow hops.

"Get used to it, Little Girl. You'll be part of all this in the future."

Frankie sat there in the soft, moody light of the long barn, taking her time milking, and realizing that she was using a stanchion for the first time in months. There had been no barn and no stanchion since they'd left Indiana back in the spring. This milking session on this particular morning, after so many months on the trail, was a step back to normal—back to what was familiar. It was about having a home again.

When she finished milking, she turned Blossom and Primrose into the back barn-lot. Pleased with how natural it all felt, feeling as if she had done it a thousand times before. Feeling more at home now, than ever.

Then, she headed back to the Conestoga; she took Trumpeter off his picket-rope and led him to the front barn-lot and released him to explore. That done, she whistled for the dogs and headed to the house, hungry after the morning's work of exploration and discovery. It was time for a meal and for coffee. It was time to fire up the big Majestic and sit down to a table.

She thought back to the last time she had sat at a kitchen table, realizing it had been the morning after Independence Day in the white cottage at Fort Kearny; it had been at breakfast, right before the orders for the hearing arrived.

While the coffee brewed and potatoes and onions and a few slices of bacon sizzled in a frying pan, Frankie sat down at the big trestle table, smelling the coffee and the bacon. Sniffing at the aroma of the onions. Making it a moment she would remember, because this was the first meal she was cooking on her homestead. *Because this is the start of my future in the meadow. This is the legacy my family gave me.*

It was, like her father and uncle always said, all a matter of getting things right from the start. *'Start it right and it'll stay right.'* Those were the words swirling through her mind at the moment. She could hear her Uncle James saying those words as clearly as if he were standing there in the kitchen.

And when she closed her eyes, she could see her father; she could picture his expression—his right eyebrow would lift a little, and then he'd give a little nod. That was his way of letting her know she was thinking right. For a moment, she could see his eyes—deep and dark, soft and bright, all at the same time. She could see him as if he were leaning back against the counter of the baking cabinet. And in that same moment, while the fresh air from the meadow swirled lazily through the kitchen, she knew what Justus Harding would be thinking. She knew exactly what both he and her Uncle James would be thinking.

They would be thinking that she had done well. That she was where she deserved to be. Her father would be nodding, telling her that she had earned the right to be here. Her Uncle James would probably be giving her one of his winks, quietly letting her know that he agreed with his older brother.

Frankie's thoughts shifted then, leaving them and the past behind, returning to the present, and then moving forward to the immediate future. Because she had work to get done. Because the Dunbars were coming to visit in a matter of days and she had her concerns about that. She had concerns about other settlers in the area, too, because there was a very good chance that folks out here on their own homesteads might decide they didn't want a ten-year-old girl living on her own. And finding a way to live her own life, on her own homestead, had been on her mind all the way up the Cheyenne Trail. But she had a plan. *Sort of a several-step plan. Sort of.*

Meeting up with her nearest neighbors had, in fact, been the first part of her plan. The first-meeting. And now, going over the meeting in her mind, she thought it had gone well. She had met Everett and Ida Dunbar the day before, late in the afternoon, nine or ten miles downriver, near the ford to their place.

Now, it was time for the next part of the plan. The reckoning-day. And that would be in four days, when the Dunbars came for their first visit. They were coming then because there'd be a full moon that night; they would stay for the day and then travel home by moonlight.

That would be the day when the truth would come out between her and her new neighbors. Because they would be assuming her family had arrived. Because Frankie had allowed for a 'slight misinterpretation' by the Dunbars. She hadn't lied to them—in fact, she had been careful not to lie—but she had explained things in a certain way that had nudged them into thinking certain things. And she hadn't helped them to think any differently.

And because of that, when she and the Dunbars had parted ways in the late afternoon, they believed they were dealing with a ten-year-old boy. They were also thinking that her family was traveling behind her on the trail.

That had been part of her plan—a plan to give them some information and to direct their thoughts in a certain way, so that she had time to prepare and get settled in on her homestead. That, she hoped, would give her time to make it look like she was doing fine on her own. She had used the full-moon night as a way to stall, so when they did visit, they'd see that she was managing well on her own. Already living in the house. Already cooking for herself. Already seeing to the livestock.

Frankie Harding filled her cup with coffee and scraped the fried potatoes and onions and bacon onto her plate. She tossed a piece of bacon to Matilda on the rug in front of the kitchen fireplace and settled herself down at the table. Started in on her first meal in her new home. *My first meal. My first breakfast.*

She looked past the collie-dog into the bedroom just beyond the pantry doorway. *My bedroom, right beside the kitchen.* She watched the daylight flickering through the lace curtains in the bedroom. Quiet. Peaceful. *That's where I'll sleep tonight.*

Her mind went back to the neighbors. The Dunbars. Nice people; nice neighbors. *Likely, they'll be my neighbors for years to come, so it'd be nice to have things go right from the start.* She grinned when she thought about the conversation the day before. Nice. Easy to be with; easy to talk to. They had been pleased at the thought of having a new family move in.

But they were going to be more than a little surprised when they and their daughter, and maybe their son-in-law, rolled into the meadow. Because they would be expecting to see a whole family. But there wouldn't be a whole family; there wouldn't be any adults. There wouldn't even be a ten-year-old boy. There would be no one in the meadow but a ten-year-old girl. They were going to be surprised all right.

But until then there was plenty of work to do. Plenty of things to do to prove that she could manage on her own. Thinking through things while she finished her meal, she decided it might not be necessary to have *everything* moved into the house from the wagon, but it would be good to be far enough along so the Dunbars would see that she was settling in and doing fine on her own.

The Dunbars seemed like fine people, but they *were* adults after all, and she *was* a kid. There was no use ignoring the fact that adults tended to think in certain ways. It was likely that the Dunbars were going to have plenty to think about and plenty of concerns about her being alone on her homestead. A child living out here on her own, probably wouldn't sit well with them—any more than it had with the soldiers who came across her alone out on the prairie. Her being alone, and traveling on her own, had been enough for the US Cavalry at Fort Kearny to decide to disrupt her life and detain her at the fort.

Frankie had no idea how many settlers were in the area, but if word was going to get out about her—and she knew it would—then everything needed to start out right. The Dunbars might be the best chance of that happening. If they believed in her, if they spoke well of her and had confidence in her, then others might follow suit.

Frankie poured water into the dishpan and washed the dishes; then she washed the dishes in the tub in the pantry, deciding to clean up Lillian Kinison's mess. And all the while, she was thinking about the Dunbars. Thinking about the way they smiled and spoke. There had been a kindness about them. They seemed thoughtful and steady. They seemed like people her father and her Uncle James and Aunt Sarah would like. So to Frankie's thinking, with a good start and honest talk, there was reason to believe it might all go well.

But there was something niggling in the back of her mind—their daughter and son-in-law. She knew nothing about the daughter; but she had seen the daughter's husband, or at least, she had seen someone that Everett figured must have been her husband. She had seen him from a distance, traveling in a farm wagon, driving a skinny mule, heading south—and even at a distance, from way up on the hilltop, there was something about him she hadn't liked.

She couldn't put a name to the feeling, but she had felt her gut tighten. Shivers had rippled up her back. If that was the Dunbars' son-in-law, then she needed to watch that end of things carefully.

Frankie shook her head, throwing off the thoughts, wanting to bring her mind back to her meadow. To her house. Because today, she was moving into *her* home and *her* homestead. And tonight, she was going to sleep in her bedroom. *In my bed.*

Frankie headed into the pantry, remembering the corner where the brooms and mops and buckets were lined up. She decided to start the process of settling into her homestead by settling into the house itself, and she would start with the easiest things first—the dusting and sweeping. A broom and a feather-duster, a bucket of water and damp rags. *Easy enough.*

While she dusted and swept and rinsed the dusty dishes and wiped down the counters and shelves, she thought through the process of emptying the wagon, thinking about the things in the wagon. Thinking about where things would go and what the priorities had to be; thinking about how her Aunt Sarah would do things.

Luckily, there wasn't much in the way of household furniture to unload; the wagons had been loaded mostly with food supplies, because Lillian Kinison had described the houseful of furnishings she left behind. So mostly, it would be crates and barrels of food, boxes of dishes, pots and pans and trunks of clothes that she would be unloading.

Once the sweeping was done, Frankie started heating water in the copper-boiler on the back of the stove. She decided to start with the bed linens and blankets from the wagon, letting them soak in washtubs of soapy water while she started unloading the wagon. Once she was done with her own bed linens, she'd start on the ones that had been left on the beds in the house.

She took a long look at the clothesline that stretched from the veranda posts on the back of the house to the outhouse at the base of the hillside. That clothesline, she realized, was going to get some serious use over the next couple of days. She knew she was going to be washing a lot of bedding throughout most of the day. *And likely tomorrow too.* But she knew she was doing it the way her Aunt Sarah would. *Start with everything clean. Make it a fresh start.*

With the bedding soaking in two washtubs, she harnessed High Boy and Black Mack and hitched them to the Conestoga; she circled them and backed the wagon until the tailgate was butted up against the kitchen porch.

With that, Frankie started making the house her own. She moved the most important items into the house first. The two violins, the tooled-leather box and the mahogany mantle clock went into the sitting-room; her Aunt Sarah's remedy-chest went into a cabinet in the pantry; her father's books went into her bedroom where they would stay separate from the other books on other shelves. She carried her grandmother's side-saddle, her own saddle and Fanny's bridle, and the McClelland saddle and bridle to the barn and settled them in the tack-room.

For the household items, she started with the small things first. Small steps and easy decisions. Bags of staples destined for the pantry, she could carry easily enough; pots and pans, coffeepots and kettles, the boxes of dishes and utensils were easily shifted into the kitchen. When she worked her way up to the boxes and trunks too heavy to move, she opened them in the Conestoga and carried armloads into the house—it meant more trips but it was easy enough.

As to the heaviest things—the barrels filled with loose cornmeal and rice, oatmeal and beans, she decided to wait—she'd figure out the exact process later.

At the end of the day, she drove the wagon to the barn and unhitched High Boy and Mack. In the morning, she decided, she'd start by unloading the farming and gardening tools, the kegs of nails, the hand-tools, the boxes of farrier equipment and horseshoes into the barn. Getting those things out of the wagon and into the barn would allow for more room in the wagon-bed to unload all the remaining crates and barrels of food.

By the time the birds started singing their evening songs and the coyotes began their yipping-and-yammering in the hills beyond her meadow, Frankie had positioned herself on the bench on her front porch. She was watching the trees and low brush on the hillside that ran behind and beyond the house, along the northwest edge of the meadow, watching the movements of the now-wild-and-soon-to-be-domesticated-once-again chickens.

Each time she sat down to rest or eat a meal during the day, she had watched the chickens pecking around under the tree branches and roots and scratching among the dead leaves on the ground. And she had seen them on and off throughout the rest of the day, spotting them scuttling and trundling around in the brush on the hillside, catching glimpses of the feathery creatures every once in a while.

There was no doubt they had become accustomed to life in the wild; like Everett Dunbar had said, they were too wild to catch. He wasn't wrong in his thinking—the chickens would have no desire to interact with humans. Not when they were doing perfectly fine without them. And just as Everett Dunbar had found out, it would be an exercise in futility to try capturing them during the day.

But during the night, it'd be a different story. Because Frankie had a few tricks up her sleeve—the same tricks that coyotes and foxes and weasels typically had up their furry little sleeves. There was a reason those varmints raided henhouses at night, and Frankie knew what it was. It was a simple enough thing and it had always amazed her that most people, even people who raised chickens, didn't know enough to work chickens at night. Clipping wings, cutting toenails and spurs, turning roosters into capons—it was all an easy business after nightfall. Because chickens in the dark of night were very different from chickens in the light of day.

Throughout the day, Frankie came up with a rough count; she figured a few more than a dozen chickens were wandering among the tree-trunks and brush. She thought there were four or five roosters, and she had spotted what she thought to be a dozen hens and pullets. From what she could see, most of the birds scuttling around in the low brush and branches were the black-and-white Dominikers—the kind typically seen pecking around most farmyards no matter where you went. But she had seen a number of Leghorns and some red hens she assumed were either Rhode Island Reds or New Hampshire Reds.

Sitting there on the kitchen porch in the late evening, with Laughing Girl and Matilda dozing in the grass near the steps, Frankie had her Cavalry spyglass focused on the hens, watching to see which branches, in which trees, the chickens were seeking out as roosts for the night. As shadows started lengthening and the evening air began cooling, Frankie watched the chickens flapping up to their chosen roosts.

As they went to their roosts, she realized there were far more than a dozen chickens out there on the hillside. Watching the activity, it looked like chickens were coming from all directions, from all over the hillside; they were coming to roost together in the low-hanging branches of the trees along the base of the slope.

Frankie grinned, thinking about her bounty. Fried eggs and roast chicken. Milk and cream. Vegetables from the root-cellar. A full pantry of essentials and staples. And more barrels and crates of staples still sitting in the Conestoga. *Not much reason to worry about starving this winter.*

Once darkness settled in, she went into the house and pulled her aunt's scissors from the sewing basket; she lit a lantern and trimmed it to a dim glow; she grabbed a burlap-sack from a cabinet in the pantry and walked to the grove of trees that had become a night-roost for her homestead's chickens. It was time to hunt and gather.

It only took Matilda a few minutes to figure out what the night's work was about, and what she could do to help. By the time Frankie lifted two of the sleeping hens from their night-roosts and lowered them into the sack, Matilda had a clear understanding of this new game her human was playing. 'Find-the-chickens, bag-the-chickens.' It was a game the collie-dog could play. And she played it well.

From the moment she caught on, Matilda became an expert at locating the roosting birds. She used her instincts and her nose to find the feathered treasures. The tawny little collie-dog prowled around the tree trunks, her head high, sniffing the air. Time and again, Frankie watched her plop her little collie-bottom down on the ground beneath a branch and stare intently up into the tree.

And each time, Frankie put the lantern down, readied her bag and waded through the grass and brush to the branch that Matilda had her eyes on. It was simple enough to lift the sleepy hens and roosters from the branches. Lift the chicken, lower it to the bag. Lift the next chicken, lower it into the bag. One at a time; easy as pie.

Four drowsy chickens in the bag and Frankie made a trip to the henhouse. She transferred her catches to the indoor roost and headed back to the trees for a refill. After three more trips, with a gain of four birds each time, Frankie figured she had a good start for her flock. Any chickens she might have missed could be gathered up on another night's hunt. *A flock of sixteen is a nice enough start.*

She was ready to quit the catching-and-bagging part of the game and get on with the next part of the job—the wing-trimming-with-scissors part. Frankie whistled Matilda in. But the collie-dog had no intention of quitting. In her mind, the game was still on; there were still chickens roosting in the branches.

Matilda had the next roosting hen spotted—she stayed where she was, sitting on her bottom, staring at a branch above her. Waiting.

Her pretty collie-tail wagging slow and steady against the ground, trusting her person would do her part of the work at hand.

It was clear the tawny little collie-dog wasn't going to stop halfway through her self-appointed job and Frankie figured that no amount of explaining was going to sway the collie-dog's mind. The reality, Frankie realized, was the half-grown pup would take it as a betrayal if she were ignored for doing her duty; Matilda's heart, Frankie knew, would be broken.

She let out a sigh and gave in. Out of nothing less than a true sense of loyalty to her faithful dog, she went back to scrambling around among the trees and the branches and the bushes; carrying the lantern and lugging the gunnysack that grew heavier with every chicken added. She kept stuffing chickens into the gunny-sack, four to a bag, and lugging the load to the henhouse. She'd lift the drowsy birds out of the sack and shift them gently onto their new roosts. Then she'd head back to where Matilda was sniffing out more hens and roosters.

She captured every chicken Matilda located, and all the while, she kept thanking the tawny collie-dog, telling her she was wonderful at chicken-hunting. And the more she praised her, the bigger the toothy dog-smile grew.

It was a little after midnight and the catch-and-bag part of the game was done. At least, it seemed that Matilda thought so. Inside the henhouse, by dim lantern-light, Frankie counted twenty-eight hens and pullets, and half a dozen roosters. And along with the compliant and dozing hens, she had one outlier—a nasty-mouthed brooding-hen with a sizeable clutch of eggs.

Matilda had located the brooding-hen in the last play of the game; she found the grouchy hen and her nest hidden among a twisted clump of tree roots. The hen, though, wasn't in a deep slumber like her companions; she was wide awake, alert enough to bloody Frankie's hands with a few well-timed and wicked beak-strikes.

To Frankie's mind, it would have been easy enough—and probably a lot wiser—to gather up the hen and eggs in the morning, when she could see better to dodge the flashing beak. But Matilda couldn't fathom leaving the hen and her nest behind. And since Matilda had established the set of collie-dog rules for the game, Frankie felt she had no choice but to comply. She had made another trip out to the trees, a special trip for Matilda's sake, just to bring the broody-hen and her clutch to a nesting box in the henhouse.

Now, sitting there in the henhouse in the dim light of the lantern, Frankie looked at the crowd of chickens surrounding her, dozing on the roost bars and pretty much oblivious to what they had just gone through. Frankie grinned, knowing the simplicity of the hunt had a lot to do with the simplicity of a chicken's brain—they were plenty smart and clever, just like all birds were—but apparently, not once the sun went down.

She took a final count—twenty-eight hens and pullets, fourteen nested eggs, and six roosters. Thanks to Matilda's comprehension of the 'catch-a-chicken, bag-a-chicken' game, she had more than enough hens.

Frankie began the next phase of the game—the trimming-with-scissors part. She went to work with the scissors, clipping wing-feathers while Matilda looked on, grinning, apparently pleased with the idea of having more livestock to add to her list of daily duties.

Trimming wings was a job that Frankie had done plenty of times back in Indiana; it was a simple task and it was peaceful enough, sitting in the low-light of the lantern. Working away with the scissors, clipping the longest wing-feathers, listening to all the drowsy chickens uttering their night-mumbles and their sleepy slow-clucks while they dreamed their chicken-dreams.

It was a necessary job, and it was painless for the chickens. And the trimmed wings would tame them down quickly, erasing any thoughts in their chicken-brains about flapping up into trees. From all her chicken-experiences while working with her boy-cousins back on the Indiana farm, she knew the trick would be to keep the flock penned for a few days, feeding them the grains and seeds they loved—corn and oats, barley and millet. They'd 'home' to the coop again quickly.

In a few days, with their newly trimmed wings, she'd be able to release them into the meadow without any worries about them returning to the trees to roost. The 'wild' in them would be gone; they'd be eager to return to the henhouse to roost every evening.

Most of her new-found flock stayed in their dopey-drowsy state while Frankie kept trimming their wing feathers. All of them except the brooding-hen; she remained a formidable foe, continuing her sharp-beaked assault on Frankie's hands and wrists. After the broody-hen drew blood several more times, Frankie started recalling the assortment of swearwords she'd learned from the troopers at Fort Kearny—words that she had learned at various times during her stay at the fort. But there had been one particular day, while she was hiding in the stable's loft, that a whole slew of new cusswords reached her ears.

And that was when she realized that soldiers had a *whole* different way of communicating when ten-year-old girls weren't around. There had been a bunch of words new to her ears that day—and a lot with meanings she could only guess at.

But now, working in the dim light of the lantern, dealing with the furious broody-hen and wiping at the fresh blood flowing from the beak-gashes in her hands, Frankie didn't really care about the actual meanings. She used every one of those mystery-words several times around. And by the time she managed to finish trimming the bloodthirsty hen, she was pretty sure she had remembered every one of the words the troopers of Fort Kearny had unwittingly taught her.

And now, in the midst of the nasty beak-strikes, along with the wing-flapping face-slaps, Frankie reached the conclusion that those particular words seemed to help a lot—they were very handy words for such dire circumstances. Somehow, hissing those words through her teeth, making sure to apply the same emphasis the troopers used, seemed to make everything better. There was something soothing about having the power to spit out those words. And somehow, it seemed like the bleeding wounds and the sharp pains were easier to endure.

When she finally finished her task and settled the hateful old rip onto her clutch of fourteen eggs, the broody-hen gave her an ugly glare and an even uglier growl. Then she suddenly changed her pea-sized chicken-mind, and went to work sorting through her clutch, turning and rearranging the eggs until she was satisfied. She uttered a final chicken-snarl and settled herself down on her eggs.

Frankie stood watching until she tucked her head down against her wing and went to sleep; she wasn't particularly happy with the hen or her clutch of eggs. Not just because of the battle of the beak, but because the eggs had no real value right now. Given the size of her newly acquired flock, Frankie didn't really need fourteen chicks that would grow into fourteen more chickens. Nor could she use the eggs for eating, because there was no telling exactly how long the biddy had been setting them—depending on how long she had been setting the clutch, there might be partially-formed chicks inside the shells.

The best way to appease both Matilda *and* old Mrs. Swingle, she decided, was to leave things as they were. Let the moody old biddy hatch out the clutch and see what came of it. She grinned at the hen on the nest of eggs, realizing that without planning to, she had already named the mean-tempered chicken; the broody old hen had earned the name of a moody old woman from back in Indiana—old Mrs. Swingle had lived on the neighboring farm.

An hour and a half after midnight, according to her father's pocket-watch, Frankie had completed the first two parts of her chicken-gathering game—the catching-and-bagging part, and the wing-trimming part. She started on the third part—the win-them-over-with-food part. She filled several feed-pans with the grains from the barrels in the feed-room and settled the pans outside in the henyard where the chickens would find them. Then she filled the low trough with water.

With the game over, Frankie stepped out of the henyard, thinking about her henhouse full of slumbering chickens. Grinning. Because come morning when they woke, the chickens were going to be plenty surprised. It was unlikely they'd remember anything at all about the nighttime game they had been involved in—all they would know for sure, is that they were suddenly in a place where the food tasted good and it was easy to come by. Given three or four days, the whole flock would tame-down and happily settle into domesticated life once more.

So. As to that end of things, Frankie had no worries. The problem was, given the size of the coop, she already had twice as many birds as she actually wanted. And sometime soon, a batch of fourteen eggs would be hatching out. That meant she'd have way too many chickens. She stared at the chicken-yard, eyeing its dimensions, grimacing at her fortune that seemed a little 'too good'.

Her thoughts went back to the Dunbars, hoping her new neighbors would take some hens and a rooster, or two, home with them. Thinking back to the conversation she had with Everett, she decided it *might* be a possibility—because he had mentioned trying to catch these. And *that* might just mean the Dunbars would want some. *If they don't, I'm gonna be eating a lot of roasted and fried chicken, and a whole lot of eggs for weeks to come.*

Clapping her hands together and swiping at her clothes after her night's work, Frankie watched a flurry of chicken-dust and feather-scraps stir into the night air. She sniffed at the chicken-smell, wondering how much chicken-poop she actually had on her clothes. She eyed the windmill pond across the meadow and grinned. *Good time and good place for a bath.*

She closed the gate to the chicken-yard, fastening it shut to protect the hens from any prowling varmints. Thinking suddenly, about how Lillian Kinison had done the opposite; she had fastened it open to endanger the chickens, leaving them to fend for themselves in the middle of winter.

Walking over to the quiet pond, Frankie tried to figure out exactly how she had ended up with an out-of-control chicken-business. She also knew exactly what she would be fixing for dinner when Everett and Ida and their daughter came for their visit. Given the number of chickens she had, there would be a couple of chickens roasting in the Majestic oven on that day.

"You're the problem here, you crazy little stock-dog." Frankie looked at the half-grown collie-dog. She raised the wick on the lantern, sending a bright and warm glow spreading across the meadow.

"In the future, try to remember you don't have to round up *every* creature you come across."

The tawny little collie-dog grinned her doggy-smile all the way to the pond; Frankie grinned back at her to show there were no hard feelings. At the pool's edge, she kicked off her boots, stripped out of her britches and shirt, and waded in. She spent some time washing away the smell of anything having to do with chickens, and then she lay back in the water, floating and relaxing while Matilda and Laughing Girl splashed in the pool near her.

When she was satisfied that she was clean and the chicken smell was gone, she washed out her shirt and trousers, picked up her boots and headed back to the house, letting the cool water drip and dry on her skin.

She draped the wet clothes over the clothesline, walked up the bedroom porch and into the door of her bedroom—the room just behind the kitchen. This, she realized, would be her first night in her own home. In her meadow. Out here all by herself in the Sand Hills of the Nebraska Territory.

For the next two days, Frankie worked and ate, and worked some more. In the evenings, she saddled Fanny or Rock, took her rifle and rode up onto the prairie beyond her secluded meadow, learning about each of the different tracks that led up and out of her home meadow.

The track she had followed into the meadow was the main entrance, wider than the others and with a gentle rise and curve that traveled up from the ford on the North Loup River. There were three other tracks—two that rose steep and twisting up the valley's side slopes—one on the eastern hillside behind the house and the other on the western slope behind the barn. The third track ran out of the front meadow and through the center of the fenced pastures in the second meadow; it continued into a third broad meadow where it branched off into several tracks trailing up the hillsides.

To Frankie's thinking, it was a handy thing to have several ways to enter and leave the home meadow. Given that each track came in from a different direction, there would never be a time she would find herself trapped in her meadow by any drifts that winter storms might leave behind—no matter which way the wind blew, at least one or two of the tracks would remain open. She didn't know if Daniel Kinison planned it that way, but that was the outcome nevertheless.

It was the same way with the house; the five doorways into the house itself, plus the entrance to the stonewalled pantry-room, offered the same solution. If some of the doors were blocked by drifting snow, there would always be other doors that weren't—there would always be a way out of the house.

The meadow in the second valley, with its four fenced pastures, was bigger than the home meadow—almost twice the size. The windmill near its center, had a pair of swinging-flues rigged to serve a corner pond in each of the four pastures. Just like in the front valley, cottonwoods, ash and hackberry trees, along with a few maples and a couple of burr-oaks were scattered in clusters along the slopes. A large grove of trees was tucked against the western hillside in the back pasture. On closer inspection, Frankie discovered several walnut trees, a handful of small apple trees and a few mulberry trees in that grove. And to her surprise, there was one sycamore with wide-spreading branches. All were trees that were common enough back in Indiana and they were all species that she had seen along the Missouri and along the Independence Trail beside Little Blue River. Sycamores, though, had been few and far between since leaving the Little Blue. *Likely, it was the birds. Probably birds carried the seeds as they traveled up the North Loup River.*

The third valley beyond that, had a meadow that was wide and open, rich with hard-grass, and a few groves of trees sprinkled along the valley slopes. There was no operating well, but it looked like Daniel had started working on one. Lumber for a wind-mill, already cut and sized, was stacked beside a low fence.

The low fence surrounded a hole that looked to be five or six feet deep. Near the fenced-in hole, she could see an area about the size of the windmill pond had been lined out. There too, Daniel Kinison had been digging, starting another retaining pond similar to the one in the front meadow. *More plans. More ideas for more livestock.*

Frankie was starting to get an idea of the area of her claim; given that Daniel had been working out here on this project, she was pretty sure that this meadow was also part of her homestead. From what she had heard of the conversations in the big house back in Indiana, she was sure that her homestead had four quarter-sections—160 acres each—which meant she had a full-section of 640 acres. And it seemed like her section encompassed all three valleys.

The workings on the future well seemed to verify it. And the handful of turkey-foot corner-stakes she located suggested the same thing. That is, at least, if she was reading them right. But when it came down to it, she knew she had very little knowledge about homestead surveys and section-marking.

She had listened to the discussions between her uncle and older cousins, and there had been talk about such things among the men of the wagon party, but she knew little beyond that. She had not paid much attention to talk about surveys and markers and acreage. Nor had she ever studied the documents and land titles for her homestead—those were all hidden in the secret place in the wagon where they had been secured when her family left their home in Indiana.

Now, she realized, it was time to start studying such things— it was time to learn about sections and quarter-sections, acres and property-lines. And section-markers. She decided that as soon as she was settled-in a little more, she'd better spend some time looking through the land documents.

Later on, if she needed help understanding those things about her homestead, she was sure that Everett Dunbar would be able to help her. If he and Ida turned out to be the kind of people she thought they were, they might just be the best people to turn to for that kind of information.

For now though, she would let things lie; she didn't want to sound like a lost little kid who didn't know where she was. She'd ask later, when they knew her better. And when she knew *them* better.

During her evening explorations, Frankie found the highest point on what she believed was her homestead; it was a hill about a hundred yards west of the second valley, considerably higher than the hills around it. She named it her Lookout Hill, and along with its useful height, it was unique in several ways. The hilltop itself was long and wide, offering plenty of space to move about while she scanned the realm of the Sand Hills from all directions. There was also plenty of room and plenty of grass for a horse to graze upon while she looked out to the far hills. And there was an outcropping of rocks at the crest of the hill, just along the southern slope.

Three large rocks and a cluster of smaller rocks. To Frankie's mind, they didn't really have any business being there, because none of the other sandy-soiled hills had rocks—none that she had come across anyway. But whatever the reason, and by whatever ancient means, they had ended up there on her Lookout Hill. She decided they would be pretty handy things; already, they had proven to be perfect for sitting on. Perfect for standing upon, while she scanned the land around her. And she discovered, they were also perfect as picnic-rocks—a perfect place to spread out whatever little supper she pulled out of her saddlebags.

She spent a lot of time on the crest of the Lookout Hill on those evenings, learning the lay of the land. Surveying the vast landscape of the Sand Hills, watching the land that seemed to move like water, flowing under the ripple of the grasses.

When she wasn't viewing the vast realm of the far hills from the Lookout Hill, she spent time riding the banks of the river that flowed through her place, traveling both upriver and downriver along the North Loup. Learning about the depths and bends and coves of her river; watching the movement of the wildlife and the game-trails along her river.

A little more than a mile upriver, she found a mass of dead trees and limbs—a huge mountain of them—that had been washed up in one of the bends of the river. Probably, Frankie decided, left there after some massive water-flow years and years before. *And likely, more wood will keep flowing into the cove every year. Getting tangled up into the base. Adding to the mountain of wood all the time.*

She felt her crooked-grin forming. The sight pleased her; it was beyond her homestead, at least according to what the section markers seemed to indicate. But since she was the last homestead upriver, according to Everett Dunbar, it was land no one owned. So she made a mental note. *Firewood and fenceposts.* She grinned. *Lots of firewood! Lots of fence posts!*

Further upriver, she found three different coves with wide bands of smooth river-rocks. Sitting on Fanny's back, eyeing the long ribbons of rock following the curves of the river—or maybe creating them—Frankie figured they must have been deposited by some ancient glacier. Or maybe some great earth-shift. Because that was how such things in landscapes happened. That would be her father's assessment of the situation. 'Wrought by some ancient circumstance,' he'd say.

However it came into being, and given what she had been seeing, the sight of the rocky coves seemed oddly out of place out here in the Sand Hills. But it *did* explain where Daniel Kinison found the rocks for the stone-buildings and the fireplaces and the garden wall. Like the cove with the mountain of wood, Frankie made a mental note of the bends of the river with the bands of river-rocks too. And she made another mental note about how the Sand Hills seemed to have all kinds of odd little mysteries and surprises.

Closer to her home meadow, there had been another surprise along the river's banks. But this time, it was a manmade surprise. Something she had first seen from her wagon-seat on the evening she arrived. She had seen rows of trees on each side of the track as she had forded the pretty North Loup River—three long rows of trees running parallel to the river bank, upriver from the ford. Three more rows on the downriver side.

When she finally had the time, she rode Rock down to the river and wandered among the rows of trees downriver from the ford. Once she saw the bark and leaves, along with what was growing on the branches, she started smiling. Three rows of nut trees—one row of black walnuts and two of hazelnuts. A dozen to each row. There were already nuts showing on a good number of the trees—not a lot, but some. And that, probably explained the two barrels holding nuts in the root-cellar. Which told her the trees were at least four or five years old, and that meant every year from now on, there would be more and more nuts. She sat on Rock's back, feeling her crooked little grin getting bigger. *That's a mighty nice thing for the future of any homestead.*

When she explored the rows upriver from the ford, she found more reasons to smile. Apple trees. Three rows of apple trees. Twelve in each row. And like the trees downriver from the ford, they were standing in their rows, lined up and looking just like soldiers at Assembly at Fort Kearny.

Figuring them to be two or three years old when Daniel Kinison planted them, Frankie thought they were probably seven or eight years old now. In the moisture and the rich soil beside the river, they had been growing fast and were already producing plenty of fruit. There looked to be a lot of apples hanging in the branches, which meant there would be plenty of apples going into the root-cellar this year. And best of all, there would be plenty more in the years to come. She grinned, picturing bins of apples in the root-cellar; picturing baked apples and apple pies and apple crisps coming out of the oven.

Munching on a ripening apple as she rode further downriver, Frankie had another surprise. She found more rows of trees—more walnuts and hazelnuts and apple trees. And two rows of young mulberry trees. All the trees in these rows were younger than the trees by her ford—maybe a couple of years younger—but they were planted in rows that looked exactly the same as the plantings on her land.

Unfortunately, they were not her trees—because she knew they were almost a hundred yards beyond the marker that designated her eastern section-line. Frankie sat there on Rock's broad back, staring at the rows, trying to figure out who had planted them. It didn't make sense that Kinison would have planted these trees beyond his own section. And yet, there was no one else who could own them—there were no other homesteads between her place and the Dunbar place some ten miles downriver. But the trees must belong to *someone*.

She rode further downriver, expecting to see signs of a homestead, maybe a small house hidden among the riverside trees. Or a dugout in one of the slopes of a hill out from the riverbank. She looked for some indication that someone had been working a claim in the area. But she saw nothing of interest except a bevy of swans swimming in the deep shade of a riverbend. She made a mental note about the swans though, suspecting they might frequent the quiet bend in the river. Because swans provided a lot of meat for the cost of a single shotgun-shell; far more than a single duck or goose.

She rode back to her meadow, puzzling over the mystery-neighbor—someone who planted trees, but had no home.

After three days, Frankie had emptied the Conestoga of all the household items. She had even managed to move the four large oak-barrels filled with corn and oats, beans and rice. She started by transferring all the grain from the first barrel into buckets and washtubs and empty crates; then, with a lot of grunting and groaning, she rolled the empty oak-barrel out the tailgate of the Conestoga, onto the veranda and into the stone-room pantry. She used a long branch as a pry-pole, and with some more grunting and groaning, she tipped it upright again. She shoved and scooted it under one of the long counters and then refilled it from the buckets and washtubs. And then, barrel by barrel, she repeated the process.

Any of the trunks and crates proving too heavy or awkward received the same treatment. It wasn't a hard process, but Frankie found it more than a little annoying. It was tedious and time consuming, and it made for a lot of trips back and forth. But in the end, it was done right and done well, and she was satisfied, And that was the feeling she wanted.

Thinking about the bare bunks in the Barracks, she carried the two narrow mattresses from the wagon and settled them on two of the bunks in the Barracks. Then she dragged a few of the heavy food-crates to use as tables beside the bunks and nailed smaller wooden-crates on the walls for shelves. She looked around her, staring at the other bunks, realizing that at some time, someday, she'd need to have more mattresses. *If I ever have men staying here in the Barracks, I'll have to get some more. Maybe make some out of corn-*

shucks. Or maybe, save up chicken-feathers. She grinned. *Well, no hurry. That's probably a long way off.*

Late in the afternoon of the third day, Frankie hitched Sunny Jim and Little Bub to the Conestoga and backed the wagon to the barn entrance. The last items in the wagon were the long planks Corporal Buchanan and the troopers had fashioned as a second-level floor in the wagon-box.

Frankie studied the hay-hook-turned-lumber-lifter that Daniel Kinison had rigged in the barn; she understood the concept, but she wasn't at all sure of the mechanics of operating it; nor, did she believe she had the strength or body-weight to hoist any loads of planks. After eyeing it for a few minutes, she decided she wasn't willing to spend any great amount of time trying it out. Not for the time being, anyway.

Instead, she decided to do what she knew—she knew how to carry boards. There was nothing confusing about it. So she started pulling the planks from the tail-gate of the Conestoga and carried and dragged them, one by one, up the loft-staircase. It made for a lot of trips—three dozen trips—up and down the stairs, but in the end, with all the planks stacked with the other lumber in the loft, Frankie was satisfied. Looking at the new planks she had added to the stacks, she felt the pleasure of the job being done, and done well. It was the last of the unloading; the last part of moving in; the last part of being done. The Conestoga was empty of its cargo. She was officially home and settled in.

So. The journey was done; she had found her homestead; she had moved into the home she had been searching for—the home that she had been longing for. Finally, she had what she had fought for. Finally, she had something permanent.

She grinned at Matilda and Laughing Girl who had been following her up and down the stairs on every trip. Beside her, or behind her, all the way. Much like they had done during the journey home— staying with her all the way. She felt tears starting to roll down her cheeks. Satisfaction. Happiness. Relief. She stood there in the loft, looking around at *her* loft and *her* barn.

Looking at the new stack of boards, her mind went to another time and another place. Back to Fort Kearny. To the Independence Day Celebration and the night of the dance. Because the planks had come from the dancefloor. Her troopers had loaded some of the dancefloor boards from that night into her wagon, using them as a false-floor in the wagon-box to create more room for more supplies.

They had spirited the boards and the supplies away from Fort Kearny, probably under the cover of night. They had been working with Mr. Wheaton out on Fort Farm Island to ready the Conestoga for her trip, working to keep it a secret. Working to protect her. Trying to get her away from the fort and the dangers lurking there.

Frankie stared at the boards, knowing her troopers would have had other thoughts about the boards too. They had ideas that went beyond the boards being used as a false-floor in the wagon for storing supplies. Their thoughts had gone beyond that immediate use—they had included the planks for her to use on her new homestead, in case she needed them. For shelter, or maybe, for livestock pens. Because they had no idea where she was going. And they had no idea what she would need when she got there.

There had been a desperate haste back then to get everything together for her. There had been a lot of unknowns, but they had done the best they could. They had loaded her wagon with supplies, trying to think of anything that would make her life easier.

Frankie swiped at the tears trailing down her cheeks. It was Corporal Buchanan and Thomas Denning who had seen to most of the planning and the loading. And Thomas Bates and Will Trask. And Travers—Septimus Travers—with the gray-brown eyes and the slow smile and the quick wink.

The tears came faster and Frankie settled herself down on the floor of the loft; she hugged Matilda tight against her. And she let the tears come.

Frankie didn't know how long she had been there in the loft, but when the tears finally subsided, her arms around Matilda's neck were salty and wet and Matilda's pretty white ruff was damp. But at least, Frankie knew, her mind was clear, and she figured her heart had done some healing too. And she knew something else—the crying sessions and her life at Fort Kearny were done. They were in the past; *this* was her life now. And here at this homestead, deep in the Sand Hills of the Nebraska Territory, was where her mind would keep clearing and her heart would keep healing. Because this was home.

Frankie wiped at the tears and wiped at her nose. There was still work to do. There were things to finish up. Because company was coming on the day after tomorrow. She stood up and trotted down the stairs.

She moved the big wagon around to the rear entrance of the barn and led Little Bub and Sunny Jim into the alleyway, pulling the big blue-green Conestoga into the long barn. Then, steadily and carefully, she backed them, easing the wagon into its very own place in the very back corner of the barn by the big doors. Easing it into its new home where it could rest after the long journey. Where it could rest after carrying the family cargo all the way from Indiana— across the prairie, across the wide Platte River, across the Nebraska Territory, and deep into the Sand Hills.

With the massive blue-green wagon settled into its proper place and the horses unhitched, unharnessed and released to graze in the summer grasses, Frankie walked back to the house with the last of her precious items from the wagon—she had the two wolf-hides draped across her shoulders and the three arrows clutched in her hand.

Two of the arrows had come from the burned-out homestead beside the South Loup River; the third arrow and the wolf-hides had come from her own little battle-ground beside the clear little creek on the Cheyenne Trail, just about a week earlier. As she walked through the meadow grass toward the kitchen porch, Laughing Girl pranced along beside her, grinning her wolfhound-grin at the sight of the wolves she had stood down. Frankie grinned back at her. Together, they had proven to be a pretty good wolf-hunting team.

The wolf-hides, Frankie decided, would look nice on the porch, one on each side of the kitchen door. So that's where she put them; she pounded the nails into the porch wall and hung the hides. The arrows, though, she wanted on the sitting-room mantel, right beside the tooled-leather box. She stood them in a row with their feathered ends down and their arrowheads up.

And then she went to work on her other treasures. The other special things she had found along the Cheyenne Trail and had brought with her to their new home. She sat down at the trestle-table in the kitchen and cleaned the glass in the gold-scroll frame she had found in the collapsed soddy in the hidden valley, way back in her first days on the Cheyenne Trail. She worked the nails loose from the frame's backing and wiped the dust and dirt from the golden scroll-work.

She had been hoping the pretty-colored map, the treasure map that had shown her the way home, would fit into the gold frame. It was the map Captain Jack Connell had given to her—the one that had traveled safely in the spyglass case all the way from Fort Kearny. To her delight and relief, it did. *It fits quite nicely. Perfect, in fact.*

She took the last drink of buttermilk from the glass beside her, grinning at her luck while she went to work on the frame again. Working at the tiny nails again, wiggling them back into their little holes to hold the wooden-backing in place.

Holding the finished product at arm's length, Frankie looked at the result. She liked the look and she was awfully happy with the outcome. And thinking about it, she decided that having the map and the frame fitting together so perfectly, really shouldn't have been such a surprise. Because in one way or another, a lot of things about her journey had come together in a perfect way. It had been that way all along. But this *was* a nice piece of luck. And it was a reminder of what her cousin Isaiah use to say. 'Everything's always fine in the end. If it's not fine, then it's not the end.'

It was late in the evening as Frankie Harding balanced herself on a chair in front of the fireplace in the sitting-room and tacked a nail into the wall above the mantle; she settled the pretty gold-frame with its pretty-colored map—her treasure map—onto the nail. Straightened it. Asked Matilda if she thought it was hanging straight. Matilda gave her toothy dog-grin and Frankie climbed down from the chair.

When she stepped back and studied the mantle above the fireplace, she liked the sight. The prettily-colored map looked perfect hanging right beside the arrows and above the tooled-leather box. The little purple bottle that had been in the dirt beside the frame in the caved-in soddy, stood on the mantle right beneath the picture and right between the leather box and the Indian arrows. They all looked fine, because, Frankie decided, they all belonged together. Those, along with the wolf-hides, were the testaments of the last leg of her journey. *So it must be the end. Because everything is fine.*

She went to bed then, knowing that she'd sleep deeply. Like the other nights, she left all the doors and windows wide open, letting the night air drift through and around the house, sweeping away everything old and stale. By her figuring, tonight, the house was officially and completely hers. Tonight, any of the old and bitter memories left behind in the house would be swept out—the swirling breath of the night-wind would move through the house and clear out everything that was old and angry.

The night-winds would flow; the prairie-winds that traveled thousands of miles across the Sand Hills would drift across her while she slept; the breezes that swept along the hillsides and rippled through the low meadows would blanket her in the night.

She went to her room and stretched out on her bed, feeling the caress of the night air rippling across the bed linens. Prairie air.

On the fourth morning, Frankie woke up thinking about the Dunbars' upcoming visit. *They'll be here tomorrow. My fifth morning.*

Before she was even out of bed, she was thinking about what she should wear, thinking about what she should make for the meals. Thinking about how she would explain everything.

She kept reminding herself how sincere the Dunbars seemed. They had been kind. Everett had even offered to show her the way to her homestead. Lying on the bed, staring out the open doorway that showed the grasses glittering with morning dew, Frankie realized she was actually more excited than worried—she was more pleased at the thought of spending time with these neighbors, than nervous about it.

Out in the coop, the oldest rooster, the Dominicker with the best adult crow, that she had named the Bugler, was crowing his head off. Frankie grinned as the cockerels made a few squawky crows. She pulled on her boots and nothing else, and walked to the outhouse. Then she strolled over to the windmill pond and relaxed in the water, scrubbed her hair with sand and soap. Splashed in a wild romping game with Laughing Girl and Matilda.

After that, she wandered over to greet Trumpeter, promising he'd go out to pasture very soon. And maybe, just maybe, he would be visiting the mares. She milked Blossom in the stanchion in the barn and released her and Primrose into the pasture with the four oxen. For a while, she stood leaning against the board fence, watching Bo and Benjamin, Buck and Billy, already well into their morning grazing, wading through the grass, filling their bellies. Looking content with what they had in front of them.

Frankie figured that in another hour, they'd settle down into the grass on their bellies and chests and start working their cuds. *You can tell your cows are on good pasture when they're chewing cud by ten o'clock in the morning.* That's what her Uncle James always said and she'd never heard anyone argue the point.

By the time she walked over to the chicken-house, the sun was showing over the valley wall. As she neared the coop, she had her first surprise of the day. Five hens and two pullets were pacing outside the coop's fence—seven more hens that had probably been roosting somewhere else on the night of the search had decided to turn themselves in. They were giving up their wild ways. At the moment, they were pacing and head-bobbing along the chicken-wire, clucking to the chickens inside the coop—apparently frustrated at not being invited to the breakfast party beyond the wire.

Frankie hesitated, worried about getting the new hens through the gate without letting the inside chickens out. It could be a tricky business, because if even one chicken still had a wild streak and decided to dash for the open gate, others might be enticed to follow.

She weighed her options and chose her strategy. She filled a grain-bucket in the feed-room, planning to get the attention of the hens inside the coop on a pile of fresh grain, while she tried herding the new ones through the open gate.

To her surprise, she found the new hens had their own game plan; something in the back of their little chicken-brains must have been stirred, because they were waiting for her outside the feed-room door when she emerged with the grain-bucket. They scuttled and squawked along in her wake as she walked to the henyard gate, their beady little eyes fixed on the bucket she was carrying.

Tiny little brains or not, Frankie could see that the allure of easy pickings must have won over any temptation for living wild and free. The moment she eased the henyard gate open, the seven latecomers crowded past her, in a desperate rush to join the flock and claim their share of the scattered grain. Matilda stood to the side and Frankie couldn't help laughing at the expression in her eyes—a look of pure disappointment that there hadn't been a rounding-up role for her.

Adding it all up, Frankie realized she had thirty-five hens and pullets now, along with six roosters of various ages; and of course, among them, there was Mrs. Swingle, the nasty brooding-hen who was more like a snapping-turtle than a chicken. And soon to hatch, was her clutch of fourteen eggs.

Checking the nesting boxes inside the henhouse, Frankie found seven fresh-laid eggs, proving the hens were already settling in; she realized she'd be getting at least two dozen eggs a day. And that made her hope a little harder that the Dunbars, and maybe their daughter, would see fit to take some of the chickens with them when they left.

Frankie watched her chickens pecking and scratching inside the enclosure, knowing she should be thankful, but still feeling a little perturbed at the size of the flock; it was way too big for both the chickencoop and her needs. She glanced at Matilda and Laughing Girl standing beside her, watching the chickens pecking their way through their breakfast of easy-pickings.

Matilda's eyes were fixed on the flock; she was smiling her doggy-smile, apparently pleased with the memory of the night-game of chicken-snatching. Frankie wondered if the tawny little collie-dog would ever come to the conclusion that more livestock actually meant more work for her. But so far, Matilda had never complained about having too many animals, or too much work.

With the outside work done, Frankie headed into the house; she pulled on a pair of britches and Captain Connell's Cavalry-shirt. She brushed and braided her hair, and then spent a good part of the morning reacquainting herself with the big cookstove and its ovens. Over the last couple of days, she had made coffee and done some frying on the stovetop, but today, she was planning on giving herself a little practice with the oven. Because tomorrow, company was coming.

First on her list were peach pies—because she loved peach pie—and she figured the Dunbars would too. And as it was, she had plenty of canned peaches—the troopers of Fort Kearny had seen fit to load cases of canned peaches into the Conestoga. They all knew she favored peaches, and they had outdone themselves; they had loaded cases, and cases, and even more cases, into the wagon-bed for her journey.

So Frankie opened several cans and got busy making peach pies. With the fresh eggs, she made a couple batches of cornbread and several pans of biscuits. She started a pot of dried beans soaking at the back of the range.

Looking to the timing of things for the next day, Frankie figured the Dunbars would start out for their visit as soon as they finished their morning chores; with nine or ten miles to travel, Frankie figured they would probably pull into the meadow sometime in the middle of the morning. Being a full-moon night, they would likely stay until dark, waiting for moonrise, then drive home by the light of the full moon. So she decided to have an early midday meal soon after they arrived. And then a big dinner in the late afternoon.

There were three skinned rabbits hanging in the stone-room—thanks to Laughing Girl's hunts along the valley hillsides—so Frankie decided to make rabbit stew in the cast-iron kettle, figuring she could leave it to simmer slowly on the stovetop through the morning while the beans baked in the oven. The stew and a platter of biscuits would take care of the early midday meal with the Dunbars.

Then, it would be a matter of keeping the oven stoked so in the afternoon, she could set a couple of chickens to roasting, with sweet potatoes and onions and squash tucked in the Dutch-oven with them. The beans would finish baking while the chickens and vegetables roasted. That, she figured, along with the cornbread, ought to be plenty for the late dinner. Then they'd have the peach pie with whipped cream and sweet-coffee for dessert.

Frankie had a strategy at work; she was thinking that preparing a couple of meals might show these new neighbors she could take care of herself. And the clincher of the whole meal deal, might just be the peach pie. Clear out here on the homesteads, at this time of year, supplies of store-bought goods would be running low. She doubted the Dunbars had the makings for peach pie.

Another part of her strategy was to load them up with butter and milk when they left, since according to Ida, they didn't have a milk cow. And she could send a basket of eggs too, if they needed them. On top of that, Frankie was thinking, that with any luck, they might just take a couple of burlap sacks of live hens.

In the afternoon, Frankie moved the three bay mares and Fanny from the open meadow into the front-pasture; she turned the Shires and the three mules into the fenced pasture beyond it and sent the other geldings, Boone, Rock, Solomon and Samson out to join them.

With all the animals out to pasture, except for Trumpeter, she climbed to the top-rail of the fence and watched her livestock for a while. They were settled in three of the four pastures, all grazing in the belly-deep meadow grass, their heads were down and they were filling their bellies. Trumpeter, the only stallion, was still in the front barn-lot.

The fencing in the four large pastures was post-and-plank, the fence-lines were neat and strong and straight. Daniel Kinison had allowed space for a broad track that ran down the middle of the valley, with two pastures to each side. In the center of the meadow, to one side of the track, stood the homestead's second windmill.

And that was where the whole business of the water-flues began. The long flue that snaked its way along the board fence toward the holding pond in the garden and the troughs in the back-lot of the barn started there. But there were two shorter flues connected to the windmill tower, too; they were rigged to swing out like wooden arms—each one could be maneuvered to fill two different ponds. So every pasture had as much water as needed.

Water-flues. Frankie knew that's what they were called; she had heard of them, but she'd never seen them before. Her family never had them back in Indiana. The flues allowed for the transfer of water, and here, Daniel Kinison had put together a whole system that would save a person from toting a lot of water buckets.

Frankie watched the windmill out in the middle of the meadow, watching the sails turning in the steady wind that blew overhead; she didn't know all the mechanics and the ins-and-outs of the windmills. Not yet. But she *had* figured out how to pull the long lever that either released the head of the windmill to turn and the water to flow, or served as a brake to lock it into place—she had figured that out two days earlier.

She had figured out some things about the garden, too—Daniel Kinison had made work easier there, too; the flue filled the holding pond, and by lifting either one of two small wooden gates in the holding-pond walls, you could release water into different sections of the garden. The water would flow right down the garden rows. All of which meant there would be no need to tote water-pails there, either. And that, Frankie decided, would be something Isabelle would think was a wonderful idea. Because watering plants in Isabelle's garden behind the little cottage at Fort Kearny required a lot of pail toting.

For a few minutes, Frankie let her mind roam back to the south, back down the Cheyenne Trail. Back to Fort Kearny. Back to Isabelle and her garden. To her Lieutenant and the Captain and Major Maxwell. To Trask and Travers, always together, always watching out for her. She felt her throat tightening and the tears rising. She pushed the tears back down. *Not now. Not when I have work to do.*

She turned her thoughts to her livestock. The animals out in the grass looked to be plenty satisfied. The oxen and Blossom had already settled down in the grass on their chests, working on their cuds, relaxed and content. Glancing up to the sun, Frankie knew it was just past ten—the grazing in both the meadow and the pasture was good.

Now, she had Trumpeter to think about; she was of half a mind to release him into the front-pasture with the mares. But she wasn't sure about the timing for breeding. Releasing him to the mares now, meant the mares would have their foals late next June, or in early July. In the minds of some horsemen, it would be better to wait and breed for the following year. Back in Indiana, her uncle liked for foals to be dropped in April and May, when the weather was mild. But the weather way out here in the Nebraska Territory, Frankie knew, might be a lot different and she had no idea what to expect.

Sitting there on the fence, thinking about it, she decided to ask Everett Dunbar for his advice. If he didn't see a problem with late June or July foals out here, then she'd turn Trumpeter out with the mares. Plus, it might be a good thing if Everett thought she was smart enough to seek advice. Anyone new to homesteading in this area— man, woman or child—would need advice about the weather.

Liking the idea about asking Everett for advice, she climbed down from the fence and headed for the chickencoop. She had some butchering to do if she wanted a chicken dinner tomorrow. She needed to have a couple of chicken carcasses hanging in the pantry today.

The next morning—the morning of the Dunbars' visit—Frankie worked on Boone's wound, just like she had done each morning. She milked Blossom and turned her and Primrose out to pasture; she fed the chickens and collected eggs. By sunup, she had the root vegetables and two chickens in a roasting pan, sitting on a counter in the pantry.

At nine o'clock, according to the mantle clock, she stoked the Majestic to the level she wanted and set the rabbit stew to simmering on the back burner.

She separated the cream and brought up the butter in a jar; she pressed the butter into the mold and poured the buttermilk into a pitcher.

Then, she washed up in her room and found herself standing in front of the washstand mirror, looking at her reflection, wondering if she could pull it all off, wondering if she could start things right. Wondering if the Dunbars would understand. *Oh, please God. Please. Help them understand.*

She changed into her blue-green dress—the dress that Isabelle had made for the Independence Day celebration. She combed out her hair and re-braided it, her mind still on Isabelle. Thinking about how beautiful and bright she had looked on the afternoon of the celebration in her own blue-green dress. Picturing her walking from the cottage with her hand on her husband's arm, picturing how beautiful they had both been. *My Isabelle; my Lieutenant.*

In the mirror, she could see tears welling up in her eyes. She let them spill out and watched as they trailed down her cheeks. Watching and waiting until they stopped. Waiting for the aching in her heart to stop.

When the tears stopped and the pain faded, she took a deep breath, wiped her face dry and turned away, looking around her room. She picked up her shirt and trousers and tucked them away in the wardrobe. And then she made up her bed. Because she had company coming.

She wandered around the house after that, glancing around the rooms, moving things that didn't need to be moved. Trying to stay busy, because now, she was getting nervous. Because there was no doubt that today was a day when she would be scrutinized and studied. The Dunbars and their daughter, and maybe their son-in-law if he was back, would form their thoughts and opinions about a ten-year-old girl living alone on a homestead. The way everything went today, would have a major impact on how she lived in this area.

Finally, Frankie decided she had worried enough. She decided to get to work and forget about her concerns. She would handle whatever might come up, as it came up. For now, though, she knew she needed to be busy and she figured she probably had a couple of hours before her neighbors drove into her meadow.

She headed out to the barn with two ideas in mind. The first idea was for an outside table on the veranda, and to do that, she needed some pulling power. The second idea would play a part in the first, and it was something she had been avoiding since she had arrived at her homestead—she needed to learn how to work a mule.

It was time to get over that hurdle. People talked about how different mules could act in-harness compared to a horse in-harness. She decided, she might as well use mule-power today; it was time to see how different things actually were.

She chose the sad-eyed Aloysius as her mule-minded instructor for the day; she brought him up from the back-pasture, walking down the center track and thinking that maybe working a mule after she had just changed into a clean dress, might not be a particularly wise choice. But it was done. And it was entirely possible the Dunbars would drive in while she was working the mule, and if that happened, she didn't want to be in a shirt and britches. Because that didn't fit with her plan. Because today, the truth had to come out.

She led Aloysius to the tailgate of the Conestoga, harnessed him, and then hitched him to the low stone-sled; she walked him up the barn alley with the sled sliding along the hardpacked dirt behind him, watching him for any odd reactions. Watching for warning signs. Trying to spot any sign he was going to erupt into some kind of mule-minded frenzy. Or maybe a sign that he was intending to go into a mule-minded balk. But she saw no warning signs; she saw no problems. She saw nothing that seemed to concern Aloysius at all.

At the front entrance next to the workshop, she tipped one of the long workbenches onto the sled, watching to see if anything about the idea or the noise bothered the mule. It didn't. Aloysius just waited, patient and sensible.

With the bench lying on its side on the sled, Frankie led her mule across the meadow, heading toward the house. Aloysius walked along beside her, bobbing his head and flopping his long ears while the sled slipped through the grass behind them. When she turned him in front of the house and eased him and the sled right next to the porch, he seemed perfectly fine with the process.

With the sled beside the front porch, Frankie tipped the bench off the sled, leaning it up onto the porch floor. Aloysius stood quietly and watched her. When she scooted and dragged the workbench, heaving and yanking it into its new position in front of the wall-bench, her mule didn't seem to mind that either. He just watched her, looking as if he were trying to tell her that if she was fine with the whole deal, then he was too.

Frankie led her sad-eyed mule back to the barn with the sled still sliding behind them and Aloysius still being patient and sensible. And once, when she glanced back at him, she realized he had put on a good amount of weight in the last week. Looking out to the back pasture, she could see the other mules were showing the same kind of weight gain. She shook her head, feeling a little silly for not noticing before now. In the midst of all the settling in, and unloading, and exploring the homestead, she hadn't stopped to assess the weight gain. Looking at the mules now, she saw that there had been a big change.

Aloysius and the other two mules, Artemis and Septimus, had shown up in her life bone-skinny and in bad shape while she had been traveling north on the Cheyenne Trail. But looking at their condition now, Frankie thought they might be more than halfway back to their true weight. The grass on the valley floor had given them most of what they needed, but the remedies and the daily ration of corn, oats and molasses had played a part too.

She made a second trip to the house, repeating the process with the sled, but this time she brought the long wagon-bench that had traveled with the Conestoga. She and Aloysius went through the same maneuvers beside the kitchen porch and Frankie settled it in front of her new porch-table.

The workbench-turned-table and the wall-bench and the wagon-bench, fit right between the kitchen and sitting-room windows, looking as if they belonged there. Reminding her of the table and benches that had been on the deep veranda of the Indiana house. Reminding her of the Sunday afternoon meals with her family on the veranda of that big white house. That memory alone made every minute of the hauling and grunting and heaving worthwhile.

Frankie stood looking at the table and benches, thinking that the idea had turned out better than she expected. It was a good thing. And there was another good thing—she had worked her first mule in-harness. It had been a fine lesson for both her and Aloysius. The mule had learned a little about her, and she had learned a little about mules. Aloysius had listened to her voice and he had paid attention to her cues, and all in all, he seemed to be just fine with the concept of cooperating.

And mostly, it seemed as though the mule was genuinely surprised that all she was requiring from him was to drag a light sled for a couple of trips back and forth from the barn to the house. Thinking about it, Frankie figured that as a former freight mule, he would have pulled heavily loaded wagons for ten-hours a day, for six or seven days a week. She stroked his neck for a few minutes after they were done; she whispered to him, thanking him. And sad-eyed Aloysius, seemed just fine with that too.

She was circling him and the sled, heading back to the barn to unhitch and unharness when both Matilda and Laughing Girl stood up suddenly; they froze in place, staring toward the front track. They growled low, giving a warning that told Frankie that someone was coming up from the ford. Frankie watched the meadow's entrance, pretty sure of what she'd be seeing in a few minutes. Likely, the neighbors had arrived.

Matilda gave her deep-throated growl and the blond-brindle wolfhound curled her lips back, showing her nasty set of fangs; she gave her wicked snarl and started stalking stiff-legged toward the meadow's entrance, hackles raised.

A moment later, Sunny Jim called out his customary greeting. An instant after that, the bay mare, Belle, neighed loud and clear, her pretty voice ringing out across the meadow.

Frankie stepped back to the porch and lifted the Henry rifle from inside the kitchen door. Just in case, it wasn't the Dunbars. She watched the dogs and she watched the entrance to her valley. Trumpeter called a challenge from the front barn-lot.

A moment later, a seal-brown mare pulling a spring-wagon came into view. Frankie saw Everett and Ida Dunbar on the wagon-seat; she could see the smiles on their faces as the mare trotted around and down, following the track into the meadow. She smiled back and waved to the couple. To her neighbors. Feeling excited and nervous at the same time—because the moment of reckoning had come.

Frankie took in a long, slow breath, leaned the rifle against the porch post and walked back to Aloysius. She twisted the lead-rope over the hames in a couple of half-hitches. She brushed the dust from her hands and her dress. Knowing it was time.

As she walked toward the wagon, she saw Everett and Ida Dunbar looking around the valley, seeming a little perplexed. No doubt, they were looking for someone else; they had been expecting to see an adult or two—and probably, a little boy about her size. And maybe, a couple of other kids.

Everett pulled his mare to a stop near the front of the Barracks. He set the brake and looked around again. No one was coming from the house or calling from the barn; no one was walking out from any of the buildings to greet the new neighbors. There was only a little girl in a blue-green dress walking toward them.

Frankie stopped in front of the mare, motioned for the dogs to stay back. She waited, watching the two people who seemed so nice. Watching the couple she had met down along the track about ten miles downriver. It was just the two of them. No daughter and no son-in-law. Frankie breathed a little sigh of relief, thinking that the day might be a lot easier if it was just these two people visiting.

Her new neighbors stayed on the seat of the wagon for a minute, still looking around. Clearly surprised. Maybe even confused—because meeting one's neighbors was a big moment way out here on the homesteads. And yet, there was no family coming out to greet them.

Finally, their eyes drifted back to her; they were still looking a little confused and a little unsure. They had been waving and smiling when they drove into the meadow, but now, their smiles had faded as it dawned on them that there was no one else. No one else would be coming out to greet them.

Frankie stepped closer to the mare's head and slipped her fingers under the cheek-strap of the bridle. She stroked the mare's face. She took a deep breath, and then she looked steadily at the two people sitting on the wagon-seat. Looking first at Everett, and then at Ida—her new neighbors. The kindness was still there. She had liked them when she met them five days ago, and today, she knew she had read them right. These were people her Uncle James and her Aunt Sarah would have liked; people who Isabelle and her Lieutenant would like. These were people who would be good neighbors to have.

"You're looking for my family. And my family's not coming." Frankie took another breath. "I think you should step down and stretch your legs. And then we should sit and talk for a while. There are things I need to tell you; things you need to hear." Frankie spoke the words quietly. Carefully. Looking into Ida's soft blue-gray eyes.

It was Ida Dunbar who asked the first question; she asked it straight-forward and gently.

"Are *you* Frankie, then?" Her eyes were soft and encouraging.

And somehow, Frankie thought Ida Dunbar looked like she was a little relieved, like maybe she wasn't so surprised after all. Like maybe, somewhere deep down inside of her, something had been niggling at her.

"Yes, Ma'am. I'm Frankie. It's short for Frances but nobody calls me that. It's always been Frankie. Frankie Harding." She looked at the woman with the gray hair and the blue-gray eyes, looking steadily at her for a moment. Letting her decide what she needed to decide; letting her have time to make her choice.

"Well then, Miss Frankie Harding. I agree with you. Maybe we *should* sit down and talk for a while. And I'm hoping you have a pot of coffee on, because I haven't had a cup in more than a month." She smiled softly. It was a smile that told Frankie that Ida Dunbar wasn't upset at all; the smile said that she was pleased with how Frankie

83

was handling the situation, even if she wasn't exactly sure what the situation was.

The tall milk tin and the low crock were sitting on the porch table where Frankie and the Dunbars were drinking coffee. Ida had brought back the containers Frankie had handed to them at their first meeting—containers that had been filled with milk and butter. And typical of country neighbors, Ida hadn't brought them back empty. She had filled them with flowers from her garden.

For almost a half hour, Frankie had been explaining everything. Explaining why she let them think she was a boy when they first met, explaining that traveling in boy's clothes usually proved to be safer. She told them she had learned to be careful about saying too much, too soon. She had learned to let people think what they might think, because it was typically safer that way.

And then she explained why her family wouldn't be coming. She told them the story, letting them know the truth. Telling them her family *was*, actually, still south—they were still back on the trail as she had told them five days ago. But they wouldn't be coming, she explained, because of the fever. Because they were buried beside the Little Blue River. And Everett and Ida understood; Ida nodded and Everett reached to pat her hand. He nodded and looked away and Frankie thought she saw tears welling up in his eyes.

So Frankie talked on, telling them how her family had died. And how she and her cousin Isaiah had buried her Uncle James and little Charles, and then Samuel and her Aunt Sarah. When they buried Thomas, she had done it mostly by herself, because Isaiah was feverish and weak by then. And she told them how, in the end, she had buried Isaiah by herself. She told them how she traveled on toward the homestead.

They listened. They understood. They asked their questions and Frankie answered them. Mostly, they asked about how she managed, how she had followed the trail, and how she handled the harnessing. And they wanted to know, how in the world, she had taken care of the livestock all by herself. And they asked about her journey, asking how she had made it so far, all alone. They had traveled out West by wagon and team, the same as she had, so their questions were drawn from their experiences, their own hardships.

Frankie talked about the fears she had lived with—the fears of having people try to stop her from coming to this homestead. She explained how she had avoided crossing paths with people as much as she could while she traveled.

She knew their concern was genuine; she also knew they had a lot of thinking to do, given what she had already told them. So she held off telling them the whole story in this one sitting; she didn't talk about the theft of her animals, nor about her river-walk in the middle of the night to recover them. Nor did she tell them about Silas Beckett. Or about the weeks the Army had detained her at Fort Kearny. Or about the legal hearing. Not yet.

Neither did she tell them about the Cheyenne Trail; she could tell they assumed she had traveled the same trail as they had—like everyone else who settled in the area, the Dunbars had come by way of Fort Cottonwood. And she let them think she had done the same. For now.

Frankie didn't intend to lie or mislead them; she answered their questions, but offered nothing beyond the basic story, because it was still too early to know *how* much was *too* much. And there was another problem lurking in the back of Frankie's mind. She still had concerns about the wagon-driving son-in-law; something about him still made her feel uneasy, and until she knew more, she didn't want him hearing too much about her. Just in case she was right about him.

So she told them there was more she'd tell them another time. They nodded; they were satisfied with the story. And Frankie figured their minds were probably full enough with what she had already told them. They had probably heard enough to hold them for a while; they already had plenty of things to mull over.

They spent another hour together talking about a lot of things while they drank their coffee—homestead things and neighbor things and weather things. And Frankie noticed a few things about the Dunbars. When they started sipping at their cups of coffee, she saw a dreamy look rise up in their eyes—which made sense, since Ida had mentioned they had been out of coffee for over a month.

She also noticed that they had been sniffing at the rising aroma from the simmering dinner as it wafted through the screen-door. And they both seemed to perk up when she told them she had a stew simmering for the midday meal. Their smiles grew when she told them about having a Dutch-oven full of chicken and root vegetables ready to roast for the evening dinner. Given their reactions to the coffee and the mention of the coming meals, Frankie had an idea that there was more to their story too. But she decided to let things be, figuring she would hear more when they were ready to say more.

When she suggested eating their meal on the veranda, Ida liked the idea, declaring the day was 'just too pretty to be inside'. Frankie led her into the kitchen and they got busy taking dishes out to the porch table.

Neither Everett or Ida seemed to mind the 'hominess' of the rabbit stew. They both had second servings and the biscuits on the platter disappeared fast. With the way Ida and Everett were eating, Frankie decided that maybe it was a good thing that the daughter and her husband hadn't come along. This way, Everett and Ida could have their fill. Because with only three at the table, there was plenty of food.

Her new neighbors carried on about the flavors of the stew, but it was the biscuits and fresh butter that seemed to please Ida the most; she explained they'd had no eggs since their last chicken died back in May. She said they had run out of flour a few weeks back. For Everett, it was the buttermilk that brought a look of pure joy to his eyes.

"It feels like it's been years since I've had a glass of buttermilk," he said as he set the glass back on the table. "We lost our milch cow back at the beginning of winter, but it seems so long ago. Seven months is a long time to be without a good milking cow."

And all the time, Frankie was thinking that there was something odd here with this couple. They seemed sensible, and they seemed to have a lot of knowledge about the land. But they were talking as if they had no livestock on their place. No milk cow; no chickens. Ida had mentioned she hadn't had coffee or flour in a long time.

It sounded as if they had been scraping the bottom of the barrel for quite a while and Frankie suspected it was all part of their untold story. But once again, she left the subject alone.

Instead, she asked them about their trip out West and their time on the prairie. And about their family. Everett talked about their three sons; all three had died—one from illness, and two in the War in the South. They said that was part of the reason they had decided to move West. To move on. They had traveled from Iowa a little more than two years ago, traveling with a group of twelve families that decided to settle in this region of the Territory. They had come West with their daughter and son-in-law, planning to homestead on adjacent claims; planning to share livestock and work the land together.

Frankie could hear an uneasiness, and at first, she thought it was about the loss of their sons in the War. But soon, she realized their real uneasiness seemed to center around their daughter and her husband. Not long after they drove in to the meadow, they had explained that 'Hugh wasn't back yet', and their daughter Rebecca, 'was busy at home and couldn't make the trip today after all'.

Now, further into the conversation, Frankie heard that their daughter 'wasn't really a social-type person' and 'she always had a hard time meeting new people'. And that it was always 'so hard on her when her husband was gone'. It became clear to Frankie that something was very wrong—but either the Dunbars didn't want to talk about it, or they didn't know how to explain it.

"Did you meet up with Rebecca's husband, Hugh David, on the trail when you came?" Everett was asking the same question he had asked when they first met on the track near their place. Something about the son-in-law and his journey south was bothering him. "You see, he was on his way to Fort Cottonwood. We ran low on supplies, so he went to buy up more. Enough to tide us over till harvest when we sell our crops."

"I think I may have *seen* him, but I didn't meet up with him. There was a wagon traveling south on one of the days I lay over. I was still south of the Middle Loup, camping off the trail quite a piece. I was up on a hill looking at the lay of the land when I saw a man driving a mule with an empty wagon." Frankie kept her words casual, being careful not to sound like she had any opinion about the man. "I was too far away from the trail to see much more than that. And he never looked my way."

"What day was that, Honey?" Everett Dunbar was nodding, thinking.

"It was on the afternoon of the day I was laying over." Frankie had to think back, trying to sort days and travel. "I wanted to push through the last twenty-five or thirty miles in one day, so I was resting the livestock. So I guess it would have been on the day before I met you."

Frankie saw Everett Dunbar looking off into the distance—not looking at anything in particular. Just looking. Clearly troubled. But he didn't ask any more questions, so once again Frankie let the subject go.

They spent part of the afternoon walking around the meadow and buildings, talking about the homestead. Discussing the produce in the root-cellar. Looking over the tools and equipment in the barn. Talking about everything Daniel Kinison had built. And everything that Lillian Kinison had left behind.

They ended up at the front-pasture fence, standing at the gate looking into the four pastures. They talked about the windmills and the flue-system for a bit. Then about Blossom and Primrose. Everett mentioned that he could see that the mules were gaining weight. And as soon as she could, Frankie started peppering them with questions about her house—about her perfectly-square house.

The way Everett explained it, each room of her house was on the corner of a different one of her quarter-sections.

"By building it that way, Daniel managed to prove-up all four quarters with a single building. He was here a few years before the Homestead Act was passed. But he knew it was in the works; I think his father was in the Congress in Washington and had some information as to what to expect. So Daniel was ready when the act went through. He and Lillian and his parents each laid claim to a quarter-section. He paid a portion up front, so he could prove up in six months instead of the five-year period. No one from the government was ever up in this region to verify whether all four of them resided on the place or not. So it all went through on paperwork."

That single explanation answered a lot of Frankie's questions in one swipe and she had more questions ready to fire at him, but Everett had his own questions. As soon as he supplied the answer about her house, he started in with questions about the henhouse and the flock of chickens.

"Did you bring those chickens with you, or are these the ones Lillian left behind?" He was glancing around the meadow, peering into the undergrowth and the trees, looking to see if there were still chickens out where he had known them to be.

"These were on the place. They're the ones you told me about."

"My goodness, Honey, how on earth did you manage to round them all up? We tried several times, thinking we'd have the use of them and keep them safe for the new owners, if anyone ever showed up. But they were so wild we gave up."

"Well, my cousins taught me a few tricks for catching chickens gone-wild. First Trick is to catch them at night. I managed to catch up a good-sized bunch of them. And once I had them in the coop, within a couple of days, more hens came in on their own." Frankie saw the expression on Everett's face, showing both astonishment and disbelief. And in the moment, seeing as they had lost all their chickens, Frankie thought there was a very real possibility the Dunbars would take some of the hens. So she laid out the situation.

"So anyway, *now* I have a problem. I've got too many birds. I was hoping you might take some home with you."

"Oh Honey! We lost our last hen three months ago. Rebecca and Hugh had such terrible luck with them." Ida's voice was quivering, and she started wringing her hands. Frankie wasn't sure if the hand-wringing had to do with the agony of losing their chickens, or with the excitement of the possibility of getting new ones.

"Well, we can start you a new flock then. It would take a load off my mind, because I've got a hen setting a fourteen-egg clutch right now."

Frankie saw the excitement in Ida's eyes, and she saw relief in Everett's. But then, surprisingly, Everett's expression changed and he shook his head. Clearly uncomfortable, clearly on the verge of saying something. He propped his foot up on a fence rail, looking out past the front-pastures again. Looking beyond the pastures, as if he was seeing something far in the distance.

"Frankie, I can't tell you how much we want to take some of those hens with us. But I think we better leave them here for now." He looked at Ida, waiting, and after a moment Ida nodded. He went on then.

"You see, it wasn't *really* just bad luck with the chickens. Our son-in-law just doesn't take care of things. And Rebecca just sort of follows along with how he does things. If we bring any chickens home, he'll insist on taking them over to their place. And in a few weeks or so, somehow, all the chickens will end up dead or gone. That's pretty much how we lost the milk cow. And two of the mules."

Frankie saw the look in Everett Dunbars' eyes and the same look was in Ida's. There was some embarrassment and some sorrow. And there was some confusion too. But mostly there was hopelessness. It was the same look she had seen in an old woman's eyes one morning way back along the Little Blue River—an old woman traveling with two families and two wagons. They had started their journey West, but when Frankie had come across them, they were heading back East; they had given up on the trail and turned around.

The leader of those two families had been a chesty little braggart who strutted around, jabbering like a magpie—doing a lot of talking, but saying nothing of value. The wagons had been wobbling and wheels had been creaking; everything in their camp had been rough and dirty and unkempt. And in the old woman's eyes, there had been confusion and sorrow; she was worn down by circumstances that didn't fit with what she knew was right.

That, Frankie realized, was what she had here in front of her; *that* was the situation the Dunbars were in. They weren't rough and dirty and unkempt, but there was confusion and sorrow. Someone had worn them out and she could see that even though they knew their situation, they were having a hard time admitting it to themselves.

Frankie decided to say something, because in her mind, the best thing she could do, the *most right thing* at the moment, was to let them know they were seeing things right.

"Then, that's why the mule he was driving looked so poorly." Frankie said it as a statement, but there was a question beneath it. And Everett didn't miss it. She watched as he stared across the front meadow, looking toward her three mules; the sad look was still in his eyes and when he looked back at her, Frankie knew the answer wouldn't be a simple yes or no. Beside him, Ida pulled an embroidered hankie from a pocket in the folds of her skirt. She dabbed at her eyes.

"Honey, what I'm thinking right now," Everett was speaking quietly, sadness cloaking his words, "is that less than a week ago, I saw you arrive with healthy livestock. They were strong and in good shape, even after a long journey. Your animals looked the way I like to have mine look. Of all your stock, only those three mules looked to be in bad shape. You explained they had come to your camp, sick and in need of care.

"And this morning when we drove in, I could tell the mule you had in harness had gained a couple hundred pounds. Looking at the three of them now, I can see their open-sores are almost healed. I can see their hides are showing some shine. There's no mistaking you've been taking care of them." Everett Dunbar paused, took in a ragged breath, and went on.

"And here you are, only ten-years-old, and yet, you're taking better care of your livestock and your home than my son-in-law and my daughter. And they're grown adults." Again he paused, and Frankie saw his hands trembling.

"Honey, it seems like everything in their lives just falls apart." He was saying the things out loud that he and Ida had probably been trying to explain away for a long time. "Their animals get sicker every week. Their equipment breaks down and never gets repaired. They've done nothing to improve their place. Our own place suffers because I spend most of my time trying to help them to get their place in shape. Every animal that they've had on their place has died except for one last mule. Even one of our mules died when it was at their place." Everett stopped talking then. He dropped his eyes to look at the ground beside his feet. He took a breath, and then went on.

"Honestly, that's just not the way Ida and I do things. We've never lived our lives this way. But it's the shape of things now. The truth of it is, we're at our wit's ends."

Everett stopped explaining; he went silent again, ducking his head and pressing his finger and thumb against the bridge of his nose. Ida had stayed quiet while Everett had been talking, and now, on the far side of him, Frankie heard Ida sniff and take in a raspy breath; she was still dabbing at her eyes.

Frankie stayed still, letting the quiet remain. Waiting. Knowing that 'speaking the truth was the first step in dealing with the truth'. Remembering that her father had told her that many times. And standing there at the front-pasture fence, she was thinking the Dunbars must really be at wit's end—because they were confiding all this to a ten-year-old girl they had just met.

After a few minutes, Everett shifted his foot from the fence-board to the ground and Frankie knew he was ready to move off this subject. The story had been told. And maybe, the truth had been faced.

The three of them started walking, heading down the center track of the second meadow, heading down to the windmill. The conversation, Frankie knew, would change and the talk would be about the windmill and the water-flues.

It was deep into the afternoon when Frankie and Ida started setting the table and putting out the dinner. They pulled the roasting-pan with the chickens and the root vegetables from the oven; they loaded everything on a platter and set it in the center of the table. They put out the bowl of baked beans and the platter of cornbread. Ida took a step back to look at the dinner there on the trestle-table.

"It just looks so pretty, doesn't it, Honey?" Ida started dabbing at the corners of her eyes again, and when Frankie slid her arm around Ida's waist—thinking that this sweet neighbor of hers probably needed it—Ida wrapped her arm around her shoulders and squeezed her tight. She dabbed at her eyes a little more. Smiled down at her and whispered a quiet 'Oh, Honey', before putting her hankie to her eyes again.

The roast chicken and vegetables clearly pleased the Dunbars, but it was the peach pie with the thick cream that surprised them and set them to giggling like school-children.

To Frankie, it seemed as if they became true neighbors during that meal. It was over that dinner that they all came to a silent understanding, knowing they would be in each other's lives for years to come. For Frankie, the relief was rising, because the Dunbars seemed to understand her situation. They knew she intended to stay there on her homestead, and they hadn't offered an opinion or an argument. They had said nothing regarding her future, and to Frankie, it all felt safe. At least, so far.

The tension of the earlier discussions faded as the time at the dinner table went on; the problems in their lives had been put aside. They sat through the late afternoon speaking about the Sand Hills and the seasons, about their garden, and about the crops that would soon be ready for harvest.

When the talk turned to her livestock, Frankie told them about her Uncle James and how he had trained the Shires. She answered Everett's questions about the oxen and their training. They talked about her Aunt Sarah and her love for the Jersey cow.

And when the discussion moved to the blood-bay stallion, Trumpeter, Frankie asked Everett about breeding the mares—since it was late in the year. His advice was to go ahead with the breeding.

"There's no harm in having June or July foals. I don't think you'll be sorry for breeding those mares now. There ain't any real difference in a colt whether it's born in the late spring or early summer. In terms of weather, June might even be easier on them." Everett Dunbar looked out to the front pasture, studying the mares while he talked. "This way, come next June, you'll have foals on the ground. And if you want the next foal-crop born sooner, then you can breed the mares on their foal-heat. That'll get the next ones on the ground in May."

Frankie nodded, liking his advice, pleased he was saying what she had hoped to hear. There was no sense in wasting a year when the mares could be growing babies in their bellies. She liked Everett's thoughts and perspective; she thought there was wisdom there, the same kind of sensibility that Mr. Wheaton out on Fort Farm Island had. And probably, it was the same as what Major James Madison Maxwell would say.

Her mind whisked back across the miles, down to Fort Kearny; she wondered where her major was now. Wondering what he would think about his prized stallion being here in her meadow—about to start spending his days in the company of a handful of fine-looking mares. Her thoughts came back suddenly to her table, in her kitchen, in her house. Ida was standing up from the table, lifting plates, speaking to her.

"Frankie, you two go on outside and do your talking about your mares and breeding. You and Everett can go ahead and move your stallion out to the pasture if that's what you decide. I'll stay in here and clean up."

When she started to protest, Frankie saw Everett flash a funny look at her. She gave him a nod, offered Ida a quick thank-you and headed outside with him, leaving Ida to herself in the kitchen. They walked across the meadow, bee-lining to the barn-lot.

It seemed to Frankie there were two things going on. One was that this man, as kind and caring as he was, had some concerns about her handling a stallion alone, especially with mares nearby. The other, she decided, probably had to do with something he wanted to talk about. And that thought had her concerned about the possible subject—because it might have to do with her being out here alone. She was worried that he would tell her that they had decided not to leave her on her homestead after all. Whatever was going on, Frankie was sure there was some kind of reckoning in the works; she just didn't know what it was.

In the barn, she pulled Trumpeter's bridle from its peg in the tack-room and walked out to the barn-lot. Everett was waiting outside the fence, watching her, but Frankie could tell that he was uneasy. A lot of stallions could be dangerous and unpredictable, and clearly, Everett had his concerns about the situation. But still, he was being respectful; he was staying back and letting her take the lead with her own stock.

Trumpeter lowered his head as Frankie approached with the bridle, just like she knew he would. She whispered her thanks to him, stroked his face, and slipped the bridle on him. She led him to the water trough, stepped up on the trough's edge and boosted herself onto his back.

She sat on his broad back for a moment, waiting for his mind to come to the reins and her hands, waiting for the feel she wanted. When she slowed her breathing, his breathing slowed, and he lowered his head—it was a small movement, but it was what she was watching for. He started working the bit in his mouth, feeling it, tasting it. Relaxing. His ears flicked back toward her and she knew she had his mind; he was paying attention to his rider, putting his own thoughts and wants aside.

When she nodded for the gate, Everett opened it, held it as they passed through. He closed it while she and Trumpeter stood and waited. Then he walked beside her and her blood-bay Kentucky Charger as they headed to the gate of the front pasture. Everett opened that gate too, and once again, he stepped back.

She rode Trumpeter into the pasture, smiling at the way he changed the moment she had him through the pasture gate. Mares! He could see them and he could smell them. He couldn't help himself—he started dancing a little jig. Arching his neck. Pawing. Snorting. Because, he *was* a stallion, after all.

Frankie snapped the reins, warning him, bringing his mind back to her. He corrected himself, because stallion or not, he had been trained to be a gentleman. He lowered his head, gave into the rein. Calmed. He waited while she slid down to the ground. She stayed beside him, stroking his neck, making him wait for her to release him. And then things started to change.

The mares had been out in the far corner of the pasture, but they had seen the activity. They knew Trumpeter and they knew he was a stallion, and now, they suddenly realized that he was in their pasture. Belle called out. Fanny started toward the gate at a trot, head up, ears forward. Nickering. And then Belle and the other mares, Easy and Silk, broke into a trot. Following the neat-footed Morgan mare, excited about having a new member in their herd.

Frankie slipped the bridle from Trumpeter's head and released him, sending him away from her. Sending him out to the mares. *His* mares, now. She watched him lift into a long, reaching trot, neck bowed, tail high. 'Strutting his pride,' her Uncle James would have called it. Trumpeter, Major James Madison Maxwell's warhorse, was putting on a show, already working to impress the mares.

She and Everett leaned against the gate, watching the formal greetings, the nose-to-nose huffing and the excited pawing. By the comments Everett made about the stallion, and then about the mares, Frankie knew he understood horses. When he commented on how she had handled the stallion, she gave the credit to Trumpeter, to his manners and his training. Everett nodded and made a few more comments about Trumpeter's qualities, talking about the kind of qualities he thought the stallion would pass onto the foals that would be born next June.

And then he quit talking; he paused. And Frankie waited, knowing that the time had come. In a moment, he would talk about the subject that had been lying just beneath the surface. She gathered herself, pretty sure he would say something about her being here alone. She knew she was going to have to talk fast if he said that he and Ida were planning on taking her with them to their place.

But then Everett Dunbar said something completely different from what she had expected.

"Frankie, I have a question to ask you, and honestly, we were going to ask it of your folks, thinking they would be here." Everett Dunbar stopped for a moment, looking out across the meadow. "But now, I need to ask you. I have a good feeling about you and I know Ida feels the same way. I know we oughta be concerned about you being here alone. And maybe, we should be stepping in and handling this a different way. But I think you have a good head on you." He paused again and took a breath.

"You handled an awful lot to get here on your own, and you've managed things well in your first few days. As good and maybe better, than a lot of adults. And whatever we might have been thinking at first, right now, I think it would be wrong for us to interfere." He paused again, gathering himself for what he was about to say.

"Ida and I need your help, Frankie. And maybe, we need your ideas. We've been getting deeper and deeper into trouble over the last few months. Ever since we saw you and learned we had new neighbors settling in, we've been talking a lot. Now that we've spent the day with you and have an idea of how you think and work things out, I'm thinking you may be able to help us with one of our problems. If you're willing."

"Mr. Dunbar, I know something is going on. I don't know exactly what it is, but I'm thinking it has to do with your son-in-law."

"It does, Frankie. It's mostly about him. But it has to do with Rebecca too."

"It may sound strange for me to say this, Mr. Dunbar," Frankie decided to spill it all, thinking it might make it easier if he knew her feelings on it. "But I knew something was wrong about your son-in-law when I saw him from the hilltop last week. So don't worry that I won't understand what you have to say. We haven't known each other for very long, but we're neighbors. And I think neighbors should work together on things."

She had said it all, and then, thinking he might worry about handing a problem to a young girl, she said something else—something she thought might ease his mind.

"Mr. Dunbar. My father was a professor and he was pretty clear about the best ways to handle things. He always said it was best to take a complicated situation and talk about the simplest thing first."

Frankie glanced behind her, looking toward the kitchen where Ida was clearing up after their dinner, realizing that Everett had chosen to discuss this out here because of Ida. Because the conversation would be too hard for her. Because this wasn't just about the son-in-law—this was about her own daughter. *That* was why she had offered to clean up after dinner, and that was why Everett had flashed the funny look at her.

"Okay then Honey, here's the simplest thing." Everett gave a sigh and turned to face her. "I need to know if we can leave our mare here. Ida and me, we think it'd be better if we didn't have her at our place. We could bring her here in a few days. We still have a mule at our place to use, though honestly, he's not in much better shape than the one you saw Hugh driving."

"Sir, that's simple enough." Frankie saw relief flood into his eyes the moment she spoke the words. "Your mare can be here for as long as you want. And I don't need to know the reason unless you want to tell me."

"Well, the truth of it is, we're worried that when Hugh comes back, he'll have a plan to move on farther west. He'll want to take Rebecca with him and she'll want to go. They'll expect us to pack up and go too. Mainly, because Hugh will want our mule and our mare. You see, it's the mare he really wants, because of her quality." Everett Dunbar wiped his palm across his forehead.

"You see Frankie, Hugh's the type of man who knows how to get his way about things. If we don't agree to go with them, he'll find some way to work things around. And one way or another, he'll end up taking the mare. And he'll take one of the mules, either his or ours." He paused again, and it was a long time before he said the next part.

"Our mare Jenny, is the last thing of real value we have. She belongs to us. Neither Hugh nor Rebecca has any claim to her. She came to us through Lillian Kinison, from when I took her down to Fort Cottonwood. But Hugh David wants her for himself.

"You see, Frankie, after we lost our sons, Ida and me felt the need to be near our only remaining child. So we've moved around with Rebecca and Hugh David. Hugh's a little shiftless and we've already followed him and Rebecca to two different places. It's always the same—everything fails and falls apart. We should have known better. Truth is, Hugh David never sticks with anything. I don't believe he cares about anything in this life except himself. For some reason, Rebecca is willing to follow him anywhere. And we've been willing to follow her." Another pause.

"Frankie, Ida and I are tired of all of this. We're older now and it's wearing us down. We like it here. We think there's promise out here and we don't want to start all over somewhere else. Honestly, we don't have enough to start over, and I'm not even sure we have enough to make a go of it if we stay here. We're already pretty live-stock-poor and without *both* the mare and my mule, I won't be able to get my crops harvested. God only knows how I'll get a crop hauled to market."

"Mr. Dunbar. I don't need to know the whole story right now. We're neighbors, so there'll be time to talk about things. I think you're right about your son-in-law having plans to leave again when he gets back. It fits with what I thought when I saw him. He wasn't paying attention to anything but himself; he wasn't watching the trail or the land or the mule. I had the feeling he was the kind of man who uses up both people and animals. I've watched other men like that; they take everything they can get, and then they move on to take from someone else."

Frankie stood beside her neighbor, leaning on the fence, looking out toward Trumpeter and the mares. Her mind slipped back in time—thinking back to the other men she had known like Hugh David. Silas Beckett was one; he had been leading the wagon party. And there was Colonel White at Fort Kearny. Both were men who destroyed the lives and the happiness of everyone around them, simply because it was easy. Simply because they could.

"I've never met Hugh David and I don't know if he'll come back or not. But I think you're right—if he does show up, he'll have it in his mind to take the mare and Rebecca and leave." Now, it was Frankie who paused. She was thinking carefully about her next words. "If your mare's over here, then what are you gonna tell Hugh David when she's not at your place?"

"I'll tell him she wandered off and I haven't been able to find her."

He said it a little lamely, like he wasn't sure it would work. Frankie thought for a minute, thinking about the kind of man they were dealing with.

"I think you'll have to tell him more than that. Give him a story with some details, so he doesn't start wondering why she hasn't come back. Tell him she got out of her pen one night and disappeared. And tell him one of the other homesteaders said there have been wolf-kills in the area—that there was one just down the trail. Tell him it might have been your mare. You're not lying because I'm a home-steader and I'm saying it to you now. I did see a wolf-kill not too far away." Frankie hesitated, dreading the answer to the question she needed to ask.

"Right now, Hugh David doesn't know anything about me, and I don't want him to. I don't need him coming here for any reason, especially if he's looking for your mare. What does your daughter know about me? Because there's a problem if she tells him anything."

"Frankie," Everett Dunbar looked down for a moment. "Ida and I decided not to tell her about meeting up with you. She's become a lot like Hugh. She's been lying and hiding things from us. And we're pretty sure she'll agree with him if he decides to take both the mule and the mare. At this point, we think she's willing to leave us here with nothing. We heard them talking before he left. Talking about Fort Laramie. Saying something about her working in the fort's laun-dry, while he works for a freighter.

"That's in our favor then." Frankie felt her shoulders relax and she was pretty sure her heart slowed down. "It'd be better to not say anything about me. No one else in the area knows about me yet, so neither Hugh or Rebecca will have heard anything. When he comes back, let him take what he wants and leave. If he has no hope of hav-ing the mare, then he may argue that he needs both mules. Put up a bit of an argument, so he doesn't suspect anything, but let him take the mule if you have to."

"That puts me in a bad situation for harvest, Honey. I'm hoping he'll decide to take his mule and leave my mule with me."

"He might leave you with one of them, and he might not. But right now, the best thing that can happen is for him to leave. There are plenty of mules left on the planet if he takes both. I have three mules out there in the pasture doing nothing but filling their bellies. The question of mules and harvesting can all be handled later."

Frankie was thinking fast. It seemed like the Dunbars could see *some* things about their son-in-law, but she wasn't sure they saw everything. Hugh David was no different than Silas Beckett or Colonel White, and if he came back with certain things in mind and found he couldn't get them, then everything could take a bad turn. Because he was the kind of man who could justify hurting someone if he didn't get his way.

So she took a chance; she told Everett about the danger to him, and she told him Ida would be at risk too. When she brought Ida's safety into the conversation, Frankie saw his eyes widen. Then he nodded.

"Everett, you and Ida drive home tonight." Frankie changed her tone, softened it, speaking carefully. Because there had to be a plan; there had to be precautions. Because she knew the damage men like Silas Beckett and Colonel White and Hugh David could do.

"Leave the mare tied to a post in her pen where I'll find her. When you wake up in the morning, the gate will be hanging open and your mare will be gone. And that's all anybody needs to know. She was just gone when you woke up. I'll bring her here where she'll be safe. And if you want, I'll put her in with these mares and Trumpeter. You might as well have her bred for next June, like my mares. You'll have a start on a nice team."

Everett Dunbar stayed where he was, leaning against the top-rail of the fence, his eyes looking far beyond the pastures of the second valley. Far beyond the third valley. Frankie waited, letting him think through everything, realizing he was having a hard time. Because there were truths being brought into the light—the truth that his son-in-law was a very real danger and the truth that their daughter was already lost to them. It was a lot to face.

And now, what little hope he had for the future was at risk—a hope that revolved around protecting a mare and saving a mule and trying to salvage the crops he had in the ground. Standing there at the pasture gate, Everett Dunbar was right in the middle of giving up a lot. Right now, he needed some new hope—he needed to see a new future. She waited for a few minutes; finally, she spoke up.

"Mr. Dunbar, there are three good using-mules standing fifty yards from you right now. They'll be stout and healthy by the time you're ready to harvest. And there are four solid oxen standing over there that need to be doing honest work. You and I both know I'll need grain for the winter. And come next year, I need to have some of my land farmed, and I know *nothing* about farming. So maybe you and me could do some trading." She watched Everett, still staring out across the valleys; she thought she saw a change come into his eyes.

"You and I can talk particulars later, but you and Ida and me, we already have a pretty good sense about each other. Don't you think we could come up with some sort of trade where I loan you the stock and you see to the farming? So you can get your crops harvested? And I get a share of grain? And you can get your crops to market?"

Everett turned toward her; she looked straight into his eyes and she was pretty sure she could see hope flickering in them. He had been listening to what she said. He started nodding. Sure enough, he was finding hope again; he was seeing a future again.

"Frankie. I think we have a solution for now. And a plan for later."

He put his hand out to her and they shook hands like they were partners. They were smiling as they walked back to the house. The evening was settling in, and over at the house, Frankie saw Ida come through the kitchen door; she stepped to the porch-table with the coffeepot and coffee cups in her hand. She smiled at them and raised her hand with the cups just a bit—a gesture said that she was glad they were coming in and that she had coffee ready for them.

102

They sat on the porch, talking as darkness settled in around them; they spent most of the time finalizing their plans. They were all in agreement that if Hugh David did return, it would be soon— so there was a need to get the mare away from the Dunbars' place as soon as possible. And doing it in secret would be the best course of action. Because nothing would be served by having anyone know about the mare leaving the Dunbar place.

There was no sense in taking a chance of being seen by some homesteader who might be traveling or hunting nearby. And especially, not Rebecca. Because as Ida said, 'if Rebecca knows, then Hugh David will know'.

Frankie wanted to move the mare under the cover of night. She had no interest in running into anyone, because in her past, she had experiences with people who showed up unexpectedly; there had been people who had seen too much and had said too much. She had learned *that* lesson with the strutting and boastful magpie-man and his family; after she had crossed paths with them way back along the Little Blue River—that simple encounter had set off a chain of ugly events.

So while they ate more of the peach pie and drank more of the coffee, they made their final decisions. Frankie would travel to the Dunbars' place late in the night. In the morning, when the Dunbars checked the pen, the gate would be open and their mare would be gone. They would tell Rebecca that the mare had disappeared during the night. Once Hugh David returned, Everett would tell him he'd seen her tracks on the riverbank and it looked like she had gone downriver.

He and Ida would say there was word around the area that a pack of wolves had been spotted—a mule had been killed the week before. Everett would say they had looked for the mare, but feared she had been chased off and killed by wolves. He would also tell Hugh there had been wolf-tracks along the river to the south on the morning after the mare disappeared.

And after tonight, the Dunbars would use dishcloths tied to a fencepost as a signal for Frankie—one cloth if the son-in-law was back; two cloths if he had come back and had gone again.

For her part, Frankie would check the situation every other night. She would watch from a safe distance—watching for the dishcloth signals, watching to see if Hugh David was there. Watching to see what Hugh David had decided to do.

And if she needed to talk to the Dunbars, she'd meet with them on their place after midnight; if *they* needed to talk with *her*, they'd tie the dishcloth to a different post.

Once the moon was up and shining across the land, Everett harnessed the mare and hitched her to the wagon. When he brought the wagon up to the house, Frankie and Ida loaded a crate into the wagon-bed—a crate filled with sacks of flour and sugar, a basket of eggs, crocks of butter and a tin of milk. Frankie added a flour-sack full of biscuits and the second peach pie. The last thing she tucked into the crate was a sack of coffee-beans from the pantry.

When Ida saw the sack of coffee, tears puddled up in her eyes and spilled down her cheeks; she hugged Frankie and squeezed her hands; she thanked her and promised she'd replace the coffee and the other things once Hugh got back with the supplies.

Frankie looked at her, realizing what she had just heard. Realizing that at least part of Ida still believed Hugh David would show up with a wagon-full of supplies. Ida was still holding out hope—and that meant there was still something unspoken. There was still something important that needed to be addressed.

Because a week ago, Frankie had seen the wagon from the crest of the hill and it had been empty. There had been nothing in the wagon to trade, nothing to barter for the needed supplies. So Hugh David would have been carrying cash money.

Frankie choked back a groan, knowing the other piece of the story. There were a lot of ways for a man to lose his money around a fort-town, and a man like Hugh David couldn't hold onto money. If he did return from Fort Cottonwood, he certainly wouldn't have a wagonload of supplies with him—he would have spent the money in other ways, for other things. For his own wants.

She stared at the tears in Ida's eyes for a moment, and then she asked the question that neither Ida nor Everett wanted to hear. She asked if they had sent money with Hugh David. The look of sudden despair in Ida's eyes told Frankie what she had suspected—the Dunbars had given Hugh David the last of their money. They would have sent it with him, counting on him to bring back enough supplies to tide them over until they had a crop to sell in the fall. Ida and Everett both nodded, acknowledging finally, the full truth.

Now, Frankie understood how dire Everett and Ida's situation was. They had been drained; they had lost everything of value. Like Everett said, they were livestock-poor; without a healthy and strong team, there would be no crop harvested from his fields. And if they *did* manage to harvest even some of their crop, their team would be worn down from the fieldwork. Fort Cottonwood, down on the Overland Road, was their market and it was three or four days away. That was a long haul for a worn-down team.

But now, there was a new hope in front of them; one that wasn't pinned on their daughter or son-in-law. There was a solid plan in the works—and keeping their mare safe and hidden was just the first step.

Part of the reason for the despair in Ida's eyes, Frankie knew, was because she didn't know everything that had been discussed at the pasture gate. Tonight, the talk in the kitchen had been mostly about keeping their mare safe. There hadn't been time to tell her about the future plans for the three mules and the oxen. Or about the harvest and the planting in the coming spring.

"There are things for you to hear yet, Ida. Everything's better than you're thinking right now. Everett will have time to explain everything on the way home." Frankie saw some of the hope come back into Ida's eyes. The *real* hope. "I promise you, Ida, everything will be fine in the end. We're not at the end of this yet, so I know it doesn't feel fine. But it *will*. I promise."

Frankie stayed where she was, standing in the silvery moonlight of the meadow, watching as the Dunbars drove out of the meadow. Going up and around on the track, traveling home into the night. She didn't expect them to get very far beyond the ford before Everett started explaining everything to Ida. They would talk about their daughter and her husband. There would be talk about the mare and the mule. About the dangers. And the solutions. And Ida would hear about the three mules and the four oxen and the trades. Before they were home, they'd have some things sorted out about their past and about their future.

Ida, Frankie realized, would probably go to sleep tonight with a new spark of hope. A real and possible hope. Maybe she'd sleep well tonight. Maybe for the first time in a long time.

Once the sound of the mare's hooves faded and disappeared into the night, Frankie headed to the barn. She readied the McClelland saddle and Rock's bridle; she slid the Henry into the scabbard, the spyglass into the saddlebags, and tied an extra halter to the saddle. And all the time, she was adding things up, thinking about the time and distance to the Dunbar place. Thinking about wagon-time compared to horseback-time.

Putting her end of the plan together, she decided to give the Dunbars a full three hours to get home in the wagon. It was plenty of time for a horse and wagon traveling at a steady road-trot for at least some of the trip. She decided to start out an hour after midnight; she wanted Everett and Ida to be home and settled in for the night before she showed up. Just to keep things going according to plan.

She went back to the house, changed into a shirt and trousers, and helped herself to another piece of the peach pie. Looking around the kitchen as she poured the last of the coffee into her cup, she could see Ida had left the kitchen spotless. That, just like everything she had seen throughout the day, showed her the kind of people the Dunbars were. Ida had left the kitchen cleaner than when she and Everett had walked in that morning. Their mare was in good shape and the harness was well-kept. The wagon was in good repair. The poor condition of the mules, according to Everett, lay squarely on the son-in-law's shoulders.

Everett and Ida Dunbar were honest and decent people and they were only in trouble because of the people they had in their lives. And *that* could happen to anyone. It could happen to a couple because of the man their daughter married, the same way that it had happened to the people of an entire wagon party because of the wagon-master they had trusted. Frankie had seen that happen, just like she had seen what could happen to an entire military post when a new commander arrived.

Tonight was the first step toward getting Everett and Ida Dunbar out of the mess they were in. They had asked for help and Frankie was going to do what she could, because it was the right thing to do. Because these people were her neighbors.

Frankie set out an hour past midnight, in the bright moonlight, with Laughing Girl loping along beside Rock. She had left Matilda at the homestead; the collie-dog's initial dejection at being left behind, had changed when Frankie told her to guard the meadow and the livestock. Matilda must have understood, because she had already taken up a sentry position on the Barracks porch as Frankie turned Rock toward the front track.

It was the first time Matilda had been handed the job and Frankie had been laughing to herself. Apparently, the tawny little collie understood the significance of the instructions, because she had a mighty serious look on her face as she settled herself on the porch; she wasn't even showing her toothy-smile. And there had been no sign of a sulk, either.

Frankie gave Rock his head and he settled into a long-reaching road-trot as they traveled along the southern bank of the North Loup River. It was the same track she had traveled almost a week earlier in the blue-green Conestoga, the same track Everett had pointed her to. It was the track that had led her home.

She listened to the different night-birds calling out their songs from the trees along the riverbanks. A mockingbird was still awake and busy rattling off a series of stolen tunes; a couple of killdeer were out somewhere in the open grassland to her right side, calling to each other.

A screech owl sent a message to the other creatures of the night, sending its string of hollow-sounding hoots into the moonlight—a funny call, that to Frankie, sounded both eerie and amusing at the same time. Before it completed its series of hoots, another owl of its own ilk replied from further downstream. And then another, even further downstream. And a moment later, two more of its kind sounded off. *A whole family of them,* Frankie thought. *Or maybe, it wasn't a family; maybe it was just a nightly argument over territory.*

She watched the land and the river as she rode. The moonlight blanketed the land, painting the grasses of the Sand Hills with ghostly shades of watery colors. Silvery-gray shadows floated amid the widespread swaths of yellow-white light from the moon. Along the river, the moonbeams cut through the treetops and filtered down through the dark branches; the shafts of moonlight seeming to twist and turn as they streamed down through the late-summer leaves, settling in light-splattered patches on the sandy banks. Their speckles of light shimmered, shining on the river's dark water, sparkling bright and bold. Flashing and flickering in the night.

The night-birds kept singing and the full moon kept shining and Frankie kept traveling. Beneath her, Rock's hooves were hammering out a soft and sand-muffled beat, solid and steady, carrying her east-by-southeast, as she traveled beside the banks of the pretty moonlight-speckled river. The blond-brindled hound ran beside her, keeping the pace, loping along in her effortless way. Grinning her wolfish-grin. *This is my homeland. My land, my home, and my life. My part of the North Loup River; my portion of the Sand Hills. My grasslands.*

She rode on, feeling the night air. Feeling the prairie-air. Watching the moonlight blanketing the land around her. Soft and shimmering. Ghostly. *And maybe, it's my moonlight. Because it's blanketing my world. Mine,* she thought, *because there's no one to argue about it.*

And tonight, this was *her* night-ride. She grinned and nodded, relishing the thought. Because she was on a mission. And it was a fine mission. Because she was doing the right thing for the right reason, for the right people. Even if it *was* under the cover of dark, riding through moonlight and moon-shadows, and hidden from meddling eyes.

Her mind went back in time, back to a night on the Little Blue River when she had been on another mission. A mission similar—in some ways, at least—to her mission tonight. There had been animals whose fate had been at stake that night too. And on that night, it had also been about doing the right thing. That night, it had been the most important mission of her life—to recover her stolen livestock—and it had turned out right. 'Right purpose and right intent always gives a right result.' Her Uncle James had taught her that. It had proven true that night and Frankie was betting it would on this night too.

It was a little more than an hour, according to her father's pocket-watch, when Frankie reached the bend in the road where she first met Everett and Ida. That had been a little less than a week ago. She had seen them coming up from their river crossing, riding along in their spring-wagon behind the pretty-headed seal-brown mare.

Frankie looked down the track to the south, eyeing the high ridge where the main track angled its way down the steep slope, taking a few sharp turns as it came through a cut in the hillside. She had driven the Shires and the Conestoga down through that cut to reach the river-flats—land that had been leveled by the North Loup River during some ancient time when it had flowed wide and harsh.

Tonight, Frankie sat in the saddle, letting Rock rest for a moment while she studied her surroundings. The moonlight showed the fork of the track that went to the northeast. That, she knew, was the track to Everett and Ida's place. The track dropped down to a ford on the river; beyond the ford, forty yards away, she could see a cluster of sod buildings standing bathed in moonlight. That place, situated on the north side of the river, was the Dunbar place.

There was another cluster of sod-buildings sitting south of the river, with its own little roadway coming straight out to the main track. Frankie remembered the place; she had spotted it when she first traveled this road. That day, she had had no idea who lived there. But she knew now.

That was the home of Rebecca and Hugh David, and to Frankie's way of thinking, it was by God's grace she had met up with Ida and Everett instead of those two. It was also by the grace of God that she hadn't met up with Hugh David on his way to Fort Cottonwood; her situation would be much different today if she had. She felt a little shudder move through her and she knew it wasn't due to the night-breeze.

Knowing what she knew now, having Hugh David as a neighbor wasn't a thought that pleased her. And sitting there in the shadows of the trees along the riverbank, Frankie was thanking God and all the angels and all her lucky stars, that she hadn't crossed paths with the Dunbars' son-in-law.

And given her own experiences with other men who weren't all that different from Hugh David, she was hoping that maybe he wouldn't come back. Because in her mind, nothing good would come of his return. Because he'd never change. He would continue to cause heartbreak and destruction in the lives of everyone around him. *Maybe, he'll just stay gone.*

In her own life, there had been Silas Beckett who looked for ways to tear apart the lives of others while he satisfied his own selfish desires. Then there had been Colonel White who took an obscene pleasure in causing the destruction of everything around him. And there had been the strutting little magpie-man who seemed intent on doing nothing worthwhile in life—a man who had been content to let his own family pay the price for his own self-centered concerns. This son-in-law of the Dunbars' was no different than those men. And if Rebecca had accepted his lead, then she would never change, either.

Looking toward the sod-house sitting beyond the track, Frankie suddenly started thinking it might be best if Hugh David *did* return. Because then he and his wife would take what they wanted and leave. If they left with everything of value, it was likely they would never return. *That, might be the best thing of all. Get it all over and done with at once.*

Looking around her, Frankie spotted what she wanted—a low rise across the river and to the west, just beyond the riverside trees. A slightly higher spot, a place that would serve as a lookout, so she could read the lay of the land.

She sent Rock across the ford and turned him back to the west toward the low ridge. She pulled to a halt near the top of the rise and stayed in the saddle, scanning the homestead on the north side of the river. She sat there for a while, seeing the Dunbar place in the bright moonlight, almost as clear as in daylight.

Studying the Dunbar homestead, Frankie thought it looked to be a nice homey place; it sat by the North Loup River, not far from a grove of riverbank trees. About half the claim looked to be planted in corn. Another smaller portion, appearing almost snowy-white in the moonlight, looked like oats.

Just above what would be the flood-plain of the river, was a rectangular sod-house. It was neat and tidy, just as Frankie had expected. A sod outhouse and a couple of other small, neat and tidy sod-buildings were clustered close to it.

There was a large fenced garden. And there was a little shed-roofed sod building that Frankie assumed to be the chicken-house— it would be empty now, because apparently, the hens that *had* lived there, had been carried off by the son-in-law. A little further away, there was a large lean-to building, built mostly of sod, but with a wood-plank roof; the front opened to a couple of livestock pens.

Frankie spotted shadowy movements in those pens. Studying them for a moment, she managed to sort out the shapes. She could pick out a mule in one pen, and in the corner of the second pen, she picked out the seal-brown mare. *Jenny. That's what Ida had called her.*

She watched the mare standing in the pen, watching her shift her hindquarters a few times. But she stayed where she was, right there in the corner. She had told Everett that if she arrived in the night and the mare wasn't tied, she would know they had changed their minds. *Yeah. She's standing tied. So. The* mission's *going forward after all.*

Now, Frankie smiled, understanding something else about Everett and Ida Dunbar; when they had a good reason and a good plan, they stayed with it. They hadn't backed out and they hadn't wasted her time.

She stayed in the saddle, scanning everything below her, trying to set everything about the homestead in her mind—the placement of the buildings, the river ford, the roadway leading into the farmyard, the river's course downstream.

Frankie was also thinking about the timing of everything. Not just the timing of *her* activities tonight, but also, the timing of Hugh David's activities. She figured four days by wagon to Fort Cottonwood, probably a stay of a day or two, and then four days back. And to be safe, add on an extra day or two for unknowns. Adding it up, probably ten or eleven days for the whole trip. The son-in-law had already been gone six days, so Frankie figured Hugh David *could* be back as early as three days from now and probably no more than five.

And there was something else she was thinking about. Once Hugh David returned and discovered that the mare was gone, it was unlikely he would just let the matter drop. Especially, if he had decided the mare was the solution to his latest problems. He would probably look for the mare. So Frankie planned on leaving evidence to match the Dunbars' story—just in case Hugh David decided to head downriver to look for hoofprints.

Leaving some horse-tracks, along with some wolf-tracks where Hugh David would find them, was part of Frankie's mission tonight. Because as it happened, she had brought the makers of horse-tracks and wolf-tracks along with her—both Rock and Laughing Girl had some work to do tonight.

She headed down the hillside, circling Rock to the north, giving the Dunbar buildings a wide berth. A hundred yards downstream she swung Rock toward the river's edge where she walked Rock around on the sandy bank, making sure to leave enough hoof-prints that they couldn't be missed; she made sure that Laughing Girl did plenty of exploring in the dirt and sand by the river, traipsing around with her big wolfish feet.

Then, Frankie rode downstream for a quarter-mile, whistling for Laughing Girl crisscrossing the river several times, going up and down and along the riverbanks with Laughing Girl loping along behind her. *Wolf-tracks among horse-tracks.*

She grinned at the thought, thinking it was a clever idea. It might not fool a top-notch scout like Corporal Thomas Buchanan down at Fort Kearny, but someone like Hugh David wouldn't study on anything for very long—he wouldn't do a good job of anything.

Finally satisfied with their efforts at deception, Frankie turned away from the river and rode out into the grass where Rock's tracks would disappear from the eyes of anyone other than an experienced tracker. Once again, she swung out in a wide circle to the north, and finally, turned toward the Dunbars' homestead buildings.

She slowed Rock to a walk as she rode into the farmyard. She felt a shiver slide up her spine, remembering another time she had been moving through the moonlight, taking a horse that didn't belong to her. That had been her last night at Fort Kearny, back when she and Rock were slipping away together, escaping unseen and unheard in the night. She had to keep reminding herself that, tonight, she didn't have to worry about being caught. Because no one was trying to catch her. Tonight, there was no great need for stealth. Because tonight, this was just play.

She left Rock standing near Jenny's pen; she took the extra halter from her saddle and slipped through the gate. She spoke to the mare, spent a little time getting acquainted, stroking her neck and back. Deciding she was an awfully nice mare; she had strong hindquarters, strong shoulders and a deep chest. And she was in fine condition—her weight was good and her hide was shining in the moonlight. She had originally belonged to Daniel Kinison, and had been in Everett's hands since January. So Frankie knew two things. First, Daniel Kinison knew a good horse when he saw one. And second, Everett Dunbar knew how to take care of his animals.

She stayed beside the mare for a few minutes more, talking softly to her and thinking about what Everett said about needing both her and the mule for harvest. Jenny was bred to move nicely under saddle, and for pulling a light farm-wagon or buggy. But she was too refined, too fine-boned, for a plow or heavy wagon.

It was common for homesteaders to make do with whatever livestock they happened to own, because there wasn't always an alternative—the work had to be done and that meant you used whatever animals you had. But this mare was no draft horse. She could be hitched to a plow or heavy wagon and she'd do the work required of her. But to Frankie's mind, it would be a shame.

Ready to get on with her mission, she switched halters—putting hers on Jenny and hanging the Dunbars' halter on the gate post. Because horses that wandered off at night didn't usually halter themselves first. Frankie didn't know exactly how smart this son-in-law was, but he might figure something was amiss if he realized the halter and lead-rope were missing along with a mare that had supposedly run off in the night.

It was as she led Jenny out of the pen, making sure to leave the gate hanging open, that she heard a strange sound. She stopped and looked toward the other pen; the sound was coming from the mule. Hugh David's mule. The strange sound was a soft wheeze it made every time it exhaled.

Frankie stared at the mule. It was in bad shape; it was bone-skinny, pacing with its head low. Watching it for a moment, she could see the ribcage shudder slightly with every breath and the flanks hollowed and sucked in deeply every time the lungs filled. Her Uncle James would have said that indicated a serious problem, something deep within the system. Something that probably wouldn't correct. *Another victim of Hugh David.*

Taking one last look at the poor mule, Frankie mounted Rock, wondering if the Dunbars had been watching her and her activities. She grinned, pleased with her work; pleased that this part was done.

She turned for home with the mare trotting behind; she whistled for Laughing Girl and headed out of the farmyard, lifting into a canter once she crossed the river.

She turned south on the main track, choosing to not follow the river-track. Thinking it better to hide her real direction. Just in case. After a hundred yards, she swung to the west, leaving the main track and cutting to the west through the grass. She traveled several miles at a swinging trot before turning north toward the river and the river-track.

In Frankie's mind, it was all about what her Lieutenant would have called evasive action. Because there was at least a small chance that the son-in-law, in his quest for the mare, might decide to ride upriver for a piece to look for tracks. And the last thing Frankie wanted was for him to see hoof-prints and wolf-tracks going north on the river track. Just the thought of Hugh David showing up in her meadow was enough to make her stomach tighten up. She forced down a wave of nausea and rode on in the moonlight.

An hour and half later, she turned Rock into the river at her ford; when she rode into her valley, she smiled at the sight. The meadow was bathed in silvery-yellow moonlight and silvery-blue shadows. The dew had fallen and the grass was sparkling with dewdrops. And as late as it was, the mockingbird was still sending the notes of its stolen songs through the moonlit night. The soft, sweet night-call of a horned owl was coming from the high trees behind the house. There was a movement in the meadow near the front pasture fence. *A deer. No, two deer.* She watched the deer for a moment longer as the deer watched her. *No, five deer. Two does. Three half-grown fawns.* Heads up. Eyeing the horses and human. Turning then and heading toward the cover of the hillside, trotting off in their high-stepping, lofty-light trot. Smooth and silent. Laughing Girl showed an interest in giving chase. Frankie called her off.

"No, Girl. Leave them. You've done enough tonight."

After putting Rock and Jenny in barn-stalls for the night, she squatted down and hugged Laughing Girl, thanking her for her wolfish duties that night. It was enough to make the brindle hound prance around, grinning her big wolfish-grin and forgetting her disappointment at being called back from a deer-chase. Then she praised Matilda for the wonderful job she had done by 'guarding the entire homestead and all the animals, all by your little collie-dog self'. The tawny little collie-dog flashed her toothiest dog-grin and nearly twisted herself in half with all her wagging and wiggling.

Walking across the meadow to the house, Frankie was smiling pretty big herself, pleased with both the day's activities and the night's antics. She washed up in the basin in her room, swung every door in the house open and went outside to sit on top of the porch-table for a while. She ate a dish of cornbread soaked in milk and drank a glass of buttermilk while she watched her valley. Listening to the night-sounds of the livestock in their pens and pastures. Soft snorts; quiet snores. Her animals were all there, all sleeping in the light of the silvery moon. And likely, Jenny was already sleeping too.

It wasn't long before Frankie heard birds starting with their pre-dawn songs, tentative at first, like maybe they were testing the coming day. Finally, feeling the tiredness overwhelm her, feeling the need for sleep after the night's mission, she walked inside the house, stripping out of her clothes as she went into her bedroom. She stretched out on the bed and let the pre-dawn air drift across her.

For the next several days, as soon as she finished the morning chores, Frankie rode the land along the North Loup River. She had already spent a good share of time upriver, following its course to the northwest, learning about the river and the land beside it. So now, she began exploring farther downriver, learning the bends and curves and coves to the southeast.

She watched the wildlife and the vegetation, the soils and the sand. She found the fords and the game-trails. She found two of her own section-markers but found more quarter-section markers than she could make sense of. She decided to wait for Everett Dunbar to help sort it all out.

Frankie also spent some time worrying about Ida and Everett. Worried about Hugh David returning, uneasy about his possible reaction to finding the mare missing. Knowing men like that could reach high levels of anger; knowing men like that felt justified in lashing out at anyone who displeased them. She was hoping that if he did return, he would take his wife—and everything else he wanted—and then leave Everett and Ida's lives for good.

She was also hoping that Hugh David's pattern would hold true—because Everett had said when Hugh David left a place, he burned his bridges and never returned. The thought of him leaving was a nice thought; the thought that he'd never come back was even nicer.

Every other night, she set off for the Dunbars' homestead, traveling in the light of the waning moon, keeping watch like she promised. Choosing to implement another evasive maneuver, she created a new path to the Dunbars, following narrow game-trails on the north side of the river. Deciding it was wiser to avoid the established track beside the southern bank. Unwilling to take any chances with Hugh David spotting any hoofprints on that track.

Once on the ridge to the west of the Dunbar place, she sat on the grassy slope in the pale light of the moon, watching the two homesteads. One to each side of the river. The first thing she always looked for was the signal—a dishtowel hanging from the corral-post. Knowing that with the sight of the cloth, she would have to be ready for any changes that would come.

And always, she stayed in place for a good while, studying both homesteads, knowing there was a value in recognizing the typical appearance, the normal activity. So that any changes signaling the son-in-law's return would be obvious. A wagon, a mule; any activity or lights in the dark.

It wasn't until her third trip to the Dunbar homestead that Frankie saw a single cloth hanging on the corral post, stark white in the moonlight, standing out against the dark fencepost, lifting and twisting slowly in the night breeze. Just one dishtowel. She sucked in a quick breath, slipped down from Solomon's back and scrunched down on the surface of the slope. It was an instinctive move—guarded and wary—because now, there was danger. *So. Hugh David is back. And he's been here for at least a day.*

Now, there was the question of whether he would decide to stay—figuring to get a share of the crops. Or whether he would just leave. And if he left, there was the question of whether he would leave one of the mules with Everett and Ida. It was likely, since he wouldn't be getting the mare like he had expected, that he would decide to take both mules, along with whatever else he wanted. Because he'd be angry. *He'll be down-right pissed.*

Thinking about the situation and adding up everything that she knew about men like Hugh David, Frankie didn't believe he would stay. Even with a crop in the ground, and even with the promise of the cash from the harvest, a man like Hugh David wasn't going to work in the fields for it. And it wasn't likely he would be patient enough to wait around for it, either. Given there was very little food left on either place, and no livestock to speak of, there wasn't much to entice him to stay.

Because pretty much, Hugh David had used up everything— there was very little left to interest him. So if he ran true to pattern, he would leave and go on to something else. And true to pattern, Rebecca would want to go with him. And Hugh David would take her along, if he still had a use for her.

Down in the pen where the white dishtowel waved in the moon-light, Frankie could see a movement in the pen. *A mule. So that's good.* She watched the mule standing along the fence. It wasn't pacing with its head low; it wasn't moving uncomfortably like what she had seen the other night. It was standing quietly, shifting to stand hip-shot occasionally. Sleeping. *Maybe that's the other mule. Everett's mule. Maybe Hugh David already switched mules. So at least, that's one good thing.*

She eyed the only other movement on the Dunbar homestead—the dishtowel flitting gently in the night-wind. Given that it was well after midnight, Frankie had no real expectation of seeing any more activity on the Dunbar place, but she spent a few minutes scanning the land and buildings. Just to be sure.

When she turned her attention to Hugh David's homestead, though, she was surprised to see lanternlight in the soddy's windows. Using the spyglass and focusing it on the buildings, she realized there was actually a lot of movement; shadowed forms were crossing in front of the light, moving back and forth in front of the window. To Frankie's thinking, it seemed to be an awful lot of activity for this late hour. So she kept her scope trained on the house.

It wasn't more than a few minutes before she saw a new light showing at the soddy, a rectangular splash of light showing bright against the dark form of the house. The front door had been opened.

As difficult as it was to pick up details, given the distance and the low light of the waning moon, Frankie could see enough to know that two people were going in and out of the doorway. Hugh David and Rebecca were walking back and forth, going from the well-lit doorway, out to the dark shadows beside the soddy, and back through the doorway. On the out-going trips, the shadowy-shapes were always larger than on the in-going trips. And that told Frankie the story—they were carrying things. Arm-loads of items were being carried out of the house and into the dark shadows beside the building.

She couldn't see exactly what was in the shadows beside the building, but she was betting it was a wagon. Hugh David and Rebecca were loading their wagon and likely, before very long, they would be driving away. Sneaking away in the dead of night when no one would see them.

Her mind shifted back to Ida and Everett, worried suddenly that Hugh David had hurt them. Or maybe, worse. Frankie could feel her heart beating faster and she sucked in a few breaths, talking herself out of rushing down to the sod-house. Chewing on her lip. Forcing herself to stay still. *Wait. Think. Add things up. Just wait.*

Frankie turned the spyglass back to the Dunbar place, searching for something—anything that would tell her Everett and Ida were safe. She could see the mule still standing in the pen, and watching it sleeping there among the striped shadows of the fence, she realized it was giving her the answer she needed. The mule was proof that Ida and Everett were safe. *Because if Hugh David did something to them, he wouldn't have left the mule behind. And he wouldn't be trying to sneak away from them in the dark. So Everett and Ida must be safe.*

Turning her attention back to the activity at Hugh David's sod-house, Frankie was still biting her lip. But now, for a different reason. Because now, she was hoping she was reading things right, hoping that Rebecca and her husband were truly leaving. Hoping they were taking his mule and the wagon, along with whatever else they wanted, and leaving. *For good. For the good of everyone.*

After what she figured was another ten minutes, Frankie watched the shadowy form of the wagon pull away from the sod-house. One mule, one wagon, two people. They headed west along the homestead's roadway and turned south onto the main track. The mule clipped along, pushed into a fast trot.

She kept the spyglass trained on the wagon until it reached the cut in the high bank; she watched as the mule, the wagon and the two people went up and over the bank, topping out above the river-flats. The mule lifted into a trot—once again, being pushed harder than a poor-condition mule ought to be pushed. And then the mule and the wagon and the two people went out of sight. Out of view. Gone.

Frankie thought about mounting up and following them for a while, just to make sure that they were truly gone. But thinking back through their hasty departure, she let go of the idea. There was no need. Because Hugh David was traveling with a purpose. Likely, being the type of man he was, he had some idea about easy money and he'd have some kind of time-frame in mind. Plus, he thought he was getting away with something—he thought he was outsmarting Everett and Ida—and that meant he wasn't going to change his mind and suddenly turn around and come back. At some later point, maybe if he and Rebecca had some sort of trouble on the way, they might come back. But not tonight. For now, they were gone.

She watched the south track for a while longer. Just to be sure she had figured things right; just to be sure they weren't coming back. And then she swung up on Solomon and headed back the way she had come, following the trail she had been using along the north bank of the river.

It was in her mind to hot-foot it home, get some sleep, pull a few things together and head back over here at daylight. Everett and Ida were going to need an explanation about what happened. They'd also need to be convinced about something else—they would have to be convinced to go along with another part of the plan. Because sitting there in the dark, watching the activity, and thinking about Hugh David and his kind, Frankie had another concern.

Everett and Ida would be safe tonight, and maybe, they'd be safe tomorrow. But to Frankie's thinking, it was possible that Hugh David might still return. If the mule dropped dead, or if the wagon broke down, he and Rebecca would be back. Which meant that for a while, there was still danger.

The sun was just showing itself on the eastern horizon as Frankie rode into the Dunbars' yard, riding Samson and leading Artemis in-harness. Everett and Ida came rushing out of the front door of their soddy, hurrying toward her, waving for her to stop. They were clearly worried about something, and once Frankie was close enough to hear, she could tell they were calling out a warning.

"Hugh came back last evening. He and Rebecca are coming over this morning." Everett was shouting, glancing toward the other homestead, apparently concerned that Hugh David and Rebecca might be on their way over.

"No, Everett. No. They left in the night," Frankie shook her head and called out her news. "I watched them load up and pull out."

Frankie pulled Samson to a stop, slid down from the saddle as she started explaining, telling them what she had seen in the night. Telling them that Hugh and Rebecca had loaded the wagon in the dark and headed out from their place, going south. She told them that she had watched them go up through the cut, that she had watched until they were out of sight.

By the time she was halfway through the story, Everett and Ida had gone silent. They were staring at her. Listening to her. Listening to the truth. And when she finished the story, neither Everett or Ida said a word. Frankie watched her two wonderful neighbors standing in front of her with the sun rising behind them; as it rose over the far hills, it gave them an odd sort of backlight—almost as if a halo had formed around them.

Standing there in the early morning light, they seemed to be swaying a little, wavering a bit. Looking weak and frail. For a moment, Frankie wondered if maybe the soft morning breeze was going to knock them over. She stood in front of them, holding Samson's reins, watching them. Waiting. Because it was all she could think to do. *Just give them time. Give them the time they need.*

She saw tears welling up in Ida's eyes; she saw Everett's face go pale. They seemed to age a hundred years as they stood there. They both looked empty. Beaten. Worn down. And Frankie kept waiting, for what seemed an awfully long time.

"They left us with nothing, then." Everett finally spoke.

His voice was so soft that Frankie wasn't really sure if he had actually said anything. But then, as he went on, his voice grew a little louder.

"It's odd. Because Hugh seemed so happy when he came here yesterday evening. He said he had the wagon sitting over at their place, plumb full of supplies. He was so proud because he'd gotten them at a good price." Everett was shaking his head. "He came in the late evening, riding the mule. He wanted to take Jenny over to their place so he could haul the wagon of supplies over first thing this morning."

"We thought maybe everything was going to be okay, after all," Ida spoke then, her hands wrapped in her apron. Tears in her eyes. "He said he had gotten more than we expected. That the wagon was full."

Frankie felt her chest tightening, feeling like someone was wringing her heart, just like Ida was wringing the corner of her apron in her hands. So there it was, then; Hugh David had played them again. They had bought into the lies he told them. They had latched onto the false hope. He must have known that some part of them would still believe what he said.

"What did you tell him about the mare?"

"Just what we decided on. I figured to stick to the story, and then if things turned out okay, Jenny could always turn up later on. If it turned out that he was going to stay on."

"What did he say about her being gone?"

"Well, he was plenty upset. Blamed us for not taking care of things. He fumed for quite a while." Everett stared at the pen where Jenny had been tied as he talked. "Then, he took her halter and lead-rope and went out looking for her. He headed downriver like I told him. He came back just before dark and said he had seen her hoof-prints along the river. He said he had seen wolf tracks too."

Everett's hands were trembling; Ida was dabbing at her eyes with the corner of her apron.

"So he believed she was gone," Everett went on. "But he was still God-awful angry. And he switched mules on me. Claimed the one he'd been using was tired from the trip and he wanted the fresher one to bring the wagon with the supplies over in the morning."

Frankie looked at the mule standing in the pen. It was plenty thin and bony, but it wasn't wheezing and huffing like the other mule that had been in the pen when she took Jenny. It might be weak and tired out from the trip south, but she figured it was probably health-ier than the one Hugh had just taken.

"What else did he take?"

"My rifle. And the handful of bullets I had left. He said his rifle had jammed and that Rebecca had heard wolves and was scared."

In all the time they had been talking there in the morning sun-light, Everett hadn't moved a step. To Frankie, it seemed like he was frozen to the spot; he stood there, looking down at the dirt, shaking his head.

"So you know for sure? That him and Rebecca took off in the middle of the night? That they're truly gone now?" Everett kept star-ing at the ground. "Him and Rebecca, they left in the wagon, with the mule and all the supplies, and my rifle? And they left us with nothing?"

Frankie knew he didn't expect an answer. Mostly, he was asking the questions out loud, maybe with a last hope that the universe would give him different answers than what he was already hearing in his head.

"Listen, Everett. There weren't any supplies. They were loading the wagon with their belongings. And then they drove away. He did what you needed him to do. He left."

Frankie felt her gut tightening as she said the words, because neither Everett nor Ida seemed to hear what she was saying. She tried again.

"Everett! However it happened, he's gone now. And he can't tear your life up anymore. He outsmarted himself. He didn't get the mare like he thought he would. And without realizing it, he took the sickest mule." Frankie paused, waiting for the news to sink in. Still not sure that they were hearing her words.

"You both know he was lying about a wagon full of supplies. He was only telling you that because he was trying to get his hands on Jenny. If she'd been here, he would have left with her in the night. Instead, he handed you your own mule. He actually gave you the *best* mule." Frankie took a breath. "Everett, your plan worked. Jenny's safe. And you have your own mule."

Once again, Frankie waited, knowing they needed some time to realize that everything had happened in the best way. She watched them, pretty sure that neither would want to leave their place, even though their homestead had just become the most dangerous place for them. At least, for the time being.

It was then that Frankie realized it was exactly the way she had been thinking last night—Everett and Ida truly couldn't grasp the danger. They were overwhelmed with everything they were hearing, and everything they had to face. They couldn't see the danger because they still hadn't admitted the truth to themselves.

They couldn't see that Hugh David might rethink things—that he might come back in a fit of anger. Blaming them about the mare; blaming them for his own losses. Neither could they see there was a strong possibility that he and Rebecca might just come walking back in a day or two—because the mule he was driving might not make it very far. He might come back to get the other mule. And he'd be angrier than ever.

Frankie glanced over her shoulder, looking out toward the track to the south, toward the cut in the high bank. Dreading the thought of seeing Hugh David and Rebecca walking on the track.

She realized it was time to push things—she needed to get Everett and Ida off this place. She needed to get them away until it was safe again. Until the danger was past.

"Listen to me. We can't trust that Hugh David isn't going to come back. If he does, he'll be seething. He'll be hoping Jenny came back, or he'll want your mule. If he's mad, he's going to take it out on you two. You *know* he will." She spoke fast and firm, trying to use the clip and the cadence that her Lieutenant and her Captain used when they wanted no questions or arguments. "We're all going to my place for a few days. Till we're sure he's gone for good."

She watched them for a moment, watching them still frozen in place. *This won't do. They have to move. They have to know what to do.*

"Ida, you go in the house and pack up enough clothes for the both of you for a week or so. Then write a note to leave on the table. Say that it's for anyone looking for you and Everett."

Frankie looked at Ida. She was standing still. Silent and motionless. Not even dabbing her eyes any more. It wasn't Hugh David that Ida was thinking about; she was a mother—her thoughts would be on her daughter.

"Ida!" Frankie spoke to her again, louder now. "We don't have a lot of time. If that mule broke down a few miles down the road, they'll be back."

Ida looked up, suddenly understanding. She nodded; she was listening now. Frankie went on.

"Say in the note that you and Everett are leaving. That you're going back to where your family is. That you're not sure if you're coming back. Something like that. Then grab what you want to bring with you, because you two and your mule, are coming to my place."

125

She looked toward Everett, still speaking urgently, trying to make sure he understood.

"Get your mule haltered while I hitch Artemis to the wagon. I'll explain more once we're out of here."

Frankie backed Artemis and hitched him to their wagon while Everett caught up his mule and tied him to the tailgate. As they finished, the soddy's door slammed and Ida was walking from the house, carrying several bundles and a satchel. Everett stowed the bundles in the wagon-bed and helped her onto the wagon-seat. Frankie climbed in her saddle as Everett climbed onto the wagon-seat beside his wife and picked up the reins.

They headed out to the ford at a fast clip, Frankie on Samson and Everett turning Artemis to follow her, with his own mule tied at the tailgate. Frankie glanced to the south, eyeing the high ridge where the track went up through the cut. *No one there. No sign of anyone.*

Just like she had done the night she had taken their mare, Frankie swung to the south on the track for a hundred yards, and then headed west across the grassy river-flats. After a mile, she slowed down for the sake of the Dunbars' mule; a few miles after that, she began angling northwest to join up with the riverside track.

They traveled quietly through the early morning. Everyone, Frankie knew, was busy with their own thoughts. There was no conversation; no discussion. The journey had begun with a sudden sense of urgency—and maybe, a little desperation. Halfway to her homestead, the urgency had been replaced by sorrow, because with the immediate danger gone, the Dunbars were beginning to realize that their daughter was gone too.

Rebecca had left—following her husband into whatever trouble he would find or create—and it was unlikely she would return. She had been lost to them for a long time and now, they were facing that reality. The sadness wouldn't be resolved on this journey. Frankie knew that. It was a deep sorrow that would have to heal over time. And for now, during the journey to her meadow, no one spoke of it.

By the time they reached Frankie's meadow, another change had come over the Dunbars; the sorrow had changed to acceptance. And with that acceptance, a certain resolve seemed to have settled in them.

They pulled to a stop at the front barn-lot and they all looked at each other, knowing that the hard part was over—the decisions had been made. The confusion and the turmoil and the danger were gone. There was safety and respite here in the valley. If Hugh David did return, looking for something more, he would never think to look ten miles upriver.

Everett helped his wife down from the wagon; Ida stood by the wheel, smoothing out her dress and apron. She looked around her, eyeing the meadow. Then she looked at Everett and Frankie; she gave them a firm nod. And then Ida Dunbar took charge.

"I'm going to the kitchen to get that stove going. I think we could all use some coffee. You two see to the stock and the chores. Then come on in when you're done."

"I think we could all use a big breakfast too." Frankie called after her, watching her walking toward the house, taking a moment on the way to reach down to ruffle Matilda's ears.

"I suspect you just made her awfully happy, giving her a free rein in the kitchen like that." Everett turned and started looping the lines on the hames; he moved to the traces, patting Artemis on his back as he went. "Once we get these boys unharnessed and unsaddled, you think maybe that Jersey cow of yours will let me milk her?"

"If you don't mind doing the milking, Mr. Dunbar, I'll see to the hens and gather the eggs."

Frankie loosened the cinch on Samson and led him into the barn. Behind her, she could hear Everett talking to Artemis, his voice soft and kind as he started working on the harness buckles. He had asked about doing the milking, but she knew it hadn't really been a question. In his own way, Everett Dunbar had told her he *needed* to do the milking—there had been a certain sound in his voice that said he had been missing that particular chore. It was no different from

127

Ida wanting time to herself in the kitchen, getting coffee and a big breakfast together. Frankie had heard that same sound in her voice too.

Once they were in the kitchen and having breakfast, Everett and Ida wanted to hear the entire story of the nighttime departure. And this time, when she explained her concerns about Hugh David returning, they listened closely. Everett and Ida talked, too—discussing the problems and the dangers they knew could come if their son-in-law returned, admitting now, that they couldn't trust either Hugh David or Rebecca.

They agreed that if something did happen to the mule Hugh was driving, it could go two ways—if he and Rebecca were fewer than two days away, they'd come back for the other mule. If they had traveled more than two days, they'd be closer to Fort Cottonwood so it was more likely they'd continue on their way there.

If they *did* have to walk back, Everett counted it as three days for them to get back to the homesteads. They would see the note, maybe stay for a day or two, but with them and the mule gone, too— Hugh and Rebecca would end up leaving; they'd probably decide to go on to Fort Cottonwood again.

"The walk'll probably do them some good." Ida said it with a bit of spit and fire in her voice, and Everett and Frankie burst into laughter. Ida stood to fill coffee cups again, and she gave a little huffing snort before continuing. "Well. If it happens like that, then they deserve what they conjured up. They were willing to leave us afoot if they could have. Let them taste some of their own medicine."

Frankie and Everett laughed harder and Ida joined in. There was a spark in Ida's eyes, and to Frankie's thinking, it was a good sign. Apparently, Ida decided she had been confused and sad for long enough. Now, she was angry and putting a voice to it. Frankie knew exactly what her Aunt Sarah would have to say about it—she'd say that spouting a bit of righteous anger was one of the signs of healing.

The Dunbars decided to stay with Frankie at her place for the time being, agreeing it would be safer. Adding things up, they all agreed that if Hugh and Rebecca *did* return, it would most likely be within the next six days. They tacked on another two days just for good measure and decided to stay clear of their homestead for eight days.

Ida, though, expressed some concern about taking advantage of Frankie's offer for them to stay at her homestead. Frankie had expected as much, and she knew exactly what to do—all she had to do was give them a mission that would override any worry about taking unfair advantage.

She said it would help her a lot if they stayed. Because, she told them, if they stayed for a week or so, they could show her things about her homestead. Everett, she said, could teach her about her land and help her locate her section-markers. And he could teach her about the windmills and the flues.

"And I've never had a root-cellar before. I need help sorting everything in the bins," she told Ida. "And I need you to teach me how to set it up for winter."

Frankie saw the quick look Ida flashed her way and she knew that Ida wasn't fooled; she knew exactly what her young neighbor was doing with all the talk about windmills and section-markers and root-cellars. But then, in spite of what she knew, Ida turned to Everett with a question.

"Eight days then?"

"Well, our place will be fine if we aren't there," Everett shook his head and gave a wry smile. "We don't have to worry about feeding livestock, because all our stock is here."

"Maybe though, if we're cautious, we could make a few trips over to tend to the garden?" Ida looked back to Frankie. "Maybe to pick what's ready in the garden? And to look things over?"

Ida sounded like she was asking questions, but Frankie knew she was just trying to get used to the thought of being away from her home. She was trying the idea on for size, seeing if it felt right. She was silent for a moment, and then she gave a soft nod.

"All right. If you're willing to put up with us." She gave her firm nod then; she had decided.

And Frankie breathed a sigh of relief. The last part of the plan to get the Dunbars out of danger was done. It had been the most difficult part, but now, finally, her neighbors would be safe. There would still be more reckoning for Everett and Ida, regarding their daughter and son-in-law—because there had been theft and betrayal and loss. The wounds to their hearts and their spirits would need time to heal. But the plan was complete, except for the week of waiting.

The three of them stayed in the kitchen, sitting at the big trestle table, talking about what Ida declared was a new start.

"A fresh start is the whole reason we came out here. Maybe we got waylaid a bit, but there's nothing saying we can't still have that dream. And this time, I think we have a chance. Because there won't be anyone to tear things down." Ida reached to pat Everett's hand. "We have a fine piece of land. We have a good garden with plenty of vegetables and root-crops. We have crops in the fields, and we'll manage to get them in somehow."

"Plus, we have our mare. And our mule. And if we can get him fattened up some, we can put him to work. Ol' Isaac, he's always been strong in the field." Everett turned his eyes to Frankie, winked at her. "And we have us a new neighbor. A good one too. She lives just down the road from us."

They kept talking and Frankie could hear the hope in their words. She could hear something else, too, and she suspected it was relief. Which made sense, because hope and relief were a lot easier to cultivate when you weren't surrounded by a fog of confusion and danger.

Neither Everett nor Ida showed any sign of despair over their son-in-law's departure, and if there was sadness over their daughter leaving them, it didn't show while they were at the table. That subject, and the sorrow that would surround it, would likely come later; it was something that would find its way to the surface when the waters calmed a bit, and then Ida and Everett would find their way through it together. Because they had lost a daughter—and no matter what shape things had taken, there would still be grief.

But now, as they started on second helpings of fried eggs and ham, fried potatoes and onions, the talk centered around what Hugh David hadn't gotten his hands on. There was a very real sense of joy that Jenny and Isaac had been kept safe from his clutches. Jenny was fine and healthy, and it was likely that, with a little time, Isaac would return to health too.

They ended up laughing about Hugh David and how he thought he had been clever enough to switch mules like he did; he believed he was getting shed of the trail-tired mule and getting the fresher one. But it pleased Everett that Hugh had actually ended up with his own mule—a mule which Everett was not really sorry to see off his place.

"That mule always had a tendency to be poorly," Everett said. "And he was a hard mule to work in the fields. He was always a bad balker and he had a dang nasty kick too."

Frankie's thoughts went back to the night she spirited Jenny away from the Dunbar place; it was Hugh's mule in the pen that night—the one with lung and digestive problems—the one that would probably never recover. Hugh had taken Isaac for his trip to Fort Cottonwood and it was Isaac that he had left with Everett when he returned. It was his own mule he had taken when he slipped away in the night.

Given the pace Hugh had set when they headed out, Frankie was sure that the mule's problems were going to get a lot worse, a lot faster; she doubted it would survive the journey to Fort Cottonwood.

The mule out there in her barn—Everett's own mule—was certainly in rough shape. And that, as Everett had explained, had to do with Hugh. Hugh David was the type of man who used livestock harshly and while Isaac had suffered under his hand, Frankie doubted there were long-standing problems in him. He needed some doctoring and some time to recover, but with some grain and some good grazing, she figured he'd be fine.

Partway through their breakfast, Everett's face had softened; a smile had been playing on his face through much of the conversation

131

and Frankie figured it was because he was seeing some light—he was seeing things from a different perspective. They had been in a bad situation, but a plan had been set in place to get them out of it. It had all worked out. And now, Everett could see that they had a chance.

Ida looked different too. The longer they talked, the more she seemed to relax. With a little more time at the table, Ida began talking about Hugh David.

"I was afraid of Hugh and his temper for a long time," she said. "For a very long time." She said it slowly, as if she were listening to the words for the first time. "I never liked him. Never trusted him. He was shiftless, for one thing. But it was more than that. He was so unpredictable and that's what scared me the most. Thinking about it now, I knew all along we were in danger." Tears started running down her cheeks. "It got to where we were afraid to disagree with him about anything. Even about things on our *own* place. Because we never knew what might set him off."

"Nothing good can come from meeting up with him again," Everett agreed, nodding. "Now, we need to come up with a plan to take care of our garden for the next week. I don't want all that produce spoiling just because we're concerned Hugh David *might* return."

So the three of them put a new plan in place. They would all go to check on the place every other day. From the rise near their ford, they would look things over to make sure Hugh and Rebecca weren't around. Once they knew it was safe, Everett and Ida could go down to their farmyard to check on their house, tend to their garden and collect the vegetables that were ready. Frankie would ride to the cut in the high bank to the south and act as lookout, watching the road to the south. And of all of them, it was Ida who liked the plan the most.

"We can still keep our place in shape and that makes me so happy. As long as we don't have to take any chances. Because it's like Everett says, nothing good can come from meeting up with Hugh again. We need him gone from our lives." She paused for a moment, looking out through the kitchen door. "It's odd how clear it is to me now. Everything has been so dark for so long. We never had a chance at being happy as long as he was near."

Something in Ida had come alive again—Frankie could hear it in her voice. Some piece that had been buried inside her was rising up. Ida Dunbar was finding her way back to herself. She was a woman who was a mother by nature—protecting and nurturing a family was a strong part of her spirit. And over time, like everything else, Hugh David had taken that from her as well; he had scared it out of her and he had worn her down.

Now, with no one working to break her down, Ida would have time to settle into herself again, and Frankie figured that everyday life in her home meadow would allow it to happen faster and easier. There was safety here. Peace and solitude. The dangers that had been in Ida's life were far away now. Whatever was left of the fears and the uncertainty, would fade with each passing day.

Frankie sat listening to Everett and Ida talking. They were talking about Jenny and their mule and about what would be ready in their garden. Everett decided he might work on the axles on his wagon and wondered if there might be some grease out in the barn he could use. Ida thought maybe she'd put some dough together and get a few loaves of bread going and wondered if Frankie thought that would be okay.

They went on with their planning and thinking and wondering, and Frankie figured the best thing to do was to just let them keep going. She knew she was grinning, because now—while they were in the midst of thinking and planning, wondering and hoping, there was something else going on—Everett and Ida were healing.

It seemed like there was always healing going on in this little meadow. She had done her own healing; it had started the moment she had driven her Shires and the big blue-green Conestoga into the valley. She had survived her sorrows and her wounds; she had survived the dangers and the pain. Now, it was time for Everett and Ida to do the same.

As soon as they finished at the table, Frankie brought out the remedy-chest, her Aunt Sarah's remedy-chest that had become her own. She had used the remedies and poultices and powders from the chest when her Lieutenant was snake-bit, and she had used the remedies on Boone when he had been wounded in battle. Now, she had another patient—Everett's mule needed some doctoring.

She selected the powders she wanted, mixed them together and added a handful of clay powder. She tossed the mixture into a pail along with a good bait of cornmeal and oatmeal from the pantry added hot water and drizzled some molasses into the mix. Everett finished his cup of coffee, and then they set off across the meadow, heading for Isaac's pen.

Frankie stood back while Everett fed the bucket of grain-mash to his mule, answering his questions about what she thought was wrong with him. She stepped into the pen and walked over to a fresh pile of his droppings, beckoning for Everett. She kicked at the pile, showing what lay within; it was churning with little white worms.

"*That's* the problem. His gut's full of them. He's slowly starving while they're getting fat and healthy off everything he's eating. I think he was probably pastured on wetlands-grass before you got him. Back in Indiana, my uncle could always spot animals that had been grazed too long on wetland-grass." Frankie watched as Everett nodded, his mind, no doubt, going back in time.

"He's so full of worms, he's probably been dropping them like this for a while. The remedies I put in his grain will flush out the rest of them, along with their eggs, once and for all. Once we get the bulk of the worms and eggs out, his gut will start healing. Then he'll start putting on weight again. His hide will get its shine back too." She grinned at him. "Isaac's gonna be fine. Probably in time for harvest."

Everett hugged her against him and held her there for a moment, shaking his head. Then he stepped to Isaac's side and stood stroking his neck while the mule worked his way through the last of the grain in the bucket.

"So Hugh's mule is afflicted with the same thing?"

"I think so. But he's probably worse off because he doesn't have the solid breeding that Isaac does. So his mule was probably worse to start with." She kept talking, thinking that Everett already knew what she was going to say. "That night when I was getting Jenny,

134

I could hear that other mule huffing and wheezing in the next pen. It's not just worms in his gut. That mule's blood and lungs are full of infection. The more Hugh uses him, the faster he'll go downhill and the quicker he'll drop dead. Hugh had that mule going at a fast clip when I watched them leaving. That's why I've been thinking he and Rebecca might come walking back in a few days. I'm not sure that mule will get Hugh David far enough down the road to keep him out of our hair."

"So. Hugh really did out-smart himself, then? By switching mules with me?"

"I'd say so. I think you're way better off than he is. He tricked himself into a mess. But I doubt he'll ever realize it."

Ida had her mind and her heart on taking charge of the house. It was work she knew—it was safe and familiar and it was where she felt comfortable. And here in Frankie's meadow, the kitchen became her domain. She ignored any protest Frankie put up; she smiled and sent her outside with Everett.

And on the second morning, she laid down the law. 'From now on, you two deal with the livestock and see to the milking and the feeding. I'll take care of the chickens. Breakfast will be on the table when you come in from your chores.'

And like Everett, Frankie learned to comply; she and Everett simply nodded and headed out the kitchen door, grinning as they went to tend to chores. Leaving the house to Ida.

After they returned and she fed them, Ida sent them out again while she stayed in the house; she began her days with a flurry of baking, moved on to starting the midday dinners. And then she started cleaning. There wasn't much, she found, because Frankie had been taught to keep a clean house. Ida had suspected as much when Frankie had talked about spending her first two days in her new home, dusting and sweeping and washing bedding.

But Ida cleaned anyway, because, besides the house, there were other buildings to clean and sweep out, and other buildings with windows to wash. She spent time cleaning in the second house that Frankie called the Barracks. She moved on to the Dwelling Place in the hillside. Then she spent some time sweeping and dusting and washing windows in the tack-room in the barn. After that, she spent hours cleaning the root-cellar—with Frankie at her side—sorting through the produce.

But mostly, it was the house where Ida wanted to be. She spent her time there doing what she needed to do for her heart and spirit. Cooking and baking. Sweeping. Washing the clothes and the bed linens. Straightening the rooms. She accepted Frankie's help when she was in the house, but she didn't ask for it. Nor did she need it.

What she *needed* was to be a wife and to run a household. That had been taken from her, because the events of the past few years had shaken her to the core. The future she had strived for had disappeared from her life. She had always thrived on nurturing and nourishing the people around her. Ida knew that about herself—her pride was in building a home, just like Everett's pride was in his land and livestock.

And here at Frankie's homestead, Ida knew she had a household to run. Here, there were meals to cook and baking to do. And here, there was a pantry that allowed for it. There were people to nurture here—two people who gladly accepted what she had to offer; two dogs that counted on the scraps she passed on to them; chickens that required her attention.

Ida could feel the peace and the confidence rising up from deep inside her, rising up from where it had been crushed. She was experiencing happiness again, a sweet happiness, that had been gone for a long time. She was smiling again. And laughing—laughing hard enough that sometimes her jaw actually ached.

From inside the kitchen, and out on the porch, Ida had been watching Frankie in the meadow and around the buildings and her livestock. Watching as she was becoming part of her homestead and blending into the life in her valley, day by day. She so clearly loved the life in her meadow, and more than that, she loved learning about it. For the last few days, during their meals and late into the evenings, Frankie had been peppering them with questions about the land and the weather and the seasons.

Now, halfway through the morning, as Ida was busy punching the bread-dough down after its first rise, bringing it together for the noon meal, she could see the activity out the kitchen window. She watched Frankie and Everett walking through the grass, heading toward the front pasture.

Ida could tell Frankie was chattering as she walked with Everett. And she was probably asking her questions; probably, working her way through a whole string of questions. And as was her way, she would be listening intently to Everett's answers, learning everything he could teach her.

Ida could feel a smile on her face as she watched the two, recognizing the feel of her old smile. It was her smile from the past—a light and easy smile. And it was Frankie who was making her smile. Because she was out there, trotting along beside Everett in the way of ten-year-olds, bouncing a little as she walked with him. Ida's smile grew as she watched, knowing Frankie didn't really need to trot to keep up, because Everett wasn't walking at a fast pace. Nor did she need to bounce. But it was her way; it was her energy, her excitement with life.

Frankie was one of those kids who picked up things quickly; Ida had seen enough to know that. And she wasn't shy about asking her questions, either.

'A *lot* of questions,' Everett had said last night after they were in bed. He had started laughing and Ida had shushed him, knowing Frankie was in her room next to theirs. 'So *many* questions,' he had whispered then, chuckling. 'But every one of them matters to her. She's not just jabbering like some kids. She just wants to know everything.'

So Everett had a new work-companion who kept him company throughout the day—trotting beside him, asking questions and making him laugh. Because, Frankie had a special way of making Everett laugh. And it was good for him.

Earlier in the morning, Ida had spotted them across the meadow at the windmill. Frankie had been standing on a crossbar halfway up the windmill tower. There was something Everett was teaching her about the windmill, something about handling a lever of some sort; she was looking down and saying something, and Everett was looking up and nodding.

And then they were both suddenly laughing. Everett pointed at something above her and Frankie was climbing and reaching and saying something to him that started him laughing even harder. Ida wasn't at all sure what could possibly be so funny about pulling levers and discussing the workings of a windmill, but they were clearly enjoying themselves. For some reason lost to Ida, they were actually enjoying working on the contraption.

For Ida, everything about Frankie Harding was fascinating. It was fascinating that this child had found her way here to the Sand Hills by herself. This ten-year-old had managed to bring the family's wagon and all the livestock across the prairie and through the hills to this valley. But somehow, in spite of all the hurdles and hardships— and there had been plenty of those—she had done it.

As the days went by, she and Everett were hearing even more of the story of Frankie's journey. They were learning what she had been through, and what she had fought against. And as unbelievable as it all seemed, the more they were around her, the more believable it all became. Some of it, Ida thought, was just because of what was inside of Frankie—it was her nature and her spirit. But much of it went back to the foundation her family had given to her.

It was just as Everett had said in the bedroom one night; it was Frankie's father, and her aunt and uncle, who had given her the right start in life. They had given her a strong foundation—they had understood her spirit and they had strived to guide and strengthen her character. They had given her a strong education and they had taught her to believe in her strengths. They had encouraged the passions they recognized in her. And most importantly, they had built a high level of resolve and determination within her. *This child,* Ida thought, *knows all about perseverance.*

With that kind of direction, Frankie had learned to adapt in life; she adjusted easily and quickly to everything going on around her. She was clear-minded about what she wanted and about what she knew was right. There were times when she talked like an adult and handled things like an adult. And yet, there was so much about her that was still a laughing, light-hearted ten-year-old.

In a lot of ways, Ida thought, Frankie was like their third son, Caleb; he had been a funny and light-hearted child, but at the same time, he had been so level-headed and clever. He had been a quick-thinker like Frankie. And like her, he had a knack for knowing how to get things done. Of all their children, Caleb was the one who could figure out how to make something happen. He could always see all the angles—he had always been beyond his years in that way—to the point that even his older brothers knew enough to listen to his ideas.

Much like Frankie, Caleb had had a strong sense about people too. He had been the first to recognize what Hugh David was like. He had warned her and Everett about what Rebecca would become if she stayed with him. And he had been right.

And now, it was becoming apparent that Everett was dealing with Frankie and responding to her, much the same as he had with Caleb. It was a comfortable companionship between them; they simply enjoyed each other. And that, was making such a difference for Everett.

In a matter of just a few days, Ida could tell he was doing so much better. The pale look to his face was gone. His shoulders were no longer stooped. There was purpose in his stride again. His spirit seemed to be rising up again and Ida knew Frankie was responsible for that. At least, for part of it.

And as she watched the pair walking and talking their way through the meadow grass, Ida knew that her own spirit was rising up, too—she could feel it at night when she lay down in the back bedroom and she could feel it when she rose in the morning. There was no doubt it was because of Frankie and these days of respite in her meadow.

Just by being who she was, just because of the spirit and sensibility her family had protected in her, Frankie had given them a way out of the horrible mess Hugh David had created. It was a situation that had been getting worse year by year. Then, month by month. Then, every week. Finally, the confusion, the tension, and the problems had been increasing daily.

Thinking about it now, Ida realized she and Everett had become aware of it, but they hadn't been able to find a way out of it. They hadn't been able to see their way clear of it. Ida smiled to herself. *But we're seeing things clearly now. We're talking each night, back there in the bedroom. We're figuring a way out of the situation we've been in.*

Frankie, though, had seen it all clearly enough. And she had seen a way for them to get out of the ugly little hell of hopelessness they had been mired in. She had made the solution so simple. So obvious. They had asked for her to help with their mare, but she had seen the real problem, the underlying problem. She had known to look deeper. It was a perspective beyond her years—it rose out of her sense and sensibility. And it was part of what her father and uncle and aunt had nurtured in her.

And now, out there in this pretty little meadow on this warm August morning, Frankie was back to being a ten-year-old child, busy learning what she needed to know. Busy adapting to this new life. Determined to find a way to live out here. And she was so *excited* about it all. No fears. No frustration. Just her lively and sensible way of handling things. Taking it step-by-step, and enjoying each minute of it. That had been Caleb's way too.

Ida finished shaping the loaves, settled them into their buttered pans and spread a dishtowel over them. She left them to rise and walked out to the porch. Thinking about making a rabbit potpie for dinner. Thinking about talking to Everett and Frankie about hunting for a deer. Thinking that venison for the table tomorrow, would be a nice thing. *Steaks for breakfast, and maybe a venison roast for dinner.*

There were rifles here at Frankie's homestead and it might be good for Everett to go on a hunt. Hunting had been limited on their place, because there had been only a handful of bullets left. Bullets had been on the supply list that Hugh had carried with him. Now, there weren't any bullets, nor was there a rifle, because Hugh David had taken it all.

Ida walked out to the chicken-house, smiling as she swung the henyard door wide, fastening it open so 'the ladies' could come out to begin their hunting and pecking. Seeking out the worms and the slugs, the seeds and the bugs. And any new-sprouting weeds they craved. *The ladies. That's what Frankie calls them.*

She started laughing, thinking about what Frankie had told her about naming her chickens.

'I'm holding off on naming them,' she had said. 'I'll name mine after you and Everett pick out the ones you want to take home. Because you should have the right to name your own. And I don't want to waste the names that I like on any that you take.' *Really, such a clever perspective. Such a ten-year-old perspective.*

So Frankie had held off christening any of the hens, except for the mean-tempered broody-hen, Mrs. Swingle. That one, Frankie explained, had already earned her name. Ida burst into laughter, remembering Frankie's description of the moody neighbor-lady back in Indiana. The name seemed natural for the broody hen. 'It just sort of popped into my mind while I was getting pecked half to death,' Frankie had admitted. So the reputation of the Indiana neighbor-lady lived on in Frankie's meadow.

Once she gathered the eggs, Ida stepped out of the coop with her basket. She waded through the hens already busy pecking around the outside of the coop and walked toward Frankie and Everett coming from the barn. Everett was carrying the milk-pail, brimful of rich Jersey milk, and Frankie was telling him a story about a soldier named Crazy Eddie, explaining about how he made her carry water with him one day and had her laughing so hard with his goofy stories that she had sloshed water out of the buckets all the way to the cook-fire. And then, she said, all the other soldiers had given her what-for because she had wasted so much water, claiming that they wouldn't have enough for a pot of coffee.

She was telling the story in a way that had Everett laughing so hard that *he* was sloshing the milk out of the bucket; finally, he stopped and put the bucket down.

"Darn it, Frankie, you're no better than that Crazy Eddie. I'm wasting milk here, like you were wasting water."

Frankie just gave him her crooked little grin, not looking particularly worried about the spilled milk. She was laughing, telling him to keep carrying the milk-pail.

"Just keep walking and sloshing the milk around like that. You'll have butter churned-up by the time we get to the house."

Plans had been made to bring in loads of firewood for both homesteads, and Frankie had the perfect place in mind. It was just after sun-up on the morning of what promised to be a hot August day, and she and Everett were bringing Bo and Benjamin up from the back pasture. They spanned and yoked them to the heavy farm-wagon, and then, with Ida sitting on the wagon-seat beside Everett, balancing a dishpan packed with dinner, they headed out of the valley. They turned upriver for a day of woodcutting.

Each day, for three days in a row, they traveled upriver a little more than a mile to the riverbend with the mountain of dead wood. And every morning, Frankie rode horseback beside the wagon, Matilda sat on the wagon-seat between the Dunbars, and Laughing Girl trotted along beside the wagon, watching for rabbits.

They spent the mornings pulling heavy branches and small trunks from the tangle of wood. They had their noon dinners on a blanket in the grass, and after they rested for a while, they went back to work, cutting everything into firewood or fenceposts. They worked until the doves and meadowlarks began their evening songs, and as the twilight settled in, Ida packed up the dishpan and the blanket, while Frankie and Everett spanned and yoked the oxen. And then they would head back to the meadow.

They stacked the first day's work—a wagonload of firewood—under the porch roof of the Barracks, protected from the weather and only steps from the house. The next day's load of fenceposts was stacked in the back corner of the barn, half for Frankie and half for Everett to retrieve as needed. The third day's load was firewood again, and that load would stay in the wagon, waiting for the Dunbars' trip home.

"It's a fine thing, Frankie Harding, to have a start on winter wood," Everett patted a few of the short logs on the last wagonload, satisfaction shining in his eyes. "It's a mighty comforting feeling knowing we're well on our way. To tell you true, Honey, I wasn't sure how I'd find the time, or the means, to cut and haul wood for the winter." Everett Dunbar stared out toward the back valleys. "It's an odd thing, but I always thought I'd have grown sons to help me with such things. And I guess I thought I'd have a son-in-law to help too."

"All we need is a few more sessions like this and we should have plenty." Frankie watched his eyes turn back to her. "Don't you think so, Mr. Dunbar?"

"I believe you're right, Miss Harding. With a few more days out there, with the saws a-sawing and the hatchets a-hatcheting, we should have some fair-sized stacks."

Frankie laughed at his word-game and he laughed with her. Partly, Frankie thought, he was laughing because she was laughing. Partly, because it was one less worry. And partly, because he was just plain happy—pleased with both the work and the wood. The work had paid off and the wagonloads of fenceposts and firewood proved it. He was building for his future.

For Everett, the woodcutting days beside the river made the biggest difference in his life. It was proof that his life was turning around. Spanning and yoking the oxen, driving to the riverbend, cutting and loading the wood—all of it was about working toward the future. The days of solid and sensible work, and the knowledge that he was accomplishing something toward his future was filling him up inside. Pride was growing in him again—a pride that came from knowing he was providing and protecting, planning and preparing. Once again, he was caring for his wife and his home.

Finally, after a long time of being lost, he was getting back to being who he really was. Along with the pride, there was something else rising up within him and Everett knew exactly what it was. It was hope; hope was coming up from somewhere deep inside. That pride and hope had been tamped down for a long time, but now, he could feel them as plainly as he could feel the ache in his muscles and the blisters on his hands. It was the work that was doing it; because it was work that was finally making sense and paying off. *This* work was taking him forward; *this* work was creating stability and building a solid foundation.

Each day, by the time Ida called them away from the saws and the axes for the noonday meals, he was tired and aching from the morning's work. And *that* was his best reward—it was proof his life was finally turning in the right direction. There was a pleasure in the hard work. Work done sensibly. Work done well.

And there was the pleasure of needing rest for his body and for his tired arms, and for his sore back. It filled him with contentment to rest in the shade of the riverside trees with his companions, eating the meal Ida had packed. It was a contentment he hadn't felt for years.

He and Ida listened to the stories Frankie told. And Frankie listened to the stories they had. They told her about their sons, laughing at the memories and describing the nonsense growing boys could get into.

Ida talked about her garden—talking about what they still had to harvest and her plans for planting the coming year. And every day, she talked about the chickens they'd be taking home, and about how nice it would be to have hens scratching around the farmyard. 'Maybe some of those Dominikers,' she decided. 'And some Leghorns.'

And every day, when Everett heard the excitement in her voice, he felt excitement in his own heart. He knew he had come home again; he was where he belonged. He had ideas and plans for his farm—ideas and plans much like those he'd had when they first arrived. But now, there were no doubts or fears clouding his vision.

They had taken up a quit-claim, he and Ida. Like Frankie's place, the buildings were already there on their homestead when they arrived. With the buildings and fences waiting for them, and two of the forty-acre fields already worked, it seemed like the hardest part of getting a homestead up and running was already done. It was supposed to have been a head-start—since they would be able to move straight into farming and planting crops.

That had been his plan and his hope on the day they drove their wagon through the ford on the North Loup and onto their place. But instead, within two years, everything had crumbled.

First, it seemed they just had a few unlucky turns and he had believed those things would straighten out. But then those things—those various things—like the livestock dying, and equipment breaking down, and Hugh David always 'needing' to be heading off somewhere, continued to happen. For a while, it seemed like everything was getting worse by the month. Then each week seemed to be worse than the last.

Looking back, Everett realized he had been trying to run the two homesteads at the same time. Working harder with fewer working teams. Always working to keep up, and then working to catch up. He and Ida had ended up doing the work of four people. When Hugh David was on the place, he did little or no work, and when he'd disappear for weeks at a time, Rebecca would sit idle, doing nothing but waiting for him to return.

Everett had seen that nothing seemed to improve and nothing was ever resolved, no matter how much work he put in. And all the things that were always going wrong that Hugh and Rebecca left untouched—the things that ended up broken, sick and dying—just kept adding up.

The point had come when he had caved in. He reached the point when he figured there was no longer any chance of getting caught up. That was the point when hope disappeared; the point when he and Ida still put on a good face, but they knew it was over. They feared they'd have to pull up stakes and leave before winter set in. That point had come in the middle of July, just before Frankie came up the track from the south.

And that night, after they met Frankie Harding on the road, he and Ida had talked. They decided it was crucial to protect the mare and keep her away from Hugh David. Because the mare, Jenny, had become the most valuable possession they had left; she was their key to survival, their only way out—with her, at least, they would have the means to leave when the time came.

And now, Everett thought, *here I am, working a team of fine oxen and putting an axe and saw to wood. Spending these days getting ready for the winter. Setting-in firewood and making plans for harvest. Planning for some kind of harvest because I'll have a team I can count on.*

Now, on the third day of woodcutting, he was lying back in the grass, watching Frankie as she laughed and talked with Ida; the two of them were laughing like schoolgirls, talking about funny little things having to do with gardens and chickens and the joys of baking with eggs and cream.

Everett watched them, thinking about the morning's work, watching the oxen settled down in the grass. Ruminating. Drowsing. Here by the riverbank, there were *neighborly things* going on; neighbors helping each other out. Neighbors cutting firewood. Cutting fenceposts. Sharing a meal. Sharing ideas and plans. He liked that he was helping Frankie out with firewood, just as she was helping them out. But Everett knew Frankie Harding was doing something else too.

He knew she was watching how he worked the oxen; she was watching how he handled them with the wagon. Young as she was, she knew how to work and she knew how to 'get in and get things done'. She had been taught that; she knew the value of it. And through all these days, while he and Ida were in and around the meadow, she had been watching to see if her new neighbors knew the value of work too.

She had never said anything about it, but it was clear someone had taught her there was no sense partnering up with anyone who didn't share the same values. Likely, her father or her uncle had instilled that in her; whoever it had been, had taught her well.

It didn't bother Everett that he was being tested. In fact, it made him smile. Because he knew the value of working hard. He, too, liked 'getting in and getting things done'. He had been taught to live that way, and that's what he had taught his own children. But somehow, in the last few years, he had gotten off track; he had put both himself and Ida in a dangerous situation by not living according to that standard.

Looking back with clearer eyes now, he could see he had known well enough that his son-in-law didn't see the value in a good day's work. But he had convinced himself Hugh David would change. He wanted to believe in the man his daughter married; he wanted to believe that eventually, Hugh David would find pride in work done well. He had convinced himself that Hugh would catch on, that he'd change for the better.

His sons, all three of them, had learned what he had taught them about work; his daughter, though, never had. The truth was, Rebecca was no better than the man she married. Everett had clung to a desperate hope that they both would come around. But it had been a false hope. And it had almost ruined him.

Frankie loved the time beside the river with Everett and Ida. They separated branches and trunks from the great mountain of wood and used the oxen to drag the wood to the grassy glade. There, they sorted it, sized it and cut it, and then loaded it in the wagon. Hard work and steady work. Working together; laughing together. They had their picnics beside the river. They worked in the cool morning air and in the hot afternoon sun. In the early twilight, they packed up and headed home, tired and happy together. Still telling their stories and still laughing together.

And each evening when they got home to the meadow, while Frankie and Everett unloaded the wagon, Ida milked Blossom. Then, while Ida gathered the eggs and Matilda sent the hens into the coop for the night, she and Everett would walk the meadow. Checking the stock; checking gates. 'Putting the livestock to bed,' Everett called it.

And then she and Ida would set supper on the table, and for the rest of the evening, they would sit at the kitchen table, eating and talking. Planning for harvest, and planning for the sale of the crops. And they planned for the planting in the spring.

Things were coming together and Frankie was pleased. She was settling in to her homestead; she and Ida and Everett were blending into their lives as neighbors. She trusted the Dunbars and they trusted her. The time in her meadow together was good for all of them.

Each night, the land of the Sand Hills was cooled by night-rains—gentle, late-summer rainstorms that washed the grasses and cleaned the land. Dark, low-lying thunder-clouds rumbled through the nights; bright sunlight and silver-blue skies ruled the days. Ida declared that it was the best thing for her garden, and after the three days of woodcutting, they started traveling to the Dunbar homestead every other day. Everett and Ida drove their wagon and Frankie took on the role of Cavalry scout, riding ahead of the wagon and the mare—looking for any sign of activity on the two homesteads.

Then, while they tended to their place, she took up her post on the high ridge where the track cut up the steep embankment, watching the main track to the south. Watching for any sign of travelers, for any trouble that might come up the trail. Watching for the possible return of Hugh David and Rebecca, and saying little silent prayers, asking God and his angels to keep them away.

With no livestock on their place, Ida and Everett had few chores to do; mostly they checked inside the house and the other buildings, looking for any telltale sign of disturbance, for any indication that Hugh and Rebecca had returned.

And then they worked in the garden picking the ripened produce, digging the ready root-crops. They filled their baskets and crates and loaded their wagon, stopping to look to the south occasionally, keeping an eye on their young neighbor out on the rise, watching to see if she had spotted trouble coming up the track.

With every trip, Ida and Everett came away with a bounty of vegetables. There were crates of beans and tomatoes and every kind of root vegetable Frankie could think of. And that made her smile, because Ida knew what she was doing in a garden, just like her Aunt Sarah had. The warm days and the nighttime rains had done their part, but in Frankie's mind, the crates and baskets filled with food told the story—Ida Dunbar knew how to plant a good garden. And she knew how to nurture one.

At suppertime in the meadow, the table was always loaded with platters of vegetables straight from the garden, both cooked and fresh. The bulk of the harvest, though, was being transferred into the root-cellar. Frankie and Ida worked together in the cool of the cellar, filling the bins and crates with carrots and parsnips, turnips and beets. They spread onions and garlic on the long counter to cure. They tied bundles of dill and sage, parsley and thyme, rosemary and basil and hung them from hooks in the ceiling.

They sorted through the bins, organizing and planning, making space for the coming produce—more of the root vegetables that were still growing in Ida's garden. And there would be the squashes and melons and pumpkins.

'And sweet potatoes,' Ida told her. 'Lots of sweet potatoes. And yellow potatoes and russets too.'

They had been smiling at each other while they worked, both happy with their newest decision. A neighborly decision. The Hardings and Dunbars would share the use of the cellar. Frankie would supply the storage space until Ida had her own cellar, and Ida would share her garden's produce until Frankie had her own garden.

On the last day of the Dunbars' stay, preparations began for the move back to their homestead. Frankie and Everett brought Jenny out of the front pasture and settled her into a barn pen, readying her for the next morning's journey. Watching as Everett worked the curry-comb through her mane, Frankie thought the sweet-mannered mare was looking a little pleased with herself. When she told Everett what she was thinking, he broke into laughter.

"I believe you're right, Honey. Seems like Trumpeter was giving her a lot of attention for a few days there, wasn't he? Maybe she's figuring out what she should be expecting come next year."

Everett turned his attention to Isaac, grooming him, and then going into the tack-room for the farrier tools. While he worked on the mule's hooves, Frankie filled a half-dozen buckets with corn and oats, stirred some sweet-treacle into the mix, and loaded them in the wagon.

"I'll replace the corn and oats, Frankie, once we start working the harvest."

"I know you will, Everett. I just figure we oughta keep Isaac on the same rations. He's gaining fast now. No sense in breaking his routine."

She watched Everett nod and she saw the smile on his face as he put his attention back to the hoof he was trimming. She knew he was pleased, but not just because she was sending the buckets of grain. Mostly, he was pleased with Isaac, because the mule was fattening up and showing some shine. And Everett was glowing with pride, because for a while, he had doubted Isaac would ever return to health.

Now, it was a different story. Isaac had been healing steadily. He was eating well; he was perking up and starting to pay attention to his surroundings again. The tired and clumsy shuffle was gone from his walk. He was a companion to the other mules in the pasture, staying near them, doing what they did. When they walked, he walked. When they decided to trot, he trotted with them, moving along at a good clip. When they galloped around, hee-hawing and acting like fools just because they felt good, Isaac joined in their antics—making noise and showing off to the world. Just because he felt good.

Over the last few days, Everett had been making a lot of comments about Isaac. One morning, he had remarked about Isaac's eyes. 'I believe they're looking some brighter now, Frankie'. And one evening as they walked back from the barn, carrying the milk-pail, he had paused and looked at Isaac standing near the pasture gate. 'Look there, Honey. I think his coat's taking on a shine. Can you see it?' When she nodded and agreed, his smile grew.

Sometimes, he just stood at the fence, looking out in the pasture, staring at his dark-bay mule. Nodding as he watched him. And Frankie would stand there beside him, nodding like he was. Grinning at him, when he grinned at her. It had become obvious that everything they had been doing with the mule had been working.

'There's no doubt about it,' Everett would say, 'that mule's coming around.'

Then, he'd nod some more and Frankie would nod too. And then Everett would wrap his arm around her shoulders and squeeze her against his side.

To Frankie's mind, it *was* just like Everett had said—there was no doubt about it, Isaac was coming around. The week of remedies and rest, the buckets of grain and molasses, and the rich grass of the pastures had paid off. He had already gained back a good deal of size and strength; he was ready to go home and Everett was excited to be taking him there.

The plan for the Dunbars' trip home was in place. Since Frankie's heavy wagon was still stacked high with the Dunbars' share of firewood, they would leave their light wagon at Frankie's meadow. On their next visit, they'd switch wagons.

"A *plenty* fine start for the winter," Everett declared, showing the same look of pride and relief that he'd been wearing a great deal lately. He patted the side of the wagon the same way he patted Isaac's side. "Dang good start, Honey. This here load has taken a lot of worry out of me."

In the pantry, Frankie and Ida packed crates and baskets with the staples they needed—staples the Dunbars had already been needing when Hugh David went south to Fort Cottonwood. They filled empty sacks with rice and oats, dried beans and peas. They tucked a dozen eggs into a keg filled with cornmeal.

"To hold you until your hens settle in and start laying," Frankie told her.

Frankie added one of the slabs of bacon, a smoked ham and a sack of flour, telling Ida they'd go bad before she could use them. And she added a tin of molasses.

"For baking, and for adding to Isaac's grain," Frankie told her. Tins of baking soda and baking powder went into a crate beside the molasses. She added cans of peaches and spiced apples. When Frankie wedged a couple of bags of coffee beans into the crate, Ida kissed her on the cheek.

"You sweet girl."

They filled milk-tins and packed butter into crocks to load in the morning. And the chickens for the Dunbars' flock would be selected in the morning; Ida would choose nine hens and a rooster, and she agreed to take along enough feed for them until the harvest came in.

With everything else ready for loading in the morning, Frankie decided to add something else. She brought out her cousin Samuel's rifle and several boxes of bullets. She shook her head when Everett protested.

"I've got my own rifles, Everett. This one belonged to my cousin, so I'm only loaning it to you. But I'm not letting you go back to your place without some kind of protection." She saw him starting to shake his head, ready to argue again. "Everett. None of us know for sure there won't still be trouble. It's our best guess Hugh David is gone for good, but we don't know for sure. And we all know that no one ought to be out here without a rifle. Besides which, Ida has been talking about venison roasts for her dinner table, and you and I never got a chance to hunt. There's a herd of deer that hangs out in those trees downriver from your place."

She saw Everett Dunbars' face soften. There was a nod, an understanding between them.

"You keep this rifle at your place and when you get a crop sold at Fort Cottonwood and have a chance to buy yourself a new one, then bring this one back. But keep it on your place for now." Frankie saw him glance to Ida and she saw Ida nodding. It was decided; they would take the rifle.

As the late afternoon turned into evening, they stayed near the house, sitting on the front porch, eating the last of Ida's spice-cake and drinking glasses of cold coffee, sweet and thick with sugar and cream. They talked about their homesteads and about being neighbors. They smiled as they discussed their plans and talked about the way their lives were coming together.

They were pleased with their start on the firewood; the wood-cutting days and the noonday picnics beside the river had been 'such good times', according to Ida, they decided there would be more of those days.

"Good neighborly-sharing," Everett called it. "A good coming-together."

There was pride in Ida's voice when she spoke about the wagonloads of garden produce filling up the bins in the root-cellar. The decision to family-share the cellar, they all decided, was a good one. And there would still be more from Ida's garden.

"Goodness, we haven't even gotten to the deep-root crops, yet. And there'll be several kinds of squashes," Ida's eyes snapped with delight. "There'll be potatoes galore. Sweet potatoes too. And pumpkins and more winter squashes. And with all the onions, we're going to need plenty of bins just for them."

Then, too, there were apples ripening on the trees beside the river—some already ripe—those would go into crates in the cellar too.

"And the nuts are coming. Walnuts will be dropping soon. And we'll have to get the hazelnuts before the squirrels start on them."

"And we got a good crop of corn and oats coming," Everett looked at the mules in the pasture beyond the barn. His mule Isaac was out there, his nose deep in the hard-grass, grazing beside Septimus, Artemis and Aloysius. "They've done plenty good this summer. The land produced better'n I dared hope for." He paused, still looking toward Isaac, and then went on. "The weather warmed up at the right time. The rains came as we needed. And now, we got teams and wagons to handle the work."

They talked about Isaac, about his weight gain and his health. The talk went on to the mares and the breeding. They could see the Dunbars' mare, Jenny, out in the barn pen and Frankie's mares out in the front pasture. Fanny and Belle, Easy and Silk. There would be a handful of foals on the ground in June and that thought made them all smile. And then Ida started talking about eggs and milk, butter and cream. And about chickens and roosters.

"Why, I'll have hens pecking around in the farm yard again. And Everett and me, we'll be waking to a rooster's crow tomorrow morning." Ida reached to pat Frankie's hand. "Oh, Honey. That'll be the nicest thing of all. There's something about hearing a rooster crowing to wake a farmyard that makes the world seem like a good place again."

"Well, you may have to wait a while for your rooster to get a full-throated crow. For a while, you're gonna be hearing more croak than crow. But as soon as your hens settle in, you'll have eggs on the table at breakfast." Frankie grinned at her. "And Blossom can keep milk and cream and butter on your table."

Sitting there at the table, sipping at the cool sweet-coffee, Frankie watched Ida's smile; it was a soft and sweet smile now—a lot different from the first day when they had rolled into the valley to wait out the possibility of Hugh David's return. Her smile was relaxed; the tension was gone. Her eyes—the soft blue-gray eyes—were calm; there was no fear or despair in them. Not anymore.

For the Dunbars, the dangerous times were past. They had fallen prey to someone who made them doubt themselves and lose sight of who they were. To Frankie's figuring, anyone could end up being a target of someone who thrived on tearing apart the lives others had built. She, herself, had suffered at the hands of men like that; she had found her way out of the danger and recovered from the damage.

And now, Everett and Ida had too. They could pick up and carry on. They had left Iowa to build a life out here and they had been working hard for it. And now, no one would be tearing it down.

The conversation had turned to the heavy wagon in front of the stone-room porch, already loaded with firewood, ready for the crates and baskets of supplies that would be loaded in the morning. For a few moments, the talk stopped. They sat looking at the wagon standing in the last of the twilight, ready for the rest of its cargo—the tins of fresh milk and the crocks of butter, the eggs and the live chickens. And *that* was when Sunny Jim called out—his voice rang out across the meadow and echoed against the valley's walls.

"Someone's coming." Frankie threw a look toward Everett. He understood. He was up from the table as quick as she was, because someone unseen and unknown was coming to the valley.

By the time Trumpeter gave his own challenge, Frankie was at the kitchen door, reaching inside for the rifles on their pegs. She had her Henry in-hand and was passing Everett the Spencer when Belle's voice rang out. Beside the porch steps, the dogs had their eyes fixed on the track at the valley's entrance; Matilda gave her throaty growl, Laughing Girl uttered a wicked snarl.

Frankie signaled for Everett to stay at the kitchen porch; she darted across the grass to the stone-room and tucked herself into the shadows of the porch, her eyes on the meadow's entrance the whole time.

She gave a quick glance over her shoulder and spotted Everett squatting down by the porch post outside the kitchen door. She heard him whispering to Ida.

"Get in the house. If things take a bad turn, go to the back-bed-room. Go out that back door and up the hillside into the trees."

Now, they watched. Waiting and ready. Frankie looked to the dogs, watching to see what they were telling her. Their eyes were still locked on the track at the entrance; Laughing Girl was walking toward the front track, stiff-legged and slow. Hackles up. Snarling, low and mean.

Trumpeter's voice rang out again; Everett's mare called out from the barn pen. And from beyond the valley's entrance, came a response—a loud, quavering neigh rang out. An instant later, a second call came from the same direction. A different call; a different horse.

Frankie glanced to Everett, saw him show her two fingers. Two horses. Maybe, a team and wagon. Or maybe, two riders. Maybe more. She nodded, turned her attention back to the meadow's entrance.

Hoofbeats sounded on the hardpacked track, hoofbeats that were picking up pace. Coming closer and coming faster. Frankie looked at Everett; he returned her look and nodded. Knowing exactly what she knew—there were more than two horses. There were a lot more.

Frankie leveled her rifle's barrel, knowing that decent peo-ple didn't barge onto a homestead without some kind of call, *some* kind of greeting. The hoofbeats continued, growing louder with the approach. Another neigh rang out from beyond the entrance. But still, no human call. No greeting.

And then suddenly, horses appeared, coming over the rise in the track—some at a lope, some at a quick trot. Heads up, ears up, neighing and snorting. Following the track around and down into the meadow. *Definitely more than two. Maybe five or six.*

Frankie had her eyes on them, trying to think fast, watching the whole group and trying to see behind them at the same time. Suddenly relieved, knowing that Everett was with her. *Another set of eyes; another rifle.*

The meadow was ringing with neighs. Loud calls from the new-arrivals as they thundered onto the meadow floor; answering calls from the horses and mules in the pastures. But no wagons. No riders. No humans. Frankie stared. *Horses. Just horses.*

There was the sound of more hoofbeats coming along the track. More hooves sounding. A moment later, cows were at the top of the track, coming around and down into the valley and following the horses, trotting along behind them. Like the horses, the cattle slowed as they reached the meadow floor. They began milling around, heads up, looking around.

That was when Frankie realized there were more cows than horses. The new horses were still neighing and some of the cows were bellowing. And from the pastures, Frankie could hear her own horses answering. In the next moment, Blossom and the oxen were all speaking up too.

Frankie stared at the scene before her. She shook her head to clear her thoughts. She whistled to the dogs, calling them to her. She turned her attention back to the new arrivals. Horses and cows. No humans. She turned to look at Everett and he was shaking his head a little, giving her a look of pure astonishment—which she figured was the same look she was giving him.

Everett seemed to recover his senses faster than she did, because he pointed toward the entrance. Frankie turned her attention back to the track, looking where he was indicating. Realizing that he was warning her, because this might not be the end of things. There might still be danger; this might all be a distraction.

Frankie waited. Watching, with her eyes on the track, trying to see in spite of the deepening dusk. Listening for any new sounds that might signal coming danger, trying to hear above the sounds of the horses snorting and the cows bawling.

Minutes passed. No humans came riding in. No more animals trotted in. No more sounds came from beyond the entrance. Looking to the dogs, Frankie could see they were no longer showing any interest in the front entrance—their only interest was in the odd collection of livestock.

The cows had stopped their loud bawling; now, there were only a few huffing snorts as they milled around the meadow. The loud and frantic calls of the horses had diminished; the loose horses were heading toward the barn pens and the pasture fences. Now, there were only nickers and snorts now—some boisterous and some curious. Friendly horse greetings as necks and noses stretched across the plank fences, reaching out and introducing themselves. Nipping and snuffling and blowing.

One of the horses, a sleek-looking brown horse was staying next to Jenny in her barn pen—the two horses were busy nosing each other across the top of the fence, nickering softly.

Frankie stepped away from the corner of the building. She eyed the herd of animals milling about in her valley and did a quick count in the fading light of the dusk. *Five horses. Ten head of cattle. No humans.* She counted a second time and heard Everett speaking to her from the kitchen porch.

"Five horses. Ten cows." He had done his own count. He looked at her, gave her a broad smile, then looked back at the livestock.

They both watched the animals for a couple more minutes, and Frankie figured they were both letting it all sink in. *No danger after all. And a whole batch of unexpected animals right in front of our eyes.*

She and Everett grinned at each other. She shrugged, and he did too. They shook their heads and without saying a word, they started walking in different directions because they both knew what needed to be done. They needed to pen the new arrivals and it was all about penning them as quickly as possible. Before the whole lot of them

157

decided to turn and go racing out of the meadow. Later, they could sort out exactly what they were dealing with.

Frankie called to Matilda as she made her way across the meadow, walking slowly through the loose herd. Everett circled in the other direction, moving toward the meadow's entrance, positioning himself to head off any animals that might decide to head back the way they had come.

When she reached the barn-lot gate, she unlatched it and swung it wide. She spoke to Matilda, talking to her about 'bringing in the animals' and Matilda was listening. Because when Frankie whistled and pointed, the little collie-dog went to work. From then on, all Frankie and Everett had to do was stay out of the way. The tawny little collie-dog went at that loose herd; she was doing what she was born to do, moving slick and fast, slipping in behind the loose animals, staying low and nipping at heels.

In a matter of minutes, she had them bunched up and moving toward the barn-lot gateway. A moment later, she had the horses and cows trotting through the gate. There had been no hesitation from the animals, not a single hitch in the whole deal—it had been so smooth and so slick, that to Frankie, it looked as though the livestock had been moved into the pen a hundred times before.

When she grinned at Everett and told him that, he grinned back at her and said they probably had.

"Maybe not a hundred times," he said as he reached her side, "but they *have* been in that barn-lot before."

And Ida, coming across the meadow from the house, agreed with him. The livestock, she said, had indeed been in the meadow.

"They've been in that pen plenty of times," she said.

"It took me a bit to realize what I was seeing, what with it being almost dark. And because it's nothing I ever expected," Everett winked at Frankie. "But I got it figured out now."

The animals, Everett said, were Daniel Kinison's. He and Ida had always assumed Lillian Kinison had sold them to someone down around the Middle Loup settlement.

"Because she said she had," Everett shook his head, looking a little surprised. "I figured the new owner had come and took them while I was taking her and the boys to Fort Cottonwood. Because when I got back from the trip, the livestock was all gone from the place. I never heard anything different. And I've never seen any sign of 'em since she left."

Apparently, Lillian Kinison hadn't sold them to anyone. Nor had she given them to anyone who might have need of them. Thinking about it, Frankie figured that was pretty much her pattern. Because it's what she had done with the chickens—she had thrown the gate open to let them fend for themselves, leaving them to live or die. She must have done the same with the livestock.

Frankie looked at Everett and Ida, knowing they were thinking the same thing. It seemed an odd way to handle things. But now, the animals were back. And in the end, it had turned out fine. She said it out loud and the Dunbars agreed. As soon as they were through shaking their heads at Lillian Kinison's odd behavior, they looked at each other. Grinning.

"Well, *this* a fine treasure, isn't it?" Ida laughed.

They stood at the barn-lot gate, studying what they had in the pen. There was the brown gelding that looked to be a perfect match for the Dunbars' mare. There were two gray mares, one with a weanling colt at her side. There was a strongly-built, buckskin-colored horse. There was a brown spotted dairy cow with a spring heifer by her side. And a bull, that to Frankie's thinking, was the same breed as the dairy cow.

"Guernseys," Everett said. "That's what Daniel Kinison liked for a milk cow."

The other cows, seven of them, were roan short-horns. Four cows and three calves—with the calves looking to be Guernsey-crosses. Which Frankie thought made sense.

For a few minutes, the three of them stood at the fence, quietly looking over the wayward herd. Frankie knew they were all thinking the same thing; they were all thinking about what Lillian Kinison had done. Finally, Everett said it out loud.

"She must have just opened the gates and let them go. Didn't care what happened to them." Everett was shaking his head.

"Why wouldn't she have left them with you? Or at least, told you about them?"

"That's the way she was, Frankie. She was a self-centered and stingy woman." Ida spoke now, looking at Frankie. "Nothing Daniel did here meant anything to her. He worked *so* hard, trying to get everything ready for his family. He built this place, trying to make it just right for her, but it still wasn't good enough in her mind. She hated it and she made sure he knew it." Ida paused for a moment and then continued.

"I tried to like her. We both tried to get along with her. But really, she didn't want to get along with anyone. She just wanted to have things her own way. When Daniel died, she wanted us to buy the stock, but we couldn't offer her anything. We didn't have the money.

"That made her mad and she got pretty huffy about it. She said she'd find *someone else* to buy them. She told us that down at Reverend Austin's churchyard on the day Daniel was buried. We checked in on her a few days later and she told us she was going back to Indiana. She needed to get down to Fort Cottonwood so she and the boys could take the stage back East. She offered to trade a wagon and team if Everett would drive her there." She paused and Everett took up the story.

"The next morning, she showed up at our house with Jenny hitched to the wagon. She had her two boys and a few satchels packed with some clothes. A box with food for the trip. Some blankets and quilts for the nights on the trail. That was it." Everett stared at the ground, shaking his head. "She told us to check on the place, but never said please or thank you. She expected us to do it. Never offered us anything for the time and trouble."

"Of course, we wouldn't have taken anything," Ida spoke up. "We planned to do it anyway. For Daniel. She never did say a word about why she gave us just the mare and not the team like she promised."

Frankie listened to the story, already knowing a little about Daniel Kinison's wife. She had met the woman back in Indiana. There had been plenty of bitterness and disgust in Lillian Kinison's voice when she talked about the homestead. There had been no sorrow in her voice when she spoke about her husband's death. There had been no words of sadness over the loss of their home. Just angry and hateful words about 'that place out in the Territory'.

"When I met her at my uncle's house," Frankie told them, "she seemed a lot like my mother. I could hear the same bitterness. I'd bet when she threw open the gates and sent the animals out, she was feeling satisfied that she didn't have to give anything to anybody." Frankie eyed the brown gelding that had been at Jenny's pen, certain that he was the teammate Lillian Kinison had promised to the Dunbars.

"Anyway, *now* you have the team she promised you. There's a wagon-tongue in the barn that probably goes with your light-wagon. And there's a light-harness and collar in the tack-room that's a match for Jenny's harness."

"Frankie, we can't take the horse. He goes with the place. Your family bought everything that went with the property." Everett's surprise was genuine.

"No, Sir. You said Lillian Kinison traded you the wagon and a team. And I remember her telling my uncle she traded *a wagon and team* for the trip to Fort Cottonwood. It's what she promised and I'm not going to help her be dishonest. That gelding is the match for your mare and he needs to be with his teammate."

As far as Frankie was concerned, the conversation was done. A deal had been made, and now the deal was done. She left the Dunbars standing where they were and walked into the barn, returning with a halter. She slipped between the planks of the barn-lot fence, taking her time, easing her way among the animals until she reached the gelding. Even after the months of roaming wild, the gelding showed he was every bit as sensible as Jenny.

Frankie stroked his neck for a moment and when she raised the halter, he lowered his head and nosed into it. She fastened the halter, led him out of the lot and down the alleyway. When she released him into the stall with his former teammate, they started nuzzling each other again.

Frankie hadn't realized that Ida had followed her, but Ida was waiting in the alleyway when she stepped out of the pen.

"They're happy to be together again, aren't they?"

"I think they are, Ida. They're teammates. It's what they know and it's how it needs to be." Frankie felt Ida's arm wrap around her shoulder; she felt the squeeze that Ida gave her. Gentle and hard at the same time.

They decided to have a late meal, even though they'd already had supper. Because, Ida declared, they should 'have a little celebration'. Because the animals had returned. They whipped up a batch of hotcakes and fried up bacon and eggs, onions and potatoes and green peppers. They cut up tomatoes and cucumbers and doused them with cream and vinegar. They sliced apples and fried them with butter and sugar and apple pie spices.

They sat at the trestle-table late into the night, celebrating the return of the livestock, and deciding exactly how to handle the new animals. There were some for which Frankie had no need; and there were some that the Dunbars could use on their homestead.

By the end of the meal, decisions had been made and deals were in the works. The Dunbars agreed to take the brown gelding—finally acknowledging he was part of the team Lillian Kinison had promised. Frankie would keep the buckskin and the gray mares and foal. And she would keep the short-horn cattle.

As far as the Guernsey cow and her calf were concerned, Frankie had no need for them. Everett and Ida, having lost their own milk cow, had a clear need for the Guernsey and her calf. And as far as the bull, Frankie had no interest in having a dairy bull on her place. But she did see a need to have it for breeding with Blossom, and eventually, with Primrose. So Frankie suggested a shared-ownership—she would retain breeding rights, if the Dunbars would keep the bull at their place for the breeding they needed.

Every animal seemed to have a natural place to go, but the Dunbars had concerns about payment for the Guernseys. And they wanted to pay for Jenny's breeding to Trumpeter.

"Honey, we won't have any cash until the sale of our crops. And there's always a chance something can go wrong with the harvest. Or with hauling the crops to market." Everett shook his head. "I don't like the thought of owing that much to you with no sure way to pay."

"Well, I've got a couple of trades in mind. If you'll hear me out." Frankie started laying out the deals.

She wanted Ida's help with planting a garden in the spring. She suggested trading the cow and calf for Ida's help in planning and planting in the spring. Ida perked up at the idea, but she had two conditions.

"I'll work with you on your garden and provide all the seeds you need, but only if we agree it's for five years."

As for Jenny's breeding, Frankie's idea was to trade this summer's breeding for a future foal from the mare.

The trades were put in place and Everett was grinning when he reached across the table to shake hands. Frankie took his hand and they closed the deal. The trades, to Frankie's thinking, suited everyone, but looking at Ida, she thought that maybe Ida was happier than anyone else. She was smiling a bright smile; her soft gray-blue eyes were shining and puddling-up with tears. Frankie smiled back at her, knowing what was making her so happy.

It was the Guernsey cow with her big and tight udder that had Ida smiling. As of right now, she and Everett owned a milk cow—and tomorrow morning—they would be taking her home. And tomorrow evening, they'd be milking their own cow on their own place. *That* was why Ida was smiling a bright smile—because a milk cow with a heifer at her side, spoke of a future for a homestead. There would be years of milk and cream and butter for the table.

Then Everett said something that made Frankie's head swivel toward him.

"There's something else you oughta know about the livestock," he said. "It's something that just occurred to me. Daniel had more beef cattle than just those roan cows that came in here this evening. I don't remember what the count was exactly, and I don't know what it'd be now. But at one time, he had a herd of something over thirty roan short-horns. Durhams, he called them. And he had plans to keep building his herd." Everett looked out the window, looking into the night.

"I'd guess the rest are out there somewhere in the hills. This is just a handful that wandered back, probably following along with the horses. Something must have been niggling in their brains, something that made them want to come back to what they knew. So there's a chance some more of those short-horns just might show up at some point."

"Thirty head of roan short-horns?" Frankie's mind was wandering out across the Sand Hills, picturing dark-red cattle grazing on hillsides and the low, grassy valleys. Thinking about Ida's words. *Well, this is a fine treasure, isn't it?*

She heard Everett talking about the lost herd, thinking that maybe soon, they should take some time to look for them. But Frankie's mind was already roaming out across the Sand Hills, picturing a herd of short-horn roan cattle. Because a herd like that spoke to a future on a homestead too.

They were all up long before sunrise. While Ida cooked up a hot breakfast, Frankie and Everett milked the cows. Both cows. After that, they went to work on Jenny and the mule, giving them a good going-over with curry-combs. Then Frankie waited while Everett groomed the gelding, talking to him quietly, getting him used to a human voice and a human hand once again.

Frankie knew Everett wanted to get to know this new horse of his, but he didn't stay with it as long as she thought he would. Because apparently, he had something else on his mind—he kept glancing to one of the pails sitting on a bench outside the milking-pen. The pail that was filled nearly to the top with good Guernsey-milk. From *his* Guernsey cow. Frankie figured he was itching to carry it to the house, anticipating the moment when he would present the full pail to his wife.

And sure enough, when they walked through the screen-door a few minutes later, Frankie saw Ida's eyes on the bucket before Everett was fully in the kitchen. Ida stood there by the stove, staring at the milk sloshing gently in the pail, knowing it was *their* milk, from *their* milk cow.

Moments later, plates were on the table, loaded with scrambled eggs and ham, fried apples and fried onions. Three glasses of buttermilk stood by the plates. Cups were filled with coffee. A platter of buttered parsnips sat next to a bowl of green beans. The blue butter-crock was sitting next to a pan of hot biscuits.

Frankie scanned the table, grinning at the array of food, understanding why Ida had out-done herself with this breakfast. Because it was their last meal together after eight days in the meadow together. It was their ninth breakfast together.

For Frankie, there was a pang of sadness that they were parting. But for the Dunbars, there was something different going on. There was excitement in their eyes—because they were ready to go home for a new start.

The food on the plates and platters disappeared fast, and this morning, nobody stayed at the table once the meal was done; no one lingered over the cups of coffee. Almost before Frankie knew what was happening, Everett was pushing his chair back from the table, deciding it was 'about time to get the team hitched'. And Ida started talking about 'catching-up some chickens'. They all slid their plates into the dishpan and headed outside.

Everett went to the barn to do the harnessing while Frankie, with Matilda trotting close behind, followed Ida out to the chicken-coop. Frankie grabbed a few gunnysacks from the shelf in the feed-room and told Ida to choose her chickens.

Ida started pointing and Frankie started catching and bagging. She liked what Ida was selecting—a nice mix of Dominickers, New Hampshires, and Leghorns. Three of each. It would be the start of a good flock for their homestead. It took only a matter of minutes to get nine of them bagged. When a tenth hen happened to scuttle by, close enough to reach, Frankie snatched it up too. As she lowered it into the fourth sack, Ida scolded her.

"That's enough, Frankie. We agreed on nine. Ten hens will be more than enough for a starting flock."

"But I still have room for three more in this bag, Ida. I was thinking you'd want at least a full dozen. Or maybe, fifteen. *Fifteen* would be a nice flock." Frankie decided to argue a bit, her mind on the clutch of fourteen eggs tucked under Mrs. Swingle. "I've got more than a dozen eggs fixing to hatch out, Ida. That's *way* too many chickens."

"No, Honey. Ten hens are plenty. And you know better than to count your chickens before they hatch," Ida smiled and shook her head. "I don't want you coming up short if that clutch doesn't hatch out well."

"But you really *should* take more, because there's twice as many people to feed on your place. I've only got me here." Frankie saw Ida shaking her head again, knowing that the logical approach wasn't working. She tried another tactic. Guilt.

"You're my nearest neighbors, Ida, and I'm asking you to do the neighborly thing here. You and Everett should do the responsible thing and help me out." Frankie gave the guilt approach a solid try, and added in a bit of whining for good measure. "I'm *only* asking you to take another five or six chickens."

"Ten is plenty, you little rascal." Ida hadn't been swayed.

Frankie groaned, knowing it was over; her earnest attempts at logic, guilt, and whining hadn't made a smidgeon of difference. It occurred to her she had been at a disadvantage to begin with— because Ida had raised four children. *She's probably had all kinds of practical experience with kids applying those sorts of tactics.*

She sighed and gave it up, accepting the reality of the size of flock she was left with. She turned back to the chickens in the coop, spotted what she wanted and grabbed up two more birds. And then another. A total of three of the young roosters would be going to a new home. She gave Ida a smug look as she lowered the third rooster into the bag with the hen and the other roosters.

"We were talking about *hens*." Frankie grinned when Ida gave her a warning look. "These are *roosters*. And I never agreed to just one rooster."

Everett had Isaac and Jenny harnessed to the heavy farm wagon with its full load of firewood; the brown gelding was tied next to the wagon-seat where Everett thought he 'could keep an eye on him, since he's still a bit fresh to all of this'.

"Jake was his name. That's what Daniel called him," Everett was thinking back, talking out loud, while they walked to the barn-lot for the Guernseys. "Full-brother to Jenny, as I recall."

"I wouldn't doubt it." Frankie looked over her shoulder, eyeing the pair. Two seal-browns; the same size; the same shape to their heads. The same temperament. "You've got a mighty nice-looking team there." Frankie watched as Everett stopped and turned to look back at the wagon. She saw him nod, more to himself than to her.

"I do. I truly do." Everett reached to tug at her braid. "And I've got a fine-looking mule too. Thanks to you, Honey."

"Thanks to *both* of us for putting in the time doctoring him. And thanks to my Aunt Sarah for her remedies. Eight days on her powders and tinctures turned him around."

Everett murmured something in agreement, but his mind was already on the rest of his livestock. His Guernseys. Frankie followed him and waited while he fashioned halters and lead-ropes from a couple lengths of rope. She stayed outside the pen while he did his own work with his own cattle. Figuring he'd rather do it himself. The cow stood quietly while he fitted her with a halter; the bull swung his head a few times and tried a half-hearted bovine-kick; he gave up his protest when Everett smacked him on the ribs with the knotted end of the rope.

Satisfied, Everett gave a few pats to their necks; Frankie swung the gate wide, watching as Everett led his bull and cow toward the fire-wood-laden wagon. The spotted heifer followed along and managed to do a prancing little tap-dance as she stayed close to her momma. Frankie swung the gate closed, leaving the rest of the newcomers inside. She followed Everett and his little parade to the wagon. The cow was showing nothing but sensible compliance; the bull was calm and quiet now, not really caring about anything except being close to the cow. The heifer stayed near the cow for reasons of her own.

167

Watching Everett leading his cow and bull, Frankie thought back over the whole event, thinking about how perfect it had all been. From the moment the animals had arrived, none of them had shown much concern over being handled and directed by humans. They had accepted the sudden change in their circumstances in what her cousin Samuel would have referred to as a very 'philosophical way'. And the night in the corral had probably helped stir their memories and settle their minds.

It wasn't a rare thing for animals to wander back to a familiar life, not rare at all for them to seek out something they had once known. These animals had come back to the meadow they had been homed to. Some memory, somewhere deep in the mind of at least one of the animals, had come forward; something had tickled a memory about this little valley and the barn and the humans. That critter had decided to come home and the others had followed. And now, in spite of Lillian Kinison and her misdeeds, everything was the way it should be. *Probably just the way Daniel Kinison would have wanted it.*

With the Dunbars' livestock harnessed and hitched, haltered and tied, caught and bagged for the journey home, Frankie and Ida started loading the boxes and baskets in the wagon. Some, they tucked under the wagon-seat; some, they wedged in among the stacked firewood in the wagon-box. It was Everett who lifted the sacks of soft-murmuring chickens, half-drowsy in the half-light of their surrounding sacks, and settled them behind the seat.

"Right here where we can keep a close eye on our new flock." He grinned at Frankie. Winked. Thanking her in his own way.

Ida and Frankie held each other. Cried a bit at the departure; laughed a bit because like Ida said, they 'would just be a little way down the road'. Ida wanted Frankie to come to their place on Sunday, six days away.

"Spend the day at our home, Honey."

Frankie promised she would. She leaned against Everett's side when he draped his arm around her shoulders, squeezing her hard. Then he kissed her on the cheek and reached to help Ida onto the wagon-seat. He climbed up beside her, took the lines in-hand, clucked to the seal-brown mare and the mule. The wagon rolled along the track, up, around and over. Frankie returned Ida's wave as the Dunbars and their little caravan disappeared over the rise in the track.

She stood scratching Laughing Girl's neck, listening to the change in the sound of the hoof-beats as they left the hardpacked track and entered the ford in the North Loup; the steady beat of hooves—horse-hooves and mule-hooves and dairy-cow hooves—started up again once they climbed up the south bank. Gradually, the sound faded as the Dunbars, and all their animals, moved farther along the trail.

"It was a *fine* visit, wasn't it?" Frankie had spoken out loud and she grinned as the blond-brindle hound and the tawny collie-dog looked up at her. Listening for words they knew, listening for any instructions. "We've got us some fine neighbors, don't we?" Matilda gave a soft whine, still listening and trying to sort out the meaning.

"Nothing, Matilda. It's nothing." Frankie stayed where she was for the next few minutes, listening now to the sounds around her. Listening to the sounds of her meadow. The birds were singing their heads off as the sun moved higher in the sky. She could hear a meadowlark declaring his personal territory; an oriole was calling out; a woodpecker was banging its beak into a tree somewhere on the slope above the windmill pool. A brown thrasher was sending his crazy, mixed-up trill across the meadow.

But Frankie was still thinking about the Dunbars heading downriver. They were heading home with a lot more than they came with. Staples for their kitchen. A sleek-looking team. A healthy-looking mule. A fine-looking Guernsey cow and heifer-calf. A good-looking Guernsey bull. A nice-looking flock of hens and a trio of aggravating roosters.

They were all traveling to a safe home and a fresh start. The Dunbars had a chance now, because there was no one to tear their home-life apart. The danger was gone. There would be comfort for them now; there would be peace.

Frankie turned away, heading toward her own herd in the front barn-lot, thinking it was time to get to know these new arrivals. She had a good idea about what she had there; she and Everett and Ida had looked them over. But now, it was just her—just *her* thoughts and impressions about *her* livestock. It was her chance to get things straight in her mind; her chance now, to bring up all she had learned and all she had been taught by her grandparents, by her father, by her Uncle James and her Aunt Sarah. By her cousins, Samuel and Thomas, Isaiah and little Charles.

She climbed up on the barn-lot fence and watched her new animals moving around. Realizing that the animals there inside the pen would be adding to the legacy from her family. She started wondering if her family could see how she was doing, wondering if maybe they could see this pretty little meadow with the perfectly square house and the long barn. Wondering if they could see that she had made it her home.

The Shires and the oxen were here, along with Fanny and Blossom, just like her family had planned. Now though, she wondered if they could see Blossom had a calf beside her. And now, there were three more mares. And a stallion and four geldings. Three mules. And a fine coop with a flock of nice chickens. And she was wondering if they could see the newest arrivals that had just returned home.

She watched her new animals. Assessing them, learning about them, looking at them the way her Uncle James had taught her to look at horses and cattle. Remembering what Thomas would have pointed out about the cattle—because Thomas liked cattle. 'Look at the size of the head; look at the top-line; look at the hips.' And Isaiah would have been eyeing the horses—because Isaiah favored horses. 'Look at the slope of the shoulders. See there,' he would have said, 'see the angle of the pastern. Mark how the hind feet track with the front feet, look to see if the hoof-prints show a good reach.'

So Frankie studied *her* cattle, *her* roan short-horns. Durhams. These weren't dairy cows; these were beef cows. Bred for meat. They were built strong and square and hefty. There were four cows, deep rusty-red, all showing roan coloring, some showing brindling. All were mottled with some white. There were three calves—two heifers and one bull-calf—all looking mostly like their mommas, but a little lighter and a little more spotted than mottled. *Probably, the Guernsey bull sired them. And probably, the cows already have babies in their bellies for next spring.*

She opened the gate that led into the barn; she kept the horses in the pen and let the cattle into the barn alleyway. She sent Matilda behind them, pushing them down the barn and out to the back barn-lot.

Walking along behind them, Frankie watched them, trying to think like Thomas. To her thinking, her cattle all looked to be strong and sturdy. All were bright-eyed. There was no lameness. The cows carried plenty of milk in their bags and the calves showed the benefit. It was a good herd, she decided. *Thomas would approve.* She closed her little herd in the back-lot and returned to the front-lot.

She climbed back on the fence and looked over her new horses. Four interesting new horses. The two gray mares were what her Uncle James would have called 'catfish-grays'. They were bigger than any of her mares and bred both for saddle and harness. Stout enough to do some heavy pulling, clearly showing some draft blood. They were a matching pair. *Probably sisters. And probably only a year or two apart.*

They were long in the back, long-legged and smooth in their walk. She thought they carried Percheron blood, maybe crossed with Thoroughbred. To her eyes, there wasn't a thing to complain about. The foal was a horse-colt; he was a dark brownish-bluish-black, and at this point, Frankie knew it'd be nothing more than a guess to say whether he'd go gray or not.

She turned her attention to the fourth horse. In the waning light of the evening and again in the half-light of the early dawn, Frankie had pegged him as a dark buckskin. Now that it was daylight, she saw something different. He was a mouse-colored dun with a stripe down his back and dark legs, zebra-striping above his knees and hocks. He was a tough-built stallion, but not nearly as big as Trumpeter or the bay mares—he was closer to Fanny's size. He was wiry and muscled, clear-eyed and clean-limbed.

And there was something else she could see about him in the light of day—the tough dun had a massive open-cut across his chest that extended deep into his shoulder, and down his leg. It was a deep wound, bigger than Boone's had been. It was a wound that was going to require a lot of work. And plenty of healing.

She moved the mares and colt into one of the barn stalls and went back to the barn-lot to study the dun. It was a nasty wound—a long and deep slash with a swollen pocket of tissue below the wound. She eyed the wound from a short distance, noting the swelling and the yellowed-pus draining down the inside of his leg. *Not a fresh wound. An older wound. It hasn't been healing, though. Probably because the motion of walking and running keeps tearing at it.*

It was bad, no doubt about it, but as bad as it was, Frankie still had some hope. Because Boone had healed up fine. It had been a little more than a month since he had come to her, and even though he would always have a scar, he showed a limp, but she didn't see anything that she thought would be a lasting problem.

With all the other animals in the lot, neither she nor Everett had paid much attention to this particular horse. But Everett *had* said that he didn't recall it being one of Daniel's. So Frankie spent some time wondering where it might have come from. From what Everett had said, there were other homesteads to the south near the Middle Loup River. Ten or twelve miles away. *So maybe it came from there.*

Looking at his shoulders and withers and along its back, Frankie could see no signs of harness wear. No saddle-marks on the withers. No sign it had even worn a halter. And there was a bit more of a mystery to the dun horse, because there was some wildness to his character. Yet even as a stallion, he was responsive to her; he didn't mind when she stepped close and started touching and poking and probing around his wound.

He seemed perfectly agreeable with what she was doing; there was no flinching, no fidgeting, no attempt to move away. He just kept watching her with a wise and curious eye. He studied her; poked at her gently with his muzzle; nudged her a few times. Not unlike what she was doing to him; he was giving as good as he got.

And that made Frankie smile. Because she liked that in humans and she thought it was a fine thing in horses too. She walked around him looking for other wounds and he watched her as she did, watching every move she made. Every bit as calm as he was curious. Attentive and sensible.

She saw no more wounds, but she saw something odd in his mane. Something that surprised her and gave an answer to the mystery—or at least, part of the answer to the mystery. Because right behind his poll, there was a thin strip of rawhide braided into his mane.

Her mind raced south across the Nebraska Territory, down to the prairie near the Little Blue River. She pictured a red-and-white pinto, the tough and wiry horse that the Cheyenne warrior, Strong Hand, had been riding. There had been a feather braided into a strip of rawhide in that pony's mane—the very feather Strong Hand had fastened to the fore-stock of her Henry rifle just before he had ridden off with his band.

There had been other Indian ponies there, too—some with feathers braided into their manes and some with feathers tied up in their tails. Brown-and-white eagle feathers, russet-colored hawk feathers, shining blue-black raven feathers. There had been bluebird feathers strung together in long strands that twisted and twirled in the prairie breeze. There had been feathers everywhere, lifting and flitting from bridles and shields and tall lances—all held in place by little braided strips of rawhide.

So. Now, she knew something about this tough, wiry dun-colored horse. He was an Indian horse. *Maybe a Cheyenne pony. Maybe not. Maybe he belonged to the Sioux. Or to the Pawnee.*

According to the pretty-colored map hanging above her mantle, those were the tribes that roamed this part of the Nebraska Territory. They were the Indian people who rode through the Sand Hills. There were the Ponca and Otoe tribes, too, but they tended to be closer to the Platte River and near the banks of the Missouri.

Frankie stood back, looking at the Indian pony, assessing things. She had more information now. A little more, anyway—or maybe it was a lot, depending on how she looked at it. She knew three things for sure. It was an Indian horse. It was wounded. It was in her hands.

What she didn't know was why he was here, instead of with his Indian. Maybe he had strayed from a herd. Maybe, he had been left behind after some battle. Or maybe, he had broken away. Whatever the reason, he had probably wandered around, found the mares and the gelding somewhere, and tagged along as part of their herd. And as of right now, he was in her meadow and standing in her front barn-lot.

She wasn't sure exactly what a white person was supposed to do with an Indian horse. She didn't know if it would be wiser to keep it here, or turn it loose. Because she didn't have any idea what the Indian owner of this horse might expect her to do. Neither, did she know whether a white person could get in trouble for messing around with an Indian's horse.

So after she stood and contemplated her odd circumstance, she decided to take some time before choosing a course of action. To do that, it might be best to step away and clear her mind. *Because, there are things here to sort out.*

The Bugler, the full-grown rooster, had been calling out most of the morning, well before it was fully light, and now, to Frankie's relief and delight, there were only a couple of younger roosters chiming in. The rooster-racket had been diminished with the departure of three of their ilk and that made Frankie smile as she walked across the meadow to the coop. Thankfully, a big part of the rooster-noise had gone with Everett and Ida when they drove out of the meadow.

Tomorrow morning, there would be young roosters doing their ratchety-croaking crows on the Dunbar homestead and Frankie doubted that Everett and Ida would mind the crowing competition. Most likely, it'd make them smile. Because there was warm comfort that could come from the sound of a rooster in the dawn. Because roosters usually meant hens, and hens usually meant eggs. Once their new flock settled into their new home, Ida would have eggs on the table every morning, and that would be something else to make them smile.

Frankie swung the henyard gate wide, fastened it open and watched the hens of her now-much-dwindled-down flock, scuttle out into the meadow grasses. Rushing and hurrying, because somewhere inside their little pea-sized brains, they knew they had a whole day of hunting-and-pecking to do before the sunset. Frankie grinned at them. *Apparently, they want to get a good start.*

She slipped into the henhouse to gather eggs, giving a wide berth to the nest-box where nasty-beaked Mrs. Swingle was guarding her clutch. She entertained a brief notion to reach under the hen to check the clutch, but an especially ugly growl from the hen caused her to reconsider. *Not really anything that I need to know about her eggs anyway. And I'm not feeling any particular need to have my knuckles bloodied up this morning, either.*

When she stepped out of the henhouse, Matilda and Laughing Girl were waiting. Watching. Anticipating. Because they knew there might be a game in the works. Because they knew that on some mornings, eggs could fall from the sky and it usually happened when their person was walking away from the henhouse. Frankie grinned as they started following her, their eyes bright and alert, glancing at her, and then looking to the sky above—looking up to the heavens, searching the sky for any falling eggs.

She tossed two eggs high, sending them arching through the air. The dogs didn't follow the flight of the eggs; they only knew that when her arm went up, eggs would come down. So they pranced and danced, glancing at the ground around them, listening for the sound. Knowing that their prize was coming.

As soon as the eggs smacked against the ground, the dogs pounced on them, lapping up the splattered yolks, sucking up the whites and crunching up the shells. Licking their dog-lips when they finished. And even after they finished with their surprise-from-the-skies, they still kept watching her arm, alert and excited—sending a few quick glances upwards, hoping for a second raining-of-eggs. Which, Frankie decided, was an example of the steadfastness of dog-hopes. Because there had never been a second egg-rain on the same day. But still, the two dogs had their hopes.

She walked toward the house, laughing at them and wondering if they'd *ever* figure out the connection between the eggs-in-her-hand and the eggs-raining-down. She had tried several times to show them the eggs in her hand and demonstrate how her hand lifted and released the eggs, so they could see what she was doing. But for some reason, their dog-brains just weren't adding it up. They had great abilities when it came to following pieces of jerky leaving her hand and catching them out of the air. But eggs, for some reason, baffled their brains.

Once in the kitchen, Frankie cut into the loaf of bread Ida had left for her; she toasted a slice in the frying pan, slathered butter on it and sat herself out on the porch table. She munched on the toast and drank a glass of buttermilk, and all the while, she was watching the wise-eyed dun-colored horse out in the barn-lot. Sorting through the situation, adding up what she knew about the Cheyenne warriors and their horses. Wondering what Strong Hand or Knife or He's Proud might want her to do if the horse belonged to them. She didn't think they would be upset if she worked on one of their horses if it was wounded. And then she started wondering if warriors in other tribes might see the situation differently and expect something else of her.

After she finished the toast and buttermilk, and after all the contemplation, Frankie realized she still had no idea about the right and wrong of the situation. At least, not from what might be an Indian's point of view. She also had no idea if the horse was actually hers now, or if it still belonged to whatever Indian had been separated from it. Because she didn't know the Indian-rules about keeping horses that just wandered up to a person's home.

She had no idea if she was supposed to go looking for the owner. And she realized, she had no idea whether the Indian owner might come looking for his horse. More than that, she didn't know whether or not that particular Indian might be upset that she had his horse penned up in her barn-lot.

All in all, it was a peculiar situation and she was wishing Everett and Ida were still around because they might have some input about handling such a circumstance. And then again, Frankie thought, maybe not. *Because, maybe they don't know anything about the Indians who might be in this area. They've never said a word about Indians, not in any conversation during their entire stay. And it might be, since I actually have some Indian friends, I might be the expert in this region when it comes to knowing things about Indians.*

There weren't any answers coming to her—not from her past experience and not from the current event. So she decided to follow her own gut. She decided she had two solid truths before her. One, she had a horse in her meadow that was wounded; and two, it had probably been dealing with the pain and infection for a lengthy period of time. *That* was the reality and taken as it was, *that* made it a moral choice. And *that,* she decided, meant she should deal with it. *And truth be told, it doesn't really matter where the horse came from.*

She decided to take care of the Indian horse the way she'd take care of one of her own horses. It all came down to the Golden Rule, and that was the only rule Frankie could think of which might apply to the situation. '*As ye would that men would do unto you, do ye also unto them likewise.' And maybe, that rule extends to doctoring some other man's horse, the way you'd want him to doctor yours. Because, after all, St. Luke was one of the Bible people that had something to say about that particular rule, and he had also been a doctor. He was the 'dear and glorious physician'.*

So she decided she'd follow St. Luke's advice and trust him to intervene on her behalf if she ended up with an Indian problem. She boosted herself off the porch table and headed for the pantry, sliding her dishes into the dishpan on the way. Her thoughts were on the remedy-chest in the cabinet; she was deciding which remedies and powders she'd need.

Once she had the chest open, she pulled out the bottles and cannisters she wanted and then sorted through the needles, hunting for the size she needed—bigger than the size for human-skin but smaller than the ones for sewing wagon-canvas. She found the right needle and she found the cat-gut for the suturing. Because, like Boone's wound, this was a long and deep gash, this wound would need to be sewn too.

She could feel her fears rising, and she tried to quiet them, trying to think back to what the fort's doctor had shown her as he stitched up Boone's wound. The inside muscle-stitches, and the outside skin-stitches. *Just remember what Dr. Gannon showed me. Just stitch it like he did with Boone.*

She mixed the remedies for dousing the wound; she mixed linseed-oil and milk together for a poultice. *Three-parts milk, two-parts linseed oil.* She added squares of cloth, strips of cloth bandages and a jar of clay to her growing assortment. When she was satisfied, she packed everything into a pail and headed to the barn-lot.

It was almost two hours until she was satisfied with the doctor-ing on the mouse-colored dun. Cleaning and debriding the wound was something she understood well enough; her only concern with *that* process was being thorough, so she took her time.

It was the stitching on the inside tissue that was the most worri-some for her. All she could think to do was to try to imitate what Dr. Gannon had done back when they had worked together on Boone. She couldn't recall all his words, but she could remember the way his hands moved as he eased the muscles together with the sutures.

So she did her best to copy him. She remembered the way Boone's muscles had jerked and twitched, so when the dun's muscles started twitching, she wasn't surprised. What did surprise her was that the Indian pony barely seemed to mind. By the time she finished with the muscles and began working the sutures into the edges of his hide, he actually nibbled at her hair. Once she put aside the needle and thread, and had begun packing the poultice against the wound, he was blowing softly in her ears and sending his warm breath down her neck and back.

Her hands were shaking and her face and arms were wet with sweat by the time she finished doctoring the wound. And when she stood up, her knees were stiff and wobbly at the same time. She mixed up more remedies—both tinctures and powders—into an assortment of grains in a pail, and then added some of the dark treacle from the can in the barn.

She offered the mixture to the dun horse and waited while he studied the pail for a few moments. He nudged it with his nose a few times and then did some snuffling and blowing at it. He seemed to be intrigued by the contents and the smells, but he was clearly concerned about the contraption.

"This is probably something completely new for you, isn't it? Both the pail *and* the grain."

Frankie spoke to him softly, just as she had been doing through the whole doctoring procedure; now, he was listening to her, eyeing her calmly like he had done all along. She doubted he knew what she was saying because she figured it was unlikely he spoke the same language as a little white girl, but he seemed to understand the tone. Finally, he nibbled and licked at the grain in the pail; then he lifted his head and worked his lips. Testing and tasting the sweetness. Working the oats and corn around in his mouth. Working his thoughts about it around in his mind.

Frankie waited, letting him sort things out, letting him work his way through what was probably a whole new experience of sweetgrain. He kept nibbling at the grain in the bucket and nibbling at her hands while she held it. He must have decided he liked it, because it wasn't long before he started eating faster—taking bigger bites and chewing faster.

And all the time, he kept looking up at her, studying her. Steady and calm. Frankie decided she liked him a lot. He was a very serious boy, and a very sensible boy. And wherever he came from, she was glad he was here. *Hopefully, if his Indian comes looking for him, he'll be glad too.*

Frankie spent part of the afternoon in the windmill pond, splashing and playing with the dogs. When they were done playing, she stretched out in the meadow grass, basking in the warm sun. She had her meadow to herself again and she hadn't realized how much she missed the solitude. So now, in the warmth of the late summer afternoon, she was making up for lost time.

While the Dunbars had been visiting, she had slipped out of the house a few times, late in the night while they slept, making her own time to bathe and relax in the water. Having company staying in the meadow had seriously damped the freedom she had become accustomed to, but lying in the warm sunlight, she knew the brief loss of freedom had been worthwhile.

Because Ida and Everett were part of her life now, and she was glad to have them nearby; they were her neighbors and they would likely be in her life for a long time. The concerns she had about other homesteaders interfering with her life on her homestead, if not gone entirely, were diminished. The last nine days had been the perfect opportunity for the friendship between her and the Dunbars to grow solid and true. As of now, the trust between her and her new neighbors ran deep.

In Frankie's mind, it was a good beginning. From the discussions in the evenings at the kitchen table, she had learned of a settlement to the south of her place. A good ten miles away, down near the Middle Loup River. The Dunbars said it was just a dozen or so homesteads down in that region; folks who had taken up claims and considered themselves to be a community of neighbors. Some of them were people who had been part of Everett and Ida's wagon party when they had traveled west. Others had already been in the area and living on their claims.

'Probably spread out over maybe a six or seven-mile region,' Everett had said. 'All folks working to prove-up their claims.'

Apparently, there had been more at one time, but a good number of families had already given up—they had pulled up stakes and left.

The center of the settlement, itself, was mostly considered to be where two of the more frequently traveled wagon-tracks happened to cross. On one corner of the crossroads was a preacher's homestead; on an adjacent corner was the preacher's church—nothing more than a long and low sod-building. But according to the Dunbars, the

Reverend Simeon Austin 'kinda holds the community together. His church gives folks a reason to come together. To visit and worship on some Sundays, when farming and weather allow'.

The farm-market for the settlers to sell crops and buy supplies, Everett had said, was down to Fort Cottonwood on the Platte River—a four to five-day trip by wagon. So from what Frankie understood, there was no actual town in this entire region. No supply store or bank or school. No post office. No elected officials, no town council, no sheriff. Nothing that resembled a town at all. Just a bunch of families living in fairly close proximity. Folks who relied on each other, sometimes for some things.

That was rather a good thing in Frankie's mind. No laws to worry about. No officials to intrude into her life. Just other homesteaders trying to prove up their claims; settlers who had their own lives and futures to think about; people who probably wouldn't go looking to disrupt the lives of other folks—not while they were busy trying to build their own lives. Lots of people might have opinions about a ten-year-old living alone; lots of people might not like the idea. But if there *was* a law that said a kid couldn't live alone on a homestead in the Nebraska Territory, there were no lawmen out here to enforce it.

So to Frankie's mind, if she was going to stay on her own homestead and live her own life—mostly, she needed to stay out of the eyes and minds of anyone who might feel some sense of obligation to interfere. As of now, she knew the Dunbars understood her need to be here. And as of now, she had no fears they would interfere.

The preacher down in the Middle Loup settlement, though, Frankie decided, might prove to be a bit of a stickler. Because preachers could sometimes take up an unyielding, and sometimes unwieldy, righteous stance. And *that* might be exactly where trouble could arise.

But as to most of the other settlers who might raise questions about her living by herself, Frankie figured that Everett and Ida would have answers for them; they would speak on her behalf and anyone questioning her situation would hear exactly what the Dunbars had to say.

As the afternoon moved into evening, Frankie bridled Black Mack and headed out to the north, rifle in-hand. She surveyed the surrounding land from the top of her Lookout Hill, the highest hill she had found—the one with the cluster of large rocks near the crest. She used her spyglass, training it in on anything that caught her eye. To the west, she saw an antelope buck, and from the size of the herd traveling with him, he looked to have a good start on gathering his females. Out to the northwest, she could see a few herds of deer— groups of does mostly, with their half-grown fawns among them.

And then, something caught her eye. Beyond the herds of deer, far out along the horizon, out north-by-northwest, she spotted a large blackish-brown patch of something out on the far hills. Looking closer, she could see more large dark patches tucked in among the hills and valleys. Several of them. And there were a lot of tiny blackish-brownish specks scattered among and around the larger patches. Both the large patches and the small patches and the specks seemed to be moving across the landscape. Moving slowly, haltingly.

She watched as the largest patch slowly weaved its way among the far hills, gradually disappearing from sight behind a long ridge. It reminded her of something she had seen when she had been traveling on the Cheyenne Trail; there had been something moving along the far hills then too—not big dark patches of somethings on those hillsides—but rather, a long line of somethings moving along the horizon. It had turned out to be a band of Indians traveling northward, looking a little like a caterpillar crawling across a great green rug.

She was watching something similar now. *Similar, but different.* It was dark, but it wasn't so much caterpillar-shaped as it was blanket-shaped. Several of the blanket-shaped somethings. It looked as though some great unseen hand was dragging a few odd-shaped pieces of cloth slowly across the land. Gently; slowly. So slowly, in fact, that there were long periods of time when the cloth looked as if it wasn't moving at all.

Clearly, the dark-masses-of-somethings weren't bands of Indians traveling through the hills and valleys. They were, rather, some great herds of living, walking somethings. And whatever they were, Frankie decided, watching them made for a fascinating way to spend her time on the crest of her hill. She slid down from Mack's back and settled herself on the highest-placed rock, elbows on her knees and spyglass in her hands. She sighted the telescope's lens on the far hills.

The shapes of the great dark cloths changed—steadily, gradually—as the great herd-of-somethings moved gradually, ever so slowly, over and around the hills. Up the slopes and down into the valleys. Drifting along the hillsides and disappearing into the draws and valleys. Out of sight, then back in sight, with the edges sometimes lagging and taking on the appearance of frayed edges of the cloth. *Fringed cloth. With strands dragging along through the grass.*

From the distance, she knew they weren't massive herds of deer or antelope. Nor were they looking like—or moving like—the great herds of elk she had seen on other days. *These* great dark cloths, made up of whatever creatures were traveling the Sand Hills, was more intriguing than anything she had seen before. *'Absolutely mesmerizing.' Isaiah would have called it that.*

Her mind drifted back to her cousin, just a few years older than her. *Isaiah.* The cousin who had always taken her riding and hunting and exploring with him. *On Fanny. His mare. His pride.* Frankie brought her thoughts forward, wondering what he would think of this odd sight out across the far hills. *Mesmerizing. Yeah, that's what he'd think.*

Frankie kept her telescope trained on the dark herds of creatures, working to focus the lens, working to clarify the object of her fascination. Trying to bring this life-form into perspective; trying to identify the darkened-forms moving across the rippling grasses, moving through the twisting waves of the rising heat-vapors. She took her time, adjusting and re-adjusting, until finally, she locked the vision into focus. Clear and steady. The sight startled her. She sucked in a quick gulp of air. *Buffalo!*

She shivered, feeling the excitement tickling its way up her spine and rippling out across her skin. There, within the circle of her lens, the great beasts were moving. Slowly, calmly. Walking; wandering; meandering. Grazing their way along the grassy slopes and through the valleys. *Playing follow-the-leader. Or maybe, following several leaders. Or maybe, they're all just following some instinct.*

Frankie Harding was grinning her crooked grin; she could feel it pulling at her lips and cheeks. She knew it was a wide grin—a happy, excited, astonished grin. Because this was something she had only heard about. Something she had never seen before. Not once. In fact, she had never seen a single buffalo before. Not down along the Little Blue River. Not around Fort Kearny. Not while she had traveled the Cheyenne Trail. But now. *Now,* she was seeing hundreds. *No! Thousands! Thousands and thousands of 'em!*

Studying the distant herds, she figured the biggest dark cloth to be almost as wide as it was long, spread across the land and rippling along slowly. Moving just like the grasses that rippled along the hillsides. Moving to the east and maybe a little to the south, slow and steady. Slow and relaxed.

She focused on the little dark specks. The individual animals along the edges of the great dark patches, watching as those great lumbering giants plodded along. Watching as they lowered their heads, reaching down to the earth, twisting their great heads as they grabbed at the grasses. Pulling up a mouthful at a time. And then, standing and gazing across the land as they chewed. Watching the land like she was watching them. They were part of the prairie, part of the hills. Part of the rolling land. They belonged out there as much as the grass and the sky.

Frankie kept her spyglass on the great herd, feeling the pleasure of the discovery. Astonished. Mesmerized by the vision within the spherical world of the lens. She realized that she knew nothing about these massive creatures, except for what she had read and what she had heard. She had heard some stories back in Independence before they crossed the Missouri—some of the people in the wagon party had talked about the buffalo herds. And sometimes, the soldiers at Fort Kearny had talked about them.

She had heard stories of their vast numbers and their great herds. And of their deadly stampedes that could mow down whole homesteads and wipe out fields of growing crops. And there had been tales from blustering braggarts like Silas Beckett who described the slaughtering of the herds by the hide-hunters—men who killed the animals by the hundreds and thousands for the money they could make from the hides.

Frankie shook her head to clear away the stories about the blood and the gore and the stench that Beckett had told—stories he told at the campfires, stories he had told to impress the men and to shock the women. She shook away the memories of Beckett's laughter as the women turned away wide-eyed and pale, leaving the campfires, retching and gagging at his descriptions.

She focused again on the faraway herd, wanting to know more about the massive beasts than just a handful of remembered tales— there was more about the buffalo and their great herds than those men knew. Far more, she thought. *These animals! These buffalo! I need to learn about these creatures for myself.*

She kept watching the far hills, still hypnotized by the slow and steady movement of the herd. Fascinated as she watched them moving with the rhythm of the land. She wondered about the time of the buffalo. About the years of the buffalo herds, about the centuries and lifetimes they had traveled the land, moving through the prairie grasses, just like they were now. Grazing. Grabbing mouthfuls of the green grasses, and then raising their heads to gaze across the land. Across the slopes. Across the Sand Hills.

Frankie stayed as she was, sitting on the rock at the crest of her Lookout Hill, watching them across the hills until they disappeared with the fading light. Watching them as they became part of the darkness, fading from her sight into the dusk and into the dark.

There was mystery out there among the hills and Frankie was quivering with the magnificence of it. There had been majesty and mystery right there within the circle of the lens; there had been silence and serenity. And there had been peace, a separate peace, as the herd disappeared into the shadowed land.

A pair of nighthawks with their white-banded wings, whipped low to the ground in front of her. Sailing in silence, swooping-and-looping back and forth along the slope of the hill below her. Frankie whistled for Black Mack, whistling soft and low, watching him as he strolled over to her. She slipped up on his back from the top of the rock and turned him back onto the flat hilltop.

She sat there on his broad warm back, still trying to see the dark patches, trying to get one last look at the great herd that had already been lost to the night. She stayed as she was, picturing the buffalo; knowing the vision was imbedded in her mind now. *Forever,* she figured. *For always.*

She let Mack have his head so he could graze while she leaned back, stretching her arms and arching her back, and then melting down into the soft curve of his spine. Lying there, looking into the night sky, thinking about the Sand Hills and the grasses that rippled and waved.

Thinking about the movement of the buffalo herd. Thinking about the movement of all the herds—the deer and the antelope and the elk. Thinking about the way the badgers and foxes, the coyotes and wolves moved through the hills, weaving their way along the slopes and down through the valleys. The rabbits dashing and dodging. The prairie chickens bobbing their heads, turning and spreading their wings, kicking and scratching at the soil.

She was picturing the hawks and eagles soaring and circling, floating in their spirals above the hills. Picturing the larks and the wrens, the flycatchers and sparrows—all flitting and flapping, dipping and darting through the long stems of the prairie grasses. *This is my life. My hills and my river. My earth and my sky.*

Frankie stayed still, listening to the songs of the night-birds, traveling through the dark skies. Their songs soft and haunting, coming from nowhere and going everywhere, all at the same time. She stretched again; she felt Mack's warm muscles moving against her back as he stepped forward in his grazing. She gazed upward, staring into the blue-black sky. *My night-sky.*

The planets were showing themselves, taking turns and appearing one by one. And one by one, Frankie named them—Saturn, Venus, Jupiter—identifying them like her father had taught her. Knowing their positions and their movement. She spotted Mars. She looked for Mercury, but realized she was late—the little planet would have already followed the sun down behind the western horizon.

Frankie watched the constellations appearing, showing themselves in a steady procession as the night-sky deepened and darkened. She saw the North Star make its appearance and she followed the handle of the small dipper on its arching path to the little square cup at its far end. She turned her attention to the southern sky. *There! Antares. The ruby-red heart of the Scorpion.* The red-giant star; the one that her cousin Samuel liked so much. *Maybe, just maybe, he still watches it. Just from a different place. From a different perspective.*

All of which made her start wondering if people in heaven, wherever that was, could still see the stars. *Or maybe, they're so much in and among them, that they don't even notice them anymore. Like the-forest-and-the-trees thing.*

Frankie waited as the night deepened. Waiting; watching. Knowing exactly what would happen if she was patient enough. And then, it happened—the stars began their descent. Coming down from the heights, slowly and surely. Steadily. Coming down to her, just like she knew they would, pulling the blue-black cloth of the universe down with them.

They came down, surrounding her. Wrapping around her, bringing her and her dark horse and the dark hills into the soft folds of the dark velvet that they carried with them. And once again, she became part of the sky and the stars. Once again, she felt the sensation—the gradual clarity—that she was *of* the universe, not beneath it.

Because, she wasn't watching the universe—the universe was watching *her.* Knowing that she was home in the universe; knowing that she was exactly where she was supposed to be. She was part of her family's dream, and her family's dream was part of her. She had come home. And she had brought her family with her—they had all come home.

Frankie stayed where she was, lying there on her dark horse's broad back, staying there deep into the night. Lying there among the stars. Resting in the dark of the moon. Realizing that in the next few days, the moon would begin its waxing phase. Realizing that she was beginning her own waxing phase. She was into this life now; living this life now. Growing within it, now.

Because she was home. She was living someplace permanent, now. Living where her family had chosen. She had taken some twists and turns, and she had taken a beating to get here. But she had gotten here anyway. And everything—every trial, every blow, every challenge—had been worth it. No one had stopped her. No one had given her a beating that she couldn't take. Nothing had stopped her from following her chosen direction; no one had kept her from traveling her path.

And now, she was here, resting on the back of one of the horses she had fought to keep. She had the comfort and peace of knowing she was exactly where she belonged. She was building the life her family wanted and she was doing it in a way that would make them proud.

She knew it in her heart and in her gut. Clarity in her mind and passion in her heart had gotten her down the road—a long way down the road. Clarity and passion had brought her here. And now, she had time to plan.

Finally, she sat up. Picked up Black Mack's rein and turned him down the slope. Heading home. Content with her discoveries—pleased with the sight of the buffalo, pleased with the dark sky and the bright stars. Pleased with her place in the universe.

Frankie woke early in the morning after her night-ride home by starlight. She was thinking about the buffalo herd in the faraway hills. The massive herd had boggled her mind. It had been her first sighting of buffalo, her first chance to watch the way a herd moved. Her first chance to observe the way a herd of the great dark beasts shifted across the grass-covered slopes, drifting its way through the valleys of the Sand Hills.

She stretched. Breathed in the cool morning air floating into her room from across the meadow. Listened to the Bugler crowing his heart out as he greeted the sun; an instant later she heard the croaking-crow of one of the younger roosters, struggling to copy the king of the coop. She listened as the Bugler sent out his flawless call again and giggled at the young cock's second attempt to master the sound—it was worse than his first. Frankie grinned and decided to start the day.

And from the start, she knew it was going to be a good day. A simple day filled with everyday homestead things. She washed up at the washstand and braided her hair; she decided to spend the early morning in her nightshift. When she went into the kitchen and stirred the banked ashes in the big Majestic stove, she grinned when the flames flared right away. *Good start to a good day.*

After adding more wood and setting coffee to brewing, she headed out the kitchen door with Matilda at her heels. Laughing Girl bounded up the porch steps, grinning her wolfhound-grin, looking like she too, was ecstatically happy with the day. Frankie grinned back at her, stopped to ruffle her ears, and then headed across the meadow with her two companions prancing along beside her.

She checked the livestock in the pastures, doctored the dun, and did the milking. At the henhouse, when she went inside to gather eggs, she found another good omen. She found a changed chicken; in the space of a single night, the nasty Mrs. Swingle had a change of heart. She had an entirely new outlook on life—the clutch of eggs had hatched out and the moody, broody hen had become an adoring and doting mother of eleven chunky little chicks.

Frankie breathed a sigh of relief. Mrs. Swingle no longer had any interest in ripping the skin off human hands; she was not issuing any nasty, blood-curdling chicken-growls and chicken-snarls. This morning, she offered no challenge when Frankie removed the three remaining eggs from the nest-box she had been guarding so fiercely. Mrs. Swingle was showing no interest in the eggs she had left behind—because her tiny little chicken-brain already knew there was no life in those three eggs.

Pulling the remaining eggs from the box, Frankie was planning to toss them away, but first, she wanted to watch motherhood in action. She followed Mrs. Swingle outside, delighted with the change in her attitude. The red-feathered hen was waddling around in the grass, cooing and chortling softly, chatting with her babies.

The eleven babies were tripping and tumbling over themselves, and each other, as they followed her, desperately determined to go wherever she went. Some chicks were scrambling and hopping and clawing, gamely trying to climb on her back; others were trying to tuck themselves under her wings. And all of them were tangling and twisting themselves around her feet. But Mrs. Swingle didn't mind; Mrs. Swingle was deliriously happy with her life and her lot.

Frankie stood smiling at the eleven little-bitty chicken-babies that seemed awfully happy to be alive; they were skittering and scuttling around in the dirt, doing their baby-peeping and baby-pecking. Doing all their baby-chicken things.

Laughing Girl watched the action for a few minutes and then trotted off to find other things to do. Matilda, though, stood beside Frankie, watching the activity with intense interest. Deeply fascinated with the fuzzy balls of baby-chicken fluff.

The real fascinating thing for Frankie, though, was the complete change in old Mrs. Swingle. She had seen broody-hens change into mother-hens before, but this change in Mrs. Swingle was a serious adjustment of attitude. Sometime during the night, the New Hampshire Red had magically transformed into an extraordinary mother, and she was awfully busy whispering and murmuring to those little kids of hers—soothing them, encouraging them, correcting them, admonishing them. She was clucking softly, cooing sweetly. Gathering them to her. Teaching them and leading them.

And all the while, she was wearing something Frankie thought looked very much like a silly smile on her beaky chicken-lips. For once, she didn't seem to mind there was a human hanging around. At one point, she looked at Frankie with a soppy look of sweet motherly-love in her beady little chicken-eyes. The old biddy had transformed—she had her babies around her and she was finally happy.

In that moment, when she showed Frankie that soppy-happy look in her eyes, Frankie forgave her for every drop of blood she had drawn. There was new and fresh life in the meadow, and whether she actually needed eleven more chickens or not, Frankie thought it boded well for her homestead. It was another sign that the future was building.

After Frankie finished the morning chores and after she fried up a breakfast of eggs and ham, she changed out of her night-shift into her shirt and britches and boots. She took her Henry rifle from the pegs by the kitchen door, readied her horses and headed out of the meadow. She was riding Rock and leading Boone; Matilda and Laughing Girl were trailing after her. Because, Frankie decided, it was a good day for an outing, and she had a few good reasons to think so.

First, she figured they were all due for a day out of the valley— her and the dogs and the horses. Second, she wanted to ride up to the Lookout Hill and see what had happened to the buffalo. There were things that she wanted to know about buffalo herds, like how far and how fast they traveled in a day, and whether they traveled in a single direction. And whether they stayed together as one herd. Or if the different dark patches ever split up to head off in different directions. And third, she wanted fresh meat, because she was tired of chicken and ham, bacon and rabbit.

She had her mind set on a young buck, which typically, wouldn't be a good idea because she couldn't eat all the meat before it spoiled—even if she shared out a fair portion to the dogs. But this, she decided, was a perfect time for hunting, because on Sunday, she would be heading to the Dunbar place. Until then she could hang the carcass inside the barn entrance on the pulley-and-hook hanging from a beam in the ceiling. It could age for a couple of days, and then she would take some of the fresh meat to Ida and Everett.

Once out of the valley, Frankie circled to the north and headed for the Lookout Hill, planning to spend some time studying the buffalo herd. And while she was there on the hilltop, she thought she just might be able to spot any deer in the area. And as it turned out, that's exactly how things worked out.

High on the crest of the hill with Boone and the dogs beside her, Frankie sat on Rock's back, watching the great herd. It was still there, out in the far hills—far to the northwest. Still looking like several great blackish-brown blankets spreading across the hillsides and dipping out of sight, down into the valleys.

She trained her spy-glass on the herd, realizing it hadn't changed much from the last time she had watched it. It was still there among the rolling hills, still looking like a dark cloth, or rather, several pieces of dark cloth. Because today, there were a great number of pieces of the great dark patch—small sections of the herd that had separated and shifted away from the main herd.

A number of the smaller herds were disappearing into the valley-folds for a time and then reappearing on hillsides. Whole segments of the herd seemed to be taking turns, first disappearing and then reappearing. But always, the sum of the great herd was moving slowly and steadily.

Watching the herd, Frankie decided the buffalo were apparently satisfied with where they were and what they were doing. They were acting a little like cattle that were well-fed and content with their grazing. *No need to hurry when you have plenty to eat. No need to get somewhere else when your bellies are getting full where you are.*

Given where the buffalo were last night and where they were now, she thought they were traveling on an east-by-southeast course. If they stayed on that setting, she figured they would come a little closer to her homestead, but still be far to the north of her place. And they'd still be far to the north even when they passed the Dunbar place. *At least, that's what it looks like now. Unless they change direction.*

She knew she had no idea how to read a buffalo herd; she had no real idea of what the buffalo might decide to do. She sat there on top of the hill, watching the herd and realizing she had no idea what went on in a buffalo's brain and no idea what might change its mind—there was no telling what might change the mood or the motion of a vast herd as it moseyed its way across the Sand Hills.

She figured that, if buffalo were like cattle, then as quiet and calm as they might be over a good length of time, they were also subject to sudden changes in mood and behavior. All kinds of things could change the minds and the actions of a herd of cows—a herd of thirty or forty cows could change behavior pretty fast if something unexpected came along. Dogs barking and chasing. Gunshots. Train whistles. Thunder and lightning.

Lots of things could set off a herd of cattle and send them running and changing directions without any great thought of where they were going, or where they might end up. Even herds of typically placid dairy cows were known to get fretted-up into crazy runs—she'd seen it happen. And since buffalo were similar bovine-type creatures, Frankie decided, it was likely they could be riled into erratic behaviors too.

She continued her watch, sitting there on the crest of the hill on Rock's back, thinking that she didn't really want a herd like this to suddenly decide to make some kind of crazed-run toward her place. Luckily, there were no train whistles out here, and probably no packs of neighborhood dogs like back in Indiana. There were wolves and coyotes, but she didn't know if a pack of wolves had any reason or desire to send a massive herd of buffalo running. There were certainly thunderstorms and lightning, but buffalo, being the wild creatures that they were, probably didn't pay any more attention to such things than deer and antelope did. But she didn't know for sure.

Frankie lowered her spy-glass, deciding there was something that she *was* sure about—given the number of animals out there among the far hills, she was pretty sure she didn't want them running, or even moseying, through her homestead and buildings. Coming fast or coming slow, it would not be a good thing. She decided to keep an eye on the herd.

Before she left the Lookout Hill, Frankie scanned the nearby hills, studying the draws and the meadows. Watching for movement. Finally, she spotted what she wanted. Almost out of her sight beyond a low ridge, a small herd of deer was grazing in the hard-grasses of a low valley. She watched the deer for a while and studied the lay of the hills and valleys around them, deciding her best course to reach them. Choosing her path.

She knew the meadow they were in; it was a narrow meadow which opened near the north bank of the river, more than a mile north of the apple trees and a bit past the cove of piled wood. There were a handful of valleys and slopes between the Lookout Hill and the meadow where the deer grazed, but she figured she could weave her way among the slopes to the north until she reached the hill bordering the meadow. From there, she'd be able to work her way around the north slope of the hillside and into the meadow toward the herd.

Satisfied with her plan, Frankie rode down the far side of the Lookout Hill and traveled through the lowlands, working her way to the far meadow.

When she reached the hill that sheltered the meadow, she left Boone and the two dogs beside the northeast slope and rode on alone, guiding Rock along the base of the hill, circling around toward the meadow side. She slid down the side of the saddle, clutching the cantle, crouching with one foot in the stirrup. She stayed hidden against Rock's side with the hill's slope at her back, rifle in-hand. Peeking at the deer from under Rock's neck.

Rock, being the warhorse he was, seemed fine with all of it; he was being his calm sensible warhorse-self. His ears showed he was a little curious with what must be a new sort of wargame to him, but he kept walking. Smooth and steady; alert and attentive. Patient. Waiting to learn what was expected of him.

As they came around into view of the low meadow, Frankie kept him walking while she scanned the open meadow, peeking under his neck. She counted eight does and a handful of half-grown fawns. A large buck stood near the females and fawns, his head high, his eyes on the horse, wary of the intruder. Two younger bucks, two points on their racks, were near the front edge of the herd, clearly curious about some strange horse walking along the edge of the meadow.

The big buck was massive, with a rack that showed a lot of age. But it was the young bucks that held Frankie's interest. She guided Rock along the base of the hillside, clinging to the saddle, watching the deer, while the deer were busy watching Rock and probably wondering why some horse was wandering around by itself.

Frankie doubted they could see anything except the saddle and maybe, a hint of something odd, hanging on its far side. She doubted they associated anything they were seeing as being human, but every deer in the meadow was watching. None were showing any alarm, and most were showing more curiosity than caution.

Within a minute or two, most of them went back to their grazing, but to Frankie's dismay, the largest buck began walking toward Rock. His head up; his antlers high. His chest puffed up. His eyes locked on the intruding horse. Frankie gave an inward groan, realizing things had just gotten complicated. Now, she would have to time things and make her shot before the old buck figured out that the odd thing hanging on the far side of the horse was a human.

She had planned on taking her time to find the best moment—and the best place—to drop to the ground and get a shot off at one of the small bucks. Now, this big buck was mucking up her plans. He was either going to get in the way of her shot, or he was going to get close enough to understand the situation.

The buck had some age to him and Frankie figured he hadn't gotten all those points on his rack without accumulating some wisdom along with them; it wouldn't be long before he figured out what was going on, and once he did, he'd send the whole herd racing away to the riverside trees and underbrush.

Rock kept easing his way along the base of the slope, while Frankie's brain was busy sorting everything out—the distance, the timing, and the tactics. She was also remembering another hunt, a hunt down on the prairie, south of the Platte River. Remembering her Corporal with the blond hair and green eyes. And her two troopers—Will Trask with the soft Southern drawl and Septimus Travers with the gray-brown eyes and the quick wink.

195

She shook her head, trying to shake the memories out of the way. Trying to shift her thoughts back to *this* hunt and *this* herd. She glanced to the buck with the huge rack—he was still approaching, angling toward Rock, getting closer with each step. His head was higher, his nose was higher; he was trying to find a scent on the breeze.

And Frankie knew if the breeze shifted even a little bit, he would likely pick up human-smell. She said a quick prayer, asking the angels-above to hold the breeze for a moment. *Just for a moment. Please. So I can get a shot. Please give me a little miracle here.*

She received an answer to her prayer. A little miracle. Sort of, anyway. Because something happened; something she hadn't expected. One of the two-point bucks had a sudden inspiration to start walking toward the older buck. The old buck stopped his forward movement; his interest shifted from the strange horse to the youngster offering a challenge. The young buck took a couple more steps and then stopped, facing the old buck. And remarkably, when he stopped, he was standing broadside to Rock. *Thank you, angels-above.*

Frankie decided things weren't going to get any easier—the young buck had just put himself right where she needed him. And not twenty yards away. She stepped out of the stirrup and plopped her bottom on the slope right in front of Rock. And Rock, being a warhorse by training, understood the rifle and her movements; he took two quick steps back and froze in place.

Elbows braced on her knees, Frankie set her aim and took her shot. The buck fell and the rest of the herd spun away, racing off, disappearing into the trees and willows along the river-bottoms. The world along the river went silent as the sound of the shot echoed itself away. Birds hushed their songs; the piercing calls of the red-tailed hawks circling high in the sky ceased. The red-winged blackbird that had been watching the proceedings and voicing his opinions, was gone.

Frankie looked at Rock—he was watching her, ears tipped forward. Nostrils wide. He gave a snort and tossed his head, rattling his bridle and reins. Then he dropped his nose to blow his warm breath against her face and Frankie was pretty sure he winked at her.

She grinned at him, then looked toward the fallen buck. It was still lying where it fell. Unmoving. She leaned back against the hillside, sinking down onto the warm grass, feeling the heat of the sandy soil against her back. She lay there, thinking about miracle-prayers and magic-bullets. Not sure which applied here; wondering if it was maybe a combination of both.

Her mind traveled across the hills, racing back, south of the Platte River for the second time in a matter of minutes. *Knife. My warrior-brother. He would believe it was magic. That's why he wanted the bullet from the dead buck.*

That had been the same day she had been hunting with Corporal Buchanan and Trask and Travers. She had never been really sure if there had been magic in her bullet that killed the deer, but Knife believed there was. His belief had been strong enough that he had used the bullet in a necklace. And once, when he and the other warriors had come to Fort Kearny's trading post, he had squatted down in front of her and let her touch it. *Knife and He's Proud and Strong Hand. My brothers.*

As far as the hunt today was concerned, Frankie decided it didn't really matter—maybe it was magic, maybe it was the prayer, or maybe, it was *pure* luck. *Doesn't matter. Maybe it was all of them working together.*

Frankie stayed in the grass for a few minutes, feeling the tickle of the grass-blades on her back and neck. She let her body soak up heat from the soil, letting her mind stay with that day and with that hunt way down south of the Platte River. Just for a while.

She closed her eyes, listening to Rock's hooves on the sandy soil as he stepped away from her. Hearing his bit-rings jingle as he lowered his head to nibble at the grass. And the jingle got her to thinking about how the noise of a bridle-bit could ruin a hunt; it had happened to her in the past, way back when she used to hunt with her cousins. She had lost a chance at a buck once because her horse had chomped down on the bit.

Today, she had actually forgotten to slip the bridle off Rock, but for some reason—due to either magic or prayer or luck—nothing had gone wrong. She sat up and looked at Rock; he lifted his head from the grass and looked at her.

"Today, Warhorse, today it all worked out fine, didn't it?" She didn't expect an answer from him, but he did give her a wise and thoughtful look before he dropped his head to reach for another mouthful of grass. "And now, we have work to do."

Plenty of work. Because the shooting was the quick-and-easy part. Now, came the dressing, the bloody-and-mucky part. She whistled the dogs in, sure that *they* would come running, but not sure at all, if Boone would come with them. There was a chance, though, that he might. Because Boone had belonged to Corporal Buchanan, and surely, the Corporal had trained his mount to come to him. *Surely, Corporal Buchanan had some sort of cue for him. Maybe, it was a whistle.*

She stood there, waiting for the dogs, wondering if she'd have to backtrack for Boone. Wishing she knew the specific whistle that Corporal Buchanan had used for him, if he had trained him to one.

It was less than a minute before Laughing Girl came racing around the far slope of the hill, with Matilda doing her best to keep up. And there, coming along behind them at a quick trot, was that big, ugly, roman-nosed, dark-bay horse.

Frankie grinned, watching him coming to her. Wondering whether he had taken his cue from her whistle, or from the dogs. Either way, he was coming along with them. He was tossing his big ugly head, with his too-big ears laid back tight against his poll; apparently, the bow-legged dark-bay was annoyed that he hadn't been included before now. Frankie laughed, knowing he would have more to say about the way he had been treated.

Sure enough, when he stopped in front of her, he reached out his too-long neck and snapped his nasty teeth at her. She had been expecting as much, and she also knew he wouldn't actually make any contact. So she didn't flinch. Which annoyed him even more. He glared at her and reached forward again, his teeth flashing and gnashing, as if he was planning to rip the skin off her face. She slapped at him, just so he would think he'd gotten a rise out of her. He threw his head up, snorting, acting shocked and surprised by her reaction.

"Knock it off Mister, or I'll smack you good." She laughed and he reached forward again, snatching at her sleeve. She slapped at him again; he jerked backwards again, acting genuinely surprised again. "Get your big ugly butt out of my way."

She sneered at him and turned away, ignoring him. She stepped over to Rock, stood on her tip-toes to slide the Henry into the scabbard, picked up the reins and walked toward the fallen buck.

It was lying where it had fallen. Dead to the world. The rest of the world, though was returning to normal—the birds along the riverbank were singing again, the hawks were calling from high in the sky. A meadowlark sent out its song. A catbird was singing from the high branches of a riverside tree. The red-winged blackbird was back and giving his ratcheting-trill. The breeze was still rustling through the grasses. The water in the pretty North Loup River was still rippling along, showing bright splatters of reflected light through the leafy shadows. Life was going on.

Frankie heard hooves plodding softly in the grass—Boone's hooves—coming from behind her. One-step. Then another. And another. Coming closer. She wasn't surprised when she felt warm breath on her neck and a hard tug to her braid.

"Boone, I swear. I'm gonna whack you silly if you keep this up." Frankie said it without looking back, but she saw his shadow as he jerked his head up and away from her—acting scared and surprised, again. She grinned and shook her head. She stepped to lift the braided-rope from Rock's saddle. Stroked the liver-chestnut's neck. Whispered her thanks to him.

"Good man. Well done, Warhorse."

Fastening the rope from the deer's hind leg to Rock's saddle made the whole dressing-process easier than Frankie expected. She let the rope and Rock's strength do the heavy work of shifting the carcass around while she cleared the entrails. Then she let the dogs have what they wanted of the inside of the buck, while she had Rock drag the outside of the buck to the trees beside the river.

Frankie selected a hefty tree limb and tossed the tail-end of the rope over it. She looped it around the buck's hind legs and tied the other end to the saddle again and backed Rock until the carcass was hanging high. While he stood in place, she led Boone underneath the dangling buck and brought Rock forward a few steps. She lowered the buck onto Boone's back, tied the carcass in place and stepped back grinning, pleased with the ease of the whole process.

By the time she was done with her work, the dogs had eaten their fill and were stretched out in the shade with their bellies tight and full. Frankie stripped down and waded into the cool water of the North Loup. She washed the blood from her arms and neck and face, then called to the dogs, wanting to rinse the clumps of blood and entrails from their fur.

When they showed no inclination to join her, she started scrubbing at the Cavalry shirt and her britches, wishing she'd had the sense to strip down before she cut open the buck's belly and started the blood-and-muck work. She groaned, mad at herself. Thinking about how it would have saved her the time and trouble of doing riverside laundry.

Once she had the bloody streaks and stains, and the mucky globs of deer-hair and prairie-dirt out of her clothes, she started twisting and wringing, working as much water out of the cloth as she could. Realizing she was probably wasting her time with all the wringing, thinking it would be easier to just ride home buck-naked. Far easier to just carry the wet clothes home and hang them on the clothesline.

Since she was already well into the process, Frankie kept twisting and wringing. When she was satisfied, she spent more time and energy pulling and dragging the mostly-wet clothes onto her mostly-wet body. She complained to herself as she tugged the wet cloth into place, then consoled herself, deciding her britches and shirt would dry fast under the August sun. Realizing that both she and her soggy clothes would be completely dry by the time she reached the meadow. So she kept pulling at the cloth, tugging the clinging material into place.

When she was finally dressed, still thinking about how much easier it would have been to travel naked, she mounted Rock. She gathered up Boone's lead-rope, whistled for the dogs and turned for home. She let Rock pick his own way along a narrow game-trail along the north bank; Boone followed with his load and the dogs trotted ahead.

She settled into the rhythm of the ride, letting her mind wander back to the evening after her hunt with her troopers, thinking about Crazy Eddie McClure and his questions about why she had removed Fanny's bridle during the hunt.

'Well Eddie,' she had explained when he asked about the bridle-less horse in the hunt, 'I was on that hillside today and all of a sudden, I decided to give you something to think about tonight. So I took the bridle off.'

That had set the other soldiers to cutting up and laughing around the fire. She had never given him a straight answer. And Crazy Eddie—the one who usually dished out the jokes—had been plenty pissed about being the butt of her story.

It had been Lieutenant Halliday who asked her about it later that night when they were in the Conestoga. She had told her Lieutenant the real reason—because even back then she'd known it wasn't polite, or wise, to mess with the mind of a Cavalry officer—explaining that it was only to avoid spooking the deer, just in case the horse chomped at the bit. She could still hear her Lieutenant's chuckle in the dark of the wagon. Laughing because, partly, he was amused at the simple reasoning. And partly, because like the troopers, he realized Crazy Eddie McClure had gotten some of his own medicine.

When the game-trail Rock followed made a sharp twist, turning away from the riverbank, Frankie knew they were nearing the rows of apple trees by her ford. And just as she and her little band left the heavy growth and moved out into the bright sunlight, her mind and attention snapped back to the present—because there among the long rows of apple trees, she saw something she had not anticipated. Something wholly unexpected.

Frankie reacted; she had the Henry rifle out of the scabbard before she had Rock to a full stop. Laughing Girl and Matilda dropped back to stand beside Rock; they were staring ahead, growling low and mean, and their hackles were up. Because there was something that didn't belong there among the apple trees, and they knew it.

Rifle in-hand, Frankie stayed still on her warhorse's back, staring at the sight and trying to sort things out. There in the midst of her nicely planted apple trees, right there on the bank of her portion of the pretty North Loup River was a nice little red mule hitched to a nice little farm-wagon. And not far from the wagon, two people—a man and a woman—were standing there. Looking at her.

Frankie knew she was staring and she knew it was wasn't a polite thing to do, but she was having trouble getting her mind wrapped around what was in front of her. The two people were doing their own staring; they were staring at her, and from the looks on their faces, they were every bit as surprised as she was.

The man was standing beneath one of the trees, and to Frankie, it seemed like an odd sight. He was tall and thin, *very* tall and *very* thin. And right on the very end of his chin, he had a tuft of a beard—a wispy, scraggly little tuft, brownish-red, and about three inches long. He had a black flop-hat on his head and he was dressed head-to-toe in black coat and trousers—clothes that were every bit as black and plain as a parish preacher's. He stood there with an apple in one hand and a basket half-filled with fresh-picked apples in the other. And Frankie thought it was a very strange sight to behold, right there among her apple trees.

The woman, holding her own basket of apples, was standing close to him. She was considerably shorter than the man and there was nothing thin about her. She looked to be fairly stout and plenty sturdy; she was wearing a light brown dress and a cream-colored linsey-woolsey apron, and from the set of her face, Frankie figured she likely wore a stern expression most of the time. But in the moment, she was looking a little grim, a little afraid, and plenty surprised.

Frankie whistled the dogs back and ordered them down. She lowered the rifle, deciding there was no real danger. Because the intent of people carrying baskets of apples tended to be a lot different than the intent of people who carried guns.

She turned Rock toward the couple and nudged him forward, thinking she probably should introduce herself. She was also feeling a considerable amount of relief that she had put her clothes on after washing up in the river. This, she realized, was one of those 'thank the holy-heavens' moments that her Uncle James used to refer to. *Nope. Wouldn't have done my reputation a speck of good if word got around about a ten-year-old girl traveling the countryside buck-naked, carrying a Henry rifle and hauling bloody deer carcasses horseback. And riding up on unsuspecting couples.*

Frankie pulled Rock to a stop in front of them, offering a friendly smile. Because it felt like it was probably a good thing to do. The couple seemed to appreciate it, because they offered a couple of smiles right back at her. The man's smile was warm and relaxed; the woman's was stiff, and anything but relaxed.

And then, a moment later, Frankie found she had an even bigger reason to 'thank the holy-heavens' that she hadn't actually ridden into the rows of apple trees buck-naked. Because during the introductions, she learned that the man who was dressed like a preacher— actually *was* a preacher. He introduced himself as the Reverend Simeon Austin and introduced the woman with him as his wife, Betsy Whitten Austin. He explained they lived nine miles south. Down at the Middle Loup settlement, he said. *So. This is the preacher and his wife Ida and Everett told me about.*

"I am a God-fearing man, Young Lady, and you have just caught me stealing apples from my neighbor's trees. I confess, I am ashamed."

The preacher-man said it in a serious and sober way, but Frankie knew he was playing at the dramatic—amusing himself and assuming it might amuse her too.

And he was right, because Frankie decided she liked his sense of humor. She was laughing as she climbed down from Rock's back, accusing the Reverend of 'leaning a bit to the melodramatic'. She used the phrase her father would have applied to the situation and the Reverend Austin burst into a relaxed and free laughter. Smiling at her, clearly pleased with her response.

Mrs. Austin appeared to be joining in the mirth, but Frankie didn't read her smile as relaxed and free like her husband's. Her smile was a bit stiffer and her mirth seemed to be a bit dulled by what she was busy studying—she was eyeing the boots and trousers and the over-sized Cavalry shirt. Clearly, the preacher's wife didn't approve of the little-girl-hunter in front of her. And certainly, she wasn't pleased with her garb.

The man—the Right Reverend Simeon Austin—was showing no sign of any disapproval at all; he seemed completely unconcerned about her state of dress. He just seemed to be happy to see her. And for the moment, Frankie decided to try to ease the mind of the preacher's wife before her fiercely righteous-and-religious heart, just stopped beating altogether from the shocking sight.

"I'm sorry I'm in such a state, Ma'am," Frankie spoke to the preacher's stout and stern wife. "But you see, wearing a dress and trying to ride a horse and getting everything all tangled up around a rifle, is just too dangerous. Hopefully, next time you see me, I'll be dressed properly and fit for company."

Frankie had spoken the words in an effort to soften Mrs. Austin's stern mettle, but she was actually thinking that 'those who get caught stealing their neighbor's fruit ought not to be so damn judgmental about their neighbor'. She was also remembering her father's guidance to 'be willing to extend the olive branch whenever you're in doubt', because, as he would point out, 'you could always take back the branch later if need be'. He had always winked when he gave her such advice, but there was some truth to it.

Her state of attire—being dressed like a boy—seemed to amuse the Reverend Austin more than offend him; he was offering a delighted little smile as he fondled a wispy little beard that sat right smack-dab at the end of his chin. Pulling at the wispy beard on his chin, Frankie suspected, was something he probably did a lot.

He kept smiling as he explained about their presence among the trees and why they were there picking apples that didn't actually belong to them. Daniel Kinison, according to the tall and lanky

Reverend Simeon Austin, had always invited them to pick what they wanted, at least for the last three years while the trees had been producing.

So each year, he said, he and Betsy came to pick apples which they'd take to share with his little country congregation at his little country church. He explained that he honestly had no idea the Kinison place had been taken over by another family. He certainly hadn't *meant* to steal from her family. And he said, he and Betsy had come to pick apples today, believing that Daniel-God-Rest-His-Soul, wouldn't have minded.

"Daniel would have thought it sensible to put the apples to good use, rather than let them go to waste. Quite honestly, we had no idea that anyone was here to put them to use." The Reverend apologized and offered her the basket of plucked apples he was holding. "Here, young lady. I believe these belong to your family."

He had a clever little smile on his face when he proffered the basket, and Frankie figured that he knew darn well she wouldn't accept them. She grinned back at him, letting him know that he was right, letting him know that they both knew what they both knew.

And then—right then and there—she made a deal with the Reverend Simeon Austin. She told him she didn't want to undo the gift Daniel Kinison had offered to him and his parish.

"Well, Reverend. Looks like you brought four baskets with you. Why don't you just count on filling up four baskets every year?" she suggested. "We'll call it my donation to your collection plate."

Simeon Austin thought it was a fine idea and it looked as though stern-faced Betsy did too, even if she didn't make a big friendly show of it. The Reverend Austin invited Frankie to come to his service on Sunday and Frankie told them she was supposed to be going to the Dunbars' place on that day. Both the Reverend and his wife nodded. Smiled. Said they knew Everett and Ida Dunbar quite well. And they said, they 'liked them so much'.

Which was what Frankie wanted to hear. Because now, after this 'meeting in the orchard', it was a good bet the Reverend Simeon Austin and his wife would drive their nice red molly-mule and their nice farm-wagon over to the Dunbar homestead sometime in the next two days. *Pretty darn likely.*

Because the kindly-seeming Reverend, and his not-so-kindly-seeming wife, would take it as their Christian-duty to enlighten their congregation about the new-neighbors-up-north at the upcoming Sunday service. To do that, he would first need to glean what information he could from Everett and Ida. So that he could be the bearer of the best and brightest information.

Once the good Reverend informed his congregation, word would begin spreading through the settlement like butter on a stack of hotcakes; it was likely that at least a few in his flock would show up at the Dunbar place for a visit to gain relevant information about the new folks.

Frankie figured she might even have a few families trickle into her meadow. *But probably not yet.* Because the church-goers would probably want to do a little digging and a little speculating first, before seeing things for themselves. They would know that Everett and Ida would be the best source for tidbits of information about this 'family with the ten-year-old girl' living at the Kinison place. *Especially now.*

Because, Frankie realized, she had just created a reputation for being a half-wild girl toting bloody deer-carcasses around the countryside, and leading a pack of blood-slobbery dogs. Because at the moment, both dogs were lying in the grass with their faces and chests half-covered with swaths of dried blood and flecks of mucky entrails. They were resting in the shade, grinning slyly at this apple-picking preacher and his God-fearing wife. And all the while, the Reverend and his wife were asking questions about anything other than bloody-faced dogs. Frankie tamped down the groan she felt rising from deep inside her. *None of this is gonna do my reputation any good.*

Mostly, the Reverend and his wife were keeping their questions polite, simple and neighborly. They were asking about her home back in Indiana, and whether the livestock made it through in good shape.

They were being careful not to ask anything that would seem nosy or pushy. But eventually, Frankie knew, they would want some real information. And until she knew more about who she was dealing with, she decided the best course was to 'lay low, ride it out, and say as little as possible'. Just like her Uncle James would suggest. So just like she had done in her first meeting with Everett and Ida, she decided to keep her answers 'honest but vague'.

So when the Reverend asked about meeting her folks, she told him her folks weren't at the homestead. They were still on the trail to the south, she said. She explained she had come ahead in one of the wagons to get things ready and sorted out. She made a point to say the Dunbars had stayed with her for the first week. To help her out, she said.

"They just went home a few days ago." She offered the information, keeping it simple and true.

The Austins seemed interested and satisfied with that explanation. But more than a few times, Frankie saw they were still throwing uneasy glances toward the bloodied-up dogs in the grass. They were also casting a few glances toward the deer-carcass tied across Boone's back. And Frankie could see Betsy Whitten Austin was still pretending not to be eyeing the garb of the new neighbor girl—still sizing her up.

Frankie suppressed a grin, because it wasn't hard to guess what subject the preacher's wife would choose for the wagon ride home. Given all the givens, Frankie decided it might be best to tip the scales a little more in her own favor. And she had a pretty good idea about what might work.

"Reverend Austin? I have a bit of a problem here. Of my own causing, Sir." Frankie tipped her head a little, trying for a bit of innocent appeal, mixed with a bit of little-girl-uncertainty. She gave it her best, hoping it would work. "I went hunting, thinking to keep some of the meat for myself and to take some over to the Dunbars. But truth is, I still have way too much. Would you maybe take a quarter? I mean, if I wouldn't be putting you out?"

"Young Lady, are you sure you want to give a couple of thieving apple-pickers yet another gift?" Simeon's eyes were sparkling in spite of the self-deprecating humor; he was clearly pleased with her offer.

"Sir, like I said, it would help me out."

The Reverend Simeon Austin gave her an odd little squint; the squint was only there for an instant, but it told Frankie he had caught on to her scheme. She saw him flash a quick glance toward his wife, but his wife's eyes were on Boone and the bloody buck lashed to his back. Betsy Whitten Austin had no idea about any scheme. *She's probably thinking about how a venison roast will look sitting on a platter on her kitchen table.*

The Reverend Austin looked back at Frankie, and Frankie looked at him. He raised his eyebrows, just a little. He nodded at her and Frankie knew her plan to improve her position in the eyes of Betsy Austin would stay a secret between them. Apparently, Frankie thought, the tall and lanky preacher saw things much the same as she did.

Frankie grinned at him, deciding right then that there were a lot of things she liked about this man. He had kind eyes and a gentle smile. He was modest and proud at the same time. He was certainly a highly educated man. And Frankie decided, he was a serious man who didn't take himself too seriously.

She liked all those things. But most of all, she liked the deep resonance of his voice. It was the kind of voice that would calm and soothe people, a voice that would easily hold the attention of a congregation. She was busy thinking her thoughts and she realized that the Reverend was standing in front of her with a funny look on his face—a look that made her think he was right in the middle of spotting things about her that he liked.

His wife, though, was a different story. Frankie figured Betsy Whitten Austin was the type of person who wouldn't offer up her friendship quickly or easily. With her, it would be a slower thing. Because, even though she smiled pleasantly enough—like a preacher's wife should—there was little doubt that she would still hold herself in reserve. With Betsy Whitten Austin, a person would have to put in some time and effort to actually earn her trust and favor.

Frankie moved Rock beneath one of the trees, stood on his back and started picking the ripest apples near the treetops. Handing her handfuls to the preacher and his wife while they picked from the low branches.

At least twice before they were done filling their baskets with apples from the no-longer-forbidden-fruit-trees, the Reverend Austin invited Frankie and her family—'when they arrive'—to 'come and see his little chapel some Sunday soon'. Each time, Frankie thanked him. And each time, she switched to another topic, not at all sure she wanted to be on public display in his church, so soon in the game.

Once they had all the Austin baskets full—all four of them—and had settled them into the wagon-bed, Frankie and the Reverend put their attention on separating one of the haunches from the rest of the deer. Betsy Whitten Austin talked about tucking some onions and turnips in the roasting pan with the venison, and thought that 'would just cook up so nice'.

The Reverend, though, was still firm in his resolve to get his young neighbor to one of his Sunday services. By the time they lifted the hindquarter into the wagon, Frankie had been invited to the church yet again.

"Just a little sod-church, mind you. It's not up to standards of the churches your family would probably know from back in Indiana."

Frankie knew it was an attempt by the Reverend Austin to gain a bit more information about her and her family, thinking she might offer more information than she had already given. *Probably hoping I'll talk a bit about my family. Probably wanting to know their background and their religion. And whether they're church-goers or not.*

She compromised, deciding to withhold the exact information he was seeking, but still yield a little bit of ground to him.

"I haven't been in a real church with my family since we left home back in April. So I think that'd be nice." She saw the Reverend Simeon Austin nod, looking pleased and confident, apparently content with the knowledge that her family *did* participate in church services and churchly-functions.

Frankie made sure to nod and smile each time he invited her, but like any good preacher—settled in his own mind and sure of his own God-fearing path—he still wasn't fully satisfied. He was beginning to show all the signs of being a-preacher-bent-on-expanding-his-flock. And at that moment, Frankie knew that all the light conversation about the countryside and the river, the apples and the venison was over. And she knew why.

The Reverend Austin was a wise man, certainly wise enough to sense some evasive action on her part—he just hadn't figured out exactly what she was trying to evade. So now, he was looking to sink his teeth into more meat than just the haunch of venison. Up to this point, he had heard only vague references to her family—about them being somewhere 'south on the trail'. He wanted answers, but he didn't want to push and intrude. Betsy Whitten Austin, however, didn't harbor such qualms. *Of course not.*

"When are you expecting your family to arrive, Dear?" It was Betsy asking the question that hadn't been asked yet. With the direct question, Betsy Whitten Austin was announcing that she was joining her husband in the hunt for information. "It seems like this is a long time for you to be on your own."

"Well. The family plan was to stock up on supplies at the fort, so that always takes some time. Plus, a supply wagon is always heavier, so travel is slower."

Frankie turned her attention to checking Rock's cinch, keeping herself busy to avoid looking at Reverend Austin. Because she could feel his eyes locked on her. He was a smart man. A clever man. He was studying the situation and sensing that things weren't exactly adding up. So Frankie switched the subject back to his worship-service invitations, which she figured he'd probably latch onto. Hoping it might redirect his thinking.

"But Ida and Everett already told me about you, and they want to bring me to your church sometime. Maybe we'll all come down to a Sunday service together. Once things get caught up around here. Once everything settles down a bit." She chattered on. "I think it'd be nice for all of us to travel down to your settlement. It'd be a nice way to visit your church."

After that, the talk drifted once again to lighter subjects, just as she had hoped. They talked about the Dunbars' place. And about milk cows. And about chickens and how they would be coming into molt soon. With the conversation going easy again, and with the venison tucked in the back of the preacher's wagon along with the baskets of apples, Frankie decided it was a reasonable time to attempt an escape. *Before I get tripped up and say too much. Before any damage is done.*

She mounted Rock and whistled for the dogs. Reached for Boone's lead. Expecting the preacher and his wife would make their way onto their wagon-seat. Which they did. They were both smiling. Betsy was thanking her for the apples, and the Reverend Austin was nodding at her, laughing and calling her 'my favorite young huntress'.

"A young Diana. A goddess of the land and the hunt." He kept laughing while he swung the red mule toward the ford and down through the trees. "Now, *who* would have believed we would find such a fine and clever adventurer way out here among these hills?"

He called his farewell over his shoulder, waving, as the sorrel mule pulled the wagon clear of the trees. "You come see us down to the settlement, my young friend. It's in a line almost straight south of here. Almost ten miles. A nice little ride if you find yourself longing for another adventure. You don't have to wait for a Sunday service. You're welcome any time."

The nice little molly-mule pulled the nice little wagon onto the track and turned down into the ford. The nice-talking-preacher was waving and laughing, and his prim-and-proper-preacher-wife was looking over her shoulder, giving a seemingly-friendly wave and a fairly-friendly smile.

Frankie waved to them and smiled her nicest little crooked-smile, thinking maybe her scheme had worked. Maybe Reverend Simeon Austin was satisfied, and maybe, Betsy Whitten Austin had softened up a bit. She was also thinking that the preacher and his wife would get a bit of a surprise when they showed up for a visit at the Dunbar place.

Because Everett and Ida would give the Austins a 'fuller account' of young Frankie Harding's circumstance. Because they all had decided that when the time came, it would be best for Everett and Ida to enlighten the people of the settlement. They knew exactly what to say and how to explain things. And Frankie was betting that the time for enlightenment was coming. Within a few days. Hopefully, the Dunbars would be ready.

As she turned Rock toward home, heading toward the entrance of her home valley, she grinned at the two entrail-eating dogs. They were giving their best bloody dog-grins, so they must be happy with how the meeting went.

She took a last look toward the very-nice preacher and his sort-of-nice wife, and turned her bold-and-bloody little parade toward home, hoping the next meeting with Betsy Whitten Austin might be a little more conventional and a little less hair-raising. For everyone's sake.

Four days later, Frankie had Fanny hitched to the Dunbars' spring-wagon. Artemis, Aloysius, and Septimus were tied to the tail-gate with their harnesses arranged in the wagon-bed. She looked over everything she had for the trip to the Dunbar place—her first trip there that was just for a visit. No rush and hurry this time; no need to watch and worry. Not this time; not now. The son-in-law and the daughter were gone; the danger was gone.

This would be just a comfortable drive downriver on a pretty August morning. Heading east into the sunrise. Going for a visit and dinner with her nearest neighbors. Taking them 'some fixings' for their table because that was the country-neighbor thing to do.

The plan had been for the heavy farm-wagon that had carried the firewood to the Dunbar place, to come back to the meadow with crates of garden produce for the root-cellar, but Frankie had other ideas. She was planning to take the spring-wagon there and back, because she planned to leave the heavy wagon at the Dunbar home-stead along with the three mules. Because harvest-time was coming. And Everett would need the wagon for the field-work, as well as the three mules.

The three mules, together with his own mule, would give Everett two mule-teams that were strong and solid—mules bred for field-work. And he'd have the heavy wagon to do the hauling. The mules and the wagon would put him in good shape for harvest, if he'd agree to use them.

Frankie had been a little worried he might change his mind about using them. She had been thinking a lot about her Aunt Sarah, and how she used to say that 'misdirected pride could rise up unexpectedly'. She had talked about the difference between 'worthy pride' and 'misdirected pride'.

And now, Frankie was thinking it was entirely possible that Everett might lean toward misdirected pride. If the three mules and heavy wagon were already on his place and ready to work, Frankie thought that he might go ahead with their original plan.

She gave the spring-wagon a last look, assessing things, making sure she had what she needed in the wagon. The Henry rifle, the spy-glass, a lantern and matches, and her Cavalry bedroll—just to be safe—just in case something went wrong on her way home in the night.

She had packed the peach pie she had baked the night before into a wooden box and tucked it under the wagon-seat. Two crates of ripe apples were settled in the wagon-bed. A good portion of the venison was wrapped in canvas and tucked into a couple of boxes beside the apple-crates.

"They'll like that, Matilda." Frankie grinned up at the tawny collie-dog already sitting on the wagon-seat. Ready to travel. Grinning her own toothy dog-smile, apparently pleased that her person was bringing her into the conversation. "Ida will get a few roasts out of that. And probably, some breakfast steaks. Maybe enough for a stew or a pot of soup. And enough scraps for a big pan of hash."

She took another look at Fanny and the three mules. She nodded, satisfied. She climbed into the jockey-box and settled herself on the wagon-seat. Grinned at Matilda sitting beside her with her tongue lolling out and her eyes shining. The collie-dog was ready for an adventure. Laughing Girl pranced in a circle around the wagon and team, giving her best wolfhound-greyhound grin. Ready to take the lead to wherever they were going; excited at the prospect of another journey.

Frankie twisted in the seat, looking around her valley, eyeing her meadow. This would be the longest stretch of being away from her home since she had first arrived—from early in the morning until late in the night. Everything was in order. The chickens were locked in the henyard for the day; the horses were in their pastures; the cattle and oxen were in theirs. Blossom and Primrose were grazing out beyond the barn. Gates were closed; doors were shut. The meadow was secure.

She lifted the reins and clucked to Fanny, sending her toward the valley entrance, putting her into her neat-stepping trot up the track. Going up and around and over.

Frankie smiled, watching the pretty North Loup River just ahead of them, flowing quiet and content between the sandy-soil banks, drifting along under the low-hanging branches of the riverside trees. She sent the Morgan mare down the track, down to the river's ford, still thinking about leaving home for the day. And thinking about returning to home in the night. Returning to her home. To her meadow.

Ten miles downriver, she crossed the North Loup at the Dunbars' ford. She clucked to Fanny as she reached the north bank, lifting her into a quick trot up the riverbank. As the wagon topped out on level ground, Frankie stared at the view in front of her. It still looked like the same little cozy homestead she had known—but there was a difference now. The place had come alive.

It was a very different picture from what Frankie had seen the last time she had visited. The place was bustling with life now—animals seemed to be everywhere she looked. She could see Isaac, hefty and healthy, grazing in the fenced pasture beside the river. Two brown horses, looking fat and sleek, grazed near him. A massive brown-and-white bull was settled on the ground nearby, resting on his chest and working his cud. Looking awfully content.

Standing in one of the pens, a pretty brown-and-white milk cow and her calf were dozing in the morning sunlight. Chickens scratched and pecked in clusters around the farmyard. From somewhere near the lean-to barn, Frankie could hear a young rooster's desperate squawk, still trying to master a full-grown crow. A calico cat scatted across the track and slipped under the garden fence.

Frankie shouted a 'hello-the-house', and watched as Ida stood up from a flowerbed along the front of the house. She gave a wild and excited wave and started hurrying toward the incoming wagon, wiping her hands on her apron and looking toward the barn, calling for Everett. She stepped aside to avoid a chicken scuttling across in front of her, chasing after some scrambling bug.

Ida scolded at the chicken, laughed at it, and then resumed her hurried walk. She was smiling a wide and happy smile—a smile that told a story of contentment and excitement at the same time. Ida, Frankie decided, looked as if she was awfully happy with her life and home.

She pulled Fanny to a stop, trying to wave at Ida and climb off the wagon-seat at the same time. She tripped on the hem of her calico dress as she stepped off the hub; she caught herself and still managed to dodge Matilda as she leaped to the ground.

Ida was still hurrying, calling for her to be careful, and then laughing as she reached the wagon. They hugged, holding each other like they hadn't seen each other in years, and laughing at themselves because they'd just seen each other a few days before.

"Oh, Honey. It feels like ages ago, doesn't it?" Ida used her apron to wipe tears from her eyes. "And, oh my, I thought you were going to topple right off that wagon. And oh, just look at this dress. Peach calico! I haven't seen this one before."

And then, Everett was coming from the barn, calling a greeting. Even from a distance, Frankie could see his broad smile, wide and relaxed. Proud and confident. A smile she had never seen on him before.

"Honey! We've been watching for you all morning," he gathered her up in a hug and kissed her on the cheek. He held her away from him and looked her up and down. "Oh my goodness, we're so glad to see you!"

"Not as glad as you will be when you see what I've brought with me," Frankie grinned at him, laughed and pointed him toward the wagon-box.

"Well, let's just see what you've brought." He smiled even bigger, gave her braid a quick tug and looked into the back of the wagon. He patted the crates of apples, and then lifted the flap of the canvas-wrapped bundle. Grinning, he beckoned to Ida. "My goodness-gosh, Frankie. We'll be having venison roasts on the table for days to come."

He was delighted with both the apples and the venison, and when Frankie reached into the jockey-box and brought out the peach pie, Ida started giggling like a school-girl.

"Oh, *look* what you've been up to in your kitchen. Isn't this just the perfect surprise?" Ida took the covered pie in one hand and Frankie's arm in the other, and started leading her to the house, laughing at Matilda as she pranced and danced around them. "Why Frankie, she seems awfully happy to be here. I think she missed us, don't you?"

"Yes, Ma'am. She's been asking about you and Everett almost every day."

Ida laughed and raised the pie-plate higher as Laughing Girl approached with her own prancing and dancing.

"You bring everything in when you come, won't you?" Ida called over her shoulder to Everett.

"You ladies just go on inside. I'll bring things in once I see to the mare and the mules." Everett was whistling as he started leading Fanny forward, heading to the nearest pen.

He said something else, but Frankie couldn't hear because Ida was walking her toward the soddy, talking about the new flower bed she was starting in front of the house.

"I always like a flowerbed to each side of the door. I think it makes a place look homier, don't you?" And before Frankie could answer, Ida was talking about the cat that had come back—a stray cat that had wandered in more than a year before, then left again when things were getting so bad with Hugh David.

"We never knew why she left, but cats do that don't they. Cats seem to wander away, but they *always* come back, don't they? No matter how long they've been gone." Then she was discussing the hens. "They're laying more eggs than Everett and I can use. And listen to those young roosters, will you? I swear, I don't know if those darned birds are ever going to learn to give a good crow." Ida kept talking, balancing the pie-plate in one hand and squeezing Frankie to her with the other. "And one of those Dominikers is going broody on me. I'm going to let her set a clutch. Meat for the winter, you know. Everett's planning on having a pen of capons as soon as possible." Ida stopped to take a breath before going on.

"And Frankie, you just won't believe how much milk Bonnie is giving. My Lord, she's got a bag on her. She's such a gentle cow. And she's a really good momma to Babe. Everett says she's carrying another one in her belly. He's so pleased about that. And won't it be a fine thing to have a brand-new calf come spring?"

Frankie kept nodding at everything Ida was saying and she kept looking wherever Ida was pointing. She wasn't even trying to respond to Ida's questions, because after the first few questions, she realized that Ida didn't really need any answers—she just needed to talk about her home and her happiness.

They reached the door of the neat little soddy, and as Ida ushered her inside, Frankie could hear Everett out at the pen, talking to Fanny. Busy explaining something to her. And just like his wife, he didn't seem to be waiting for any answers; he was just talking out loud while he unbuckled the hames and gathered the leathers.

When Frankie glanced back, right before Ida closed the door, she saw that Laughing Girl and Matilda were out with Everett, too— they were sitting on their bottoms right beside him, watching and listening while he worked with the harness, their tails swishing back and forth on the hardpacked dirt. It didn't look like they were trying to answer any questions either. Mostly, it looked like they were just listening politely while Everett was talking out his happiness.

The three of them sat in the cool air inside the sod-house, drinking coffee and working on their plates of peach pie. Frankie listened as Ida and Everett talked about 'the visitors they had'. It was exactly as she had figured it—the Reverend Austin and his wife had come by the Dunbar homestead two days ago. 'Just to do some visiting,' the Reverend had said. 'Just checking on my flock.'

"I was betting they would. I figured they were a little worked up." Frankie was trying to stay calm, because there was good reason to have concerns. Because it wasn't a rare thing for preachers to have their own ideas about what sort of influence they should have within a community—and usually, they could quote some piece of scripture that would support whatever outcome they wanted. Frankie had seen it before—preachers had a way of being pretty righteous about having some level of 'God-given permission' to do whatever they wanted, in whatever manner they had already decided was best.

"Well, Honey, they were a little worked up, but not necessarily in a bad way as far as your situation." Everett Dunbar leaned forward, patting Frankie's arm. "We don't think the Reverend Austin is looking to interfere. He was maybe just a little hot-under-his-collar because he wasn't the first to know. You see, the good Reverend is used to being the first to know about anything going on in the area. So you already being there on your homestead and us knowing before he did, well, that took him by surprise."

Ida reached across the table, took Frankie's hand and squeezed it. Frankie felt her heart slowing a bit and the tightness in her gut going away. The thought that she might be taken in as an orphan and end up living at the home of the preacher and his wife had occurred to her more than once over the past several days.

"Honey, Ida and me, we told Reverend and Betsy the story about your family dying of the fever and you coming on alone, just like we all decided. But we *did* change it a little." Everett spoke to her slow and steady. "We didn't *plan* on changing things, but when we were talking with the Reverend, it kind of made sense. We told him and Betsy that you were family of ours. We didn't lie exactly, but we said things in a *certain* way."

218

"I mentioned to him that I have people back in Indiana," Ida took up the story. "Some of my mother's family lives there—so that's true enough. And we explained that your folks back in Indiana decided to buy the Kinison place and come out here to live. Which is true enough too."

"See, we're not lying," Everett took up the story again, "because Ida *does* have relations back in Indiana. And we thought if the Reverend decided to connect Ida's family with your family, then it might not be a bad thing."

Frankie grinned at them. "So you kind of did with Reverend Austin what I did with you? Back when we first met?"

"Well, yes. I guess we were just following your lead. But we had good intentions too. Just like you did." Ida squeezed her hand again. Then she patted it. She started chuckling. Then they all started laughing, and Frankie figured they were all thinking about 'the road to hell being paved with good intentions'.

"And there's another piece to this, Honey. Because Ida and I decided you *are* family to us. So if the Austins and other folks in the settlement come to believe Ida and I have a family member, a young cousin, who came out here from Indiana, then they'd be exactly right." Everett gave her a little wink.

"So we told the Reverend what happened to your family, and we said you'd decided to come on to the homestead by yourself. On account of you having no one left back in Indiana." Ida picked up the story again. "We told him that was one of the reasons why we had been staying with you. *And* that we were going to be keeping a close watch over you."

"We didn't tell him and Betsy much more than that," Everett stepped in. "But we *did* tell them that we felt there was a need to protect you. Because there were men around the forts and on the Overland Road, who had tried to get hold of you for some bad purposes. Ida told them that because of that, you had learned that sometimes, it was safer to dress in boy's clothes."

"*That* seemed to settle some things for Betsy. Some of that stiff judgment of hers—about you being half-wild and dressed-up like a boy—faded away right about then." Ida started laughing and Frankie and Everett joined her. It was a nice thing to imagine Betsy Whitten Austin's stiff countenance fading away.

When they were done with the laughter, Frankie realized the Dunbars' story was done too. Now, she realized, Everett and Ida were waiting for her reaction. They were hoping she was happy with the story as they had changed it. Hoping they were right in calling her 'family'.

Frankie nodded and smiled, wanting them to know they had done a wonderful thing. She stood up and hugged them—first Ida and then Everett. The deal was sealed between them. They were not just neighbors anymore; they *were* family.

"I think you told them exactly right. If we're family, then no one will think they have a right to step in and interfere. And since I have family here, it takes the wondering and the mystery out of it."

"I should warn you that Reverend Austin and Betsy expect us to bring you to his church one of these Sundays." Ida stood up and poured more coffee and kissed Frankie on her head as she reached across to fill Everett's cup. "We don't need to do it right away, but it might be a good idea not to let it sit too long."

"I kind of suggested that to him after about five of his invitations. I told him you two were going to bring me the first time. I think he's an understanding man and a nice man, but I don't think he's a particularly patient man when it comes down to his church and the invitations he gives out." Frankie thought back to his repeated suggestions and she remembered the way his tone became a little more insistent with each mention.

"I think you've got it pegged right, Honey. His patience might wilt a little if it goes longer than what he's got in mind." Everett ate the last bite of his pie and then went on. "And you showing up with us some Sunday might go a long way toward showing folks that you're with us. That you're connected to family out here. Ol' Simeon Austin knows we stayed with you for a time, and he knows we'll be trading livestock back and forth and sharing work between our places. That'll all go toward making it look like everything's settled and working out fine."

Frankie was thanking her lucky stars, along with God and all his angels, because the concerns she had—the concerns from her very first days alone, way down on the Little Blue—had just lifted and floated away. She had a better start than she had dared hope for, and she had better neighbors than she had ever imagined. The Dunbars had not only put out word about her being family—they had explained about men who might be looking for her, men with dangerous intent. And because of that, she had a good chance of being protected by everyone around the region. Now, it was unlikely that word about her would ever go beyond the settlers in the area.

The Dunbars had helped her in a big way and she told them that. They were family to her too. And she told them she had known that from their first meeting out beside the North Loup. She had been cautious, she said, but she had known. And by the time she was done saying it, Frankie felt the tears welling up in her eyes.

They finished their talk and they finished their coffee and pie. And then Ida wanted to show off her garden. So they walked through her garden together. Looking around her as they wandered between the rows, Frankie was amazed, because Ida truly knew how to make plants grow. Everything in the fenced garden was producing wildly— the vegetables, the herbs, the flowers.

Ida talked and explained and pointed, and Frankie listened to her words and looked wherever she indicated. She was surrounded by vegetables—a great variety of vegetables, both the above-grounds and the root crops—and she was also seeing a fine assortment of herbs and flowers.

The scents of the plants and soil, and the fragrances of the different flowers, were sending Frankie's mind back to the fenced gardens in Indiana. Here in Ida's domain were the same kinds of plants and herbs that her Aunt Sarah had always grown. Ida was talking about the different herbs, talking about which ones she liked for the different meals she cooked, but Frankie's mind was going in a different direction. Because here in this garden were herbs that could go into her remedy-chest. They could hang in the root-cellar to dry, and then they could be crushed into powder with the mortar and pestle.

When Ida paused, Frankie reminded her about the remedy-chest she had pulled out when she and Everett had doctored Isaac. When she told Ida about the different plants that could be used for poultices and tinctures—some of the very flowers and herbs Ida had been growing—Ida's interest was piqued.

"Oh, Honey. We can work our gardens together. I didn't know you knew anything about the healing-plants."

"Mostly, I know how to plant seeds and pull weeds. And I know how to pick the produce. Pretty much I know how to do the stuff that requires grunting and lifting. But I don't know how to plan a garden. And I don't know when to plant what or which plants should go where."

Once again, Frankie's mind went back to the garden in Indiana. She could see the long and narrow gardens—three long fenced-gardens, standing side-by-side. The familiar fragrances came back to her. And suddenly, for just a moment, she could see Isaiah pulling weeds in the row next to her. She could hear the groan he always made when he would stop and straighten up, stretching; she could hear her Aunt Sarah humming the hymns she loved.

Frankie shook her head, leaving Indiana and her aunt and that garden behind, coming forward in time, back to Ida and this garden.

"My Aunt Sarah always tended to the planning and rotating. My cousins and me, we were the field-hands. That's what my father and Uncle James called us."

Ida laughed and told her that's exactly what Everett called himself. She pulled Frankie against her side, hugging her tight.

"Memories always come back when you're in a garden." Ida paused and her eyes took on a faraway look for a moment. "I think it's all the smells. And for me, it's the feel of the sun on my back as I'm bending over the rows, doing the weeding and picking."

"My Aunt Sarah used to say that every time she put her fingers deep into garden soil, she felt like she was a little girl again, working beside her grandmother in *her* garden. She learned to grow herbs and plants for her remedies and medicines in her grandmother's garden. Her grandmother taught her all about gardening and plants and making remedies."

"Well, Honey," Ida's eyes returned to the garden around them, coming back to her own plants on her own homestead. "Don't you worry. We'll see that you have all the herbs you want. I always grow plenty. And you have that lovely garden with the rock walls. I'll help you get that going in the spring. Between both gardens, you'll have all you need. You just start pointing out the plants you want."

So Frankie started pointing and explaining, and Ida started marking the plants by pushing tall sticks beside each one that Frankie wanted.

"This way, we'll remember to harvest extra seeds for you."

They followed the rows up and down, and when Frankie pointed to a plant, Ida would push a stick into the ground and tell her the common name. And for most of them, Frankie could tell her the Latin name—the names her Aunt Sarah always used.

About the time they finished walking through the garden rows and marking their plants, Everett showed up. He wanted to show Frankie around the homestead, around *his* part of the domain. He saddled Jenny and Frankie swung up on Fanny and they spent the early afternoon riding through the fields and along the river.

They rode the perimeter, talking about the planting and the weather and the soil. He showed her his field crops; two fields of corn, one of oats on his quarter-section. And the same crops on the quarter-section on the south side of the river.

There was a soft smile on his face as he talked about the standing crops and Frankie thought back to the strained look he had when he and Ida had first come to stay at her place. Back then his face had carried the strain of uncertainty and the weight of the unknown. All that was gone now—the uncertainty was gone, the unknown no longer existed. Everett Dunbar had hope again. He was looking across his fields as they rode along, seeing his future on his homestead.

There was no doubt he was pleased with the coming yield the fields showed; he had good reason to have hope for the harvest. The Reverend Austin had talked about the settlers in the area planning to harvest together this year, sharing their teams and equipment and traveling from one homestead to the next until all the crops were in. Then they'd form a wagon party and haul the crops to market down to Fort Cottonwood.

And that, Everett said, was the guarantee he needed; now, he knew he'd be able to get his crops in. First the oats; then the corn. Everett nodded as he spoke, his eyes scanning the expanse of corn growing beside them as they rode along.

Frankie saw the look in his eyes. It was a look of peace that comes over a person when things start falling in place. It was the look that comes when hope changes to promise.

"Now that I have a team of horses and the mule, I can be part of the harvest crew. We should be able to get both crops in. And maybe even those across on the other quarter-section." Everett looked across the river. "Hugh and Rebecca's quarter."

"Do you think Hugh will come back for his crop on his claim?"

"Well, to be honest, it's not his claim. Ain't Rebecca's either. That quarter-section is actually in Ida's name. You see, Hugh and Rebecca went ahead of us to Omaha. The plan was for each of them to file for a quarter-section. And we thought they had. They talked like they had taken their two claims. But after a few days along the Overland Trail, Hugh told us they hadn't filed."

"Why not? That would've given the four of you a full section."

"Well. Hugh said he didn't want to tie up his name on this land. That was the reason he gave, anyway. He thought something better might come along. He figured the two quarter-sections that Ida and I had would be enough for both families. So we didn't have a lot of choice. We ended up deciding that he and Rebecca would live on the place to the south of the river and work those fields, and me and Ida would live and work the quarter on the north side."

"Did they work it? Or did you?"

"Well, *I* did." Everett was looking down at the ground, shaking his head. "Hugh was always off doing something. Off traveling somewhere. And Rebecca tends to stay shut up and by herself when he's gone. She doesn't do terribly good when he ain't around. So me and Ida, we saw to the field work."

"So it's your land *and* your crops?" Frankie grinned at him.

"By all rights, I guess. But truth be known, Frankie, I'm not sure how much acreage I can handle. With Jake and Jenny and Isaac, I have a team with a spare, so I can switch around. But if I put in with the harvest crew, it's gonna be a lot of steady farm-work. Isaac should handle it fine now that he's healthy, but I'm worried about wearing the horses down. And my wagon isn't going to handle much heavy hauling. Hugh and Rebecca took the big wagon we brought for the heavy farm work."

Frankie heard his words, and she heard nothing that said he was expecting anything from her. She knew Everett Dunbar was being careful—he wasn't the kind of man who would take advantage of any-one. He had seen the three mules and the harnesses she brought with her, and no doubt, he remembered the conversation at her pasture gate—the conversation about three idle mules standing out in her pasture. It was exactly the reason she had brought all three mules and harnesses; it was why she was planning to leave them and the heavy wagon. But Everett Dunbar wasn't going to assume anything.

And it seemed like his pride might get in the way—it was exactly what her Aunt Sarah had said about misdirected pride rising up in a man unexpectedly. Worthy pride was one thing, a good thing; misdi-rected pride was a sad and maybe even a damaging thing.

To Frankie's mind, Everett had a sizeable crop growing on his land and it could make for a solid future for both him and Ida. And the deal she and Everett had discussed was still in the front of her mind. In the moment, sitting there on their horses among the fields, Frankie started worrying that things were taking a wrong turn.

"Everett, I don't know much about farming, at least not much beyond what a crop in a field looks like. But I *do* know I need grain this year and I need land planted next year. So here's my thinking," she took a deep breath. "I think you're right about wearing down your horses with the kind of field-work you're looking at. Especially if you go in with the harvest crew. I have three good working mules.

You've got one. That makes two teams of stout mules." Frankie saw that Everett Dunbar was listening and she saw that he was trying not to interrupt her.

"I think I have enough corn at home in my crib to feed my animals this winter. But I'd like more, just to be safe. And I'll need more oats than what I've got. I'd like to barter with you for all that. If you use my mules with Isaac, and my heavy-wagon, you'd have what you need to work with the crew and get all your crops in. You'll have plenty for your place. And for my share. And to send to market."

Frankie paused for a moment, knowing Everett was uncomfortable about using her mules.

"Everett? Can't we go ahead with the trade we talked about? A trade that fits for both of us?" She paused again, watching Everett pulling at his lower lip. He was thinking. He was considering things. He was working things out in his mind and maybe getting closer to agreeing. Frankie decided to lay everything out.

"My Uncle James always said you should use equipment for the purpose it was made for, and you should use animals for the purpose they were bred for. You're right about the horses you have. They aren't made for pulling a plow through a rough and choppy field, or for pulling a heavy wagon loaded with harvest. Not for day after day, and mile after mile. Those three mules and Isaac were bred for that kind of work.

"You know your spring-wagon will break down in a year if you work it like a heavy field-wagon. There are three good mules and a heavy work-wagon sitting in your farmyard right now. And there are four oxen eating grass in my pasture if you need them."

"Now that I have a good team, Frankie, I feel like I was taking advantage of you to go ahead and use yours." Everett stared across the acres of corn in front of him. "I'll see you still get a fair trade in grain. I ain't forgetting that Ida and I have chickens, a milk cow and calf, a bull, and a driving horse that came from your place. All that still needs to be squared up."

Frankie could see he was struggling with something and it wasn't just the mules and the wagon. And it wasn't the idea of the barter. He was having trouble with the idea of things working out right. He was struggling because the solution was too easy, too simple. She looked out across the acres of corn tassels stirring in the hot breeze.

"We already settled on a fair exchange for all those animals, Mr. Dunbar, so that's not part of this conversation. But you spoke the truth when you said your horses aren't built for heavy field-work. You have a pair of horses born and bred for riding and steady pulling. You can go ahead and put them to work in the field and they'll dig in and do the work. But handling the harvest the way you're thinking, means that by next year, you'll have two horses that'll be worn down or lame. And probably, your mule too. You'll be right back where Hugh had you. Excuse me for saying so, but you were around him long enough that you got in the habit of thinking like he does."

Everett Dunbar said nothing; Frankie sat on her horse next to him on his. Watching him. Waiting. After a long while, she spoke again, thinking maybe he needed to hear what another man would say.

"My father thought foresight was one of the finest qualities a person could have. He used to say that foresight was the only thing that outweighed education. I think my father would consider you to be somebody with foresight. And I think he'd say it wasn't easy to hang onto the ability to see ahead, when you're around somebody who destroys that in everyone."

Everett nodded. He looked up into the sky and Frankie thought he might be saying a little prayer. She spoke again, softer this time.

"Using my mules and wagon means you'll be protecting your horses and your wagon; you'll still have a good team of healthy horses and a good wagon that you need on this place. Trading me a share of grain for using my mules and wagon means you'll be paying out some of your harvest to me. But by working with the crew, you'll be harvesting three times as much. And you'll be helping me out with something I can't do on my own."

They rode on then, heading toward the western corner of the corn field, riding side-by-side. Saying nothing. They turned the far corner and were on their way back to the house, when Everett

Dunbar pulled his mare to a stop; Frankie reined in, knowing something had just happened.

Everett sat on his mare, looking out across the Sand Hills to the east. Looking downriver. Sitting quietly. Teary-eyed.

"Do you know what, Honey? I just realized I've been in a trap. I *have* lost my ability to look ahead. Somewhere over these last few years, I started thinking like Hugh David. The first day we were at your place, I told you that Ida and I didn't tear things down like Hugh and Rebecca were always doing. And now, I'm realizing I've been leaning that way." Now, it was Everett Dunbar who drew in a deep breath before he went on.

"I know what you're saying is right, and if I heard someone else planning to do things the way I was talking, I'd point out exactly what you just did. But I swear to heaven, somehow I haven't been able to see it in myself."

"None of us can see ourselves clearly all the time." Frankie scanned the slopes of the hills to the east, looking to where he was looking. "It's hard to see things when they're up too close. It's like trying to read a book when it's pressed right up against your nose. I think that's why I like the prairie and the Sand Hills so much. Nothing's pressed in too close. And there's the solitude too. It lets me think clearer. My father used to say that solitude lets you breathe deeper and think wider. The Sand Hills are all about solitude."

"It seems like I've forgotten a lot of the experiences I've had in my life. It's like I forgot to think like myself. I just let Hugh take over because it was easier to get along with him. I didn't know I'd lose part of myself by doing that. Now, it feels like I'm remembering who I am. And it seems like everything is getting clear again." Everett reached between the two horses, reaching to squeeze her arm. "New things and better things are coming to me and Ida. And you're one of those things, Honey. It's only been a few weeks since you've been here, but you're awfully precious to us."

"Well. It's like you and Ida told the Reverend and Betsy. We're family." Frankie was still looking out into the hills. "Mr. Dunbar, I think family is about having someone who can help us find ourselves when we get lost. I don't think family has anything to do with being blood relations. I'm beginning to believe that it's rare when the members of a real family are born under the same roof."

"Since we're family, are you going to keep calling me *Mr. Dunbar*?" Everett smiled at her. Frankie smiled back.

"Ohh, I think I'll probably just keep switching back and forth between Everett *and* Mr. Dunbar. Depending on the day and my mood."

"Well then, I'll just switch back and forth between using Frankie and Honey. I suspect we'll get along just fine that way."

They sat on their horses for a while longer and then Everett said something about Ida probably having dinner on the table. They turned their horses toward the farmyard and moved off at a fast trot. Laughing.

PART II

HARVEST MOON

Frankie had spent much of the late afternoon and evening on the crest of the Lookout Hill, just as she had been doing for the last several days. Continuing to watch the herd of buffalo grazing its way through the Sand Hills; it was still taking its time, still up in the north, coming out of the north-northwest. Still moving gradually to the southeast.

The buffalo had been moving steadily over the last five days, and Frankie had them figured for being about fifteen miles away. She had been watching them every day, studying their path and direction. Learning a little about how they lived and moved among the hills.

Some days she could see the herd moving together, looking like a great brown-black swath of cloth made up of thousands of buffalo. On other days, the animals were spread out in groups and clusters, sometimes in the hundreds, sometimes in clumps of tens and twenties. And always, there were single animals dotting the far hills and lowlands.

And on one day, the greatest part of the herd seemed to have disappeared from the earth, gone from her sight. She had watched a few dozen clusters of buffalo grazing along the slopes of the grassy hills for most of the afternoon, but she knew that the great mass of the herd was still there; it was out there, somewhere, hidden among and between the rolling hills. And in due time, later on the same day—or maybe on the next day—she knew the great herd would begin to reappear. Gradually re-amassing. Re-forming. Reappearing. Coming together as the great beasts worked their way through the grasses, grazing their way across the land. Grazing and dozing and walking. And then grazing some more.

For the last two days, it had seemed to stay in the same place, almost motionless. She thought it was a sign that the grass must be especially good whenever the herd lingered, grazing in the same wide valley for days. Eventually though, the buffalo would move forward again, continuing their journey, spreading out, spreading up and across the hillsides.

Frankie took her eyes away from the herd as the sun began dropping from sight behind the far hills to the west. She sat there on the big catfish-gray mare that had once belonged to Daniel Kinison—one of the sister-mares that had come with the other livestock that night.

She had been riding both of the mares, taking them out in the early mornings or late evenings. They were both nice mares; each showed a sweet sensibility. She had searched for names for them for quite some time and finally, she had settled on Adeline and Ada. Nice solid and sweet names for two solid and sweet mares. She reached down to play with the wisp of mane at Adeline's withers, smiling as the mare returned the favor and swung her head back to nuzzle her rider's bare toes.

From the far side of the hilltop, came a squeaking little snort—Frankie and Adeline both turned to watch Adeline's colt playing at one of his baby-horse games. Flint was pawing at the ground, giving huffy little snorts, trying to conjure up some excuse to go into a pretend-spook. Suddenly, just like Frankie expected, he gave a squealing-snort and launched himself backwards, acting as if some terrifying beast was emerging from the ground beneath him.

The colt bolted in pretend-fright, racing across the hilltop, giving a few wild baby-horse bucks on the way. Frankie grinned. It was the same game. Same imaginary beast for the fourth time.

She left Flint to his games and looked back to the western horizon, watching the twilight colors developing within the gathered ribbons of clouds, watching the colors evolve and deepen. Naming the hues as they appeared. Dark purples and deepening blues, rich crimsons and bright bloody-reds. Fiery oranges and deep apricots, shining peaches and glistening pinks. *Eight, so far. Eight distinct colors. Sky-colors.*

From three different directions beyond the crest of the Lookout Hill, Frankie could hear the evening chatter of coyotes; their yip-yippings and their yammerings echoed across the land, bouncing between the slopes of the hills. Around her and below her, the nighthawks were already starting their sweeping flights, swooping and sailing and soaring like they did every evening. It was the start of their night-flights, their silent search for flies and bugs and other winged-insects that flitted among and above the hillside grasses.

Frankie had watched the hunt of the nighthawks before—it went on every night as the dark birds with their white-banded wings began their search for food on the fly. Dipping and swaying and tilting along the length of the hillsides, they reminded Frankie of light-footed dancers on dancefloors, but this was a dance on the grasslands. It was the dance of the nighthawks, a swift-moving, soundless night-dance—a beautiful swirling dance, teeming with smooth dips, sleek turns and masterful spins—their very own version of an airborne waltz.

Meadowlarks were following their own evening routine, sending out their last songs and offering what her Aunt Sarah called 'a final farewell' to the light of the sun. Above her, Frankie spotted the evening flight of mourning doves; they were flying by, flapping hard and fast as if someone, or something, was chasing them. Hurrying to the tree line along the banks of the North Loup. *Heading for the trees. Birds on a mission; birds of a feather.*

Frankie followed their line of flight, watching their frantic flapping. Grinning as she listened to the hurried strings of chortles—their frenzied little calls to each other, urging each other to 'hurry-up, hurry-up, hurry-up, hurry-up'.

Once the fast-flapping doves, with their frantic little squeaky-calls reached the treetops among the leafy branches, they'd rest-up for a few minutes before fluttering down to the sandy riverbank. They'd water-up for the night and then flap their way back into the high branches of the tree, select their roosts, and become their calm little selves again.

Then they would begin their forlorn little cooing-songs—the evening vespers of the doves—the same sweet and soft songs the

Bible spoke about in the Song of Solomon. 'The time of the singing of birds is come and the voice of the turtle is heard in our land'. The turtle that the Bible spoke of, was the turtle-dove, her Aunt Sarah had explained. Another name for the mourning dove.

Frankie watched as a few straggling flights of doves arrived riverside to water-up and roost; her thoughts trailed back to her first camp on the Cheyenne Trail. The evening flights of doves had led her to her campsite that first evening. She had watched them on their evening journey, flapping their way to water-up and roost for the night; she had turned her team and followed the path of their flight, letting them lead her away from the trail and behind a long hill. Back to a little hidden valley.

She had stayed in that valley, recovering after the turmoil and trauma of her last days at Fort Kearny. She had spent her days healing in the hidden valley, exploring the pretty little glade with the ground-spring and the old dugout-soddy. It was in the tumbled down soddy where she found the little purple bottle and the gold-scrolled picture-frame that were now on the mantle in her sitting-room; two little treasures that had come all the way up the Cheyenne Trail with her, traveling to a new home.

Frankie turned her attention back to the northwest, training her telescope on the buffalo herd out in the Sand Hills. Wanting to see it one more time before she lost sight in the darkness. Realizing suddenly, that if the herd continued on their southeasterly path, eventually, they'd move beyond her vision. That, she decided, would be a sad day. Because, when she thought about it, the herd had become a friend of sorts—something of a kindred spirit—sharing the vast lands of the Sand Hills with her. Living within the grasses; living within the landscape. Being part of this world with her, this world of hilltops and valleys and blue skies.

She watched the great swath of the dark herd until its darkness blended with the dark of the land, disappearing as the night settled down onto the distant hills. Finally, when it was too dark to see across the land, she sighed and gave up her vigil; she sent a silent promise to her herd, assuring them that she would return tomorrow. That she'd see them again.

Twilight had become dusk and in the fading light, Frankie gave a whistle, calling to the dogs on the slope below her, busy exploring rabbit-trails and gopher-holes; she turned Adeline down the hillside with the colt trotting along near them, prancing his little feet and tossing his little head—pretty confident that the whole world existed for his own little needs.

He pawed and bucked and kicked; he sent showers of sandy soil skyward as he burst away in quick little sprints, only to come prancing back, tossing his little-boy head and twisting his little-boy body, knowing within himself that he was the fastest-of-the-fast and the strongest-of-the-strong.

Frankie laughed out loud, watching him dashing off in a headlong race with the dogs. Head down and tail up, hard little hooves churning on the hardpack of the track. The last of the light was fading as she reached her meadow, so she never saw whether it was the horse or the hounds that won the race. But the colt circled the meadow and came dashing back, showing-off as he danced a few high-stepping circles around his momma and her human. Watching him, she knew Flint didn't really care who came in first; he was feeling plenty proud of his performance and no one else's opinion mattered at all.

He darted off again, dashing around the meadow in the very last of the light, and watching him, Frankie decided she had named him well. He was tough as nails, as solid as a rock and as hard as flint. So she'd given him the name. Flint. He was still in his baby-color, but he was showing signs that in the spring, the dark black-brown coat would shed-off and become the same catfish-gray of his dam and her sister. *Probably it's the Percheron bloodline. That'd explain the rich gray.*

But whatever his bloodline, Flint was growing fast; he was clever, quick to learn and fast to understand. And he was a show-off— an incessant show-off. He spent his days strutting his stuff, prancing and dancing, cavorting. Kicking at the sky and pawing at the air. He was pretty sure that everything and everyone in his world was watching him all the time. Frankie grinned at him, watching as he finished his last dash across the meadow, ending his run with a string of four high-bouncing bucks. All in all, he seemed awfully impressed with his own impressiveness.

As they headed to the barn-lot, Flint led the way, still strutting, still stepping high and proud, convinced in his own little heart that he was showing his mother exactly how it ought to be done.

Frankie settled them into a pen for the night, then walked to the windmill pool, stripping out of her clothes on her way. She pulled her braids loose as she waded into the water, dunked herself, and started washing away the dust of the day. Once she was satisfied, she lay back, floating and relaxing in the water that still held the warmth of the hot afternoon.

When the dogs joined her, bouncing into the water to play, she splashed with them for a while. Then, clean and cool and fresh for the night, she headed to the house, barefoot and naked, sashaying through the meadow's grass, pretending she was a nighthawk. Twisting and turning, arms spread wide like nighthawk wings. Loving the cool of the night; loving the dark air swirling around her.

She waltzed her way along the back of the Barracks and behind the stone-room, twirling as she headed to the back corner of the house. Then she danced her way across the porch floor and through her bedroom door. She tried to mimic the cooing-song of the doves while she pulled on her nightshift, pulling it down over her damp body, tugging as the cloth dragged and grabbed at her damp skin.

In the kitchen, she dished up cornbread and the leftover venison from the midday meal; she gathered up the pie-plate with the last piece of apple pie and a cup of lukewarm sweet-coffee. She headed out the kitchen door and settled herself on the front porch bench.

She ate her dinner and finished the remains of the pie, sitting on the darkened porch with the glow from the kitchen lantern slanting through the doorway and angling across the porch floor. She stayed there long after she finished her supper, listening to the night-sounds. The prairie-night sounds. The night-song of the Sand Hills.

Beyond the meadow, out on the higher land, killdeers still gave their shrill-staccato calls. Somewhere in the hillside trees behind the house, a great-horned owl sent out his solemn song—speaking his mind and sounding awfully sad and lonely. A moment later, another owl answered and Frankie smiled to herself. *Not too lonely. Because his mate's letting him know she's close by.*

Coyotes called, yipping their messages back and forth to each other. Then there was a strange and eerie cry—a long, sharp and shrill cry—sounding like a woman's pained and hopeless wail. Frankie listened again, feeling little tickling-shivers slipping up her spine. She recognized the cry—it was a sound she had heard once from her bedroom window in the white house back in Indiana. Her cousin Isaiah told her what it was—it was the haunting high-wail of a female fox. A vixen searching for a mate. Inviting him to visit; begging for him to come. Beseeching. *A vixen's call.*

Frankie stayed quiet, listening. The faraway wail came again. An odd cry; a faraway human-sounding cry. Ghostly. And a little terrifying if you didn't know exactly what you were hearing. Vixen night-cries had been to blame for a whole lot of ghosts-stories and tales of haunted forests and riversides—the sound of a she-fox calling for a mate on a dark night could be a spooky thing.

She heard a long string of assorted bird-songs coming from the biggest hackberry tree on the hillside beyond the pool's edge. *The resident mockingbird.* She grinned. Because like most mockingbirds, this one never seemed to understand the rules of nightfall and sleep-time. She listened to him running through his personal repertoire—all songs that he had stolen from other birds during the days, so he could entertain himself in the nights. 'A perennial thief or a relentless borrower, depending on your point of view.' That's what her cousin Samuel always said about mockingbirds. Frankie thought it over. *Maybe it all depends on the point of view of each of the individual birds he took his songs from.*

Frankie wondered about it for a moment, wondering if any of the true bird-owners of the songs ever confronted the mockingbird about using their songs without their permission. She decided to leave the issue with the birds and she headed into the kitchen.

She washed the dishes, and then wandered back into the cool bedroom. She stretched out on the bed linens and drifted off to sleep, pretty sure that she'd be dreaming about buffalo herds in the distant hills and birdsongs in the treetops.

The milking was done, the eggs had been gathered and the chickens were already out of the coop, busy scratching in the meadow and pecking along the hillside behind the henhouse. Frankie was in the kitchen, smiling because she had already done all the morning chores and she was still in her nightshift. There was a light and free feeling to the sleeveless nightshift that was so much nicer than the heavier nightgowns used during the winter months. She liked the freedom and that's what had her smiling. Because here in her meadow, she could use what she wanted and she could wear what she wanted, whenever she wanted. *No required uniforms here. No bugles ordering anyone out of bed. No one making schedules that needed to be kept.*

She was busy at the stovetop, making what she wanted for breakfast, because no one had made the decision about what should be on the breakfast table, either. So she put together a breakfast of fried eggs with a hash of venison and potatoes, squash and onions. She decided to fry up some apples in butter and sugar and cinnamon, too, just because she wanted to. And because there was no one around to say anything different. And no one was going to suddenly show up in her meadow today, either. Because everyone in the region was busy. The harvest had begun.

That's why the Dunbars hadn't visited her for almost two weeks—they had been working the harvest with the rest of the homesteaders. And with the use of the heavy wagon and the four mules, Everett could contribute to the community effort. Everyone expected the oat harvest to be done today or tomorrow, and with tomorrow being Sunday—if the harvest was over—Frankie expected the Dunbars would be driving in for a visit.

The field harvesting was a community effort, and once the crops were ready, the settlers down along the Middle Loup River—down where the Reverend Simeon Austin lived and preached—began the fieldwork together. They'd move together as a working crew—a harvest-party of neighbors—going from place to place, taking their wagons and equipment along with their teams of horses and mules and oxen.

They'd work the oat fields at each homestead together, cutting, threshing, and sacking the oats; and then stacking the straw. Then they'd move on to the next place. The men would work in the fields, and the women would see to the meals. And then, it would all start over for anyone growing wheat—the harvest-party would once again travel from place to place. Then the corn harvest would begin.

Since Everett and Ida were working with the other homesteaders, their fields would be included in the community harvest. Everett's eyes had been shining at the reality that he would be harvesting his first strong and solid crop this year—the first time since he and Ida had settled on their place. The weather had been right, the soil had proven rich, the fields were full. What pleased him more than anything else, was that with the harvesting crew, he would be able to harvest the crops from both quarter-sections.

Once all the crops were harvested and Everett had his crops in, he would bring Frankie her share. He would hold back what he needed for his own stock, along with the seed he needed for spring planting, and the rest of the crops would be hauled to the market at Fort Cottonwood. There, he and Ida would sell and trade their grain.

Some men would drive their own wagons; some families would hire neighbors and young men to take their wagons and act as their agents; sometimes, whole families would go with their wagons. It would become another community project with a common goal of selling crops and stocking up with supplies for the coming year.

It hadn't been so very long ago that the Dunbars had serious doubts about getting their crops in. More than that, Frankie knew they had been looking at the very real possibility of going under— they had been planning for the possibility of having to pull up stakes and head back to Iowa. But now, that was in the past.

Now, they were assured of a solid return this year, and there was the likelihood of a good planting and harvest for next year. As Ida saw it, they had the fresh start they wanted. The last time Frankie had seen them, right before they were heading out to join the harvest crew, Ida had said that finally, they had the homestead they wanted.

'We have the fresh start we wanted,' Ida's eyes had been soft and sparkly at the same time. 'And we've got solid prospects.'

'It's all turned around. We're going to be fine now, I can feel it in my bones,' Everett had said. 'Better than fine, really. Everything just came together'.

All of which had reminded Frankie of her father's words, words she had heard him say many times. 'When wrong people leave your life, wrong things stop happening.'

There was no doubt in her mind that his words applied to the Dunbars' situation. Everything in their lives had been falling apart; their future had been crumbling. All it took for Everett and Ida to stop spiraling into ruin, was to let their daughter and son-in-law walk out of their lives. Letting those two go their own way was the wisest decision Everett and Ida could have made.

Frankie finished at the stove, dished up her plate, filled a coffee cup and headed out to the porch table. She settled herself cross-legged on the tabletop and started working her way through the eggs and hash while she watched the on-going dispute between Mrs. Swingle and Matilda.

It was a battle of instincts between the mothering-hen and the herding-dog. It had started earlier in the morning—there had been a lot of squawking and barking all through the morning. And now, from her perch on the porch table, Frankie could see that some sort of chick-custody argument was going on between the hen and the collie-dog.

With chores done and no other immediate plans, Frankie decided to watch the show. She was comfortable where she was; the sun-heated wood of the tabletop was warming her bottom through her nightshift, which she decided was a nice contrast to the cool morning breeze on her face and arms.

Ever since the chicks had hatched out, Mrs. Swingle had been doing her mothering-duty and keeping tabs on her lively little flock, teaching them and training them. For some reason, Matilda had been struck with a mothering instinct of her own, and that maternal-instinct had somehow become entangled with her herding-instinct. As a result, Matilda was busy trying to gather the chicks and herd them over to her favorite sunny-spot on the kitchen porch.

Mrs. Swingle was a dutiful mother, and she had been spending all her time teaching her brood the finer points of hunting-and-pecking and soil-scratching. This morning, like all the other mornings, she was waddling along, calling for her babies to follow, intent on taking them to the trees along the hillside. To their credit, the chicks were doing their best to follow. But Matilda was throwing a wrench into the works; she was intent on taking custody and control of the tiny flock. But the dedicated Mrs. Swingle wasn't having it.

Frankie was fascinated with the situation and she was more than a little curious as to what the actual outcome of the bickering would be. Because she knew from personal experience, that Mrs. Swingle was more than capable of drawing blood. But then again, the old hen was dealing with a young collie-dog, quick on her feet and three-times the hen's size. So Frankie kept eating her breakfast while she kept an eye on the odd little battle of basic instincts.

The hen grew crankier and the dog grew more dogged; the chicks, caught in the midst, grew more confused. And probably, Frankie figured, more than a little dizzy with all their scurrying and hurrying as they scrambled back and forth, trying desperately to comply with the opposing demands.

The running battle went on for a good ten minutes and Frankie was considering rescuing the chicks from their dilemma when suddenly—through some secret language apparently understood by both herding-dogs and mother-hens—a silent compromise was reached. A treaty had been struck.

From what Frankie could figure, the terms of the treaty awarded Matilda, the interloping-collie-dog, a single chick; Mrs. Swingle, the-true-and-rightful-guardian, was awarded the remainder of the brood.

The righteous old hen marched haughtily away with her remaining ten chicks, and Matilda carefully picked up her prize—smiling the best doggy-smile she could manage with the fluffy-feathered chick filling her mouth—and carried her prize up to the porch and laid it gently in Frankie's lap. She gave Frankie her toothiest-smile, more than pleased with her award.

Frankie did as Matilda expected and cuddled the chick in her hands, stroking it until it quieted. Then Matilda nudged her hands, ready to reclaim her prize—she carefully lifted the fuzzy-yellow prize from Frankie's lap and walked to a sunny patch on the porch floor. She turned a couple of circles before curling up on the sun-warmed wood. And then, she nestled the chick between her front legs.

The chick kept trying to leave and the tawny collie-dog kept nosing and nudging it back where she wanted it. Carefully. And gently. But doggedly. Each time it tried to slip away to catch up to its sibling-flock, Matilda lifted it and settled it back between her legs.

Eventually, the chick gave up. It admitted defeat and surrendered; it hunkered down and simply accepted the attention being offered. Matilda cuddled the baby, snuffling and sniffing it, grinning a self-satisfied doggy-smile all the while. She kept licking it and bathing it, until Frankie decided the chick looked like nothing more than a soggy little mess of downy dog-drool.

Finally, Matilda was satisfied with the cleaning. Apparently, the chick was too—it snuggled itself deep into Matilda's pretty white ruff, tucking itself under the collie's muzzle and dozed-off in the heat of the late morning sun.

Out on the grass beside the steps, Laughing Girl had been working hard to ignore the whole custody battle. She rose from her nap, stretched her long greyhound legs and her long wolfhound back; she glanced around and sauntered over to a different sun-warmed location by the edge of the porch. The blond-brindle hound flopped herself down, rolled herself over and stretched out on her back. She gave a long groan and a soft sigh and started drifting off to sleep again, leaning against the edge of the porch with her long skinny legs pointing straight up to the sky in that funny way that the long-legged coursing hounds were wont to do.

Frankie stared at her, studying the lean and sleek wolf-hound-greyhound body, suddenly realizing it wasn't looking *quite* so lean and sleek anymore. She started counting back through the past weeks, trying to figure exactly how long it had been since her night-flight from the fort. Counting the weeks since Mr. Wheaton had placed the hound inside her wagon. Recalling his words—he had talked about the hound's wounds and the fights she had been in.

Suddenly, Frankie understood the reasons for the dogfights; the hound had been in season; she had been fighting with the other bitches. *So. Laughing Girl's carrying puppies. She's pregnant!* Frankie grinned. *Not a bad thing. Not at all.*

Because, to Frankie's thinking, having more of these coursing hounds around her homestead would be a fine thing. Because Mr. Wheaton had said the hound would protect her place; he said she'd have no trouble with wolves or coyotes with one of these hounds roaming around her homestead. So far, there had been no trouble from either coyotes or wolves.

Frankie was in the middle of wondering how many wolf-hound-greyhound pups she might get in a litter, when Laughing Girl was suddenly twisting herself up from the ground; she scrambled to her feet, growling her ugly growl and showing her ugly fangs. Her hackles were up and her eyes were fixed on the meadow's entrance.

An instant later, Matilda lunged to her feet, giving her deep guttural growl. Leaving her chick to sleep in the patch of sunlight. Matilda's eyes were locked on the track at the entrance, too; her growl was getting louder as she backed up, moving closer to Frankie.

Sunny Jim called out from the gelding's pasture; Trumpeter offered a challenge from the front pasture—his call rang out, echoing between the valley's slopes. Her horses had picked up the scent of horses in the air—horses that didn't belong.

Frankie stepped closer to the kitchen door, reached around the door-frame for her Henry rifle. Someone was coming up the track and it clearly wasn't the Dunbars. Given the way the dogs were acting, there were strangers out there. Close by. There had been no sounds of a wagon, no sounds of anyone coming up from the ford. If any homesteaders were coming to visit, there would likely have been a call. A shout to announce their arrival—a 'hello the house!'

She stood watching, listening. She felt her skin crawling; knowing suddenly she was being watched. She could feel it. Laughing Girl's gaze shifted to the hillside behind the barn; her growls growing louder. Matilda was shifting her attention back and forth, her eyes moving from the front track, to the barn's hillside, and back to the front track.

The birds in the trees on the hillsides had stopped singing; a flock of sparrows erupted from trees along the slope above the barn. In the barn-pen, Rock was standing at attention, his head high, staring toward the front of the meadow. The dun horse was in the pen next to his, was frozen in place, his eyes locked on the entrance.

It seemed like an awfully long time to be waiting and watching, but Frankie had no real idea of anything else she could do. Because she knew she was being watched. She didn't know by whom, and she didn't know by how many, but there were people out there watching her meadow. By keeping an eye on the two dogs, she knew someone was out by the front entrance, and someone else was up in the trees on the hillside behind the barn. And she knew there could be other watchers—in other places—that neither she nor the dogs knew about.

Frankie shifted her position a little, stepping closer to the corner post of the porch, giving herself a little more cover. A little more protection. But from exactly what, she had no idea. She stayed still, watching and waiting. Trying to add up what she knew and what she didn't know. It was unlikely that some neighbor had come for a visit, because anyone in the area would be at the big harvest to the south. Besides which, someone coming for a friendly visit wouldn't be lurking around in the trees on the slopes above her meadow.

So far, she knew there was potential danger in at least two directions. What she didn't know, though, was whether there was danger in the hillside trees along the back meadows, or whether there was danger on the hillside behind the house—and she didn't know of any way to check that situation without leaving her present position and losing her view of the two known dangers.

Frankie felt a groan rising from low in her throat. Adding up everything had done her no great good—it had only established that she was in a bad situation. And that, was making her feel more than a little nauseated. She did the only thing that she knew to do—she kept the stock of the Henry pressed against her shoulder, watching and waiting.

She stayed as she was, listening to the slobbering growls of the dogs. Watching Laughing Girl's spittle dripping to the ground. Watching drops of Matilda's slobber splatter on the porch floor. Thinking it was a little odd that she was noticing drops of dog-slobber while she was right in the middle of danger coming from what might be several different directions. *Such an odd thing to notice things like that at a time like this.*

Frankie gave her head a shake, trying to turn her attention back fully to the situation at hand. And that's when she saw the movement.

The first sign of trouble was on the hillside above the barn, back among the trees. Frankie's eyes locked on a strange little movement. A single feather flitting in the breeze—a feather that wasn't attached to a bird. She watched for the odd movement again, knowing there was nothing normal about a single feather moving on its own among the branches and leaves. Birds were always flitting through the trees, their wings flashing and flickering among the branches and leaves. But not a single feather. Not like that.

It happened again—the gentle flitting of a feather showing among the leaves. And then, quite suddenly, there was a different kind of movement. The movement of horses. Horses and riders among the trees; riders with feathers in their hair; horses with feathers hanging from their bridles and manes. They were easing down the track on the hillside. *Two horses. Two riders. Indians and Indian ponies.*

Frankie lifted the barrel of the Henry, pointing it toward the riders. Just in case. Then suddenly, without quite knowing why, she was swinging the barrel toward the front entrance—an instinctive move, done without thinking.

An instant later, it proved to be a wise move. A group of horses and riders came into view, following the front track into her valley. Following it around and down to her meadow. *Indians! Warriors!*

Their faces were painted. Stripes and circles were painted on their arms. Feathers were hanging in their braided hair and feathers were flitting and twisting, tethered to weapons—rifles and lances and bows. Feathers and colored-cloth streamers were hanging from the bridles and dangling from the manes and tails of painted war-ponies.

Frankie lowered the barrel of the Henry, understanding suddenly there was no sense in bringing the rifle into play. There was no reason to fire off a shot. Because she knew she couldn't shoot every Indian in sight without getting killed herself.

She glanced to her own feather on the fore-stock of her rifle—the white and brown-speckled eagle feather that Strong Hand had fastened there. She wondered if the spotted feather would mean anything to these men, wondered if it would gain her any favor. Because it might be a handy thing if these warriors took notice of it and saw value in it—it might be her only hope, because she had no clear way out of the situation before her.

In the next moment, as the warriors rode down into her meadow, she realized there was no actual threat from them. *Not yet.* They didn't have their weapons up; no rifles or arrows were pointed at her. They were just riding into her meadow; they didn't seem to be looking for a fight. *Not yet, anyway.*

Frankie was already well aware she wasn't in any position to stop the warriors from doing whatever they wanted to. Mounted and armed as they were—the warriors could do as they wished. The situation, Frankie realized, could turn ugly real fast. There was no sense in helping it go that way. Her safest course, she decided, would be to wait and see what they had in mind. It had worked before; it had worked on the day she stood waiting on the blue-green Conestoga, watching a group of Indians riding up to her—the first time ever that she had seen Indians. Maybe it'd work this time too. She lowered the barrel of her rifle.

She spoke to the dogs, firm and clear. Calling them off. Calling them to her side. Telling them to be quiet. Calming the situation for the moment. And all the time, she had her eyes locked on the riders.

The main party paused once they reached the meadow floor; the two hillside riders circled around the front barn-lot and joined their companions. All the warriors paused for a moment, speaking softly among themselves. They reined their painted ponies, turned them toward the house, then walked their ponies forward, coming right toward her, right toward the corner of the kitchen porch where she was standing.

Frankie waited, the barrel of her rifle pointing to the ground, watching the warriors coming across her meadow. Moving steadily. Seeming oddly casual about it. Taking their time. Some of them were glancing around the meadow, eyeing the buildings, scanning the hillsides. But most were watching her. Quiet. Fierce. As their ponies walked steadily toward her. Eight ponies; eight warriors.

And then Frankie saw it. A little surprised she hadn't spotted it already. A black-and-white pinto. It was there at the front of the band of warriors. It had a circle of yellow paint around one of its eyes and blue painted hand-prints across its chest and shoulders. She knew the horse—she'd never seen it painted like it was today, but she knew it. She'd seen it before. Three different times.

And right behind the pinto, there was a buckskin. She knew that horse too. It had a lightning-strike of black-and-yellow, zig-zagging down its neck and front legs. The painting was new to her, but she recognized that horse too.

She started grinning—she knew warriors on their backs too. *Motåhke and E-Menóhkahe.* Knife and He's Proud. *My Cheyenne warriors! My brothers!*

Frankie lowered the butt of her rifle to the porch floor; she stood there in the morning sun in her white nightshift, the spotted eagle-feather tied to the fore-stock of her rifle lifting and dipping in the morning breeze. She waited as Knife and He's Proud and the six other warriors rode straight to where she stood. The tips of their lances shimmering in the sun's rays; the feathers and strips of bright red flannel dancing in the breeze.

She watched the men as they approached, watching the way their dark skin glistened like bronze in the bright sunlight. Remembering that coppery-bronze shimmer; she had seen it before. She had been watching warriors riding toward her on that day when she had been standing in the jockey-box of the Conestoga.

The paint on their bodies and their horses was new to her—never before had she seen warriors with their faces masked with paint, and their bodies marked with the stark and colorful designs. She took in a sudden breath, realizing how very fierce and unnerving the scene would be if she didn't know the men behind all the paint and feathers and weapons. But she *did* know them.

The black-and-white pinto stopped a few steps from the kitchen porch. Frankie stared at the warrior on the black-and-white pinto—her eyes on his eyes. Motåhke's eyes. Knife's eyes. The Cheyenne warrior sat his horse in front of her, looking fierce and dangerous—black paint covered his cheeks and forehead; from the corners of his mouth, over his whole jaw and down into his neck, he was painted white. Yellow lightning-strikes angled down his temples to the corners of his eyes; bands of black and red paint circled his arms; yellow streaks of lightning shot down his arms.

The last time she had seen him, he had been wearing a buckskin shirt and he had been squatting in front of her on the street at Fort Kearny. He had been smiling at her. Today, there was no shirt; today, he was sitting on his warhorse, looking wild and terrible. Today, there was no smile. But he was still Knife. She had claimed him that day; she had called him *na-htataneme*. My brother. And he had accepted her claim; he had called her *na-semahe*. My sister.

Frankie took a step closer to the edge of the porch, closer to the Cheyenne warrior on his piebald pony. He was looking at her; staring at her. Frankie grinned, tilted her head, watching him. Watching his eyes. Waiting.

He looked straight at her, ignoring the dogs' growls that had been increasing in volume as he had ridden closer. His eyes drilled into her and Frankie figured that if she didn't actually know him, his face would be a fearsome thing to look at.

"Na-semahe. Ne-toneto mohta-he?" Knife spoke to her and then he waited.

The meaning of his words came forward in her mind—he was calling her sister and asking how she was feeling. He, too, remembered that same day; the day they had claimed each other.

All the words spoken that day were suddenly swirling around in her mind. She heard again the rhythm of the Cheyenne language. Her mind was flashing back to the three times she had met up with Knife and his companions. The first time, she had been standing in the jockey-box of the Conestoga—that day she had faced Knife and a man named Strong Hand and the warriors who rode with them. Then the second time—the day of the deer hunt with her troopers. And there had been a third time—the day at Fort Kearny in front of Sutlers Store, when Knife and Strong Hand had recognized her; Corporal Buchanan had been there, squatting beside her in the street and translating for her.

Now. Here in her meadow. Standing on her kitchen porch, Frankie's mind was racing back to the fort, back to the conversation; she could hear the words Corporal Buchanan had given to her, the words he told her to use. He's Proud had been there that day, acting as a translator for his companions. And he was here today. And Frankie thought that was a lucky thing, because He's Proud could translate for her—because He's Proud spoke English.

"Na-htataneme. Na pevo mohta." 'My brother. I'm fine.' Frankie was nodding, happy he had found her. Happy he had come.

She glanced to He's Proud, knowing she would need his help, because very soon, she would be running out of words she knew. For now though, she wanted to keep talking, using the words she remembered. Wanting to show He's Proud and Knife that she still remembered some of the Cheyenne language—that some of their words were still inside her and part of her. She saw He's Proud nod, a slight nod; he already knew what she was thinking; he knew what she would need.

"Ho-esta Hesta Ka-ėškóne, ne-náestse." 'Fire Heart Child, come here.' Knife spoke to her, beckoning from his pony's back.

Frankie went over to edge of the porch, walking to him just as he had asked, suddenly remembering Bill Wheaton's words, the advice he had given on her last night there on Fort Farm Island. 'Don't be afraid if Strong Hand's people find you. They'll just be watching out for you.' He'd said something else too. 'That damn Knife, as mean as he is, he'd lay down his life for you.'

She leaned the rifle against the porch post. She stepped off the porch, stepped over to his horse. And then she did the same as she had done with Corporal Buchanan—she reached her arms up toward him.

"He-ama." 'Up.'

Knife laughed and leaned down, gripped her arms and lifted her to the withers of his horse. He sat her in front of him, grinning at her. She looked into his eyes and grinned back at him. She asked him how he was, using a few of the Cheyenne words she remembered. He laughed and answered her. He patted her leg, smiling broadly.

Frankie looked at the other warriors around her; she saw their surprised expressions and she understood what was going on. They had just watched a little white girl tell a Cheyenne warrior what to do. And he had done it. She realized that it didn't matter what tribe someone belonged to, white or Indian—because confusion, surprise and amusement all looked exactly the same, no matter what the tribe or the language.

Several of the warriors burst into laughter, watching this companion of theirs—a serious-minded warrior, a man who rarely smiled—sitting with a little white girl on his lap, just because she had demanded it. But it was He's Proud's expression that delighted Frankie; he was watching the whole scene and his eyes were snapping with amusement. He may have been surprised to find her here, but he wasn't surprised to see the way Knife was treating her. He had seen it before.

Knife had questions for her, because whatever he had expected when his band of warriors found the valley, he had not expected to find her. Frankie listened to his words, watching as he swept his arm in a half circle, indicating her valley, her meadow, her house. She didn't know his words but she was pretty sure he wanted to know why she was here, and how she had come to be here.

She beckoned to He's Proud and asked him for the words she needed. He moved his horse closer, leaning in. He explained Knife's questions in English and when she gave him the answers, he started translating for Knife. And that's when Frankie stopped him, telling him she wanted to tell Knife herself.

"Give me the words. I want to say them. I want to speak them. I need to learn how the Cheyenne speak."

He's Proud smiled at her and said something to the others that made them nod. It made some of them chuckle. But they were all pleased with what He's Proud told them. Frankie looked up, met Knife's eyes and grinned at him, because he was grinning at her. Every bit as pleased as his companions.

The warrior who was known for being so dangerous, was smiling as he stroked her hair. Understanding what she wanted and why she wanted it. He lifted her braids, showing them to the other men, saying something that made them smile bigger and nod some more. And laugh a little.

"He told these men that you are his sister, who loves the Cheyenne people and sees the world like a Cheyenne. Because Fire Heart Child has the eyes of our people."

"E-peva'e tsexė-ho'ėhneto." 'I'm glad you came.' Frankie smiled, nodding to Knife, searching her memory for other words Corporal Buchanan had taught her.

Knife slipped down from his pinto, lowering her to the ground with him, keeping his hand on her shoulder. Almost, Frankie thought, as if he didn't dare let her go. *Almost like he's afraid I'll disappear.*

He squatted down in the grass near the edge of the porch, motioning for her to stay with him, wanting to keep her near. He spoke to the other warriors then, and He's Proud moved close to her side; he spoke softly.

"Knife," he said, "is telling the others about you."

Knife told the story of how he and Strong Hand had found her far away on the prairie, traveling far to the south of the Platte

River. On a vision quest, he said. Alone with her great wagon and her four black horses. Giant horses, he explained, calling them ho-haa mo'éhė-no'ha. 'Very-much-horses.' He told his companions he was her brother, because she had claimed him at the soldiers' fort. She had claimed him and Strong Hand and He's Proud as her brothers. And Knife said, she was his sister.

The others had all dismounted and they were relaxing in the grass beside her and Knife. Frankie watched the warriors around her, some squatting on the ground near them, some sitting cross-legged, some relaxing and lying sideways, propped on their elbows.

There were Cheyenne warriors here with her, but Frankie could see there were other warriors in this group. Men who were different. The beading on their buckskin shirts was different; the shapes of their faces were different; their words were different.

She asked He's Proud about them and he told her they were friends of the Cheyenne; they were of the Oglála tribe. They spoke the language called Lakotah and they were brothers to the Cheyenne. They were hunting with them, scouting and tracking together for their people.

And then, Knife started talking again, and He's Proud stayed close to her, speaking low and steady, keeping her in the conversation. Explaining things as well as translating—telling her more than just what the men said; he was giving her a deeper understanding of the men and their conversation. He's Proud was teaching her, leading her into the world of the Cheyenne.

Frankie listened to Knife's words, hearing his inflections and his tone, speaking quickly and loudly as he told his stories about how she had stolen her animals from white men by following the river at night. He laughed as he told the story of the deer hunt with the soldiers.

Sometimes one of the Cheyenne men reached over to her, touching her shoulders or fingering her braids and saying she wore her hair like their children. They murmured among themselves. Smiling at her. 'Eyes of our own people,' they said.

These warriors, He's Proud said, had already heard of this little white girl long before they found her here. They knew she was the one who gave her magic to Knife—they knew it was her bullet, from her rifle, that Knife wore at his throat. They knew she was the little white girl who had the 'very much horses', who traveled the prairie alone and unafraid. They already knew of Fire Heart Child.

He's Proud kept translating, speaking for the men as they asked their questions. Like Knife, they asked about her journey to this valley. To this river. They wanted to know why was she here, and they asked where her people were.

Frankie gave He's Proud her answers and he gave her the words so she could repeat them. He was patient, giving her the words and repeating the sounds when she needed help. Correcting her pronunciation, teaching her the inflections. The warriors were patient, too, listening to the twice-told answers—hearing the answers first from He's Proud as he gave her the words, and then hearing her repeat them. They waited, smiling, while she kept asking for the pronunciations and worked to duplicate the sounds of the new words.

The whole time, Knife kept his hand on her. On her head or arm or shoulder. Or resting on her thigh. A soft touch. Steady and firm. Gentle. Almost, Frankie realized, like an ownership, almost like he was proving that he was her brother and that she belonged to him.

They all sat there on the grass in front of her house, Frankie and this new band of warriors who had come to visit. They talked and she talked. He's Proud kept translating and the men kept waiting patiently, giving her the time she needed to find her way through the words and learn their language.

Among these people, she realized, it was a show of respect. They wanted to learn about her and her life. And they wanted her to learn about them. Because these men who roamed the grasslands, who lived this life—these men who traveled wherever and whenever they pleased—had decided to spend some time with her.

Frankie didn't know how much time had passed, but she realized the warriors had been talking and relaxing with her for well more than an hour; like anyone else who might visit, she realized she

252

should feed them. Because they were her guests. Because Knife and He's Proud were her brothers.

She went into the kitchen and brought out a skillet of cornbread and a crock of butter. When she divided it among them and showed them how to slather the rich Jersey butter on their cornbread, they grinned. The combination of flavors pleased them and they reached out to her, patting her arm and shoulder. They spent the next few minutes using their knives to spread dollops of the butter on their hunks of cornbread, savoring the flavors, speaking about the *ve'kea-hanoo'o* and the *heóve-amėške*—the 'sweet food' and the 'yellow-grease'—among themselves.

While they were eating, Frankie spent the time studying them, trying to see the differences between her Cheyenne and the Oglála men. Looking at the beading on their buckskin shirts and the way their moccasins were made, she could see the differences. The designs in the paint on their bodies were different too. She looked out to the ponies grazing in the meadow grass, studying the roans and the buckskins, the pintos and bays and grays.

There were differences there, too—differences in the blankets draped on their backs, differences in the surcingles and in the bows and arrows and lances fastened to them. Looking at everything, Frankie could see the differences—the painted ponies and the weapons of the tribes were different, just like the warriors of the two tribes were different. But still, they all blended together.

A red-and-white pinto there among the Indian ponies reminded her of the pinto Strong Hand rode. She turned to Knife and asked about Strong Hand. He-kóne Mósėstotse. Asking why her brother who had fastened the spotted-eagle feather to her rifle, wasn't among this band.

"He is with the people of his father," Knife told her. "Lame Horse's people live far to the southwest, beyond the great flat river. His mother and her family still live there."

"Strong Hand," He's Proud said, "will be happy we found you. He has searched for you across the lands of his father's people. Everyone in Lame Horse's band watches for you."

"That's why we are surprised to find you here," Knife told her. "The soldier-scouts believed you were far away to the west."

"The Cheyenne heard Fire Heart Child had left the soldiers' fort," He's Proud explained. Our friend, White Man On The Island, told us to hunt south of the fort called Cottonwood, west of the fork in the great flat river."

"You have kept us busy, Fire Heart Child." Knife reached around her shoulders and pulled her back against him, rocking her, chuckling. "Our people have grown tired in their hunt for you. But now, we have you. We found you far from where we searched."

Frankie took the teasing as he meant it, she giggled as he held her, tickling her sides, scolding her for causing them such trouble. He's Proud continued with the story, telling her that the horse-soldiers had been searching for her in those lands. That they still searched for her. And Frankie listened, understanding it was Bill Wheaton on Fort Farm Island who told them where to look. *So. He still believes I'm out beyond Fort Cottonwood. And the Cavalry believes it too.*

She felt the relief flooding through her, realizing she was safe here in the Sand Hills. Nobody at Fort Kearny had any idea where she was. Which was exactly as she had hoped. *No one followed me that night. No soldiers. No Indians. No white-men. None of the dangerous men like Colonel White or Silas Beckett.*

Any searches for her were far from her homestead. Far from her quiet little meadow. They wouldn't find her. Her thoughts traced back to her Lieutenant and Isabelle at Fort Kearny in the little white cottage—the cottage that sat all by itself—at the end of the street. She thought about Captain Jack Connell. And Septimus Travers and Will Trask. She thought of Corporal Buchanan—her brother, just like Strong Hand and Knife were her brothers. And there was Sergeant McCallister with the gentle Irish lilt in his voice, who had held her and sang the soft Irish songs to her when she was hurt so badly. *They're all still wondering, then. Probably, still worried.*

Frankie knew the tears were starting to rise, the sorrow was coming up from deep inside her. The hurt and the pain of losing them felt like losing another family.

And then Knife jostled her and her mind returned to the meadow. He rocked her against his side again, teasing her about how she had eluded them—talking about how she was 'as clever and wise as a prairie-wolf'. He tipped his head back, laughing at his own astonishment when he had first seen her this morning. He made a face at her, making an exaggerated look of astonishment—trying to make her laugh.

Because, Frankie realized, somehow Knife knew something had made her sad. She broke into a grin. He grinned back and then began asking her questions again, and the other men were joining in with their own.

"Now," He's Proud said, "they want to hear about the night Fire Heart Child escaped from the soldier-fort."

So Frankie told them, describing how she slipped out of a window at night. She told them she crossed the fort in the dark and stayed in the stable, hidden in the hay in the stable-loft. She talked about how she watched and waited for two days. And when it was safe, she rode away from the fort, escaping on a stormy night.

When she told about taking her Lieutenant's horse, to take him away from the fort commander, the warriors laughed loud and long. They thought stealing a horse from the Cavalry, and especially from the fort's chief, was a wonderful thing.

The warriors kept asking for more of the story, so Frankie went on with her tale. She talked about meeting up with White Man On The Island on the stormy night. And she told them how she had followed the river west, until he quit watching. Then she had turned north across the grassland and let the storm and rain cover her trail.

When she told them she had searched for the old trail of the Cheyenne people, they became quiet and exchanged glances. Knife's grip around her shoulders tightened; he pulled her against him, holding her hard and strong. He spoke quickly to He's Proud, his voice low. The other men spoke too, keeping their voices soft, nodding to each other. Their expressions had changed; they were watching her in an odd way.

To Frankie's surprise, He's Proud didn't translate their words, and even when she asked, he refused. He said they were speaking of 'the ancestors'.

"Our grandfathers used that passage through the land, Fire Heart Child. But no more. Only the spirits travel that path now."

It didn't seem like anyone was inclined to tell her any more than what He's Proud had said, so Frankie thought it might be a wise thing to leave the subject alone. It seemed like it was a discussion for these men, and maybe not for little white girls.

So she told them how she had come to this meadow. How her family had come from their old home in the East. She talked about traveling here after they died, traveling alone. Because, she explained, this valley was a hidden place that had been waiting for her. It was her home now.

She said her people at the fort, her soldier-family, must not know where she was. They loved her and protected her, but there were men at the fort who weren't her friends and wanted to harm her. And there were other men, white-men who weren't soldiers, who would still be hunting for her. So no one could know where she lived.

He's Proud and Knife looked at each other, nodding. Not seeming at all surprised by the story she told, and Frankie realized they had probably heard the story. Probably from the Otoe people who worked for Bill Wheaton—White Man On The Island. She knew the Otoe and the Cheyenne were friendly with each other because they had a common enemy—the Pawnee. So probably the Otoe had told Strong Hand's band about Beckett and the beating. And maybe about Colonel White too.

Knife's arm was still around her, but now, there was something different—the teasing and the rocking and the tickling had stopped—now, his arm felt protective. Now, there was safety there against his side and under his arm.

Frankie had always felt safe here in her meadow, from the moment she had driven the big blue-green Conestoga into the valley. Now though, there was actually a greater safety. Mr. Wheaton had been right—these men, Knife and He's Proud and this band of warriors, would protect her. They would tell no soldiers or white-men where she lived.

Knife asked her more questions about her journey from her home far to the east, and asked about her family. She told him about the fever and how she had buried them beside the Little Blue River, and then she explained about the soldiers he had seen her with and how they had taken her to the fort to protect her.

Then, Knife wanted to know about her painted-wagon and the black horses, the 'very much horses'. When she told him the wagon and horses were still hers, that they were here with her, he grinned and stood up, talking to the other men.

They all walked with her to see her four Shires. Once in the pasture, there were murmurs and cooing sounds from the men as they looked at them. They stroked the necks of her Shires and reached their hands to their backs and withers, delighted by their size. Of the group, only Knife and He's Proud knew of them, and Frankie could tell that Knife was taking it upon himself to show them off to the others.

They walked through the other pastures and among her animals; the warriors talked about the oxen and their brindle coloring—painted like the grasses of the land, they decided. They studied her other horses—the mares, they decided, would give fine colts for war-horses. They admired Trumpeter, stroked his sides and shoulders—murmured softly to each other about him, nodding and grinning.

When Frankie lifted the halter from the fence and put it on the stallion and told Knife to ride him, he grinned wildly. Pleased with the offer. He swung up on the blood-bay and began reining the stallion and moving him through the pasture. Trumpeter complied, responding to his touch; he pranced, dancing and stepping high for Knife; he gathered himself when Knife asked it of him and when Knife leaned forward, the stallion charged forward, launching as if in battle. Trumpeter was being the warhorse he had been bred to be; he was being everything a Kentucky Charger should be.

There were whoops and high-chirps from the other men as Knife turned Trumpeter toward the center of the pasture. Frankie watched the stallion moving for Knife; the rider on his back might have different signals, and he might have a different style and seat than the big bay was used to, but Trumpeter seemed to know he had a fighting man on his back.

The Kentucky Charger was feeling the courage and the knowledge of his rider and he was figuring out what the man wanted. The warhorse and the warrior were both enjoying the moment—galloping, trotting, turning and spinning—moving together with strength and spirit. Strong and sure. Their power combined in smooth and graceful action. Sleek and swift movement. Quick and certain response. It was a beautiful show.

When Knife brought the blood-bay stallion to where Frankie stood, he was wearing a wide and relaxed grin that Frankie had never seen on his face. If a grin from a Cheyenne warrior was the same as a Cavalry officer's, then Knife was truly pleased and impressed.

He slipped down from the stallion's back and stood next to Frankie while she pulled the halter and released Trumpeter to return to the mares—to his mares that had been racing and bucking around the pasture, excited and delighted by the action. Playing and cavorting and flirting with the stallion. And Trumpeter, true to his second purpose in life, headed back to his herd, snorting and grunting, calling out to the mares with his loud ringing neigh. Racing to run beside the mares as they raced across the pasture.

Frankie and the warriors watched as the stallion circled the mares, snaking his head low, nipping at their hocks and flanks. Bringing them back into his control, reminding them about who he was. And then, he chose a mare; he singled her out and moved her away from the other mares. He moved her where he wanted her, turned her and halted her.

And when he rose up and mounted her, the warriors broke out in laughter. Giving their whoops and high-chirps again. This too, was part of the show, and in their minds, it was a good ending. Knife was still grinning his wide and relaxed grin. Proud of this stallion of Ho-esta Hesta Ka-éškóne.

They were all walking back to her house, when the Oglála men stopped suddenly. They were looking at a different horse now; they were staring at the mouse-colored dun standing in the shadowed doorway of the barn-stall.

And in the next instant, everything changed. The laughter and grins stopped. One warrior shouted, pointing to the dun stallion; he spun to look at Frankie, his hand pulled a long-bladed knife from the sheath at his belt. He was moving toward her, anger and rage on his face.

Frankie felt hands on her arms, the grips hard and harsh. He's Proud was pulling her backwards, pulling her away from the men, urgent, asking her why the horse was with her. And Knife was in front of her, shouting at the Oglála warrior, facing off against him.

There were shouts on all sides of her, voices loud and angry. Arguments erupted. The warrior with the knife in his hand was waving it, pointing toward the barn-pen, pointing toward the mouse-colored horse. The shouting was growing louder.

Frankie couldn't understand the words and He's Proud wasn't translating for her, because he and Knife were in the midst of the angry scene. She could tell there were two sides—the Cheyenne arguing against the Oglála—and it had to do with the dun horse. There was no doubt the Oglála knew the horse, and as the pointing and shouting continued, she was pretty sure the dun belonged to one of them. It was also pretty clear from all the shouting and pointing and knife-waving—pointing at the horse and knife-waving at her—that there were questions about why the horse was here.

She watched the exchange for a moment longer, and then decided to step in. Because all the pointing and waving wasn't resolving things. Frankie jerked away from He's Proud and ducked away from Knife's hand as he grabbed at her in an attempt to keep her away from the Oglála warriors.

"Hova'åhane! Ne-náestse." 'No! Come here.' She looked to the Oglála man holding the knife. Beckoned for him to follow as she walked toward the mouse-colored pony in the pen. To her surprise, and more than a little to her relief, he followed her. It didn't surprise her at all that Knife and He's Proud moved quickly to walk beside her, staying close to her.

When she reached the pen's gate, Frankie motioned to the Oglála man and led him into the pen. The dun horse emerged from the shadows of the barn doorway, his ears up. She motioned for the warrior, pointing him to the dun horse. He eyed her for a moment, studying her, and then turned to the horse.

The Oglála warrior reached his hand to the horse, spoke quietly. The Indian pony moved to his hand; his ears forward, snuffling, reaching with his nose. The warrior stroked the horse's neck and his shoulder. His hand trailed down and stopped next to the wound.

Frankie turned, looking for He's Proud, needing his help, thinking that she didn't want to spend a lot of time with the double translation right now. He's Proud was already in the pen, right behind her.

"You say the words to him, now. Tell him the horse came to me. That he found my home because he was sick and he needed my help." She waited while He's Proud talked and the Oglála warriors listened. Everything was quieting, settling.

"See here? See where he was wounded?" Frankie squatted down, placed her hand on the dun's chest, tracing the wound up and along his shoulder. "The wound was deep inside him and the muscles were dying. Rotting. So I've been taking care of him. I've been waiting for his warrior to come and find him. When he's healed, he should go home with his warrior."

The Oglála warrior squatted down next to her; he touched the stitches; his fingers traced the length of the cut. He stood then, staring at Frankie once again; Frankie stood up and stared back at him. Waiting to see what would happen.

She had done the best she could—she had told him the truth about the horse. And now, she was standing before the warrior, thinking that the truth ought to mean the same, no matter what language you spoke. And apparently, it did, because just a few minutes before, he had been ready to do her some real harm. But now, she saw his face soften.

Knife stepped into the pen; he started speaking quietly to the man who knew this mouse-colored horse, and He's Proud squatted down next to Frankie, translating Knife's words. She listened as Knife told his Oglála brothers about the white soldier and the snake-bite, telling them that the other horse-soldiers had known he was dying. So the soldiers found Fire Heart Child and she healed the man from the snake's poison. She helped him and he had lived. Now, this horse had found her and *he* was healing.

And that was the moment when the tension in the dun horse's pen cleared; that was when all the warriors relaxed and started grinning and nodding. The anger was gone as quickly as it had erupted.

Frankie decided it was time to turn the talk to other things. Safe things; things that would make people smile. She leaned close to He's Proud, knowing what she wanted to do and asking him for the right words. She whispered to him, knowing exactly what would help now that the shouting was over. He's Proud spoke softly, telling her what to say.

"Na-haeana. Na-mésėhe-tano. Ne-haeana-he?" 'I'm hungry. I want to eat. Are you hungry?'

She left the pen and walked around to the front of the barn; she swung one of the doors open and pointed to the dressed deer hanging from the rafters. Both the Cheyenne and the Oglála men broke into grins. The knives came out again, but this time, there was laughter. Frankie went to the rope, beckoning to the men, showing them how the rope ran to the pulley and to the hocks of the buck.

As she started untying the end of the rope, one of the Oglála men took the rope from her hands and lowered the carcass. Two men reached for the buck as it came down; they had their knives slicing, and in a matter of minutes, they had the hide stripped from the carcass and began the butchering.

A couple of the warriors headed toward the windmill pond; they picked the place for a cookfire and when they started gathering wood, Frankie beckoned to Knife. She headed to the stack of firewood along the side of the stone-room and Knife went with her, walking beside her with his hand on her shoulder. Staying close.

As some of the men began threading strips of venison onto sticks and propping them against rocks, leaning them over the fire, Frankie headed to her house. Grease from the meat was spitting in the flames by the time she returned with the big wash-pan packed with a pitcher of Blossom's milk, tin cups, biscuits and two apple pies.

She offered the men cups of the rich Jersey milk which, to her surprise, they didn't like at all. But when she handed them another crock of butter and the biscuits, they grinned at her, nodding, remembering the butter on the cornbread; they started slathering the butter on the biscuits. Then they started slathering it on their venison strips and they liked that even more.

But it was the slices of apple pie that pleased them the most. As soon as she started handing pieces to the warriors, apple pie became their new favorite food; they were laughing and patting her shoulders and arms, while they ate their way through the two pies—pies that Frankie had made, anticipating the Dunbars' possible visit the next day. She didn't mind though; she could make more pies. But she might never again have the chance to see Cheyenne and Oglála warriors having what she figured to be their first taste of apple pie.

While the men were busy eating the venison and the biscuits and the pie, Frankie sat down beside Knife. He's Proud settled down on her other side, translating for her, telling her what the men were saying about the food and about her home here in the hidden valley. They were talking about the vé'ho é-måheo'o, 'the white-man's house' where she lived. They were talking about all her horses, but mostly about the ho-haa mo'éhė-no'ha, the 'very-much-horses' and her stallion.

But mostly, from what Frankie could hear, they were talking about hunting and shooting. And they were laughing at each other, telling stories on each other, poking fun at each other. And to her mind, nothing about the time around the fire was all that different from the meals at the cookfire on the prairie with her Lieutenant's troop.

As the men went on with their talk, He's Proud leaned closer to her and explained about the uproar concerning the dun horse. It had belonged to the father of the Oglála chief named Šungíla Hóta, 'Gray Fox', He's Proud said. His father had been scouting for buffalo, and a war party of Pawnee had surprised them. The Pawnee killed Gray Fox's father and the other Oglála men, and they took all the Oglála horses—the mouse-colored dun horse among them. Today, when Gray Fox saw his father's horse, he believed the Pawnee had given her the horse; the Oglála men thought that she must be a friend of the Pawnee. *That* was the reason for the anger.

To Frankie, it all made perfect sense—the shouting, the tension, the knives pulled from sheaths. And now that she knew Gray Fox's story, she told her own story—the mouse-colored horse's story. She told He's Proud how the dun horse had come to her meadow one night, traveling with a herd of other horses that lived here. She talked about the gaping wound across the stallion's chest and she explained how she had been doctoring it. She told He's Proud she hadn't known where it came from or who it belonged to, but she had taken care of it anyway—because it was the right thing to do—because it was wounded and sick.

She told He's Proud to tell Gray Fox he could take the horse with him now, or he could leave it here and she would keep doctoring it. Then Gray Fox could come back for his father's horse after it was healed.

He's Proud turned and spoke to the Oglála warrior, but he wasn't using Cheyenne words—he was using Gray Fox's language. Frankie listened to the Lakotah words, hearing a rhythm different than the Cheyenne language. That the words were different didn't surprise her, but the flow and the sounds were different, the inflections were different too, and that intrigued her.

Across the fire, Gray Fox had been listening to the story. The other men had stopped talking and were sitting silently. They too, had been listening to what the little white girl had to say about the buffalo horse. When He's Proud finished the story, Gray Fox turned to look at her. Frankie tried to hold his stare and couldn't; she dropped her eyes and felt her hands beginning to tremble.

And then, to her surprise, He's Proud leaned down close to her and spoke softly into her ear. He told her she had done well—she had offered a gift to the Oglála warrior and when she looked down, she showed the men she was humble. That was a good thing, a polite thing, he said. It honored the one who was receiving. He patted her shoulder, told her she was becoming a good Cheyenne-girl.

It was a relief to Frankie, finding out she had managed to blunder into a behavior that pleased the men around the fire. Her hands quit trembling and she took in a deep breath. There were lines here—certain things that *should* be done and certain things that should *never* be done—just the same as there were lines at the fort. There had been an Army culture she had to learn; now, there were Cheyenne and Oglála cultures she needed to learn. Beside her, Knife shifted position; he nudged her arm and put his hand on her knee.

"E-peva'e." He told her. 'It was good.'

Knife spoke to her and He's Proud translated. Her brother told the story of their battle with a Pawnee band two days ago. They had been looking for a buffalo herd when they saw the Pawnee riding in the hills, so they left off their hunt and followed the Pawnee, watching to see where they camped. That night, the Cheyenne and Oglála warriors had 'painted and danced for war', Knife said.

"Yesterday, we attacked them and we taught them what true warriors can do." He paused for a moment, and Frankie realized that Cheyenne story-telling allowed for dramatic pauses just like white-man stories did. "We sent the stinking Pawnee running back to their homes of dung-and-filth." He leaned closer to Frankie and she saw the corner of his lip lift in disgust as he told her his opinion about the Pawnee way of life. "They live in dark mud-and-stick tunnels like moles and river-rats."

The warriors laughed at his words; agreeing, and snorting their disgust. 'How easy it had been,' they said, and *their* lips lifted in sneers too.

"The stupid Pawnee need to stay in their mud-lodges where they will be safe. Where their women can protect them. Now, we will hunt again," Knife told her. "We scout for a buffalo herd so our people can hunt. Our families need the buffalo meat for the winter."

He told her there had not been enough buffalo. The Cheyenne and their brothers, the Oglála, were hunting together because the people of their villages would all need more meat and robes for the cold months.

Frankie looked at Knife with her crooked little grin, knowing that what she said next would amuse him. She asked He's Proud to translate.

"Tell Knife that I need him to do a trade with him. Because I need him to make something for me."

Knife listened to He's Proud's words and then turned to her. Looking amused, just as she expected.

"What do you have to trade, Little Sister?" He looked around the fire, pretending to be astounded; making the men laugh. "What does this little-white-girl have to trade with such a great Cheyenne warrior like me?"

Frankie knew he was teasing her; it was the same tone that Dr. Gannon at the fort would have used when he made deals with her. She stood up, gave him a glare—a teasing glare—and trotted over to the house while the warriors busted up laughing. She crossed the porch and ducked into the kitchen door, knowing the Indians were watching her—they were waiting to see what the little-white-girl was up to. She returned to the fire with her trade items clenched in her hand. She held out her hand to Knife, showing him four wolf-teeth and the three bullets.

Knife took them from her and started examining them; Frankie sat down, wedging herself into her place between him and He's Proud.

"I want you to make these bullets into a necklace. Like the one you have." She reached to tap the single lead ball he wore on a braided rawhide strip around his neck, the one from the buck he had seen her shoot. "But I want the wolf-teeth in it too." She told him she thought her fight with the wolves was a good thing to remember, and she wanted to have the teeth and the bullets as a necklace.

Knife showed the other men what she had given him and several of them moved to study what he held in his palm. Knife gave her a funny look, squinting at her. Then he asked her for the story.

So she told the story of how she found the dead mule and how the two wolves had risen up from behind it, intent on killing her. When she pointed at the wolf-hides by the kitchen doorway, Gray Fox and another man stood up and walked to the kitchen porch. They stayed by the kitchen door for a few minutes and when they returned, they brought the two hides with them.

The wolf-hides made a couple of trips around the fire, passing from hand to hand as the men examined them. There were a lot of murmurings and exchanges and Frankie was beginning to think she had asked for something that wasn't right. She asked He's Proud, but to her surprise, he ignored her and continued speaking with the warriors.

Frankie waited, listening to the exchange, a little confused and more than a little worried; she could understand almost nothing, but it seemed to be a serious discussion. Finally, impatient with the waiting and annoyed at being ignored, she pushed at He's Proud. But it was Knife who responded to her, laughing at her impatience; He's Proud was laughing along with him as he began translating once again.

"I will make this necklace you want. It's good medicine for you. I don't need a trade from you," Knife told her, smiling and patting her knee.

"But I *have* something to trade. I can give you buffalo."

Everyone went silent. Neither the Cheyenne nor the Oglála moved.

"Tosa'a?" 'Where?' Knife was eyeing her.

"Tseohe." 'Here.' Frankie knew the exact word and she didn't wait for He's Proud's help.

"Tone'še?" 'How far?' Knife spoke again.

"A'e. Kahkése." 'Near. A short distance.' She used some of the words she had heard earlier, over by the porch.

All the warriors sat up a little straighter. Listening, now. The laughter and teasing had stopped.

"Tóhkomo?" 'A few?' Knife looked a little unsure, a bit confused. Frankie knew he probably thought she had seen a few buffalo in some valley. Or maybe, he thought she was teasing, like a child would do.

She turned to He's Proud—needing his help, needing more words now. She told him what she needed to say and He's Proud hesitated for a moment, glancing around at the men. Then he gave her the words, speaking softly to her. Frankie repeated them, telling the warriors what they needed to know.

"Haesto. Haesto. No'ka-måhtóhtoa-måhtóhtó-nó'e 'Many. Many. Thousands.'

He's Proud was staring at her, still unsure. All the men eyed her for a moment. Then they looked to Knife—because he knew her best.

Knife leaned forward, looking into Frankie's eyes; he spoke to her gently, asked her if she was playing. Asked if she was teasing them. He patted her thigh and told her that if she was having fun and teasing them, then it was okay. It was good for her to tease them. Because they had teased her. They had all been laughing.

Frankie stood up, shaking her head, suddenly upset that they thought she would play at something so important. She knew how important the buffalo were; she knew the herd meant food for their families. She spoke to He's Proud, asking him to tell Knife she wasn't playing a little girl's game; she told him to tell the men she wanted their families to have more meat for the cold months.

"Tell them I understand it's important." She knew she was almost shouting. "Tell them I can show them where a great herd is. They can see the buffalo for themselves."

She turned as He's Proud started the translation, heading to Rock's pen, breaking into a trot, hurrying away so the warriors wouldn't see her tears of frustration and embarrassment. She shook her head, trying to shake off her tears, and her fears—fears that the men didn't know that she understood the buffalo were important.

Frankie could hear the discussion back at the fire, and she knew they were listening as He's Proud explained; she also knew they were watching her as she went into Rock's pen.

Rock stood quietly as she bridled him and when she pulled down on the reins, he lowered his head like the gentleman he was, waiting patiently as she boosted herself onto his neck. He raised his head at the right moment, lifting her so she could slide down his neck and onto his back. She gave him a quick pat on the neck, whispered her thanks to him, because he was a warhorse and he was taking care of his rider. Because he had done it before.

And she was also breathing a sigh of relief, thankful that it had gone smoothly. Because there had been other times when she'd messed up the timing and ended up flopping to the ground on her bottom. Today though, it had gone well; she hadn't ended up on the ground with all the warriors watching.

She turned Rock around, leaned down to unlatch the gate and sent him out of the pen and toward the track at the meadow's entrance. If they had been doubting her before, now suddenly, the warriors of the Cheyenne and Oglála understood she was serious. They were on their feet, catching up their horses and swinging onto their backs; they were laughing and whooping, yipping in anticipation. The painted ponies started dancing, whirling and swirling and spinning in the meadow grass, kicking up dirt and sending dust curling high into the air.

Rock started dancing too, pulling at the reins and pawing at the ground. Frankie knew he was caught up in the excitement; she grinned, because now the men were ready to follow her anywhere if she was, indeed, going to lead them to thousands and thousands of buffalo.

They turned their horses and swept up the track behind her, following her; they thundered out of the meadow with Knife on his pinto, riding close at her side. Riding within arm's reach. Frankie grinned, knowing her Cheyenne brother was being protective, ready to catch his little white sister if she had trouble staying on her mount.

As they surged out of the meadow and onto the grasslands, Frankie was thinking fast; she wasn't sure the Lookout Hill would still offer a view of the herd—because the herd had been nearly out of sight the night before. Thinking there would be a better view from a hill further north, she led the warriors around the base of the Lookout Hill and onward, through several long valleys.

After traveling a little less than a mile, she turned Rock up the slope of a long, steep hill. Dust and dirt flew as she and the eight warriors reached the crest and pulled their horses to a sudden stop. She swung her arm to the north, pointing right toward the buffalo herd across the rolling hills.

She stared and gulped in a breath. Because there to the north, out among the far hills, there was nothing. Nothing. Only the hills and the far-away grasses. The herd wasn't there; the buffalo were nowhere to be seen.

The hills beyond were bare; the slopes where the herd *should* be, stood empty of everything except the grasses and the afternoon sunlight. *No dark cloth. No smaller dark clumps. No dark specks. Nothing.*

Frankie stayed still on Rock's back, squinting in the bright sunlight, scanning the faraway hills, desperate to see something, desperate to see any sign of the dark blanket of the buffalo herd. She felt her stomach knotting up, wondering if the Cheyenne and Oglála men would think this was her idea of a joke. She wondered if they would believe they had fallen for the little-white-girl's silly little trick. She started wondering if the warriors would use their knives on her, or if they'd just beat her with their hands and fists. *Or maybe, they'll just decide to shoot me full of arrows.*

The warriors sat there beside her, all eight of them sitting there on their ponies with the wind silently sifting through their feathers and fringes. Looking out to the north hills where she had pointed. To her surprise, they weren't showing any signs of being angry; they weren't snorting in disgust or glaring at her. Oddly enough, it didn't seem like they were even doubting her.

They had believed her when she stomped off to her horse, ready to prove she wasn't a child playing a game. They had trusted her and followed her. And now, here they were, sitting on the hilltop on their tough and wiry horses, their eyes fixed on the land to the north. Their hair and the manes of their horses lifting and flitting in the midday breeze; the eagle feathers and hawk feathers and raven feathers were all fluttering as the Cheyenne and Oglála warriors sat beside her, still trusting her. Even though the great buffalo herd—thousands and thousands of them—was nowhere to be seen. *Cripes! How does a whole goddamned herd just disappear in one goddamned night?*

She stayed quiet, but she had a lot of words swirling around in her brain at the moment—swearwords. Choice swearwords. Cusswords she had heard from the stable loft at the fort, cusswords the troopers below her had been using.

For a moment, she wondered if she said a few of the choice words out loud, right there on the crest of the hill, if He's Proud would be able to translate them. And then she wondered if the Cheyenne and Oglála had swearwords. And she wondered, for a short moment, whether He's Proud would teach her the Cheyenne words if she asked him. Because she didn't know if little Indian kids were prohibited from saying swearwords like little white kids were.

Then, her mind returned to the high hill and her companions sitting on their ponies beside her. Her mind returned to the far-off, grass-covered hills—the hills now barren of buffalo. The hills with no buffalo grazing on their slopes. Anywhere.

The black-and-white pinto shifted position, side-stepping closer; she felt Knife's knee press against her leg. She glanced at him, feeling a sense of relief, knowing her brother was right beside her. He, like the others, was watching to the north. Watching out to the far hills. Eyes searching. All of them, scanning the land where she had pointed, like maybe they thought a big buffalo herd was suddenly going to appear.

Frankie stayed as she was, sitting on the broad back of her liver-chestnut warhorse, there in the midst of the buff-colored grasses on the top of a high hill, under the prairie-blue sky. Nervous. Sick to her stomach. Confused. Trying to appear confident. Because the last thing she wanted was to look like she was doubting herself. Beyond that—beyond trying to appear confident—she had no idea what else she could do. Because this was a strange predicament.

Because the buffalo she had been watching for several weeks had vanished completely. All of them. Every last one of them. She didn't know where they were. Or how to get them back. And she didn't know how to explain it to the warriors beside her. She groaned inwardly, wondering what she'd look like if the warriors left her here on the hilltop, stuck full of arrows. *Probably, I'll end up looking a little like Aunt Sarah's pincushion.*

She was pretty sure it wouldn't happen, because she *had* shared her food with them. Because they had, after all, sat at her cookfire, eating her venison and her apple pies. Surely that friendly act would count for something. And thinking a little more about it, she was pretty sure Knife wouldn't let anyone hurt her. Because he *was* her brother, after all. And he *had* protected her earlier over the big misunderstanding about the dun-horse.

But still, these wonderful men might be more than a little disappointed in her for getting their hopes up. And *that* thought, the thought of disappointing these new friends, was making her feel a little nauseated.

There was a sudden movement among the warriors on the far side of Knife, and when Frankie looked, several of the warriors were standing on the backs of their ponies. She stared, shook her head, and stared some more. It had been such a simple and subtle thing for them to go from sitting on their ponies to suddenly standing on their backs. It had been a quiet, effortless shift of position—they had simply put a hand on the withers of their horses and leaned forward. And as simple as that, they were standing up. It had been so casual and easy that Frankie wasn't sure how they managed it. And right then and there, she decided she was going to have to learn to do that.

Beside her she saw Knife eyeing her, giving her a funny look, as if he knew exactly what she was thinking. And then, one of his hands was moving to his pinto's withers, and the other was reaching to grip her arm. The next thing she knew, she was standing on Rock's back and Knife was standing behind her, keeping her steady.

She stood there on Rock's back, feeling Knife's arm circling her ribs, keeping her back pressed against his chest. She stared out across the land, surprised at the changes in the landscape, astonished at the new and better view that an extra few feet of height offered. Understanding exactly why the warriors had shifted their positions.

All the men were standing on their horses by then, and all of them were watching the land to the north. Still watching; still patient. Apparently, Frankie decided, they were still trusting the little-white-girl. Apparently, they were confident she wasn't playing a game and teasing them.

They all stayed as they were, surveying the world, standing high in the prairie air with the prairie-breeze curling and swirling around them. Feathers flitted and twirled; manes and tails rippled and flowed. Time passed. And still, the men watched. Patient and calm. Waiting.

Frankie watched. Losing patience. Starting to fidget and fret. Worrying. She felt Knife's grip tighten around her chest. His hand stroked her arm, reassuring her. Calming her. Because for some reason, he wasn't worried; because he seemed to know something that she didn't. Frankie tilted her head up, looking at him, wondering what he knew.

"Don't worry, Fire Heart Child. The herd is there. You spoke the truth. We know." It was He's Proud; he was speaking to her, standing on his own horse's back on the far side of Knife's pinto. He knew something too. They all knew.

"Nėheohe!" 'There!' It was Gray Fox, the Oglála warrior. He pointed. A tiny dark blotch appeared in a cut between two hills. Frankie squinted, her eyes following along Knife's outstretched arm, looking toward the hills where his fingers pointed. She stared into the distance. *Yes! There! Nėheohe!*

She glanced up, looking to Knife again, this time, seeing delight on his face.

"E peva'e." He looked down at her. Smiling. 'It is good.'

"E peva'e." She repeated the words and nodded, looking out to the faraway buffalo herd. She felt his hand squeeze her shoulder.

"Haáhe, Ho-esta Hesta Ka-ėškóne. Hotóá'e. Ésevone. E peva'e."
He gave her the new words, his smile grew. 'Yes, Fire Heart Child.
The buffalo. The buffalo herd. It is good.'

For the next half hour, Frankie and her eight warriors watched
as the tiny dark blotch grew. They watched it grow, spreading out
slowly, ever so slowly, until it became a large dark blotch—a broad
patch of dark cloth, spreading out along the hillsides and valleys.
They watched as the front-edge of the brown cloth slowly rippled
along with the grass, moving up and along a hillside. Watching the
buffalo. The *hotóá'e*. Watching the buffalo herd. The *ésevone*. Then
the buffalo herd began to spread across two hillsides. Then it spread
further, covering the slopes of even more hills. *The dark cloth. And
dark clumps. Little dark specks everywhere.*

Frankie breathed a very quiet sigh of relief. She squinted, staring at the dark ripple of the herd, growing gradually as more buffalo moved into view. Step by step. The dark herd—thousands and
thousands of bulls and cows and calves—was moving and spreading
across the grasses, in and around the cuts and draws. Slow, very slow;
calm and steady. *No'ka-måhtóhtoa-måhtóhtó-nó'e*. Thousands. She
smiled, letting the words roll around her tongue. *Haesto no'ka-
måhtóhtoa-måhtóhtó-nó'e*. Many thousands.

There was a beauty in the deep blackish-brown herd of great
animals as it was growing, flowing—slowly blotting out the ripple
of the grass. Consuming the prairie; covering the Sand Hills, wading through the valleys and the meadows and the slopes. Those animals—those great dark beasts—were part of the prairie, part of its life
and breath. Its history and its story.

Frankie leaned back against the warm chest of her brother, gripping his forearm with both her hands. Stood there with him, relaxed
and happy. Content now. Proud. Knowing that *this* was a good gift
for these warrior-brothers of hers. *This* was what they had been seeking; *this* herd, this ésevone, would feed their families. *Haesto no'ka-
måhtóhtoa-måhtóhtó-nó'e! Many thousands!*

She felt Knife move and she looked up at him; he was grinning down at her, looking at her like he knew exactly what she was
thinking.

And suddenly, she felt other eyes upon her. Beyond Knife, she saw Gray Fox, the Oglála warrior; he was standing on his pony while the prairie wind twirled the feathers hanging with his braids. He was looking at her; looking into her. His eyes quiet and calm. Looking at her as if he knew everything about her; looking at her as if he understood her better than she understood herself.

She held his stare; she looked into his eyes and realized that he *did* know everything about her—just like he knew everything about the prairie and the grass, the water and the sand, the rocks and trees, the horses of his ancestors, and the buffalo that fed his people. She suddenly realized that she understood him, and that she was starting to understand his people. He nodded, ever so slightly, and then looked away.

They all dropped down on their ponies' backs then; they turned their horses down the slope of the hill, going back the way they had come. There had been no spoken word, no signal or sign given, but all nine riders moved in the same instant—Frankie and her eight warriors.

To Frankie it seemed as smooth as any movement the Cavalry troops had ever made on the maneuvers field; it was all of the same thought, all of the same energy. They had all turned their horses in unison and were heading back to her meadow.

It was as they approached the river and the rows of apple trees that Frankie realized everything about her day was changing once again. Because once they reached the track that led up and over and into her valley, the warriors pulled to a halt. Once again, there were no words, no command given. No discussion. They had brought her home to her valley. And now, they would leave her.

Knife leaned sideways from the back of his pinto, reached and touched her shoulder.

"Na semahe." 'My Sister.' He spoke the words softly. Looked into her eyes. Nodded. "Nė-sta-vå-hóse-vóomåtse." 'I will see you again.' And then he turned his black-and-white pinto to follow the others.

He left her behind. Leaving her there, sitting on Rock on the track to her meadow. He and his band of warriors disappeared into the grasses and the brush and branches along the riverside trail, leaving only the sounds of the rustling leaves behind them.

Frankie watched her eight warriors riding away. Single-file. Quietly; steadily. He's Proud had told her they had come from the east, scouting for buffalo. She had shown them the great herd far to the north. Now, they were riding west-by-northwest, traveling upriver. They would ride into the rolling hills—they would go deep into the Sand Hills, far out to the lands where their families were waiting for word of the buffalo herd that they would follow and hunt—buffalo that would give them food for the long winter.

She waited, watching the path of the North Loup River, eyeing the breaks in the tree line, watching for the open places where the trail showed itself, free from the cover of trees. She caught sight of them once more as they followed the trail up a low slope. They crossed a long ridge, riding their painted ponies through the fringe of the grassy hilltop, and then they began their descent down the far side of the hill. Still moving quietly, steadily. And then they were gone. They vanished like the soft-swirling heat-vapors curling up from the ground, twisting among the grasses and floating away, as weightless as whispers.

Frankie stared and shook her head, looking again, wondering for a moment if the day had really happened; wondering if it had all been a dream. Wondering whether there had really been eight Cheyenne and Oglála warriors in her meadow. Wondering if her brother Knife had really found her.

Frankie rode back to her valley alone, feeling lonely for the first time in a long time. She followed the track up and around and down, and when she rode into the quiet of her home meadow, the smell of the dying cookfire and slow-roasting meat tickled at her nostrils. The last of the roasting venison remained on the spit above the cooling embers.

Laughing Girl and Matilda greeted her at the base of the track, racing in circles around Rock, grinning their dog-grins. She grinned back at them, laughing when Matilda cut loose with a string of excited yips. It was a rare thing for the little collie-dog to make noise like that, and Frankie decided that maybe the dogs were happy to have the meadow returning to normal. *Or maybe, they're just hoping for a share of the meat still on the spit.*

She slipped down from Rock's back, pulled the bridle from his head, releasing him to graze in the meadow. She walked over to the fire and lifted the haunch of venison from the spit. As she walked to the house, she pulled a couple of pieces of meat loose from the roast and tossed them to the dogs. The wolfhound gulped hers down without a tooth ever touching it; Matilda snatched her piece from the air, chewed and swallowed, and then trotted off toward the house, her pretty little collie-tail waving in the air.

Frankie followed the collie's path, grinning, knowing exactly what she had on her mind. Sure enough, by the time she reached the porch, Matilda already had her chick nesting between her front legs, nestled into her white ruff; she was busy licking and grooming it, and the chick—soggy little mess that it was—sat there obediently submitting to the washing, struggling to right itself each time the collie-tongue toppled it sideways.

As she went into the kitchen, Frankie could hear the late afternoon bird-songs coming from the treetops around the meadow. And singing right along with them was the resident mockingbird. He was full into his business of taunting every bird in the valley, mocking them by singing their personal songs right back at them.

Frankie listened for a moment, wondering once again whether the other birds took it as a personal insult, or whether they saw it as a compliment. She decided that for the most part, birds seemed to be pretty philosophical about things; they probably just rolled their eyes when the mockingbird started up. It'd be like birds, she decided, for them to take all the teasing and copy-catting in stride.

She went to the pantry and looked into the basket of apples on the counter; she selected a couple of handfuls and started peeling them. Planning dinner for the Dunbars' visit the next day. If they came. If harvest was done. Fresh bread, she decided, along with reheated spit-roasted venison, roasted turnips, sweet potatoes and parsnips. And two fresh apple pies.

"Where do you think Daniel Kinison got all the logs for these buildings? I haven't found any stands of trees that these logs could have come from. Not within ten miles of here anyway." Frankie lifted the pot of hot coffee from the stove and leaned to fill Everett's cup. She walked around the table to fill Ida's cup, and then her own.

"Oh Honey, they didn't come from anywhere close to here. Three big, long-haired Swede brothers had some kind of sawmill set up along the Niobrara River," Everett sipped at his cup, then reached for the plate of pie that Ida handed him. "Way up north and west of here. They were contracted to cut and deliver timber for the government—for a string of forts the Army planned to build. A Fort Sully, up on the Missouri, was one of them. One or two others closer than that, I think.

"The brothers had their mill set up and they knew well enough how to handle logs. And how to build with them. I guess they did the same thing back in Sweden. Anyways, they were in the midst of a stall with the government, as to whether Fort Sully would need more buildings, or maybe, the fort was going to be moved to another location. And there was something about building onto Fort Randall too. I think the War in the South was causing a lot of the hold-up. But Daniel came across the Swedes down to Fort Cottonwood and got to talking with them. Ended up contracting with them and had them hauling in loads of logs all winter long."

"That's a lot of logs to haul, especially with the winter snows." Frankie was clearing plates from the table with Ida.

"Well, I'll tell you, those big Swedes knew how to use the snow." Everett was drinking his coffee, thinking back over what he had heard. "They cut the logs to the size Daniel wanted, when they were up at their mill. Then used teams of oxen—long hitches of big black oxen—to sled the loads across the snow. Those big Swedes would stay here for a few days and help Daniel set them into place. They'd head north again and be back the next week with more logs."

"How far did they have to haul them?"

"It was seventy or eighty miles, I expect. Maybe more. But it didn't matter to them because of the hold-up with the government contracts." Everett pointed over toward the smaller log-building.

"The first thing those Swede brothers did was build that little log house you call the Barracks. That's where they stayed whenever they came here. When the weather warmed, they used a big, heavy, four-wheel log-truck with iron tires on the wheels four inches wide so it wouldn't bog down in the softer soils. I saw it once. Those brothers had six black oxen hitched to it. Claimed it could carry seven tons."

"That had to be a lot of money for the logs, plus all the hauling." Frankie reached for Ida's plate, dishing up another piece of pie.

"Daniel came from money," Everett sipped at his coffee and kept talking. "Family money. He had trained as an engineer of some sort. I'm thinking maybe construction engineering. And he had some type of architectural schooling too. But he really just wanted to work with his hands. I think Lillian came from money too. Ida and me always thought Lillian married Daniel expecting he'd drop the whole idea of homesteading at some point. He never did, though. He was *so* proud of this place. And he was so happy building it. He was sure if he built everything just right, Lillian would end up loving it." Everett paused, thinking. His mind on the past. "She never did like it, though." He took a slow drink from his cup.

"Anyway, those Swede brothers knew how to get things done. Seems they built plenty of log houses back in Sweden, and by damn, they were good at it. Daniel kept coming up with more ideas for buildings and they just kept bringing more loads. Those big brutes barely spoke a word of English, but somehow, they understood Daniel and what he wanted.

"There was only one disagreement that I ever heard about. The Swedes thought the fireplaces should be in the center of the buildings and Daniel didn't like the idea. They went around about it, and finally Daniel relented. Later on, he told me he was glad he had.

"It was probably a year later that the Swedes gave up on the government contract. Likely because of the hold-up on the forts. But Daniel said they started having trouble with some Indians up near their mill. They knew they were being watched and they got a bit spooked—probably worried about losing their long blond hair to scalpings. But whatever the reason, they moved on.

"Daniel said they talked about leaving everything and just pulling out. I believe that Daniel bought those two gray mares off them and at one time, he said something once about wanting to buy some of those black oxen, but I guess that didn't happen. Daniel heard that they headed out toward Fort Laramie, with an eye toward working on some of the forts being built along the Bozeman Trail. Later, he heard something about them going on to California. But wherever they ended up, they were a big part of building this place."

Everett talked a while longer about the building of the homestead and about Daniel's plans, but Frankie knew it wouldn't be long before the conversation took off in a different direction. Because she had seen both Everett and Ida casting glances to the windmill-pond across the meadow, eyeing the cookfire with its spit. So Frankie waited, offering up nothing.

And then, sure enough, the conversation about the logs and the Swedes came to a stop and for a moment, Everett sat drumming his fingers on the table.

"Frankie, we're worried about what that campfire over by your windmill means. There's a lot of signs that Indians were here. Did you have trouble?"

"No, Sir. Some Cheyenne people I know came to visit yesterday. I knew them from back when I stayed at the fort. Even before I was at the fort."

Frankie eased into the subject. She had thought about it last evening, because she was pretty sure the subject would come up; she had decided not to go into much detail about the visit from her Cheyenne and Oglála brothers. Because usually, white folks had their minds made up about Indians. And given what she had heard from most of the people in the wagon party, and from a lot of the soldiers at the fort, the subject could get tense.

279

"You have to be very careful with Indians, Honey." Ida spoke up. "You can't allow them to just hang around your home. It's not safe for anyone, Frankie. And certainly not for you being alone here."

"That's not what's going on here, Ida." Frankie turned to Ida, working to keep her voice steady and quiet. Knowing there was a real danger lurking below the surface of the conversation—handling this the wrong way could mean that the Dunbars, the Reverend Austin, and others in the region might decide she shouldn't be allowed to live alone. Not with Indians showing up at her place.

"They may seem friendly at first," Everett stepped in. "They can turn on you in an instant. Even if they're *acting* friendly. And they're all thieves. They'll start taking things from you. Everyone knows they'll steal you blind."

"Everett, these men are my friends. They take care of me; they've *always* watched out for me." Frankie watched Everett; she saw that his jaw was set. Looking back at Ida, she saw that her hands were clasped tightly together. Their minds were already made up.

"They got you to feed them, didn't they? That's what the campfire was about." Everett was talking again, his voice urgent. "Next time they'll want more. Next time they'll start making demands."

"They just came for a visit," Frankie gave her answer, but she was already sure the Dunbars wouldn't hear her explanations. "They didn't ask anything of me. I offered them food because I wanted to give them a meal. Just like I have food on the table for you today. Just like we have dinner together when I'm at your place."

"Frankie. Those are *men. Grown* men. And you're a girl," Ida waded in again, speaking firmly, and Frankie could hear the fear beneath her words. "They can do things to you, Frankie, and you won't be able to stop them. You may want them to be your friends, but you don't understand what they can do. And you have no idea what they might be planning."

"Ida. These aren't just some Indians that wandered in to steal things. Or to get food. I've known these men longer than I've known you and Everett. Knife and He's Proud are brothers to me. They would never hurt me. And *no* one will ever hurt me if they're around.

They were just visiting me yesterday. They were just making sure that I'm safe."

Frankie watched Ida's face, searched her eyes for any sign of acceptance. She saw none. And Everett wasn't accepting any of it, either.

"Honey, these men are not like white-men. They want something different from you."

Everett's voice was a little louder and Frankie could hear rising anger in his words. She realized that in a moment, his objective would change—he would stop trying to reason with her. His fears would push him to fight for control and he would start requiring compliance. He had been a father to four children and his parenting instincts were bound to come forward.

So now, before it was too late, Frankie knew she had to break the pattern of their thoughts—of what they had been told to believe— or there would be a problem between them. And that would be the beginning of more problems. Because if any of the other settlers heard from the Dunbars about 'Indians hanging around her place', she'd have all kinds of problems.

"Everett. Like I said, these people are my *friends*. It doesn't matter whether they're white or not. They haven't hurt me or beat me. White-men did those things to me. Not one Cheyenne or Oglála man has *ever* laid a rough hand on me. And none of them would allow anyone else to treat me that way. They're part of my life. They're my brothers. And they're welcome to visit me here at my home, just the same as you are."

"Frankie?" Ida reached to touch her arm, patted it gently. Imploring her to understand. "Honey? What would your mother and father think of this?"

"Ida, my mother would have beaten me for having Cheyenne as friends as quick as she would have beaten me for having you two as friends. Or for any other reason she could come up with. As for my father, since you brought him into this, he'd be proud of my friendship with these people. He'd want to understand them and he'd like sitting at the fire and talking with them. He'd be happy that they protect me and watch out for me. I think it would ease his mind to know that I'm safer on my homestead because of them."

There was silence then. Everett and Ida sat quietly, and Frankie figured it had a lot to do with what she had said about her father. They had asked about her father's perspective, and in an odd way, that had actually been the undoing of their arguments. Because whenever her father had something to say on a subject, it was pretty much inarguable; it was rare that anyone could really contest her father's point of view, because he was always so precise when he laid out his opinion. 'Clear discernment and honest insight', he had called it. And it had just come in awfully handy.

Frankie waited, telling herself to stay quiet. Telling herself to give them time. She could tell the Dunbars were thinking about the situation and it seemed that maybe, just maybe, they were thinking a little differently. They still weren't comfortable with the friendship as she had described it, and they clearly weren't comfortable with Indians being on her place. But they had heard her words, and they had heard her father's words. And so far, they weren't rejecting them.

And it seemed clear that even if the subject changed, Everett and Ida would continue to mull things over. *Probably for the rest of the day. And probably on their drive home. And then, probably for the next week.*

She also knew there would be more conversations about it. *There'll have to be or it'll become a rift between us.* Because already, Frankie realized, there was tension growing in the kitchen—the silence was starting to harden.

And then, quite suddenly, everything changed—the tension faded as Matilda walked into the kitchen. Everyone turned to look at the tawny little collie-dog walking through the door, stepping carefully, holding her head high with her pretty little white muzzle tipped up. She was holding something in her mouth.

"Now, what's she up to?" Ida had her attention on the dog, her brows knit together, confused at the sight.

Frankie, though, knew exactly what was going on. Matilda had decided to show off her pride and joy to the visitors—she was walking across the room, her tail waving slowly, proudly. She put her pretty little muzzle into Frankie's lap and laid her chicken-baby gently into her waiting palms. The collie-dog stepped back, sat her little bottom down on the floor and smiled her toothy little dog-smile.

It wasn't the first time; it happened several times a day. Matilda had been feeling the maternal desire to show off her baby to admiring eyes, and Frankie knew exactly what to do. She thanked Matilda, and then she cuddled the little rooster-chick; she cooed over it, ooh-ed and ahh-ed over it, spoke to Matilda about the beauty of her baby. She handed it to Ida, and Ida followed Frankie's example. Across the table, Everett watched, more than a little confused.

After a few minutes, Matilda whined and Frankie took the chick and placed it on the floor in front of the tawny little collie-dog. Matilda lifted the chick carefully and gently; she turned, carried it outside and headed toward the sunny spot on the porch.

"What was *that* about?" Everett was still confused, but he was laughing.

"She's raising it as her puppy. Mrs. Swingle got tired of rescuing her clutch of chicks from Matilda and finally made a trade with her— she gave Matilda a single chick for her very own, on the condition that she'd leave the rest of her brood alone."

"I've never seen the like of it." Ida was laughing hard, wiping tears from her eyes. "But she *is* acting like it's a puppy and not a chick. How are you going to get it back to its mother?"

"I don't know that I will. I think it'll cause more problems if I try. The hen, the dog and all the chicks were exhausted from the back-and-forth that was going on. This seems to be the treaty they managed among themselves. So I'm thinking I should just lay low and ride this out. It isn't really my battle anyway."

"You'd never guess that things could be fine like that. But they seem to be doing just fine." Ida was still laughing.

They all watched the dog and her chick, lying in the warm sunlight in front of the door, napping in peace. And out in the front meadow, Mrs. Swingle was leading her brood around, clucking and chattering and chuckling, content with her own lively collection of clever little chicks.

Frankie knew the subject about the Indians was closed for the time being. There was no doubt in her mind there would be future discussions, but the tension was gone for now. Matilda and Mrs. Swingle had helped settle things, at least, for today.

Two weeks had passed and Frankie was sitting on the crest of the Lookout Hill, once again watching the buffalo herd. The ésevone. But today, she was deeply disappointed—because the scene out on the far hills was very different. There was no great herd anymore; there was no great dark cloth spreading across the far hills. Now, there were only small patches of dark cloth to be seen—just small clumps and clusters of buffalo that had stayed together through the hunt, or had come back together afterward. The great herd, the massive herd of no'ka-måhtóhtoa-måhtóhtó-nó'e', 'thousands and thousands', was gone.

The hunt, Frankie knew, must have happened the day before, and she was kicking herself for missing it. Annoyed because it has probably happened while she was spending the afternoon cleaning the alleyway of the barn. *Crap! The barn could have waited.*

Even though it would have been only a distant view through her spy-glass, she had wanted to see it. She had planned for it; she had been tracking the herd's movements each evening since her warriors had left, waiting to see when the warriors brought their families to the herd. She had watched for Cheyenne and Oglála families. It never occurred to her that she wouldn't spot them.

But they had been out there, somewhere. They had been there in the hills near the buffalo herd, and somehow, the Cheyenne and Oglála families must have circled around the herd. Because the hunters had turned the herd during their hunt, turning it and sending it back to the northwest. Probably, Frankie figured, to keep the buffalo away from the Pawnee lands to the east. Because, she knew, the Cheyenne and Oglála despised the Pawnee; they fought them at every opportunity and they would have no interest in sending the buffalo onto the lands where the Pawnee lived and roamed.

So now, the massive herd that had been gradually moving to the southeast, was farther to the northwest, close to where she had first seen it weeks ago. Twelve, maybe fifteen miles away. The hunt was over; the buffalo were done with their running; and now, the distant groups of buffalo—the clumps and clusters—were grazing quietly and gradually joining up again. Eventually, the way Frankie had things figured, they would become one massive herd again. Because all herd animals knew there was safety in numbers.

And even now, while she was watching through the evening, she could see the smaller clusters becoming bigger clumps. Little patches of dark cloth were becoming bigger patches of dark cloth.

Most of her interest though, was not on the faraway herds; her real interest was much closer. Because out to the north, and a little to the west of where she sat on the hilltop—some ten miles away—something very different was happening. There were buffalo up there, too, but they weren't moving and grazing. They were lying in the prairie grass—dozens and dozens of them were there, lying motionless.

Through the lens of her telescope, Frankie could see tiny figures moving around the fallen beasts; people were out there—her Cheyenne and Oglála people were out there on the grassy slopes. They were walking and riding and leading horses, moving back and forth among the fallen beasts, moving from one animal to another, doing the work that came after the hunt.

Frankie watched them, trying to soothe her broken heart—broken because she had missed the chance to see the hunt. Still breaking, because she was missing out on the aftermath of the hunt. Watching the tiny figures, she wondered about Knife and He's Proud. She wondered about Gray Fox, wishing that his father's buffalo horse had recovered enough to go with the warrior. *He could have hunted on his father's horse.*

She watched the faraway scene as the sun began settling down to the horizon. The Cheyenne and Oglála had found the great herd. They had turned the herd and they had their hunt. Frankie sighed, surrendering to the reality—she had missed it all. Now, the families of the warriors were finishing up their work for the day; they had been butchering and cooking and drying their meat. And tomorrow, they would continue their work.

Frankie spotted the dim glow of their distant fires as the evening deepened into twilight. She was surprised for a moment as she saw one of the fires growing in size, growing bigger than she expected. Much bigger. And then she recalled He's Proud's words; he told her the families would dance by the light of fires—they would dance, he had said, deep into the night.

'We will celebrate when the hunt is done, Fire Heart Child. And we will speak of how you called to the buffalo for our families. We will tell the story of your hilltop.' He had reached to squeeze her thigh, smiling at her as they had ridden down the hillside.

Now, Frankie was considering riding to the north. She wanted to go, to watch, to see everything that was happening. To see it up close. To be with her brothers and their families. *Just ten miles or so. I could ride out there tomorrow.*

She shook her head, clearing the thoughts from her mind. Because she wasn't at all sure about what might be welcomed by the Indians, or what might be considered an intrusion. She didn't want to insult these people and push into their lives. This hunt was their business; it was about their survival and comfort. It had nothing to do with a little-white-girl.

So Frankie decided to stay at her meadow and wait. She'd stay in her own life and leave the Cheyenne and Oglála people in theirs. She'd wait, because there was a chance that Knife and He's Proud would come for another visit. *Now that the hunt is done, maybe they'll come back. And maybe, now that the dun horse has had more time to heal, Gray Fox will come for him.*

And in the meantime, she decided, there were some things she could do to make everything more comfortable for her brothers. She pictured the cookfire beside the windmill pond where they all sat and talked and ate together. If they came back, she knew they would stay out beside the fire, because for whatever their reasons, they wanted nothing to do with her house or the other buildings. But she could make things more comfortable by the fire; she could show them that they were welcome at her home. *Just in case they come to visit again.*

The next morning, Frankie put harnesses on Sunny Jim, High Boy and Little Bub. She gathered up chains and three of the log-tongs that hung on the walls of the shop and two big canvas bags. She climbed up on Sunny Jim's broad back, took hold of Little Bub's lead-rope and headed upriver with Laughing Girl trotting ahead in her usual scouting position. Matilda trotted dutifully behind.

Today, up at the woodcutting camp, Frankie had business to tend to; she had a plan to teach herself the art of applying log-tongs to logs, and chains to log-tongs, and then hitching harnesses to the chains. She already knew how to work with ropes and chains on branches and limbs and small tree-trunks. Back when they had their woodcutting picnics, she and Everett had used ropes and chains to pull tree-trunks and branches from the mountain of wood.

It had been easy enough to wrap the ropes and chains around the trunks and branches and pull them free from the massive pile of wood in the river's cove. It had been only a short-distance to haul the wood out to the open grass beside the river where she and Everett had cut the branches and treetops.

But today, it was a different situation; she had no interest in hauling or cutting fenceposts or firewood. It was the large logs lying around the site that she was interested in—all the hefty trunks that had been left behind after the cutting and trimming. The eventual plan was for those big logs to be cut with two-man saws, and then split with wedges. But today, Frankie had other plans for three of them.

She wanted to drag three of those big logs to the meadow to use them as benches beside the cookfire. And she knew that dragging those stout logs over that distance—a little more than a mile—would require more than just a few wraps with a rope.

It would have to be a very different process, which was why she had harnessed three of the Shires. And that's why she brought the chains and the log-tongs. She wasn't at all sure she knew exactly how to do what she was planning. But she was pretty sure she could figure it out. She had never used the tongs before, but she had seen them used.

She'd seen men using them behind a team of horses a couple of times back in Indiana. Mostly though, she just remembered the end result of the process—the horses pulling and the logs dragging—because back then she had been more interested in running and playing around the woodlot with her cousins. She hadn't been watching all the fastening and the hitching and the team-work. And now on this bright and sunny morning way out in the Nebraska Territory, she was wishing she had paid more attention to the whole log-securing process.

Once at the woodcutting site, Frankie practiced setting the tongs into a few of the fenceposts still stacked in the grassy glade. And then she spent some time playing at being a horse. After dragging fenceposts around in the grass for a while—and after some stumbling and tripping, and some sudden jerks and jarring halts—she learned there were certain angles and lifts necessary for a log-hitch that were very different from the angles of a wagon-hitch. Without enough lift, the front of the fencepost would catch and ram against everything in its path. And without the right angle to the traces on the harness, the pull on the collar and hames would be hard on the horse.

Satisfied with her practice session with the fenceposts, Frankie turned her attention to the heavy logs. She walked among the branch-bared tree-trunks, studying them, sizing them. Picturing them beside her cookfire. Finally, she selected three that suited her—three that were about eight feet long and stout enough to work as benches.

Frankie did a fair amount of positioning and repositioning with the hitches and the harnesses, and after some hints from High Boy, Sunny Jim and Little Bub as to how they preferred things, she hooked the trace-chains to the log-chains and did a few short pulls.

Satisfied with what she had, she grabbed on the harness and hames and climbed onto Little Bub's back. She turned him and headed downriver, traveling slow and steady, with the log dragging behind; High Boy and Sunny Jim followed along, dragging their own logs. She spent the time, watching both the dragging trunks and the track ahead of her, keeping her eyes peeled for anything a dragging log might catch on.

All told, it had proved to be a pretty simple process, much easier than she had expected. Watching the tree-trunks slipping effortlessly across the slick grass and sandy soil was a pleasant thing to behold. Little Bub followed the game-trail beside the river, walking along easily, dragging his trunk without any great effort or concern.

Sunny Jim was equally unconcerned as he trailed along behind; he spent some of his time tossing his head and flopping his long fore-lock up and down, amusing himself as he dragged his own log. Because that was just the way Sunny Jim was; he had always been proud of his long and beautiful forelock. And he had always liked flopping it up and down and side-to-side. 'Just like a school-girl tossing her tresses,' her cousin Isaiah used to say.

And High Boy, being the serious and eternally hard-working horse that he was, brought up the rear, keeping his mind on his work and his eyes on the trail in front of him.

Laughing Girl led the procession and Frankie could see Matilda behind High Boy's log, bringing up the rear. She was trotting dutifully along at the end of the little parade, her tongue lolling out of the side of her mouth, tired from her day of exploring the river-bottoms and the woodcutting camp.

When they reached the rows of apple trees, Frankie pulled her parade to a halt, stopping the horses under the tree branches, her eyes and her mind on the apples on the highest branches. While the horses nibbled at the grass, she took turns standing on the horses' backs, reaching for the highest apples and filling the canvas packs.

Frankie was working to fill the last pack when she heard a warning growl. Glancing toward Laughing Girl, she saw the big hound staring through the rows of trees, looking toward the ford. She leaned down, lifted her rifle from where it was lashed to the hames and stood up again, watching the ford from Little Bub's back.

Through the foliage of the apple trees, she could see something moving on the river's south bank—something that was moving down the bank and into the water. A moment later, through a break in the leaves, Frankie watched a nice little wagon with a nice sorrel mule climbing up the north bank. And there on the wagon-seat was the Reverend Simeon Austin. And there beside him, was the formidable Betsy Whitten Austin. Once they topped the riverbank, the Reverend turned the mule upriver, following the track toward the rows of apple trees, trotting along at a nice little clip.

Frankie gave a quiet groan, waved at the preacher and his wife, and decided that Betsy Whitten Austin was probably never going to have a good opinion of her. *Here I am, sweating and dirty, wearing boys' clothes again. I'm dragging logs around the prairie and standing here on a horse's back holding a rifle on a preacher man. Crap!*

She whistled for the dogs, calling them to her side; she took in a slow breath and shrugged her shoulders, resigning herself to the reality. *Last time, it was a bloody deer-carcass. This time it's just log-dragging. At least there's no blood-soaked carcass or bloody-mouthed dogs this time.*

"Well, hello again, Young Lady!" The Reverend Simeon Austin pulled his mule to a stop beside the outer row of trees. He seemed to be in a fine mood. "I saw the horses out here in the trees, and I suspected we might find you here, clambering among the treetops." He was grinning broadly, clearly delighted and amused with what he was seeing before him. Clearly pleased to see his young neighbor engaged in a whole new creative activity.

Betsy Whitten Austin, sitting there beside her husband, didn't seem to be nearly so delighted. Not at all. Nor did she appear to be amused. Her expression suggested that her suspicions had just been confirmed—their new little-neighbor-girl was showing signs of being a little loose in the hinges.

But she did offer a nod and a smile, though to Frankie's eyes, she didn't appear to be putting a lot of heartfelt emotion into it. In fact, her face looked pretty stiff and tense, and there was an odd twitch under one of her eyes as she sat there assessing the scene before her.

Frankie decided once again, to pretend like she hadn't noticed—her mind slipping back to her father's counsel about extending olive branches whenever possible.

"Well, hello again, Reverend. Mrs. Austin. How have you been? It's another fine day for a meeting out here in the apple trees. Did you come for more apples?" Frankie smiled at him, deciding that she truly liked this man. As for his wife, things would probably have to settle out over a span of time.

"Well, we certainly wouldn't turn down any apples you might be inclined to offer. But no, we were out and about, visiting in the area and we decided to drop by to say hello." He wrapped the lines around the brake-rod and stood up in the jockey-box, arching his back and stretching before he went on. "We had the occasion to visit with Everett and Ida Dunbar some time back. We had a lovely dinner at their place. Had the occasion to admire their livestock. And as a matter of fact, our conversation turned to you and your homestead once or twice."

"Yes, Sir. I expected that would happen. I hope I didn't come out too badly."

"To the contrary, my young friend, you fared quite well." He laughed, relaxed and easy, and Frankie had a feeling he knew exactly what her fears had centered around. "Quite well, indeed." He winked at her as if he was purposely choosing to put her mind at ease.

Frankie dropped down to sit on Little Bub's back, smiling as she watched the Reverend laughing and realizing that just listening to his voice—his soothing bass-baritone voice—made her feel happy. So she told him that, and it made him tip his head back and laugh up toward the sky. And Frankie decided his laughter was nice too. And then Betsy began laughing too, and to Frankie's surprise, it sounded light and friendly.

And when they were done laughing, Frankie decided to take the leap, figuring she might as well dive in, because it was obvious the Austins hadn't been 'visiting in the area' and 'just dropping by to say hello'. Because her homestead was the end of the line; there was no one else living out this way to visit. So the preacher and his wife had come all this way just to see her. Because likely, the Reverend Simeon

Austin had decided it was his Christian-duty to make his own decision about her circumstances going forward.

So Frankie nudged Bub toward the wagon, easing him closer and being mindful of the logs dragging at the end of the chains. She handed the Reverend Austin the canvas tote she had just filled. And then she invited them to dinner.

"We'd be happy to accept and proud to sit at your table," Betsy Austin said. "If it won't be too much trouble."

"No, Ma'am," Frankie replied. "No trouble at all. As long as you're okay with what I have waiting on the stove. There's too much for just me, anyway."

With that, Betsy gave an approving little smile—just a little smile, with just a hint of approval—and Frankie figured she had just passed some kind of test.

She reined Little Bub clear of the wagon and started leading her little log-brigade toward the track to the meadow, following it up and over and around, with the Reverend's nice little molly-mule pulling the nice little wagon along behind.

Frankie said a brief and silent prayer as she led her parade into her meadow, thanking the Lord that she had the means to feed these people some passable food. Sitting in the big stove's warming-shelf, was a pan with several roasted prairie-chickens, with turnips and parsnips and carrots tucked into the pan. Right above it on the pie-shelf, was a fresh-baked peach pie. *I might just come out looking okay.*

She explained about the logs while she and the Reverend unhitched her horses and his mule, slipped their bits, and walked them over to water-up in the shade of the windmill-pond.

"I want to have the logs for benches by the fire." She left everything about the visiting warriors out of her explanation. She'd had enough trouble calming down the Dunbars on the subject of visiting Indians; she didn't want the whole settlement down by the Reverend's place getting riled up. *No sense in having word of Indians floating among the other settlers' minds.*

"It can be a fine thing to sit out in the open around a fire at night," the preacher said that much and made no mention of Indians.

So maybe he hasn't heard about my visitors. She breathed another silent sigh of relief.

"Maybe some evening you'll be visiting and we'll spend some time trying out my new benches."

"I believe that might make for a fine evening, Child. I truly do."

While they were seeing to the horses and talking about benches and cookfires, Betsy Whitten Austin had wandered over to the chicken-house; she was looking at the chickens and she called out, saying she thought it was 'such a fine henhouse'.

Frankie thanked her, calling back from the pond, asking if she'd toss the hens some grain, thinking she might as well put the woman to work. Because keeping her hands busy and her mind on the hens might keep her from settling her disapproving eyes upon other things.

"Young Lady, the Dunbars had so many fine things to say about you. Some *really* fine things. And during the harvest, they spoke a bit about you too." The Reverend Austin stood in the cool shade under one of the hackberry trees, his deep voice soft and thought-filled. "To be honest, Betsy and I have been concerned about you and your circumstances. Being here alone, such as you are. But today, by the look of things, I can tell Everett and Ida were right about how they saw things."

"Everett and Ida are part of my life, Sir, and I'm happy they are. They've made my life here easier." Frankie wanted to put the focus back on Everett and Ida, thinking it might be better to keep his mind and his words on them—at least, until she had a better feel for this preacher-man, along with any plans he might have.

"Frankie Harding, that's just what they said about you. I have to say, I haven't seen them so happy in a long time. You're good for them; I think it's good you're here."

Frankie plucked a handful of the hackberries from the tree branches and handed a few to the Reverend; she popped some into her mouth, grinning as Simeon Austin followed her example. He chewed them, grinned at her, told her he had never tried them.

"Well, they make a good pie, kind of a pudding feel to it. Like a pumpkin pie. If your wife does any baking."

293

"Oh, Child. My Betsy does more than her fair share of baking. I'll have to tell her about this. Hackberry pie. I had no idea."

They left the Reverend's red mule and the three Shires in-harness and released them to graze in the meadow. As they started walking toward the house, Betsy joined them. She was looking around the meadow and taking in the surroundings, but Frankie saw her eyes flicking back toward the henhouse and the clusters of chickens scurrying to the coop, their eyes and minds on the handfuls of grain she had tossed in the henyard. Betsy Austin's mind was on the chickens and Frankie was pretty sure where the subject was going to go.

"Your hens look awfully nice Frankie; you take good care of them. I see you just had a hatching too."

"Yes, Ma'am." Frankie waded in, thinking that there might be another opportunity to soften Betsy Austin a bit. "I don't suppose you need any chickens at your place? With the hatch-out, I need to cut my flock."

"Oh, Frankie. I'd be glad to have a few hens. I'm down to three now. But what I *really* need is a rooster. Our old rooster didn't make it through the winter and a fox got the other two last month along with some of the hens. If I had a rooster, I could start building a flock again.

"You'd be the answer to one of my prayers if you'd take one of my roosters. I'm getting awfully tired of them fighting for best crow every morning, all morning long." Frankie grinned at her and Betsy Austin reached around her shoulder and squeezed her close to her side.

"Well then, I'd be pleased to serve as an instrument of the Lord's answer to your prayer." They both burst into laughter as they walked on toward the house, with Frankie suggesting that 'maybe we'll just have to find a burlap sack for your trip back home'.

At the porch, Frankie said she wanted to 'wash up a bit after hauling logs', and invited the Reverend and Betsy to 'have a look around the place, if they wanted'. She knew that's what they really wanted to do anyway, and it was right in-line with what she wanted. She wanted them to see she was settled in and doing well—since that was the *real* reason they were here. They smiled and said they'd 'like that just fine', and 'take your time and don't rush on our account'.

She went to her room to wash off the day's grime and dust, glancing through the windows occasionally to keep an eye on her visitors while they wandered around the meadow. They stopped at the barn-lot to look at Blossom and her calf for a while, and then they walked over to the front-pasture fence to watch Trumpeter and his mares for a bit. They moved down the pasture track to look into the pasture where Solomon and Samson and Boone grazed with High Boy and Black Mack, and with the three mules Everett had brought back after the harvest. They stayed for a while at the fence where the oxen and the herd of roan Durhams were pastured.

Frankie combed out her hair, braided it fresh, and had just changed into her blue-green dress, when she spotted the Reverend and Betsy walking toward the rear entrance of the barn. They'd see that the barn was neat and tidy; that the horses in the stalls were well-situated. *Good. Let them see that everything's in order.*

She was in the kitchen, setting the table when she heard the Reverend and his wife coming up the porch steps. From the look Betsy Austin gave her when she stepped into the kitchen, Frankie knew the dress and the show of getting 'dinner on the table' had erased at least some of the doubts that remained in her punctilious mind and her righteous heart. Betsy Austin's face lightened up considerably; her critical countenance faded as she launched into helping to ready the dinner.

Several times Betsy remarked about the beautiful dishes and the clean kitchen as she worked with Frankie. And when Frankie glanced to the Reverend, there was no doubt that he had been observing the changes in his wife's expressions too. She saw the wink he threw her way—a private little wink meant just for her.

He smiled broadly at her, tugging lightly at the tuft of a beard on the end of his chin and Frankie knew he understood exactly what she had been up to; he knew the fresh dress, the clean kitchen and the table laid full of plates and dinner-platters had won his wife's favor. And he knew she had planned it that way.

Frankie couldn't help winking back at him. This, she knew, was a secret that would stay between the two of them.

Partway through the dinner, Frankie was thanking the Lord, and all her lucky stars, because it seemed as though the meal had been blessed even before the Reverend Austin had officially asked for it. By the grace of God, the prairie-chickens and the root-vegetables came out of the roasting pan warm and tender. The biscuits were fluffy. And the peach pie brought wide smiles to the faces of the preacher and his wife.

Frankie knew the bounty of food on the table—and full and happy stomachs—had gone a long way toward stabilizing their relationship. And the tour the Austins had taken around the meadow and out to the pastures, seemed to have helped settle their minds too.

It was likely now, Frankie figured, that the Reverend Austin would be putting out word to his congregation that the young girl living up on the North Loup was doing just fine. He'd be able to say that he'd seen it for himself, he'd also be able to assure folks that the Dunbars were keeping an eye on her, and he'd probably tell them that he and his wife intended to keep a close watch on her too. Because, Frankie realized, it was very likely the Reverend Austin and his wife would be 'just dropping by to visit' quite often.

Today's visit by Reverend Austin had been a good thing. 'Fortuitous and fortunate', her father would have said. Her Aunt Sarah would have said it was 'serendipitous'. 'Auspicious' is what Captain Connell at Fort Kearny would have called it. Because now, no one was going to interfere; no one would try to take over her life; no one would be putting forth any arguments about 'Christian-duty'. Not now. Because the Reverend Simeon Austin wouldn't allow it— the Reverend had already made up his mind. Frankie could see it on his face.

And along with everything else—the clean dress, the clean kitchen, and their tour around the place—Frankie knew that sending along a burlap-sack with a rooster and a few hens would only help her cause.

The conversation around the table never lagged; they never ran out of subjects. They talked about her four black Shires, and the four brindle oxen, and about what Betsy declared were 'truly beautiful mares out in the pasture'. They spoke of how she seemed to be settled in, 'just like she belonged here'. The Reverend asked about her father. And then about her Uncle James and her aunt and cousins. And with a soft and earnest voice, Betsy asked for the story of their deaths down along the Little Blue River.

The Reverend Austin talked to her about all the books on the shelves and asked her about her education. He asked about the violins in the sitting-room, and she told him and Betsy about playing with her father and uncle at the dances and weddings, the fairs and church-socials, back in Indiana. And that made him smile. And then he asked her to play for him and Betsy. So Frankie agreed.

They carried their plates of peach pie and their cups of sweet-coffee out to the porch table and Frankie stood in front of the porch, barefoot in the grass, as she played her father's violin. She played several of the songs she loved, playing soft and sweet, sending the notes into the prairie breeze, to drift up through the leaves and the limbs of the shade trees.

First, she played the sweet strains of "Sweet Evelina", letting her mind travel back to the dancefloor at Fort Kearny, remembering the gentle hands of Captain Jack Connell as he led her through the dance. She moved into the song of "Annachi Gordon", holding back her tears as she pictured her Lieutenant and Isabelle dancing across the wooden floor. She played the love song of "Annie Laurie", and finally, she played the sweet strains of the "Cliffs of Dooneen", her first dance with her Lieutenant. She sent the notes high into the sky, rising to meet the hawks, calling and keening, as they soared in their circles high in the heavens.

Once the Austins had heard her offering of music, they asked for music of their worship and their devotion. Frankie had expected as much and she complied, playing the hymns the Reverend and Betsy requested; by what she figured to be more of God's grace for the day, she happened to know the very hymns they wanted her to play. She played to their pleasure, quite sure that God and his angels were doing her yet another favor today by inspiring the Austins to choose songs she knew—which probably made her look to be a stronger 'fellow-Christian' to them than she actually was.

And while she was playing the church-songs, Frankie kept thinking that the Lord must be sitting back in heaven and having fun today—keeping Himself entertained with the job of working things out for her. Because He certainly had been answering her prayers, and pretty much, He had anticipated everything she needed. Even before she sent her requests up to Him.

But there was another prayer Frankie was sending up to God— along with any angels who might be listening. She was fervently praying that a large band of Cheyenne and Oglála warriors would not suddenly come charging into her meadow on their tough Indian ponies—covered in dried buffalo-blood and brandishing blood-dripping buffalo-haunches. And toting raw buffalo-hides smelling to high-heaven.

That, Frankie decided, would certainly catch the preacher and his wife off-guard, and she wasn't sure how she would *ever* work her way out of that kind of surprise. As it was, *that* prayer was answered too, because no warrior-hunters came racing into the valley during the afternoon.

The Reverend and Mrs. Austin were pleased with the dinner; they were pleased with her homestead and how she was living. And as the afternoon wore on, they showed signs that they were content with her character and her ideas. And they were definitely pleased with the violin-playing.

And while she had been playing, Frankie had noticed the preacher tugging on his beard. A lot. It seemed the Reverend Simeon Austin had a habit of working his long, slender fingers into the wispy little beard there on the end of his chin. And whenever he was doing that, Frankie was pretty sure he was mulling over some developing idea. She was also pretty sure that she would hear something about the idea he had been mulling before he drove out of her meadow.

It had her curious, but not worried. Because today, the three of them had come a long way into an honest and sound understanding. That was a good thing, she decided. A very good thing. Because this couple had a lot to do with the minds and leanings of the community. Because if the preacher who was leading the community was content with her situation, then it was likely that the community would also be content. And that, would go a long way toward keeping her safe on her homestead.

The Austins readied themselves to leave late in the afternoon, and when Frankie stepped into the feed-room and emerged with a burlap-sack in her hand, Betsy's smile softened yet again. To Frankie's delight, Betsy selected the young Dominicker rooster with the loudest mouth—and the Bugler didn't look at all disappointed when he saw her lowering the cockerel into the sack. And when she pointed out what looked to be a smirk of pleasure on the older rooster's face, the Reverend Austin burst into laughter.

Frankie snatched up a trio of hens—a Leghorn and two of the Dominickers—and settled them in the sack with the young rooster. Betsy offered a protest, saying that the gift of the rooster was enough.

"The hens'll keep him company on the trip down the road." Frankie made a quick snatch and managed to grab a Hampshire Red by a leg; she tucked that hen into the bag too. She grinned at Betsy, happy enough that she had just reduced her flock by five.

Betsy laughed and tried to protest, but she was wearing a bright and relaxed smile. The truth was, Betsy Austin was more than pleased and wonderfully satisfied. And in Frankie's mind, that was a very good thing—it was a perfect end to the visit.

The Reverend Austin and Betsy climbed onto the wagon-seat, and then the Reverend did what Frankie knew he would do—he once again invited her to attend his church and meet his congregation.

"*One* of these Sundays, I *assume* I'll be seeing you in my chapel," And this time, his invitation carried a little more weight than all his previous invitations—his voice carried the tone of a Cavalry officer issuing an order. "And soon."

Frankie nodded, smiling to show compliance. The Reverend Simeon Austin, wasn't satisfied. He didn't relent; he took his case a little farther.

"And *when* do you think that might be, my young friend?" He looked her in the eye. Straight in the eye.

Frankie understood the look. He would not tolerate a sidestep any more.

"Ida and I were talking about your church just the other day." Frankie offered the information. "They want to be the ones to bring me to my first meeting."

"Well, I'll be watching for you." He took his time arranging the driving lines in his hands. "And maybe, you'd consider bringing your violin when you come."

And that, Frankie realized, was the idea he had been mulling over as he had been stroking his wispy little tuft of a beard—he had plans for her and her violin. If not right away, then at some later point.

She stepped back from the nice light-wagon that was hitched to the nice molly-mule; she smiled her crooked little smile. Nicely; sweetly. Showing that she was ever-so-pleased-to-be-asked. And she let it go at that.

They drove off, up and around and over the track, and Frankie took in a great breath and released it slowly. The visit today, together with whatever Everett and Ida had said to the Austins, meant that now there was a strong base of understanding and support for her. Today had been the turning point; she would be staying on her homestead without anyone interfering. *This was a big step today. This visit settled things.*

Frankie went into the house, changed into her britches and shirt, and headed out to the meadow. She hitched High Boy to the chains and tongs again and dragged the logs into place at the cook-fire. Then she led him into the barn, hitched him to the stone-sled, and spent some time loading rocks from the pile behind the barn, using them to create a large oblong stone-ring around the firepit. She loaded the sled with firewood from the stone-room stack and off-loaded at the far side of the fire-ring, back against the hillside.

Finally, she went to the Conestoga and brought out the iron-forks and the iron spit-rods from her days on the trail, along with the cookpots and pans. She finished her work, stood back and studied her campsite.

The makeshift cookfire had become a permanent camp right there in her meadow. It would be there when her Cheyenne brothers came back; that way, they would know she had made a place for them at her home. She didn't think it would be long before they came.

It was early in the morning, four days later, when Frankie spotted a different movement out where the buffalo hunt had ended—the very thing she had been waiting for. Watching for. A long line of dark specks began moving to the west and she knew what it meant; the work after the hunt was done. The line of specks were the Cheyenne and Oglála families; they were moving on, following the buffalo once more—they would follow the great herd to hunt again.

He's Proud had explained it to her. They would approach the herd and plan their hunt. After the hunt, they'd butcher the fallen buffalo and hang the long strips of meat on standing-racks to dry. They'd work on the carcasses and the newly stripped hides. And then, when they were done with the work and the meat had dried, they'd follow the herd and hunt again. So they could add more to their stores of food for the winter. Because, He's Proud told her, that was their way.

Frankie watched the long parade of dark spots, pretty sure that it was the main body of the Indian families. But she was watching for something else. Holding out hope, because she remembered Knife's last words to her. *Nė-sta-vȧ-hóse vóomȧtse.* His promise that he'd see her again.

She was hoping it meant he'd see her after the hunt. *Maybe.* She let the thoughts run around in her head as she moved the lens of her spyglass around the hills and valleys in the distance. *And maybe, Gray Fox will want to get his father's buffalo horse. That might be another reason for them to come.*

She spotted another movement. A separate movement. As the great line of horses and riders moved to the west, it looked like a small cluster of horses and riders was turning southward, moving away from the long parade of riders. *Maybe.* She rotated the lens of her spyglass, focusing on the cluster. *Yes! There! Haáhe! Nėheohe!*

There in the spherical world of her telescope's glass, she saw a small group of riders, moving through the late summer grasses among the slopes of the hills, traveling to the south and a little to the east. Coming in her direction. They were still far away, but they were coming toward her homestead.

Frankie grinned. They were coming. She swung onto Boone's back, and sent him down the hillside at a faster pace than she knew she should. But Boone didn't seem to mind; his head was up and he was taking the slope easily. Willingly. *Probably, feeling the excitement.*

Because Frankie was excited. She had been waiting and watching and hoping. And now, it was happening. And now, she had a lot of work to do and only a matter of hours to do it. Company was coming and she wanted to be ready for them.

She wanted to bake three or four pans of cornbread and several batches of biscuits. She had butter to make. She wanted to start the cookfire in the pit and fill her biggest cast-iron kettle with vegetables and set it to simmering so there would be a stew ready when her visitors arrived.

Plus, there was the big copper pot that should be loaded with apples and cinnamon and sugar—she'd let that sit in the coals to cook down through the day. Originally, she had planned on making several pies, because the warriors had been delighted with the apple pie during their last visit. But the more she had thought about it, the more she realized that it was the taste of the sweet-cooked apples that pleased them—coming in the shape of a pie had nothing to do with it.

So she had decided not to spend time making pie-dough and baking pies, when bowls of cooked apples would bring the same pleasure.

She had gone for a hunt the evening before, planning to try for a buck to have hanging in the barn entrance, but something had scared the herd before she had even made her approach. So she had no venison for her guests. But she did have rabbits—there were seven rabbits, dressed, but not skinned, hanging in the stone-room, ready for the spit. Thanks to Laughing Girl. So she could roast the rabbits on the spits if there was a need for meat.

But it was her fervent hope there would be no need to roast the rabbits. Because she was hoping her friends would bring buffalo meat with them; she was hoping to have her first taste of buffalo. Hoping. But she wasn't counting on it. *Because the Cheyenne and Oglála families probably dried the buffalo meat already. Because they'll need it for winter.*

Once she reached the meadow, she turned Boone toward the millpond, her mind on getting the fire going. There would be apples to peel, vegetables to ready for the cookpot. She slid off Boone's back before he was at a full stop, her thoughts on the tasks ahead of her, thinking that she could have everything ready, or cooking towards being ready, by early afternoon. Then maybe, she would have time to return to the hilltop. To watch her Indians traveling to visit her.

Frankie had been watching the distant activity, watching the cluster of riders working their way through the far hills. She had been on the crest of the hill for most of the afternoon, sitting on one of the big rocks in the hot sun, stripped down to her bare skin, feeling the sun's heat settling deep inside her. Reveling in the light; basking under the cloudless sky. Pleased with the way the sun was turning her skin to the rich, brown-tone of the earth and the curing grasses. Turning her skin to the color of the Cheyenne people's.

There were other times when her skin had been colored by the sun—back in Indiana when she played outdoors with her cousins. Spending the summer days running in the pastures and hunting by the river and running along the roads. Back then her face and hands had always turned dark from the sun—much to her mother's dismay. Because to her mother's thinking, it wasn't feminine.

But *never* had Frankie seen her whole body turn the golden-brown. Not like what was happening now. Because now, during these sunny days, she was spending plenty of time riding around horseback without a shirt on—just like her cousins used to do. And she was spending plenty of time lying buck-naked, napping in the sun-soaked grasses on the hot afternoons—just as she had done back at her camp in the little hidden valley on the Cheyenne Trail. And now, her whole body was turning the pretty tan-brown; she decided she liked the smooth color of her 'summer-skin'.

She had touched Knife's arm when she was sitting beside him at the fire, touching the beautiful deep bronze color of his arm, contrasting it to the golden-tan color of her own arm. He had watched her as she held her arm next to his. He had smiled softly and patted her arm.

He had spoken then, pointing to her eyes and then to his own. He had wrapped his arm around her shoulders and pulled her tight to his side, telling her she belonged to the land of his people. Her love of the land was in her eyes, he had said, it was in her heart now and it would always be there. Her skin was already like his, he said.

He told her he knew why she had come from far away: she had come here on her own vision-quest, because this was the land she was born for. He told her that he and Strong Hand had known she was following her vision when they found her beyond the great flat river, traveling with her very-much-horses. All the men in the band that day had known she was traveling her own path.

'It was a good vision,' Knife had said, 'it was a good path, because it led into the land of your brothers.' He's Proud had translated everything Knife said and his eyes had been shining when he spoke the words. Knife's words were his words, too, he said.

And now, sitting on the crest of the Lookout Hill, Frankie had her attention on the small band of riders coming her way, still moving south-by-southeast, gradually approaching the North Loup River. They were out there among the Sand Hills, following a path of their choosing, riding slowly. Steadily. Weaving in and around the hills. Coming along through the low valleys, angling toward the river. *Coming to my homestead.*

Frankie shivered with pleasure, knowing they were coming this way for one reason—they were coming to see *her*, to spend time with her. Because they called her one of them. She studied the small group of riders through the telescope, trying to spot certain riders that she knew would be there. She focused the lens on the horses, thinking that she'd be able to recognize the Indian ponies before she could name the riders. Finally, she singled them out. The black-and-white pinto was there. *Knife! He's coming! Just like he said.*

And Gray Fox's bright bay was there, walking beside Knife's pinto. After another moment, she picked out a buckskin. *He's Proud!* There looked to be eight other horses carrying riders. And four horses carrying packs.

She stayed there on the hill, watching. Waiting for the group to get closer, wanting a better view of the riders themselves. Half an hour later, when she honed-in on the small band, she could pick out more details. *Sure enough. Knife and Gray Fox and He's Proud. And six other men.* And to her surprise, two women were there; they were riding along with the nine warriors, leading the four packhorses.

Frankie redirected the telescope's lens, refocusing so she could take in the breadth of the land they were traveling. So she could measure the distance between the band of travelers and the river, and estimate the distance between the riders and her meadow.

The band kept coming, still moving steadily and unhurried. Purposefully. She watched them for a while, studying their pace, timing their movement and the distance. Figuring they'd reach the banks of North Loup, probably just north of the cove with the mountain of wood, in a little more than an hour. *So I should have plenty of time.*

Frankie whistled for her dogs. She swung up on Boone's back and rode down the hill, lifting him into a lope once he reached level ground. Heading back to the meadow. She was thinking if she hurried and got everything ready, she could ride upriver and meet her friends. Maybe somewhere beyond the woodcutting cove.

But first, there were some final things she needed to do—like checking the stew she had simmering in the pots at the campsite and getting Gray Fox's horse ready. And getting some clothes on. *Because company's coming. And greeting visitors buck-naked probably wouldn't be considered a polite thing.*

Once she reached the meadow, she turned Boone into the geldings' pasture and headed into the house. She glanced into the pantry, looking at the dishpans of cornbread and biscuits and the crocks of butter waiting on the countertop. Smiling. Knowing her friends would smile when they saw her carrying the pans and crocks from the house.

She headed to her bedroom, washed her face and arms and slipped into her blue dress—the blue one with the white-satin trim that Isabelle had made for her. She laughed at herself as she re-braided her hair and tied the braids with the matching blue ribbons, realizing she was dressing for these visitors the same as she would if the Dunbars were coming for dinner. Or if the Reverend and his wife were coming. She opted for bare-feet. *No sense in going too far with dressing-up.*

Frankie took a last look at herself in the mirror, laughed a little at her efforts to dress for the occasion and headed out through the kitchen. She tripped over Matilda and managed to catch herself before she tumbled to the floor; she gathered herself, laughed again, and trotted and skipped out to the barn.

Samson and the dun horse were waiting in stalls, watching as she came down the barn alley, heads up and ears forward, acting almost as if they had been expecting her. She bridled Samson and slipped a rope halter on the buffalo horse, feeling her fingers trembling with excitement as she fastened the halter in place. She wanted to meet Knife and the others along the river so they'd know she had been waiting and watching for them.

Her plan was to be leading the dun so she could present him to Gray Fox—so he would know for sure she wanted him with his rightful owner. She had been working on the mouse-colored dun all along, feeding him sweet-grains, working to get weight back on him and working to get his hide shining.

She had pulled the last of the stitches from the wound three days ago; she had been rubbing cornmeal and clay on the wound for the last two weeks, working on the scar, trying to slough-off any proud-flesh that was forming.

She was happy with the result—there would probably always be a jagged line of darker hair where the wound had been, but the scar-tissue was barely visible. The muscles lying under the wound were supple, there was no pulling or binding. She had ridden him several times up to the Lookout Hill. She had trotted him and let him lope through the low valleys. There seemed to be no lameness; none that she could see; none she could feel in his stride. In her mind, he was as good as new—but ultimately, it would be Gray Fox's judgement that mattered.

There in the alley of the barn, the tough dun danced a bit at the end of the lead-rope as Frankie boosted herself onto Samson's back. She looked at the Gray Fox's buffalo-horse, grinning at him, knowing he was feeling the excitement in the air; his eyes were bright with anticipation. She nodded to herself, pleased with what she was seeing.

Even in the low light inside the barn, she could see that his hide was shining. Every hair was in place; his dark mane and tail were rippling and flowing, moving like silk—the daily grooming sessions had done that.

The sun was working its way toward the horizon as Frankie headed up the track, riding bareback and barefooted on Samson, leading the tough mouse-colored dun, with Matilda and Laughing Girl trotting behind. She figured she had three hours before the sun dropped out of sight and she thought the timing was perfect. *Plenty of time before dark. Plenty of time to meet up with them and ride*

back to the meadow. Plenty of time before dark to have a meal at the fire.

She left the track and turned Samson toward a low slope just to the north, beyond the lines of apple trees. She halted there on the rise, watching the riverbank, looking for the travelers, pretty sure her friends weren't very far away; they would have been moving steadily, coming ever closer during the hour she spent in her meadow getting things ready.

She could see where the North Loup took its sharp turn, creating the bend where the mountain of wood was. *Somewhere along there.* She watched that area, looking for movement among the trees where the trail ran close to the riverbank. *Maybe. By now, they must be somewhere close to the woodcutting camp.*

"Néheohe!" She said the Cheyenne word, saying it without even thinking. "There!"

She had seen a flash of movement among the brush and trees along the river. *There they are! Just beyond the bend in the river.*

It had been a quick movement—a flash of white-and-black. Just for an instant. She grinned, and then felt her grin growing. *A piebald. Knife!*

She watched the place, waiting to see something else. Looking for another movement or color to verify they were there among the riverside trees and brush. A moment later, she saw another a flash of color. Red. *Cloth, then. There they are! Working their way downriver. Coming to see me!*

Frankie reined Samson and sent him down the front slope of the low rise, angling toward the river trail. Grinning. Resisting the urge to put her horse into a hard gallop. Thinking slow-and-steady would be better—slow-and-steady, the same pace as her friends.

Halfway down the slope, Laughing Girl came bounding up from the brush along the river, looking awfully proud of a rabbit she had in her mouth. The hound reached Samson's side and danced on her hind-legs, offering up her latest catch. Frankie leaned down from her mount's back, taking the rabbit by the hind legs. She thanked the hound; told her she'd done well. But in truth, she was feeling as though she had a bit of a problem. Because she wasn't at all sure whether it was appropriate, or polite, to ride up on a band of Indians holding a dead rabbit in her hand.

Thinking about her white friends and how they might react, she decided it depended solely upon the individuals—the Dunbars probably wouldn't mind at all. But it certainly wouldn't put a smile on Betsy Whitten Austin's face. As to the reaction of the Cheyenne and the Oglála people, Frankie decided she'd have to take the chance. Because she didn't have the heart to throw the rabbit away in front of the big brindle hound—it would only confuse her and muddle-up her wolfhound-greyhound mind.

Because the truth was, the whole rabbit-snatching thing was an awfully handy way of putting meat on the table and Frankie didn't really want to discourage the hound from her forays into the rabbit infested river-bottoms. And anyway, she had no doubt if she tried tossing the dead rabbit to one side, the hound would just grab it and offer it up again. So Frankie kept the rabbit in hand and rode the rest of the way to the river's side.

Once she reached the shady trail along the river's tree line, she turned Samson upriver; the dun horse tucked in behind her and Matilda brought up the rear. Laughing Girl, though, bounded ahead and disappeared into the trees and brush of the riverbank.

Fifty yards further upriver, Frankie pulled her procession to a stop, reached into the pocket within the folds of her dress-skirt, feeling for the tobacco-twist. Sighing when she felt it, relieved she had remembered the gift for He's Proud—a gift for all times he had translated for her. She felt a tug on the lead-rope and glanced back at the dun—his head was up; his nostrils were flared. He was sucking in air, breathing in the scents the breeze carried. His ears were tipped forward; his eyes were locked on the trail ahead. *He knows. His people are near. He's already picked up the scents. And maybe, the sounds.*

Frankie touched her heels to Samson's side, starting up the trail again, only to pull to a sudden stop after a few strides. She groaned. The big grinning hound was back, standing on her hind-legs again, dancing and offering up another rabbit. Frankie leaned down, again; reached for the hind legs of a second rabbit. *Dammit!*

She arranged the four hind-legs in her hand, getting a better grip. Looking at her loot. Knowing she was grimacing a little as she thanked Laughing Girl once again, trying *not* to make too big of a deal out of it this time. Thinking that too much praise might inspire the big hound to go on yet another hunt.

The rabbit-snatching was a fine thing, but the timing today wasn't exactly what Captain Connell would have called 'auspicious'. She tried to look at the bright side and offered a little prayer, thanking God and her lucky stars that at least the dead rabbits weren't dripping blood all over her blue dress. Because with Laughing Girl's kill-tactics, there was never any blood.

Frankie continued following the game-trail among the trees and willows of the riverbank, feeling the day cooling as the sun lowered itself toward the western horizon. The leaves rustled above her and the grasses made a soft whisking sound as the horses moved through them.

She had gone no more than a quarter mile when she saw movement ahead—a subtle flickering among the low branches and the trunks of the trees. Horses moving quietly among the low branches and brush. Once again, Frankie resisted the urge to kick into a faster pace; she held Samson to the steady pace, thinking it was probably wise not to go bursting into a band of Indians traveling, steady and unsuspecting, along a quiet river.

A moment later, she saw the dogs lift their noses, sniffing the air, sensing the approach from upriver; she whistled, spoke to them, ordered them to stay back. And then, suddenly, the band of Indians came into view seventy yards in front of her—they emerged from the tree line, riding out into the sunlight on the grassy game-trail. Knife was in the lead, riding his black-and-white pinto, his eyes on her, looking straight in her eyes. *Motåhke!*

The riders behind him had their eyes on her, too, and none of them seemed even slightly startled to see her. Because, she realized, they had probably known exactly where she was all along. *They were probably watching me before I ever saw them. Because it's their way.*

Frankie pulled Samson to a stop, side-stepped him to the edge of the trail. She waited, watching as Knife and the band approached her. She sat a little straighter on her horse's back, shivering, feeling the excitement rising from deep within her. She watched her brother's eyes and grinned when she saw his smile—a smile she recognized. *Knife's smile.*

His horse started walking faster, leaving the others in the band behind. The other riders of the band moved their horses out from the single-file line, out into the grasses so they could see her ahead on the trail. They were watching her, laughing and nodding, chattering to each other. Someone there among the riders said her Cheyenne name.

"Ho-esta Hesta Ka-ėškóne." 'Fire Heart Child.'

Frankie could see others pointing toward her. Someone called out her name again, and then, there was more laughter. She could hear all of it. She could see all of it in her broader vision—but her eyes were on Knife, watching him as he watched her. Watching his face, and realizing that this time, there was no war-paint on his face. This time she was seeing his face. His eyes and his smile. Just like the first time she had ever seen him.

He stopped his pinto when he reached Samson's side, his knee touching her leg. His face was still, his eyes on hers. He nodded. A slight nod, ever so slight. Barely there.

"Pave-éšeeva, Ho-esta Hesta Ka-ėškóne. Ne-pevo-mohta-he, na semahe?" 'It's a good day, Fire Heart Child. Are you feeling good, my sister?'

Frankie picked up the greeting, understanding his words. She knew how to answer.

"Na-pevo-mohta, na-htataneme." 'I'm fine, my brother.' She smiled at him, proud of her words.

"Na-ho'ė-ho'ohtse." Knife spoke, nodding to her. His smile widened.

"He says he's come to visit." He's Proud was suddenly beside Frankie, easing his horse next to her on the opposite side from Knife.

311

He had come up with the rest of the band, and now, the others—the warriors and the women and the packhorses—were crowding closer.

"E-peva'e tsexė-ho'ėhneto." 'I'm glad you came.' She spoke to Knife, remembering other words from the last visit. And then, looking at all the people gathering near her, she spoke again. "Ne-haeana-he? Ne-tåhá-mėse-ma!" She asked if they were hungry and said they should all come to eat.

There was laughter, and the others of the band moved up closer, nudging He's Proud aside as they moved in. Laughing, excited and happy. Talking to her, asking her questions. And Frankie suddenly realized she had herself in a mess because now that she had spoken some of their words, they seemed to think she had a better handle on their language than she actually did.

He's Proud managed to work his way back to her elbow again, speaking to her. Telling her that the others in the band were talking about the yellow-grease.

She started laughing at the idea that the butter had caused such excitement. She told them that she had plenty of the yellow-grease. They would have the heóve-amėške. And when she used the Cheyenne word for butter without He's Proud's help, her new friends laughed louder. And with He's Proud translating, she told them they would have rabbit too. She repeated the word for rabbit when he said it.

"Vóhkoohe." She held up the two dead rabbits as proof, which made them laugh even louder. One of the women—a broadly-built, bulky woman who was jiggling with her laughter—reached to take them from her. She held the rabbits up, holding them high for every-one to see and called out 'vóhkoohe', again. All of which brought up more comments and louder laughter. Lots of smiles; lots of chuck-ling and giggling.

He's Proud leaned close to Frankie, explaining they were excited about the rabbits.

"They are tired of eating so much buffalo meat," he said. "They want to eat the meat of the rabbits tonight. They have plants to eat, too, plants they collected during their ride to visit you."

"Tell them I have a great pot full of plants already cooking. And I have more rabbits to go on the fire." Frankie grinned when she saw the look of pleasure on He's Proud's face—he was smiling as he trans-lated her words, and Frankie was thinking that maybe he was tired of the buffalo meat too. "Tell them they should all come with me. We should all go to my home."

And then, there in the midst of all the talk and chatter, Frankie saw something new—something she hadn't noticed before. The sight made her smile, and she knew it was probably her best and biggest smile of the day. Maybe, in a lot of days. Because she could see a young girl riding double behind the woman holding the two rabbits; Frankie could see her peeking around the woman's buckskin dress. Behind them, riding on one of the packhorses, there was *another* little girl.

Frankie sat there on Samson's back, startled at the sight, staring at them—looking from one to the other. Watching them. Not at all sure what she should do or say. She figured them to be about her age; they both had long black braids, and they had black eyes that were shining with excitement. And both of them were smiling at her.

And in that moment, Frankie realized she hadn't been around any girls her age in months. And as she thought about it, she realized that she hadn't had any little girls for friends for a *very* long time. Not since she lived in Indiana. *And now, I have two of 'em!*

The girl on the packhorse started giggling; she cupped her hand over her mouth, her dark eyes snapping with laughter. Then the one riding double with the woman started giggling too. So Frankie started giggling too, and when the little girl sitting on the buffalo-hide on the packhorse waved at her, Frankie waved back. Which made all three of them giggle even harder.

Frankie's attention shifted when she saw the Oglála warrior, Gray Fox, ride his bay pony next to Knife's. Gray Fox spoke to her, greeting her in Cheyenne; and she answered him, using the Cheyenne words she knew. Then she smiled at him, knowing it was time—the buffalo horse should go back to his rightful owner.

She backed Samson a couple of steps and reined him to circle around Knife's horse, leading the dun buffalo-horse. She reached out, putting the lead-rope into the Oglála warrior's hand. She looked into his eyes and nodded at him. He studied her for a moment and nodded. Understanding why she had brought the buffalo-horse to him. Knowing she was honoring him. Knowing she was honoring his father.

He slipped off his bay horse and led the dun a few steps away; he stroked the dun's neck, and then ran his hand down the pony's throat. He squatted down in front of the dun's chest and his fingers went to the scars—first, to the long horizontal one across the chest, then to the long jagged one that ran along the shoulder and down the leg.

Two other Oglála men—men that Frankie hadn't seen before—joined him, examining the healed wound for themselves. They talked among themselves, speaking quietly in their language while they slid their hands along the chest and leg of the mouse-colored pony—touching his chest, pressing their fingers into the skin and the tissue beside the scars.

Frankie watched them, realizing that everyone around her was watching too. Everyone had grown quiet. The talk and laughter had stopped; the chattering and giggling had ceased. Somewhere among the horses, there was a snort. Another horse stomped the sandy soil. From the tree branches beside the river, leaves rustled and birds sang and flitted among the high branches. But from the people, there was no sound.

It made perfect sense. Because this was Gray Fox's time; it was about him and his father and the buffalo-horse. She felt, rather than saw, He's Proud side-step his horse closer to her; he leaned close and started talking to her—explaining everything, talking soft and low, exactly the way Corporal Buchanan used to do.

The three men looking over the buffalo-horse were speaking in the Lakotah language, he said. He told her they were surprised and pleased to see how the buffalo-horse had healed. Gray Fox was telling the other men that the wound had been a deep and open wound. A wound that had not healed because it had been a rotted-muscle wound.

Gray Fox, He's Proud said, was telling them that Fire Heart Child had been working to heal his father's horse. And now, the wounds had healed; the rotten-tissue had gone. Fire Heart Child had made the wounds heal.

The Oglála men stayed where they were for a few minutes more, speaking softly, continuing their examination of the scars and the muscles beneath and around the wound. Then they stood. As everyone watched, they walked around the dun horse, running their palms along his back and sides. Lifting his feet and bending his joints. They led him, watching him walk.

Finally, Gray Fox turned to Frankie and began asking questions, and Frankie waited while he talked, listening to the words of the Oglála warrior. Listening to the rhythm of the Lakotah language—a rhythm that was so different from Cheyenne. Then, she listened to He's Proud as he translated the words and questions.

"He asks if Drum is strong again. He says the muscles and skin feel strong. He asks if there is weakness in his shoulder and his leg. He wants to know if you have ridden him. And whether he runs lame."

Frankie listened to what He's Proud conveyed, understanding Gray Fox was being polite and respectful—he was asking her for answers he could actually learn for himself. It *was* his horse, after all, and all he had to do was ride it.

He's Proud explained that Gray Fox was honoring her; he was asking for her knowledge. It startled Frankie a bit, and He's Proud told her it was an important thing that Gray Fox was choosing to do. He said, it was as important for her to understand his intent as it was for her to understand his words.

She was startled again when she heard He's Proud use the same word that Gray Fox used when he spoke about the dun horse. Čhánčhega.

"It's the Oglála word that means 'drum'."

"Drum," Frankie said the Oglála word softly. "Čhánčhega." Realizing that for all the time he had been with her, she had never known his name. She had never even known he *had* a name. This sensible and wise-eyed dun-horse was named Drum.

As to the business of turning Drum over to Gray Fox, Frankie knew she needed to say the right words, because the Oglála warrior was assuming nothing—he would not simply take possession of the horse. The horse she had found and doctored, the horse that had been his father's prized buffalo-horse, had been in her hands. Now it was her choice as to whether he would go back to Gray Fox's hands.

She turned to look at Gray Fox, spoke directly to him, knowing He's Proud would be relaying her words to him as she was speaking. Knowing also, that everyone would be listening to her answers—they would all be listening for how the little-white-girl returned the respect. Because this—at this very moment—was the actual hand-over.

Frankie told him about Drum, once again telling the story of how he had come to her meadow with her own horses. She told the story because He's Proud had said that the story was important. All the people would want to hear it. So she talked of the sickened muscles and the dead-skin and of the remedies and powders she had used. She told him Drum was wise and clever and that he had let her do her healing work. And now he was strong and powerful again.

She told Gray Fox she had ridden his father's buffalo-horse out in the hills and let him run. She said she didn't know if he was strong like he *used* to be, because she hadn't known him before he was wounded. And she didn't know how an Oglála buffalo-horse was supposed to run—because she was just a little-white-girl. But she had ridden him just two days ago, and to a little-white-girl, it seemed like he had run fast and hard.

"Take your horse and run him through the grasses. Let him show his warrior whether he has speed and strength again. He can show you better than I can tell you. You know your buffalo-horse better than I ever will, Gray Fox."

She spoke the words, selecting them carefully, trying to show the respect the Oglála chief deserved, conveying the horse back into his hands; trying to show that in her mind, the horse had never belonged to her. She had only cared for him—and now, she was returning him.

Frankie was trying to find the right words, so no one would have any question that she saw Drum as Gray Fox's rightful horse. Beside her, as he translated her words into Lakotah words, she saw a slight smile on He's Proud's face. Barely a smile. But enough that Frankie knew she had chosen the right words. To her other side, she saw Knife turn his head to her—it was only a slight movement—but she saw his eyes. He was pleased.

Out in front of her, Gray Fox stood at Drum's side. Looking at her. He tilted his head, considering what she had said. Then he nodded at her. His eyes softened, and he gave her another nod.

The Oglála warrior turned and swung onto the dun's back—smooth, effortless. He turned Čhánčhega toward the grass-covered hills to the north; the two Oglála men turned to their own horses, swung onto their backs and followed Gray Fox and his buffalo-horse.

Knife leaned toward Frankie, patted her thigh. Tickled her behind her knee.

"It is all good. Gray Fox will learn about his buffalo-horse. But now I am hungry. We have come to visit. Now you must feed us." He laughed, saying it loudly, making sure everyone could hear his words. "Fire Heart Child has much food and many rabbits waiting for us at her fire. We must hurry now, because my belly is growling like the bear when it leaves its winter-sleep."

Frankie heard everyone burst into laughter; they all started chattering, and the woman who held the rabbits lifted them above her head again and called to the others. He's Proud was laughing at the woman's words too.

"Their bellies are heavy with buffalo meat," he said. "They are happy you have more rabbits and food at your fire. They want different food in their bellies."

They turned their horses back to the riverside trail, with the whole band following her on Samson and Knife on his pinto. All heading toward her meadow. A moment later, Frankie felt someone slip onto Samson's back, right behind her. Small legs tucked in behind her own legs and a belly pressed against her back. Small hands slipped around her waist. The little girl who had been riding behind the woman with the rabbits had switched horses. She started giggling, and Frankie did too.

Her name was Heóvė-stséa-vo'ėstste, 'Dandelion'. He's Proud said she was his daughter. And the woman who was so delighted with the rabbits was his wife, Meno'ke. Which, he told Frankie, meant 'Willow'.

The smiling woman named Willow was anything but slender or willowy like her name suggested. She had a broad face that matched her broad body; her smile was broad, too, and Frankie thought she might just be the happiest person she had ever come across. Even her eyes had a happy smile in them, and every time she laughed, her whole body jiggled. Her buckskin dress had what looked to Frankie like little white stones sewn in neat rows and they all shook and waggled every time she laughed.

She reached to touch one and asked He's Proud about them. He told her they were elk-teeth; Willow laughed even harder at the idea that Ho-esta Hesta Ka-ėškóne didn't know what elk-teeth were. And the more she laughed, the more she shook, and the harder the rows of pretty elk-teeth waggled.

Frankie grinned at her and Willow smiled even bigger, and then she started laughing harder. The rows of pretty white teeth all started waggling again, slapping and glistening against the buckskin dress.

Right then, Frankie remembered the twist of tobacco. She pulled it from the pocket of her skirt and held it out to He's Proud, telling him it was a gift. To thank him for translating for her. And for teaching her. He smiled and patted her shoulder, clearly happy and very surprised with the tobacco.

"Péeono'e," he told her. "Tobacco." He looked over his shoulder, smiling broadly at the other men.

But Frankie was distracted; she was breaking into ticklish giggles as Dandelion started running her fingers along the satin-trim of the dress. The Cheyenne girl was giggling, too, and chattering to her mother and the other woman as she stroked the cotton dress-cloth; the two women were laughing at what she said, and when Dandelion leaned down to tickle Frankie's bare-feet, she and the women started laughing even harder. Apparently, Frankie decided, bare feet must be amusing.

318

She rode to her home valley with Knife riding beside her and Dandelion riding double with her. As they passed the rows of apple trees, she reined Samson toward the trees and plucked apples for her new girlfriends—handing one to Dandelion and passing one back to the girl on the packhorse. Frankie bit into one and the girls did the same. They broke out in smiles and giggles, and then everyone close to the trees began reaching to pick apples.

Apples were being passed around and the people of the band were biting into them, smiling and laughing and saying the word, má'xeme. When Frankie asked He's Proud the meaning, he said it meant 'big-berry'. That made Frankie wonder if the Cheyenne and Oglála people had ever eaten apples before. And that got her to wondering where exactly they would have gotten them, if they *had* eaten them before.

And then, Frankie and the band of Cheyenne and Oglála were trotting their horses along the home track, riding up and around and down into the meadow as the day went into twilight.

Glancing behind her as the band of Indians started dismounting and unpacking their belongings, Frankie felt a shiver of excitement shimmy up her spine. Partly because it was exciting to have her Cheyenne and Oglála friends visiting, and partly because she was fascinated with the idea of having two little girls visiting her.

Suddenly, she had two girlfriends in her life. Dandelion was almost exactly her size and she had a husky laugh that made Frankie feel warm all over. The other girl was Gray Fox's daughter and her Oglála name was Čhán Šiyóthanka. 'Wood Flute'. Her mother was the second woman, and she was called Čik'ala Thawinyela. 'Young Doe'.

Wood Flute was shorter than Dandelion, and Frankie figured she was maybe a little younger; she was also a little shy, and she was much quieter than Dandelion. Both girls wore buckskin shirts that were beaded all around their necks and down their sleeves. They wore breechcloths like the men, but without any leggings. On their feet, they had prettily beaded moccasins.

It was a matter of minutes for the Cheyenne and Oglála to settle into the meadow. The men pulled the packs from the two packhorses, and then released all their horses to graze in the meadow. Then Knife and He's Proud took the new warriors to the back pastures. Frankie watched them, deciding to let them go on their own, thinking that Knife wanted to show the newcomers the ho-haa mo'éhė-no'ha. The 'very-much-horses'. And the vé'ho'é-otóva'a. The 'white-man's buffalo'.

Willow and Young Doe went right to work at the cookfire; they built up the fire and had the big pot of vegetable stew bubbling in a matter of minutes. It didn't take them much longer to have the two rabbits gutted and skinned and on the spit. And when Frankie ran to the pantry and returned with the other rabbits—all seven of them—the faces of the two women lit up and within minutes, those went on the spit too.

By the time the men came to the fire, Frankie—with a few helpful and timely arm-pulls from Dandelion and Wood Flute—had already learned to stay back and let the two women do what they knew how to do. Apparently, the men had learned long ago to keep out of the way; they sat themselves around the fire, leaning against the logs, laughing and talking, and looking pretty relaxed and a little lazy compared to the two women bustling about.

It was when Frankie brought the crocks of butter from the stone-room along with the dishpans piled high with cornbread and biscuits, that the men suddenly showed a new level of energy. They had their hunting knives out and began reaching for the breads and slathering the 'yellow-grease' on the breads.

After a moment of watching the process, Willow and Young Doe, Wood Flute and Dandelion followed their example. There were grins and plenty of laughter as the two women and the girls learned about the flavor blends of baked sweet breads and butter.

A few minutes later, to Frankie's surprise and delight, Willow pulled a long slab of meat—fresh meat—from one of the packs. Frankie stared at the meat and felt the air whistle past her teeth as she sucked in a breath. *Buffalo meat!*

She moved closer, watching as Willow worked with the long slab, twisting and spearing it onto one of the long iron rods; she settled the rod onto the iron-forks and in less than a minute, the cookfire's flames were flaring and hissing. Juices and fat from the dark red meat were dripping and drizzling onto the coals.

Frankie stayed near the fire, eyeing the buffalo meat as it cooked, watching as the women turned the long rod occasionally, watching as the flames kept spitting and sputtering. She had seen plenty of meat roasting over a fire, and she'd seen flames hissing and spitting before, but this wasn't just beef or venison or rabbit on the spit—this was *buffalo meat* that was causing all the hissing and spitting and sputtering. This was a wild and wonderful meat, that until now, she'd only heard about. Up until now, she'd only ever *thought* about eating buffalo meat. *And now, it's right here cooking over my fire. In my meadow! On my homestead!*

The aroma was filling the air and Frankie was picking up a stronger and meatier smell than she'd ever known. A smell that was rich and thick. It was a mesmerizing aroma that hung in the air, overpowering the smells of the roasting rabbits and the stew in the pot. She stepped closer, sniffing at the rising aroma, bending forward.

And suddenly, she realized she had leaned too far; she yelped and scrambled as she fell forward—fighting against gravity, trying to regain her balance. Knowing it was already too late, already aware that she had lost the battle. Knowing she'd end up in the flames and the coals.

She heard one of the women yell. A hand grabbed her wrist, a harsh grip, and she was being yanked away from the flames. Laughter broke out. The harsh hold on her wrist softened, an arm wrapped around her waist. Her feet left the ground; someone was lifting her. And suddenly, she found herself sitting in Knife's lap. Safe.

"Fire Heart Child? Did you decide to climb on the spit with the buffalo meat?" Knife was grinning at her.

His voice sounded serious but his eyes were laughing; his arms were wrapped around her. Rocking her, reassuring her. He's Proud was having trouble translating Knife's words because he was laughing so hard, just as hard as everyone around the fire.

"No. I was just trying to smell the buffalo. I never smelled buffalo meat before." She was surprised as everyone around the fire burst into a new round of laughter as He's Proud told them what she had said.

Willow and Young Doe were chuckling, and Wood Flute and Dandelion had broken into a string of giggles again. The men, though, were laughing the hardest—they were leaning back against the logs and really laughing. And that sent Frankie's temper flaring; she felt the indignation rising. She twisted in Knife's lap, looking to He's Proud and tried to offer an explanation. Trying to make the laughter stop.

"But I've never even *eaten* buffalo meat before. It's not my fault I haven't smelled it cooking."

The men *really* started laughing at that. And Willow and the two girls were no better—they broke into wild and boisterous laughter right along with the men. But not the woman named Čik'ala Thawinyela; Young Doe didn't laugh at her. She just smiled sweetly and reached to pat Frankie's belly and said something that sounded a lot like she was reassuring her that 'it would only be a little while'. And when He's Proud translated, it wasn't far off.

By the time Gray Fox and the two Oglála men returned from their ride out among the hills, the dishpan of cornbread and biscuits was well on the way to being gone. The bowls Frankie brought from the house had been filled with the vegetable stew again and again. She began to think that maybe the vegetables *were* actually a very real craving among these people. Maybe they *had* been eating too much of the heavy buffalo meat.

The women seemed to understand something about it, because they were continuing to add in the roots and wild onions that they brought in the packs. When Frankie showed an interest in what their mothers were adding to the stew, Dandelion and Wood Flute decided to teach their little white girlfriend the Cheyenne names of the plants and roots going into the pot.

They started naming everything for her—horses and bridles and trees and birds and grasses and sky. They kept quizzing her on every name they offered. They giggled and teased her whenever she struggled to pronounce the words. They taught her Cheyenne words until she was breathless from trying to keep up with the lesson and their laughter.

As the twilight deepened into dusk, they all tired of the naming game. The two girls decided to play other games and Frankie followed them, doing everything they did—running in the grass, wrestling and rolling together like a passel of puppies. They laughed at each other and tickled each other. They dashed around the windmill and the pond; they darted through the trees and ran up and down the hillsides.

To Frankie's surprise, the girls grabbed handfuls of food from the bowls by the cookfire whenever they wanted and kept running and playing. She was delighted to follow their example, realizing that for children of the Cheyenne and Oglála, there seemed to be no rules about when to eat. There was no set dinnertime. So like her new-found friends, she grabbed biscuits from the dishpan and hunks of jerky, and kept running and playing, laughing and giggling.

When they tired of all the dashing and darting and wrestling, the three of them huddled together near the fire, still laughing and giggling. When they got in the way of the women working over the pots, they each garnered a few light and loving whacks with wooden stirring spoons, or sometimes, a light smack with a gentle hand.

It wasn't lost on Frankie that there were no frowns or shouts of disapproval, no scoldings from the mothers. Just smiling corrections and a few amused shakes of their heads. Just sweet acceptance and affection. It delighted Frankie; it was so different from the ways of most of the white mothers she had known. And it was *very* different from her own mother's behavior.

These mothers were kind and gentle; they were sweetly stern and patiently firm when they needed to be, but mostly, there was only a loving amusement. Willow and Young Doe treated her with the same sweet regard they showed their own daughters; they gave her the same soft smiles and the same tender touches. And for the first time in a long time, Frankie realized she was feeling like a ten-year-old girl again.

It was after the sun had gone down and the dark had settled in, that Frankie saw Knife motion to her. He was still sitting by the fire, leaning back against one of the logs, and now, he was beckoning to her. Relieved to have a rest from all the laughter and giggling, she went to him. When she squatted down next to him, wondering what he wanted, he wrapped an arm around her and pulled her over to sit close against his side. Then he pulled his knife from the sheath at his waist.

She watched as he leaned forward, reaching toward the long slab of buffalo meat still dripping juices down onto the flames. He sliced off a strip of the meat and as Frankie watched in the yellow-orange light of the fire, Knife pulled a chunk from the strip. He paused for a moment, waiting for the meat to cool. Then he gave Frankie a sidelong grin and spoke a single word—the word that still sounded magical to Frankie's ears.

"Hotóá'e." 'Buffalo.'

And then, he put the taste of the prairie into her mouth—he pressed a piece of the buffalo meat between her lips. She bit into it, tasting it. Savoring it. Rolling it around in her mouth. *Buffalo meat!* She pressed her teeth into the chunk of meat, chewing. *My first buffalo meat!* She let the flavor sit in her mouth, tasting it, thinking it tasted a little like beef. *And a little like venison. Maybe a little bit of the tang of wild duck.*

She swallowed and broke into a smile, grinning wide. Her look must have said more than she realized, because everyone around the cookfire broke into loud and delighted laughter.

"Hotóá'e!" She put all the magical sound she could muster into the word and everyone laughed harder.

Knife kept her beside him, feeding her the buffalo meat—one piece at a time. Cutting off hunks too hot for her fingers, holding them with his own fingers until the meat cooled enough for her. He fed her, piece by piece, taking care of her like the big brother he was. He kept feeding Frankie pieces of buffalo while the others around the fire ate the vegetable stew and the cooked apples and the roasted rabbits.

Once Frankie's taste for buffalo was satisfied and she told Knife her belly was full, he pulled her into his lap. He sat cross-legged, wrapping her within his arms, his chin resting on her head. Beside them, He's Proud held Dandelion in his lap while he translated for Frankie, speaking in soft tones, sharing the conversations of the men and women around the fire.

Everyone sitting at the fire was talking. The conversations had become soft and quiet; the laughter changed to chuckles and smiles. The Cheyenne and Oglála people were relaxed and content, resting after the meal. *Their bellies are full too.* Frankie looked around the fire, studying this new family of hers. Watching the people of the Cheyenne and Oglála tribes. *They all came to visit. And they brought buffalo meat to me. The meat of the great Hotóá'e.*

She felt herself smiling as she said the word to herself. Practicing the word. Remembering the sound. *Hotóá'e.* Letting the four syllables roll around in her mouth and her mind. Letting the reverent sound of the Cheyenne word mix with the solid sound of what He's Proud said was the Oglála word for buffalo. *Tatanka.*

Frankie nestled deeper into Knife's lap, listening to the stories of the buffalo hunt, and when she asked questions, the men gave her their answers. Kindly; patiently. They told her about finding the herd and they explained the strategy of the hunt. They told her about tactics of the chase in the same way the soldiers of Fort Kearny talked about the tactics of battles. They gave the reasons, and they told her all about the why's and how's of the hunt. The questions from the little-white-girl, Frankie realized, didn't irritate them; the questions made them smile. They were pleased that she asked.

It wasn't long before Knife began telling the others about Hoesta Hesta Ka-ėškóne and her wagon when she had been far to the south on the prairie. He told them how she stood up to him and Strong Hand when they found her—how she had been ready to fight nine Cheyenne warriors. There was plenty of laughter and there were questions about her great wagon and the four black horses. The ho-haa mo'éhė-no'ha. 'The very-much horses.' And about her rifle and her shooting.

And after Knife told the story of the hunt with the soldiers, the warriors asked her about the deer she had shot when she hunted with the soldiers. She told them about the trick that the soldiers had tried to play on her and how she had turned the trick back on them, the warriors broke into laughter.

That was when Knife tapped the necklace at his throat—he spoke softly to the warriors as he touched the bullet that rested on his chest. The tone of the story changed; the warriors' voices went soft as they asked Knife their questions. He's Proud didn't translate the quiet conversation for her, and Frankie thought they were probably discussing the magic that Knife believed was in the bullet. *Probably it's warrior-business and not really ten-year-old girl-business.*

She stayed in Knife's lap, sitting silently, listening to the soft voices. Leaving them to their business while she and Wood Flute made faces at each other from opposite sides of the fire.

Then, there was talk about the soldiers and questions about her escape from the soldiers' fort and her journey to the north. And there were many questions about the attack by the two wolves, and the wolf-hides hanging beside the kitchen door. That was followed by soft murmurs and more talk—talk that Frankie thought must be serious, because He's Proud didn't translate any of that for her, either. He gave her the word for wolf, hó'nehe, but then he turned his attention to the conversation with the other men—a conversation where the word hó'nehe was being used a lot.

Frankie sat quietly, taking her cue from the two girls and their mothers. She was satisfied enough with where she was at; it was a comfort to be sitting in Knife's lap like she was, tucked back against the warm solid wall of his chest and belly, reminding her of being nestled into the big rocking chair with her Lieutenant in the white cottage at the fort.

The heat from Knife's body was at her back and the heat from the fire was in front of her; the meat of the buffalo had warmed her inside. The firelight was blurring and the voices of the warriors were fading. She squinted, trying to see better; she kept shaking her head, trying to stay awake, annoyed that she was starting to fall asleep. Because she really wanted to listen to the men while they talked.

She kept forcing her eyes to stay open as she listened to the rhythm and the flow of the language, hearing the pauses and the halts, the whispers and the lifts. The Cheyenne words mingled with the Oglála words; the music of the two languages floated through the air with their own movement and patterns, lifts and falls. Their own special tempo and inflections, steady and smooth.

There was a cadence, a pulse within the words that belonged to the grasses and the skies of the prairie. It was a rhythm and a pulse and a pace that was taking her beyond the fire, deep into the earth and the history and the past. It was a tempo and a ripple and a vibration that swept her back in time, long before the evening. Long before the morning. It was taking her back to times that happened long before the hunt and before her journey. Before her time at the fort. And before the time in the white house in Indiana.

It was a sound and a pounding that resonated deep within her—constant and steady—moving like the buffalo, flowing like the grasses, sweeping like the wind through the Sand Hills.

The men's voices seemed to be traveling far and away from her. And then, the voices were gone. Everything became dark and quiet. There was only the smell of the fire and of the smoke. The smell of the grass and of the hair of the buffalo. The smell of the prairie and the smell of the Sand Hills. The smell of home. And she slept.

Frankie stirred, hearing muffled sounds and hushed giggles; she could feel tiny tickles on her belly and little puffs of sweet breath against her neck and back. More giggles. And then, little-girl fingers were poking her navel and flicking at her earlobes.

She opened her eyes in a world of dim and filtered light, wrapped within a thick and heavy buffalo-robe that held the scents of the prairie—the fragrance of the grass and the earth, of the land and the sky, of the fire and the smoke. And there was the sweet scent of the two children who had slept beside her and cuddled with her through the night.

And now, Wood Flute and Dandelion were giggling beside her; Frankie started giggling, too, waking in the midst of a wonderful tangle of little-girl arms and little-girl legs. The silly giggles turned into silly laughter as they scrambled out from the dark and warm burrow of buffalo-robes, tumbling out onto the grass.

The three girls were shrieking with laughter as they erupted into the morning light and Frankie was wondering exactly how she had gotten there; she had only the vaguest memory of Knife standing up. A memory of being carried in his arms; a memory of his soft murmurings of sweet Cheyenne words. She remembered him settling her into the soft and furry world of curly buffalo hair, nesting her down between her two sisters.

She was remembering the moments in the dark of night, but she didn't dwell upon it for very long, because she was thinking about the one thing she knew for sure—a marvelous thing—she had been laughing when she opened her eyes, and she had been playing when she woke to the world.

Dandelion and Wood Flute were on their feet and running the minute they were free of the buffalo-robe and Frankie was right beside them; they dashed past the women working at the cookfire, they charged past the men leaning against the fireside logs. They ran out into the meadow, startling the Indian ponies out of their quiet grazing, racing to the far side of the meadow, across to the base of the hill beyond the henhouse. Her sisters dropped down, squatting to relieve themselves.

So Frankie followed their example. What did she need with an outhouse today? And when they started running and laughing again, running back across the meadow toward the windmill pond, Frankie was running right beside them. And Matilda and Laughing Girl were bounding along with them. When Dandelion and Wood Flute began stripping off their shirts and breechcloths while they ran, Frankie started pulling off her dress, tugging at the buttons, working to free herself from the restrictions of the cloth.

They never slowed; they launched straight into the water of the windmill-pond, yelping as they hit the cold water, yipping their delight in the morning. As they splashed and romped, Matilda and Laughing Girl joined them in the water games, their excited yips and barks every bit as loud as the girls' shouts. And to Frankie's surprise, no adult seemed to care about the noise and splashing.

The women stopped their work beside the fire and straightened up to watch them splashing in the pool. After a moment, they turned back to their stirring-sticks and the cookpot, shaking their heads and laughing. The men watched them for a few minutes, and then turned back to their conversation. But no one scolded them; no one cautioned them. No one called them away from the pond; no one hushed them or complained about the noise. *Apparently*, Frankie decided, *it's the Cheyenne and Oglála way. Which is a lot nicer than the white way.*

The girls scrubbed each other's bodies with handfuls of the sandy soil; they scrubbed their scalps and hair, unwinding each other's braids and finger-combing handfuls of sand through to the ends. They dunked each other under the water, and they rose to the surface again, sputtering and shaking their heads. Shaking the sand and the water from their hair. Again and again, they ducked under the water's surface, splashing and swirling, giggling and laughing.

When they finally came out, no adult seemed to care about their naked, brown bodies. When they flopped naked on the buffalo-hides, rolling in the long soft buffalo hair to dry themselves in the cool early morning air, no one seemed to care about that either. No one told them to 'cover up' or to 'get some clothes on'. And in Frankie's mind, it was all a fine thing.

They were still on the curly-haired hides in the early sunshine, arms and legs out-stretched, gathering the sunshine to their bodies, when Frankie suddenly had an idea. She jumped to her feet and raced toward the henhouse with Matilda romping along; Wood Flute and Dandelion raced after her. Frankie was thinking about the hens and the eggs. *Eggs! Eggs for our breakfast!*

She slipped into the henhouse and came out with a handful of eggs; she handed them off to her sisters and disappeared inside again, emerging once again with more eggs. Dandelion and Wood Flute were delighted, their bare feet danced in the meadow grasses and their brown bodies spun in circles. They hopped around, surprised at the thought of the clumsy and silly birds giving their eggs to their little white sister. And very surprised at the size of the eggs. It was all a wonderful magic to them.

And when nine eggs, brown ones and white ones, were presented to Willow and Little Doe, the women thought it was a wonderful idea too—they cracked the eggs open and dumped them into the pot of stewing vegetables. It was a new idea to Frankie, but it seemed like a good one. Stew-poached eggs, cooking there among the root-vegetables from the cellar and the wild turnips and wild onions and cattail-roots, suddenly seemed like a wise and wonderful thing to do.

The three girls stayed naked for most of the morning; they ran and scampered around the meadows, rarely walking. When Frankie ran into the alleyway of the barn, she was surprised to hear both girls protesting; she was bewildered by their concerns about entering the long building; she stood inside the doorway, beckoning and beseeching, and finally, after a good amount of coaxing, Wood Flute and Dandelion relented. The three of them darted past the workshop and raced down the alleyway past the horses in the stalls, past the farm wagons and the Conestoga, and out the back doorway. They ran on, dashing past the rock walls of the garden and beyond the corncrib, swerving to head out to the center-track between the pastures.

She pointed to Blossom and Primrose and tried to explain about the yellow-grease coming from the cows, but even with a mixture of both Cheyenne and English words, she couldn't seem to explain things well enough. As it was, neither Dandelion nor Wood Flute seemed to care—all the new sights and the laughter and the running seemed to be enough for her Cheyenne sisters—so Frankie let it drop.

When she showed them the four brindle oxen, the girls gave little gasps of amazement. The Shires, with heads twice the size of the Indian ponies and hooves almost as big as the cookpot, startled and scared them. But when Frankie ducked into the pasture through the gaps in the plank fence, they followed. And after a few more gasps and a lot of grins and giggles, they started fondling and petting the giant horses, just like their new sister was doing.

Then, the three of them raced back down the center-track and down the length of the pastures, and when they reached the cookfire, they were still laughing and shouting. Dandelion and Wood Flute had all kinds of stories to tell, and when they started jabbering about their adventure to their fathers and mothers and uncles, there was more laughter.

Frankie stood back and listened as He's Proud translated what he could, and from the sound of the girl's explanations, it sounded like they had a pretty clear understanding about what Frankie had shown them.

Frankie had been watching how the men and women ate from the big stewpot; sometimes they used the long wooden spoons and shallow bowls made from portions of what looked to be portions of animal shoulder bones. But it was a pretty regular thing to simply reach into the steaming pot and fish out pieces of buffalo and chunks of vegetables with their fingers. After watching the method a few times, she made a few valiant attempts to snatch pieces from the hot stew.

The heat of the simmering contents was her undoing; she kept trying, but the steaming fluid was too much. Again and again, she came up empty-handed. She kept trying, determined to meet the challenge, trying to apply the same casual ease that her new family displayed. But whatever pieces she *did* manage to grab, she ended up releasing as she jerked her hand back, yelping from the heat.

Finally, Knife took pity on her and lifted her back from the fire and the pot; he settled her in his lap and started picking chunks of meat and vegetables from the stew for her. He held the pieces, letting them cool, and then shared them with her—feeding her piece by piece—just as he had with the roasted pieces of buffalo. Casual and attentive, taking care of her as if it was something he had always done. Feeding her; eating some himself.

Around the cookfire and the big stewpot, the men and women were talking and telling their stories and Frankie nestled down in Knife's lap, sitting like a naked little bird while he kept selecting pieces of food from the pot, sharing his meal with her.

Across the fire, Gray Fox sat with Wood Flute, his arms wrapped around his daughter, keeping her warm while they sat in the shade in the cool morning. He was talking with the other men, but Frankie could see he was tucking bites of food into Wood Flute's mouth the whole time. The Oglála girl smiled across the smoke at Frankie, and Frankie smiled back. *This is Cheyenne and this is Oglála. And this is family.*

Then, the mothering started. Willow and Young Doe dug into leather bags, found what they were looking for and stood up, motioning for the girls to follow them. They sat the three girls down on one of the buffalo-robes and started combing through their hair. They each worked on their own daughters first, and then they both went after Frankie's hair.

And it didn't take long for Frankie to realize they had no intent of doing a less than a thorough job. They had no qualms about raking through her hair with the carved combing sticks and she was pretty sure the combs were ripping right through her scalp and into her skull.

Wood Flute and Dandelion had a great time mimicking the grimaces Frankie made as those two mothers worked on her hair; the girls really cut loose with laughter when Frankie, feeling the sting of their betrayal, shot a few scowls at them.

The braiding that the women did was beautiful and tight; the braids hung straight and clean in a way that Frankie had never seen. They wove slender leather strips into her braids and laced in beads at the bottom. From their gestures and from what words she could pick out—and with a few helpful words from He's Proud—Frankie realized they were telling her the leather and the beads would help her hair to grow faster and longer. Because apparently, for the Cheyenne and Oglála people, *long* braids, and not just *braids*, were the desired goal.

A moment later, Frankie was startled when she saw the women and the girls looking behind her; the four of them stood up and stepped back. She looked over her shoulder to see Knife walking toward her; he had no smile for her now—he didn't look at all kind and relaxed, not like he had been while they were eating together.

Frankie stood up quickly, suddenly wary, watching as he approached with He's Proud and Gray Fox at his side. When Knife stopped and beckoned to her, Frankie felt Willow's hand at her back, giving her a gentle nudge. She complied and stepped forward as Knife squatted down. He beckoned again, wanting her closer. She stepped up to him, feeling the soft curly hair of the buffalo-hide tickling at her feet.

She stood stock-still. Unsure; still wary. Trying to keep her hands and knees from trembling. Waiting. Sensing something important was happening. Realizing no one in the meadow was talking now; there were no conversations; there was no laughter, no light chatter.

Her warrior brother reached out his hand to her, opened his fingers, showing her what he held. Frankie stared at a strand of braided rawhide on his palm. She recognized the wolf-teeth; she saw the pieces of dull-gray lead. Three bullets. She closed her eyes, feeling tears rising, knowing her brother had made the necklace for her. This was his end of the trade. He was honoring her; thanking her in his way.

She felt his hands reaching around her neck, felt his fingers working the rawhide strings. She opened her eyes while he was tying the necklace at the back of her neck—looking at his eyes, looking at his forehead and his cheekbones and his jaw-line. Smelling the scent of his body and the bear-grease on his shoulders and arms. *My brother. My necklace.*

When he was satisfied, Knife leaned back, studying the necklace and eyeing her the same way she had been eyeing him. Then he tapped her chest where her heart was; he said her Cheyenne name softly. Gently.

"Ho-esta Hesta Ka-ėškóne. Na-semahe" 'Fire Heart Child. My sister.'

333

"He is offering you a gift, Fire Heart Child." He's Proud whispered. "A spirit-gift. It carries wolf-medicine. From the wolves who offered themselves to teach you a lesson for this life."

Knife smiled at her. He said nothing else, but he held his hand against her chest, his palm over her heart. Then he stood up, and Frankie watched her brother and the other men walk to where their ponies grazed in the meadow. She watched as Knife bridled his black-and-white pony, watching as all the men bridled their ponies. And it was as they swung up on their ponies that she saw they all carried weapons. Rifles in-hand; quivers and bows strapped across their shoulders and backs.

She watched, mesmerized by the motion and the movement of the men and their horses—smooth and swift and effortless; they reined their wiry ponies and thundered out of the meadow. Racing up the track, racing up and around and out of the valley. And all the while, she realized, she had been fingering the gift that Knife had fastened around her neck. The gift he had made; the symbol of her wolf-medicine.

Frankie looked down at the necklace lying against her chest, resting at the base of her neck—the necklace of black and white and blue beads, three gray bullets, and four white wolf-teeth—all woven and braided into a thing of beauty. He had done this for her; he had made what she had asked for. And it was beautiful.

The women turned back to their daughters and Frankie found herself lost in fascination again. Young Doe fastened a breechcloth around Wood Flute's waist and Willow was doing the same for Dandelion; they slipped soft buckskin shirts over the girls' heads; they handed the girls their beaded moccasins. The two girls plopped themselves down on the buffalo-robe and started pulling on the moccasins.

And suddenly, Frankie was feeling a little a little wary. Because the girls were grinning slyly at her the whole time, as if they knew something she didn't know. A moment later, she found out they *did* know something she didn't know. Because suddenly, it was Ho-esta Hesta Ka-ėškóne's turn.

Willow beckoned to her; Frankie complied cautiously, watching as Willow dug into a drawstring bag. She watched as the Cheyenne woman took out a bundle of soft yellow-tan leather—she shook it and straightened it, showing Frankie a dress made of buckskin, fringed and beaded. Frankie reached to touch the dress, feeling the leather that had been tanned until it was soft and supple.

Willow grinned and nodded, pleased with Frankie's reaction; she broke into her big laugh that shook her whole body. Dandelion and Wood Flute started giggling and hopping in place, happy that their white-sister was happy. Frankie glanced at them, grinned at them, but she hesitated, unsure about what she should do.

And then, Willow pulled her close; she lifted the silky-soft leather dress, with all its fringes and beads, above Frankie's head and lowered it, settling it down onto her shoulders and arms. Young Doe reached out, straightening the dress as it drifted down around her waist and hips. Smoothing it, stroking it gently into place. Straightening the fringes.

"Vó'kaa'e," Dandelion said, pointing to the white, sun-bleached horned skull that Daniel Kinison had hung on the Barracks wall long ago. Frankie stared down at the dress, understanding—it was made from the hide of an antelope. She stroked the silky leather, astonished with the beauty, thinking it was every bit as beautiful as the shirts Dandelion and Wood Flute were wearing. She touched the quills and beads around the neck; she ran her fingers down the sides, feeling the soft-tan of the hide, feeling the fringes rippling lightly between her fingers.

She took a few steps away from the women, feeling the antelope-hide dress swaying softly against her sides, sliding against her back. The fringes tickled at her knees and wrists, moving and flowing like the grasses of the prairie.

And when Young Doe beckoned to her, calling her back to the buffalo-robe, Frankie went to her, staring at the beaded moccasins she was holding. Young Doe motioned for her to sit, so Frankie sat down and watched as Wood Flute's mother eased the moccasins onto her feet. She felt the thick leather soles against the bottom of her feet, felt the soft supple leather of the tops against her ankles.

Frankie stared at the pattern of the beads and traced her fingers along the beads—beads of orange and red, yellow and white—sewn into pretty rows and arches across the leather that reminded her of prairie sunrises. Her tears were rising as Wood Flute and Dandelion squatted in front of her, pulling the leather laces into place, tightening each moccasin. Giggling and grinning, happy for this little-white-girl. Happy for this sister of theirs.

She lost the battle of the tears, and when they welled up and started streaming down her face, the girls wiped at them with their fingers and palms, laughing and petting at her shoulders. When they were satisfied that the tears had stopped, the girls stood up and followed their mothers toward the fire.

Frankie scrambled up, following them, unsure once again as to what was happening; surprised that they were all moving suddenly and quickly. Apparently, there was work to be done. She watched the women begin to shift belongings around, watching as they rolled and tied the buffalo-robes. Then they were putting the cooking tools and the knives and spoons and the carved burl-bowls into pretti-ly-painted parfleches.

Willow's and Young Doe's movements were smooth and swift and practiced, and suddenly, Frankie realized what it all meant— her Cheyenne and Oglála people were leaving. Realizing suddenly, that they would go and she would stay. Realizing that before very long, they would follow the track up and around and out of her little meadow. Understanding suddenly, that in a short time, she would be standing here all alone in her meadow.

Dandelion and Wood Flute were moving quickly too. Frankie could see that they knew what was expected of them; they knew exactly what to do. They were moving as swiftly as their mothers, their actions just as efficient—doing what they had done many times before.

When they trotted out toward the Indian ponies still in the meadow, Frankie trotted after them, helping them halter and bridle the horses. But as soon as they brought the packhorses to the campfire, Dandelion and Wood Flute began passing bundles and bags and equipment to their mothers. And Willow and Young Doe were lifting and settling the bundles and bags onto the backs of the pack-ponies.

Frankie knew it was best to stay out of the way. Because they were all moving quickly and they clearly didn't need a little-white-girl in their way. So she stood back, letting her fingers play in the long fringes of her antelope-leather dress as she watched the little camp disappear. Watching as her new family prepared to leave.

Everything was packed up and tied up, all of it fastened on the horses in what Frankie figured was not much more than five or six minutes. And just as the women finished their work, Frankie heard the sound of hooves pounding on the track beyond the meadow's entrance.

A moment later, the band of warriors came ripping into the valley on their spotted ponies. They swept past the women and girls and when they pulled their horses to a hard stop at the front of the barn, Frankie suddenly understood why they had left the meadow with their rifles and bows ready. They had gone hunting. A deer carcass was strapped to the back of one of the ponies—the men were replacing what their band had eaten on their last visit.

The time it took the warriors to hang the deer left Frankie's mind spinning—it took less than a full minute. They had barely pulled to a stop at the barn entrance before Knife was leaning from the back of his pinto, grabbing the end of the pulley-rope and flinging it to Gray Fox. Gray Fox fastened his end of the rope to the deer in the time it took another man to untie the carcass from the horse.

The instant he finished, Knife and He's Proud slid off their ponies, using their body-weight on the other end of the rope to hoist the carcass upwards. Knife tied the line to the barn-hook, leaving the buck swinging in the barn entrance, hanging exactly where the other deer had been when they had last visited.

Gray Fox walked over to one of the packhorses, his mind already on something else. He lifted one of the rolled buffalo-hides from its back, tossed it over his shoulder and motioned for Frankie to follow him. He carried it to the porch at her kitchen door; he laid the hide down and squatted in front of her, his hand on her shoulder.

He spoke to her in his language and He's Proud was beside her, speaking softly, translating Gray Fox's words. Gray Fox said he was happy she had cared for his father's buffalo-horse. The horse, he said, ran with the same speed and strength he had when his father rode him. The buffalo-robe was his gift to her, he said; but this buffalo-robe, he explained, was not from *this* hunt. He would return and bring her a buffalo-robe from a lead bull from this hunt—a buffalo that was of *this* herd that she had brought to the Cheyenne and the Oglála people. It would be the hide from the biggest and best lead-bull. That, he said, would be his gift to her.

Gray Fox said he would come to visit her many times. And when she came to visit his people, she would live with his family in his lodge. She was Fire Heart Child, who had called to the buffalo, who could kill rabbits without leaving a wound. She was, he said, his little-white-girl who could heal horses.

Frankie stood staring at him, and then she looked down, staring at the ground unable to come up with the right words. He stood then and walked to the horses. He swung up on his bay pony and rode out of the meadow, leading his father's buffalo-horse. The other warriors followed him. The girls, already on the horses behind their mothers, gave her a final look over their shoulders.

Knife held his horse back while the others rode up the track, riding around and out of her sight. He pointed to her and said the words softly.

"Na-semahe. Nė-sta-vå-hóse vóomåtse" 'My sister. I will see you again.' He sent his pony up the track in a hard gallop. Then he was gone.

Frankie stood watching. Waiting to see if he would come back. Waiting to see if any of them would come back. Wanting desperately for them to return. But there was no sound of horses coming back. Her dogs trotted over to her, standing next to her for a moment, and then they began sniffing at the buffalo-robe.

She watched the dogs for a moment, then walked into the house and back to her room. She slipped out of the silky-soft dress because she didn't want her tears to stain her beautiful gift. She folded it carefully, then she loosened the ties on her moccasins and laid them on the dress. She stretched out on the bed, lying face-down. The morning air drifted in through the porch door, circling around and sweeping across her as she cried. Suddenly realizing that she was alone again. All alone. And she was feeling a pain in her chest. She knew what she was feeling. It had a name. It was called lonesome.

The tears came up from somewhere inside her and she let them come. She let the tears flow; she felt the pillow dampen. Then she turned to her side, pulled the quilt up in a bundle and hugged it against her chest. She stared out into the meadow, looking toward the track where her people had gone. Her Cheyenne people and her Oglála people. The tears came again and she closed her eyes.

Frankie woke in the early afternoon, still hugging the bundled quilt against her. She stayed as she was on the bed, watching the hillside out her bedroom door, listening to the sounds of the valley. No shouts and laughter of her new sisters. No Cheyenne words or Oglála words coming from beside the cookfire. She heard the sweet and earnest song of a wood thrush. Then the faraway caws of a flock of crows. *No. Too harsh and hoarse for crows. Ravens, then. Must be a flock of ravens.*

She lay there on the bed, feeling the afternoon breeze drifting across her bare belly and chest. Clutching the crazy quilt with one hand; fingering the soft-tanned hide of the soft antelope-dress on the edge of the bed with the other hand. Listening to the flock of ravens. Listening to their calls growing fainter as they moved off. *No. Not a 'flock' of ravens. An 'unkindness' of ravens. Father called them that. It's the group-noun.*

Frankie listened to the last of the raven calls. *Then what's the group-noun for crows?* She thought for a while, trying to remember, picturing her father in his library, trying to hear his voice.

Remembering suddenly. *A 'murder' of crows. A group of crows is called a 'murder'.*

She grinned, remembering his voice and the smile on his face when he told her that.

'Why do they call them that?' She asked him, and she must have had a funny expression on her face because he'd been amused.

'I don't know, Sweet Girl; I've never discovered the origin, nor the reasoning, behind that particular designation.'

'Well then, why is it an unkindness of ravens and a murder of crows? Why can't they just be a flock, or a bevy, or a flight? Like other birds? What do they have against ravens and crows?'

'I have no answer for you on that question either, My Sweet.' He had reached out his hand, waggled his fingers at her, beckoning to her. 'Come now, before we find ourselves lost in a lengthy concatenation of your questions. Instead, we should see what your aunt has prepared for us at table. Let us away, Child.'

They had walked down the long hallway in the big white house, her father holding her hand—with her laughing at his use of unwieldy words and old English phrases, and with him amused by her laughter. Her mind whisked back to that time, to that home—the big white house where her aunt and uncle and cousins lived—where her father had moved them. *Just me and him. And not her.*

Frankie could remember well enough the day they had moved, just after she had turned seven, leaving her mother to live alone with her anger and spite. It was after her father had learned about her mother's violent rages—she could still see the look on his face when he had first seen her arms and chest and back. His expression had changed as his fingers touched the older bruises and traced the fresh welts.

She had never seen anger in his eyes before, but there had been anger in his eyes *that* day—his whole face had been clouded with anger. He had stood up suddenly; he took the carpet-bag—the pretty flowered-tapestry satchel—from her closet and he started packing her clothes. They walked out to the carriage house together. She stood to the side, watching while he hitched the old gray gelding to the carriage. *Prince Charlie. That was the old gelding's name. Bonny Prince Charlie.* And then, they drove off.

They had driven across the county to the big homeplace—to the big white house with the wrap-around veranda. Her Uncle James and Aunt Sarah had swept the front door open and welcomed them. From that day on, their home had become home for Justus Harding and his daughter. That had been a wonderful day.

Frankie let her thoughts stay on that day, revisiting the time and the event. Revisiting her father. Letting her mind stay for a while in Indiana in the white house that sat on the knoll above the river. It had always been a second home to her—the welcoming house—where her grandparents had lived with their son James and his wife Sarah and their four sons. *At least, until her grandparents had passed on.*

Her father had spoken to her later in the week, telling her that she wouldn't be going back to the other house. Neither of them would be returning to live there.

'We'll be living here from now on.' He had taken her chin in his hand, held it firmly and gently. 'I will not have you treated that way. Never again.' He had said more, too—he explained everything he believed she should know; he talked to her until he was sure she was content with the change.

And she had been *more* than content with the change. Because in that moment, everything had changed for the better. They lived there in the big house with her Uncle James and her Aunt Sarah and her four cousins—Samuel and Thomas, Isaiah and Little Charles. Her life had become wonderfully calm and wonderfully exciting, all at the same time.

She had always played and run with her cousins whenever she visited the great house. But now, that became her life—she ran and raced through the farm and the fields with her cousins; she roamed the forests and the riverbanks with them; she climbed trees and rode horseback and hunted with them. Every day. They played together and did their chores together; they romped and wrestled and laughed together.

As always, she spent part of her days in her father's classroom at the teaching academy. She listened to her father as he taught his classes; she learned what his students learned. The rest of the time, she spent in the house and the dairy barns and the horse stables. She helped the hostlers at the stage-stop in front of the main stable, and she tagged along with her Uncle James while he trained the coach-horses.

When her Aunt Sarah was in the kitchen and in the vegetable gardens, Frankie worked beside her. In the herb gardens and the drying sheds, she helped with the preparations of the herbal powders and tinctures; she learned about the salves and the remedies and the medicines. When her aunt traveled to homes to treat illnesses and injuries, Frankie went with her, working at her side; she was at the bedsides with her aunt, watching and learning when babies came into the world. And watching and learning when the elderly left it.

Frankie brought her mind back to her own home, releasing the thoughts of Indiana and her family back in the big house; she rolled to her back and stared at the slats in the ceiling. Running her fingers against the little thread-balls of the hobnail bedspread. Staying where she was for a few more minutes. Listening to the birdsongs from high in the treetops on the valley's hillsides. Hearing the hammering of a woodpecker, pounding his beak into some tree trunk. Picking up the occasional bursts of hen-clucking from the henyard.

Out in the front pasture, she heard one of the horses nicker. She heard Blossom lowing from the back barn-lot. *She's wanting some help with her milk. Her udder's probably tight. Primrose probably hasn't taken enough milk from her and I didn't milk her last night or this morning.*

Frankie grimaced at the thought, surprised she hadn't gotten to the milking; but understanding how it happened—given everything else that had been going on. *It's not so bad, really. Because Primrose has been nursing. That'll have eased most of her discomfort. But still, she could use a milking.*

Beyond those sounds though, beyond the normal sounds of the homestead, there was nothing else. No other sounds. Everything was quiet. She stretched and sat up. Took in a slow breath and released a quiet sigh. She swung her legs off the bed, rubbed her hand across the soft folds of the antelope dress. Fingered the beads.

Finally, she stood and walked to the kitchen, glancing to the dishpan on the counter. Remembering how it had been piled full of biscuits and cornbread. It was empty now. The butter-crocks beside it were empty. She stepped out onto the kitchen porch and scanned the meadow. It was empty too.

The meadow was silent; the laughter was gone. So were the buffalo-robes and the weapons of the warriors. And the fringes and the feathers. The painted ponies were nowhere to be seen. No one was sitting by the fire-ring. There was just silence. Her friends of the prairie had gone away. Deep into the Sand Hills.

She squatted down to run her hands across the soft curls of the buffalo-robe that was still laying where Gray Fox had left it. It was her first buffalo-robe. Something she'd never had before; something she'd never imagined having. She looked over to the barn, looking at the pen that stood empty now. Drum was gone—Čhánčhega was gone from the meadow. He was back among his people; he had gone back to the life he knew. He would be chasing buffalo again. *Probably in a few days. Once the families catch up to the herd again.*

Matilda bounded up on the porch with the chick, following close behind, freed from the stall in the barn where Matilda routinely stashed it when she needed to roam or work unencumbered with a tagalong chick. Frankie ruffled the collie-dog's ears and reached to give the chick a boost up the last step onto the porch. Then, she stood up, looking over to the cookfire, watching as a little wisp of smoke rose from the ashes, curling up, and then drifting away. Disappearing as it followed the soft afternoon breeze. Gone.

No one was at the cookfire now. The logs and the ring of stones were still there and the iron forks were still in place. The spit was there with the big empty iron cookpot hanging on its hook. But there were no people there; her Cheyenne and the Oglála were gone. Their words, the soft Cheyenne words and the heavier Lakotah words, were gone too.

Frankie squinted at the grass near the fireside logs—there was something over by the campsite that didn't belong, something sitting in a small pile beside the stacked firewood. She was confused, trying to think of what she had left there. *My dress, I left that there. But nothing else. I sure didn't leave a pile of things sitting there.*

She walked across the meadow, eyeing the oddity as she approached. Close enough, finally, that she could see what made up the neat little pile. She saw rawhide boxes and leather pouches and hides—all things that her Cheyenne and Oglála families had left behind. She squatted down, touching the items gently, running her fingers over them. Realizing that Willow and Young Doe must have put them there while she was at the kitchen porch with Gray Fox. *They left these here for me. Gifts. Gifts from my family.*

A blanket of small hides stitched together was lying across the top of the pile. Dark-colored fur, rich and thick—deep brown with a tinge of gray. *Muskrats, maybe? Probably.* A pouch made from rabbit-hides, trimmed with blue, yellow and green beads. One of the rawhide boxes was filled with buffalo jerky; the other with pemmican. There were leather pouches filled with wild onions and wild turnips; others filled with the roots of cattails and smart weed and prairie primrose. And wrapped in pieces of buffalo-hide, there were slabs and strips of buffalo meat.

And there was more. There was another pair of moccasins, different from the soft and fancy-beaded ones in her bedroom with the dress—these were made of heavier leather, plain and tough. *Everyday moccasins, like everyday boots.* There was a bridle that was round-braided, beaded and beautiful—like the ones that He's Proud and Gray Fox used on their own horses.

Frankie stood there, looking at the wonderful gifts. Standing naked, in the way that young Cheyenne girls could, with no one scolding or correcting or criticizing. Her thoughts went to her time with this new family of hers—the loving smiles, the gentle smiles.

She stood where she was, continuing to stare at the gifts from the Cheyenne and Oglála. Fingering the necklace that hung around her neck—the necklace Knife had made—the wolf-medicine necklace. Three bullets and four wolf-teeth and the black and white and blue beads. It rested softly, gently, powerfully, against her skin.

These people, she realized, were her family now. And they would be back. They had told her so.

Frankie let Solomon set his own pace on the way back home from the Reverend Austin's church, and mostly, the big chestnut wanted to travel at a fast road-trot. It was a natural gait for him and it was probably one of the reasons Captain Connell had favored him as his Cavalry mount. The strong trot, plus the bright chestnut coloring, the blazed face and the tall white-stockings, gave him an element of flash that made him stand out among most other horses.

Captain Jack Connell was a true horseman, and Frankie knew he always looked for performance and true quality in a mount—and not necessarily appearance. But if he did manage to find the performance and confirmation qualities that he favored in a mount, and there also happened to be some flash, he wouldn't mind. He'd see it as a bonus. And Solomon had all those; he was everything a solid horseman could want.

At the moment, as Solomon was taking her along the north-track in his smooth road-trot, Frankie was happy enough to be heading home. It had been a full day, filled with a lot of people and activity and noise. First, there had been the Reverend Austin's Sunday service, and then, there had been the community's Harvest Picnic in the churchyard.

The harvest celebration on that mid-September day was an annual event for all the settlers in the region, but for Frankie the event had been her first. The day had actually been two firsts for her—her first Harvest Picnic, and her first time among the people of the settlement. Since all the families in the region had heard about the young girl living alone on a homestead, Everett and Ida and the Austins thought it wise for her to meet the whole community in one fell swoop. So all the curiosity, concern and speculation would be put to rest at once. And while Frankie knew the wisdom of the plan, it had still been a strenuous day—a day with a lot of people and a lot of activity around her all at the same time.

And that was the very reason Frankie had chosen to ride her own mount instead of traveling in the Dunbars' wagon; it was all part of her own plan—a plan that would allow her to slip away and head home if the day became tiring. Which she had thought likely.

Everett and Ida had stayed at her place Saturday night, and in the early morning, they had all traveled to the settlement together; the Dunbars in their spring-wagon and Frankie riding Solomon beside them, using her grandmother's side-saddle to accommodate the new pink dress Ida made for her after the harvest trip to Fort Cottonwood.

Traveling with the Dunbars had been a good choice; Frankie had been glad enough to arrive at the gathering in the company of her closest friends, because Everett and Ida made all the greet-ings-and-meetings go a lot easier. The Harvest Picnic would draw all the people of the Middle Loup settlement, plus more homesteaders from miles around, and even though Frankie had been prepared for a crowd, it had still seemed like an awful lot of people—because it was more people than she had been around since she had left Fort Kearny.

They were her neighbors, and even though there had been a lot of them milling around the churchyard all day, Frankie had liked meeting them. They were good people, hardworking people, who were busy settling onto their homesteads and learning to live in this new land that was far different from what they had known.

These people of the Middle Loup settlement had spent the year working the soil and planting their fields. They had harvested their crops and hauled them to market. And today, the Harvest Picnic had given them a chance to celebrate the bounty of their harvest after they returned from selling their crops. They set aside their work for the day to come together there in the churchyard. Visiting and laughing, catching up with their friends, enjoying the time with their neighbors.

Overall, Frankie was pleased with the day. It had given her the chance to meet the settlers in the area, and it offered them the opportunity to meet the young girl they had been hearing about. So any mystery and speculation that might have been still swirling around among the homesteaders in the region, was over.

So the event had served its purpose for her. And it had also allowed her to fulfill her promise to the Reverend Austin—she had visited his church as he asked. She had seen his cozy little sod-church and she had listened to his sermon.

But now, as she was heading home, letting Solomon take her away from the crowd of people and all the chatter and laughter and noise, she was still thinking over the day—the whole long day.

The actual arrival at the church that morning had surprised Frankie, because it had been oddly comfortable. She had ridden Solomon beside the wagon as Everett drove his team of sleek and shiny seal-browns into the churchyard. He had been waving at the folks walking around the grounds, smiling, happy to see everyone there. And also, clearly proud of how his life was going. Proud of his wagon and team; proud of his new clothes; proud of the way his wife looked in her new dress.

And it hadn't taken Frankie long to realize he was also proud of the chance to show off the 'young cousin' that he and Ida were keeping watch over. The people of the Middle Loup settlement had heard plenty about the young girl living on the old Kinison place. They had heard she had traveled to this region alone; they all knew that her family had died of the fever.

Everett had helped Ida down from the jockey-box, and then he had reached to lift her down from Solomon. Within moments, he was walking 'his young cousin' around, introducing her to everyone who approached them. Acting just as proud of her as if he had invented her himself.

Frankie had stayed at his side, saying the polite 'glad to meet you's' and 'how do you do's', as required. Nodding and smiling, as required. Feeling a lot like she had felt back at Fort Kearny when she had walked around the Parade Grounds beside Lieutenant Halliday.

She thanked the ladies when they complimented her on her dress, telling them Ida had made it for her, and then agreeing with them that 'yes, Ida had done such *lovely* hand-work on it'.

And when the men had commented about 'her fine gelding' and saying things like 'awfully fine horse there, Young Lady', Frankie explained the horse had once belonged to a friend of her family's. She thought it explained things well enough, and maybe managed to settle some of their curiosity about how a little orphaned homestead-girl came to be riding around on such an impressive mount.

Ida had stayed close beside her too, telling the ladies about how she was 'keeping such a nice house there on her homestead', and saying that 'oh my, she's such a wonderful cook'. And she 'certainly knows how to make that big kitchen stove do her bidding'. And Ida also made a point of talking about the four apple pies Frankie had made for the picnic.

'Picked the apples from her own trees, put the pies together, and baked them up all on her own. Just to share them today.'

Ida was keeping herself busy trying to say anything that might quiet concerns anyone had about Frankie Harding's circumstances. It was a lot of talk about all the 'lady-like' activities going on at her homestead, but Frankie knew Ida was, in her own way, directing every woman's mind. She was working to build confidence about how the new neighbor girl was managing her own life. And from the approving nods and sweet-smiles of the women gathering around, it was clear she was doing a good job of it.

It wasn't long before Frankie realized someone else was competing with Ida. Betsy Whitten Austin had worked her way to her side and she was stepping in and doing much the same as Ida. She, too, was talking about how young Frankie Harding was 'just doing so fine'. Betsy Austin was busy talking about her spotless home, and about the hens and the henhouse, and about the beautiful Jersey milk cow. About her big kitchen stove, and about how 'adept she was' at cooking and baking and making butter.

And all Frankie could think to do was to stand there between the two women and let them go at it. Because there was definitely a competition going on. Both Ida Dunbar and Betsy Austin were vying for bragging rights about the girl on the homestead to the north.

It hadn't really surprised Frankie that Everett and Ida stayed close to her side seeing to introductions and making sure she was comfortable among all the strangers. Frankie had expected that—it had been the plan. But it had surprised her that firm-minded and stern-faced Betsy Whitten Austin had also become one of her strongest allies for the day.

Betsy Austin had even made a point of insisting that she 'come and have a quick look inside the chapel before the service'. So Frankie went inside the Reverend Simeon Austin's church, hand-in-hand with the preacher's wife, while everyone else kept wandering around the churchyard—visiting and laughing and enjoying their neighbors.

Frankie had been more than a little surprised at the church building itself; it wasn't like any church she'd ever seen, but she had been delighted with it. It was a humble sod building, quiet and solid and unpretentious. It was long and low, with a double door at one end and three windows set in each long wall. The pews were nothing more than long benches of neatly stacked blocks of sod—lined up in rows on each side of an aisle that ran right up the middle of the chapel.

And even before the service, Frankie could see that the people of the congregation had already spread their blankets and quilts on top of the sod-pews. Certainly as a means of protecting their skirts and britches from any dirt and dried bits of grass and roots from the sod blocks. But also, Frankie figured it was an attempt to reserve the seats of their choice.

At the front of the church, there was a hand-made wooden pulpit on one side of the room and a potbellied stove on the other. The only wooden chair in the church stood near the pulpit—a chair for the Reverend's use. Frankie figured it was probably so the Reverend wouldn't be walking around at the front of the church, preaching his heart out, while his backside was covered with sod-dirt and dried-grass from sitting on a stacked-sod seat.

Thinking about it, Frankie decided it was probably a good idea; it would be a hard thing for a man of God to maintain any level of

349

dignity—no matter how good he was at preaching—if he was walking around in front of his congregation with clumps of dirt and scraps of grass hanging from the seat of his black preacher-pants.

Once she and Betsy Austin emerged from the dim and cool interior of the sod-church, Frankie realized that yet another competitor had stepped into the game of showing-off-the-young-homestead-girl. The Reverend Simeon Austin clearly believed he and his wife had home-rights and home-rule when it came to introducing this young neighbor to his own congregation. He made his move, and he and Betsy managed to edge out both Ida and Everett. Frankie felt bad for the Dunbars, but there wasn't much she could do about the situation. Because the Reverend Austin had a definite advantage—he was, after all, standing on his own turf, being there in his own churchyard.

In his kindly way, the gentle preacher kept finding reasons to lead Frankie away from the Dunbars' sheltering arms, taking her over to this group, or that group. He talked about her homestead and her fine livestock. He bragged about the buck she had been packing home the first time they met, and how they had 'dined on fresh-killed sage-hen on another visit'. He claimed she was 'as fine a huntress as the goddess Diana could ever claim to be.'

He told the story of meeting in her apple orchard, confessing to being caught stealing 'the forbidden fruit' from her trees. And when he boasted about her talent with a violin, Frankie saw the knowing and slightly-devilish smile and wink he threw her way. It occurred to her that the smile and wink seemed a bit wicked for a preacher to be using on a Sunday morning, and once again, she had the odd feeling that the preacher still had some idea turning around in his mind—an idea that somehow involved her and her violin.

Frankie had been anticipating a crowd at the Harvest Picnic, but it was still a surprise to see how many homesteaders were actually there. There were far more people in the area than she thought; she counted about sixty-five people which, when she thought about it, was probably only about ten or twelve families, besides the Dunbars and the Austins.

By listening to the talk around her, and by fitting in a few of her own questions, she learned that most of the families had farms near the Middle Loup River. Some had traveled as far as fifteen miles. Mostly, there were families with varying numbers of children, but there were a few unmarried men in the group too.

There were three or four men whose names Frankie didn't hear, but there was a man with the last name of Hyatt who seemed to show a lot of interest in Solomon. There were three brothers with the name of Hargan who seemed to be somewhere in their late teens; they all kept finding reasons to approach her, and two of them said something about having a 'pretty new neighbor'. But inevitably, they seemed to forget what they wanted to say and they ducked away—elbowing each other, blushing, and stumbling over their own feet.

And there was one man there who had only one arm; he spent some time talking to a few of the other men, talking about the weather and the spring planting. Frankie had seen him standing alongside the man named Hyatt, both of them studying Solomon together, and probably discussing other horses too. It wasn't long after that, when Frankie saw the one-armed man leave the churchyard, walking off to the south by himself before the Reverend's service started, and long before the picnic got underway.

Thinking over the day as Solomon trotted for home, Frankie decided there had really only been a couple of tense moments for her. One had been just as Betsy Austin finished showing her inside the chapel—as they exited, a red-haired lady had started clanging a little hand-bell, calling to all the children in the churchyard and herding and hurrying all of them inside the chapel. She had been talking about a Sunday School session, and how they would 'learn lots of new verses to recite, and have the chance to learn about being good disciples for the Lord. Frankie had cringed at the thought, suddenly worried about any possible expectations of her being included in the children's Sunday classroom. To her relief, no one had sent her inside with the other children; she had remained outdoors walking and talking with the adults around the churchyard.

After an hour or so, there had been another moment of tension—as the doors to the sod-church opened and the Sunday-schoolers poured out. It was at that point, as the adults started filing into the church for the Reverend's service, that Frankie had feared she was going to be left outside with the children, left to do their running and playing. Once again, Frankie had breathed a sigh of relief as Betsy Austin took her arm and ushered her into the chapel right along with Ida and all the adults.

Frankie had given a quick prayer of thanks to the Lord and His angels as she walked into His house—feeling a gush of gratitude that she hadn't been left to romp and play with the children of the settlement. Because, in her mind, nothing good could come from anyone seeing her in noisy and frivolous play with the other children. Not on her first appearance among the homesteaders of the region. Not when so much about her future could be affected by what the neighboring homesteaders saw today.

As Betsy guided her and the Dunbars to the front of the chapel, right up to the front sod-bench, Frankie noticed she was the only child among the grown-ups. And when she took her seat between Betsy Austin and Ida for the Reverend's service, she suspected it wasn't an accident. Likely, the Reverend and Betsy, Ida and Everett had planned it that way.

The service and the sermon fascinated her, mostly because the Right Reverend Simeon Austin could talk up a storm without ever getting loud or fearsome. No bullying; no fire; no brimstone. No admonishments to fear the Lord; no warnings about the wrath of God. His words were a testimony about trusting in God's love, respecting God's word, and walking through life in a way that honored God's wishes for mankind.

The Reverend Simeon Austin's words were kind and fierce at the same time. His message was strong and encouraging, passionate and steady. Compassionate and generous. It was a service that made Frankie proud that she knew the man. His voice had a grounded quality to it, deep and rich and resonant. And always, his words were honest and humble there in that sod-house of God. Everything within the modest building made from the very earth that God had created, was solid and respectful—the people, the preacher and the sermon.

While the children of the settlers were outside in their own world of frolic and play, where even the babies and toddlers were in the hands of the older children, Frankie sat inside the earthen walls of the Reverend's chapel, listening to the depth of his message— his words were clearly meant to build peace and faith within this community.

And to Frankie, the Reverend Austin's mission was clear—way out on the prairie, way out in the Sand Hills between the Middle and North Loup Rivers—the Reverend was building a community. He was starting from the ground up, literally. And he was following a righteous path. He was starting it right, which usually meant, it would continue right.

Out in the churchyard after the service, while Frankie stood among a cluster of her new neighbors, the Reverend Simeon Austin had made a point to ask her what she thought of his 'little sod church and its humble beginnings'.

"I was listening to your words during the sermon, Reverend, and I was thinking about how you're building a community out here. My Uncle James always believed that starting on the right path, meant you would stay on the right path." She paused for a moment, knowing everyone around them was listening—which, she realized, was exactly why the Reverend had asked her his question. "And that's what I think you're doing here, Reverend."

The Reverend Austin had rocked back a bit on the heels of his brogans, his eyebrows raised; he had stared at her, tugging on the wisp of the reddish-brown beard on the end of his chin. He had given her a slow nod. Then he had hugged her to his side.

"You know, my young friend, I was feeling a bit guilty. Thinking I had, perhaps, overlooked your needs. You see, I was worried that by inviting you into the service, I had cheated you of the opportunity to play with children of your own age. Now, I'm thinking God had His hand in this, because I truly needed to hear what you just said. I was blessed to have you among my congregation today."

"Sir, when I walked out after your sermon, I was thinking that I was blessed. Thank you for allowing me to listen to your words."

Frankie felt a kiss on the top of her head and looked up to see Betsy Whitten Austin smiling at her. It wasn't one of her surface-type smiles; it was a warm smile, coming up from deep inside of her. Heart-felt. There was a sudden silence among the cluster of people and Frankie decided it was time to change the subject.

"How is that loud-mouthed little rooster doing for you Mrs. Austin?" She looked up at Betsy's smiling face.

Betsy Austin broke into a hearty laugh; she shook her head as she began leading Frankie and the people clustered around them toward the row of plank tables—tables purpose-made for the day—all standing end-to-end—holding all the platters and pans and baskets of shared foods.

Betsy Whitten Austin started telling the story of how the rooster had taken a liking to flogging anyone and everyone who crossed the farmyard. And with that tale, everyone around them started nodding and laughing and talking about contrary farmyard animals they had known; it seemed as though everyone had a story to tell about flogging-roosters and broody-hens and cranky-kicking milch cows.

Frankie had seen her chance to slip away; she went to where Ida was spreading out their blanket on the ground and opening the basket-lunch.

It had been an afternoon of families enjoying the picnic lunches they brought for themselves and sharing in all the extra plates, platters and baskets of food that had been brought for the great Harvest Picnic. The plank tables groaned under the weight of the harvest's bounty—a great variety of foods. Platters of baked potatoes and squash, turnips and beets and carrots, bowls of baked beans and buttered parsnips. Baskets of breads and dinner-rolls. Pans of fried chicken and fresh-butchered pork. Spice cakes, and chocolate cakes, sweet-potato pies and pumpkin pies, bread-puddings and cobblers, doughnuts and tea-cookies. Everything that was part of the year's harvest from all the homesteads.

Frankie's apple pies brought out smiles, because as Frankie learned, none of the homesteading families had any producing apple trees. Some had planted whips over the past few years but most had been lost to the whims of the weather. Any trees that *had* survived, were still too young to bear fruit.

So when Frankie handed out little canvas packets of apple seeds along with the plates of apple pie, there were more smiles. And that was when the Reverend Austin took advantage of the moment and offered an addendum to his morning behind the pulpit—he declared that the apple seeds spoke of the future.

'We should regard the gift of the apple seeds,' he had said, 'as a timely sign, as a signal of harvests to come.'

Once they had eaten their lunches, the children of the home-steads started up with their games again—running and playing, yelling and shrieking. And the adults spent a lot of time and energy, scolding and shouting at them in futile attempts to quiet them.

Surprisingly enough, a good number of those same adults had also encouraged Frankie to run and play—apparently, deciding that she too, should be part of the running and yelling and shrieking. And Frankie had been thinking about how that meant that she too, would become one of the targets of all the scolding and shouting.

And that thought had made her a little nauseated, because she had no desire to be any part of it. It was all so different from the excitement and spirit that had been in her meadow just days ago. These were not Cheyenne and Oglála children—the play with the Cheyenne girls had been child-like and relaxed and free. This play in the churchyard was frantic and forced, childish and contrived.

It wasn't long before the Sunday School lady approached Frankie, excitedly suggesting that she should join her 'little Sunday School scripture sessions' on the Sunday mornings. Frankie found herself stumbling for an answer, and to her surprise and relief, the

Reverend Simeon Austin stepped in to rescue her; it was his gentle hand that gripped her shoulder and leaned her back against him, a gesture that felt a little protective, and maybe, a bit possessive.

"I'm sorry but, *no*, Mrs. Gingery, I'm afraid I can't let you have *this* one in your Bible-study brood. I feel the need to have this young lady assessing my message in my services. That is, if you don't object, Miss Harding."

She knew the Reverend was working to offer her a graceful way out of the Sunday School invitation, stalling things on her behalf. And in that moment, Frankie found both an answer to his question and a polite way out of her dilemma.

"No, Sir. I wouldn't object to having the chance to hear your voice and your message again. That would be the most important reason I would travel here on a Sunday morning. As long as I can sit next to Mrs. Austin in the front row. Right where I can see you."

The Sunday school teacher laughed; the preacher laughed; the people standing around them laughed. And when Betsy Austin smiled and nodded, Frankie knew she had just killed two birds with one stone.

First, she would never have to run and play with these children, nor find herself sitting in Sunday School scripture sessions with them. And second, she was now in a solid friendship with both Betsy Whitten Austin and the Reverend Austin. She had the firm footing she wanted in this community—a guarantee that she would be staying on her homestead.

And now, as Frankie rode to the north, letting Solomon follow the north track home, she realized something else. Throughout the entire day, no one had spoken a single word about her circumstance. No one had asked a single question about her living-situation on her homestead. No one asked about her family and what had happened. No one had been cutting questioning glances at her.

All that meant that word had traveled through the community. The people of this far-ranging community had heard the story of

Frankie Harding—and they had heard exactly what the Dunbars and Simeon and Betsy Austin wanted them to hear. The speculation had been halted before it had a chance to start.

There would still be talk—Frankie knew people well enough to know that—but it would be soft talk, instead of hard and cold gossip. Now that everyone at the picnic had met her, talked with her and observed her, she was part of their community. These people had accepted her circumstances and they had given no sign they would interfere.

The Reverend Simeon Austin had watched Frankie Harding ride the tall chestnut into his churchyard, trotting beside the Dunbar wagon, and in that moment, his world had brightened a bit. He couldn't keep his smile from growing when he saw his young neighbor from the homestead to the north. And today, her dark eyes were bright, her smile was sweet, and her face was radiant. The blush-pink of the dress she wore reflected the blush on her face as she scanned the gathering of people across the churchyard.

He could tell she wasn't particularly comfortable with what must have seemed like a great many people—people who were strangers to her. But as Everett lifted her down from her saddle, Simeon Austin could see her gather herself, readying herself to face the circumstance with a calm resolution.

In the Reverend Austin's mind, Frankie Harding was an enigma. Young and wise, sweet and tough, trusting and wary. And later, when he had seen her there inside his church, watching him from the front pew, he found himself unnerved by her intensity and her focus. There were no other children among his membership who showed her level of interest. She had sat alert and attentive through his sermon; she had shown an understanding and acceptance that went far beyond her years.

Even her response to his question out in the churchyard after the service, suggested she had not only listened to his words, but her thoughts had gone far beyond his message and his sermon. Somehow, he realized, young Frankie Harding was well aware he was on a mission that went beyond the sod-church standing at the crossing of two tracks on the prairie. Somehow, she already knew what no one else in this far-flung community seemed to recognize.

She was looking ahead, seeing what he was seeing; she understood the reach he desired—his dream to touch lives far beyond his work in the sod-church out here among the Sand Hills. She had said as much when she spoke about 'starting right to continue right'. Those may have been the words of an uncle, but she knew exactly how to apply the concept; she also understood the impact of the concept.

The very first time they had met out among the apple trees, Simeon Austin had watched his young neighbor assessing his wife. Frankie Harding had seen beneath the stiff and unsmiling surface, and she had understood Betsy's concerns. She had found the way to calm Betsy's discomfort and ease her beyond her judgements. This child, who had traveled the prairies alone and had fought her battles to reach her home, understood how the human heart worked. And she knew exactly how to fill the human heart and strengthen it.

The gift of the rooster and hens had not been just about 'building a flock of chickens', no more than the dinner and the fresh dress were just about 'a neighborly obligation'. The Reverend Austin knew full well what had been in Frankie's mind. It had all been about getting beneath the stiff and unyielding surface of Betsy Whitten Austin—Frankie Harding had known exactly how to find Betsy's soft smile. And she had known how to fill Betsy's heart.

When he had asked Frankie to play the violin for them, she could have refused and avoided the session with the violin. But she had used the opportunity and the music to build a trust and a relationship with his wife, as well as with him. This child—young and small, confident and sure—missed nothing.

The truth was, Simeon Austin knew, Frankie Harding was already reaching deep into his heart and it had been only a month or so since he had met her. In fact, he had actually only been around her a matter of hours. But there was something building here—something about his work and something about the future.

Simeon Austin didn't know what it was, but something was beneath the surface. All he could think to do was to simply keep his heart open. Because Frankie Harding was in his life now, and she was in Betsy Whitten Austin's life too. And only time would tell.

A week later, Frankie was standing by the front barn-lot, rubbing Laughing Girl's ears as the dog leaned against her side. She watched as the Dunbar wagon headed up the track and out of the valley with the four brindle oxen lumbering along, tied to the tailgate. She whistled for Matilda and called to her.

"Come back here. You don't need to fret over the oxen. They'll be back when Everett's done plowing." She laughed as she saw the collie-dog's head drop and her tail droop, disappointed because some of her animals were leaving and there had been no herding involved. Clearly dejected because there had been nothing she had been asked to do about it.

Bo and Benjamin, Buck and Billy were heading to the Dunbar place to spend time in Everett's fields. She smiled as they followed the wagon up the rise, thinking about how long it had been since they had worked in a field.

She saw Ida turn, half-standing in the jockey-box to give a final wave as the wagon started down the far side of the track and disappeared from sight. She waved back and saw Ida's smile just before she sat back down. She was a happy woman; it showed in her smile.

In fact, all three of them were happy and smiling. They all had good reason to be pleased, because their trades for livestock and planting had been settled. The future was taking shape.

The Dunbars had arrived early in the morning, just a bit after full sunrise, and they had all spent most of the day gathered around the porch table, drinking coffee and eating the noon meal and working through dishes of peach cobbler while they visited through the hours, talking and laughing about the Harvest Picnic and the church service. Talking about the long tables of the shared food and about all the people who had been there in the churchyard.

The conversation had moved on to plans for preparing the ground for spring planting. With farm stock available to him, Everett wanted to work more acres on his place; the deal he offered was half of the crop in exchange for the use of both the oxen and the mules— the oxen to break the sod in the fall and the mules for planting in the spring. To Frankie's thinking, it was a fair deal for the Dunbars *and* for her—a deal that would build on the future for both homesteads.

There was a new level of confidence in Everett as he talked about his plans, and Frankie knew a good part of it had to do with the good return on the crops he had taken to Fort Cottonwood. All their plans and work had started to pay off, and now, Everett and Ida were trusting in their future again. Because now, the harvest was over and the crops had been sold.

For weeks before the Harvest Picnic, the men from the area homesteads had traveled from farm to farm, going from field to field, sharing their time and their teams. Spending the days cutting and threshing. Stacking the straw and bagging the grain. The women and children had followed the men to the different farms—some women cooking and setting out meals, some threshing and bagging beside the men. And then, eighteen wagons loaded with oats, wheat, and corn, had left for Fort Cottonwood. Heading to market for sale and trade.

Both Everett and Ida had traveled to Fort Cottonwood with the other settlers. They took Frankie's heavy farm-wagon and the catfish-grays, Ada and Adeline, to haul half of their sell-crop. And they had hired one of the Hargan family's wagons to haul the other half.

It had been a hard decision to not use the Conestoga and the Shires for the trip to Fort Cottonwood, because the whole crop could have been hauled in that single wagon. But Frankie and the Dunbars had decided that sending the big wagon and team to Fort Cottonwood still posed a serious risk—all the soldiers along the Overland Road would still be on the lookout for a massive blue-green Conestoga with a hitch of four black Shires.

For a similar reason, the mules couldn't be used because their belled-tails would draw attention. Because Frankie's three mules still showed the bells on their tails, and mules with bell-shapes cut into their tail-hair typically were owned by the Cavalry or freighting companies. Eyebrows would lift and questions would be asked if a team of bell-tailed mules were seen hitched to a farm-wagon loaded with crops.

Frankie had been at the Dunbar homestead on the morning they headed off to the mustering place at the Middle Loup River. Everett and Ida had been grinning like kids going to a circus as the two gray mares headed across the ford. For Everett, the excitement was about having a good harvest; it was about having wagon-loads of grain to sell and trade, and then returning with wagons of supplies and cash in hand. *That* would be proof for him of a year's work done well.

The excitement for Ida, though, had more to do with the thought of once again having the supplies she needed. Because she'd have her shelves and cabinets and cupboards filled with what she needed to nourish and nurture the people she loved. For her, *that* would be proof she was living her purpose.

Frankie had tended their place while they were gone, traveling back and forth between her home and theirs—the same as she had done while they worked with the harvest crew. It had all been part of the plan that the Dunbars and the Reverend Austin had suggested—having her stay back during the harvest, and again for the trip to Fort Cottonwood.

The Dunbars and the Austins used the harvest time, and the trip south, to spread word among the other homesteads about young Frankie Harding and her circumstance. And that was why there had been such a strong show of acceptance by the homesteaders when Frankie made her first appearance at the Harvest Picnic.

So Frankie had stayed behind, taking care of the Dunbar homestead; it had been eleven days of waiting for the wagons to return. And when the catfish-grays finally pulled into her meadow, the smiles on the Dunbars' faces were bigger and prouder than when they had begun their journey. They left with two wagons full of grain and they returned with two wagons full of supplies.

The Dunbars had what they needed for winter, and they had money to set aside. They brought Frankie the supplies she wanted, and Everett's eyes had been shining as he put her cash-share in her hands. The Army at Fort Cottonwood had bought all the crops—with several hundred soldiers and hundreds of horses to feed, it was a guaranteed market for the homesteaders. And the commander at Fort Cottonwood had not been tight-fisted; the grain was needed and the US Army was a willing buyer.

So today, throughout their visit, the three of them had reveled in their recent success and the peace of mind that came with it. And now, having sold the crops and purchased supplies, Everett was keen to settle on a plan for farming in the next year.

They had lain out ideas for opening up new fields—planting forty acres on Frankie's homestead and an additional forty on Everett's place. This fall, he wanted to turn the sod on both places. In the spring, he would plant corn and oats on both places. The deal that they already had in place for livestock and crop-sharing had worked well. Now, they were applying a similar plan going forward. Both she and Everett were pleased with the plan, and Ida was content with it too.

But mostly, Frankie figured, Ida was content because she had her pantry full and her sewing baskets over-flowing. She had returned from Fort Cottonwood with all the material and dress-making goods that she could justify. And hearing her talking about her sewing projects had given Frankie an idea about something else, something that would add to Ida's contentment.

She led Ida to the back bedroom and showed her what Lillian Kinison had left behind in the dressers and the wardrobes and trunks. There were four crates of clothing and cloth that Frankie had sorted through. When she suggested Ida take the crates, Ida's eyes had teared up.

"I'm sorry Ida, I should have thought of it before." Frankie shook her head. "I looked through what Lillian left behind and picked out some of her biggest boy's shirts and trousers that I could use. But I don't have any use for the other clothes. Or hers. Or Daniel's either. But they should be used somehow. Maybe to be remade to fit someone else. Or for quilting."

"Oh, Honey. I never thought about it either." Ida didn't waste any time. She started digging into the boxes, lifting items. Assessing, thinking, planning. Humming. Clucking. And to Frankie's mind, sounding a little like the hens out in the meadow.

"We should take some of these boys' clothes down to the church. Betsy will know which families can use them. And maybe, some of the women will have need of Lillian's dresses. Anything that folks don't need, we'll use for quilting."

They spent the better part of an hour going through the clothing and the bolts of cloth. Ida sorted and organized, considered and supposed. She was thinking and deciding and speculating about what should be done with the various items.

It didn't take long for Frankie to realize that Ida didn't really need help with all her deciding and speculating as she worked her way through the crates. So Frankie sat herself on the bed and listened to Ida making her decisions, waiting until she had everything organized and packed up again.

They sat down to the noon-meal of antelope steaks with sweet potatoes, turnips, beets and onions, baked corn-pudding, and a platter of sour-cream cucumbers. And as soon as they were done with the peach cobbler and their coffee, Everett went out to hitch his team of seal-browns and Frankie went for the four oxen. By the time she brought them up from the pasture, Everett had the yokes loaded in the wagon.

They said their goodbyes and made plans for Frankie to visit them the following week. Everett and Ida settled themselves onto their wagon-seat and drove out of the meadow with the four oxen trailing along. There was no mistaking the expression on Everett's face; he was looking awfully proud and pleased; probably, Frankie decided, because he had his plans in place.

Ida was looking pretty proud and pleased herself, likely because she had four crates of clothing and cloth in the wagon-bed. Those crates of material, together with all the cloth she had purchased at Fort Cottonwood, meant she was already looking forward to a winter's worth of sewing projects.

Two hours later, Frankie was scooping feed for the chickens when she heard Matilda and Laughing Girl growling; when she stepped out of the henhouse, she saw both dogs watching the front track. Within a couple of minutes, a team of dapple-grays came down into the meadow at a smart and quick trot, pulling a buckboard with a pair of bright bays tied at the back. Frankie whistled for the dogs, ordered them back, and walked over to greet the two men on the wagon-seat.

At first sight, the men looked a little rough and Frankie found herself wishing she had her rifle in her hands. One was wearing a gun-belt with what Frankie thought was a Navy Colt, and the other had a shotgun beside him.

She took a breath and kept walking. They stayed on the wagon-seat—one was smiling and the other wasn't. The one who was smiling, Frankie recognized from the Harvest Picnic. She had seen him paying a lot of attention to the Dunbars' team and even more to Solomon. She remembered that his last name was Hyatt and she thought he went by William. But the man on the seat beside him was someone she had never seen.

"Good day, young lady. We thought we'd stop in and welcome you to the area. Are your folks around?"

It was the unsmiling one who was doing the talking and Frankie decided to cut through the small talk right then. Either they would deal with her honestly or they could turn around and go 'welcome' some other neighbor to the area. Because the smiling-man, William, had been at the picnic, which meant he knew full-well she didn't have any folks around the place. And, he would have told the unsmiling-guy. So that's exactly what she told the unsmiling-man.

All of which seemed to set both of those men back a little on their wagon-seat and made them drop their jaws a little bit too. Frankie stood and watched them, a little surprised at herself, but very aware that what she had just said had come from her gut. And right now, she was trusting her gut.

Those men—one looking to be in his young twenties and the other maybe ten years older—sat looking at her for a moment. Then they looked at each other. Then they looked back at her. The unsmiling-man, the one who wasn't William, spoke up again.

"Well, you just caught us up with a hard yank on the jerk-line." He waited, like he was expecting a reaction, and when Frankie stayed quiet, he spoke up again. "If you would allow it, I oughta offer an introduction. This is my brother William, and some folks call me GW. But you can call me Tipp, if you want, because most folks do. Our last name is Hyatt, and we have a couple of homesteads about three miles south and east of Reverend Austin's church."

He grinned then. Frankie figured he was either embarrassed with the game they'd played at or embarrassed because they'd been caught at it. Frankie didn't know for sure which it was, but she suspected it was the latter.

She introduced herself then, and the smiling-one named William admitted they had already known her name—and he admitted he had already heard about her situation regarding 'her folks not being around'. And then he said he'd seen her at the church picnic.

"We come today, hopin' to see you and your place. And maybe, to visit a bit." William laid it all out fairly and simply. "And we're awfully sorry for startin' things off on the wrong foot."

William Hyatt had said all of it with such sincerity, that Frankie broke out laughing. It seemed like once the Hyatt brothers were caught in a ruse, they just dropped the whole act and laid everything out in the open. And when she started laughing, they started chuckling, because all three of them knew exactly what had just happened.

Then, the one called GW or Tipp, depending on what a person preferred, admitted he had been thinking that today on their visit, he might just get her in the middle of a trade.

"I had planned on walkin' away with the best end of the deal. And now, I'm feeling a bit ashamed. An' a whole lot sorry." He said it, grinning at her and not looking all that sorry about anything. Mostly, he just looked amused with himself.

Frankie squinted at them for a moment, and then gave them her crooked grin, wanting to show that she had no hard feelings, because these two seemed a bit like some of the soldier-boys she had known at the fort.

"Well, Tipp. Neither of you needs to feel ashamed or sorry. Because I wasn't going to trade with you anyway. So you couldn't have taken advantage of me even if you'd tried."

She laid that out on the table and the Hyatt boys started laughing again, still maybe a little embarrassed, but mostly, because they seemed happy that there were no hard feelings.

"Well, Miss Frankie Harding. Do we have to trade you something for a cup of coffee, or could we just ask for it? Being as we're neighbors." William stepped down from the wagon and he put out his hand; he shook her hand and said he was proud to meet her.

When Tipp came around from the other side, he offered a handshake too, and Frankie knew they were on solid ground. She also figured it might be wise to stay on her toes whenever Tipp Hyatt started talking about trades.

They sat at the table on the front porch and Frankie gave them coffee to start with. And then she gave them a late afternoon dinner of fried antelope steaks and leftover roasted root vegetables. They were pleased enough with the meal, but the minute she put dishes of peach cobbler in front of them, she learned that any dessert with peaches was favored by the two Hyatt brothers. They made a point of mentioning their love of 'peach-anything' several times while they oohed and aahed and ate their way through their dishes of the cobbler. And Frankie realized that she had just found the way to the Hyatt brothers' hearts.

She learned a lot about those brothers while they all sat together at the front porch table. She found out that they *had been* soldier boys and that they had fought for the Union in the War in the South. William had been taken prisoner and held in a Confederate prison camp in Georgia. Andersonville, they said. Somehow—though they never said exactly how—Tipp and two of his other brothers, had 'snuck down into Georgia' and helped William escape.

Even with her questions about it, they didn't go very deep into the details, though William *did* explain that his three brothers 'had to escape *into* the prison, in order to help him escape *out* of it'. Frankie figured if anyone else had claimed such a thing, it would have been nothing more than a tall-tale. But having known these boys even for such a short time, she decided they were maybe just wild enough, and crazy enough, to manage such a thing.

After the escape, or the *escapes*, depending on how you looked at it, the three brothers had taken William back to the family home in Council Bluffs, Iowa.

"He was in pretty bad shape. So we got him healed up and then got him fattened up a bit," Tipp explained. "And then, me and William come out here to the Nebraska Territory to take up claims."

William's interest seemed to be mostly in farming and family, but Tipp's was more toward horses and horse-trading. Frankie had a feeling there was more beneath the surface with Tipp, but he was the type of man who played his cards close to his chest.

To Frankie's surprise, both men perked up when they saw the two violins in the sitting-room, and that got them telling tales about how both of them—along with two other brothers back in Iowa—had always played at dances and socials and fairs.

"On account of everyone always wanted the four Hyatt boys to kick up some tunes." Tipp said it, and William just grinned and didn't disagree, so Frankie figured it was probably true. "Of course, along with the dance music, a good share of the folks just wanted to see what kind of fight the four Hyatt brothers could get ourselves into, and then watch to see how we'd get ourselves back out of it."

When Tipp added that, William didn't disagree either. And again, she was thinking about the wild side of these two brothers, figuring that if two more brothers were added to the equation, things probably could get rough at the dances.

After dinner, the Hyatt boys wanted to see her livestock, and mostly, they wanted to see her horses. The sight of the four Shires surprised and delighted them, and when Tipp started hinting at a trade for the Shires, Frankie shut his ideas down fast. With that possibility gone, Tipp approached the idea of a different trade.

"I'll trade you those two excellent bay geldings," Tipp pointed at the two bays tied to the buckboard, and then turned to point toward Trumpeter, "for that one bay stallion there in your pasture.

William rolled his eyes. Frankie snorted and said 'no'. Tipp spat on the ground. He shook his head and laughed, saying that he 'just had to give it a try'. Frankie told him not to feel *too* bad, because maybe they could trade something in the future. Because she had a hankering for good, solid bay mares.

They stood at the pasture gate watching Trumpeter out in the pasture with Fanny and the three bay mares and the two catfish grays. After a few minutes, William said he'd like to see the bay stallion up close, Frankie whistled Trumpeter over to the fence.

Both men made a big deal over him and Frankie could tell Tipp was getting itchy about talking-trade for him again. She could tell that William had seen the same thing and she grinned when she saw him jab his elbow into his brother's side. It was a hard jab—good and hard—and she knew William was giving his older brother a clear warning to leave the subject alone. But Tipp just couldn't let it go.

"Frankie Harding, I'm about to die of mortal confusion here. You just said you've got a hankerin' for good solid bays. I've got a team of five-point bays standin' tied to that buckboard over there. An', they're just aching to go to work. I'll trade *both* of those fine horses for this one horse standin' right in front of us."

"No, you won't. You could have twenty teams standing out there and all of them together wouldn't equal this horse. That'd be like you offering me twenty nickels for one twenty-dollar gold-piece. You and I both know that." Frankie gave him a glare that was partly teasing and partly serious. "So get your mind off of that. And what I said is that I'm looking for good bay *mares*. And that's a team of geldings you have, so they're of no interest to me. And as far as working teams, I have all I need. Each team suits a purpose and they aren't up for trade. So. You ever want to talk about trading horses with me, we'll be discussing bay mares. And they'd better be good ones."

"Tipp, you have *met* your match. She said you couldn't take advantage of her, and you can't. She's two steps ahead of you, big brother."

William laughed as he sent tobacco juice in an arc over the top plank of the fence, and Frankie realized that for whatever reason, William Hyatt actually seemed pleased that she was holding her ground with his big brother.

As they strolled around the meadow and through the barn, Frankie learned something else about the Hyatt brothers—they did a lot of the section-surveying for the government, and for homesteaders. After talking a bit, they agreed to survey her section and quarter-section lines. And when Frankie said she wanted to fence in the northeast quarter and part of the southeast quarter, beyond her valley slopes, William nodded and said they could handle the job.

"We'll come back in a week or two with all our paraphernalia. Once we get the transit and click-wheels and standing-rods here, Frankie-Girl, we'll get it all lined-out for you in no time." William smiled at her, nodding. "We did the section-surveys for Daniel maybe four years back, but we want to check those again. We don't figure to charge you for checking our own work, but we'll charge you for lining-out and marking the quarters."

"We'll hire on two of the Hargan boys and the two Gingerys to do the fencing." Tipp stepped into the conversation. "They're always looking for work outside their family homesteads and they can do good work, if someone like William keeps an eye on them. I expect you still have a stack of planks up in that loft. Daniel had a sizeable stack at one point."

"Yessir, the stacks are still there in the barn. And, I've got a stack of new-cut fenceposts in the barn too. And, I brought more planks with me when I came north."

"Well, damn. I'll just bet you did. It don't surprise me at all that you've got yourself situated and ready." William burst out laughing.

He was finding humor in her revelation for some reason that Frankie didn't understand, but she didn't mind that he was amused; it usually boded well for a deal in the making if everyone was in a good mood. William went on, once he quit laughing.

"We have a few sizeable stacks we brought up from the Otoe sawmill downriver from Fort Kearny. We can bring 'em up from our place to finish out anything you might need. We'll total things up once we sort through the numbers and supplies. But don't you worry, we'll take care of you."

"You know, Little Miss Homesteader," Tipp laid an arm across her shoulders and Frankie saw him wink at his brother, "if you was to mention you were plannin' to throw together another peach cobbler on the day we show up to work, we might just find a few more ways to shave down your bill."

"I was just about to ask you if you'd rather have peach cobbler or peach pie." Frankie grinned at Tipp, playing his game with him. Making him laugh. Tipp gave her braid a yank.

"Either," Tipp had a big grin on his face. "Now, William, ain't this a fine way to conduct business?"

"It is." William grinned at her and winked. "So Frankie Harding? Do we have ourselves a deal then?" He held his hand out, ready to seal the deal.

Frankie nodded and reached out, shaking his hand. They had a deal.

The Hyatt brothers climbed into their spring wagon and Frankie watched as Tipp wheeled the dapple-grays around toward the meadow entrance. William gave her a nod and his brother snapped the team on their ribs with the end of the whip a few times, while he pulled their heads back with the lines. Frankie knew what he was doing—he was just getting them in a frazzle, wanting them to dance a bit. Showing them off a bit. Then he cracked the whip above their heads and had the grays in a hard gallop before they had even reached the top of the entrance track, with the five-point bays galloping right behind.

She sat down at the porch table, grinning, knowing what her Uncle James would have said about handling horses like that. 'Only a wild idiot wants his horses to act like wild idiots.' She grinned, thinking that maybe the two brothers weren't as much idiots, as they were just a bit wild. Or a lot wild. But even so, she liked them. And she liked that they would be seeing to the surveying and the fence building.

And that got her to thinking about her homestead. Adding things up and realizing that her life was coming together in a nice way to end the year. She had all the winter-feed she needed—she had held onto half of her share of the crop for that. And as far as paying the Hyatts for the survey and fencing, she had the cash from the sale of the other half of her crop that Everett brought back from Fort Cottonwood. That cash would be more than enough to pay Tipp and William. And so far, there had been no need to use any of the money she had in the tooled-leather box, or in the waterproof packet in the Conestoga. None of that money had even been touched.

She had food-stores for herself. There was a good amount of firewood cut and stacked and plans to add to the stacks. The hens were supplying her with plenty of eggs for eating, and enough to set aside for the winter. Blossom was providing all the milk and cream, buttermilk and butter she could use.

There was a large doe antelope hanging in the barn. Three mallard ducks and two rabbits and two grouse were hanging in the pantry. And there was plenty of game for any more hunting she wanted to do.

Everett was preparing more land for planting crops in the spring. She had a root-cellar full of produce and Ida would be working on her garden with her in the spring. And the Dunbars had just brought her more supplies from Fort Cottonwood. All told, right now, she figured she had enough food to feed two whole families for the winter and beyond, if she needed to.

And there was more good news. There were some other things about her homestead Everett had told her—and a few things the Hyatt boys had mentioned.

First, her meadow was protected from most of the heavy weather. Tucked down deep into the valley, below the prairie itself, she had a natural protection that the hillsides and trees provided. The winds and blizzards that whipped across the Sand Hills, would mostly blow above her two front meadows, and William thought most of her third meadow would be protected too. The angle of the valleys, the height of the hillsides, and the sheltering trees, had all been in Daniel Kinison's mind when he selected these quarter-sections.

Second, according to Everett, she had more land than she thought. He believed Daniel Kinison had been buying up more quarters each year, all along the river. And the Hyatt brothers had just confirmed it. They knew it for fact, William said, because they had done the surveying. Everett also doubted that Daniel had told Lillian about all he was doing, because it would have started her on another rampage. He thought it unlikely that Lillian had paid any attention to the specifics about all the claim documents.

'Knowing Lillian,' he had said, 'she wouldn't have cared about any details. Once Daniel died, she probably just issued orders to her parents' attorney to sell anything and everything to do with the homestead.' That, he said, was what she had told him she planned on doing. William Hyatt had said much the same.

'We carried paperwork for Daniel on more'n just the home section. As I recall, there were a number of filings. Given how thorough he always was,' William had said, 'there'll be land documents showing the full claim. If you don't have 'em or can't find 'em, then the federal land offices will have records. I know that for a fact. Because more'n once, when I was traveling to Fort Cottonwood, Daniel sent documents with me to send on to the land office in Independence.'

Frankie made herself a plate of biscuits and gravy and settled herself on the front porch for the evening. Deciding to put pen to paper and lay out some plans. Because now, finally, she could actually put pen to paper; because now, she had packages of paper and boxes of pencils, ink bottles and pens.

They had all been on the list she sent with Ida on the trip to Fort Cottonwood. Oddly enough, no one in her family had included them when they loaded the wagons for the journey West—somehow, they had been over-looked and forgotten items. And they were the things she missed the most.

She started writing her ideas and plans—and specifically the idea that had been forming in her mind for a couple of months. It was an idea in the back of her mind that just lately had been coming forward and taking form.

The idea of breeding and raising horses. It had started with Bill Wheaton's words the night she escaped the fort. That was the night that, along with the geldings—Boone, Samson and Solomon—he had put Trumpeter and the three bay mares in her hands. Standing there in his long barn on Fort Farm Island in the dark of night, he had told her that she had learned everything she needed to know about raising horses from her Uncle James. His words had stayed in her mind.

He had said she could raise horses as well as anyone. Over time, if things came together and if she had the right people to count on, Frankie figured she could do just that. With Trumpeter and the three mares, she had the start of a truly good bloodline. And when the time came, she would have a ready market. The Army. With all the frontier forts that the Army would be building in the territories, there would be a constant need for Cavalry mounts.

That idea had been growing in her mind ever since she had learned about Daniel Kinison's plan. He had been thinking in terms of beef and she had been thinking in terms of horses. But now, with Daniel's herd of roan short-horns, she could do both.

Bill Wheaton on Fort Farm Island had given her the start of the bloodline for Cavalry mounts, and Daniel Kinison had given her the start with beef cattle. Because along with the roan short-horns already in her pasture, there was a bigger herd of cattle roaming somewhere out in the Sand Hills that had been eating and breeding and dropping their babies each spring. Everett thought there had been thirty head a couple years ago, which meant that the herd could be well over fifty now. Frankie grinned at the thought. *And this spring, there'll be even more.*

The Army would always need horses and cattle—horses for mounts and beef for the fort kitchens. And even though it would be a number of years down the road—because it could take years to establish the foundation herds—Frankie figured she needed the time anyway. She would have to be older, so there would be no danger

373

of the Army detaining her or taking her away from her home. And she'd have to wait until all the dangers at Fort Kearny were gone—both Colonel White and Silas Beckett would have to be long gone. But eventually, she could be selling beef and Cavalry mounts to the Army.

She looked out to the back meadow, studying her little herd of beef cattle. Letting her thoughts roam out to the Sand Hills, picturing the other herd of cattle—a bigger herd—heads down, grazing steadily. *All I have to do is find them. Maybe in the spring.*

Her eyes moved to the front pasture, to Fanny and the three bay mares and the two catfish-grays. And Trumpeter. In the spring, it was likely there would be bay-colored babies out there. There would be time to search for more broodmares—good bay mares—to build a solid herd. She'd be able to build a reputation for raising good solid bay horses. *Horses with strong legs and tough hooves. Horses that are prairie-bred and prairie-raised. Horses that are conditioned and trained to the land and the weather out here. Horses bred in the Nebraska Territory instead of back East.*

Frankie's mind kept moving forward and her hand kept moving the pencil. Thinking and planning. She could feel her grin growing. *Because the Cavalry will always need well-bred horses. Sensible and fast and strong. And the forts will always need beef. A guaranteed supply of beef. There's a future here.*

While she was in the middle of thinking about horse-breeding and cattle-herds, she noticed Laughing Girl trudging around in the grass near the kitchen porch—her belly large and hanging low. She was restless and panting, stopping occasionally to stare at Frankie at the porch table, then pacing some more. Several times, the big hound climbed the porch steps, lowered her bulky-body to the wooden floor to lie down in the patch of evening sunshine that was slanting across the porch. Then moments later, she'd rise to pace some more. Groaning as she stood, glancing over to Frankie, looking a bit confused and befuddled.

Finally, Frankie gave in; she laid down her pencil, pushed the papers aside. She called the hound to her. She hugged Laughing Girl's head, talked low to her, rubbed her sides. She held the big hound's head in her lap, rocking it back and forth. Cooing to her, trying to comfort her.

While she was busy soothing Laughing Girl, Frankie saw Matilda trotting across the meadow, coming from the barn with the rooster-puppy tagging along behind. The collie-dog was heading to the stone-room porch, her eyes on the open door.

"*Don't* you take that rooster into the house, Matilda."

Matilda slowed her pace, dropped her head. She stopped and glanced toward Frankie with a look conveying both disappointment and annoyance. Even from the kitchen porch, Frankie could see when Matilda finally accepted the ruling—the collie-dog gave a disgruntled sigh and headed over to a corner of the stone-room porch, with her rooster-puppy scuttling after her.

Frankie turned her attention back to Laughing Girl, watching as the big wolfhound-greyhound began her pacing again. *Looks like there'll be new-born pups in the meadow tomorrow.*

PART III

INDIAN SUMMER

Frankie kept Rock in a slow and steady lope as they traveled along winding game-trail on the north side of the river, shunning the main track beside the south bank. She was taking the 'back way' from the Dunbar's homestead relaxing on the ride home late Sunday afternoon. Smiling as she rode, pleased with the day, pleased because it had been a very productive visit. Pleased because she and Everett had spent time sorting through her land documents—the legal documents that provided proof of ownership of the homestead claim in the Nebraska Territory.

Before leaving Indiana, her Uncle James had stashed a wax-sealed packet of documents in the wall of the Conestoga; he had shown her and his four sons everything in the watertight packet, and he had shown them the hidden compartment in the wagon. He had extracted promises from each of them to keep the documents hidden away and protected from the eyes and hands of strangers. There would come a rightful time to pull them from the compartment, he had said, but it wouldn't be during the journey. It would be after the journey and after they had taken up the claim; then the documents would be needed to verify boundaries and prove ownership.

It had been a hard decision for Frankie to pull the packet out of the hidden compartment of the Conestoga today, and harder still to make the choice to show the documents to Everett. She had protected the packet and its documents from the day she had left the six graves by the Little Blue River; out of necessity, she had been the sole guardian over the packet holding her family's dream.

Today, finally, she had worked up the courage to show the documents to someone else. It had made sense, though, because she was, after all, done with the journey and she had taken up the claim. And now, she needed to verify boundaries, just as her Uncle James had said. She had taken the papers to the Dunbars because it was time to study the documents; it was time to look through the homestead claim and the land titles, so that she could be certain about exactly what belonged to her.

As they studied the documents, they learned that there was more land than just the original section, just as Everett and the Hyatt brothers had believed. Daniel Kinison had, indeed, bought up more acreage—more half-sections and quarter-sections. The deeds showed that he had paid outright for the additional land.

According to the titles, her Uncle James and Aunt Sarah had purchased two full sections and two more quarter-sections. Lillian Kinison had sold all the land to James and Sarah Harding. And there on the titles, along with the names of her uncle and aunt, were five other names. Samuel Harding, Thomas Harding, Isaiah Harding, Frances Harding, and Charles Harding. So as Everett said, everything was set in stone. The titles made it all clear.

Everett wanted to see the section-markers that Tipp and William Hyatt had shown to her—the markers they had set while Daniel Kinison was still alive. Markers, that William had insisted, designated her total claim.

'Honey-Girl, I *know* these are all part of your holdings,' William had said while they were riding horseback on the land so he could show her all the markers. 'You need to look over your documents and make sure all these sections show. They would've been on-file at the land office back in Independence some two and three years ago. You may not have heard all the details when your folks were discussing things, but if Lillian sold this homestead, then I'm certain these parcels woulda been included.'

And now, as she rode Rock along the riverbank, Frankie realized a lot of things. The third valley that was linked to the two front valleys, was indeed hers. The Lookout Hill *was* on her land. The other rows of walnut and hazelnut trees, the apple and mulberry trees she had found downriver, actually *were* her trees—planted by Daniel Kinison on the land he owned. Now, on the land *she* owned. There was no mysterious homestead downriver along the North Loup, after all. It was all part of her homestead.

To Frankie, it felt like another part of her life had come together. She understood more about her claim; she was truly standing on solid ground now. She smiled at the play on words and turned her thoughts to the coming week. Because everything would be even more solid then. Because Everett and Ida were coming to her homestead next Sunday, and Everett said he wanted to see the placement of all her markers for the sections and quarter sections.

Once they had a chance to look over the lay of the land, they could decide which forty acres, on which quarter-section, to farm. He planned to start breaking ground as soon as they decided where to plant in the spring. Come harvest, she would take half of the crop for providing the land and livestock, while Everett would take half for providing the labor and the seed.

As to the placement of her land, to Frankie's eyes, it looked as though the North Loup ran through some portion of six of her quarter-sections. As William had pointed out, she was living on a homestead that would always have access to water, which meant she'd have plenty of water for any and all the livestock she could raise. And as Tipp said, she truly was in a fine position for the future.

Frankie was reveling in the November day. The weather had cooled in the middle of September like it should have. There had been a few nights of frost that, to her liking, had crisped the apples remaining on her trees. And to Ida's liking, the frosts had set her winter squash and pumpkins. But now, the days had gone warm and bright, becoming what felt like a second summer—it was what Tipp called an 'Indian Summer'. So named, he said, because it was the last chance for the Indians to do their hunting and raiding before the hard-winter set in.

She didn't know if that was actually true, because she didn't know whether the Cheyenne and the Oglála saw things that way or not. But no matter what name might be applied to the warm and balmy days, she was enjoying them. She was delighting in the warm sunshine and the softly-shifting west-winds. So much so, that as she approached her meadow, she decided to savor the sun for a while longer. She turned Rock toward Lookout Hill and sent him into a strong lope up to the crest.

Going up the slope, she started thinking about the November days and the dates, and realized her birthday was coming soon. Realizing suddenly that she would be done with the whole ten-year-old thing; she'd be turning eleven. *Finally!*

Frankie grinned at the thought, feeling a certain amount of relief. Because, she was thinking, her year as a ten-year-old had been a long and hard year. *Not gonna be all that sad to be done with it.*

She had been twice-orphaned that single ten-year-old year. First, her parents—her father back in Indiana last fall and her mother in late winter. And then her uncle and aunt and cousins on the trail coming out West in May. And really, she had loved and lost since then—because when she left Fort Kearny, she had lost yet another family. She had lost her Lieutenant and Isabelle, her Sergeant and her Captain. Her Corporal and Dr. Gannon. Septimus Travers and Will Trask. And all her other troopers. With all those people gone from her life, she realized that she had, in a way, been orphaned again.

Her time as a ten-year-old had been about traveling too. A lot of different ways of traveling—because the whole year had been one long journey. Not just the trail from Indiana to her homestead, but a long journey inside herself too. She was thinking about the day her father died. And then about the last day she had spent beside the Little Blue and the six graves. That had been the day she had chosen her own direction and path, the day she had chosen to find her way home. She had found her way here—it had been a long, twisted path, but she was here, now. And it was where she belonged.

Frankie settled herself on the highest rock near the crest of the highest point on her land, the highest point anywhere near her homestead. She let Rock graze while she sat surveying the land around her, watching the curing grasses of the Sand Hills—the yellow-brown waves of the Indian Summer grasses as they rippled and rolled along the hillsides. The air was moving in warm, sultry currents, drifting and swirling across the hilltop—almost as if the Lord-Above couldn't quite decide how, or where, he wanted to move the air.

She turned her attention to the distant lands, looking to the world to the north scanning the land until she saw the dark clusters and dark little specks among the far hills. *Nėheohe! There! Hotóá'e. The buffalo.*

They had come from the west and Frankie figured they were a remnant herd, separated from the great herd during the hunt. She had been watching them for the past week, watching as they moved northward over the last few days. Traveling slowly, meandering among the hills and valleys. *Apparently, in no great hurry. Apparently, satisfied with the grasses.*

It was a small herd, just a pocketful, compared to what she had seen earlier in the fall; it was nothing like the herd she had shown to Knife and He's Proud for their families. This herd looked to be about a hundred or so. *Probably eighty or ninety. Probably, a wayward bunch that broke off from the great herd after the hunt.*

Moving north like they were, Frankie knew they would reach the Calamus River in a few days. The pretty-colored map hanging above her mantle, showed that somewhere to the north beyond the herd, the Calamus River flowed. And further north, there was another river, a bigger river that cut through the land—the Niobrara River. The 'spreading-water river', according to the Cheyenne. It flowed from the mountains in the west, all the way to the Missouri River to the east.

From the black-rocky place, the mo'óhtá-vo'honáaeva, out in the west, where-toward-the-sun-disappears, the éše'hė-tsé-tåhaše-ta'enėse. Across the lands of the Sand Hills, the Heséovo'e Vósotótse. Flowing to the east, to the sun-where-it-rises, éše'hė-tséxė-heseme'enėse. Then across the lands of the Pawnee, the Ho'néhetane. All the way to the Missouri River, the É'ometåå'e.

She played with the Cheyenne words, practicing the sounds, letting the rhythm play on her tongue, her eyes on the lands to the north. Those rivers were beyond her vision and beyond the view of the spy-glass, but they were out there, flowing through the Sand

Hills. Eventually, she would travel to them too. *Just like the buffalo. Someday, I'll travel north and find them.*

She watched the small herd, as fascinated by the massive beasts as ever. Every time she looked at the buffalo-hide Gray Fox had given her, her mind wandered out to the far hills where the buffalo roamed, sleeping and grazing and wandering. The hide itself fascinated her, giving her an idea of the true size of the animals that roamed the prairie.

Watching the small herd, she toyed with the idea of traveling to see them, desperately wanting the chance to see them up close. She shook her head, shaking off the idea. It would have to wait. Because right now, there was a very real need to get ready for the winter. Because, she didn't want to dash up there to look at them and have to dash right back.

When she *did* travel to see a buffalo herd up close, she wanted enough time to watch them. Maybe several days. Or maybe, a week. She wanted to see them close-up; she wanted to study them and learn about them. And right now, with winter coming on, she couldn't spend a number of days on a lengthy trip. She consoled herself, trying to convince herself there would be other buffalo and other seasons.

Looking to the north again, she saw that the buffalo herd had disappeared. She glassed the area with her telescope, looking to where she'd last seen them, trying to locate the small herd again. Finally, she saw a few of the telltale dark spots in a low-lying area. *Down in a valley, now. Tucked away behind a hill.*

Watching through the scope, she could see movement, changes in the distance between the spots. With a little more time, more of the dark spots came into her view. *Yeah, they're still there. Twelve miles away, maybe farther. Not far. But too far to spend any real time with them.* Frankie turned Rock down the hillside and headed back to her valley.

Back in her meadow and in the barn alleyway, she pulled the saddle from Rock, turned him into a stall and walked up the alleyway to the first stall—the one across the side alley from the tack-room. Laughing Girl was there with her litter. Three girl-pups. They were bounding and bouncing around in the stall, yipping their puppy-yips and grunting their puppy-grunts. Still chubby in their puppy-faces and fat in their puppy-bellies. Fierce and fearsome in their own puppy-minds.

She stepped over the plank that kept them in their own puppy-pen, for now at least. She sat down in the midst of the pack; she talked to them and murmured to them; she let them paw at her and gnaw on her and nuzzle her; they crawled on her and over her and around her. They were pretty little females; one silvery-white, one pale-blond, and one was a dark blond-brindle.

A week ago, when Ida had been here in the barn, she had stepped into the pen and settled down in the midst of them. Her eyes had been shining as she held them and talked to them. She had spent a lot of time with them, tickling and petting them, laughing light and easy the whole time. And by the time Ida had stepped out, Frankie had seen that she was favoring one of the pups—Ida had fallen in love with the pale-blond pup—the runt of the litter.

And now, sitting in the midst of the moiling mass of puppies, Frankie decided that the blond girl-pup would go to the Dunbars' home. A growing pup, one that Ida could dote on, would be a nice thing. A growing wolfhound-greyhound pup that would learn to protect the Dunbar homestead. That, Frankie decided, would be a good idea.

Laughing Girl was pleased with the lot of them; she was a firm mother. Gentle, attentive and alert. But she didn't coddle her pups. She let them figure things out for themselves when they got into trouble—and they seemed to be very good at finding plenty of trouble there within the stall. They'd start yowling blue-murder every time they got themselves caught in a corner or stuck under one of the stall planks. The big hound would take notice, but once she was sure there was no real danger, she walked away and let them get out of the mess of their own making.

For a while, Frankie had watched Matilda closely, concerned the collie-dog might see the pups as a new avenue for her own mothering instincts. She wasn't sure how Laughing Girl would feel about the collie-dog confiscating any of them. Matilda did visit the puppy-pen frequently, taking on what appeared to be the role of a doting aunt. But as it turned out, she was still devoted to her little rooster-puppy, and it was still devoted to her. So Frankie's concerns had come to nothing.

The next morning, they hitched the catfish-grays to the heavy wagon and while Ida drove the wagon upriver to the woodcutting camp by the cove, Everett and Frankie spent their time on horseback—Frankie on Rock and Everett on Jake—riding out to study the section-markers. It was as Everett had it figured; Frankie had the home section—a full six-hundred-and-forty-acres—with the house at its center; she also had a half-section to the east and a half-section to the west. Plus, she had a quarter-section to each side of those. The configuration meant that six of her ten quarter-sections had the river running through them.

To Everett's thinking, Daniel Kinison's plan had been to start with the river property and fill in to the north with more quarter-sections. And to Frankie's thinking, it had been a good plan. And now, *her* plan was to continue with Daniel Kinison's plan.

Frankie had heard her Uncle James and her cousin Samuel talking a lot about the Homestead Act, and from what they said, she knew most of the people taking up claims in the Nebraska Territory were choosing to settle in the eastern part of the territory. Mostly along the Missouri River and spreading out along the Platte River.

If it was as her Uncle James had said, most of the homesteaders would be drawn to that region for some years to come. But there would come a time, he said, when there would be a push to settle on homesteads to the north. He figured the real settlement of the Sand Hills region of the Nebraska Territory would be ten or fifteen years away. And based on that line of thinking, he had believed purchasing the Kinison place would be a good plan.

It took foresight to see that getting yourself settled in and buying the land you wanted, before a wave of settlers came in, was the best way to build for the future. And apparently, Daniel Kinison had had that foresight.

So as she and Everett rode from marker to marker on that sunny morning in early November, Frankie thought that it would make a lot of sense to continue to buy land as Daniel Kinison had been doing. She didn't have any idea exactly how she could do that at this point in her life, but it was a plan for the future.

After they had located all the section markers, Frankie and Everett rode upriver toward the dead-wood cove. There, Ida was waiting with a noon-day picnic laid out on quilts spread out on the grass. They spent the next couple of hours enjoying the meal and the sunny afternoon; they talked about the sections and the land itself, and finalized their plans about farming and crops.

The quarter-section to the east of her home section, a quarter-section back from the river would become her crop land. Everett wanted to start turning it as soon as possible, wanting to put forty acres under the plow to have it ready for spring planting.

Everett had been using Bo and Benjamin, Buck and Billy to work more of Ida's land—the quarter-section across the river to the south of their home—working one of the back-forties behind the sod-house where their daughter and son-in-law had lived. As soon as he finished that plot of land, he would bring the oxen back to work Frankie's land. Then, he said, he'd be done with the land until spring planting.

Frankie knew Everett was doing more than just planning the work; he was planning his life. She could hear it in his voice. He was living and thinking like the man he was—a man who knew the land and the weather, the crops and the livestock. He was doing what he loved.

And looking at Ida sitting on the quilt, eating one of the apple hand-pies she had packed for their lunch, Frankie knew Ida Dunbar was living the life she wanted. She had her home neat and tidy; she had her cupboards full. She cooked and baked until her heart was content. She milked her cow and churned her butter; she cared for her chickens and gathered their eggs. She had her sewing and crocheting and embroidery. And like most of the women on the other homesteads, she worked beside her husband in the fields when he needed another set of hands.

The three of them talked about all those subjects while they ate their dinner beside the river. They relaxed there beside the North Loup, sitting on the quilt on the sunny Indian Summer afternoon, talking about their homesteads.

Once they were done eating, they spent a couple hours hauling and dragging branches and limbs, laughing and telling stories while they cut and chopped firewood. They loaded the wagon with the wood and hitched the catfish-grays; Frankie mounted Rock, and Everett and Ida climbed in the wagon, and with Jake tied to the tailgate, they all headed back to Frankie's meadow.

When they reached the rows of apple trees, they stopped to pick some of the apples still hanging on the branches. Frankie stood on Rock's back, tossing apples to Everett. Everett handed them to Ida. And Ida arranged them in the dishpan that had held their dinner. Once the pan was full, they resumed their journey, with Ida talking about making an apple crisp and Frankie teasing her to make more of the hand-pies.

"Because they make more sense. Because you can carry them around easier than toting a whole pie." Frankie was laying out her argument. "You can carry a hand-pie on horseback a lot easier than toting a whole pie-plate."

"That's a pretty weak argument, Honey," Ida was laughing at her. "I've never even seen you riding a horse and 'toting a whole pie'."

"Well, that proves my point. It'd be a hard thing to do. That's why I don't do it. But a hand-pie would be a nice thing."

"Sounds to me like you're just trying to get Ida to do some extra baking for you," Everett waded into the discussion.

"Well-l-l, yeah." Frankie made a face at him. "And I don't need *you* interfering. I'm thinking that if she agrees to make some, she can teach me at the same time. Because I've tried making them, but they just fall apart at the seams."

Everett ducked his head, shaking it slowly and laughing. And then, as the wagon rolled up the track, around the curve and started down into her home valley, he pulled the team to a sudden stop. He stared ahead. Ida gave a sudden gasp. Frankie pulled Rock to a halt. She was staring, too, just like Everett and Ida.

Frankie grabbed for the stock of her Henry in the scabbard; from the corner of her eye, she saw Everett standing and reaching for his own rifle. Rock shifted beneath her, alerting to danger—his head up, his muscles taut. One ear back, listening for her voice, waiting for a cue. Because below them, there in the meadow grass, was a band of Indians. They were there on their spotted ponies facing the two dogs crouching in front of them, their hackles raised, their growls loud and ugly. Laughing Girl and Matilda were doing their job—they were holding the intruders at bay.

In a single instant, the warriors reined their ponies, spinning to face her and the Dunbar wagon. Frankie stopped her hand on the rifle-stock, leaving the rifle in the scabbard, watching the warriors in front of her. No Indian was pulling a weapon. *No weapons in their hands. No shouts; no yells; no threats.* They were just sitting there on their ponies, ignoring the dogs and just looking at her. *A dozen warriors. Maybe more.* Looking as if they weren't surprised to see her. Looking as if, maybe, they had been expecting her.

Frankie's mind was racing, trying to understand the situation before her. Trying to watch Everett and trying to watch the band of Indians—all at the same time. *Not a war-party. No war-paint. No weapons ready; no raised spears; no arrows notched on bows.* She eyed the warriors, their clothing, their hair, their faces. *Not Oglála. Not Pawnee. They're Cheyenne.* She spotted several packhorses. *Maybe a scouting party. Or a hunting party.*

But it didn't make sense—because along with the packhorses, there was something that didn't fit for scouts or hunters. There were two horses with long poles rigged to their sides and tied above the withers—poles that dragged on the ground behind them. She had never seen them before, but she knew what they were. *Travois. But they're what families use when villages move. Not for a raiding party. Not for a hunting party. Packhorses. Travois. Warriors on horses. But no women or children. No families.*

Frankie threw a glance toward Everett; he was standing in the jockey-box, rifle in-hand with the barrel pointed down. Trying to hold the team. Trying to watch her and the Indians, both at the same time. She shook her head at him, hoping he'd understand not to bring the rifle into play, hoping he'd wait until she figured this out. Knowing that a single wrong move—some sudden motion—could set off an ugly series of events.

She scanned the band of warriors again, her confusion rising. Because she was here in her own meadow, on her own homestead, and she had no idea what to do. And in that moment, there in the midst of the men and horses, she saw something happening. She saw a movement—a calm, steady, deliberate movement. A red-and-white pinto was weaving its way through the mix of horses and riders, coming right toward her; she looked at the rider and broke into a grin. She knew the rider! *Strong Hand! Strong Hand's band!*

"He-kóne Mósêstotse! Pave-éšeeva, na-htataneme!" Frankie called to him, shivering with excitement. "Ne-teneto mohta-he?" 'Strong Hand! It's a good day, my brother! How are you?'

Frankie gave a quick whistle to the dogs; she called to them, ordering them back. She reined Rock and sent him down the track, riding toward the band of warriors. Riding toward Strong Hand, scanning the rest of the men and horses. Searching. Hoping. And finally, she saw what she was looking for. *Yes! There!*

A warrior on a black-and-white pinto was easing his way through the band of warriors. *Knife!* And there, coming along behind him, was a man on a buckskin. *And He's Proud! My warriors! My brothers!*

She and Rock had just reached the bottom of the track, when she saw every warrior reaching for his weapon, watching the Dunbar wagon. They were lifting their rifles and bows, pulling arrows from their quivers.

Frankie twisted in her saddle, looking over her shoulder. Everett was still there in the jockey-box, still standing, his rifle still in-hand.

But now, the barrel of his rifle was up; he was leveling it and moving to take aim.

"Everett! *Stop!*" Frankie stepped Rock to the front of the wagon. She held her hand up to Strong Hand, signaling him, desperate for him understand. "*Everett!* You *have* to listen to me! You *have* to trust me. These are my friends. Lower the rifle and sit down. As soon as you do, everything will be fine. *Everett! Please!*"

To her relief, she saw Everett do exactly what she said. He was still unsure, still afraid, but he was doing what she told him. Behind her, Frankie felt the tension fading; she looked away from Everett and glanced back at the Cheyenne men.

They were lowering their bows and the barrels of their rifles were tipping down. The tension was gone; it lifted and moved off with the breeze, flowing silently up the eastern slope of the valley. Everything calmed. Feathers and fringes flitted in the late afternoon breeze, tiny metal cones on buckskin shirts were jingling softly, sending bell-like tones into the meadow air.

Frankie reined Rock, turning back to Strong Hand and the Cheyenne. The danger was gone and Strong Hand's eyes were on her again; Frankie could see the smile in his eyes. Off to one side, she could see He's Proud on his buckskin, skirting around the other riders. He pulled his pony to a halt next to Rock, sidestepped his mount, shifting close to her. Positioning himself so he could interpret for her and for his people. He reached to touch her shoulder.

She turned her attention back to Strong Hand, back to the brother she hadn't seen since July, back before Independence Day, on the morning when he and Knife and He's Proud had ridden into Fort Kearny to trade for tobacco at the Sutlers Store.

"E-peva'e tsexė-ho'ėhneto, na-htataneme." 'It's good that you came, my brother.'

She spoke to him again and he smiled at her, and he nodded. She talked on, using more of the Cheyenne words she knew—telling him that she was happy they had come to her home. That she was glad that Knife had brought him and his band to visit. She grinned, seeing the look in his eyes and knowing that he was pleased she was speaking Cheyenne—he was well aware that He's Proud was providing her with very few words.

Strong Hand moved his pinto next to Rock; he reached to touch her forearm. Then he touched her cheek. He smiled as he reached to tap the wolf-tooth necklace resting at the base of her neck. He spoke to her then, his eyes locked on hers. Beside her, He's Proud was speaking low, translating.

Strong Hand said he was proud of his little sister. He had heard of the necklace, and Knife had told him of her wolf-medicine. He had heard of the great buffalo herd she brought to the Cheyenne and Oglála. He had learned of Gray Fox's buffalo-horse and how the horse had come to her and she had healed him. Gray Fox, Strong Hand said, had spoken of her as a daughter.

As Frankie listened to Strong Hand's words, she was also listening for any sound from behind her—any sound from the Dunbar wagon—worried about what Everett might decide to do. Knowing that if he suddenly feared for her safety, or for Ida's, things could turn deadly.

She knew she could trust the Cheyenne; she knew exactly what to expect of them. It was Everett and Ida she doubted right now, because there was a good chance Everett would try to take command of the situation. There was a chance he'd bring the rifle up again and decide to order these men away from her home. It would be his protective nature rising up, but she doubted the Cheyenne men would see it that way. They would see it as an insult and a threat, and everything would turn real ugly, real fast.

So there in the midst of all the Cheyenne and English words, Frankie was trying to think of a way to turn everything around, trying to think of a way to set everything to a fresh start. She looked to Knife sitting relaxed and easy on his pony; he was smiling at her, relaxed and calm. And suddenly, she knew exactly what to do—and she knew Knife would help her. She slid down from Rock's back, walked the few steps to Knife's pinto. She held up both arms. Reaching for him.

"He'ama, na-htataneme."

He gave her his amused, indulgent, big-brother-smile. He leaned down and lifted her to his horse's withers, settled her in front of him facing forward. He looked around to his companions, grinning at them; he spoke to them, saying something that sent them into loud laughter.

He's Proud translated; Knife, he said, had confessed to the other warriors that Fire Heart Child owned his heart. He could not refuse anything that his little white sister asked for. He's Proud was speaking louder now, and Frankie knew he was doing it purposely, because he, too, understood the confusion of the two people on the wagon. He was speaking loud enough for them to hear, being respectful to the Dunbars, knowing Knife's words and the laughter would calm their fears.

A moment later, Strong Hand slipped down from his pony and walked over to Knife's horse; he reached for Frankie, lifted her down and stood her next to him and rested his hand on her shoulder.

Frankie knew what he was doing; it was time for introductions. She pointed to Everett and Ida and told Strong Hand they were her people; they were part of the village of white people who lived all around her. She moved her arm in a broad sweep, indicating the lands beyond her valley.

"They care for me," she said, "they help me. They are my people. My family. So they should be your family too."

At her side, He's Proud was speaking her words loud enough for all the Cheyenne to hear; the warriors were nodding, looking at each other as they listened. Understanding about the two people sitting on the wagon. Strong Hand was looking straight at Everett, assessing, judging.

"His name is He-kóne Mósèstotse," Frankie spoke to Everett and Ida, talking to them about the man beside her. "It means Strong Hand, and he's a leader for his people."

She went on, explaining that he had been her friend for a long time. That he was her brother. Then she pointed to Knife.

"His name is Motåhke. It means Knife," she told them. "He's my brother too. They were my brothers even before I was at Fort Kearny." She reached to her side, put her hand on He's Proud's arm. "His name is He's Proud. E Menóhkahe. He helps me learn Cheyenne. He talks for all of us."

Then Frankie saw what she had been hoping for—sitting there on the wagon-seat, Everett nodded to her. And then, he nodded to Strong Hand. It was a slow nod, but his eyes were soft and gentle; there was acceptance in them. He understood. She felt Strong Hand's grip on her shoulder soften.

Strong Hand and Everett looked at each other and Frankie thought she saw a nod pass between them. Maybe. Maybe just a slight nod. Everett moved his eyes to her and Strong Hand pulled her closer to his side. Just a little. The two men understood that she was their bond. *It's done. It's all safe, now.*

She told Everett and Ida about He's Proud and about his wife, Willow. She talked about his daughter Dandelion, and about Wood Flute. And she told Everett and Ida that they were her sisters, explaining that she played with them when they came to visit. She told them Willow and Young Doe, Wood Flute's mother, made the beautiful antelope-skin dress, for her.

He's Proud stayed beside her, squatting down, keeping his hand on her arm, speaking her words to the warriors around her. He was making sure everyone knew the little-white-girl's words—making sure, in the way he knew best—that there was peace among all the people in the meadow.

Ida was desperately trying to watch everyone and everything at the same time. She had never been near Indians and she was terrified that there would be an eruption, that there would be fighting and killings. She had heard enough stories; she was sure that Frankie, as well as she and Everett, were in serious danger.

But as she was watching the men in front of her, she realized her fears were fading. The Indian warriors, like her and Everett, had just been surprised. They had only lifted their weapons—the bows and arrows and rifles—after Everett had lifted his rifle. These men had started no fight; there was no blood being shed; there were no shrieks and screams. No warclubs were being waved; no tomahawks had been brandished.

Only a moment or two had passed, before Ida realized she was seeing exactly what Frankie had been trying to tell them all along. These Indians had just come to visit her; they had just stopped by. No different than people from the church might stop by her own homestead. As she watched, Ida saw the smiles on the faces of these men who were considered wild and unpredictable. More than that, she saw the smiles in the eyes of these men who looked so fierce—so fierce and so splendid at the same time.

She watched how they treated Frankie; they were treating her the way uncles would treat a favorite niece. They were her doting uncles, or as Frankie claimed, they were her older brothers. Doting on her and delighting in her. The warrior who had indulged Frankie, had grinned sheepishly when he reached to lift her to his horse. He adored her. He didn't even attempt to hide it.

Knife. That was his name. He had been so proud when Frankie walked to him, seeking his attention. He hadn't been embarrassed by the laughter of his friends. He had actually been boasting; he had been showing her off to his companions. Ida had heard what the translator said—the words Knife had used sounded just like her own brothers' words back when her boys were little. As young uncles, they had carried their nephews around, too—adoring them, indulging them and boasting about them.

Frankie had always used the words 'friends' and 'family' and 'brothers' when she talked about these people, and now, Ida realized it had all been truth. She was seeing it. These men, Knife and Strong Hand, adored her; they were gentle and sweet with her. They were behaving no different with Frankie than she and Everett did; no different than the Reverend Austin and Betsy did.

But now, even though her fears for Frankie's safety, as well as their own, were gone, Ida was feeling uncomfortable. She was feeling overwhelmed, realizing all of a sudden that she had no idea how to act. She had no idea how to talk to these people; she had no idea what to do. So she stayed as she was, sitting beside Everett on the wagon-seat, watching Frankie with these people. She found herself smiling as she saw Frankie's excitement.

Frankie's dark eyes were shining as she was jabbering away, grinning that crooked little grin of hers as she stood beside Strong Hand, talking to him and stroking the red-and-white pinto that he rode. Strong Hand and the others were laughing as the horse nibbled at her clothes and hair. The man who was translating walked over to the wagon; he explained about the laughter and about the horse that was nuzzling Frankie.

"He is Strong Hand's warhorse. He is a mean-minded horse," he said. "He has no patience with people. He only allows Strong Hand to touch him. That is the reason for the laughter. Because he likes our little sister."

Ida looked at the man explaining the scene before them, a man who should be frightening her—a man with feathers hanging from braids and wearing a buckskin shirt with rows and rows of beads sewn into it. From everything she had been told, an Indian warrior was supposed to be wild and fearsome. Dangerous and deceitful and deadly in their dealings.

But Ida was suddenly realizing that she wanted very much to talk with this man; this warrior, who was supposed to be so dangerous and deceitful, was taking care of her and Everett. There was such kindness in his eyes; he was showing such respect by explaining things to them. But all she could do was smile and nod, because she couldn't think of what to say. Not because she was afraid now, but because she was overwhelmed with the way he was trying to bring them into the company of his people. *Because really, it is such a great kindness he's offering.*

His words were helping Everett too. Ida could tell he was calming down; there on the wagon-seat beside her, he was already relaxing with the idea of these men being in Frankie's meadow. *Not a lot. But some. He did nod to Strong Hand. And now, he's nodding as this man is talking. He's trying to be cordial.*

Ida started breathing easier; she felt her lungs filling with the warm afternoon air. She realized it had been no more than a few minutes since they had driven into Frankie's meadow to come face-to-face with a band of wild Indians—dangerous warriors with their long black hair and their feathers and buckskin clothing. Some nearly naked, sitting on their half-wild horses with bows and rifles and spears in their hands. It seemed as if the meadow had been filled with danger. *But now, it seems fine. Everything's going to be fine.*

Ida looked around at all the Indians and their ponies gathered in the meadow. The men and the horses and the pack-animals. It seemed fine now. Everything that had been whirling around in her mind—all the fears she had, all the dangers she had supposed—were no longer present. And it had all happened within a matter of minutes.

With his hand on her shoulder, Strong Hand turned Frankie, guiding her toward the packhorses. He led her past the horses with the packsaddles and walked her to the horses rigged with the travois. One travois, Frankie could see was loaded with buffalo-hides, rawhide boxes and leather pouches.

But when Strong Hand turned her to the other travois and shifted a flap of a buffalo-robe to one side, Frankie almost jumped back—it wasn't boxes or pouches that were lashed onto this travois. Whatever she had expected, it wasn't what Strong Hand revealed when he lifted the corner of the thick hide.

A woman was there on the travois, lying nestled into an assortment of furs—a Cheyenne woman. It wasn't Young Doe or Willow. This was an older woman, a woman she didn't know. And there was a child beside her, a toddler, tucked in next to her. The woman was awake; the toddler was asleep.

Frankie squatted down beside the travois, already understanding why Strong Hand and his band had come to her meadow. The woman and the toddler were sick—their faces and necks and arms were covered with reddish-purple sores and large, dark-purple patches.

She smiled at the woman, reached out slowly to touch her arm. The skin was hot and wet. She reached past her to touch the cheek of the toddler, already knowing what she'd find. *Same. Fever.*

Frankie sucked in a breath; she knew the feel of fever. Her mind flicked back to the shady riverbank of the Little Blue River. Back to her Uncle James and Aunt Sarah and her cousins. To *their* fevered bodies. And to the six graves. Then to the Conestoga and her Lieutenant and the snakebite. And *his* fever. She steeled herself, clenched her jaw, willed those thoughts back to the corners of her mind where they belonged. She put her thoughts on the two people in front of her, trying to think like her Aunt Sarah. Trying to assess things like her aunt would.

The child was sleeping, but it was a fevered sleep—a pain-filled sleep. The breathing was ragged, the skin was wet and clammy with sweat. The woman was much the same as the child. *But her breathing is rougher. More ragged. Her breaths are shorter and she's sweating heavier. Aunt Sarah would have called it 'profuse sweating'.*

The woman's mouth was bleeding. Her gums and lips were red and oozing blood. The blood was normal in color, the expected red— dark, crimson-red blood. *Blood from the surface areas, then. Good. Not a bright and pinkish-red. Not a frothy bubbly-red. Not from the lungs, then. That's good.*

From behind her, Frankie could hear He's Proud's voice.

"The woman is called Hevovetásono. Whirlwind." He said the Cheyenne words softly, as if he was afraid of waking the child. "She is Strong Hand's mother. The child is his daughter Hóh-keehso. Little Mouse."

He paused when Frankie motioned to him, needing the silence while she felt for the pulse at Whirlwind's wrist. She counted pulse-beats, first. Then she felt for each of the three different pulses—one under each of her three fingers. Feeling for the three beats—the quick-pecking one, the steady-ticking one, and the flowing-rolling one. She went to the other wrist, feeling for the other three pulses.

'Three pulses on each wrist,' her aunt would say. 'Six different pulses. The body will tell you about six organ-systems if you feel the rhythm.'

So Frankie did as her aunt had taught, listening to the messages from the body, listening through her fingers to the information about the inner workings. Feeling the pulse of life flowing inside—the life-pulses of the body were speaking of any weaknesses or low function in its organ-systems.

Here, under her fingers, she could feel the weaknesses in two of the pulses of the woman's right wrist—the pulse that spoke of the liver, and the pulse of the digestion in the stomach and intestines. They were halting and weak, out of rhythm and out of balance. At the woman's left wrist, the pulse that spoke of the heart and the blood itself, was halting and heavy.

She heard He's Proud telling her about the last few months—about the declining health of Whirlwind and Little Mouse. And about others in the Cheyenne villages out on the land beyond Fort Cottonwood. They, too, had sickened.

"Strong Hand brings his mother and daughter here to the home of Fire Heart Child," he said. "So Fire Heart Child can heal them." He went on to explain that all of Lame Horse's tribe decided to leave that land. "All the families travel here. But Strong Hand rode ahead with Whirlwind and Little Mouse. The rest of the band follows, but they travel slower."

And suddenly, Frankie had no great interest in the story; she had heard enough. She was seeing enough to know what was wrong with the woman and the little girl. The symptoms had already told her what she needed to know. The pulses had verified it.

Frankie stood up and started giving orders to everyone around her—orders to get the cookfire going, to get water heating in the big cookpot, and to help her move her patients. He's Proud started relaying the orders, and to Frankie's ears, he sounded a lot like a Cavalry sergeant, calling out the orders. In the next instant, the Cheyenne men were swinging off their ponies.

Knife knew exactly what she wanted; he was heading to the fire-ring, saying something to another man and pointing to the buckets sitting by the windmill pond. Knife, Frankie knew, would see to the fire and start heating water. Strong Hand reached for the lead-rope of the horse and headed where Frankie pointed, taking his mother and daughter toward the Barracks.

As the travois slid past her, Frankie glanced at the worn ends of the long poles skidding through the grass, understanding it had been a long journey for these people—in more ways than one.

She started walking toward the Dunbars and their wagon, knowing exactly what she needed from them—and not at all sure whether she'd get it. Because dealing with the Cheyenne warriors had been the easy part; now, she had to deal with Ida and Everett, and that might prove to be a hard row to hoe.

Everett and Ida were still sitting on their wagon-seat, still watching and waiting. Still unsure; still unsettled. Frankie could see it in their faces and in their eyes. She went to the side of the wagon where Ida sat—because Ida would be the one to convince. Ida would be making this decision, whether Everett realized it or not.

She spoke to both of them, but her eyes stayed with Ida. She told them she had no time to explain everything; she told them she needed their help and she needed to know if she could count on them. If not, she said, then it was best that they leave—they should just go. If they *were* willing to help, then she needed them to follow her lead and do exactly what she said.

"The woman is Strong Hand's mother and the child is his daughter. They've been sick and it's been going on for months," Frankie told them. "But, Ida, I know what's wrong. It's scurvy. It's not contagious, so no one else is in danger. But at this stage, it's serious for them. There's been no help from the tribal doctors or from the Indian Agency doctors." She told them all that, and then she told Ida that the little girl needed help right away.

"Ida, I *know* how you feel about the Cheyenne people visiting me, but I need someone who can hold this baby girl and spoon-feed her. The rest of the band is coming in a few days, so there'll be other women to help once they get here. But until then I'm going to have my hands full working on Strong Hand's mother. Ida, I haven't had much experience caring for babies. And right now, I need someone who knows how." Frankie hesitated, suddenly desperate for Ida's help. "Ida, she's only two years old. She's just a baby."

Frankie watched Ida, afraid she would refuse, afraid the beliefs she and Everett had about Indians would make them turn away. For a moment, Ida gave no answer; she stayed as she was, sitting stock-still on the wagon-seat. Then suddenly, she stepped out of the jock-ey-box and started climbing down from the wagon.

"Let me see this baby. *Poor* child. Poor, *poor* child. You just tell me what we need to do." Ida headed toward the travois and the Barracks. "And give Everett some work to do."

Everett didn't need to be told anything. As soon as Ida stated her intent, Everett was climbing out of the wagon and motioning to a couple of the Cheyenne men; they began taking firewood from the wagon and carrying armloads for the cookfire. Other men helped Strong Hand shift his mother and daughter into the Barracks.

Frankie called to Everett, telling him she needed apples and sweet potatoes, squash and pumpkins from the root-cellar.

"And any other root vegetables you can get to the kitchen. I need crates of them, because we need to cook them down. Stoke up the stove in the house. And Ida and I need a bunch of the folded flour-sacks from the cabinet in the pantry. And dishpans of hot water." She ran to catch up to Ida, calling over her shoulder. "And get sweet potatoes and squash cooking in the pot at the cookfire."

They went into the Barracks to begin work on Whirlwind and Little Mouse, and behind her, she could hear He's Proud talking and translating; he was following Everett everywhere, translating Everett's instructions. Ida called for Everett to start heating kettles of water in the kitchen, and together, she and Frankie began the pro-cess of washing their patients—cleaning both their bodies and their bleeding wounds.

Ida and Frankie took turns, one working on their patients in the Barracks while the other was busy peeling and dicing the vegetables and fruit in the kitchen. They had squash, turnips, sweet potatoes and beets roasting in the oven, and sliced apples frying in skillets. They planned to cook the vegetables and apples until they were soft, and then work them into soft mashes. Mashes that would be spoon-fed; mashes that were dense with nutrients; mashes that would begin to turn away the scurvy. Because, Frankie knew it was the nutrients that would halt the scurvy and reverse the symptoms.

While she was in the kitchen, Frankie spent some of her time working with the food and some of her time sorting through her remedy-chest, selecting the powders and tinctures and remedies that would speed up the healing and soothe the lesions.

At one point, while she worked by the stove, Everett made his way through the kitchen, toting the big rocking chair from the sitting-room. He had decided to take it to the Barracks.

"I figure we'll be needing this out there," Everett declared as he angled the chair through the door. "That baby's gonna need rocking." He grunted a bit as he cleared the door and started across the porch. "Rocking's good for babies."

Frankie wasn't sure if he was explaining it to her, or if he was telling himself, or if he was announcing it to the world in general, but she stayed quiet. Because Everett had made his own peace about the Cheyenne being in the meadow, and now, he had his own ideas about what needed doing. And Frankie wasn't about to interfere. Because apparently, Everett decided that none of this was about Indians or white people anymore. As of now, it was about a sick child, and apparently, he believed the child needed to be rocked.

Ida was rocking Strong Hand's daughter, spoon-feeding her applesauce and singing quietly to her. Frankie was working on Whirlwind, slathering salve onto her sores and pressing clay-packs on the seeping cuts. Through the Barracks window, she could hear the sound of wagon-wheels and horse-hooves on the main track. She had told Everett about a large patch of prickly pear against one of the hillsides, north of the riverbank and Everett and He's Proud and several other warriors were heading out of the meadow.

'I need baskets of those cactus pads. The patch is in a narrow draw near a sandy blow-out. Almost halfway between our places.

Where the river bends sharp at the cove with the sandbar. The patch is probably fifty or sixty yards north of the bend.'

So Everett and his companions were on a search-and-find mission, planning to bring back bushels of the cactus pads.

'Once you're back,' she had told him, 'peel the pads and cut them into pieces and get them boiling in the cookfire kettles. Cook them down and keep adding sugar until you have something that looks and tastes like green applesauce.'

Everett and He's Proud had been listening, nodding to her and to each other. She had handed Everett a bag of sugar and told him to hurry. Then she had gone back into the Barracks to her patients. And now, the white-man on his wagon and the Indian warriors on their ponies were heading out together, talking and laughing like they were old friends, with He's Proud translating back and forth.

Strong Hand though, stayed in the meadow, staying close to Ida as she cared for Little Mouse. Knife remained in the meadow, too, staying near Frankie while she worked on Whirlwind. The two men roamed in and out of the Barracks, stepping inside the doorway, or standing on the porch. Mostly, silent. Just waiting.

Ida spent most of her time with Little Mouse, cleaning the bloody diarrhea, crooning softly and singing to her. Rocking her and stroking her hair. Soothing her. And when Strong Hand hovered close to the rocker, Ida reached to pat his arm, soothing him too. She patted his shoulder and cheek, smiling at him, comforting him. Reassuring him, promising him that his daughter would be fine, that they'd get her well. Most of Ida's words, he didn't understand—but he understood her heart.

When Ida asked Frankie for the little girl's name, Frankie told her 'Little Mouse', and then, to Frankie's surprise, Ida asked for the Cheyenne word.

"Hóh-keeheso." Frankie told her the name and that was the name Ida used when she spoke to the child in her arms. Ida was speaking her first Cheyenne word, using it to talk to the little girl who studied her, staring at her with her dark eyes. Ida was using the name the little girl would know.

It made Strong Hand smile. He looked at Frankie as he listened to Ida whispering the name to his daughter. His smile softened, knowing what Frankie knew—that Ida Dunbar was deep within another world. She was deep into the care and compassion of motherhood; she was caring for someone else's child the same way she had cared for her own children. Ida, Frankie knew, was healing her own hurts and pain while she was soothing the hurts and the pain of Hóh-keeheso—the daughter of this man she had once feared.

Twilight had faded and the dark of the dusk was settling down into the meadow when Frankie heard hoots of laughter coming across the front meadow, coming from the group of men at the fireside. She knew what it was—He's Proud and six of the Cheyenne men were working beside Everett, busy cleaning and scraping their way through the bushels of the prickly-pear pads. They were telling their stories and tales, and from what Frankie could hear, it sounded as if they were working hard to amuse Everett, working hard to keep their new friend laughing.

Three other Cheyenne warriors had ridden out of the meadow earlier, weapons in hand. When they returned, they had a bull elk sectioned and lashed across the backs of two packhorses. They hung the meat from the barn rafters using the rope and pulley that He's Proud showed them. The butchering started and within minutes, strips of elk meat were twisted onto the spit and sizzling over the flames.

From the kitchen porch, Frankie watched the butchering at the barn entrance with some interest, impressed with the size of the elk. Realizing that it was giving probably twice as much meat as a deer. She had eaten elk meat once, back on the trail beside the Little Blue River when men from the wagon party had come across a small herd. She liked it better than venison, and thinking about that had her wondering why she had never hunted elk out here. Because she had seen plenty of elk herds. *Two horses to pack it home, instead of just one. Or maybe, use the heavy farm-wagon. Or maybe, the rock-sled.*

Frankie turned back to the work inside the kitchen, returning to the work she and Ida had been doing while Whirlwind and Little Mouse slept. Baking cornbread and biscuits. And cooking down more apples and carrots and parsnips.

She and Ida talked about the scurvy while they worked, with Frankie explaining the recovery would happen fast—because scurvy would begin reversing as soon as the right nutrients entered the body. The remedies and tinctures and salves from her remedy-chest would ease the discomfort and help the body, but it was the vegetables and apples that were the true medicines. Because correcting the nourishment was enough to bring the disease to a quick halt.

The worst of the deep and hot joint-pain would reduce quickly, she told Ida, most of it within a day and a half; the diarrhea and the bleeding in the gums and the teeth would resolve to a great degree by two to three days. The discoloration of the skin and the seeping sores on both Whirlwind and Little Mouse, Frankie knew, would be improving daily.

Within a week, most of Whirlwind's skin lesions would be fading away. The sores on Little Mouse would probably disappear in half the time—because children almost always healed faster than adults. The toddler who had been moaning in pain every time her limbs were moved or jostled, and who refused to move on her own, would be out of pain and toddling around in a day or two.

During the first day and night, Ida and Everett took turns holding and rocking Little Mouse with Strong Hand looking on. By the second morning, Ida was hard-pressed to get *any* time with Little Mouse. Because Everett was smitten. He was enamored with the Cheyenne girl, captivated by the dark eyes staring into his. Captivated by the sweet face, by the small fingers that reached to clutch his shirt and twist at his buttons.

Around noon, he had to drag himself away from Little Mouse; he reluctantly hitched his team, planning to travel to his own homestead to see to the livestock and do chores. He listened to instructions from Ida, hearing that he was to bring mint and basil and parsley and kale from her garden, along with any beets and turnips he could dig. He started for home with two Cheyenne men riding their ponies beside the wagon, going with him to help gather the food.

"And be sure to bring the green tops too." Ida called to him from the Barracks porch, adding that he was to bring any carrots and parsnips still in the ground. "And bring along any tomatoes you can find. Ripe ones or green."

Because once Ida understood what had happened with Whirlwind and Little Mouse, she started thinking of every possibility for getting fresh vegetables and fruit into their bodies.

Anticipating that more of the Cheyenne on their way to the meadow would show various symptoms of scurvy, Frankie and Ida were roasting more of the squash and pumpkin from the root-cellar. They had sweet potatoes and carrots, turnips and beets roasting in the oven. More apples and more of the prickly pear were cooking down on the back burners and out at the cookfire.

By evening, Frankie was also thinking about the people she needed to feed—not just Whirlwind and Little Mouse and the Cheyenne warriors—but the Cheyenne families who were on their way. There was the elk hanging in the barn, but with more than a dozen people in her meadow already, it was disappearing fast. From what He's Proud had said, it seemed like a lot of families were coming.

She assumed the men who rode out with Everett would probably hunt on their way back; now that it was evening, there would be herds of deer and antelope moving down to the river bottoms. But in Frankie's mind, there was a need for more than what they might bring in.

That was when she realized the obvious; she knew where there was plenty of meat. She left Ida to the kitchen work and went to talk with Strong Hand and Knife. She sat down beside them in the grass near the Barracks and asked her questions. With He's Proud translating, she learned the whole village was coming. More than a hundred, Strong Hand told her.

"Lame Horse's people, the people of Strong Hand's grandfather, will travel to a winter camp far to the north of the great flat river," He's Proud explained. "They will spend the winter with Gray Fox's people in the black-rocky place." He spoke the Oglála words, Pahá Sápa, and then used the Cheyenne name. Mo'óhtá-vo'honáaeva. "But now, they come here. When Whirlwind and the others are healed, they will go to the Oglála village."

So Frankie spoke to Knife and Strong Hand about needing more meat to feed all his people. Knife smiled at her, assuring her that they would hunt.

"We will feed Strong Hand's people, and we will feed you and your people."

When Frankie asked if he wanted to hunt buffalo, Knife shook his head and answered her.

"There will be no buffalo now, Fire Heart Child. The buffalo are many sleeps to the west now."

"No, Brother. I can send you to buffalo."

Frankie told Knife and she waited while He's Proud translated. The information got Knife's attention, and Strong Hand's too. Knife laughed and patted her shoulder; he spoke rapidly to Strong Hand. Strong Hand kept his eyes on Frankie, watching her closely, his eyes hard and piercing. Frankie sat still, unmoving, watching him right back. Waiting for him to decide. Knife kept a hand on her shoulder while he spoke to Strong Hand. He's Proud crouched down close to her, translating, bringing her into the conversation.

Knife was telling Strong Hand not to doubt Fire Heart Child; he explained how she had called the buffalo for the scouts and how she had given rabbits to the families for their fires. 'Rabbits,' he said, 'that were dead but hadn't been killed.' He was telling Strong Hand that she had wolf-medicine—that she knew what the wolves knew. That she could bring buffalo to feed the people. Strong Hand shook his head and spoke.

He wasn't doubting Fire Heart Child, Strong Hand said. He knew she would do what she said. He did not doubt that she could send them to buffalo, because he knew her strength and her medicine. He said he was watching her because he wanted to understand the reason she worked to care for his people. And for his mother and his child. He did not doubt her, Strong Hand said again, he only wanted to understand her.

He stood and asked Frankie to show him where the buffalo were. She stood and with Knife and He's Proud and the others following, she walked to the dirt surface of the track. She drew in the dirt, showing them where the buffalo were. Explaining that they would be straight to the north, waiting in a wide valley. Less than a half day's ride.

He's Proud asked her how many.

"Na'nóhtó-nó'e. Nóhaso, no'ka-måhtohtó-nó'e." 'Eighty. Maybe a hundred.' Frankie told him. There would be enough buffalo to hunt so they could feed the people who were coming, she said, and enough meat to take with them for their journey to the black-rocky place.

The men talked then, speaking quietly among themselves, speaking too softly for Frankie to hear and using plenty of words she didn't understand. After a few minutes, Strong Hand walked toward the fire, beckoning for her to follow. The other men joined them and they settled down around the fire. There was no more talk among the men; there was just silence. Everything had become serious and still.

Frankie could see that Strong Hand's eyes had a different message now. There was nothing light and easy about them, now—his eyes had become serious and still. He motioned for her to sit beside him. When she complied, he reached around her and shifted her closer to his side. He nodded to her. Then he rested his hand on her thigh.

She settled in against him. Trusting her brother, He-kóne Mósėstotse. She glanced to Knife, to Motåhke. Trusting him too. But understanding that now, quite suddenly, everything had changed.

"Stay where Strong Hand wants you, Fire Heart Child," He's Proud was behind her, whispering. "It is important that you stay next to him. The men are speaking of the buffalo and of the hunt. They will smoke and speak of things you don't understand. But stay beside him, Little Sister."

Frankie's mind was flitting across the meadow, thinking about the work in the kitchen, about her patients in the Barracks. Ida was working with Whirlwind and Little Mouse. The sickness was already easing in both of them. *Ida will take care of things. She has things in order. She knows I'm over here.*

She turned her attention back to the fire and to the men around her. She stayed beside Strong Hand, with Knife sitting on her other side. He's Proud stayed behind her and she did exactly as he instructed her—she stayed at Strong Hand's side, staying quiet. She listened to the warriors talking and listened to He's Proud as he explained what he wanted her to know.

And all the while, one of the warriors—a man named Charging Crow—worked over a flat board, speaking softly, his voice rising and falling in a sing-song pattern. Calm and reverent. The board he used was round and worn, rubbed down to a saucer in the middle, the rim painted with designs of running animals, zigzagging lines, and curls of blue smoke.

Frankie watched as he placed tobacco and bearberry leaves on the board and began cutting and crushing them, then mixing them together. He reached into several parfleche packets and brought out different leaves and bark, added them to the mix. He's Proud told her the names, reciting them softly—mullein-leaf and deer-tongue leaf, red-willow bark, red-sumac leaves and sweet-grass.

Once Charging Crow had everything blended, he began speaking steady and low, whispering soft and slow. He balanced a long, narrow leather bag in his hands—a bag painted in yellows and greens and blues with strips of fur and fringes and long tufts of hair fastened along the bottom-seam. He held it high, his voice lifting into a steady cadence as he pulled a long wooden shaft from the bag.

Frankie stared at the shaft, realizing she was seeing one of the smoking-pipes she had heard about long ago—way back in Indiana— from a story her father had read to her. *A James Fenimore Cooper story. The Last of the Mohicans. Chingachgook. He had a long-shafted pipe. A ceremonial pipe.*

Now, her eyes were riveted on Charging Crow's every movement; she leaned forward, trying for a better look at his medicine-pipe, wanting to touch the beads that spun in spirals around the shaft. Beside her, Strong Hand pressed his palm down on her thigh; Knife moved his arm in front of her, blocking her. Gently; firmly. Keeping her where she was.

She stared at the beads—tiny glistening beads of red and black, yellow and white. She watched the pearl-white flashes of tiny animal teeth and shining black shimmerings of animal claws. A bird's foot, with its sharp talons clutched together, dangled from the bowl of the pipe. The bowl itself, made from a rust-red stone, was carved in the shape of a buffalo's head. Wisps of long buffalo hair drifted down from the neck of the bowl, twisting, tangling with a cluster of black feathers. *Crow feathers.*

Frankie shifted closer to Strong Hand; her eyes were still locked on the man named Charging Crow; she watched as he tamped his blend into the red-stone bowl with a long white stick. *Bone. Or maybe carved antler.* He had pulled the tamping-stick from its own narrow leather bag. A bag decorated with quills and strings of tiny feathers laced together. *Porcupine quills. Sage-hen feathers.*

She watched him light the mix in the bowl, listened to the words he spoke, and then listened to the soft and quiet song he sang.

"The pipe-filling song," He's Proud spoke quietly into her ear.

The pipe began a journey around the fire, passing from one warrior to the next. Frankie could smell the scent of the tobacco traveling through the air as the pipe passed to the hands of each man, calmly and carefully. Quietly. Everything silent except for the soft song that Charging Crow sang. She watched as each warrior pulled the smoke through the pipe and breathed it back into the evening air.

And then, she smelled another fragrance; a different scent was floating through the air, a new scent that was rising from tied bundles of leaves, smoldering and smoking beside the fire. *Sage. Or maybe, juniper. Or cedar. Or maybe, all of them.*

Frankie couldn't tell what the scent was for sure, and she didn't want to ask, but she could see the scented smoke was being lifted and guided by the warriors—some using their hands, some using feathers. They were waving the smoke into their chests and up and around their heads. They were breathing the smoke, accepting it into their bodies, into their skin and eyes, nostrils and mouths.

"They welcome it, Fire Heart Child. It clears and cleanses. It opens them to the power of Spirit." He's Proud was saying the words as Knife and Strong Hand began sweeping the smoke through the air, using their feathers to bring the smoke to her. Bringing the scent in and around her body and up across her face and hair. Then they were lifting it up, sending the smoke away into the sky.

Frankie stayed silent and she stayed still—feeling the soothing scent pass into her nose and lungs. She breathed it in, feeling it wrap around inside of her. She could feel the scented-smoke swirling in her mouth and nose and eyes. Circling in her lungs.

She shivered and leaned against Strong Hand, pushing closer, wanting his body's heat. She could feel Knife to her other side; she felt the warmth of his arm around her back and shoulders. Her eyes began watering, her breathing slowed. Her head was tipping forward and rocking back. The firelight was swirling; the flames were rising high into the sky; the smoke was spinning and spiraling upward.

Then everything was hot; heat was coming from everywhere. Heat from the fire, heat from her brothers beside her. Heat rising from the earth below and settling down around her from the sky above. Hot air and hot smoke were circling around her, making her dizzy. Sweat was dripping from her forehead. Her eyes were watering. Then, burning.

She rubbed at her eyes, trying to open them. Trying to stay awake, but her head kept tipping forward and she could feel the sleep pulling at her. Her eyelids were burning and heavy. Aching to stay closed. So she closed them for a moment.

She dreamed of the buffalo, of the dark beasts. Of the great herds that roamed the far-away grasses of the far-away hills. She saw buffalo running and racing, coursing and chasing. Flowing like the winds, blowing and drifting and shifting across the land.

She watched the great shaggy beasts running through the grasses. Dark beasts, green grasses, blue skies. Charging through the low valleys, surging across the slopes. Snorting and blowing and bellowing. Their hooves pounding; their muscles rippling; their eyes shining. They raced on and on. Running through the land of the Cheyenne. Of the Pawnee. Of the Sioux and the Cree.

She dreamed of the flames of the fire and of the scent of sage and cedar. She saw the sweet-smoke rising from the red-stone; she watched the smoke lifting and sifting, swirling and curling above the stone bowl. Watching it through water-blurred eyes, watching it drift upward, skyward, twirling and twisting. Rising up, rising high. Rising far beyond the reach of the flames of the fire. Whisking itself upward, spinning high in a twirling and swirling dance, rising through the branches of the hillside trees.

Slowing, then. Pausing, then. Waiting, then. The sage-and-cedar smoke lingered. Searching. Seeking.

Choosing, then. Turning, then. Moving, then. The sweet-scented smoke swirled. Twisting, then. Traveling, then. Floating north. Flying north.

She dreamed of warriors. She watched them rise. She watched them follow the trail of the twirling swirls of the scented-smoke. They shouted and laughed and leaped to the backs of their ponies. The painted ponies danced; they pranced beneath their riders, spinning and swaying like the swirls of smoke.

Then, they ran; they raced. Running through the land. Running through the grasses; running through the hills. Racing. Racing to the dark cloth; racing to the dark beasts.

She heard the distant cries of eagles and hawks circling in the skies; she heard the wolf's quavering call. The cries and the calls, coming again and again. Echoing. Leading. Luring the riders.

The painted warriors rode. The painted ponies ran. Following the call, following the cries. Following the scent of the smoke.

She dreamed of the buffalo. Running. Of the ponies. Running. Of the elk and the deer and the antelope. Running. The grasses rippled. The dust rose. The birds flew. The clouds soared and the winds blew. The earth shook and shuddered. Hooves thundered. Buffalo hooves; horse hooves. Hoof-beats. Drum-beats. Thundering. Beating. Pounding. Sounding.

She dreamed of the sounds of the Sand Hills; she heard the song of the Sand Hills. The ancient songs; the ageless sounds. The rhythm and the beat on the prairie dirt. The sounds of the land and the sky and the earth. Loud and soft. Far and near. Soothing. Calming. Quieting.

She dreamed. She drifted. She floated above the land. Above the hills; above the grass. Flowing and rippling and rolling.

Then. She was walking. Walking among the buffalo. Walking slow among the dark beasts. Soft among the great beasts. Touching them. Feeling their heat. Feeling their warmth. Feeling the waves of their hair.

She dreamed as they pushed against her. Nudging her. Moving closer. Surrounding her, holding her. Leaning against her. Their breath warm; their eyes bright. Her fingers tangled in the soft hair, wrapping in the silken and swirling curls.

She pushed against the buffalo, pushing against its side. Pushing against its hide. The buffalo shifted. The dream drifted. It lifted. It left.

She woke to the world.

Not a buffalo; but a buffalo-robe.

She pushed at the robe, rolling it away from her.

The light from the mid-morning sun flashed bright in her eyes.

Frankie sat up. Surprised. Confused. Trying to remember; trying to understand. She looked around the fire. Charging Crow was no longer sitting with his saucer-board with the smoking-blend. Strong Hand was gone. Knife was gone. No warriors sat by the fire.

Instead, two women were there. Sitting side-by-side. Sitting on one of the logs with steaming bowls in their laps. The aroma of simmering stew and the roasting meat of the elk filled the air.

It didn't surprise Frankie to see Ida sitting there; but she didn't expect to see the other woman. Whirlwind was right there, sitting beside Ida; Strong Hand's mother was looking straight at her.

Frankie blinked, and then she blinked again. Shook her head and squinted. Wiped at her eyes. And still, Whirlwind was there. The Cheyenne woman was watching her, her eyes steady. Her smile was soft.

Frankie stared at her. The sickened gray-tone was gone from her face; the harsh lines of strain and tension were gone. The dark purplish-patches and the open sores were still there on her face and arms, but the woman who had been in the Barracks, sick and sweating, joints aching and body-sore—appeared to be fine now. After two days in the meadow, being spoon-fed the mashed vegetables and fruits, Whirlwind was sitting up on her own; she was there across the fire. Clear-eyed. Softly smiling. Frankie grinned at her.

"Hevovetåsono! Ne-toneto-mohta-he?" 'Whirlwind! How are you feeling?'

"Na-pevo-mohta, Nå-htona. E-peva'e." 'I'm fine, my daughter. It's all good.' The woman smiled, looking steadily at Frankie, studying her. She spoke again, her eyes soft.

"Na-mo'onaha, Nå-htona. Na-pevo-mohta. Ne-a'éše!"

"Whirlwind calls you her beautiful daughter. She says she is well, and she thanks you."

Frankie twisted around in surprise—He's Proud was right behind her, leaning back against the log, next to the buffalo-robe where she had slept. He was sitting there as if he had been guarding her while she lay sleeping, curled up within the heavy robe.

Whirlwind had more to say and as she spoke, Frankie heard a few English words tucked in with the Cheyenne words. From his place behind her, Frankie could hear He's Proud's voice relaying all her words, making sure there would be no misunderstandings. Because, Frankie knew, that was the mission of a translator. *To protect the message.*

411

"She tells you she is still hurting in her joints, but she is healing. She feels good inside. She says the heavy-sleep has left her. She is happy it has left her granddaughter too." He's Proud leaned forward and tapped Frankie's shoulder. He pointed toward the chicken-house, knowing she hadn't looked beyond the cookfire.

Frankie followed his point. Everett was out there in the meadow, coming from the henhouse, several eggs in each hand; he was walking slowly, walking in short steps—baby-steps. Frankie couldn't help smiling. *Baby-steps.* Because Little Mouse was there with Everett, walking between his legs, each little arm wrapped around one of his legs, circling his knees. She had a chicken egg clutched in each little hand.

Everett's head was down, his eyes on the toddler, watching as she was busy stepping along with his steps. Her short little legs stepping her little-girl-steps while Everett was moving along, slowly and patiently, helping her balance and move forward. Little Mouse had her head tipped up, looking at him with a wide and happy smile. Her dark eyes were shining and she was busy jabbering to him in Cheyenne baby-talk about something she seemed to think was *very* important.

And Everett was busy smiling and nodding at her, talking and making faces of surprise, laughing and chuckling at whatever she was saying, even though Frankie doubted that he had any real idea what Little Mouse was chirping about.

Frankie looked to Ida and they both burst into laughter, knowing the same thing—neither Everett nor Little Mouse had any idea what the other was saying. But it clearly didn't matter to either of them. Little Mouse was babbling and Everett was smiling, and they both seemed completely satisfied with the discussion. And meanwhile, Matilda and the rooster-puppy were trailing along behind them, making themselves part of the parade. From the toothy-smile on Matilda's face, it was apparent that she was happy about it.

The angle of the shadows on the ground told Frankie it was well into the morning—she had slept through the night and through most of the morning. And other than He's Proud and Everett, there were no men in the valley. None of the warriors were around; none of the Cheyenne ponies were grazing. Even the packhorses were gone.

Everyone had been busy with the morning while she had been sleeping; they had been getting things done while she had been sleeping, wrapped up in the buffalo-robe.

She looked to He's Proud, asking him where everyone was, upset she'd been sleeping and had missed the warriors' departure. Suddenly worried they had left for good. He's Proud stroked her hair, shook his head.

"No, Fire Heart Child. You were not sleeping. You were in the spirit dream. You were dreaming of the buffalo. You dreamed to show the hunters where to find the herd. You took them far into the hills to the north." He smiled softly at her, understanding her concern. "The hunters rode out before the sun, so you could lead them to the buffalo."

Frankie looked at him, confused that he knew about her dream, confused by his words. She looked to Whirlwind—Whirlwind with the soft and wise eyes—and saw the Cheyenne woman looking at her, nodding. Whirlwind knew; she understood exactly what He's Proud said.

"Your heart traveled to the buffalo, Daughter. You have done your work for the hunt. Let the men bring the meat for the people. Your place is here beside me and my granddaughter."

Whirlwind turned back to Ida and to whatever conversation they had been having. Frankie knew better than to argue or question, because Whirlwind had explained what she thought was important to her white daughter. She had spoken as a mother, and whether white or Cheyenne, the tone had been that of a mother who was done with the subject. When Frankie glanced to He's Proud, she could tell he was done with the subject too.

She watched Whirlwind and Ida, smiling as she saw Whirlwind patting Ida's arm and speaking softly to her, using the mix of Cheyenne and English. Ida, for her part, seemed to understand what was being said, because she was nodding and chuckling. And from the way they both glanced in her direction, Frankie assumed their conversation had to do with mothers knowing that sometimes little girls needed to be told what-was-what. There was a special language between women of that age, women who understood life in the same way. Women who had the same experiences that went with their years—even if they had lived their lives in very different worlds.

Whirlwind and Ida, Frankie realized, were speaking a language that went beyond the Cheyenne and English words—they had both raised sons and daughters, and now, they were both of the age of grandmothers. They were older women who knew common and shared things; they could sit and talk comfortably whether they were at a kitchen table holding cups of coffee, or beside a cookfire, holding bowls of steaming vegetables and broth.

Everett and Little Mouse finally reached the cookfire after getting sidetracked a few times on their way to the fireside—so bugs and twigs on the ground could be examined by little-girl fingers. It had been a slow walk at a toddler's pace, the pace of a little Cheyenne girl with sore and aching joints. But when they arrived, Little Mouse displayed her newly-found treasures clutched in her hands. She handed the two eggs to her grandmother, and then settled in beside Ida and helped herself to chunks of sweet potatoes and turnips from her bowl.

While Little Mouse ate, Frankie squatted down in front of her, tickling her, making her giggle and laugh, as she squeezed and moved her joints and looked at the sores on her lips and gums. The bleeding had stopped; the oozing sores were already healing. It had been a fast healing process. Frankie had heard the stories about the speed of recovery from scurvy, and she had been hoping for as much. But she was still surprised. Still pleased.

When Little Mouse tired of Frankie's examination, she beckoned to Everett, telling him to come with her. When he complied, she positioned herself at his knees again and directed him toward the barn, her mind set on other places to explore and more treasures to discover.

Frankie turned to Whirlwind and did a little prodding and pressing on her joints. She could see that her lips and gums were starting to heal; the sores on her skin were looking softer; the dark, harsh coloring of the lesions had lightened; the bloody-oozing was gone. It was all starting to clear.

She nodded and smiled at Whirlwind. She told her the remedies had helped to speed up the healing, but it was the vegetables and fruits that had done the real work. He's Proud stayed close, giving her the words she needed as she explained to Whirlwind about the sickness and why the plants had been the medicine for her. They talked about the plants and roots that grew on the land there where Lame Horse's people lived, the sheltered land where the Cheyenne and Arapahoe people had been living in the warm months. They had traveled to those lands and lived there for many summers.

According to Whirlwind though, many things had changed. The white-men had taken much of the land where Lame Horse's people had always roamed, especially the land along the rivers. And *that* was the land where the greatest variety of plants grew. The lands beyond the rivers were vast, but also dry and desolate.

And that, Frankie realized was where the problem began; the Indian's life and travel on the land, and their use of it, was being limited. The great variety of plants, especially those that grew in the rich soils along the rivers, weren't accessible to Lame Horse's band anymore. At least, not the same as in years past. They could no longer set their villages along the riversides, because those lands were being settled and farmed now.

As she and Whirlwind talked about the plants that grew on the more desolate lands, it seemed to Frankie that prickly-pear would be the best solution for Lame Horse's people. She told Whirlwind about cooking the pads of the prickly-pear, cooking them with honey.

"Eating prickly-pear the way we're cooking it over the fire, that'll keep away the spots and the aching sickness. All the people should eat it."

He's Proud was helping her with certain words, but Frankie was surprised at how much she could explain herself. The Cheyenne words were coming faster to her now, and with the English that

Whirlwind spoke, they were speaking easily, understanding each other and requiring very little help from He's Proud.

By the time Everett and Little Mouse returned from their adventure walk through the barn and pastures, Little Mouse was ready to eat again. Ida filled a bowl with the steaming vegetables and when she gave it to her, the little girl turned to Everett—she held the bowl up to him, her eyes shining with love and sweetness. She led him over to a place on one of the logs and sat down to eat with him; she ate the spoonfuls he held for her, and she ate tidbits he offered her from his fingers. And she snarled at anyone who attempted to interfere.

Little Mouse was making it clear that no one but this wonderful man with the fascinating eyes, this man who just had to be touched and patted again and again, would be allowed to help her eat from her bowl. And Everett was lost to her charms; he would tolerate no intrusion either. He sat on the log with *his* Little Mouse, *his Hóhkeeheso,* and tolerated no interference—she was his little girl and he was the only one who would be feeding her.

Frankie wondered for a moment what Strong Hand would say to that, but she knew when he rode in and saw his daughter giggling and smiling and toddling around, there would be no problems. One of the *good* things about working with scurvy cases was that the healing solution was simple. But the *best* thing about it, was the swift reversal of symptoms—the quick recovery could look miraculous. When Strong Hand came in from the hunt, he would see something he hadn't anticipated—not this soon, anyway.

Everett spent the afternoon walking Little Mouse around the meadow, slowly, methodically, while her body continued healing and the aching pain left her joints and muscles. She milked the cow with him; she made butter with him; she opened and closed gates with him; she petted the horses with him. She gathered eggs with him, leading him over to the henhouse every hour or so, just to hunt for the wonderful eggs. She sat on Black Mack's back while Everett led the ho-haa mo'éhė-no'ha everywhere she wanted to go, while she called out to everyone at the fire, shouting out about her very-much-horse.

Everett spent most of his time in a sweet-talk exchange with his Cheyenne shadow, finding great amusement in her dealings with the chickens. Once she understood the chickens had the work of making the eggs to give to the people, Little Mouse took to giving the hens a good Cheyenne talking-to whenever the egg-hunts proved fruitless.

Ida and Whirlwind worked beside the fire, tucking more root vegetables into the coals and adding more vegetables to the kettle. And every hour or so, the two women would walk around the meadow and out along the river. Joints moving, blood-flowing; that's what Frankie prescribed and Ida took her seriously.

Frankie spent a good amount of the afternoon in the kitchen, baking more cornbread and biscuits. Because more people were coming—dozens of families—and she knew that dishpans full of the breads wouldn't last long. She had pumpkin and squash roasting in the oven that would become a sweet buttery mash; on the back burner of the stovetop, she kept apples cooking down for applesauce. Partly because Whirlwind and Little Mouse still required them, and partly, because there were others among the Cheyenne who would likely have the sickness too.

When Laughing Girl, who Frankie suspected was looking for any excuse to remove herself from the rough-and-tumble puppy-stall, showed up at the kitchen porch with a hefty rabbit hanging from her jaws, Frankie took it over to the fire and handed it to He's Proud. He skinned and gutted it, and when he was mounting it on the spit, the hound returned with yet another rabbit. He's Proud reached for it, laughing about the hound's success and started the whole skinning and gutting process again.

While pans of breads were in the oven, Frankie made cups of sweet-coffee for Ida and Whirlwind and He's Proud. He's Proud had no great interest in the coffee, but Whirlwind thought it was grand. And as Frankie headed back to the kitchen and the oven, she was grinning, thinking about how it was a very different world here in the meadow—very different than just a month ago.

Everett was doting on a Cheyenne toddler; the two women were fast friends, chatting and keeping company over cups of coffee beside the cookfire. The world of Everett and Ida Dunbar was deeply involved with the world of the Cheyenne people; their two worlds had come together.

Later in the day, as twilight was coming on, as the clouds in the sky along the western horizon were turning to a rich fiery orange, He's Proud and Frankie rode out to the Lookout Hill to watch for Lame Horse's people.

"Charging Crow traveled to the west this morning to meet Lame Horse's band. He will send most of the families north to meet the hunting party. They'll help butcher the buffalo," He's Proud told her. "But Wild Bird, Nåhahé-ve'keso, will travel here, to be with her daughter and Little Mouse.

"So Wild Bird is Strong Hand's grandmother?"

"Yes, his grandmother. Né-ške'éehe." He gave her the word and went on. "Lame Horse was her husband. He died many winters ago. Wild Bird still lives, but she is an old woman. Lame Horse's people travel with her to Fire Heart Child's home.

Frankie and He's Proud stayed on the crest of the hill for more than an hour, letting the horses graze behind them while they scanned the western hills, watching for the traveling band. They sat on the rocks together and spent most of the time talking about the Cheyenne people and their language and He's Proud taught her more of his language, giving her more words and phrases.

He corrected her when she mispronounced them, and teased her when she misused them. And in the way of strong and gentle teachers, he always offered praise and encouragement. He's Proud was leading her forward in life, adding to who she was. Guiding her much the same as her father had. The same as her Uncle James and Aunt Sarah had.

Late in the morning of the next day, they arrived. Frankie watched an old woman leading a small band of Cheyenne into the meadow. She rode a bony old buckskin pony with a proud eye that suggested he had no inkling of his age or infirmity. Which was pretty much like the old woman—clearly no one had told either the woman or the buckskin that they were old. And no one treated them like they were. The old woman slid down from her skinny buckskin as easily as any warrior—she stood beside her pony for a moment, looking around her, eyeing all the buildings, studying the chicken-house. And then, she fastened her eyes on Frankie.

Frankie stood rooted to the ground, unable to move and unable to look away. The old woman, she knew, must be the woman He's Proud told her about. It was Wild Bird.

Nåhahé-ve'keso. Whirlwind's mother and Strong Hand's grandmother. The woman who had been the wife of old Lame Horse, the chief of this band. She found herself fascinated by the Cheyenne woman, and looking at her, Frankie figured her to be about two hundred years old. *Easily. Or maybe, three-hundred.*

Wild Bird's face was narrow and long; it was deeply-wrinkled and craggy, and her skin was such a rich, deep bronze-brown that it looked as if it had been carved from a block of wood from a walnut tree. But Frankie thought she was beautiful. She smiled at the woman, and then smiled bigger when the woman started walking right toward her. Behind the woman, other horses and riders were coming down the track into the meadow—the Cheyenne who had followed this old woman of the prairie into the valley.

Frankie was aware that they were dismounting, that they were looking at her and looking around the meadow, but she wasn't looking at them. Her eyes were locked on the old Cheyenne woman. *Nåhahé-ve'keso. Wild Bird. Strong Hand's grandmother.*

She watched the woman coming toward her, carrying a heavy stick with a burl-knob on one end of it. It must have been intended as a walking-stick, but this woman was using it for everything *but* that. She was looking over her shoulder at the people behind her, holding it by the burl-knob on its end, waving and pointing the tip in all directions, barking out commands and orders. To Frankie's ears, she was doing so with all the gusto and clarity of Cavalry officers when they pulled their sabers during drills.

And those people—all the Cheyenne who followed her down the track into the meadow—started moving fast. They got busy doing whatever it was Wild Bird was telling them to do. And all the while, old Nåhahé-ve'keso kept walking toward Frankie. Speaking Cheyenne, saying some words that Frankie knew and some that she didn't.

Frankie listened for He's Proud's voice, knowing he'd translate for her—but when she looked to her side, he wasn't there; he wasn't behind her either. He was over by the packhorses, scrambling like everyone else, hurrying to do whatever the old Cheyenne woman had told him to do. So Frankie stood where she was and waited until the woman was in front of her.

Nåhahé-ve'keso reached out a hand every bit as gnarled and wrinkled as her face; she patted Frankie's arm several times and said a single word. She nodded, and then reached to pat Frankie's cheek and said the same word once again. Nå-htona. Frankie had heard it before; it was the word Whirlwind had used for her. Strong Hand used it when he talked about Little Mouse. Nå-htona. The old woman was saying 'my daughter'.

And in that moment, Frankie knew she belonged to this woman and the woman belonged to her. She had just been adopted into this woman's heart—she was a daughter to her now. Frankie felt her heart opening up.

"Ne-a'ëše, Né-ške'éehe." 'Thank you, my Grandmother.' Frankie said it without thinking, without hesitating, without hunting for the words. The woman smiled a huge smile and Frankie was afraid in that moment that the old woman's face—with all its deep wrinkly-cracks—was going to shatter and break apart. But it didn't.

Her smile was soft and warm, her expression was full of delight. The woman patted Frankie's arm again.

She turned suddenly. Looking toward the barn entrance, listening. Frankie knew what she had heard. The husky laughter of Little Mouse was coming from the alleyway, echoing from inside the barn. Old Wild Bird watched as her great-granddaughter walked out of the barn with a firm grip of ownership on Everett's pantleg.

A few steps beyond the barn door, the two-year-old spotted the old woman standing in the meadow; she started dragging Everett along, heading toward the old woman.

"Ke'éehe, Ke'éehe!" She was hollering the Cheyenne baby-word for her grandmother and pulling at Everett's pantleg. She finally released his pant-leg, and achy joints or not, she did her best toddler-run toward her grandmother. She was laughing and calling, and Wild Bird was calling to her; she stooped to grab her great-granddaughter into her arms. The words and laughter and caresses flowed.

A moment later, Wild Bird caught a movement over by the fire; she turned to see her daughter. Her face broke into a wider smile, watching Whirlwind walking toward her, walking carefully, but still with the easy grace of the Cheyenne women. Old Wild Bird's face softened again. When she had seen Little Mouse running toward her, the web of wrinkles on her face had softened considerably; now, her face actually lit up.

The fear and concern that had been there in the midst of all the hard wrinkles were gone; now, there was only a soft joy. The agony that had been woven into the craggy pattern of wrinkles had disappeared.

The noise and activity around the packhorses were still going on; the new arrivals were still unloading the travois and the packs; they were still moving fast, going about their business. Frankie started toward the fray, curious about the bundles being laid out in ordered piles. And that was when she saw two people who brought joy and delight to her own face.

Willow was there. Big and beautiful Willow was standing beside one of the packhorses, smiling her warm and wonderful smile. Laughing her wonderful body-jiggling laugh. And right beside her was Dandelion. Dandelion who was already grinning at her, her shining black eyes snapping with excitement. Frankie gave an excited yelp, and then she was running and hurdling over piles and bundles, rushing to her own reunion.

Once she and Willow and Dandelion had their moments to greet each other, Frankie decided to pitch in; she started reaching for rawhide packets and leather bundles as they were being passed and toted. Within a few minutes, she realized that mostly, she was being pushed aside. Politely and gently; but firmly. Everyone was stepping around her, passing things over her head, patting her shoulders and shifting her out of the way.

Frankie realized she was spending more time ducking and dodging than doing any real lifting or carrying. Clearly, these women and men had their way of doing things, and clearly, she was in their way.

Needing something to do, she looked toward the crowd of people near the fire, suddenly thinking that Ida and Everett would need introductions; they would need some guidance and help so they would feel comfortable with all the new people arriving in the meadow. But He's Proud was already there, and Whirlwind had gone back to Ida's side. Together He's Proud and Whirlwind were busy making introductions and supplying explanations, and Everett and Ida were listening and nodding and smiling. Laughing. Greeting these newly arrived people like they were family.

He's Proud was staying close to Everett, talking and pointing, explaining about things he thought Everett should know. And the women crowding around Ida, were talking about Whirlwind's health and about the food stewing in the great kettle. Old Wild Bird was there, too, and Little Mouse was being passed around like a puppy.

Frankie watched the crowd by the fire, knowing she wasn't needed—not by Everett or Ida, not by any of the women at the fire. And not by the other women and men busy with the work of unloading and unpacking.

And then suddenly, Dandelion was beside her, pulling at her arm, pulling her away from the work of the unloading. Frankie followed the tugs and pulls, laughing at Dandelion's idea to leave the work to her mother and the others. Because Dandelion wanted to run through the meadow, wanting to see the ho-haa mo'éhė-no'ha. The 'very much horses'. So Frankie went with her, dashing toward the front-pasture gate.

She took a last glance over her shoulder and saw that Wild Bird was back to her stick-waving and command-calling—the women of the band were moving quickly and the men were moving as fast as the women. Apparently, when Wild Bird's stick was swinging and pointing, the Cheyenne warriors were perfectly capable of doing women's work. Already, the packs had been stripped from the horses; the travois were unloaded, and the long poles had been lifted from the horses' withers and settled to the ground.

And then Frankie was running beside Dandelion, dashing through the meadow past the buildings. Heading through the front gateway and down the track to the back pastures, racing to see the very-much-horses. They ran along the track, laughing and giggling. Enthralled with each other's company again, basking in their sisterhood.

When Dandelion saw the Shires, she 'ooh-ed and ahh-ed' over them just like she had the first time she'd ever seen them. She petted their faces and stroked their necks; when they lowered their heads, she reached to scratch behind their ears. She patted the mules and then decided she needed to pet each of the geldings.

When Boone nipped at her braids, Dandelion pinched his lips; when he laid his ears back and snapped at her hand, she laughed and stroked his cheek. He snorted, and Dandelion laughed. And Frankie laughed; Boone had met his match. Once again.

Then, they squeezed through the plank fences to pet the four oxen and Blossom and Primrose. Dandelion giggled and talked about the vé'ho'é-otóva'a. The white-man's buffalo. They crossed the track so she could greet Trumpeter and each of the mares.

When Dandelion had seen everything she wanted to see, the two girls made their way back to the front meadow and when they arrived, it was clear to Frankie that decisions had been made and plans were in motion. There was a tall conical skeleton of long slender poles standing at the base of the hillside, right between the front barn-lot and the cookfire. Women were working on the structure, adding more poles, leaning them into the standing-structure.

Frankie understood what was happening; she had seen drawings and paintings of Indian lodges in books and magazines. But she had never seen a real one. Now she was grinning, delighted that one was being erected right in her own meadow. Right before her eyes.

"Wild Bird's home," He's Proud told her. "Her tipi. Xamáa-vee'e."

When Frankie went in closer, after ignoring Dandelion's warning, she found herself ushered away by one woman after another. There were seven women making that tipi grow right before her eyes and not one of them wanted her anywhere near the work they were doing. Even Ida, who had been included in the project and was laughing and teasing with the women, pointed her away.

For Frankie, being excluded from helping erect the wonderful creation, was a personal affront. It was beyond her understanding and liking, but her complaints and protests made no difference; none of the women paid her any attention. Dandelion kept pulling her back and trying to soothe her feelings, but ultimately, it took He's Proud to convince her that she had no say in the matter. According to him, little-white-girls didn't know how to build tipis, and he made her understand the women weren't going to tolerate any interference.

Finally, she accepted the truth, but not with any grace or dignity; she made a serious show of sulking, but it gained her nothing; nobody gave her any attention and no one changed the rules for her. She relented and plopped herself down on the ground beside Dandelion to watch the process—to watch what turned out to be an amazing process.

The women worked with practiced precision and astonishing speed. It was a wonderful thing to watch as the massive half-circle of a dozen buffalo-hides slid upward, wrapping around the framework of lodgepoles. The women eased the giant skirt up the poles, and then stood on each other's shoulders to reach the top, adjusting it into position for a perfect fit. The front edges of the hides were overlapped and fastened together with sharpened sticks, stitching the hide-cover together, right up to the high crisscross of the poles.

"Séhpa-tó'óheo'o," Dandelion said.

"Fastening-things. Lacing pins." He's Proud translated.

Two long, narrow poles were fastened to flaps of hides near the top of the lodge, poles that could be shifted and tilted to change the position of the flaps.

"Hoóhtsenáheónó'e. Smoke-flap poles." He's Proud told her. He went through the motions with his hands, showing her how the pole and its flap would be used to change the shape and size of the smoke-hole at the top of the tipi.

A moment later, a hide-door was settled in place across a low opening in the lodge.

"Always, the door faces to the East," He's Proud said. "Éše'hė-tséxė-heseme'enėse. The-sun-where-rises."

While some women pounded stakes into place around the bottom of the tipi, others began carrying the piles of buffalo-robes and bundles of hides inside. More armloads of buckskin bags, raw-hide-boxes and a whole slew of parfleche-packets were taken into the lodge. And then, quite suddenly, the work was done.

It had been only a matter of minutes since she and Dandelion had come trotting back from the pasture tour. Minutes since He's Proud had given her the talking-to; minutes since she had settled down in the grass beside her Cheyenne sister. *Not even fifteen minutes.*

Frankie took in a breath, astonished at the sight—the lodge was there. The Xamáa-vee'e was standing sturdy and strong, right there in her meadow. Looking a little like a sculpture. Like a piece of art. Beautiful in its sensibility. Complex and simple at the same time.

She stared at the tall poles that rose up sturdy and strong, tilting inward, leaning into each other under the hide-walls, creating what looked like a crown where the tips emerged at the top.

Paintings adorned the tipi's slanted walls, wrapping around the lodge. Colored horses ran in circles around this Cheyenne home; lightning strikes of blue and black streaked across the hides; painted suns of yellow and red were shining brightly; footprints of deer and buffalo, badgers and bears, traipsed in crisscrossing trails across the stretched hides.

It was while Frankie was studying the wonders of this new-standing structure in her meadow that Willow came over with pieces of pemmican and jerky. Frankie figured Dandelion's mother was trying to make up for making her stay away, but when Willow gave her head a light rap with her knuckles, Frankie knew it was a stern correction. She knew exactly what the rap was about—it was about her sulk. Because her arguments and complaints had disrupted the women's work.

She had disrupted the cooperation there among the Cheyenne as the lodge went up. Everyone else had their minds on creation and cooperation. But her thoughts had been on herself—and nothing good had come from her behavior. Among these people, there was no time for sulking or arguing. It wasn't the Cheyenne way.

Frankie dropped her head, stared at the grass, ignored the pemmican and jerky in her hands. She could feel the heat of a blush rising up as the embarrassment swept over her. Dandelion read the look on her face and started giggling; she made a pouting-face, mimicking her white sister.

Finally, Frankie started giggling too, giving-in to Dandelion's teasing and the insistent tugging on her sleeve. She allowed herself to be pulled backward on the grass, tipping back and surrendering to the wave of giggles that always came with Dandelion's tickling games. The shame disappeared, lost in the midst of the silly laughter and the wild rolling and twisting and wrestling.

Somewhere in the middle of the giddiness, Frankie heard Whirlwind's call and saw her beckoning. She quit the game, scrambled to her feet and trotted over to where Whirlwind waited beside the lodge. The woman who had called her daughter, motioned for her to follow; she led the way through the flap-door into the tipi.

Frankie stepped into another world. Old Wild Bird was there in that world, moving around in the magical half-light within the lodge, arranging rawhide boxes against one of the lodge walls. She looked at Frankie and moved to greet her.

"Ésė-stsehnėstse." 'Come in and be welcome'. The old woman patted her on the shoulder and Frankie looked around at this wonderful home, knowing Wild Bird and Whirlwind and Little Mouse would be sleeping in this wonderful new lodge.

She leaned against Wild Bird as the old woman pointed to the objects around the tipi, speaking softly in the rolling rhythm of her language. Frankie listened to the names, looking to the objects. Repeating the words, letting the sounds and the syllables roll around on her tongue. Wild Bird waited for her to repeat the words, teaching her both the Cheyenne language and the Cheyenne way of life at the same time.

Frankie decided the lodge was a perfect home, clever and cozy and comfortable. With the sunlight hitting the buffalo-hide walls, everything inside was drenched in a soft buttery-glow, reminding her of her time living under the canvas top in the Conestoga.

There were skirts of leather fastened to the inside walls and piles of hides for beds; other hides were spread on the ground. Packs and stacks of belongings were all neatly sorted and organized around the sides of the lodge. Leather bags and pouches hung from the tall poles. In the very center, a ring of stones surrounded a pretty little fire-pit. And Frankie thought that was perfect too. *For warmth and light. And maybe even for some cooking, right in the middle of this pretty little home.*

Dandelion was standing just inside the door, holding the flap open, laughing at Frankie again—teasing her and copying her expressions of surprise and delight. Frankie made a face at her and they took off running, chasing across the meadow. Behind her, Frankie could hear Ida laughing above the chuckles of the Cheyenne women and men.

When they returned to the cookfire, they grabbed what food was offered to them and flopped down beside He's Proud to eat their meal. Ida was sitting between Whirlwind and Willow and they were talking back and forth about the food; Ida was talking about cooking the prickly-pear cactus and He's Proud supplied what words they needed.

Everett was wandering around with Little Mouse once again, and Frankie watched them for a while. Little Mouse was doing an awful lot of baby-chatter and Everett was doing an awful lot of head nodding and agreeing. It was impossible, she decided, to figure out exactly who was following who, and who was teaching who.

Late in the afternoon, Everett and Ida hitched their team, intent on heading home to tend to the animals and chores. Now that the sickness was handled and the danger was past, Frankie figured they would stay home for a few days; she walked beside Ida on her way to the wagon and started to thank them for all their help. But Ida interrupted her, explaining that Everett wanted to spend the evening and early morning getting everything caught up—because they planned to return the next morning.

"Because Everett has to see to his special girl, you know." Ida glanced over to Little Mouse sitting with her grandmother. Ida added that she wanted to spend more time with the women. "Would that be okay with you, Frankie? If we came back so soon?"

Frankie grinned at her, hugged her, laughing. Thinking back to how the Dunbars had always been uneasy at the thought of Indians visiting her—they had argued awfully hard against them being here in the meadow.

"To tell you the truth, Honey, I don't believe I could keep Everett away, not with his little sweetheart still here." Ida laughed at the expression on her face. "I know, Frankie. I *know*. I was just thinking the same thing. Everett and I have had quite a change of heart, haven't we?"

Once the Dunbars were climbing onto the wagon, it became clear that Little Mouse was surprised at the sight—and more than a little confused. She watched Everett climbing up on the wheeled contraption; she stared, astounded, as the wagon pulled onto the track. And then, she was scrambling out of Whirlwind's lap. Everybody watched as the two-year-old started following her favorite person as he turned his team up the entrance track.

Little Mouse's expression of disbelief that he was leaving without her faded, replaced by look of desperate determination. She started following the wagon in the best toddler-trot she could muster.

"Ne-náestse, ne-náestse, ne-náestse." 'Come here, come here, come here.' She was waving and calling for him. Confused and pleading. Begging for her wonderful man to come back. As Everett turned on the wagon-seat, watching his little girl trotting along behind, hollering for him to come back, it looked like his heart was breaking.

The adults around the fire called for Little Mouse, laughing at her determined march, but Frankie was pretty sure Hóh-keeheso was going to keep going, no matter how many people called to her. It was He's Proud who settled things; he called to Frankie and motioned toward her horse, while he bridled his.

Frankie bridled Rock, managed to swing up on him Cheyenne-style—without flopping back to the ground on her bottom—and followed He's Proud. They headed toward the front track, riding toward Little Mouse as she trotted and stumbled along after the Dunbar wagon, still calling desperately to Everett in her husky little voice.

As they approached the two-year-old on the track, He's Proud leaned low from his horse and plucked Little Mouse up from her determined little march. They caught up to the wagon and He's Proud passed Little Mouse across to the wagon-seat. Everett gathered her in his arms and settled her on his lap; Little Mouse's desperate pleas turned into excited chattering, sounding a little, Frankie thought, like a baby-bird chirping in its nest.

Everett and Ida and Hóh-keeheso were ecstatic with the turn of events. Laughter erupted around the cookfire as the wagon rolled over the rise and out of the valley with Frankie and He's Proud trotting beside it. The little procession crossed the ford and turned downriver, heading to the Dunbar homestead. While Little Mouse and Ida and Everett chatted up a storm, He's Proud talked about Wild Bird and the journey from the Cheyenne village far to the south and west.

Wild Bird, he said, along with another woman and a medicine man, had been caring for Whirlwind and Little Mouse since late in the summer, but like others in the village, they had been getting sicker day by day. Two old men and a child had already died.

When Knife had shown up with word about Fire Heart Child, he told the story of how she had healed the buffalo-horse for Gray Fox and Strong Hand remembered how she had healed the soldier with the snake-bite. That was when Strong Hand decided to bring his band here, so Ho-esta Hesta Ka-èškóne could heal his mother and daughter.

The rest of Lame Horse's people prepared to travel to the north, too, deciding to travel to the home of Fire Heart Child. Later, they would go to Mo'óhtá-vo'honáaeva, 'the black-rocky place', the Black Hills, for the winter.

So Wild Bird had come with the band; she came to see this little white girl her grandson called 'sister'. She came, believing the sickness was too great; she believed she would arrive to find her daughter and the grandchild had died. She had not expected to see Little Mouse running to her, He's Proud said. And she had not expected to see Whirlwind walking to her.

"Wild Bird understands about the food," he said. "And she knows the land where Lame Horse's band was living doesn't give them the plants they need. Early in the summer, the plants were already dried and shriveled from the sun and the heat. She says she won't return to that land. It was the land of her husband's people and she has no love for it. And this sickness has shown her that it isn't good to live there anymore."

He's Proud patted Frankie's leg as they rode together. He said she was helping his people.

"Knife says you are of the Cheyenne people. Wild Bird believes that too. She believes you lived among our ancestors and you have come back now. She dreamed of it while she traveled to the place where Ho-esta Hesta Ka-èškóne lives."

Frankie listened, trying to understand everything He's Proud was saying, overwhelmed with the importance of what he told her. Knowing he was speaking of the lives and the beliefs of the Cheyenne. He's Proud smiled at her and patted her thigh again; he rode beside her, keeping his hand where it was. Frankie realized she had nothing to say, and for now, that seemed fine. He expected nothing from her; he seemed satisfied with her silence.

They rode for an hour behind the wagon, hearing the chatter and the laughter coming from the wagon-seat. Everett was teaching Little Mouse to handle the reins and Little Mouse realized she had the power to move the two horses and 'the rolling thing' with her two little hands. She thought it was a marvelous thing and once she decided she had the hang of it, she started discussing the whole process with everyone.

She chattered about it to Everett and Ida. And she told the two horses in front of her all about it. She twisted in Everett's lap, hollering over her shoulder, explaining it to Frankie and He's Proud. Then she told the sky and the birds. She even explained it to a rabbit, shouting the news at it when it bounded across the track in front of the wagon.

Halfway to the Dunbar place, Everett pulled the team to a stop and stood to hand Little Mouse to He's Proud. She settled into his lap, still chattering and chortling about this whole adventure, satisfied with the road trip and understanding now that her marvelous friend would come back to visit her in the morning.

The riders turned west and the wagon kept going east and Ida called over her shoulder, telling Frankie they would be at the meadow by mid-morning. Frankie grinned at her and gave a final wave, thinking about how much had changed in the minds of the Dunbars in a matter of months; their former ideas about the people who spent their lives roaming the prairie had changed. The people of this Cheyenne band had become dear to them.

While Frankie and He's Proud rode back home with the sun in the west shining in their eyes, he quizzed her, throwing out Cheyenne words that he had taught her. Testing her. Wanting to know what she was remembering. Satisfied with what he heard, he started teaching her about his people, telling her of their villages and how they lived and traveled.

He told her of the Oglála and of the other Sioux tribes. He told her of the ways they were like the Cheyenne—and of the ways they were different. He spoke of the other tribes that lived out on this part of the prairie, the Pawnee and the Ponca and the Otoe. And the Arikaree—known as the Cree—who sometimes traveled to these lands, even though their lands were far to the north. And sometimes Crow warriors traveled far from the west, from far beyond the black-rocky place, to fight and steal horses. He told her what his people thought about the soldiers and their forts, and about the white people coming into the land.

Frankie listened to every word, determined to remember everything he was saying, and realizing she wasn't just *hearing* the explanations and the stories—she was beginning to feel them. She was feeling and understanding the heart behind his words—it was what her father would refer to as the context and the purpose. It was the way her father always wanted her to learn; he had spoken about the value of hearing more than just words and their meanings—he always wanted her to hear and understand the deeper part beneath the spoken words.

She realized something else. He's Proud was speaking more and more in Cheyenne, using fewer English words as he spoke with her—more and more of his explanations and descriptions were in the Cheyenne language. She noticed she wasn't really paying attention which language he was using. That, she knew, was because He's Proud was a good teacher, much like her father had been.

Like her father, He's Proud was very aware of her level of comprehension; he already knew which of the different words and subjects she was grasping, so he was picking and choosing exactly when he could speak entirely in Cheyenne. He knew when he could mix the two languages to push her understanding. And he knew when he needed to revert to using English.

Frankie recognized his strategy; she understood He's Proud was gifting her with both his time and his heart. She told him that, and she talked to him about her father and how he had taught the same way. He's Proud looked straight into her eyes; he studied her and then nodded.

"That is why I teach you, Fire Heart Child. Because you choose to learn. You can see ahead and you can see that this will matter in

your life. You understand it will matter to the Cheyenne people."
He reached to touch her shoulder. "When I first saw you at the soldier-fort, I knew you wanted a teacher and not a translator."

Little Mouse, napping against He's Proud's belly, stirred and grumbled; she pushed tighter against his belly and continued sleeping. He's Proud, Frankie realized, had known that Hóh-keeheso would sleep; he knew he would have time to school his young companion. He's Proud, Frankie decided, rarely did anything by accident. Just like her father and her Lieutenant and the Captain, He's Proud had foresight; he was always very aware of how things would take shape.

Half an hour later, when they reached the river's ford, Dandelion was there, playing in the water. She told them there was word about the hunting party.

"Blue Feather has come today. He says it was a good hunt and there are many buffalo." She reached for Frankie's arm and swung up on Rock's back behind her. "He was happy to see Whirlwind is well. He waits to see Little Mouse."

When they rode into the meadow, the man who brought the news was walking away from a palomino-pinto mare in the herd of ponies grazing in the meadow. He's Proud pulled his horse to a stop beside him and Frankie listened while they spoke.

"The families who went out to the hunt will come tomorrow," he said. "It was a good hunt. There is meat for our people. Much meat." He was speaking to He's Proud but when his eyes turned to Frankie, she recognized him.

The man's name He's Proud said, was Otá'taveenóvá'e. 'Blue Feather'. Frankie remembered him from her very first encounter with the band of Cheyenne early in the summer; he had been one of the nine warriors who had approached her when she was traveling on her Conestoga, south of the Platte River. She had stared at him that day; even in those moments of uncertainty while she stood in the jockey-box of the wagon, she had thought he was the most handsome of all the riders. Today, she was staring at him again, thinking the same thing.

He had a beautiful face, fierce and soft. A broad forehead and wide cheekbones. A strong and square jaw. Gentle and wise eyes. The taut line of his bow-string stretched across his chest. A quiver of shimmering red fox fur held a cluster of arrows against his back. A strand of tail-feathers of a red-tailed hawk dangled along the length of his long braids, their coppery-red sheen shining bright against his bronze-red skin.

On that day, Blue Feather had been sitting in front of her on a palomino-pinto mare. Even his mare had caught her eye—Frankie thought it was one of the prettiest mares she had ever seen. That same pretty mare was here in her meadow now.

And now, Blue Feather was smiling at her. *Pretty smile, pretty eyes.* Frankie smiled back. He greeted her, using her Cheyenne name, speaking the words softly. She felt herself blushing, feeling the heat flushing up her neck. *Handsome smile, handsome eyes.*

She recovered from her blush enough that she managed to return his greeting, but she heard herself stumbling over the words—not exactly sure whether the stumbling had to do with the unfamiliar language, or the wave of shyness sweeping over her. Her mind flicked back to the last time she had the same feeling. *Independence Day. That afternoon on the Parade Grounds.* The same wave had swept over her when Captain Jack Connell had approached her looking so very handsome and dashing in his dress uniform. *A sweet-crush. That's what Isabelle called it.*

She had heard Isabelle and her Lieutenant talking in the sitting-room of the cottage early the next morning. 'Just a sweet baby-love, Frank Dear. Our Frankie's in love with her Captain.'

Frankie brought her thoughts forward, back to the moment in front of her, trying to block the idea of 'a sweet-crush' out of her mind. Trying to tamp down the shy-blush and the prickly hot-skin feeling. She managed to blurt out a question, asking Blue Feather about the hunt. He smiled at her, quietly and kindly, almost as if he knew what she was feeling. *He probably knows just like my Captain did.*

He answered her question, saying once again, that it had been a good hunt.

"Many buffalo fell. Our people will eat well." He spoke then about Whirlwind, talking about the sickness being gone from her. And he thanked her for caring for his mother.

He dropped his eyes then, releasing her from her stare. He stepped closer to He's Proud on his horse, reaching to lift Little Mouse from his lap, waking her as he did. When she opened her eyes and saw Blue Feather, she gave a big grin and clapped her hands together. She patted his face with both hands and her eyes flashed with delight. She looked around the meadow and over to the cook-fire, calling out to everyone, shouting to tell them how happy she was. Because her uncle was here.

And suddenly, Frankie started putting everything together. Realizing Blue Feather was Strong Hand's younger brother. He, too, was Whirlwind's son. He was old Wild Bird's grandson. She watched as the handsome warrior wrapped his arms around Little Mouse, his smile growing as he listened to her jabbering; he was fascinated and delighted at the change in the child.

After a moment of her jabbering and wriggling in excitement, he put her down on the ground and watched her do a toddling run over to her grandmothers at the fireside. She was still excited, still jabbering, still calling out how happy she was that her uncle had come to visit her.

Blue Feather turned his attention back to Frankie, flashing another handsome smile; Frankie managed to tamp down another rising blush. Days ago, he said, Little Mouse had been in pain. She had been unwilling to move. Now, he said, she was running and laughing. She was happy and well again.

He's Proud filled in some of the words for her, but Frankie picked up most of what he said. She told Blue Feather the sickness came from not having the right foods. Little Mouse was healthy again, she said, because she was eating the right foods.

Blue Feather touched his fingers to her knee and Frankie felt the heat from a fresh blush flow across her face. She ducked her head, listening as he turned to He's Proud, saying Ho-esta Hesta Ka-ėškóne

435

was humble, that she was humble as a Cheyenne girl should be. And just about then, Dandelion started tugging at her arm, impatient with all the talk, insisting they should ride back to the river.

"Because the water's cool, Sister. Come on. Let's go. Now. You can talk later."

Frankie turned her face away from Blue Feather, managed to avoid another hot blush, and turned Rock's head toward the meadow's entrance. *Yes. The water will be cool. And that will be a good thing.*

All the way to the ford, Frankie teased Dandelion about being bossy and Dandelion accused Frankie of being afraid of the water. When Rock waded out into the river, they elbowed and pushed at each other until they both ended up in the river, splashing and shrieking in wild play. Rock left the water to graze along the riverbank, looking up occasionally to eye the two girls roiling and churning in the water, watching his person for a moment, then returning to his grazing.

When they finally crawled up the riverbank, stripped out of their clothes, and spread themselves out in the sand and the sun to dry, Frankie laughed at the expression in Rock's eyes. He was watching them in his sensible warhorse way, looking maybe a little surprised at finding himself standing guard over two naked little brown-bodied girls who had been splashing and flopping around in a river. Looking at his eyes, Frankie thought he was a little astonished—as if he had never seen such a thing before. She realized then that in all his years as a Cavalry mount, he probably hadn't.

When the cool of the early twilight settled in, they scrambled onto Rock's back and returned to the meadow with their cold, bare bottoms on his warm, bare back, carrying their cold, wet clothes in little damp bundles. They trotted into the meadow, giggling, tickling and poking each other, riding past everyone at the fire, heading toward the barn pens. They slid off Rock, turned him into a pen and spread their damp clothes along the board fence, then they raced over to the cookfire in search of warmth and whatever food might be waiting.

Frankie watched Dandelion pulling food from the cookpot, reaching straight into the steaming liquid with her fingers. She wanted to follow her example, but hesitated, already knowing her fingers couldn't tolerate the heat of the pot's contents, and pretty sure it wasn't wise to try again. Blue Feather saw her dilemma, laughed, and beckoned to her.

She went to him and let him pull her down to his lap—and just as Knife always did—he selected choice bits from the stew, holding them for her until they cooled. She took the food he offered while the talk went on around her, watching the people around her. Watching her family. *Her* Cheyenne family.

Tucked in against Blue Feather's belly, Frankie watched Wild Bird stirring the stew. She watched Whirlwind rocking Little Mouse in her lap. She smiled, watching the way Willow's whole body shook and jiggled with her laughter. Watching the way He's Proud sat with Dandelion nestled into his lap. *Family. Real family.*

Frankie released her mind, freeing it to travel back to other times, back to other places. There had been nights in the big white house in Indiana when her Uncle James rocked Little Charles to sleep by the fireplace. There had been nights when she had nestled into her father's lap in the rocker. There had been quiet laughter with that family and there had been loud and hilarious laughter too.

And at the fort, there had been times when she curled up in the rocker with her Lieutenant, resting quietly in his arms. There had been evenings when she and Isabelle curled up on the settee together, hemming blouses and skirts, and Isabelle had been laughing so hard she had been shaking.

Family. Calm evenings; quiet nights. Firelight. Quiet conversation. Quiet laughter. Love. And this was the same. This family. This evening. This fireside. Rocking. Talking.

Frankie stayed silent, watching the men and women around her. Listening to their conversation, listening to the lifts and pauses and the musical rhythm of their words. Listening to the Cheyenne language and the Cheyenne words.

The conversation went on while everyone filled their wooden plates and dishes from the cookpot; they talked about the hunt and the buffalo meat, and about the families that would be arriving the next day. About lodges that would go up beside the river.

"Many people, many lodges," He's Proud told her, filling in words for her.

As the cold air of dusk settled down in the meadow, Willow began rummaging in a rawhide bag. She called both girls to her as she pulled several bundles of soft leather from the bag, separated out a leather shirt, tanned soft and supple, and slipped it over Dandelion's head. She reached for another length of the soft leather and slid it between Dandelion's legs, lifting it up and around her bottom and fastening it at her hips.

Frankie reached to touch the breechcloth, feeling the soft leather. She asked for the Cheyenne word.

"Henova'e he'tohe?"

"Nėhpėsó'ė-hestótse." 'Cover-up thing.' Willow answered, and then Dandelion broke out in laughter, surprised that she didn't know such a thing.

Still laughing, Willow beckoned to Frankie, holding another 'cover-up thing' in her hands; she reached to slip the tanned leather between her legs and fastened it at her hips. Frankie gasped, loving the whole clever idea. Loving the feel of the soft-tanned hide hugging her around her waist. Without thinking, she did a little foot-stomping dance, delighted and excited. She hugged Willow and she hugged Dandelion and stepped back, twirling around. Laughing because Whirlwind and the others were laughing at her.

Willow interrupted Frankie's twirling when she tapped her shoulder; she was holding up another buckskin shirt, motioning for Frankie to hold up her arms. Frankie did as she was told and the big soft-smiling woman slipped the shirt over her arms. The silky-soft leather slid down her shoulders, gliding down to her waist, drifted down over her breech-clothed bottom. Fringe at the bottom edge of the shirt floated and swayed, tickling her thighs like prairie grass.

Frankie giggled and started whirling and hopping, sending the long fringes swirling and spinning. She laughed louder, loving the tickle, loving the feel of the soft-tanned leather wrapping against her shoulders and waist.

She hugged Willow and Dandelion again, and then hopped and danced her way over to Blue Feather; she tipped herself toward him, expecting him to catch her. He did. And he laughed as he pulled her into his lap, laughing like everyone else around the fire. Laughing at the little-white-girl, amused and pleased at her delight over the clothes.

Snuggling into his lap, Frankie began examining the rows of quills that circled around her neck and shoulders, deciding it was just like having a necklace sewn into the shirt.

"Heškóvetsée'e," Blue Feather told her. 'Porcupine quills.'

Which, to Frankie, sounded more like 'porcupine feathers'. *But then the Cheyenne words aren't always exact when they're translated. Because Cheyenne words are more of a description. Not a certain term.*

She thought about some of the words while she studied the fringes and quill-work. Thinking about how a wagon wasn't actually a wagon—it was *amó-eneo'o*. A rolling-thing. Thinking about how the breechcloth wasn't called a breechcloth—it was *nėhpėsó'ė-hestótse*. A cover-up thing.

Along with the pattern of quills, there were two pretty ivory-white pieces, long and hollow beads, as long as her fingers, sewn side-by-side at the front of the neckline. Made from bone, Blue Feather explained. And an ivory-white wedge-shaped piece, solid and heavy, that was hanging right between the bone-beads. A buffalo-tooth, Blue Feather said, from a buffalo he had killed. It was his gift to her, he told her, because she sent the great buffalo herd to his people. He had asked Willow to put it on this shirt for her.

Frankie had been twisting around on his lap, trying to examine the new buckskin shirt, trying to listen to the explanations and nibbling at the food he handed her. But now, she stopped and turned, looking into the eyes of this man who had given her such a fine gift. This man who had brought this buffalo-tooth for her—from his buffalo-kill.

She smiled at him, searching his eyes. Looking deeply for the first time. He was always quiet; he always stayed back and observed. He always thought about things in a way that was different than most people. Blue Feather, this brother of Strong Hand's, was a lot like the trooper Thomas Denning. And he was a lot like her cousin Samuel had been.

She understood him suddenly; she turned around in his lap, wrapped her arms around his chest and pulled herself tight against him. Blue Feather accepted it; he kept her there wrapping his own arms around her, his cheek pressed down on her head. He spoke softly to her and the words Frankie heard were the Cheyenne words for thank you. She heard him say the Cheyenne words for buffalo and Little Mouse and Whirlwind. And after that, she didn't listen for more words; she just stayed still and quiet. Because that's what he would understand.

Frankie slept in the lodge that night beside Dandelion, with Little Mouse curled up between them. She woke up to Dandelion's tickles in the dim and golden-glow of morning sunlight cast across the stretched hides of Wild Bird's home. The three of them tumbled out through the hide-flap door, still tickling and wrestling and giggling. Whirlwind smiled at them from across the firepit, looking up as she shifted the coals beneath the cookpot.

"He's Proud and Blue Feather rode out," she told them. "Long before little girls wake up. Long before the sun rises. They ride to meet the hunting party, to ride back with the families."

The three girls sniffed at the warming food, grabbed pieces of cooked meat that Willow handed them and dashed to the windmill pond. They scrubbed the sandy-clay into their hair, bathed and splashed and dunked each other. And before long, to Frankie's surprise and delight, Willow, Whirlwind and old Wild Bird joined them, bathing and washing their own hair. Joining in the laughter and splashing and dunking.

To Frankie's amazement, it was Wild Bird who had the most remarkable skills in the water. The old Cheyenne woman could disappear for astonishing periods of time under the surface of the water. Then suddenly, she'd break the surface in the most surprising places—sometimes across the pool, or sometimes, rising up directly behind someone, shrieking like a wildcat and sending everyone into wild screams and laughter.

Frankie lost all sense of time. The water flew in every direction, sparkling and shimmering like little diamond-droplets in the morning sunlight. The pool and the meadow became a wild and rollicking world filled with the yelps and yells of little girls, the laughter and shrieks of women, the barks and howls of the two dogs. And more than a few surprised snorts from Indian ponies approaching the pool for their morning water-up.

Finally, the six of them climbed out and collapsed on the bank of the pool; they lay in the grass, soaking up the rays of the morning sun just like they had soaked in the pond. Then they returned to the fireside—the women pulled on their buckskin dresses and returned to their work over the spits and kettles. The girls wrapped themselves in soft hides and trade-blankets. They crowded near the fire, cuddling together by the heat of the growing fire, waiting and watching while Whirlwind filled their wooden bowls with the steaming splendors from the cookpot.

Wrapped up in a red Hudson Bay blanket, Little Mouse toddled around the meadow, touching things and saying words and being very busy with everything she saw. Every so often, she would walk over and study the food Frankie and Dandelion had in their bowls. She'd select and eat the pieces she wanted, and then she would wander off again to busy herself with something else.

For Frankie, there were eggs to gather and milking to do, so Dandelion and Little Mouse tagged along to help her with the chores. It wasn't long before Frankie realized that for them, it was more about pointing and giggling than it was about doing anything helpful. It also turned into time for them to play with the scrambling and tumbling puppies, releasing them to puppy-romp and puppy-race in the meadow.

She left Dandelion and Little Mouse to the puppy-play; she took the gathered eggs to Willow and toted the milk-pail to the house to set the cream to separating. When she headed back to the cookfire, she carried a jar of the cream from the day before, shaking the jar as she walked. She sat down by the fire to listen as the women chatted back and forth, but the chatter soon stopped; their attention was on the jar she was shaking.

So Frankie showed the women the secrets of bringing butter out of cream and the more she explained how the heóve-améške, the yellow grease, would appear, the more intrigued Wild Bird became. Willow and Whirlwind had talked about the yellow-grease, but it was all new to the old woman.

She kept stopping Frankie in the midst of the cream-shaking to examine the contents, doubting that the yellow-grease could suddenly appear as Fire Heart Child had promised. Finally, the bright yellow-flecks of the coming butter showed themselves, shining and flickering in the midst of the whirling cream. Appearing magically, only to float away and disappear again. Elusive, but promising.

Frankie shook the jar for half a minute more until she felt the buttery-clump thumping against the inside of the jar. When she poured the buttermilk into a cup and dumped the ball of butter into one of the bowls, Wild Bird's face lit up. And after she tasted it, she was sold on the whole idea of the white-man's buffalo.

"Véhoé-otóva'a. E-peva'e." She grinned her mostly toothless-grin, speaking about the goodness of domestic cows. Willow and Whirlwind tasted the buttermilk, smiled, pleased with the flavor. Wild Bird dug her finger into the hunk of butter, pleased with the taste of the yellow-grease and, more than pleased, with the magic of the shaking jar.

When Everett and Ida rolled into the meadow in the late morning, there was a dishpan full of cornbread and another of biscuits riding on the wagon-seat with them and within moments of their arrival, Wild Bird had dollops of butter going onto every bite of cornbread. Ida sat down with her lady-friends and Everett followed the direction Frankie indicated—he headed to the barn, going to look for his favorite little girl.

A few minutes later, the two of them came out of the barn, glued to each other. Little Mouse had her fingers latched onto Everett's pantleg and she stayed at his side, grinning and jabbering the whole time he was working to unharness his team. He was explaining every-thing he was doing, talking in English. And she was busy chattering in Cheyenne, telling him everything she thought about it.

Frankie ran out to the back pasture, racing hand-in-hand with Dandelion who decided that once again, she needed to see the 'very much horses' and the white-man's-buffalo with stripes-like-grass. There was peace in the valley for almost another hour, and then everything changed.

Matilda started barking and Laughing Girl set to baying; both dogs were running toward the meadow's entrance, giving their warn-ing. A moment later, some three dozen Indian horses and Indian men charged into the meadow, with Strong Hand and Knife in the lead. The warriors were yipping and laughing, stripped down to their breechcloths, bows and quivers of arrows at their backs. Sleek and bronzed and wild. Part of the land and the sky. Part of the Sand Hills.

Once again, Frankie decided it would have been a terrify-ing sight if she didn't actually know them. The horses whirled and swirled, snorting and dancing, rearing and bucking—half-wild with excitement. The men were calling out the news of the buffalo hunt, boasting and bragging, waving their bows and lances. Shouting and laughing, putting on a show for the watchers in the meadow. Calling out about 'a good hunt' and 'many buffalo' and 'food for our people'.

A moment later, Strong Hand pulled his red-and-white pinto to a hard and sudden stop. The spinning and shouting came to a halt. His face froze as he saw Whirlwind sitting by the fire. He stared as she stood up.

He reined his pinto hard, swirling his horse in a circle, his eyes casting across the meadow. Searching for someone else. Finally, he halted his horse—his eyes on the track at the back-pasture. Everett was there in the gateway with Little Mouse, squatting down beside her, his arm outstretched. Pointing to direct the little girl's attention toward the commotion at the meadow's entrance. Pointing toward the red-and-white pinto.

It took Little Mouse a moment to see what he was pointing at, but when she did, she broke into a wide-open smile. She left Everett's side in a toddler's version of an all-out run with her arms waving gleefully, calling out with a string of husky little yips and chortles.

Strong Hand sent his pinto into a full run, leaned down from his pony's side and plucked her from the ground as his pony skidded to a halt. He had her on the horse's withers, holding her tight to his chest. Laughing at her and with her. And Little Mouse was busy hugging his face and patting his chest and shoulders. Calling out to everyone in the meadow, boasting about finding her father. She was waving her arms and telling everyone how happy she was.

Strong Hand's eyes searched the meadow again—stopping when he saw Frankie. His eyes locked on her eyes. Frankie held his gaze, understanding the look he was giving her. Understanding when he nodded to her. She dropped her eyes and when she looked up again, he had reined his pinto toward the cookfire, riding to where his mother stood.

Two hours later, another group of Indians showed up at the homestead—four older men and a band of young men rode into the meadow. Men who Frankie had never seen before; men who had never been in her meadow. They came down the track slowly and quietly and stopped their mounts at the bottom of the track, waiting while Strong Hand walked toward them.

Frankie counted eleven of the younger riders—all looking to be in their teens—older than her, but younger than her troopers at Fort Kearny. They were busy looking around the meadow, grinning and doing a lot of pointing and talking amongst themselves.

The four elderly men, though, had a very different demeanor. Calm and no-nonsense, with a high level of dignity. They did a quiet survey of their surroundings with smooth glances across the meadow. But mostly, they had their attention on Strong Hand and the discussion at hand.

She kept an eye on the cluster of men, wondering what was happening. Wondering what the conversation entailed—because it was a quiet and serious discussion. A few minutes later, it was over; a decision had been made. Strong Hand swung up on his pinto and rode out of the meadow with the elders beside him and the eleven young men following.

Within a matter of minutes, a new sound came floating through the air. A soft and rumbling sound; a throbbing, pulsing, patterned sound that seemed to come from everywhere and nowhere. Haunting and mysterious, steady and strong. *Drums. It's the beat of drums.*

Shortly after the drums began, Frankie heard the voices of men singing with the beat of the drums, their voices rising and falling, blending with the pulsing drums in what sounded like a mix of chanting, keening and crooning. The haunting song seemed to ripple and wave like the grasses, lifting and dipping like the grasses. Moving and weaving its way across the hills. Traveling across the land. Reaching into the skies. Calling out to the universe.

Frankie wasn't sure how long she stood there, frozen to the spot where she had first heard the beat of the drums and rhythm of the songs—astonished, mesmerized, mystified. Apparently, it had been long enough for Blue Feather to mount his palomino-pinto and ride to where she stood lost in the sound. He pulled his mare to a stop beside her and beckoned.

"Ne-náestse, Ho-esta Hesta Ka-éškóne. Come here, Fire Heart Child." He spoke to her using both Cheyenne and English words; he reached his hand to her. "Come. There are things you should know."

Frankie grabbed his forearm and he swung her up behind him; he turned his mare to the track and headed out of the meadow, riding toward the sound of the drums. He rode along the low ridge that bordered the valley and stopped on its crest. He reined his mare, standing her sideways, giving Frankie a clear view of the grassy-flats, just beyond the apple trees. They looked down on the broad and flat meadow that stretched to the north bank of the river.

Frankie watched the scene on the grassy-flats. The four elders beat their drums, keeping their steady beat and singing their steady song. And beyond them, out in the grass, the young men danced. She watched the young men dip and duck, circle and sway in the steps of their dance. Their every move timed to the beat of the drums and the rhythm of the song. Stepping and swirling and twirling. Sometimes swift, sometimes slow. Sweeping their legs across the grass. Circling this way; circling that. Stepping quick, then stepping slow. Stepping high, then stepping low.

And always the song; and always the drum. Steady sound; steady pound. On and on the elders sang—sending their message, sending their song. Notes flying high, notes swinging low.

Frankie sat behind Blue Feather, lost in the rhythm of the dancers. Lost in the sound of the song. Feeling the drumbeats. Moving in her heart and flowing in her blood. She leaned against Blue Feather, feeling the heat of his back, feeling the beat of his heart. Feeling the thrum of the drums.

The rays of the sun were warming the land of the river-flats, warming the soil and sending heat-vapors spiraling, lifting and weaving up through the grass-stems. Twisting and curling into the air.

And the young men danced; their bodies swayed. Twisting and twirling. Curling like the vapors; swirling like the vapors; dancing like the vapors. Bending and dipping and flowing in the grasses, moving with the grasses, swaying through the grasses. Stepping fast; stepping slow. Stepping high; stepping low.

And always the songs and always the drums. The pounds. The sounds. The heat of her skin and the beat of her heart. On and on. The singers sang and the dancers danced.

"This is É'komó'eo'he'evohomóhestotse. The Grass Dance." Blue Feather said the name of the dance and laughed when she leaned back, staring at him. Surprised at the length of the word. He made her say it several times, smiling at her mistakes. Encouraging her. Patient until she found the rhythm in the word. Patting her on the leg when she finally had it.

"The Grass Dancers come to prepare the campsite for the people. Their dance-steps lay the grass down. It's our way, Ho-esta Hesta Ka-ėškóne." Blue Feather's voice was soft and low, almost a whisper; he was speaking in English mostly, but slipping into Cheyenne words when he knew she would understand them, letting his words flow gently. Telling her the meaning and the secrets of the Grass Dance.

Frankie listened as he went on, pulling herself tight against his back, feeling the ripple of his ribs, hearing his heart still beating with the drums. Blue Feather paused, letting her watch the dancers laying down the grass with their sweeping steps. First, with their moccasin-steps, and then with the backs of their legs. Dipping low, swinging low to spin their sweeping circles. Circles in the grass; circles for the lodges. Then he spoke again.

"We ask the earth for a place to rest; we honor this land and the grass by protecting it. The dancers lay the grass down gently with their steps. The words of the song and the beat of the drums guide the dancers, so the grass will bow down and lay low. So the roots of the grass will stay strong and the life within the stems will still flow. When we leave, the grasses will rise again. The grasses will reach to the sky again, and it'll be as though we never passed by."

There was a movement and sound behind them; Frankie kept her eyes on the dancers, but she knew Strong Hand had come to join them. He brought his pinto beside Blue Feather's horse to watch the Grass Dance with them.

He spoke then and Frankie listened to his voice; Blue Feather translated for her.

"The movement of the dancers mimic the movement of the grass, Little Sister. Even the fringes on their sleeves and leggings move like the grass. And always, they tell a story as they dance. They tell their own story of how they move through the grass. They tell of how they use the grass to cover their movements. Of how they stalk their prey through the grass. And, of how they come up from the grass to strike their enemies." Strong Hand rested his palm on her thigh, smiling when she looked to him. He talked on.

"This dance will make these young braves better warriors. Their movements become fast and smooth. Their balance becomes true. Their muscles grow strong and hard, so their horses will move easily under them. The speed of the horses will be true and their turns will be sharp and fast—because they will feel the strength in the legs and bellies and backs of their riders. Because they dance, the Grass Dancers will ride better—they will hunt and fight better. The old men sing their songs and they play their drums, and all the while, they watch the Grass Dancers. Tonight, they will speak to the young men about their weaknesses, and the young men will become better dancers and stronger warriors."

Sitting there with her brothers, watching the drummers and the dancers, Frankie realized she had lost all track of time. There in the afternoon, there on the rise overlooking the grassy-flats, the rest of the world had faded away. All sound had become a drumbeat and a song. All movement had become grass.

The elders kept drumming while the Grass-Dancers kept dancing; the beat of the drums and the words of their songs swirled, spinning around the dancers, spreading out across the land until Frankie was quite sure that the Sand Hills, themselves, were pulsing with the sound. The grasses of the hillsides dipped and swayed as the Grass Dance went on. The dancers circled—spinning and swirling, twisting and twirling. Stepping high, then stepping low. Stepping fast, then stepping slow.

The afternoon went on. The sun stayed hot. The heat-vapors kept rising and Frankie knew she was lost in the sound of the song and the beat of the drum. Leaning against Blue Feather's back, pressing her cheek to his skin, she listened as his heart throbbed with the beat of the drum—keeping time, keeping pace. Deep in her chest, her own heart was pumping, thumping in time with the beat of the drum.

The singing stopped. The drumbeat stopped. The Grass Dancers stopped.

"It is done," Blue Feather said. "Now the people will come and set up their lodges. The grass will lay low and give the people a place to rest."

Three hours later, the rest of the families arrived, riding into the camp-site in the early evening. Before the sun disappeared behind the far hills, thirty-four lodges stood on the wide meadow where the Grass Dancers had 'laid the grass down'. Walking along the riverside track with Dandelion, heading toward the village of lodges, Frankie was delighted with the sight.

Just beyond the apple trees, the massive lodges stood, strong and regal in the fading light of twilight, looking as though they had always been there. Looking as though they belonged. Some of the tipis rose up from the grasses, standing in the fading light, backlit by the rays of the setting sun. Others were settled in among the low brush and riverside trees, looking as if they were tucked in for the night, half-hidden in the dappled shade of the riverbank trees.

Behind them on the track, Frankie could hear Whirlwind and He's Proud talking to Ida and Everett, explaining everything that was happening in the village, describing how things were done and why. Occasionally, she could hear Willow's voice offering more explanations. And sometimes, old Wild Bird spoke up. And always, there were questions from Everett and Ida.

For Frankie, walking into the village was entering another world; there were new sights and new activities—things she had never seen, things she had never imagined. Fresh buffalo-hides from the hunt were already staked out on the ground. Massive hides—twenty and thirty times the size of the rabbit and racoon and fox-hides that she and her cousins had worked with back in Indiana. Tall tree-branch racks were standing in place, already being loaded with thin strips of buffalo meat that would dry in the sun.

Cookfires seemed to be everywhere and the stews in the cook-pots were already steaming and bubbling. Spit-sticks were straddling the fires, laced with strips of buffalo meat. The aromas of the stews and the roasting meat drifted through the encampment, filling the air and filling Frankie's nostrils.

There were calls and greetings coming from all directions and Frankie was having her cheeks patted and her shoulders petted everywhere she went; everyone in the village seemed to be smiling and laughing. Women were slicing buffalo meat into strips and steaks, dumping handfuls of wild turnips and gathered greens into their pots.

Women and children were pounding wooden pegs into the ground—some for lodges, some for the buffalo-hides. They were talking soft and talking loud. Calling to each other; teasing each other. Sharing stories and telling tales. And always, there was the laughter.

Outside the lodges, war-shields were fastened to tall tripods of long tree-limbs—each shield facing to the west, soaking up strength from the rays of the sun. Lances leaned against the tripods; war-clubs and tomahawks, bows and quivers of arrows were hanging from the tripods. Feathers flitted in the fading light. Cloth-streamers flew. The bright metal of tiny cones and long lance-tips glistened in the flickering light of the cookfires.

And everywhere, Frankie saw the Cheyenne kids—they were running every which way, darting and dashing between the lodges, laughing and calling to each other, carrying armloads of whatever the adults handed them. They watched her as she passed; she saw their smiles; she saw the shy waves; she heard the bashful giggles.

Children were slipping up to her, darting close enough to touch her arms or tug at her sleeves—then running away, laughing and shrieking with excitement, chattering about the little-white-girl in their village. One of them would call out her Cheyenne name. 'Ho-esta Hesta Ka-ėškóne!' Then there would be more giggles and chatter and shrieks of laughter.

All of it seemed wonderfully right—the sights, the smells, the great lodges with their patterns and paintings, standing in the evening light. The smoke from the cookfires rising. The aromas of the roasting meat swirling through the evening air. Women calling to her. Children running and laughing.

450

For Frankie, it felt right. Comfortable. Familiar. It felt like she was home, as if she was finally where she had always wanted to be. From her first meeting with Strong Hand and Knife on the prairie, south of the great Platte River, *this* is what she had longed-for.

She had watched the warriors turn and ride away on their spotted ponies that day; they had left her and her wagon; they had moved silently through the belly-deep grasses until they disappeared among the rolling hills. Disappearing into the prairie itself. She had known then, somehow, that there was a life they lived that she wanted to know. And *now*, that life was here. All around her. *This* is what she had been yearning for back then, back before she even knew it existed. This was that life; this was the life she was *supposed* to know.

Frankie watched as the Cheyenne people greeted Whirlwind, touching her sores, patting her shoulders and arms. And she saw some of the women walking toward Ida. Smiling and calling to her. Beckoning to her. Chattering happily; surrounding her. Welcoming her. Welcoming this white-woman into their midst—this white-woman who had cared for Strong Hand's child, this white-woman who had cared for his mother. The story had spread through the Cheyenne village.

When the cluster of women led Ida away, taking her toward their lodges, Frankie saw that He's Proud and Blue Feather continued to walk beside Everett. They were talking with him, pointing at things around the village. Speaking, Frankie assumed, about the buffalo-hides and the tripods with the shields and weapons. *No doubt, they're talking about the man-things.*

And as they walked among the lodges, it wasn't long until Little Mouse found Everett and latched onto him again. Within minutes, there were four or five other little Indians following Everett, holding onto his hands and clutching the cloth of his trousers and shirt-sleeves. Shadowing him everywhere he went. Staring at him. Bouncing and dancing around this wonderful man who seemed to belong to Little Mouse.

Knife and Strong Hand had joined the group on the walk through the village, and as the group dispersed, the two warriors kept Frankie between them, continuing the tour, wandering among the lodges.

Women were working beside the fires, stirring mixtures in cookpots and turning meat on spits. Some women were slicing long thin strips from slabs of raw meat and adding them to the drying racks. Others were bent over the buffalo-hides staked out on the ground, scraping away at the hides, cleaning and smoothing the surfaces, each using their favored tool. Frankie spotted some women using broken knife blades; others worked with curved rib-bones or flat shoulder-blades that had been carved and sharpened. Some were using flint-stones that had been chipped and shaped for the task.

Many of the women were gathering plants and tubers and roots along the river, or digging wild onions and turnips near the base of the hillsides. Because they had heard about the reason for the sickness. Because now, the plants they needed were abundant in the soils of the river flats and the riverbanks. Now, they had the cure growing beneath their feet and at their fingertips.

And everywhere Frankie looked, there were the horses. Horses were standing tied by lodges; horses were walking; horses were trotting. Some were being taken to the river and some were being turned out to the herd that grazed beyond the lodges. Young horses; old horses. Horses of every color—sorrels and bays, blacks and grays. Solid colored horses and mottle-colored horses and spotted horses. From every direction, Frankie could hear horses nickering and neighing, squealing and snorting. Today, she realized, the broad grassy land of the river-flats had become a land of Indian dances and Indian ponies.

For a while, Dandelion stayed with Frankie, walking along with her and Knife and Strong Hand. Showing Frankie the village, giving her the Cheyenne names for everything she asked about. Then she would dash off to run and play with clusters of Cheyenne children. She would then flit back to be with Frankie for a while; then she was off and running again.

Frankie, though, wasn't about to leave her place between her two warriors. It reminded her of walking with her Lieutenant and Captain Connell on Independence Day at Fort Kearny. She stayed beside Knife and Strong Hand as they led her among the tipis, and it wasn't long before she realized everybody in the village seemed to understand that she belonged to the two warriors.

It seemed to Frankie that the Cheyenne people were awfully excited that the two warriors were walking her through their village. The women touched her cheeks and fondled her braids. They commented about her dark eyes. 'Her braids are beautiful,' they said. 'Cheyenne eyes,' they said. They touched and stroked the breechcloth and shirt that Willow had made for her; they admired the beading on her shirt; they fingered the buffalo-tooth that Blue Feather had given her; they talked about the shirt being from an antelope.

'From a female antelope,' they said, nodding, assuring her it was a wonderful thing. 'It will make you clever and quick-thinking and fleet like the female antelope.'

They examined her necklace with the wolf-teeth and bullets; they all seemed to know that Knife had made it for her; they smiled and nodded and spoke about the two wolves she had battled. It didn't surprise Frankie that everyone in the village already knew she had worked with the sickness of Whirlwind and Little Mouse. It did surprise her, though, that they knew the story of the wolves. *News travels fast among these people. Just as fast as it traveled at Fort Kearny.*

It seemed to Frankie that every woman wanted her and her brothers to sit at her family's fire and eat from her cookpot. And as soon as they left one cookfire, another woman at another lodge called to them, waving them over to *her* fire. And always, Strong Hand and Knife would comply, leading her over to each woman who called.

Always, they sat to eat with the woman and whoever else was at her lodge. And always, Strong Hand introduced her to the women and the men of each lodge—telling her about their family, explaining how they were related to him, or sometimes, how they were related to one of the other families she had met.

After they visited for a while and ate the food offered to them, they would continue on their walk, only to be called to another fire in front of another family's lodge. And once, when Frankie hesitated at the idea of sitting at yet another fire, feeling like she was already filled-to-the-gills with all the stew and buffalo meat she could eat, Knife stooped down and spoke quietly in her ear.

"We cannot insult them by refusing," Knife whispered. "When they offer you a place at their fire, they are offering their hearts."

So Frankie complied, grimacing a bit at the thought of eating more food, but loving the warm welcomes. Loving this life in the Cheyenne village. Over and over, she thanked the kind women for the food they offered. She thanked them for their kind words about her shirt and necklace and braids. She smiled when they spoke about her eyes. And always, she remembered the guidance Knife had given her—she ate what the families shared with her, eating until she was ready to pop.

Strong Hand and Knife would then lead her on through the village. Sometimes, they would stop to point out a certain lodge, or show her a shield on one of the tripods—talking to her about the paintings and their meanings. There had been glorious battles, bold and brave deeds, strong and courageous acts—the paintings decorating the lodges and the weapons, told the stories.

Strong Hand told her about the different families and many of those families were his relatives.

"These people are of Lame Horse's band. They are Wild Bird's people. And mine. They are Cheyenne, but there are Oglála here too."

"And Knife's people, too?"

"No. Knife's people were of a different band. But he lives among us now. He is of this band now, because his people are gone. So he is my brother. And he is Blue Feather's brother and my mother's son."

"My people died of the white-man's fever, just like Strong Hand's wife and his sons." Knife spoke quietly, explaining. "So Lame Horse's people are my family."

"Your whole family died? Your whole band?" Frankie watched as Knife nodded slowly, and then she looked to Strong Hand.

"And your wife, too? And you had little boys?"

"Yes," Strong Hand looked at her for a moment, pausing as if he was deciding how much to say. "My wife was called Sweet Water Woman. My sons were called Black Beaver and Night Bear. When

454

the fever came, Black Beaver had seen three winters, but Night Bear had seen ten."

"So Night Bear was my age when he died." Frankie stared at Strong Hand, her eyes locked on his.

"Yes. The fever took many of our children," he spoke softly.

"My family died of the fever too. That's why I was traveling alone when we found each other on the prairie. So that makes us family. Because we all know the same sorrow."

"We are brothers and sister since the time at the soldier-fort, Fire Heart Child," Knife was speaking now. "You spoke the truth then. We all knew the truth on that day."

And that was the moment when everything felt like it was too much. Frankie felt a heaviness in her shoulders and suddenly, it seemed like there was noise everywhere. People everywhere. All the new sights and all the new sounds. Everything new and different. Everything moving and spinning around her. The present and the past surrounding her.

Knife saw. He understood. He was, after all, her brother. He squatted down beside her. Looking in her eyes, hushing her. Waiting; giving her time. Talking softly in the sing-song way of the Cheyenne language, his voice low and quiet. He held her close. Slowing down all the whirling around her. Because he understood. It was all good, he told her, but there had been much that had happened in the day.

When the world stopped spinning, when her mind stopped swirling, when nothing seemed so overwhelming anymore, they walked on. Strong Hand pulled her tight against his side and kept her there while they walked. *He knows just like Knife does.*

They walked on and Frankie realized the Cheyenne women weren't calling out to them now. They weren't waving and beckoning for them to come to their fires anymore. *They understand too. They know. These people of the Cheyenne always know.*

It was long past sundown when Frankie started back to the meadow, walking arm in arm with Wild Bird. Ahead of them Ida and Everett walked with Whirlwind and Willow and a group of other Cheyenne and Oglála women. Dandelion was beside Ida, holding onto Ida's arm, watching her like she always did, fascinated with her hair and her eyes and her clothes.

Charging Crow's wife, a woman named Hemene, 'Mourning Dove', slipped up to Ida and spoke to her in Cheyenne, shy and quiet; she laid a shawl over Ida's shoulders—a shawl made of softly tanned rabbit-hides.

"She wants you to have this gift. To keep the evening cold from your shoulders," Whirlwind translated for Ida and tears rose in Ida's eyes. Hemene nodded and smiled, patting Ida's shoulders. Ida patted her hand, smiled back at her, and they walked the rest of the way along the track together. Understanding each other in a way that went beyond their lives and backgrounds.

Everett walked along, surrounded with the pack of little boys that had claimed him as their own; Little Mouse wasn't bothered by the flock of boys hopping and bouncing along with her and her favorite person, because in her mind—since she was in charge of the wonderful man with the wonderful eyes—she was also in charge of all the boys. She was actually ecstatic with the circumstance; she rode on Everett's hip, waving her arms, pointing and calling out instructions to the boys, telling them where to be and where to move.

And Everett was no less ecstatic. He was smiling and laughing while the boys were shouting and dashing and jumping about. Ida and Frankie smiled at each other, each knowing what the other was thinking.

"He looks," Ida said, "like he's leading a parade of wild prairie children."

Once back in the meadow, Ida and Frankie went to the kitchen and started stewing more apples and mixing more cornbread batter, readying food for the next day. Because suddenly, they had a lot of visitors to feed—visitors who relished the sweet breads and the spiced apples.

Dandelion, though, wasn't at all content with the situation. She was deeply troubled that her wonderful sky-eyed woman had gone into the house with Fire Heart Child. Both Ida and Frankie tried to include Dandelion, but no amount of beckoning and encouragement could convince her to enter the house; she would only go as far as the edge of the porch, watching the activity in the kitchen from a safe distance, leaning to peer through the doorway, calling softly to Ida.

Frankie was teasing Dandelion, mimicking her expressions whenever her friend called to Ida and pointed to different objects in the kitchen. Ida would spot what Dandelion was interested in—a china cup, a candlestick, a crocheted doily, the white ceramic pitcher. She'd stop her work to take the item out to the porch; she'd sit down on the porch step and let Dandelion hold and examine the treasure.

Since Ida was out on the porch much of the time, Frankie decided that Ida seemed to be getting out of a lot of the cooking and baking chores, so she made a point of teasing Ida about that too. But Ida, didn't seem to care the least little bit; she just smiled at Frankie and laughed with a dreamy-look in her eyes, not unlike the dreamy look Everett had when he was parading with his wild prairie children.

That night, Frankie and Dandelion slept in the lodge once more, spending the night sleeping beside Wild Bird and Willow. Everett and Ida stayed in the back bedroom of the house. Whirlwind had walked back to the village to stay with one of the families. Little Mouse, the last time Frankie had seen her, had been with her father.

Frankie thought about all that as she drifted off to sleep, listening to the night-sounds drifting in through the lodge door. In a Cheyenne camp, she realized, everyone did what they wanted; they went where they wanted. And somehow it all worked. The families each had their own lodges—their own homes—but the children roamed where they wanted, and were welcome wherever they visited.

The Cheyenne people visited with each other and worked with each other and cared for each other. It was all an unspoken cooperation that was natural and easy. Everything was handled simply and effectively. Everything was done well.

The next morning when Frankie ran to the river with Dandelion, it looked as if all the children of the village were there. She counted twenty-three kids, of all ages, playing in the water together; boys and girls were rough-housing in the deepest water, all buck-naked, and no one anywhere had a problem with that. All the youngest children—including Little Mouse—were playing close to the riverbank, splashing and squealing in the sandy-bottomed shallows.

Frankie followed Dandelion's lead and stripped down to bare skin like everyone else. They dashed into the river to join the others in the melee of splashing and swimming and diving. Laughing and yelping with the cold shock of the water. Teasing and dunking each other. When the wild excitement of the play quieted, they released their braids and scrubbed their hair and scalps. Dandelion and Frankie finished their scrubbing, rinsed off, grabbed up their shirts and breechcloths and ran naked, racing like rabbits, back to Wild Bird's lodge in the meadow.

The meadow itself, was teaming with activity. Ida was busy adding vegetables to the pot and Whirlwind was plunking chunks of buffalo meat into the steaming liquid. Little Mouse had found her way back to the meadow and had already attached herself to Everett again—along with five naked, or mostly-naked, Indian boys.

Little Mouse and the boys were trotting along with Everett, watching while he fed the chickens and gathered eggs. They were part of the cow-milking and the milk-pail carrying. They tagged along while he tended to the windmills and the water-flues. They pointed and giggled and laughed in their excitement over the oxen and the 'very much horses'. At one point, Ida pointed to the sight of all five boys and Little Mouse riding on Little Bub while Everett led him around the pasture. All with their legs splayed out flat on the broad back of the 'very much horse, all wearing wide and happy grins. And all the while, Little Mouse was busy giving the boys directions and orders and whatever explanations she decided they needed.

When Willow called to Frankie and her daughter, the girls plopped down on the buffalo-robe where she pointed and Frankie once again endured the torture of the hair-combing and scalp-scraping. This time Whirlwind worked at her hair, while Willow worked on Dandelion. Over by the fire, Frankie could hear Ida laughing, amused with the trial-of-torture she was being put through.

Just as the braiding was done, Knife, Strong Hand and Blue Feather rode into the meadow. Knife walked to Frankie, hoisted her over his shoulder and tickled her into a giggling frenzy while he toted her to the cookfire. He settled her down in his lap near the simmering cookpot and started picking out pieces of the buffalo meat, sharing them with her like he always did. Frankie grinned up at him and he grinned back. She nestled down against him, trying to soak up the heat of his body.

Everett's wild boys followed him to the fireside, grabbing handfuls of parched corn and chunks of cornbread, while Everett loaded up a bowl from the pot. Once the boys were satisfied that Everett would stay by the fire where they could find him later, they took off, running up the track and out of the meadow. Frankie watched them racing away. *Heading for the river. Or maybe, the village. Heading to play their games or hunt for rabbits.*

A few minutes later, Wild Bird stood up and jabbed Knife in the shoulder with her walking-stick. She tossed a buckskin bundle at him and pointed to Frankie. Knife jumped into action, and for a moment, Frankie was ready to jump along with him. Because like everyone else, she knew when Wild Bird began wielding her stick, she expected action.

Knife, though, knew exactly what the old woman wanted; he reached for the bundle and shook out the breechcloth and antelope shirt. Apparently, Wild Bird had seen her shivering. Her warrior-brother started working the shirt over her head, but it wasn't lost on Frankie that he kept glancing over his shoulder, keeping an eye on the stick in the old woman's hand.

Everyone around the fire was chuckling at the way he had snapped into action to do Wild Bird's bidding and even Frankie was giggling as he tied her breechcloth in place. But she was amused for a different reason. Because she knew that every single person who was laughing at him, would have moved just as fast if the old woman had pointed her stick in their direction. They all knew Wild Bird's stick

459

could do a lot more than just 'give a little shoulder-jab' if someone didn't move fast enough to suit her.

There had been times when even Strong Hand jumped as fast as Knife had; his status as leader of the band meant nothing when his grandmother shook her stick. Because the truth was, there wasn't a single battle-wise warrior in the band who would consider arguing with Wild Bird.

In the middle of the morning, five girls came running from the river-camp, wanting to see the valley where Fire Heart Child lived. Frankie and Dandelion jumped to their feet, running to show them everything they wanted to see; they went off on their meadow tour in a girlish cluster—one white girl and six Cheyenne girls—all giggling and chattering, wrapped together in a web of companionable arms.

The newly arrived Cheyenne girls were mystified by the buildings, peering into the vé'ho'é-måheo'o, the 'white-man's house' from beyond the porch. Out on the track between the pastures, they were enthralled with the very-much-horses and the roan cows and the striped oxen. They hesitated at the idea of entering any of the buildings, but with some encouragement and teasing, they ended up following Frankie and Dandelion into the barn.

They trailed after their tour guides, hushed and uneasy as they followed them down the long alleyway, walking past the corner workshop, past the puppy-pen, past the line of rolling-things, until they reached the milking-pen in the far corner. There, they studied the white-man's buffalo that gave the yellow-grease with stunned fascination.

There was no amount of encouragement, though, that could entice them into any of the other buildings. The chicken-coop, with the fenced-in birds, held their interest, but there too, they remained outside while Frankie gathered a few newly-laid eggs. They grinned and giggled as they carried the eggs over to the cookfire; they waited by the stone-room porch while Frankie disappeared through the doorway. It was when she re-emerged with a jar of skimmed-cream from the pantry's separating-pans that things got exciting in the meadow.

As Frankie approached the cookfire, Wild Bird stood up, motioning to her. The old woman confiscated the jar from Fire Heart Child and proceeded to show the Cheyenne girls the wonderful magic she could perform. Her old eyes snapped with delight as she began shaking the jar with her gnarled old hands. From that moment, Frankie realized that the butter-making was the old woman's domain—she loved enthralling her audience with her magic.

Wild Bird worked the jar tirelessly and when the yellow flakes started glittering and swirling, the girls pointed; when the ball of yellow-grease appeared right in the middle of the milky-white cream, everyone around the cookfire burst into laughter. They were all delighted with the unexpected event; even the warriors were awestruck by what Wild Bird created in that marvelous jar.

The real wonder of the whole process became clear when Ida started swiping dollops of the yellow-grease on cornbread squares and began passing them around. Buttery smiles were showing on the faces of the newly arrived Cheyenne. It wasn't long before the five Cheyenne girls dashed off, taking the news of Wild Bird's wonderful 'yellow-grease' back to the people in the riverside camp.

To Frankie's thinking, the news about the yellow-grease had actually spread like greased lightning, because it wasn't long until every woman from the village was in the meadow, relishing the sweet flavors of the butter and cornbread. She and Ida headed to the house and started making more cornbread and biscuits. They sent Dandelion back to the fireside with another jar of cream and Wild Bird displayed her magic skills to a new audience.

By late-morning, when the sun began to throw off heat like a true summer day, Everett harnessed and hitched his team for a trip back home. He had animals to tend to, chores to do, and instructions from Ida to hurry back with some of their cornmeal and flour. When Frankie protested, talking about the barrels and barrels she still had in the pantry, Ida ignored her and waved Everett toward the wagon.

After the few minutes of arguing with her, Frankie finally caught on—Ida had it in her mind that these people were her guests too. It was firm in her heart to offer them food from her home. Because Ida always nurtured the people she cared about. So when Ida called out after Everett, naming additional things for him to bring back, Frankie held her tongue.

"Bring a bag of coffee and one of sugar. And more eggs," she called after him. "And all the separated cream too. Put it in a crock and let it churn in the wagon on the way back. Oh! And before you leave, bring my sewing basket and my crochet bag from under the wagon-seat. I have some needlework I need to start on."

And when Everett left in the spring-wagon pulled by Jenny and Jake, there were five little Indian boys going along for the ride and calling out about the amó eneo'o. 'The rolling-thing'. One chattering little girl with a wide grin was sitting on Everett's lap, her hands on his hands, explaining to the boys how she was making the 'rolling-thing' roll. Blue Feather and Charging Crow rode their ponies beside the wagon, and Everett was laughing all the way up the track. Up, over and around.

An hour later, Frankie heard shouts and laughter coming from the track beyond the entrance; twelve boys and five girls were running into the meadow; one of the kids was carrying what looked like a sewn leather bag. It took Frankie a moment to grasp what was in the works. *A ball! A game!*

The kids from the village had come to play, and suddenly, the game was on. Frankie watched the game, eyeing the action, realizing that whatever the game was, it seemed to involve a lot of fast-running, quick-dodging, and solid body-slamming. After a couple of minutes, she figured out the general idea—it was a little like 'tag', and a little like 'keep-away', and a whole lot like the street-brawls that she had heard about that used to go on in Dobytown near Fort Kearny. Within the first few minutes of play, she could see blood flowing from one player's nose and from the mouths of two others. One player's knee was dripping red with blood.

Frankie grinned and headed for the fun; Dandelion, to her surprise, had already run the other way—she had run away from the action, dashing toward the safety of the adults by the fire. Frankie gave a quick glance in the direction of Dandelion's retreat, thinking that she must be too scared to join in—because it was clearly a rough game. An instant later, her mind was in the game and she found herself swept into the rough play.

It wasn't a hard game to figure out; there were no teams. It was just an all-out battle for the leather ball, and pretty much, it was every-man-for-himself. The kid who had the ball was '*it*' and that's who everyone was after. And '*it*' was supposed to keep the ball away from everyone else. But most crucial to the game was that, while it was important for each player to fight to get the ball for himself, it was *just* as important to keep everyone else from getting the ball— thus, furthering one's own chance of getting it for himself.

There wasn't any hand-hitting or fist-punches, nor was there any biting. But to Frankie's eyes, it seemed like anything else was fair-game. Anything you could do with your hands, elbows or shoulders, with your hips, knees or feet was fair-play. In fact, it was required if you intended to stay in the game. Head-butts and body-slams, kicks and jabs, shoves and pushes and pulls—all were applied skills. And mostly, they had to be applied in the midst of running and turning, twisting and dodging. And all at full speed.

The game, while fast and furious, seemed simple enough to Frankie. Get the ball and keep it. And if you didn't have the ball, keep anyone else from getting to whoever was running with the ball. But it didn't take her long to realize that she was having no success. She was being yanked and pulled, thrown and slung across the grassy surface of the meadow with stunning regularity; she was spending a great amount of time either flying through the air, or scrambling up from the ground after landing.

At one point during her flurry of short-flights, she saw, to her surprise, that Dandelion was in the game after all. And also to her surprise, Frankie could see nothing that suggested she was afraid of anyone or anything. Dandelion was playing the game well and she was playing hard. She was wild and willing, fleet of foot, and skilled in her tactics.

Frankie, for the part, was stumped; she was feeling desperate and inadequate, confused and frustrated. Again and again, she found herself reeling across the dirt and grass, watching as the other kids played on past her. She did the only thing she knew to do—scramble to her feet and go at it harder. Because, she figured, her years of keeping up with her cousins—her three older boy-cousins, all faster and stronger than her—should give her some kind of equal standing in *this* game. But it seemed like the harder she played, the farther she was flung.

Quite suddenly, at the end of a series of involuntary somersaults across the meadow grass, just as she was scrabbling and scrambling to right herself, Frankie felt a pair of hands grip her arms. She was plucked up from the grass and tossed across a shoulder. In that moment, she realized she was being carried toward the fire. Away from the running and shouting and laughing. Away from the other kids at play. Away from the battle-for-the-ball. She pushed and jerked to free herself; she twisted around to see who dared. *Strong Hand!*

He was toting her across to the cookfire, toward the adults—taking her away from the other kids in their wild and reckless game. Frankie was stunned. Horrified that she was being taken out of the game. It was clear that the grown-ups had seen her failings and decided she wasn't good enough to play—they had decided to take her out before she got hurt.

Frankie felt the tears rising. Tears of shame; tears of humiliation. Fears that she would start crying if they kept her away from the play. She *knew* she was getting banged up; she *knew* she was bleeding. But she didn't care. She *knew* she could do better; all she needed was for them to give her a little more time.

And that's what she was telling Strong Hand. She was hollering it at the top of her lungs, using what little air she had left to try to make it clear. She kept twisting; she kept pounding on his back. Yelling at him to let her go; hollering that she was strong enough and brave enough. Shouting that she wasn't hurting; insisting that she wasn't wounded.

She could hear the adults at the fire laughing and when she felt a second set of hands grab her flailing legs, she knew it was Knife. She also knew he was laughing at her, just like all the other grownups, so she directed a few kicks at him. She managed to spit out several handfuls of choice swearwords—a few in Cheyenne and a whole slew of them in English—while she struggled against her tormentors.

Knife only laughed harder, and Strong Hand joined in with him. By the time they reached the fire, all the adults were howling with laughter. Their grins were growing; their laughter kept getting louder. And all of it was making Frankie angrier. Because no one was listening to her. Because no one cared about her agony at being pulled from the game.

She was about to start swinging her fists, ready to do anything to get away and get back to the game. Ready to do anything to prove she wasn't a failure. And then, suddenly, Whirlwind was beside her. Speaking to her, telling her to wait. To stop fighting.

Frankie felt Whirlwind's hands reaching around her waist, stripping off her breechcloth. Strong Hand was pulling her buckskin shirt over her head. Knife started rubbing something on her legs. Then Whirlwind was rubbing something on her back and shoulders and arms. And all the while, Strong Hand kept her in his arms, restraining her and laughing the whole time.

He's Proud was calling to her from where he was standing with the others, watching and laughing; Frankie could hear him calling to her, telling her to wait till they were done.

"Hold off your war-dance, Fire Heart Child. Wait with your fight until you are back in the game." The more he explained, the harder everyone around him laughed.

About then, Frankie realized that Strong Hand and Whirlwind and Knife were actually working to help her—they were greasing her up. It suddenly dawned on her why Dandelion had come late into the game. She had run to the cookfire, but not because she was afraid. But because she knew enough to strip out of her clothes and grease up. Which was what all the other kids knew.

Frankie saw it now—it was awfully hard to grab the opposing players and fling them aside when they were slipping through your fingers. She realized they were all as slippery as greased pigs, and not one of them had a shirt that could be grabbed, or sleeves that could be snatched and pulled.

She stopped struggling against Strong Hand's grip. And as much as she wanted back in the game, she settled down enough that Knife and Whirlwind could finish their task with their wonderful handfuls of grease. She understood it now. *They're on my side!*

She let loose with a wild screech, shrieking like a warrior going into battle; she arched her back, straining to rejoin the game—this time, she realized, she'd have the same advantage as the other players. She was still twisting and turning, but she let Strong Hand and Knife and Whirlwind continue with their slathering while she watched the game out in the middle of the meadow. Desperately afraid it would all end before she could prove to herself—and to everyone—that she wasn't a miserable failure at this Cheyenne game.

She could see that, so far, the game was still going on; the players were still doing battle for the ball. Strong Hand held her against his chest as Knife rubbed the last of his grease on her ankles, and Whirlwind spread her last handful of grease on her chest and neck. Then they were done. They released her. *Finally!*

Frankie hit the ground running. She left Strong Hand and Knife and Whirlwind standing where they were; she left all the adults standing by the fire, still laughing at her. Frankie didn't care about them now; she didn't care a lick about their laughter.

She raced back to the game, her disadvantage gone. She flew into the game with a wild howl and a reckless fury. Running like greased lightning. Ready to do battle for the ball.

It was only a matter of minutes before she realized the struggle was gone. The frantic frustration was gone. The clothes that had aided her enemies were gone. Her skin was shiny and slick; she was greased to the gills. Now she was playing the same game as her opponents. Now she was playing like a Cheyenne kid. Now she was racing and dodging beside her opponents, learning the moves and maneuvers that allowed her to stay on her feet and to go for the prize.

She was learning to apply the body-slams and the wicked-kicks, learning to ram with her shoulders and shove with her elbows. No longer was she at the mercy of the easy grabs; no longer was she easy prey for the players. No longer were they pulling and yanking and slinging her to one side. Grease, she decided, was a wonderful thing.

No longer was she engaged in the frantic and futile attempts to grab and pull her competitors as they had been doing with her. Now she was going after '*it*', and she was laughing and shrieking and howling with the excitement and joy of the game. Because now her *feet* were flying across the grass—instead of her *body*. She was turning and twisting, ducking and dodging with the best of them.

Frankie knew she wasn't the best player on the field; she could see the kids who *were* the best, and there was no doubt that they *were* good at the game. They were *very* good. But now she was going after them—competing with them, playing with them. She was getting knocked and pounded, banged and battered aplenty, but she was giving it back too.

When the game was over—when everyone was spent—Frankie was happy. Excited. Panting like the others. Grinning like the others. Then there was a shout, and the whole passel of them turned toward the track out of the valley. Racing for the river. And Frankie raced with them. Howling like a wolf and screaming like an eagle. Just like the rest of them.

Dandelion was lying stretched out across the laps of Willow and Whirlwind, getting all her lumps and bumps, her blood and her bruises, seen to. She was lying belly-down and mostly asleep, with a half-smile on her lips. Frankie was having a rougher time of it; Strong Hand and Knife were giving her a going over too, but to Frankie it didn't feel at all good—they were digging their brawny fingers and palms deep into her muscles and joints, squeezing and gouging.

From the feel of it, Frankie was pretty sure they were trying to tear her muscles loose from her bones. But every time she protested, Strong Hand just pushed her face down against his buckskin leggings and smothered her complaints. So she tried lying quietly for a while and contented herself with muttering under her breath, and occasionally, yelping out loud when the poking and prodding went too deep.

All around her, everyone who had watched the games seemed to be having a great time at her expense—they were busy telling Blue Feather and Everett and Charging Crow, who had just returned from the Dunbars' homestead, all about the game.

Frankie was pretty sure that, except for Everett, they had all seen plenty of those games and she didn't think all the laughter and fun-making about her tumbles and sprawls across the meadow-grounds were necessary. No one seemed to care about what she thought of their talk, and when she decided to voice her opinion, Wild Bird's stick rapped lightly against her ear. And with that, Frankie decided she'd better leave them to their stories and let them say whatever they wanted.

She realized she was learning more and more about the Cheyenne people every day, and she was learning even more while she was stretched out and at the mercy of her two brothers. She realized Dandelion wasn't yelping or hollering while Willow and Whirlwind were working on her. None of the other Indian kids had made any kind of fuss over their game wounds. And even with the littlest kids—none of them ever cried or complained or pouted about anything.

The only raised voices that went on there in her meadow, or in the village beyond, were yells and shouts of excitement and happiness. Among these people, everybody laughed at themselves as much as they laughed at each other, and usually, from what Frankie could see, everyone laughed harder at themselves than anyone else.

She thought about all that, and then decided to settle down and just listen to the talk around the fire; she heard the others describing her spins and somersaults; she watched them howling with laughter once again, with tears in their eyes, as they recalled how she had been 'flying and dipping like a swallow through the prairie sky'.

And finally, Frankie started grinning as she heard how her far-flung flights were gaining distance and height with each telling. She started giggling at the absurdity of the descriptions, and right about then, she realized the digging fingers and pressing palms of Knife and Strong Hand, didn't feel nearly so deep and rough. The resistance in her body, she realized, was fading along with her resistance to the tales of the game.

Somehow, Strong Hand must have known; he must have felt the difference, because he started tickling her sides and her ears. He bent down to nuzzle her neck a couple of times, whispering sweet Cheyenne words in her ears. And while the others continued laughing at the wild stories, Frankie stayed as she was, stretched out across her two warriors' laps; she let the sweetness of these people fill her brain and her heart.

At one point, she turned, twisting to look up into Strong Hand's eyes. He dropped his eyes to meet hers, and she saw them soften; there was a depth of generosity and kindness there, and it brought tears to her eyes. This was a man who loved her, a man who was teaching her and leading her. He was giving her his culture, and he was welcoming her into his life. These were *his* people, and he was sharing them with her; he was teaching her what was important to them, teaching her what was expected and respected. And what was rewarded and revered.

Complaining and protesting and self-indulgence didn't work well anywhere in life—Frankie already knew that—but here, among these people, it not only didn't work, it didn't belong. It wasn't tolerated because those kinds of behaviors created divisiveness and problems. Those behaviors couldn't exist if there was to be harmony and joy and cooperation such as she had seen in the village along the river.

So she lay still, soaking in the deep healing that was coming from the fingers and hands of these brothers she loved; she stayed quiet, accepting the gentle healing of the laughter and mirth around the cookfire. *This is family.*

Ida had been watching Frankie from the time the Indians had arrived and she'd been seeing things in her young neighbor she had never seen before. At times, she had been astonished at the strength of purpose Frankie showed, and thinking about it, Ida realized she was seeing exactly what had brought this ten-year-old across the prairie after losing her family. There had been times Frankie stepped forward and handled events with as much clarity and purpose as an adult. Other times, she scrambled and raced around the meadow, playing and laughing as a ten-year-old should.

She had watched Frankie deal with the crisis that appeared in her valley just days ago, watching the healing process that had changed the lives of Whirlwind and Little Mouse. It had been a wonderful thing to see; a profound thing.

Scurvy wasn't a rare situation; Ida knew it was a fairly simple treatment. But she also knew that not everyone would have understood what the problem was. There had been cases of scurvy back in Iowa—soldiers returning from the War—when, even doctors had not seen the condition for what it was. The diagnosis was often missed, especially because of the various stages of the disease.

But Frankie had been clear-minded—and she remained clear-minded through the whole process; she had seen the symptoms of the two cases in an advanced and dangerous stage—but she hadn't missed the underlying cause. She had never once been swayed; she never doubted herself. And that meant that no one had doubted her; no one in the meadow had questioned what she was doing.

None of the Cheyenne questioned whether she would be successful. They already had trust in her before they started their long journey; they trusted her enough to bring their sickened family members to her. They had seen no reason to begin doubting her once they were in her meadow.

Ida realized something else and it surprised her more than a bit—neither she nor Everett had doubted Frankie either. From the moment Frankie explained what she needed from them, there had never been a glance backward. She and Everett stepped into a strange and unknown world once they decided to follow her lead. Looking back, Ida knew everything Frankie required, directed, and demanded of them—and of everyone in the meadow—had been exactly right.

The aunt who taught her, had taught her well. She had given Frankie such a strong foundation that confidence flowed out of her. And now, Ida found herself hoping the aunt was looking down from the heavens and could see what she had formed and instilled in her niece.

Right now, as Ida sat at the fire watching these Cheyenne caring for their children, she realized they were sharing their own children with two white people they knew nothing about. And it was Frankie, Ida knew, who opened that door for both her and Everett.

There had been other people who, in their ignorance, had put a hardness in her own heart. And in Everett's. The casual chatter and the callous stories told around the evening fires on the trail West, had spread a cold distrust and hate toward Indians—a hardness founded on fear. Ida knew she and Everett would have carried that hardness and fear a long time if all this hadn't come about.

Her thoughts went back to 'all those in heaven above'; she was thinking, once again, about what heavenly guidance must have been directed their way, for all this to come together. She and Everett had done a lot of healing since they had been around Frankie. And looking at the people clustered around the cookfire, Ida decided something else—when it was all added up, there was a lot of healing going on in Frankie's meadow. A lot of different kinds of healing.

Ida was thinking about where she and Everett would actually be, if Frankie hadn't set her mind on finding her own homestead; she was wondering about these Cheyenne families and what would have happened if someone hadn't given Frankie the strength of purpose, and the drive to set things right. She was wondering where things would be if someone hadn't nurtured her in a way that allowed her to reach out to other people and touch their lives.

Because touching other people's lives was what Frankie thrived on. Those parts of her character and personality had been protected and encouraged by the people who raised her and guided her. *That* was what had been paid forward and played out in this little valley.

She smiled as she watched young Frankie Harding, lying stretched out across the laps of the Cheyenne warriors—a little sunbronzed girl. Sleeping. Peaceful and content. Trusting.

A week ago, Ida knew, she and Everett would have been shocked and distraught, stunned and displeased—terrified even—at just the thought of this child running around with the Cheyenne children. Horrified at the sight of her dressed only in her breechcloth and buckskins. Running wild and excited and naked in front of these people, in front of these Cheyenne men and women—the very people she and Everett had tried to turn her against.

Ida found herself smiling at the men who held Frankie while she slept—the same men who cared for her and protected her while she was awake. Her mind went back to the day Frankie had shown the gifts the Cheyenne had given to her.

That day, Frankie had shown them the buckskin dress made from the hide of an antelope doe. Frankie had shown it proudly, but Ida remembered her own hate for it; she had tried to ignore the soft beauty of it, the elaborate and remarkable quillwork. The sight of it had actually made her angry—she had feared the gift had been used to seduce the ten-year-old into believing the Indians were her friends. She feared the beaded dress had been used to lure Frankie into blind friendship and trust—a 'pretty little thing' to trick a little girl.

Now though, Ida had only admiration for the dress. It was a gift of beauty. The quillwork and beads, the careful stitches, all the hand-work that had gone into the leather to bring it to the soft and supple flow—all of that made it so beautiful. In truth, it had been gift of time and self, a gift from the hands of women who loved Frankie as much as they loved their own children. It could only be a gift of love—a gift no different than her own handwork.

Because Ida had been doing needlework whenever she had been able to fit it in. She was in the midst of crocheting gifts for both Little Mouse and Dandelion. Gifts she wanted to send with them—pretty things, made with her own hands, with careful stitches. A gift of time and self.

From her place on the log-bench near the fire, Ida watched the two warriors coddling Frankie, letting her sleep, their hands stroking her back occasionally. Ida shifted the ball of crochet-thread on her lap; she kept her fingers moving in the practiced rhythm, twisting and turning the ivory-colored thread about her fingertips. She was making crocheted-collars for the girls' soft buckskin dresses. Simple and elaborate gifts that would speak of the love she felt for them.

Not unlike the beading and quillwork that had been stitched into the deerskin dresses and moccasins.

Around her, the women were watching her hands dipping and turning, watching the thread wrapping and knotting into the intricate webbing; they were clucking their tongues as the crocheted lace developed within her hands.

When Ida explained to the women how they would be used, the women's eyes started sparkling; they were tittering with excitement and assuring Ida they would help stitch them onto the dresses. Their excitement grew as they added their own ideas, discussing the beading they would do along with the crocheted designs.

And in that moment, Ida knew she would be crocheting a lot during the cold nights of the winter. Glancing around her, she made up her mind. *So many women and girls will want crocheted pieces. I'll have them ready for the next time they come. As soon as I'm done with a collar for Dandelion and one for Little Mouse, I must make one for Hemene. For Mourning Dove.*

Ida whispered the Indian name and smiled. It was Mourning Dove who had given her the rabbit-skin shawl—she had settled it around her shoulders as they walked together in the evening.

'Hemene wants you to be warm,' Whirlwind had translated Mourning Dove's words. 'She wants you to stay warm even after we are gone.'

While she worked with the thread in her fingers, turning and rolling the crochet-hook, showing the Cheyenne women how she was leading the fine white thread along its intricate course and pattern, Ida was thinking about Frankie. Smiling even now, as she remembered the sight of Frankie's little sun-browned form darting and dashing among the brown bodies of all the other children. Radiant and glowing. Wild and free. Unrestrained and unabashed. Running and racing across the grass of the meadow.

Ida understood now. This was Frankie's balance; this was her release. This wild and reckless abandonment of restraints—the fast, fierce and furious play—was pure childhood. It was every bit as intense and purposeful as the adulthood Frankie had to accept in so much of her life—all the duties and responsibilities and planning she had taken on, all the serious endeavors and journeys she had been on, all her struggles and travels. There had to be a means of staying balanced, and this—this wild and rollicking interlude—was her saving grace.

Ida said a prayer while she sat on the log by the smoking cook-fire, her hands still moving quickly, swift and sure, in their practiced art of the thread-and-hook. She was praying Frankie could keep running wild and free with the other children, running and playing, as boisterous and as reckless as she needed to be. *Please God, give her these times to be a child, to act like a child, to be as free as a child can be. Let that be a balance for all the hard and the heavy and the harsh.*

That was her prayer while she looped and turned and twisted the thread between her fingers. She was watching Strong Hand, the leader of this band of Cheyenne, across the fire; she watched his hand, calloused and dark-skinned, gently stroking the back of the tired girl napping in the cool of the late afternoon.

She watched Everett too. He was walking among the buildings and fences and gates with his parade of little Indians following closely. The five boys were all so very happy, and so very serious, about the work they were doing with the man they had named Haaenóve-tane.

Ida smiled, thinking about how she had burst into laughter when Frankie translated it as 'Happy Man' or 'Playful Man'. And when she finally stopped laughing, Frankie had informed her that she, too, had a Cheyenne name. E-Hahpeno'e. 'She Sews'. All of which delighted Ida, because as Frankie said, once these Cheyenne people were gone—once they traveled to their winter village—they would tell stories around their fires in the evenings. They would tell their stories about She Sews with her twisting threads and Happy Man with the rolling-thing that horses pulled.

Out and around the meadow, Ida could see Everett walking from one chore to the next with his 'little sweetheart' and his 'busy boys' tagging along, buzzing around him like little worker-bees. The five boys were aged from about four to seven, all from various families, and each one more handsome than the last. Their dark eyes were snapping with excitement and their bright teeth were flashing with their constant smiles and laughter.

It reminded Ida of the days back in Iowa when Everett would go about his chores on their farm with their own boys tagging along. Following their father wherever he went. Bouncing and skipping; bursting with their boyish ideas and plans. Chattering and chirping like little birds. Peppering him with their questions. *Back when they were young. Back when they were alive.*

But this was different now. Because this wasn't a young father struggling with the weight of his work—needing to feed his family and trying to make ends meet—always busy and worried and hurried. *This now,* was Everett's time to be a grandfather, and not a father. The pressures of a young man supporting his family were gone; *this* time, *this* day, was his 'just reward' for living a good life and being a good father. For being a good man.

These children who were hugging him, holding him, clinging to him, adoring him—these were the children who were giving him the glory of being a grandfather. The Cheyenne had named him well. He certainly was 'Happy Man'.

He was reveling in the presence of these children—and, of these people. He was learning the language; he couldn't help but learn it. He was learning to speak Cheyenne from the children, hearing the words of the toddlers and the young children. He was required to point and gesture and form the words just as they did.

These times with these wonderful children, Ida knew, would live deep in her husband's heart. Everett had been a strong and loving father, and a good and steady role-model. He had raised his children well. Raising his sons and daughter well, and easing them into adulthood with a strong foundation, had been Everett's life goal as a man. *That,* in his mind, had been his life purpose.

When he lost his sons, one by one, early in their manhood, he had started losing himself. Following that, when their daughter had no care or concern over the losses within their family, Everett had died a little more inside.

Rebecca, from an early age, seemed to have a spiteful flaw in her character. She took a certain joy in hurting people and causing pain—and when she showed no sorrow over the deaths of her brothers, it had hurt Everett at a deep level.

But now, along with all the other kinds of healing taking place in Frankie's meadow, Everett was healing too. As Ida's fingers worked the ivory thread, she watched Everett with the children. She could see the change in him; she could tell his old wounds were healing. The healing had begun on that first day while he rocked Little Mouse on the Barracks porch. He had seen the trust in Little Mouse's dark eyes. And in those hours, he began to understand that the flaw in Rebecca's character was not because of a lacking within him.

And here, today, Everett and Little Mouse were still together. They were holding each other; cherishing each other. Little Mouse rode in his arms, on his hip, on his shoulders. She delighted in his attention; she adored him, worshipped him, treasured him. And the gaggle of 'wild little prairie boys' idolized him too; they marveled at him; they held onto him. They relished his company; they copied his walk. They watched his eyes and they listened to his words. They laughed and they teased with him. They patted his cheeks like he patted theirs.

And now, as Everett returned to the cookfire, so did his parade. Those six Cheyenne children stood waiting while he settled himself on a log-bench with his wooden bowl. They insisted on sharing his food; they took what they wanted from his bowl, smiling and giggling, choosing the morsels they wanted. And all the while, Little Mouse was busy pointing and directing and issuing orders about who could be closest to Happy Man. And who could share his lap. And for how long.

Ida watched Strong Hand. Little Mouse's father was watching the scene with delight. He was laughing with the others around the fire, because they were all concerned that Happy Man was probably going to starve to death, because there was never any food left for him in his own bowl. Behind the teasing though, Ida could see the look in Strong Hand's eyes. Strong Hand, she knew, missed nothing. He knew exactly what was happening for Everett; he was sharing his child with her husband because he knew exactly what was needed.

476

There was a moment when Ida caught Strong Hand's eye. He locked eyes with her, and then Ida saw him nod; it was barely a nod, barely a movement, but she saw it. Ida smiled at him, nodding at him. Thanking him.

Each day, early in the mornings, the Cheyenne women took Frankie with them as they searched for plants and roots. Some, they would use for cooking; some, they would dry and pound into powders for medicines. They were happy with this land, both the grassland and the stretches along the riverside; they talked about the land they had just left—land that had suffered from drought, land that no longer gave them the plants they needed. Here, they were finding the plants and roots and tubers they wanted and they were busy filling their pouches.

Frankie followed along with them, watching and listening, trying to remember everything these women were showing her. She had always wanted to learn about this land; she had wanted to understand and to know the Sand Hills. And now, they were her teachers, and this was her classroom. So she followed them, digging in the soils where they pointed and stripping the leaves from the plants they indicated. Listening to their words, learning about the uses of the plants and roots and the remedies they would make.

And always, Wild Bird was beside her, acting like her own personal instructor, wielding her stick and giving a gentle rap when she thought her little white granddaughter wasn't listening or paying attention. Then smiling and nodding, patting her arm and her back when she was doing well.

Frankie was stunned by the variety of plants and tubers along the river and among the grasses. And she was surprised with how many plants could still be found this late in the year. Wild onions and turnips, garlicky-smelling tubers, wild carrots. They gathered prairie-clover leaves to dry for tea. They dug the tubers that to Frankie, looked like small sweet potatoes; He's Proud called them groundnuts, and said the Cheyenne called them *aí'is'tom i-misiš'tuk*.

Several times, the women laughed with delight when they uncovered nests where field mice and ground squirrels stored great handfuls of what Mourning Dove called *maka'ta-omnicha*, and He's Proud said were Lakotah peas. They looked a little like lima beans to Frankie and she realized she had been eating them from the stewpot at the cookfire all along—the women had gathered them from the soil along the river while they traveled to her meadow.

The women would fill their leather pouches, scooping out huge handfuls at a time. But always, they left a good portion of the stored food for the hoarding little creatures when they covered the nest again.

"The mice store much more than they need, so we take a share and leave a share for the mouse too," Whirlwind explained.

There were dozens of other plants and roots they were gathering, and Frankie was stunned there was so much she had been blind to, so much food in the grasses and along the river that she had never known about—plants that had been at her feet, all along.

And as they prowled deeper into the shaded growth of the river's edge, there were even more plants to learn about. Plants growing among the roots of the brush and trees, and under the fallen branches and trunks; plants clustered under piles of leaves, hidden and growing in the low-light.

The Cheyenne women showed her mushrooms of the autumn— far more varieties than just the spring mushrooms she remembered from the Indiana riversides. She had spent spring mornings with her aunt, gathering the morels and other mushrooms from the groves along the river, back in Indiana. But here along the riverbanks, there were autumn varieties she had never found before. The women showed her how to lift and separate the fallen limbs and the rotting bark of dying trees to find the treasures.

There had been drawings and paintings of mushrooms in books within her father's library, so Frankie knew some of the names, but now, she was seeing the living mushrooms growing, tucked in among dying cottonwoods and fallen hackberry logs—some, growing half-buried in piles of shaded leaves.

They found the white shaggy-mane mushrooms, the turkey-tail mushrooms, and the radiant yellow-orange chicken-of-the-woods. They found lion's-mane and chanterelles. They found oyster mushrooms growing like stacks of dinner-plates up the sides of poplars and ash and hackberry trees, with a scent that reminded Frankie of licorice candy.

Twice they found giant puff-ball mushrooms, perfectly white and perfectly round, each as big as a woman's sunbonnet. They fascinated Frankie—she marveled at the way they sat nestled, quiet and serene, in the grays and browns and greens of the deep shade, each one glowing bright and white, seeming to radiate light from within. Looking almost, she decided, as if some wandering sorcerer had hidden his glowing orbs there among the mosses and leaves.

Frankie was spending the time with these wonderful Cheyenne women, listening intently to their instructions for drying and preparing the foraged plant. And it wasn't long before she realized that she was understanding the Cheyenne words, no matter who was speaking to her. He's Proud hadn't been translating very much for her over the last day or two. And this morning, she wasn't even missing him because when there was something that she didn't understand, the women went back over the words slowly. They motioned; they gestured; they drew pictures in the dirt. They repeated things. They encouraged her and praised her. Always, they found a way to make sure she understood.

He's Proud had been her first teacher, but now, these wonderful women were spending hours each day teaching her. And much like He's Proud had been doing, they were teaching her more than just how to speak Cheyenne—they were teaching her the culture and customs of the Cheyenne. While they were showing her the plants and talking about how and where they grew, they were also telling her the Cheyenne stories about how the Great Spirit had created the plants and the creatures of the land—how they had come into being. The women were teaching her to be Cheyenne.

And Frankie was pretty sure they knew exactly what they were doing, because it seemed to be a common purpose among them—and once she realized that Whirlwind wasn't translating for her, she was sure of it. Whirlwind, Frankie realized, wasn't giving her any English words; she was purposely staying back like He's Proud was doing; she was staying quiet while the other women taught her.

Every day after the foraging, there were the games. The Cheyenne children showed up in her meadow with the sewn ball of leather and played the same game they had played on the first day. The minute she heard the shouts of the kids coming up the track, Frankie would dash to the fireside with Dandelion, stripping out of her clothes on the way, going for the grease before she got into the game. Lesson learned.

Each day after the play, she walked away with fewer bumps and bruises—never again as sore as she had been after the first game. And after the wild and furiously fast games, she knew enough to stretch herself across the laps of Strong Hand and Knife to let them work with her wounds and muscles. Lesson learned.

By the third day, Frankie realized the experienced kids had been going easy on her—because suddenly, the game seemed faster and harder. By the end of the game that day, it was obvious that the older kids had been coddling the little-white-girl, being patient with her while she developed the skills and learned the tactics. Lessons learned.

It was a tolerance and a kindness, much the same as she and her older cousins had afforded young Charles back in Indiana. Patient and careful with him at first, then as he learned the games and played better, they had expected more of him, required more of him. Frankie figured the same thing had been going on here.

And sure enough, on the fourth day, when the game started, it became abundantly clear that no one was cutting her slack anymore. It was getting really rough out there in the meadow grasses.

By the fifth day, because they had seen her improve and toughen into the game, everyone expected her to be ready for all-out play. They were pulling no punches; the slamming bodies and ramming elbows and knees hit home plenty of times. 'Rough and wild play' as previously defined in Frankie's mind, didn't begin to describe it.

She didn't care, though. She took the hits she had to, and suffered the slams that came her way. And she was giving as good as she got. No one was being careful and patient with her now. If there was yet another notch they could take the game to, then she would take that on too. Because she was reveling in the glory of being one of them, of being a Cheyenne kid.

Playing the game on the fifth day, Frankie applied all tactics she had learned—the physical strategies, the starts and stops, the rolls and the ducks, the spins and the dodges. And she was also grasping the mental strategies—strategies that needed to be adjusted depending on who possessed the ball. Much of it was about what her Lieutenant referred to as 'pre-emptive moves'; it was about anticipation and foresight.

During the five days of play, she had learned a lot about the kicks the Cheyenne kids could dole out—she watched and learned as much as she could during the games. But it wasn't enough. There were certain skills she didn't have, and she knew that if she had to learn them during the games, it would be a drawn-out and painful process. What she needed was some dedicated instruction and Frankie knew exactly where to find that.

After the fifth game, Frankie stalked over to the cookfire; she walked past Strong Hand. She walked past He's Proud. When she approached the log bench where Knife was sitting, he grinned and reached for her, ready to pull her across his lap, ready to work on her battle-wounds. She shook her head and reached for her clothes. She pulled on her antelope-skin shirt and breechcloth, then she turned to Knife. To her brother. because she knew he could help. She looked him in the eye and told him what she wanted.

"I need to learn the kicks and the body-fighting, Brother. Teach me the Cheyenne way to fight."

His eyes narrowed and he leaned back against the log. He shook his head and said he wouldn't show her unless she could tell him what she had seen and what she already knew. He said she had to prove to him she had already studied things and knew what she couldn't do.

"I know, Brother. I've seen. I know what I need to do. I know what the kicks look like. I know what they feel like. I just don't know how to do them."

He raised an eyebrow; he studied her eyes for a moment, and then he nodded. He stood up and stretched. Grinned at the others by the fire. He turned and began walking toward his pinto grazing beside the barn pens. Beckoning to her as he walked away.

"Come then, Little Sister. We'll find out how much you don't know."

Frankie followed him, waiting while he bridled his pinto. He fastened a surcingle and flipped a blanket across the piebald's withers. Slipped up on his back. Frankie grasped Knife's forearm and swung up behind him. Behind her at the fire, she could hear the other warriors calling out to Knife—and even though she didn't understand all the words—she understood enough to spot the irony in their jokes.

They were warning Knife to be careful; to be wary of the dangerous kicks of the Fire Heart Child. They advised him to do a lot of ducking and weaving. They told him not to scream too loudly from the pain of her kicks. Knife answered them in kind.

"I'm not afraid of her. I'm bigger than she is, so I have more blood to spill. So I can outlast her."

She felt him pat her knee; she felt his back shaking and she knew he was chuckling to himself. She ignored the comments and the laughter of the men, understanding it was the humor of the Cheyenne—they always seemed to find amusement in the way things actually weren't.

Frankie leaned against Knife's back, feeling his skin against her cheek, smelling the scent of his body and of the bear-grease. It was a scent she thought might exist nowhere else. It was a scent found here on the prairie. The thought made her smile bigger. *The scent of my prairie-people.*

Knife turned his horse's head toward the steep track that wound up the slope behind the barn, on the east side of the valley. He leaned forward; the pinto surged forward, upward, following the path and charging up the steep bank. At the top of the hillside, they burst out of the dappled shade of the trees and into the bright sunlight of the prairie. They turned north, heading away from the valley and out into the open world of the rolling Sand Hills—away from her home valley and the people.

They traveled at a steady lope—Frankie and her brother and his black-and-white pony—weaving among the hillsides, following the valleys. Going farther, deeper into the hills, far out into the prairie. Far from the eyes and ears of the others. Moving through the late afternoon, moving through sunlight and shadows. Out of sight and out of mind.

Frankie knew he was taking her away from what she knew. He was doing it on purpose, because Knife didn't do things on a whim. He was taking her far from what she knew, so her mind would have nothing to hold onto—nothing except her teacher and the lessons he would offer.

There had been plenty of jokes and teasing as they left the meadow and Knife had joined in the laughter—but ultimately, this was a serious business. The other warriors knew it; Knife knew it; and Frankie knew it. The farther they rode, the more she started wondering if maybe she had gotten herself into a mess. She began to think that maybe she wasn't really ready for what she said she wanted; she was thinking maybe she made a mistake.

Then Knife's hand was on her knee again, patting her leg as if he was reassuring her, as if he knew her thoughts. And she realized, suddenly, he probably knew exactly what she was thinking. Because he always knew.

Knife worked with her through the afternoon and into the evening. Frankie did as he required and followed his instructions, trying to forget she was already tired from the game. She refused to complain, determined not to ask for leniency. She didn't want an easy way out; she had asked Knife for this lesson, so she said nothing about being tired. And neither did he.

He worked her hard for an hour before letting her rest for a few minutes, then worked her for another hour. He was patient; his explanations and commands were clear and softly spoken. He was exacting and unrelenting—he expected her best and he expected it all the time. And Frankie knew it.

He made her kick and spin; he had her twisting and whirling, dropping, ducking and swirling. He taught her to lead with her heels and drive the kick with the power of the muscles along the back of her leg.

When she resorted to using toe-kicks, he warned her about the dangers of using her toes; when she didn't grasp the logic, he let her hurt herself a few times. He let her hop about, holding her toes in her hand and yelping with pain until she understood. After she learned that lesson, he taught her to drive for the hard kicks, teaching her to land the far-reaching and hard heel-kicks.

Like the brother he was, he teased her; laughing at his little sister, mocking her when she fell short of his requirements. He grunted approval when she met his expectations; he scowled and frowned and snorted in disgust when she failed to please him. He let her make her mistakes, and when she hurt herself, he let her learn from the pain she brought on herself.

He worked her until he was satisfied. He made her repeat her moves, her swings, her kicks. Again and again, and again. And again. Always leading with the heel; always striking and advancing. Always assessing and thinking; always gauging the target's strength. Learning the strength she needed to put into the kicks; learning how to increase the speed in order to increase the power.

He took the kicks on himself when she needed the understanding of contact. He took the kicks as they became harder and harder. He bore the strikes as her speed increased and the power increased. He took what was required of him to teach her what he knew would be necessary in a true fight.

Knife was teaching her to be Cheyenne; Strong Hand and He's Proud and Blue Feather—all the others who had been there beside the fire—knew exactly why he had ridden out with her today. They all knew he was teaching Fire Heart Child to fight like a Cheyenne. They knew his mission and his reasons. Because they knew the stories—they knew what had happened in the stable at the soldiers' fort. They had all heard about the white man who had beaten her.

And now, because of the stories and the happenings, Knife would not slack off and allow her to be less than what he thought she could be. He was teaching her the skills and the knowledge that she needed to play at the children's games—she wanted to learn the skills and the tactics, the timing and the techniques for the games. *That* was the immediate need she had; *that* was her driving desire. He knew she understood it all as a game, and he allowed her to think that. For now.

But there was a greater purpose of the games; these children's games would save the lives of these children someday—these games would serve them later, when they were adults. Because *this* was where the children of his people learned the moves; this was the way it would become instinctive. They were learning all the skills and strengths and tactics that would become great protection for them later. That was the reason he chose to teach Ho-esta Hesta Ka-ėškóne.

Finally, he let her rest again. She flopped down on the ground beside him and they drank water and waited. Quieting their breathing; letting their hearts recover. As dusk settled and the birds sang their last songs, he motioned to her and led the way high up one of the slopes. He beckoned to her as he settled down into a windblown pocket in the hillside; he pulled her down beside him in the sheltered patch of sun-warmed sandy-soil, a sandy nook where the grasses had been washed out by the winds that coursed and curled along the slopes of the Sand Hills.

Knife stayed beside her, silently watching the land around them, keeping watch over the child lying beside him on the sandy soil. The child who was exhausted now. Sleeping now. Pressed against his side.

He let her sleep, feeling the warm little puffs of her breath playing against his skin. He was satisfied with what she had learned, because one of the ways he could protect her was to teach her to fight for herself. He knew of her time at the soldiers' fort, the one called Kearny. He knew of the care and protection the horse-soldiers had given this child. He even knew of the lieutenant—the one she had called father—and he knew of his devotion to her.

But Knife had heard of the other things too, things that had happened when he had been far away, far beyond the great flat river. Far to the west among Lame Horse's people, out on the dry land where Wild Bird and Whirlwind lived. Everyone in Strong Hand's band had heard of the danger she had been in at the soldier's fort. They all knew of the fort's chief, the Bloated One, and of what he had done. And they knew of Greasy-Headed One, the man called Beckett, and of how he had beaten this child.

Knife didn't understand the rules and the laws of the fort, but he knew this child had been in danger because of those rules and the Army's laws. He knew the story of how she had escaped from the fort, how she had gathered all her animals and her great painted wagon one night and disappeared into the land. No one from the fort had seen her. She had disappeared into the prairie-night like a prairie-wolf, protecting herself when no one else could.

There were people among the Otoe who worked for White Man On The Island who knew the story of Fire Heart Child. They, too, had been far away when she escaped from the soldiers' fort and disappeared into the land. But they knew that White Man On The Island had helped her on the night of the great storm—he had seen her cross the great flat river and he had seen her travel along the northern riverbank, traveling to where the sun disappears. No one had seen her again. Like the prairie-wolf, she had gone into the land.

Knife's mind wandered back to the days and nights after she had escaped. He and Strong Hand, and many of the Cheyenne, searched for her. Just as the soldiers had. But Ho-esta Hesta Ka-ėškóne had chosen her own way. Like the prairie-wolf, she had drifted away, silent and unseen.

What intrigued him and Strong Hand—and especially Wild Bird—was that Fire Heart Child had chosen to follow the trail of their ancestors. The Cheyenne people had long since stopped following the trail of the old ones; they chose not to travel it now—because now, Fort Kearny stood in the middle of the ancient path.

The Pawnee never traveled it either, because they knew the spirits of the ancient Cheyenne still lived along the trail; the Pawnee were afraid of the ancient Cheyenne spirits who still traveled the trail. The Pawnee might choose to quickly cross the Cheyenne Trail if they needed to, but they would never follow along its course. Because they had good reason to fear the Cheyenne, both living and dead. Just like they feared the Sioux.

Knife knew also that white-men no longer used the Cheyenne Trail. Few whites even knew it had existed; most of them saw the land as dangerous and disputed. For many years now, his people and the Oglála, and other people of the Sioux Nation used another trail far to the west. The Cheyenne Trail was a forgotten way; it was untraveled now.

And yet, Fire Heart Child had known to follow it; she had traveled it quietly, unseen by the Cheyenne. Unseen by the Otoe or Pawnee or Ponca. No one had seen her pass through the land north of the flat river. This young woman-child had traveled the trail of the old ones, alone and unafraid. She had been protected by wolf-medicine that allowed her to travel unseen across the land.

Wild Bird believed she had been guided by the ancestors; she said the ancestors had known of the vision quest of Ho-esta Hesta Ka-ėškóne, and they had set her on their ancient path. They had sent her wolf-medicine to keep her safe, Wild Bird said. Because, she said, Ho-esta Hesta Ka-ėškóne had the healer's touch. And because, she could speak to the buffalo. Now, all the people of the band were protecting her. Just as he and Strong Hand and He's Proud were.

Knife smiled, watching Fire Heart Child as she slept beside him. He was thinking ahead now, thinking about the time when the people of Strong Hand's band would join with the other bands for the winter months. There would be talk of Fire Heart Child; there would be talk of her wolf-medicine. Stories would be told of how she followed the path of the ancestors, and how she called the buffalo, and how she had healed the sickness of Strong Hand's mother and daughter. Word would travel to other bands and all the Cheyenne would keep her hidden from the whites. Gray Fox and his Oglála would watch over her because, they too, would hear the stories.

But for now, Knife had it in his mind to give her a different kind of protection, because if she had known what she learned today, the Greasy-Headed One would not have been able to beat her as he did. And Knife knew there was more to do; he was not done with his lessons for her. Strong Hand, he knew, would have more to teach her too.

Frankie woke in the morning, lying tucked up against Knife's ribs and belly, with the scent of the grasses in her nostrils. The clean air of the Sand Hills was filling her lungs and the cool morning breeze was tickling along her skin. They had spent the night there in the sandy blow-out and when she opened her eyes, she realized that sometime during the night, Knife had wrapped her in the blanket from his horse; he had kept her there beside him, warm and safe, wrapped in his arms.

The memory of the long afternoon and evening came back to her. Looking down the grassy hillside at the little swale of hard grass, she took in a slow breath—that was where Knife had worked with her and taught her to the point of exhaustion. Beyond exhaustion.

She shivered a little. Partly from the cool morning breeze sifting through the grasses on the slope, and partly from the thought that the hard lessons might continue now that there was daylight. Another shiver coursed through her and she felt Knife stirring beside her. She stilled her movements, thinking it might be better for her sake if he slept a little longer—just in case he had ideas about resuming Cheyenne-fighting lessons.

It didn't work. He was awake. He sat up, grinning at her. Pulled her to a sitting position, leaning her back against his chest. Tucked the blanket around her again. He reached to his side for a leather pouch and pulled out a handful of jerky. He handed her a piece and leaned back against the hillside, propped up on his elbow. Grinned at her again.

"Are you stiff this morning, Little Sister?" His eyes danced with devilment.

"Are you sore from all my kicks, Brother?" She answered with her own question, sneering at him.

"What kicks? Did you deliver any kicks yesterday? I saw you hopping like a baby-bird among the grasses yesterday, holding your toes. But I saw no kicks."

Frankie could feel him shaking with laughter as he hugged her tight to his chest. He was pleased with her and with the teasing, he was letting her know that she had done well. She tucked herself into his arms, chewing on the dried buffalo, enjoying the time with him. Feeling a little relief now, knowing there would be no more lessons today. Without actually saying the words, he told her he was satisfied with what she had learned.

She watched as Mo'é'ha, Magpie, grazed quietly below them. The piebald was content with the grass he was in, but he paused every few minutes, raising his head to look to the surrounding hillsides. Always alert and watchful. Then he'd look to where she and Knife sat, eating their jerky and a few handfuls of cold roasted turnips and onions from the leather pouch. Magpie would eye them, then scan the meadow again. Then he'd drop his nose to graze again.

Frankie was confused about his name, knowing it referred to the annoying and noisy black-and-white birds. The magpie's color matched the pinto's color, but she knew the Cheyenne word had nothing to do with the actual colors themselves. The word was about movement.

When she asked Knife for an explanation, he smiled, pleased that she was developing a grasp of the depth of the Cheyenne tongue; pleased that she was understanding the intricate form that thought and words took on when they were spoken together.

"The word speaks of black and white without using those words, Sister. It is a picture-word for the mind. It is about black and white, but it speaks only of the flight of the magpie. Of the black and white flight that moves the same as the wind-blown grass. That is how Magpie, the horse below you, moves through the prairie."

Knife watched the child beside him; he watched her jaw muscles moving as she considered his words.

"So it isn't a language just about what you see or what's in the mind. It's about what is known and lived. It can speak of *how* we know and *feel*, not just of *what* we know."

Frankie said the words, looking out to the lands to the east, thinking about his explanation. She saw his nod and his half-smile. She was feeling something change inside her, something was rising inside her. Something was rising up from the warming earth below her that was becoming part of her—something that felt warm and soothing.

"That is the truth of our tongue, of our words. The Cheyenne language comes from what lies inside you, not what leaves your lips. He's Proud has taught you well. You are learning to live with our language, not just to speak words."

She felt Knife's palm cupping the back of her head. She could feel the strength and the warmth in his hand, the same strength and warmth that was always in his eyes. It was the way he had always looked at her—she could remember his eyes from the day they first met on the prairie. She had been standing on the seat of her great blue-green Conestoga and he had been sitting on Magpie, staring at her while she held her Henry rifle in her hands, refusing to give it to Strong Hand.

She told him what she remembered from that day and Knife leaned back against the sand and smiled.

"Yes, sister. I knew even then, you would be in the lives of my people. I knew you would come to know my heart. Your eyes told me. We watched for you and your trail after that day, so we knew you were continuing on your path."

He closed his eyes and was silent for a few minutes. Frankie waited, knowing he had more to say. After a moment he went on.

"You are of two worlds, Fire Heart Child. Wild Bird says that your life connects both worlds. The world of the ancestors and the world of our people living now. You bring their lives together and you honor both. The ancestors watch you and guide you. They watched you on your path. They sent the spirit of the prairie-wolves. They let you speak to the buffalo.

Frankie watched him stand up, smooth and graceful, without a sound. He lifted her to her feet and they walked toward his horse. The piebald took one last mouthful of grass and walked toward them, meeting them, turning to accept the blanket and the bridle. Knife slipped up on the pony's back and as Frankie took his hand, he pulled her up behind him.

They rode back to her home; she rode behind him on his pinto, holding onto his waist and he spoke to her about what he had taught her and about what she had learned. And he spoke of the caution she must use.

"You must choose the strength of your kicks. You must use your kicks and your strength with wisdom. You must always know your purpose."

In that moment, Frankie knew Knife was speaking about the difference between playing in games and fighting for life. He was telling her that her clarity of her purpose, would put the right level of power and depth and drive into her kicks. He had, she suddenly realized, taken her beyond the game. Far beyond the game.

When she asked about it, he nodded and told her all the other things he had been thinking about through the night.

"I was teaching you beyond the games," he said. "So you can protect yourself. So you will be safe when I'm not here. When there are no Cheyenne warriors around you." He was quiet then; they rode in silence for a few minutes. Then he spoke again.

"There is more you must learn, Little Sister. There will be more training. And the training will be much harder than yesterday. I'll work you harder and teach you more. And Strong Hand has lessons to teach you too. We'll both work you harder."

She nodded and tightened her arms around him. She held him harder.

Things were changing in the riverside village. As she and Knife rode in from the hills early that morning, Frankie could see a lot of activity among the lodges. As Magpie wove his way along the path, she saw women shifting things around near the cookfires, adding foods to the cookpots and stringing strips of meat onto spits. Waving to her. Calling out in Cheyenne.

"Pave-éšeeva, Na-néso!" 'Good day, my child!'

"Ne-teneto mohta-he, Ho-esta Hesta Ka-eškóne. Ne-haeana-he?" 'How are you, Fire Heart Child? Are you hungry?'

"Ne-náestse! Motåhke! Ho-esta Hesta Ka-eškone! He-méséestse! 'Come here! Knife! Fire Heart Child. Come eat!'

Frankie waved and called back to them. Telling the women that she was feeling good today. That she was already full. That she and Knife had already eaten. She shouted back to them, agreeing that it *was* a very good day. Today, she could pass by and there was no insult. Because introductions had been made.

"Héehe-e! Ta-náestse! Né-sta-va-vóomåtse!" The women waved them on, smiling and laughing. 'Yes. Go on. I'll see you later!'

"Héehe-e, né-sta-va-vóomåste!" Frankie nodded and smiled and waved as they rode on. And as Magpie continued to weave his way among the lodges, Knife kept poking her with his elbow. He was laughing and warning her the women had it in their minds to fatten her up.

"You'll end up being as big and round as Willow if we stop and eat every time a woman calls you to her fire."

Frankie told Knife to keep Magpie moving and she jabbed her fist into his rib each time he reined Magpie, pretending to turn him toward one of the cookfires.

"You and Strong Hand got me belly-sick because of all the cookpots we stopped at. I don't want to get all that started again." She poked him harder as he pretended to turn Magpie again. "I don't need fattening up at anyone's fire."

They rode on with Knife making a few more half-hearted attempts to rein Magpie when other women called to them; Frankie kept jabbing him harder and Knife kept laughing louder.

And as they moved through the village, Frankie could see that of all the changes going on, the most obvious was the large pile of wood standing in an open space among the tipis. A large and tall pile that was much bigger than the small stacks of wood near each cookfire. It confused her because the Cheyenne and Oglála people didn't use a lot of wood on their fires; they kept their fires small, burning long and low. And from what she could see, the big stack of wood, which already seemed plenty tall, was getting higher all the time—Indian kids were running up with armloads of wood, constantly adding to the stack. They dumped their loads, waved at her and Knife, and then ran off again. Apparently to search for more wood.

The kind of work being done to the buffalo-hides staked out on the ground had changed too. The women weren't scraping the hides now; apparently, the scraping-process was done. Now, the women were involved with a whole new process—something Frankie had never seen before. The process involved some kind of stinking gray muck in rawhide containers beside the hides. Frankie could smell the muck as she and Knife rode by and she decided the stench coming from those containers gave a whole new meaning to the old phrase about 'stinking to high heaven'.

She watched the women slathering handfuls of the smelly muck on the skin-side of the buffalo-hides, surprised that they didn't seem to mind the smell. Because they were laughing and telling stories and amusing each other while they rubbed the stinking mess into the hides. They paused in their work to call out to Frankie and Knife, looking as though they were wearing gloppy-gray mittens when they waved to them.

Frankie found herself astonished at the power of the stench—even after Magpie had carried them well beyond the smelly containers and the gloppy-handed women, the smell was still in the air around them. She scrunched up her nose and wiped at tears in her eyes and found herself wondering exactly how long that smell might actually stay with a person who had been up to the elbows in it for a good part of a day. And that was when Strong Hand rode up.

He looked at her and broke into laughter. Frankie figured he was laughing at the expression on her face, because after he recovered from his laughing-fit, he started mimicking her nose-scrunching and eye-wiping. He said he felt bad for Knife, because Knife was riding in front of her and couldn't see the faces she was making.

So Strong Hand began doing his best impressions of the little-white-girl's reaction to the stench, for his brother's benefit. Knife doubled over with laughter too. And when Frankie gave Strong Hand her nastiest snarl and glare, Strong Hand did his impression of that too.

Once Strong Hand quit making faces and both men stopped laughing, he reined his horse closer to Magpie. He leaned close to Frankie and asked her if she wanted to stay with the women so she could help with the tanning. Frankie didn't hesitate when she shook her head and instantly realized her mistake in answering so quickly, because both of her warriors burst into laughter again. Doubling over, again.

In Frankie's mind, she had done about as much with buffalo-hides as she wanted to. She had been helping with the scraping of the hides for a couple hours each day, thinking she might learn a better and easier way of scraping hides. She didn't learn much about scraping hides that she didn't already know. Her arms got tired just like always and she probably gained some muscle strength, but she gained no new knowledge.

It had been hours of scraping and scraping and scraping, and about all she got out of the experience was a chance to spend more time with Dandelion as they knelt side-by-side, scraping the sticky gummy-bloody guck from the massive hides. It had, though, afforded her the opportunity to learn more of the Cheyenne language. And listening to the Cheyenne women talking, had taught her something else—apparently, Cheyenne women spent a lot of time being annoyed with the laziness of Cheyenne men.

But given what was being done with the hides right now, Frankie was very sure it was nothing she needed to learn. She had no need or desire to learn anything about the process of tanning that involved the gray muck made from animal brains. At least, not now. She was pretty sure she wouldn't be going into the buffalo-hide tanning-business in the near future.

Strong Hand and Knife were still bursting into their silly fits of laughter because Strong Hand kept glancing over at her, and then demonstrating her expressions for Knife. She decided to ignore both of them and ducked her head under the quiver of arrows on Knife's back. She buried her nose against his buckskin shirt—still amazed that the stench of the gray brain-muck was wafting through the air around them.

Her warriors kept their ponies walking and their laughter died down once they were beyond the lodges and away from the hide-tanning. Frankie unburied her nose when Strong Hand changed the subject. He began quizzing her about what Knife had taught her. When he wanted to know if she learned to fight like a Cheyenne girl, or was she still going to fight like a little-white-girl, she decided to ignore him again.

She turned her attention to the arrows tucked into Knife's quiver. She ran her fingers along the smooth shafts, tracing the bands and spirals of paint. Black spirals and red bands. It was when she reached between the horses to touch the arrows in Strong Hand's quiver, that he gripped her arm and pulled her across to his pony's withers. The conversation between the men stopped as they guided their horses toward the rows of apple trees beside the river.

Frankie ducked her head, realizing that she had crossed a line by fiddling with the warrior's weapons—understanding that she had made a big mistake. The two men pulled their horses to a stop under the trees; they dismounted and Strong Hand led the way into the rows of trees. He and Knife settled down in the grass and he motioned her to sit between them. She sat down between her brothers in the dappled shade of the last leaves on the apple trees, waiting for a scolding, knowing she had been disrespectful.

As it turned out, she had figured things wrong—there was no scolding. Strong Hand and Knife placed their bows and their quivers of arrows on the grass beside them. And the lesson began.

Frankie felt a shiver of excitement ripple up her spine—this was going to be another lesson. A very new kind of lesson. One by one, they handed her their bows, talking to her about each one. They told her about the woods that were used—Strong Hand's of vénóhó'kóhtse and Knife's of mótó'e. Chokecherry and ash.

She smiled, recognizing the words. The women had taught her; they used those same woods for making cooking utensils and as fastening-pins used for piecing the lodge-hides together above the doors.

Frankie drank in the words, listening to the story of their weapons. Listening as the two men talked about how their bows had been carved and scraped, soaked and bent, shaped and smoked and smoothed. All to strengthen them and tighten the fibers in the wood. Always to honor the spirit of the wood. All to release the power.

Then, they taught her about their arrows. They showed her the paint and the designs and explained about the different colors and designs on the arrow shafts. When Knife showed her how the feathers on the arrow-shaft were positioned and angled, she watched his fingers move along the shafts of the different arrows. Hotamemenó'éstse, he said. *Dogwood.* Strong Hand's arrows, he explained, were made from wood of the chokecherry. *Again the vénóhó'kóhtse.* She stroked the wood feeling the polished silkiness of the hardwood, thinking the feel was every bit as smooth as the varnished surface of her violins.

Strong Hand talked about the arrowheads—some shaped from stone, some made from metal; he showed her how the angled position of the arrowhead related to the notched-end of the shaft. The arrows for battle had arrowheads that would fly and strike with the arrowhead horizontal—to pierce between an enemy's ribs. The hunting arrows flew with the arrowhead striking vertical. Frankie grinned at him, understanding. *Because animal ribs sit vertical when the animal stands or runs. Human ribs are horizontal when standing or riding. Because whether in war or on a hunt, you're shooting for the chest and the heart.*

Knife stood up and settled his quiver across his shoulder. Motioned to her. When Frankie stood, he handed her his bow; he showed her how to notch the arrow and told her to draw the bow-string back. She pulled, groaned with the effort. Failed to accomplish the task. She pulled harder, groaned louder, and grunted a few times. And still failed to make the draw. Her brothers laughed, apparently not at all surprised that a little-white-girl couldn't draw the bow-string.

When she glared at him, Knife took the bow from her, grinning. He aimed high and Frankie watched as he sent an arrow into the prairie sky. By the time it reached the height of its flight and began its curve to return to earth, three more arrows had chased after it. By the time the first arrow sliced into the earth five feet from where they stood, a total of six arrows had shot into the air and followed its path.

Frankie had seen the movement and heard the whispering-strum of the bowstring as Knife shot each of the seven arrows, but she hadn't fully realized what he had been doing. Now, she stood and stared at the seven arrows clustered closely together, not six feet from where she was standing. Seven flint-points in the ground, seven dogwood-shafts standing vertical, fletched-feathers vibrating in the afternoon air. It had all happened in a matter of seconds. Seven arrows cutting through the air. Swift and sure. Seven arrows piercing the surface of the earth. Silent and deadly.

When she looked at Knife, he was grinning at her, his eyes shining with wicked amusement; behind her, she could hear Strong Hand's chuckle and she knew he was laughing at her surprise.

"*There*, Fire Heart Child! *That* is what a warrior can do with the spirit of the ash tree." Strong Hand beckoned her to his side again, motioning for her to sit. "The spirits of the trees send their strength into the wood for the warriors. So our weapons can give food and protection to our families."

Knife pulled his arrows from the earth, lifting them gently, brushing the soil from the arrowheads, before returning them to his quiver. He gave her a grin as he sat down beside her—looking a lit-

497

tle wicked and a little amused—and Frankie knew it was probably because she had stood there in open-mouthed surprise, staring at the arrows in the dirt.

The lesson continued and Frankie kept listening as her warriors kept talking and she kept thinking back to her concerns about getting a scolding for being disrespectful. Realizing now, that in her brothers' minds, her interest in their weapons had been a sign of her respect for them. They had seen her interest and used it as an avenue to teach her more about their people, as well as their weapons. The lesson today had started because their little sister had touched the arrows Knife carried—that had become a pathway to take her even deeper into the life and the ways of their people.

Frankie's mind flicked back to her first meeting with these warriors, back to the prairie south of the Platte River. Back to the time when she had first realized she knew nothing of the people who roamed the prairie; she had known nothing about the people who lived their lives under the prairie skies and among the prairie grasses. She had realized back then that other than a vague knowledge of a few tribal names, she knew nothing about the tribes themselves.

But now, her time to learn had come. These families and these people were spending time with her—the children and the women and the men were all spending time during their visits, teaching her what she had yearned to understand.

Her brothers had taught her about their weapons, and now they continued with the lesson. They began talking about their hunts and the buffalo. They talked about how their families followed the great herds and traveled the prairie lands.

And when He's Proud and Blue Feather and Charging Crow rode up, they slipped off their ponies and sat down in the grass too. The lesson which began with two teachers there in the dappled shade of the apple trees, became a lesson with five instructors.

The conversation broadened as He's Proud went beyond the lesson about the Cheyenne nation; he started teaching her about the different peoples of the Sioux nation. He spoke of the Oglála people and of the Húnkpapha and the Sičhángu and others who spoke the Lakotah language. He told her about some who spoke Dakotah, naming the Sisíthunwan and the Yanktonai, and of others who spoke Nakotah. All the same language, he said, but different. There were changes in the way the language was spoken—with different sounds and rhythms. Even some of the words and the meanings changed.

The four men talked on, speaking about the weapons and the great battles and chiefs of both the Cheyenne and Sioux people. They spoke to her of other Indian nations—the Arapahoe and the Pawnee. The Kiowa. The Shoshone and Crow. Blackfeet and Arikaree. And Assiniboine. They told her of the difference and of the sameness. They told her of their fights and of their wars against each other. And of times they joined together and fought together.

Frankie soaked up the information, listening to the history and the stories, the travels and the trails. She was filling up with the words and explanations they were giving her. Pleased that they were teaching her; proud that they were teaching her.

She felt tears welling up in her eyes. A sudden fear rose from inside her—a fear that she would forget what they were telling her, that she would fail to understand the importance of something they might say. Strong Hand stopped the talk and the descriptions—he cupped his hand under her jaw, making her look into his eyes. He made her talk of her tears and the fears, making her explain. She told her Cheyenne brothers about her fears of letting them down; she told them she was afraid of forgetting what they were telling her. Afraid of not fully understanding.

They looked to each other. Nodding. Understanding. It was Blue Feather who lifted her onto his lap and wrapped his arms gently around her. They all sat silent while Blue Feather held her.

It was several minutes later when Strong Hand began speaking to her, softly, carefully, quietly; he told her why they were teaching her. He said they knew their words would be safe inside her. Their words, he said, would stay in her heart. They would rise up when she needed them. She shouldn't worry about remembering them because she was listening with her heart, and she was hearing what was in their hearts.

Everything she was hearing, he explained, would go deep inside her and become part of her. It would live there. When she needed what she had learned—it would take the form of words again. He reached to pat the side of her face. Gently; softly. The men stood up and Blue Feather lifted her to the back of his palomino pinto. Vohké-eše'he, Blue Feather told her. Her name, he said, was Crescent Moon.

The men walked along the track, leading their ponies, heading to her meadow. Their talk was low, their voices soft. Frankie felt herself settling inside, feeling the sway of the pinto mare's walk, listening to the quiet flow of the Cheyenne language as the men talked among themselves. She was not trying to hear their words now; she was sated for now. She was full of Cheyenne words for now.

She tipped her head back, watching two hawks spiraling high into the blue of the prairie sky, riding the currents, riding with the heat of the sun warmed soils. She leaned back, lying on the back of the pretty pinto mare, watching the slow circles of the hawks.

Frankie was sitting beside the cookfire with Wild Bird and Whirlwind, listening to their talk about the buffalo-hides and the drying meat, a conversation that made sense to her because they were words and subjects she knew. And after a while, the conversation changed and she started hearing different words about subjects she had never heard discussed before. He's Proud and Whirlwind gave her the words and meanings she needed, because suddenly the conversation was about the big pile of firewood in the middle of the riverside village. There was talk about the fire that would burn through the night; there were words about dancing and celebrating.

While the talk went on around her, Frankie busied herself at the cookpot, hunting for pieces of buffalo meat; Charging Crow and Strong Hand teased her, mimicking her faces and yelps as she grabbed at chunks of meat floating in the hot broth. She put up with their teasing and started mimicking the way they were laughing at her.

When Knife came to the fire he reached around her, pulled a large chunk of meat from the pot, and sat back against the log-bench, pulling her down beside him. He pulled the chunk apart, handing a piece to her and eating the other piece. He gave Strong Hand and Charging Crow a triumphant sneer. A moment later, noise erupted on the track just beyond the entrance to the valley.

Shrieks and yells in the midst of thundering hooves. Frankie scrambled out of Knife's lap, half-choking on a mouthful of meat as she watched a group of riders surge into the meadow. She stared at the riders racing down the track, whooping like a raiding party. *Not a raiding party! Not warriors! Not wild and fearsome enemies! Kids were on those Indian horses! Cheyenne kids!*

She let out her own shriek. A joy-filled shriek, because she could hear them calling her name—they were calling for Fire Heart Child to come ride with them. To come do battle for the arrow. *The same kids, but some new game! A horseback game!*

The kids were hollering for her to hurry; their ponies were dancing and prancing, fidgeting and fighting against the reins that held them in place; they were rearing and pawing, spinning and snorting while their riders were waving and shouting.

"Come, Fire Heart Child. We have a new game for you! Come on!"

And there in the midst of them, Frankie could see Dandelion on her flea-bitten gray, stripped down to her breechcloth like the other children. She was grinning and calling for Frankie to hurry—laughing at her, taunting her—while her gray pony reared and stomped, cavorted and kicked. All the kids were shouting for her.

"Why are you sitting at the fire with the old people, Fire Heart Child?"

"Are you afraid to do battle with us?"

"Do little-white-girls know how to ride warhorses?"

The Cheyenne kids were still shouting. Teasing her. Daring her. And Frankie was dancing on her feet. Spinning around. Shaking with excitement. Letting out her own shrieks and her own war-whoops. Calling back to the kids on their ponies; telling them to wait. Telling them she was coming.

This was something new and exciting. This was a *new* game. And *this* one, was all about horses. Whatever the game was, and however it was played, she knew it would be played hard and fast and wild.

"*I need grease!*" She shouted it out loud to no one in particular, shouting it out to the world as she started to strip down. She yanked at her buckskin shirt, tangling her fingers in the fringes and her arms in the sleeves. Knife and He's Proud were already on their feet, nodding and laughing, knowing exactly what to do; they grabbed her up and pulled the shirt over her head; they laughed harder and stilled her hands as she started pulling at her breechcloth.

"No! No, warrior-child. Leave that. Your battle is from horseback today."

They were already slathering her arms and torso with grease and laughing all the harder as they smeared the outside of her legs with the grease while she danced and twisted, reaching to help, struggling to hurry the process.

"No, little-white-warrior. Not on the inside of your legs. No grease against the horse." Knife grabbed her hands, stopping her in mid-swipe.

"In battle, you need to grip with your legs," He's Proud's voice was shaking with his laughter. "We don't want warriors sliding off their war-ponies."

Frankie could hear Whirlwind and Ida over by the fire. She could hear Everett, too; they were all rocking with laughter and Whirlwind was calling out.

"Fire Heart Child dances like a warhorse. All the ponies will be jealous."

The mention of war-ponies sent Frankie into a panic. Grease she had; there was plenty of grease going on. But her crying need now, was a horse—she had no horse for the game. Her mind flashed to King Richard's cry in Shakespeare's play. *A horse! A horse! My kingdom for a horse!*

She scanned the back of the meadow while Knife and He's Proud finished spreading the grease on her calves. She could see Rock in a barn-pen, watching the action at the meadow's entrance; Fanny was in the front pasture, pacing along the fence, calling out to the tangle of swirling Indian ponies across the meadow. Both could be trusted—

they were both strong and fast and willing. But Frankie realized she didn't know exactly what was required of a horse in this new game.

Frankie was pretty sure Rock's warhorse skills would be valuable, but she wasn't sure if his massive size, compared to the tough and wiry war-ponies, would help or hinder. Fanny was closer to the size of the Indian ponies, plus she had the same kind of agility, but she didn't have the fighting and battle skills that Rock had. *Boone, then? Maybe Boone's my best bet. He's fast and fearless. He's quick like a cat. Maybe Boone.*

Another fear was rising. Because she wasn't at all sure the Cheyenne kids would wait much longer—they were already on their dancing ponies, all stripped-down and greased-up and waiting. While Knife and He's Proud were busy slicking her arms, the Indian kids were still beckoning and waving, shouting for her. Whooping and hollering to the highest reaches of heaven. And to Frankie's ears, they didn't sound all that patient—at any moment, they might tire of waiting and race off to play the game without her.

"And I don't even know what horse to use!" She realized she was shouting out loud, shouting it to the world as another wave of panic swept through her. She could hear Everett and He's Proud burst into loud laughter. Charging Crow was squatting on the ground, laughing hard. Even Ida was laughing.

Frankie heard Strong Hand's voice coming from somewhere behind her. Calm and steady. Speaking to her as he walked toward her. Following closely behind him was his red-and-white pinto. His warhorse. The horse he called Ma'ô-hóohe. Fox.

The stallion looked ready for battle; he was dancing a jig behind Strong Hand, tossing his head, tugging at the single rein in Strong Hand's grip. He was blowing and calling out to the dancing and swirling Indian ponies—calling out a challenge. Sweat was already showing dark on his neck.

Knife grabbed Frankie from behind, gripping her by an arm and a thigh; he half-lifted and half-threw her onto the back of the red-and-white warhorse. She took the rein from Strong Hand and in the same instant, he slapped his pony's rump, sending him lunging forward.

Frankie tried using the warhorse's single rein and it took a few turns and spins for her to learn what Fox knew and what she didn't. For a moment, she was sending different signals than he expected, and she was getting different responses from him than she planned on. But somewhere in the midst of the quick twists and turns and twirls, she found the feel; suddenly, she understood what Fox needed from her.

The other kids waited impatiently, watching and waiting while she learned to manage her first Indian warhorse. Once they decided she knew enough, they turned their own ponies toward the entrance and raced out of the valley, shrieking like demons. Frankie gripped with her knees, leaned forward over Fox's withers—the warhorse crouched, and then he launched forward. He took off with the power of a gunshot. And Frankie went with him.

Fox moved with the same power-filled surge and action as both Rock and Trumpeter, and as they topped the rise at the meadow entrance, Frankie was thanking the angels in heaven that she had learned from those two Cavalry warhorses. Otherwise, she would have been left behind, spinning on her bottom in the meadow dirt. As it was, Fox was racing up the track, already making up the distance between her and the other players. In a matter of a few more strides, the pinto had her in the midst of the other riders, and luckily for Frankie, he knew the game. Because the game was on.

From what she could figure in the first few minutes of the flurry and fury, this game was a lot like the other one—only this one was played from the back of a horse. The twists and turns, the body slams, the pushes and pulls were still part of the game; the shoves, the blocks, the kicks and the jabs were still in use, but now, horses were snorting, hooves were pounding, manes and tails were flying.

The biggest difference was that the sewn-leather ball had been exchanged for an arrow, and now, 'it' had an arrow that he held aloft. All the players were racing to snatch the arrow from 'it's' hand, and 'it' was riding hell-bent in an effort to keep the prized arrow. They raced across the land of the Sand Hills, over the hills and through the dales. Fighting to unseat the competing riders, racing after the holder-of-the-arrow, in pursuit of the prize.

To Frankie's mind, it *was* the same game—except they were riding instead of running—and a whole lot of the focus was on staying horseback and not ending up on the ground under the pounding hooves. But it wasn't the fear of injury motivating the riders to stay aboard—it was the shame of being unseated. Every bit of this game, no matter what else was going on, was about the pride of horsemanship.

This, Frankie realized, was more of a battle than a game—it was a wheeling, swirling, twirling, racing battle. A hellbent battle-for-the-arrow with the war-ponies playing as hard as their riders. The ponies were ducking and dodging, fleet and swift and strong. Because in this game, the horses were the legs of the riders and the horses knew the game every bit as well as the yelping and shrieking warrior-children on their backs.

It took Frankie a few minutes to understand that Fox was every bit as wily and clever as his namesake. And it took Fox a few minutes to understand her. He was swift and sure-footed, quick in his mind and in all his movements. She could feel the power and the wisdom of his actions. He was teaching her the game, and he was guiding her more than she was guiding him.

And like a true warhorse, she knew he was protecting his rider. Twice, within the first few minutes of the game, he swerved to keep her safe on his back—he had corrected for her—ducking and leaning beneath her, helping her recover and rebalance. And all the while, he was racing at break-neck speed; he was watching her back and watching the other riders and their mounts, all at the same time. He was wheeling and swerving and spinning in his fight to keep her safe.

And then, there was a sudden instant when they became one— she and Fox came together—and in that instant, they both knew exactly what to expect of the other. Frankie felt it in her mind and heart; she could feel it in her legs and back and arms. She threw back her head and sucked in a great lungful of the prairie air and let out a shriek—a loud and wild and reckless shriek that seemed to come out of every bone in her body.

She gave another cry, startling herself with the fury—knowing suddenly, that it was the screaming, roaring war-cry of the Cheyenne. A battle cry had risen from her bones and joints, from somewhere deep in her belly, from somewhere deep in the depths of her lungs. She flung a grin at the rider next to her, a boy about her age who was racing beside her on his own spotted pony; when she let loose with another wild shriek, he grinned back at her and let loose with a cry of his own.

Frankie gave herself to the game and Fox surged forward, sensing he had been released from his duty as caretaker; now, he swept into the game with a new power and a savage fury. He was taking his rider into battle with a different kind of ferocity, his head low, his ears flat, his hooves digging into the sandy soil as he charged across the grasses.

The arrow-held-high game moved fast and furious; it swept the players far beyond the bounds of her home valley. The riders zipped across the land of the Sand Hills, zig-zagging through the low-lying meadows, soaring over hilltops; they ripped along ridges and churned through the sand-filled blowouts; they twisted along the riverbanks and surged through the river waters.

Wherever the holder-of-the-arrow went, they all went. For Frankie it was a mix of playing tag, follow-the-leader, keep-away, and a horse-race—all rolled into one fiercely dangerous game. It was fast and fleet; wild and reckless. No one slowed; no one quit. And Frankie was in heaven.

Three times the game swept off the prairie and thundered down the path that twisted through the village, charging past the men and the women who stood and stepped back, watching and cheering the riders. Three times, they swept along the river, turned up the track to her home valley—they raced up and around and down into the meadow, yipping and yelping and shrieking. Charging and chasing. Reckless and dashing and daring. All for the sake of the arrow-held-high.

They stampeded past the on-lookers—showing-off their skills, showing-off their speed. Brash and bold and brazen. Riding as Cheyenne warriors. They were fiery and fierce; they were wild and proud. And they all had their eyes on the arrow.

Swept up in the swift torrent, Frankie was being forced to use everything she knew of horses and horsemanship; she was using her body and her strength, her muscles and her memory. She was using everything she learned in her early years from her grandmother; everything her father and uncle taught her; she was drawing from everything she learned from the Captain of the Cavalry, and her Major. And she realized, she was using every muscle and every movement Knife taught her—because what worked on the ground, worked from the back of a horse.

By the third trip down into the meadow, Frankie and the red-and-white pinto were moving together, battling together, relying on each other. Trusting each other. The warhorse understood her movements and her signals, and Frankie understood his; he understood her intent and her intent became his. They were weaving and swerving among the other horses and riders—bold and brave and balanced. She was focused on the arrow-held-high, and he was focused on getting her within reach. They moved as one, flowing together. Fighting together.

The Right Reverend Simeon Austin wasn't quite sure about what he was seeing. Right there before his eyes—just beyond Frankie Harding's apple trees—there was an entire Indian village. And for all the traveling he had done out here in the Nebraska Territory, out here in the territory of the Indians, he realized with some amazement that he had never seen an Indian village. Not an Indian village like this one. He had seen the homes of the Pawnee tribe—the massive long-houses of mud and branches and sticks near the Missouri River, long dark mounds that sat in settlements surrounded by their crops of corn and sorghum. But *this* village was different.

This was of the stories he had read and the tales he had heard; *this* was a village of the buffalo-hide dwellings—the famed and storied tipis of the nomadic warrior tribes. The cone-shaped dwellings were standing before his eyes, sturdy and strong, each adorned with a crown of tall, slender poles rising through the top of the stretched hides. Proud and majestic dwellings, all painted with bright and beautiful and bold designs.

This village before him, sitting on what had been a flat expanse of grass-covered land, was a wild and almost mystical piece of lore, looking as if it had risen right from the paintings of frontier explorers. This village and these people, Simeon Austin decided, belonged in the art of Albert Bierstadt. Here before him was a village of the wandering people that graced the paintings of George Catlin.

And in the moment, the Reverend Simeon Austin realized he had a whole host of emotions coursing through him—fear and excitement, wonder and concern, awe and astonishment. Betsy, sitting right beside him on the seat of their light farm-wagon, was staring at this unexpected vision, as astonished as he was with the sight of the unexpected village of unexpected people. She was clutching his arm, her eyes wide. Her face pale.

The Right Reverend Austin was also experiencing serious confusion; for a man who always knew exactly how to handle any matters at hand, he suddenly had no idea what he should do. He had no idea if there was reason to fear for his wife's safety, and for his own. Neither, was he sure if he should have concern for Frankie Harding— because there was no way to know what fate might have befallen her. This village had somehow sprung up on this broad meadow right on her homestead and Simeon Austin had no idea how it had happened.

He scanned the scene in front of him, trying to sort out the thoughts and emotions whirling through his mind and his chest. He was aware of his fears, but most of all, he was confused—because along with his fears, he was enthralled with the mystical apparition of the Indian tipis and the scene that seemed to float before his eyes. The people of this village were out there, moving among the cluster of conical lodges—walking and working, carrying and cooking. Young children were running and chasing, shouting and laughing.

Quite suddenly, all the activity stopped; suddenly, all the people of the village were standing and watching the wagon and the mule. They were staring at him and Betsy. Then they were calling and pointing and shouting.

A cluster of children, small children, appeared from among the tipis; they began approaching the wagon, crowding around a man—bouncing and trotting and hopping beside a man Simeon Austin recognized.

The Reverend stared at the man walking with the children, laughing with them as they tugged at his trousers and pulled on his hands. And quite suddenly, and quite surprisingly, the fear that had been in Simeon Austin's mind and heart were gone. The scene before him, the Reverend Austin decided, was not unlike the image of Jesus among the little children.

"There! Everett Dunbar. Look at him." The Reverend reached to pat his wife's hand, pointing to direct her attention to the man approaching them. Everett Dunbar was smiling, carrying an Indian child on each hip and surrounded by a bevy of bouncing youngsters. The children were smiling and laughing—and at their companion's urging—they were waving wildly to the newcomers in the mule-drawn wagon. And to the Reverend, it looked to be an enormous delight for every one of them.

Everett Dunbar stopped with his gaggle of giggling children beside the wagon-seat. He stood there among the children with a smile that was bigger than Simeon Austin had ever seen from him.

"Welcome, Reverend," Everett gave a polite nod. "Hello, Mrs. Austin. Would you like to meet some of my young friends?"

The Reverend Austin stared, realizing suddenly that Everett Dunbar was in his true element. Two children in his arms, seven clustered around him. Some still bouncing and giggling; some shy, hiding and peeking around Everett's pant-legs and waist. Some were working up the courage to touch the mule. Others were patting the

509

wagon wheels and calling out the same Indian word over and over, seeming to be quite happy with the newly-arrived wagon.

"Well, Mr. Dunbar, I would never refuse a chance to meet *any* of your friends. Might I assume our mutual friend, Frankie Harding, has a part in all of this wonderment?"

"Who else could bring such delight into our lives, Reverend?"

Simeon Austin burst out laughing at the obvious truth, delighting in the excitement and joy surrounding him. Betsy was laughing, almost giggling, as the children, some fully naked and others in various states of dress, put aside their shy ways and began climbing onto the wagon. Everett passed one of the children, a happily chirping little girl, right into Betsy's lap.

"We ought to head down to the meadow. And we probably ought to get there quick. Frankie's not there at the moment, but she'll be coming in soon. And there's going to be a whole lot of commotion coming with her." Everett had a funny look on his face as he made his suggestion and Simeon Austin didn't miss it. "It might be best to have both you and your wagon out of the way when things start popping."

As Everett put his hand to the mule's bridle and started leading the way to the meadow, the chattering little Indian girl on Betsy's lap suddenly became very serious. She called out to Everett in her language, demanding his attention. Everett, to the Reverend's surprise, knew exactly what she wanted—he turned and reached for her, catching her almost in mid-air as she leaped from Betsy's lap. And just as quick as Betsy's lap was empty, a bright-eyed, grinning little boy crawled up from behind the wagon-seat and settled himself onto her lap.

Betsy, fully beyond her initial astonishment, burst into delighted laughter as a second boy, a chubby-faced little boy, clambered onto the wagon-seat and wriggled down between them. Simeon Austin smiled down at him and the boy flashed a wide and happy grin at him, his black eyes sparkling.

As Everett led the mule up the track, the Reverend Simeon Austin turned and looked over his shoulder, greatly amused with the wagonload of bright-eyed, black-haired children of the prairie. And

510

as his nice little molly-mule pulled his nice little wagon around and down the track into Frankie's meadow, Simeon Austin had another surprise. Frankie Harding's quiet little valley wasn't quiet anymore.

It was a changed scene. An Indian lodge stood by the mill-pond. Indian women, working at the cookfire, stopped to watch the arrival of the wagon. Indian men, lounging in the shade, rose to their feet. Indian ponies grazing in the meadow—ponies of every color and size—raised their heads to eye the mule with its wagon-load of laughing and chattering children.

And there in the midst of a clutch of women near the fire, Simeon saw Ida Dunbar; she was waving to them, holding a ball of crochet thread in one of her hands. And as Betsy returned her wave, all the children in the wagon took it as an invitation to do the same—they began waving wildly to Ida. And the little girl in Everett's arms was swinging her arms and waving both her hands at everybody.

Once in the meadow, Everett insisted on moving the wagon far to the side of the meadow, close to the barn, before bringing the mule to a stop. Seeing their expressions of confusion, Everett gave Simeon Austin a reassuring nod as he gave Betsy a hand down from the wagon.

"You'll understand my reasoning in a bit, Reverend. But for now, I just want you out of the way."

Everett's bevy of beaming children clambered down from the wagon and clustered around him as they all walked toward the fire. Ida met them halfway, with the Indian women in their beaded deerskin-dresses walking along with her. Simeon watched the Indian women greeting his wife, offering shy and sweet smiles, giving soft touches and gentle pats to Betsy's shoulders.

The greeting party began moving Betsy toward the cookfire—and if ever there was a time his Betsy would be feeling standoffish, Simeon figured it would be now. But none of those kindly women were giving her an opportunity to hold back—she was being welcomed by them and coddled by them. And by the time she had been ushered over to one of the fireside logs, Betsy was smiling as sweetly as all the women around her.

And then—just as Simeon Austin and Everett reached the fireside—the world erupted. Blood-curdling shrieks and yells and whoops came from beyond the meadow's entrance. The sound of thundering hooves filled the air. An instant later, half-naked children and half-wild Indian-ponies pounded into the meadow. The ponies that had been grazing quietly in the meadow grass were suddenly dashing from the middle of the meadow, darting toward the valley's hillsides. Screeches and shrieks echoed through the valley.

As they swept into the meadow for what she thought was the sixth time, Frankie heard yips and yells coming from the crowd at the fireside. But the calls and the cheers were different this time. This time, everyone at the fire was calling for the arrow; they were shouting for a winner. This, she realized, would be the last sweep into the meadow—the game was coming to an end. Twice the arrow had changed hands during the running-battle and now, a new holder-of-the-arrow was racing toward the far side of the meadow, his prize held high above his head. The game was ending and Frankie knew her chance at the prize was fading. *No! Not yet!*

Her eyes locked on the arrow, locked on the prize that had eluded her. It was tantalizingly close; it was teasing her, tormenting her. Beckoning to her. She wanted the arrow; she wanted the win. All she had to do was snatch it before it was lowered.

Halfway down the meadow, she saw her chance—there was a sudden opening as the riders began reining their mounts, swerving and slowing as the pasture-fence loomed. Frankie lay low, pressing tight against Fox's withers, grabbing his mane halfway up his neck. She leaned, ducking away from the last grabbing hands of her closest foes. Fox dodged between the careening horses and Frankie felt him surging beneath her. He saw what she saw; he wanted what she wanted.

They were both watching the arrow; they both were sizing things up. Frankie knew what Fox knew; they could both see the fence-line looming, the closed gate to the center track right in front of them. She knew Fox could get her to the holder-of-the-arrow—he could get her close enough to snatch the prize. But the fence would be too close; there would be no time to stop.

Frankie eyed the distance to the leader's horse, gauging the distance from her hand to the hand that held the arrow. She felt Fox's muscles tighten against her thighs; she saw his head lower and stretch forward. He dodged another horse. He changed leads. One of his ears flicked back and Frankie knew he was waiting for her decision. There was still room to stop, but in two more strides, there'd be no turning back. Frankie saw his ear flick again—he needed her to make the call. She did.

She yelled her answer. She gave her war-cry; she leaned forward and leaned out, far to the side. Leaning further than she knew she should. Reaching. Daring the earth and gravity to take her. Her eyes locked on the arrow; her eyes on the prize. Her warhorse swerved, lowered his shoulder; leaned under her and shifted, then lifted to bring her upright in the instant of her reach. She snatched. She felt the arrow-shaft slap into her palm.

"Na-a'eno!" She shouted, yelling high into the skies. *"It's mine!"* Clutching the prize.

She felt Fox's shoulders lifting; she felt his hindquarters driving. He was leaving the ground and Frankie was righting herself, crouching forward onto his withers. Shifting her weight, helping her horse.

They were into the jump. Into the air. Over the gate. Reaching for the earth. Landing. Fox galloped down the center track. Slowing to an easy lope.

Frankie felt his muscles soften; she felt his legs find their stride. She straightened on his back; she squared her shoulders. Her arm still raised to the sky, the arrow still held high.

Far behind her, Frankie could hear the calls and yells echoing through the valley, bouncing off the hillsides. The men were sending their whoops and yips across the meadow; the women were singing their high-pitched li-li-li-li's. The other riders were circling their sweating ponies on the meadow side of the fence; they were cheering and adding their own shrieks and whoops to the uproar.

Frankie slowed Fox, circled him, and headed back along the pasture track. Back toward the meadow and the other riders. As they approached the gate, she set Fox's pace and strides. She leaned, gripped with her thighs and knees, lifted the rein. Fox took the jump. Smooth and collected. Floating over the gate. His head was up; his ears were up. And the arrow was up.

Fox carried her through the cluster of horses and riders; he trotted, stepping high and tossing his head, whipping his tail. Their former foes were laughing and hollering; reaching to tap her shoulders and her arms. Acknowledging her win. Dandelion was there on her flea-bitten gray, smiling, her dark eyes snapping with excitement. More taps on her shoulders. More grins and shouts. The yips and yells continued; Indian ponies danced and spun.

And Fox was prancing. Spinning and dancing. Frankie understood what he was doing. He was strutting—the warhorse had won the battle and he knew it. So Frankie let him strut; she let him cavort, arching his neck, tossing his head. Gradually, she guided him toward the man who had separated from the crowd of onlookers—the man who was walking toward her. Her brother who had loaned her his horse.

There was an easy smile on Strong Hand's face. His eyes were on her and Frankie could see his pleasure and his pride. When he stopped at Fox's head, he stroked his horse's cheek, ran his hand along his sweat-dripping neck. He then put his hand to her leg, squeezed her thigh. He held her eye; nodded at her.

"Na-htataneme." 'My brother'. Frankie returned his nod. Met his eyes. She held her arm out, holding the arrow out to him. For him. "He-kóne Mósėstotse. Na-htataneme." She said his name, called him her brother again, and placed the arrow in his hand. She gave him the prize; she thanked him. Her eyes were smiling and so were his.

The shouting had quieted; the people had given her time with her brother. But now, there was a shout. Then several more. Somewhere behind her, somewhere out in the meadow among the other riders, Frankie heard Dandelion calling to her. Calling for her to come with them. Then they were all calling for her.

"Ne-náestse, Ho-esta Hesta Ka-ėškóne! Vese-tano, Semahe!" 'Come, Fire Heart Child. Hurry, Sister.'

The other riders—the warrior-children—were calling for her to go to the river with them. They wanted to swim, to cool off. To cool the horses. They were calling to her.

Frankie grinned and glanced toward the fire. She saw Knife watching her, standing near the fire. She saw Ida waving. Everett was there with Little Mouse in his arms, and Little Mouse was busy waving both of her hands at anyone and everyone. And there was the Reverend Simeon Austin. He was standing there in his black frock-coat, grinning at her and laughing, tipping his head down to listen to what Everett was telling him. And Betsy Whitten Austin was there too. They were both watching her.

Frankie gasped at the sight—the Reverend Austin and Betsy were standing right there in her meadow. They had watched her riding on a whirling Cheyenne warhorse, half-wild and more than half-naked. And raising holy hell. She groaned, knowing there was no way to undo any of it. Knowing that all the ground that she had gained with them, might now be lost.

And suddenly, all she could think to do was smile; she grinned at them, giving them her crooked grin. Her happiest grin. Because right now, she didn't really care. She had ridden a warhorse into battle and her warhorse had carried her through the rolling Sand Hills and kept her safe. Together, they had done a wonderful thing; they had won the arrow.

The shouting from her wild-riding comrades came to her ears again. Frankie flung a look over her shoulder; her Cheyenne friends were waiting, laughing and calling to her while their horses were dancing and spinning—pulling at their bridles, dripping with sweat and eager to be off again. Frankie pictured the river; she pictured the kids and horses splashing in the water. The battle had been fought; the war was over. And now, the cool water of the river was waiting for them.

She was in a quandary, unsure of what to do. Wanting to ride to the river with her friends, but wanting to stay with Fox and Strong Hand. Strong Hand understood; he laughed and made the decision for her—he pushed Fox's head in the direction of the other horses. He nodded for her to go. Told her to go.

Frankie glanced at him, nodded. Obeyed. She leaned across Fox's withers, leaning in the direction of the Cheyenne kids as they raced out of the meadow, heading to the river. Beneath her, Frankie could feel Fox's hooves digging into the soil, tearing up the ground to catch up to the racing ponies.

It had taken a few minutes, but it had become clear to the Reverend Simeon Austin exactly why Everett Dunbar had been wearing the sly and devilish grin. A few minutes after Everett moved the wagon well away from the entrance, away from the middle of the meadow, it had all become abundantly clear. There had been a sudden uproar coming from beyond the valley, a cacophony of yells and screams, and the thunder of what Simeon Austin thought must be a thousand hooves. The yells and the shrieks grew in volume, coming closer, ever closer.

All hell broke loose as a hoarde of Indians and horses came ripping and roaring down the track and into the valley. Simeon Austin stared, stunned and astonished, watching the children on horseback. Indian children. Racing and screaming like demons.

It was a game, Everett explained, pulling him closer to the cookfire and farther away from the wild ride. Closer to the people clustered there, all of them watching the game. Men and women on their feet, laughing and shouting. Yipping and yelling. Cheering the game and the riders.

The horses and riders raced, swerving and careening around the meadow. Chasing and charging. Zigging and zagging. They circled and swirled, and then they swept up the track and out of the meadow. Gone again, as suddenly as they had appeared.

The howls of laughter and shouts from the crowd around the cookfire continued, and the Reverend—his initial shock and surprise gone—was laughing too. He was delighted with the furious flurry and the spectacular sight. It had been a rare and remarkable ride. Children of the Cheyenne. Wild and wonderful. And Frankie Harding had been right there in the midst of the charging riders.

Simeon Austin had seen her—she'd been right in the middle of the flurry and the fury of the mad dash, riding side-by-side with the Indian children. She had been in the middle of the game, in the midst of the madness. He had seen her face. Determined, fierce, focused. Laughing, light, full of glee. Free.

Twice more, over the next fifteen minutes, the riders charged into the valley, and twice more Simeon Austin watched the wild and glorious scene. And still, he was astonished at the reckless abandon, stunned at the amazing agility and the wondrous courage of these children of the prairie. The ponies were fleet and the children were fearless; they swept through the meadow, spinning and swirling like so many dust-devils. It was the rollicking joy of competition and camaraderie.

And Frankie Harding was riding among them. He watched her in the midst of play. Her maneuvers were quick and nimble and clever. She rode the red-and-white pinto with grace and balance and beauty. She swayed and reached and swerved, using her horse as an extension of her own body. A centaur in this century. And all the while, she was laughing, eyes flashing, jubilant with unbridled joy.

He watched a third incursion, hearing a Cheyenne man named He's Proud saying that it would be the final surge into the valley. It was a race down the center of the meadow, a last determined scramble for the arrow held aloft. The holder-of-the-arrow was in a mad and daring dash, approaching the meadow's far end at break-neck speed. Impossibly fast and impossible to catch. He would be victorious. No riders could catch the leader and take the arrow because the end of the meadow and the barrier of the fence-line were looming.

Then Simeon saw the red-and-white pinto swinging and swerving. Dodging. Darting and twisting. He saw Frankie leaning low, tip-

517

ping from the horse's side. Reaching beyond reason; defying the laws of gravity.

Simeon Austin gasped; he heard a collective groan from the cluster of people beside him. Because everyone—both Cheyenne and white—knew it was too late. They all knew that snatching the arrow now, in the final fleeting moment, meant there would be no time to recover. They all knew the girl on the red-pinto pony was increasing her speed when she should have been slowing; she was leaning forward, when she should be leaning back and pulling up.

And then, in a single instant, Frankie Harding's hand snatched at the arrow and the pinto leaped. The pinto launched into the air. Horse and rider rose, sailing over and across the rails of the fence. The arrow clutched in her hand—held high and pointing to the sky.

They landed, slowed and circled, and the Reverend Austin watched as Frankie loped the marvelous little pinto back toward the front meadow, her face shining with the glory of the game. Her crooked little grin lighting up her face. He saw her direct the pinto to the fence again, sending her sleek steed over the same gate—this time the jump was measured and steady and smooth. Graceful and proud. The captured arrow still in her hand, still pointing high to the prairie sky. The horse cavorted and pranced, arching and dancing.

The Reverend watched as Frankie sidled her horse toward the fire, moving to meet the warrior walking toward her. When she reached his side she leaned from the horse's back, handing the prize to the owner of the horse she rode. Placing the captured arrow in the warrior's hand.

Simeon watched the exchange. Knowing it was the mark of Frankie's honor. Humility. She gave the trophy to the man who had honored her with his steed. She nodded; he smiled. She leaned and sent the pinto to follow the other children, the other players. They charged out of the meadow and the warrior watched, standing there, holding the arrow in his hand.

The sun was setting and the moon was rising, as the Reverend Austin drove his mule along the north bank of the river following the Dunbars to their homestead. Ahead of him, he could see Betsy sitting on the Dunbars' wagon-seat with Everett and Ida; the three of them were talking and laughing, and he knew the conversation would be centered around the happenings in Frankie's meadow.

The plan was to spend the night at the Dunbar place and head home in the morning. And Simeon thought it was a good plan. It was a good thing for Ida and Betsy to have each other's company; they enjoyed each other. Always had. If they lived closer to each other, they'd likely visit daily. As it was, Simeon Austin liked to promote any chance for them to spend time together. And right now, he thought their time together was especially fortunate. Because there was much to discuss about the day.

In his own mind, the Reverend Austin had seen it as a wild and glorious day, a wondrous day. As to Betsy and her mindset, he wasn't so sure. There had been an appearance of acceptance on her part throughout the day; she had seemed amenable and open-minded—if more than a little astonished at times—to the activities through the afternoon and evening.

He knew his wife well enough to know that her gracious and accepting behavior throughout the day could have been nothing more than just that—gracious and accepting behavior. Whether that response was genuine or not, was still to be seen. Because Betsy had a well-honed ability to appear to adapt to an immediate circumstance; it was her later response that would matter.

If she did have any lingering problems or concerns about the day of astonishing affairs, they likely would be centered around Frankie's involvement. And if that were the situation, the Reverend feared that there could be repercussions for Frankie. Then there would be repercussions for him, because if it came down to it, he would be defending Frankie. Because he would defend her right to stay right where she was, on her own homestead, Betsy Whitten Austin's opinion notwithstanding.

Simeon Austin kept watching the three people on the wagon ahead of him, pleased so far, with what he was seeing—the conversation was light, the laughter was almost constant. It all boded well. *We have the discussion going on right now. We'll have the evening conversation at the Dunbars'. And then we'll have a night to sleep on it. Tomorrow will tell.*

As those thoughts turned around in his mind, he was also in his own light conversation with Frankie Harding. She and the young Cheyenne girl, Dandelion—as beautiful and unassuming as the yellow flower of the prairie—were riding their horses beside his wagon. She was still dressed in Indian garments, still wearing the breechcloth, and now she was wearing a marvelous buckskin shirt, dressed much like her riding companion.

But now, Frankie was back to being the young homestead girl he knew so well, quite different now from the wild child who had been riding so furiously, so fearlessly, in the reckless and rollicking game. She was there, riding sedately beside his wagon, quiet and calm, speaking to him, soft in voice and wise in thought. Speaking to him of her love of these friends of hers—these Cheyenne people. Telling him of their visit, of how they had traveled to her home, and of their coming journey which would take them to the land where they would spend the winter.

After the wild horseback game, he and Betsy had stayed by the fire, talking with the men and women, He and Betsy had tasted their first roasted buffalo meat and had eaten from bowls of steaming vegetable stew. And when the children returned from the river, calm and clean after their furious game, he had watched the families sitting by the fire. He had seen the gentle love, the great affection these people had for Frankie—there had been a quiet beauty there—gentle touches, laughter, tender caresses.

All the children there by the fire had been coddled and fed and fussed over. Hugged and held in laps. And Frankie had been there among the other children. The Cheyenne people called her Fire Heart Child, and they cherished her every bit as much as they cherished their own children. They coddled and nourished her. They held closely; they teased her gently.

The women mothered her. They wrapped her in furs against the evening chill; they braided her hair; they smiled, laughing.

Affectionately. Gently. And the men watched over her as well. Protective and alert. Seeing to her needs. They made sure she ate well and enough. And then, they fed her more. There was laughter at her antics, along with a sweet indulgence, along with the same loving smiles for her as for all their children.

Driving to the Dunbar homestead, Simeon Austin knew he had become fascinated by these people; he also realized that none of what he had seen throughout the day matched at all with what he heard from other white people. There had been kindness and laughter. There was fierceness and protectiveness. There was pride and duty. And there was harmony.

The two girls rode a little more than halfway to the Dunbar place, and then they turned their horses to head back to Frankie's meadow, with Frankie promising to visit him and Betsy at their home.

"Soon," she said, and she had called to the wagon ahead. "And maybe you can teach me to make your spiced donuts, Mrs. Austin."

The two girls turned back to the west and he had continued east, following the Dunbar wagon. A moment later, the Reverend saw Everett motioning to him, pointing to the crest of a hill. There on a hill, almost out of sight in the growing dusk, Simeon Austin could see a rider. A single Cheyenne warrior.

"A watcher," Everett called over his shoulder. He explained that the warrior would stay back and out of sight, but he would see the girls safely home.

Simeon Austin smiled at the sight, realizing there, once again, was yet another indication of how these people cherished the children they had stewardship over. There on the crest of the hill was another sign of how fiercely protective they were. Quietly protective. Fierce and gentle at the same time.

For the rest of the ride in the wagons, and for the greater part of the night, Simeon and Betsy listened to the stories of the other times the Cheyenne had visited Frankie's meadow. And they heard of the reason for *this* visit—the sickness. They listened as Ida told about the healing work Frankie had done, of the devoted care she had given these people. And the Dunbars spoke of the trust the Cheyenne people had in her skills.

He and Betsy listened as Everett and Ida spoke of the love they had found among these people. They heard about the children who shadowed Everett. And Ida told about the old woman, Wild Bird, who ruled over the men with her stick. There was a lot of laughter and joy as the Dunbars told their tales.

They talked about the strength of the love between Frankie Harding and these people; they talked of the women who cherished her and cared for her, and of the men who acted like uncles to her. And of the warriors who Frankie called her brothers—the men who watched over her, protected and guarded her—the men who had been watching over her long before she arrived at her homestead. And now, all the people of this band of Cheyenne watched over her. They visited her home. They fed her; they clothed her; they cherished her.

Ida smiled as she talked of the joy that came alive in Frankie when she was surrounded by the Cheyenne children. She spoke a long time about the bright excitement that always rose up in Frankie when the Cheyenne came. Ida described how Frankie played and thought and talked like a child of ten when she was among these people, and Simeon Austin could not disagree. Frankie, Ida believed, could actually be the child she really was while she was among the Cheyenne families. Because they allowed it and encouraged it.

To Simeon Austin's mind, Ida was right. He could see that Frankie's time among these people provided a necessary balance. Much of the time, the events in Frankie Harding's life required her to live and think like an adult, to respond and react with a high level of maturity. But during these weeks, Frankie had spent time as a child. These people had been able to reach a part of Frankie, that out of necessity, had been tamped down.

And to Simeon's surprise Betsy—his own Betsy, who could be so immoveable and so rigid—was agreeing, nodding as Ida spoke. She acknowledged that she had seen the same thing during the afternoon. She had been worried about Frankie, Betsy confessed, concerned about all the responsibilities and duties and obligations Frankie carried. The burdens she took in stride. And the hurt and the pain she had survived.

'This,' Betsy was saying, 'was such a good thing.' This, she said, was a part of life Frankie would have never found again, if not for the Cheyenne people. She hoped these people would stay longer because, she believed, Frankie needed them.

Simeon watched as his wife talked and he knew he was staring at her. He was also thinking that the Lord was certainly doing some fine work here. And a good amount of His works seemed to have a strong beginning in Frankie's meadow.

That night Simeon Austin slept deeply, dreaming of Frankie, dreaming of this wild-child, riding the red-and-white pony across the land. Dodging and weaving. Flying and floating over the prairie. Effortlessly. Laughing wildly. Free from pain. All the hurt and all the wounds washed from her spirit. Healing. Strong.

In the dream, she rode the horse past him. Racing past him. Watching him. Looking into his eyes. Knowing him; knowing all that was in him. She would bring him gifts, she said; she would point his path. Then her arm outstretched. She *was* pointing—pointing ahead, as if, showing him the way. Watching his eyes. Expectant. Grinning. Because, she said, she knew his pride and she knew his path.

'You will travel,' she said. She shouted it, laughing and nodding, riding on the back of the painted pony. Proud. Excited. Reining the pony, swerving, racing away. Easily. Swiftly. '*This* is your dream,' she called out. 'This is *your* dream.'

He woke. He was laughing when he woke from his dream. Thinking of the young girl racing across the prairie. Free of pain. *That* would be his prayer for Frankie Harding. He offered the prayer then, asking for that.

'Release her from pain, My Lord. Release her body and spirit from any bonds. From any limitations. Give her strength.' He paused in his prayer. "And give me strength, O Lord, to always pray and to offer praise to you.'

He lay there then, lying in the dark of the night-world as the silver-blue light of the moon drifted through the glass pane of the window. There within the earthen wall of the Dunbars' home. There within the earthen home. There within the night. There among the grasses that rippled along the slopes of the Sand Hills.

Frankie sat on the top of her Lookout Hill watching through the lens of the telescope, searching the sunlit hilltops and the blue-shadowed slopes of the Sand Hills, wanting one last look. *One last sighting, please God.*

Aching now, deep in her heart; knowing she had seen the last of them. They had disappeared into the grasses of the prairie, into the curves and the hillsides of the prairie. Into the Sand Hills. *They're gone.*

She had ridden beside her Cheyenne people when they left early that morning, headed to the northwest, leaving to go to the lands where they would spend the winter. They were gone out of her life now. She kept scanning the lands to the northwest. *No movement. No line of horses and riders.*

The celebration dances had stopped late in the night—the dances had gone long into the night—celebrating the return to health, the return of the buffalo, the success of the hunt. All that was over now.

Frankie had worn the beautiful antelope-leather dress Willow had given her after the first buffalo hunt; she had danced in her dress beside the women in the flickering and flashing light of the great fire, dancing in the dress that had been made by the hands of the Indian women. The soft and supple leather had swirled and swayed on her body, the fringe had flipped and flowed with the movements of the dance.

The women led her, taught her—Whirlwind and Willow took her hands and stepped her into the circle. They taught her the 'step, toe-step, step' of the dance, so her feet could move to the rhythm of the drums, to their beat and their hum, to their throb and their pulse and their pound. The sound of the drums had moved her feet, luring her feet into the rhythm of the dance.

There in the dark of night, in the flash and flare of the flames of the fire, she had celebrated with the Cheyenne people. They had celebrated with her; they taught their dances to their Fire Heart Child.

Now, sitting on the hilltop, with the warmth of the sun on her back and the warmth of her horse's sides against her legs, Frankie was recalling the beat and the rhythm of the drums; once again, she was feeling the sway and the movement of the Nemá'ó-homó'ėhestótse, the Round Dance.

The earth had moved last night as the women did the Round Dance; the whole world had been spinning and turning and throbbing. The land of the Sand Hills had been shaking with the dance, the grasses and the soils had shifted and swayed with the power of the circle.

Frankie had been shifting and swaying with the circle of dancers. She had become the circle of dancers. She had become the prairie itself—merging and blending with the rhythm of the songs and the beat of the drums, floating with the breeze and flowing with the breath of the prairie air.

She danced with Dandelion and the other girls. And she danced with the women. She wore the swaying-soft dress and the beautifully-beaded moccasins the women had made; she wore the feathers the women put in her hair; she wore the strips of otter-fur around her braids. She danced with the bracelets they fastened to her wrists and the cuffs they tied to her ankles—the cuffs with metal cones that jingled and rang like sweet bells in the night.

The men of the Cheyenne had watched. Strong Hand watched, smiling and proud. Knife danced beside her in one of the dances. Step-stepping beside her. Foot-then-toe, foot-then-toe. Moving beside her, teaching her the soft steps. Foot-then-toe, foot-then-toe. His hand resting on her shoulder, guiding her, traveling with her. Taking her through the dance. His pride; her pride. She had looked to his eyes and he had smiled, knowing her heart. Brother and sister. Smiling. Dancing together while the people of the Cheyenne watched.

The night had deepened, the drums had played and the sky and stars had descended. Surrounding them; cloaking them; joining them. Frankie sat between Strong Hand and Knife—between her brothers—listening to the drums, hearing the chants. Feeling the sounds and the songs rising up from the earth, floating up from the soils of the Sand Hills.

As the night deepened, the darkness wrapped around her; the sounds had softened, the sights had blurred. The dancers seemed to be slowing, floating and drifting away. She was swaying. Her eyes heavy, her vision fading.

There had been a different movement then. A slow shift. A lift. Drifting in the cool of the night. She felt the warmth of a warrior's arms. Strong Hand's arms. The firelight had faded; the throb and the thrum of the drum was gone. She closed her eyes again. Feeling the night air. Floating through the night air.

There had been a new rhythm then; a cadence of step and stride. Moving through the night. Arms warm around her; skin warm against her cheek; breath warm on her forehead. Soft Cheyenne words to her ears. Softly spoken, softly murmured, softly whispered in the night. Strong arms, gentle arms. Holding her, wrapping her. Taking her home.

Then, the quiet and the warmth; the soft swirl and deep curl of the hair of the buffalo-hide. Safety and sleep. Soft touch and gentle grasp. Hands holding. Sisters. Sleep. Quiet and deep.

This morning, when she had awakened, lying warm beside Dandelion under the heavy folds of the buffalo-robe, the smell of the smoke and the scent of the buffalo had been strong in her nostrils. All of it familiar, all of it normal. All of it comfort.

Frankie remembered emerging from beneath the heavy warmth of the hide, into the daylight and into the day. And she remembered how her world had begun to change. Because the families were preparing to travel.

She and Dandelion had gone into the water of the windmill pool and when they came out, Willow and Whirlwind settled them on the buffalo-hide. There by the fire, cloaked by its warmth, they had combed and braided their hair. And Frankie had suddenly realized it was the last time; it was a last moment that would become a last sweet memory. Because her Cheyenne family was leaving.

She had walked among the ponies and the packs and the piles, wearing her breechcloth and the new shirt Whirlwind had put over her head—a shirt that her Cheyenne mother had made for her—a soft-tanned buckskin shirt, dyed the color of the autumn leaves with rows of pretty stitches and a yoke of brown and blue and white beads.

The women loaded the packhorses and the travois, happy and laughing. Excited. Chattering about the journey ahead of them. Talking about the path that would lead them to their friends and relatives waiting for them in other campgrounds. But none of their laughter and chatter had made Frankie happy.

She hadn't been laughing about their journey and their path. Because her heart had been breaking again; the deep pain was rising up from deep in her chest. As she walked among the women, they patted her on her back; they smiled at her; they spoke sweet and warm words to her. They tried to help her smile. But it didn't help. Not at all.

Little Mouse had been following Wild Bird as she went to find the eggs. She then followed the old woman into the barn, going to find the creature called Blossom, the creature the color of a fawn. And when they emerged through the doors of the barn, Little Mouse danced and pranced along beside her great grandmother, peering into the bucket of milk the old woman carried.

Frankie had taken the pail from old Wild Bird and carried it to the stone-room and poured it out in the pans to separate. Then she roamed into the kitchen, trying to do the normal things, the home-stead things—talking to Matilda, opening the windows in the kitchen and her bedroom. She started a fire in the stove, poured water into the coffeepot, ground up some coffee-beans. Started coffee brewing. Trying to keep her mind on the simple things, the daily things, so she wouldn't think about the loss that was coming. Because there *would* be loss. Because the Cheyenne—her Cheyenne—were leaving.

The Cheyenne had come with sickness and they were leaving with health—the aching joints, the pain, the bleeding, the red-purple sores, the limp muscles, the loose bowels and unrelenting fatigue. All the sickness was gone now.

And there was another happiness for the Cheyenne people—there was new meat from the hunt. There had been buffalo and a hunt that they hadn't counted on, so there was meat for their journey, and meat to add to their winter stores. The Cheyenne people were happy. For the Cheyenne it was a time to celebrate. For Frankie, it was a time to grieve.

When she worked up the courage to emerge once again from the house, she had followed Dandelion's bidding, riding with her out to the lodges by the river. And once there, she watched as the village came down faster than it had gone up. The women had been moving fast. The proud and beautiful lodges were gone; the lodgepoles had been repurposed for the travois; the lodge-hides were bundled and loaded and ready for the journey.

And then, quite suddenly, the entire village and the Cheyenne people—her people, her family—had begun their journey. They trailed away to the northwest; they would follow the path of the pretty North Loup River upstream for several days. Then they would turn north-by-northwest; they would head across the land, going to the Mo'óhtá-vo'honáaeva, to the black-rocky place, to meet up with Gray Fox's band.

Frankie had ridden along with the families, riding bareback on Boone, riding beside Dandelion and Willow. The women were still talking about the journey and the relatives they would see and all Frankie could do was trail along with them, trying to hide her sadness, trying not to pout—because it wasn't the Cheyenne way.

Far ahead of the families, she could see Strong Hand, He's Proud, and Blue Feather riding with other warriors. And she had seen one warrior turn his horse around—a warrior riding a black-and-white pinto—had been riding back toward the main band of travelers. Knife.

She had watched him and Magpie, coming closer, his eyes on her. As he rode by her, he motioned for her to follow. She had turned Boone and followed him back downriver, riding past the long line of families. As she passed by the men and the women and the children, they reached out to her, touching her arms and patting her legs as they passed. Speaking words of the Cheyenne tongue, words that spoke of love and of pride. Of friendship. Of staying warm during the cold times. They said sweet words to her and they called to her. Na-semahe. Nå-htona. Ho-esta Hesta Ka-ĕškóne. Sister. Daughter. Fire Heart Child.

She had followed Knife because he told her to, because he was her brother and she wouldn't argue with him. She had tried to smile; she tried to hold the tears inside. And once they were past the line of travelers, he beckoned for her to move up beside him.

He had spoken to her then, speaking of his love for his sister, telling her to remember what he had taught her. Telling her to be safe at her home. Then she remembered her gift for him, and she had reached into her pocket for the pearl-handled penknife; a penknife from Sutlers Store at the fort; a penknife just like the one her Captain had given to her.

She put it in the hand of her brother. He held the penknife and studied it; he opened and closed the blade and smiled at her. He touched her shoulder. Nodded. Then he turned Magpie and lifted into a lope to catch up to the line of horses. Leaving her sitting there on Boone.

Frankie had stayed there, watching as Knife swung his black-and-white pony to the side of the line of horses and riders and loped beyond them, riding to catch up to Strong Hand and the other warriors out in the lead. Then, she had turned Boone and continued downstream.

So now, the Cheyenne were gone and Frankie sat there on the high hilltop, feeling the prairie sun beating down on her back, feeling the emptiness and the loss. She scanned the land before her, staring out across the rolling land of the Sand Hills, looking for one last sighting. Watching to the northwest. But she could see no sign of them. *Nothing. They're gone.*

They were already well on their way, following a path of their choosing, a path that would take them to their new home. Frankie eyed the ocean of grasses before her, the rippling waves of the hills that reached to the horizon. Staring across the vast land before her. There was no indication that a band of more than a hundred Cheyenne had just traveled across the hills. There was no trail; no road. They had disappeared into the land; they had gone back to the prairie.

Frankie knew their destination. They were traveling to the Mo'óhtá-vo'honáaeva. The Black Hills. The dark-rocky mountains that Strong Hand and He's Proud told her about; the sheltered land that Whirlwind and Willow had been talking about. There, the Cheyenne would spend the winter, deep in the black-rocky hills with the Oglála; they would find the camp of Gray Fox and stay with his people, wintering within the protected valleys of the Black Hills.

She spoke the words, saying the syllables carefully, with due reverence. Because He's Proud had told her it was a sacred place. The Black Hills. A place of spirits and ancestors. Mo'óhtá-vo'honáaeva, the Cheyenne words. Pahá Sápa, the Oglála words. Two peoples; two names. Same place.

She had sent her Cheyenne with gifts. She had given Knife the pearl-handled penknife. She had given the men some of the twists of tobacco she had brought from Fort Kearny. She had given the girls colored ribbons for their braids. To Dandelion, she had given the china teacup—the one her sister had asked Ida to show her again and again, while she was peering into the kitchen doorway. She had given Willow an ivory hair comb—one of the two her Aunt Sarah had in the little wicker hamper.

The Dunbars had left the day before the dancing, heading to their home to catch up with their work after the days spent among the Cheyenne. And the Reverend Austin and Betsy had gone with them. So now, there would be emptiness in her meadow. And in her life.

Frankie had known she would feel the loss. And she knew she would grieve for the loss of yet another family. And she knew when she was done grieving, she would move on with her life. The winter would come, and then the spring. And with the spring, would come the greening of the grasses. And maybe, her Cheyenne family would return. Maybe, sometime, they would come again to hunt the buffalo.

She took one last look to the northwest. Saw nothing. She turned Boone down the hillside, reining him toward the river and toward her meadow's entrance. She rode up the track, over and around. Matilda was there; she came trotting up the track to meet her person, her white-tipped tail wagging happily.

Frankie grinned at her and the tawny collie-dog grinned her toothy dog-grin right back. Boone followed the track, trailing down into her home valley. And as she rode into her quiet little meadow Frankie brought Boone to a sudden stop. She sat there on his back, staring. Astonished with what was there before her.

Wild Bird's lodge was still beside the windmill pond. The old Cheyenne woman was there beside the cookfire, using her stick to stir the ashes. She looked up from her work; she smiled at Frankie, calling to her, beckoning. Telling Ho-esta Hesta Ka-ėškóne to come and get food from the pot. There was buffalo meat, she said.

Frankie kept staring. The woman called to her again, beckoned again. Frankie turned Boone toward the fire, thinking back over the morning. Because when she had left the meadow to go out to the village with Dandelion, she thought the women were taking down Wild Bird's lodge. She had been wrong. *Because Wild Bird's here. She's staying.*

"Come!" The old woman called to her, laughing at her, understanding her surprise. She was pointing toward a stack of packets and hides by her lodge door. "There! See your gifts, Fire Heart Child."

Frankie slid down from Boone's back and went to Wild Bird. She knelt down by the stacked goods, touched her fingertips to a folded piece of leather. Soft leather. Brain-tanned leather. Wild Bird's hand was on her shoulder and patting her back, telling her to look.

So Frankie looked, lifted the folded leather. It was a dress—one of yellow-tan buckskin with a yoke beaded in blue and white; and, there were leggings that fastened at the knee and moccasins too. All the same yellow-tan color. All heavier leather than her antelope dress.

"Deerskin," Wild Bird said, "to keep you warm in the cold months."

Frankie ran her fingers over each item, feeling the soft-tanned leather, marveling at the beadwork. She spotted a cluster of arrows leaning against the lodge wall—a dozen or more—each one different. Each with its own paint and colors and pattern. *Arrows. Different arrows from different warriors.*

There was a knife in a beaded rawhide sheath. A necklace of buffalo-teeth. Mittens of marten-fur. There were rawhide cases of pemmican and jerky. There were two buffalo-robes. And there was a blanket made of elk-hide—tanned soft and supple and painted on the skin-side with pretty-colored horses running in a wild race, circling around the edge of the hide, spiraling their way into the hide's center.

"To keep you warm during the time of the cold moons, Granddaughter." She felt Wild Bird's hand on her shoulder again. The old Cheyenne woman had an odd smile on her wrinkled old face. It was a smile that looked a bit expectant, as if she was waiting for something. *Probably, waiting for me to finish going through this pile of gifts. Waiting for what I say.*

But it wasn't that. Frankie discovered exactly what it was a few minutes later, after she arranged the gifts into neat and smaller piles so she could carry them to her house. It was when she stood up and smiled at Wild Bird, and then followed the old woman's eyes. Looking across the meadow over to the house. To a spot right in front of the kitchen porch.

Frankie knew she must be wearing her own odd look, because Wild Bird broke into her cackling laughter. Because there, tied to a porch post, stood a red-and-white pinto. Frankie found it impossible to move her feet; impossible to move at all. All she could do was stare. The pinto's head was turned, looking right back at her. As if he was waiting for her. *Ma'ô-hóohe! Fox!*

Strong Hand had found his way to thank her. He had brought his daughter and his mother to her and asked her to heal them. Just as she had healed her Lieutenant from the snake bite; just as she had healed the horse of Gray Fox's father. Now, his gift to her was standing beside her door.

Fox was his great pride. His warhorse. The horse he trusted to carry him into battle. He had put her on his prized warhorse for the children's game, and now, he was gifting the same horse to her. Frankie crumbled to the ground looking at the war-pony, understanding the generosity and the magnitude of the gift.

Wild Bird sat down beside her, holding her. Rocking her in her arms. Speaking to her of Strong Hand's love for her, speaking of his pride in her. Speaking of his need to protect Fire Heart Child who had become his own sister.

"Fox," Wild Bird said, "will protect you when Strong Hand cannot be with you. This is what Strong Hand wants." Then the old woman spoke to Frankie of her own love for her, for her white granddaughter.

"I will stay with you," she said. "I will stay with you for the time of the hard moons. To teach you more of the Cheyenne ways. And of the ways of the old ones."

She said they would live in the meadow together and she would teach her about the animals and the birds and the plants of the land around them. And about the people who traveled these lands. She would stay with Fire Heart Child who had cared for Whirlwind and Little Mouse. That, she said, would be her gift.

Frankie stood up, wiped at her tears; she walked across the meadow grass to greet her Cheyenne warhorse, the red-and-white pinto that carried her to win the arrow-held-high.

And late in the day, after she and Wild Bird gathered eggs in the evening and after they had milked Blossom—just as twilight came on—Frankie rode Fox out to the Lookout Hill. She lifted him into his strong and steady lope, letting him surge up the hillside, feeling the powerful stride of a warhorse that would carry his rider to safety, feeling the strong and steady lope that he could maintain for hours.

He was her warhorse. Her protector. A horse that would not leave her behind as long as she was alive. Strong Hand had honored her; this red-and-white Indian warhorse was a fine gift. The finest he could give.

She sat on Fox's back there on the crest of the hill, looking to the northwest again, knowing her Cheyenne family was long-gone. The people of the Cheyenne band who had come to visit her, the people who had come to stay with her at her homestead, were well on their way to the Black Hills now. Traveling to the black-rocky place.

And now, sitting there on the hilltop in what her father would have referred to as being 'in the gloaming', she knew her Cheyenne people would come back; they would return after the winter months, sometime in the early spring. They would come for Wild Bird, so she could travel with them again during the warm and easy days. And they would come to see their little-white-girl, because she was their family too.

Frankie was sitting on the milking stool in the dim morning light in the barn when she felt a sharp rap on the back of her head. It didn't hurt very much, but it certainly wasn't something she had expected to happen while she was milking a cow. Before she could lift her head away from Blossom's flank, she got another rap—a sharper one that smacked against her ear.

She spun around on the milking-stool, throwing a quick look over her right shoulder and got a third smack. This one whacked her left shoulder and it was considerably harder than the others. She saw Wild Bird standing behind her, glaring at her.

"Ta-náestse! Énanótse!" 'Go away! Let go of it!' The old Cheyenne woman's voice was sharp and she swung her knobby stick at Frankie again. Another blow, a sharper blow, connected with the back of Frankie's head. "Ta-náestse!"

Frankie yelped and twisted around on the stool, ducking to the right.

"Ne-ve'nėheševe!" 'Don't do that!' She saw the stick swinging again and tried ducking again. Too late again. She caught another rap on her shoulder. *Dammit!*

She tried blocking the next swing and caught the blow on her forearm. *Dammit! Dammit!*

As Wild Bird leveled her stick again, Frankie tipped herself backwards off the milking-stool, feeling no shame in diving to avoid the next smack. She scrambled to the side, crawling and scrabbling like a crab.

"Ne-tonéševe?" 'What are you doing?' Frankie was still scrambling, yelling at the old woman, watching the movement of the swinging stick, angry over the hits that had already landed.

Wild Bird jabbed the stick at her, then swung it to point at the cow. She then raised it again like she was fully intending to bang the brains out of the little-white-girl's head. Frankie kept scrambling backwards, shocked and indignant.

From the corner of her eye, Frankie could see Blossom watching the whole scene from her stanchion—curious, but not particularly concerned. Primrose, though, was apparently pleased with a little early morning excitement—she was busy bouncing and bucking and kicking her way around the milking-pen.

And Frankie was busy trying to time things so she could get to her feet and manage a quick retreat. She was halfway to standing when Wild Bird jabbed the stick again, telling her for the fifth time, to leave the cow and the stool and the pail alone. Frankie shouted at the old woman, telling her she could have them for all *she* cared. And that was when she made a serious mistake—she reached out and grabbed the end of Wild Bird's stick.

Just like that. Without thinking. And suddenly, Frankie found herself looking straight into Wild Bird's cloudy old eyes—eyes that looked every bit as surprised and shocked as Frankie was feeling.

And in that moment, Frankie's mind started racing as she tried to assess what had just happened. She hadn't even planned on *touching* the old woman's stick, and now, quite suddenly, she was *holding* onto it. A wave of nausea swept through her gut; she came to the sudden realization that no amount of talking was going to get her out of this. Because it was a serious dilemma.

The idea of maintaining her grasp on the stick was terrifying enough—but the idea of letting go of the stick was far worse. She knew she had just done something akin to lunacy among the Cheyenne people. She had just grabbed Wild Bird's stick, and she was pretty sure that no one in the entire Cheyenne Nation would dare to do that. Not even Strong Hand, himself—the leader of the band—would consider grabbing his grandmother's stick if she decided to swing it his way.

Considering Wild Bird's age, Frankie was pretty sure she could outrun the old woman. *Because she's probably two hundred years old. Or maybe, even older.* So for the moment, she thought her best bet might be to simply let go of the stick and start running. *Probably.*

Except that escaping the current situation wasn't all there was to it. Because there would be the aftermath to deal with. Because Wild Bird would see this as deliberate insolence and it was unlikely she would simply forget the little-white-girl's disrespect.

And that, Frankie knew, meant she would have to give the old Cheyenne woman a wide berth for some time to come. Because the Cheyenne stick could still rise up and come down again. *And probably when I least expect it.* She realized there was no telling exactly how long she'd need to be watching her back. *Weeks, maybe. Or months, even.*

In the moment, Frankie could only see two options—paying the price and taking the pain of punishment now, or enduring the shame of running like a scared rabbit and living with the lingering dread of that wicked stick coming down on her at any given moment. It was then Frankie realized the wisest and bravest thing would be to face the consequences right now; the most noble course was *not* to run.

But in the exact instant, when she saw Wild Bird's eyebrows shift from the raised position of 'surprise' to the narrowed position of 'now-you've-done-it', Frankie realized that she didn't feel like being wise and brave; she didn't want to be noble—she wanted to run. So she did.

She dropped her hold on the stick; she scrambled to her feet, darted through the milking-pen gate. She made a wild dash for freedom and safety, running toward the barn door, racing like a greyhound and leaving Laughing Girl in her dust. Behind her, she could hear Wild Bird's voice calling out, saying something about the cow and the barn and the stick, but Frankie had no interest in slowing down to listen and translate.

Once outside, she gulped in the fresh air of the meadow as her legs churned through the grass. She was feeling a little surprised at her speed, until she suddenly realized she wasn't just a ten-year-old anymore. She was eleven. Her birthday had come and gone. *Hah! I'm running on the legs of an eleven-year-old, now.*

Frankie said a quick prayer of gratitude and kept running, managing to throw a quick glance over her shoulder. Fully expecting to see Wild Bird coming after her. *Nothing! Not yet!*

She reached the house and leaped onto the porch, thanking God-and-the-angels-above for the extra speed that came with being eleven years old. She launched across the wood floor in a single bound, ducked through the kitchen door and slammed it shut just after Matilda squeezed in. Collapsing to the floor, she leaned back against the door, pressing against it and listening for any sounds that meant Wild Bird was racing after her. She listened.

"Nothing!"

She listened for another moment. No sounds of a chase. No Cheyenne words being shouted and coming closer. No sound of moccasins on the porch-floor.

"Nothing!"

She grinned, still impressed with her newly acquired speed. She thought back. *Yes! On the day Knife taught me to fight.* That *was my birthday!*

Frankie was thinking about her birthday and still grinning about having the legs of an eleven-year-old, as she stood to peek out the kitchen window. Watching for any sign of the old Cheyenne woman. Thinking about all the hours of training that Knife had spent teaching her to protect herself, and realizing it hadn't done her *one speck* of good. None of it could be used against this old woman who wielded the wicked stick. *All that work for nothing. Dammit!*

She shook her head in dismay and kept watch. Waiting. She felt safe enough in the house—Wild Bird had never even approached the house. In fact, none of the Cheyenne had shown any desire to set foot in the house. Whirlwind and Little Mouse had been in the Barracks, but only while they were at their sickest. After that, they never again went inside. So she was pretty sure Wild Bird wouldn't come in the house after her. *Probably not.*

Frankie stayed by the window, still peeking out through the lace curtain, looking toward the barn. And then toward the tipi. Then toward the barn again. Biting her lip. Considering things. Deciding there was a possibility that Wild Bird might decide to enter the house after all—because the old woman who had shunned all the buildings at first, seemed to have no problem going into the barn and the chicken-house, now. Once she decided she had good enough reasons to enter those buildings—the reasons being the milk-and-butter and the eggs—she no longer hesitated.

So. It was entirely possible that the chance to whack a disobedient little-white-girl on the head might be a good enough reason to enter *this* building. *Maybe while I'm cooking at the stove and not watching. Or maybe, while I'm sleeping.*

Frankie decided to stay in the house. *At least for the time being.* She spent some time arranging her newest arrows from the Cheyenne warriors on the wall above the sitting-room mantle, grinning as she recalled what her warriors had told her when she had shown them the arrows she had found.

'Ho'néhetane,' they had said.

'Pawnee,' He's Proud had explained.

'They are all Pawnee arrows,' the Cheyenne warriors told her.

They pointed to the painting and design of the arrow she had pulled from the hindquarters of the dead mule. Strong Hand said the arrow belonged to Black Turtle, who was a loud and crazy Pawnee.

'Black Turtle,' Strong Hand said, 'lives his life like a squirming worm. He lives in the mud-and-stick tunnel-houses of his people along the great muddy river to the east.

'The É'ometāā'e,' he called it.

'The Missouri River,' He's Proud explained.

And when Knife declared that managing to shoot a mule in the butt was probably the best shot Black Turtle had ever made, all the warriors had erupted into laughter.

After that, there had been many more stories and there had been a lot of nasty Cheyenne words that the men used as they spoke about the Pawnee. That had made Frankie grin—she had started practicing the new and choice words right then, tucking them away in her memory. Wanting to be sure to have them on reserve, ready and waiting for whenever the right moments and circumstance presented. Because, she decided, it could be a very handy thing.

Thinking about it now, Frankie decided she had learned at least as many colorful and handy words in that single conversation, as she had learned while she had been at the fort. Even more than she had learned on that one day while she had been hiding in the stable-loft, listening to the troopers talking about Colonel White.

While she lined up her new arrows and fastened them to the sitting-room wall, eight to each side of the pretty-colored map in its gold-scroll frame, she practiced her new Cheyenne swearwords— working on her speed and delivery—and trying to train her lip to lift-and-curl in a snarl. Trying to mimic the expression on Knife's face as he spat out the words. It was, she recalled, an especially nasty snarl that seemed to show up whenever he was talking about the Pawnee in general, and Black Turtle in particular.

Once she had positioned the arrows to her liking and spent time practicing her Cheyenne swearwords, she went back to the window and scanned the meadow again. She studied the Cheyenne lodge tucked away in its spot by the cookfire, wondering where the old woman had gone. She could see no sign of Wild Bird, but she could see the milk-pail, full almost to the brim, sitting out in the meadow grass about halfway between the barn and the house.

It was sitting right where Wild Bird always put it whenever she milked Blossom, leaving it there so her little-white-granddaughter could take it into the white-man's lodge. The pail looked innocent enough, sitting there in the meadow grass—just like always. *But today, it might just be part of a trick. It might just be a ploy to get the little-white-girl out in the open.*

Frankie kept her eyes moving around the meadow; it all looked quiet and safe but she figured it could still be a trick. *Quite possibly.* Because Wild Bird had lived plenty of years and had plenty of time to have a sizeable assortment of sneaky tricks up her buckskin-sleeves. *Yeah. It might be a trap. The pail might just be bait.*

But she could see no sign of the woman sneaking around the meadow, and there wasn't really any hiding place close to the pail. Unless, Wild Bird was hiding behind the far wall of the stone-room. Frankie thought everything over, came to the conclusion she was probably over-reacting. *Probably.* She hesitated. *But still...*

She considered the over-reacting idea for a moment longer and decided not to take any chances. She slipped through the kitchen, tip-toed across the stone-room and peeked out the window along the far wall, straining to look down along the foundation. *Nope. No old Cheyenne woman there.*

She decided to slip out, snatch up the bucket and hightail it back into the house before the milk spoiled, or before one of the dogs got into it. She eased the stone-room door open, scanned the meadow again; she dashed across the porch, raced across the patch of grass, snatched up the pail and darted back to the stone-room. Gasping for breath. Amazed she hadn't sloshed more milk from the bucket than she had. Glancing out to the meadow, she could see no sign of the old woman. She breathed a sigh of relief. *Nothing! Nowhere!*

But now, she had a bigger problem—Wild Bird would be expecting to get a jar of the cream that had separated from last evening's milk. The old woman's self-assigned task was to make the butter and she took her job of bringing cream into butter very seriously; if she didn't get the jar of cream in short order, she might see it as another disrespectful act and get even angrier.

Frankie paced, and watched, and paced some more. Finally, she decided to take whatever lumps might be coming. The waiting and not knowing, was as hard as what she had gone through back at Fort Kearny when she had to stand against Captain Connell's wall while he shaved and she waited for the whipping.

After skimming off the cream to fill the jar, Frankie started the long walk over toward the Cheyenne lodge, the jar of cream in her hand, more than a little worried about what Wild Bird might do.

"Né-ške'éehe." 'My Grandmother.' Frankie waited. No answer. She called again. "Né-ške'eehe?" Still no answer.

She had no doubt Wild Bird was in her lodge, so, unsure about what else to do, she sat down cross-legged in front of the tipi and waited. She sat there in the grass, looking down. She waited. And while she waited, she let her mind drift southward, back to Fort Kearny and to her Captain's quarters. Back to the morning when she had to stand watching and waiting while he took his time, working his razor along the strop, then watching her in his mirror while he shaved.

Suddenly, a shadow fell across her. Wild Bird was there. Standing right in front of her.

"Granddaughter. Why did you behave like that?"

"I didn't want to be hit."

"A little Cheyenne girl wouldn't behave like that. It was disrespectful to an old woman."

"I'm *not* a little Cheyenne girl. I wish I was, but I'm *not*. I'm a little-white-girl and this little-white-girl doesn't *want* to be hit with a stick."

There was silence then. For what seemed like an awfully long time. Finally, Frankie spoke again.

"If you want to milk the cow, then you can *tell* me that. I would be proud to have you milk that cow. But this little-white-girl wants you to talk to her and not hit her with a stick."

"Come." Wild Bird picked up the cream jar and walked away, heading to the fire.

Frankie followed her and sat down beside her.

"Who was the woman who hit you?"

"My mother. She hit me. When my father found out, he took me away from her. We went to live somewhere else."

Frankie didn't know where the tears came from, or why they were coming now. Because it had been so long ago; more than four years, now. It had been back before her father died. He had taken her away to live at his brother's home and she had lived with him there, in the home where her Uncle James and Aunt Sarah lived. She had lived there with her four cousins and had become part of their family. And finally, it was all fine—she was happy then, and everything about her life had become easy and good and exciting.

But now, the tears were coming and the old woman was petting her and cooing to her. Holding her and rocking her. And without Frankie explaining anything more, the old woman—the Cheyenne woman who looked to be at least two hundred years old—seemed to understand everything. Frankie closed her eyes, feeling the gnarled old hands stroking her, holding her head on her lap. And somehow, the old woman was taking away the pain.

All the hurt that Frankie knew, all the pain that was supposed to stay deep inside her and never trouble her again, was suddenly rising up from her heart. Because Wild Bird had her wisdom and her ways—and somehow—the old Cheyenne woman found the hidden pain down in the deep spaces of her heart. Somehow, the old woman was calling to the pain; somehow, she called for it to rise up. And then, somehow, she was sending it away.

Frankie closed her eyes. All the sights of the world disappeared; all the sounds of the world faded away. There was only the gravelly voice of Wild Bird singing a soft chanting-song, her voice soft and quavering. She was singing of love gone and pain released. Singing of hurt flying away. Singing of pain traveling far away. Far beyond the clouds.

It was a dream then, Frankie thought, a soft, blue-tinted dream. She could feel herself lifting. Drifting upward. The blue air of the sky flowing around and through her fingers. Through her hair. Blue against her face.

There were blue birds then—blue birds flying and calling, circling and spiraling through the sky. Sailing and soaring across the sky. The songs of the meadowlarks surrounded her—thousands of meadowlarks raising their heads, tipping back—sending their songs out to the world.

A robin walked through the grass, tilting its head—reaching down into the earth, leaning back, pulling and straining and tugging

542

at an earthworm. Finally, it drew the worm up and out from the deep soils, bringing it up, bringing it out from the heart of the earth.

Hawks floating high, drifting away. Eagles circling, gliding, wheeling. Columns of great birds rising, twisting and twirling in spirals, silvery-white spirals—shimmering and flickering like faraway pieces of confetti—rising to the highest part of the sky, calling and singing a chortling song; rising until they disappeared into the blue heavens of the prairie sky.

The dream left her then—Frankie watched it rising with the birds, lifting and drifting away, disappearing with them into the deep blue. She heard the gravelly words of Wild Bird.

"Stay still, Child. Stay here. Stay still." So Frankie stayed still. Waiting. Quiet and still.

Frankie woke in the middle of the night, looking at patterns of soft light and shadows flickering and shifting above her. Soft and strange and silent. She stared at the show of pale lights and shadows. Wondering; unsure. She rubbed her eyes, watched it some more. Finally, realizing that it was the firelight and moonlight and moon-shadows, all intertwining, all flickering and flitting against buffalo-hide walls. There was a soft movement beside her, and in the dim glow of the low burning fire, she could see Wild Bird next to her. Sleeping. Breathing soft and slow. *Ohh. Wild Bird's lodge.*

Outside the walls of the old woman's home, beyond the buffalo-hides, Frankie could hear the night sounds. The soft sounds of the night. Sounds she knew—the sounds of the prairie. The night-song of the Sand Hills.

The sweet song of the breeze whispering its way through the low grasses, whisking softly through the high branches. Somewhere across the meadow, the horned-owl called for its mate. Far away beyond the valley, a killdeer called.

Beside her, Wild Bird was breathing slow and steady and soft. Frankie smiled. The whole earth was breathing quietly tonight.

Frankie breathed in the night air. Filling her lungs with the sweet air. Softly. Quietly. And she slept again.

Two days later in the middle of the morning, Frankie watched through the kitchen window as Everett and Ida rolled into the valley, the team of seal-browns pulling the spring-wagon down the track. Everett slowed the horses for a moment as Ida pointed to Wild Bird's lodge and called out to the woman tending her fire. They waved and exchanged greetings, and Everett clucked to Jenny and Jake, sending them forward and on to the barn.

For a moment, Frankie was surprised to see the Dunbars' arrival, and then suddenly, she realized that it must be Sunday. Realizing suddenly, that she had lost all sense of time—the days, the weeks had all been a blur while her Cheyenne family had been visiting. She waved from the porch, grinning, excited to see them, smiling because this part of her life had settled in, again. This was her normal, again.

Ida waved as she climbed down from the wagon-seat, clutching at the rabbit-fur cape around her shoulders—the gift from Mourning Dove. But there was no smile on Everett's face. From where she stood on the porch, Frankie could see the sorrow in his eyes.

The last time they had left for their homestead, they knew that the Cheyenne families would be leaving, so Everett had certainly known better than to expect to see a little Cheyenne girl running to greet her Happy Man today. And he would have known that there would be no troop of wild little prairie boys romping around. But no matter what he had known, the meadow was still a very different place today. Everett Dunbar was feeling the full loss as he surveyed the meadow.

Frankie headed across the grass to greet them—half-skipping, half-trotting—calling out and asking if they were surprised to see Wild Bird's lodge.

"Wild Bird decided to stay here for the winter!" She slipped around in front of the team, pointing for Everett to look to the pasture where the geldings were. "And you should go see my new horse!

Strong Hand left his pinto for me. As a gift!" She was jabbering—she knew she was—but she was trying to find some way to make Everett smile. "Isn't it such a wonderful thing?"

She reached Everett's side of the wagon and hugged him as he stepped down; he held her longer and harder than ever before and she let him, knowing he was hurting. Knowing he was feeling empty.

"You know they'll come back to visit again, don't you? You know Little Mouse will come back?" She whispered the words into his ear as he held her; he loosened his grip, leaned back and looked at her. Tears welled up in his eyes, and then he smiled a soft tremulous smile.

"Yes, Honey. You're right. Thanks for reminding me." He kissed her forehead, glanced toward the Cheyenne lodge and hugged her again. "Yes, they'll be back. And meantime, we have Wild Bird to tell us her stories."

When she hugged Ida, Ida held her for a long time, too—softly, almost carefully. Frankie stayed against her, feeling the warmth of the rabbit-fur shawl, feeling the fur tickling her nose. Waiting until Ida released her. There were tears in Ida's eyes too. Tears that were happy and sad at the same time. Tears that spoke about the love she had for people she never thought she could love. She nodded at Frankie with a look that said they were both thinking exactly the same thing.

They talked of the lighter, easier things for a moment—talking about how warm the rabbit shawl was. And then about how the Indian Summer was over.

"Yep," Everett said as he worked at the buckles on his mare's harness. "Mornings are brisk now. Evenings are cooling off quicker." He directed his next words to his wife, pointing toward the back of the wagon. "Don't forget about the crates in the wagon-bed."

"Oh dear, yes. Don't let me forget to go into the cellar, Honey. Everything's been so different lately that I lost all track of my home-stores. I haven't been paying any attention to what I'd used. I had to make a whole list of what I need."

Frankie nodded, grinned at her, knowing they were all doing a lot of chattering. Partly, because they were happy to see each other again. Partly, because they were happy that things were normal again. And partly, because they were trying not to think about why the valley was so deafeningly quiet now.

About then, Everett said he 'supposed he'd better go take a look at this new horse Frankie's got herself', and he headed off toward the pasture lane. Ida gave Frankie a knowing look and Frankie nodded back—both knowing that he needed to have some time to himself. Because for him, the meadow had changed the most.

"It'll take some time for him to adjust to his Little Mouse being gone."

"It always takes me a while to adjust every time they leave." Frankie watched Everett opening the gate and starting down the track between the pastures. "This time, with Wild Bird being here, it hasn't been so bad."

Ida sat with Wild Bird for a while and Frankie brought sweet, milky coffee and a platter of warm bread and butter out to the fire. Everett was still out in the pastures; Frankie saw that he had spent some time around Fox. But Fox, being the warhorse he was, considered the little-white-girl to be his person—and that being the case, he had no great interest in being sociable with anyone else.

Watching from a distance, Frankie saw Everett had done his looking and assessing of Fox at a respectful distance. And then, he turned his attention to the Shires and the mules, walking among them, stroking them, fiddling and fussing with them. Even though there was nothing to really fiddle or fuss with.

After that, he went to the barn and from the sound of things beyond the entrance, he'd been fiddling and fussing around in the workshop, too—all in his private effort to adjust to the changes in the valley. Finding his own way to accept the emptiness and the quiet. Seeking his own way to deal with the loss of these new loved ones. Because others he had loved, had left and never returned. It was likely, Frankie figured, he was trying to remind himself that *this* time, *these* loved ones would come back.

Once he fussed around in the barn with whatever he found needed fussing-with, he had gone over to the stall-turned-puppy-pen and let the pups loose. And the three pups did what they always did. With none of the grace or speed or free-flowing agility of their mother, the pups made a mad-dash for the barn entrance. It was the same circus every day—they raced out into the meadow in their puppy-ways, scrambling and scrabbling, tripping and stumbling over their own oversized puppy-feet.

It was always hilarious to see the mad-scramble and it had been a source of great amusement for the Cheyenne women when the younger Cheyenne kids set the pups free each day. The wolfhound-greyhound pups had spent the afternoons running with Cheyenne children and racing circles around the Cheyenne ponies in the meadow.

Today was no different. Frankie watched the three pups race into the meadow, acting as if they believed a whole new world was waiting just for them. Everett, she could see, was watching the reckless run of the pups from the barn entrance; he was doubled over, laughing at the sight, laughing as if he'd never seen it before. Lost in the moment. Frankie smiled to herself, pleased, because Happy Man was back to himself.

The three pups were full into their wild run, grinning their wolfhound grins, putting their best efforts into their puppy-clumsy race, doing their best to run like their grey-hound hearts told them to. Their lack of coordination didn't seem to put the slightest damper on their outlook on life—they saw life as something that held wild adventures just for their purposes. As a result, they were wildly excited about everything around them.

Frankie watched the trio of pups—the white one, the brindle one and the blond one. Behind her, she could hear Ida and Wild Bird laughing. They, too, were watching and waiting. Every one of them was anticipating the coming event; they all knew what would happen. Very soon, in the midst of their rollicking puppy-run, the pups would spot one of the objects of their affection; they would spy Matilda dozing in her favorite spot, lying in the warm sunlight on a corner of the pantry porch.

The three of them had unrestrained puppy-love for the tawny little collie-dog; they worshipped her with their excited little puppy-hearts, and whenever they saw her, they would fall all over themselves, and each other, for the chance to reach her and greet her.

It was about to happen now, because suddenly, in the midst of their wild play, the white pup spotted Matilda drowsing in the sun. On some unspoken cue, the whole puppy-pack swerved and bee-lined for the corner of the pantry porch. Their legs went faster and their grins grew bigger; they launched themselves onto the porch floor and Matilda got a rude awakening. She disappeared into the midst of the frenzied greeting as the pups romped and rolled themselves all over and around her.

Matilda, Frankie knew, had actually brought it all on herself, because at one point, she had showered her love and affection on the pups, every bit as devoted as Laughing Girl. But now, with their recent growth-spurt and their puppy-sharp teeth and puppy-sharp toenails, they had become too much for her.

At the moment, Matilda was working to free herself from the tumbling turmoil; she was scrambling, snapping and snarling, working her way out of the moiling mass of puppy-legs and puppy-tongues. Ultimately, the tawny little collie-dog managed to loose herself from the frantic frenzy and made a desperate and undignified retreat.

She dodged free and dashed around the corner of the Barracks. Circling around to the back of the house to seek the quiet safety of the bedroom porch. The audience at the fireside cheered for her, but the pups didn't care—because they knew that other wild and wonderful adventures awaited them. Once again, they turned their attention to the open meadow and launched into another tumbling, stumbling puppy-race.

Beyond their episodes of wild and reckless exuberance, Frankie was actually proud of them. Laughing Girl had thrown a nice litter, each puppy every bit as nice as the next. The silvery-white pup showed her wolfhound blood in her coat of long bristly hairs sticking out everywhere, and in every direction—she gladly accepted human attention but she made no effort to seek it out. The largest pup was a blond-brindle like her mother, but much darker in color and showing a squared muzzle and a heavier head—she was as boisterous in play as her siblings, but with people, she was shy and standoffish.

Then there was the runt. She was pretty in her face; her coat was as blond as the lightest color in her mother's coat. She had a sweeter inclination toward people than her littermates and she seemed to be very clear about exactly how sweet and lovable she was—and she had figured out exactly how that worked with the humans.

And today, she showed her true spirit. She had played hard with her sisters, but when she tired of that activity, she left the wild play and headed for the humans at the fireside, fully confident she could make herself welcome among them. And today, it was Ida she had her sights set upon. The runty little blond pup plopped herself down, splaying her little wolfhound-long puppy-body across Ida's feet and got busy licking Ida's ankles with her long pink tongue; she was grinning a proud and contented grin, apparently pleased with her new self-appointed occupation.

The pup ignored Ida's meager attempts to dislodge and discourage her; the runty-pup had no intention of relinquishing her post. And to Frankie's eyes, it didn't really look like Ida was trying very hard to send her away. When the blond pup was satisfied with her ankle-cleaning activity, she dozed off, still splayed across Ida's feet—and Ida didn't seem to have a problem with that either. In fact, Frankie realized, Ida didn't seem to have an issue with either the puppy-adoration, or the puppy-slobber.

Most of the talk around the warm fire on that cool autumn day was about Little Mouse and the five little boys. Some though, was about Strong Hand and Knife and Whirlwind. Some was about the buffalo hunt and some was about the sickness.

Frankie kept busy translating, surprised once again with how much she actually understood when Wild Bird spoke. Only a few times did she find herself stumbling over the meanings and needing to question Wild Bird. There was much talk about the children's games, and Wild Bird talked a lot about the night of celebrating—describing the measured dances of the women and the wild dances of the men for Ida and Everett.

Wild Bird talked about the land her people were traveling to—and about the rivers the band would cross to get to the land of the black-rocky place. She talked about the protection of deep valleys and the forests of the black-rocky place, where Strong Hand's band would winter.

The old woman reached to pat Frankie's arm, speaking then of the valley of Fire Heart Child.

"This valley," she said, "will be a good place to spend the days of the hard-faced moons," She explained. "Fire Heart Child has much to learn about the ways of her family." And then, she grinned with a mischievous glint in her eyes. "This is a good place to be," she told them, "because the white-man's buffalo will give us the yellow-grease. And the walking-birds will give us their eggs. There are many good reasons to stay." She patted Frankie's arm again and went on talking.

Her people, she said, would come back and find her late in the winter, maybe when the grasses began to turn green again. Until then, she would stay with her granddaughter. Strong Hand had decided that during the warm months, his band would stay near the land of the Heséovo'e Vósotótse. The Sand Hills. They wouldn't travel back to the land across the great flat river, Strong Hand had decided, because there was dryness there, and the food on that land was no longer good for them. Because, too many of the vé'ho'é were living there now.

Frankie heard Wild Bird use the Cheyenne word for white-men. Vé'ho'é. The spider-people—people who were all wrapped up in cloth that was woven together like a spider's web.

"Our band," Wild Bird said, "will stay on the lands north of the great flat river."

Everett and Ida were smiling as Frankie translated those words and she knew why. Because if Strong Hand's band stayed in the land of the Sand Hills—then they would probably visit the meadow more often. And that thought pleased Everett and Ida.

Frankie ducked her head, smiling as Ida talked about her love for the rabbit-fur shawl Mourning Dove had given her, and about her pride in the buffalo-robe Whirlwind had given her for her home. She talked about her plans for the crocheting and the embroidery she wanted to do—so she would have gifts ready when the Cheyenne families returned.

Ida kept talking and Frankie kept grinning, because this was all so different from the discussions the Dunbars had with her in her kitchen a few months ago. Back then, they had been warning her to stay away from the Cheyenne.

The four of them stayed by the fire that day, staying beside Wild Bird and eating from her cookpot. The old woman told them stories of the ancestors and of the years of the hard winters, talking about the winters of 'terrible-snows' and winters of 'no food'. And she talked of the winters of plenty, saying that this year would be like those—the times of the hard-moons would be easy times and the Cheyenne families up in the black-rocky place would have plenty of food.

Hours later in the early evening, while Everett hitched his team, Ida and Frankie went to the root-cellar and filled the crates with everything from her list. Once Ida had settled herself on the wagon-seat, and as the three pups were romping and playing around the wagon wheels, Frankie grabbed the little blond pup. She boosted the wriggling little body into Ida's lap.

"She's the smallest in the litter, Ida, but she's the smartest. She's going to need you to keep her attention directed toward good things." Frankie could see the tears welling up in Ida's eyes. "You'll need her around your place to keep the wolves and coyotes away."

Ida hugged Frankie from the wagon-seat, leaning down and kissing her on the head, all while keeping a firm hold on the twisting and wiggling puppy. Everett gave Frankie a nod and a smile, looking as if he wasn't all that surprised they were taking a puppy home; he glanced toward Ida and his smile grew. He slapped the reins on Jenny and Jake, turned them and sent them toward the entrance. Before they were even out of the valley, Frankie could hear Ida chatting happily to Everett, already trying to decide on a name for the runty-pup.

Frankie headed back to Wild Bird's side at the fire, wading through the two wagging and wiggling pups that were flipping and flopping around her ankles. The old woman was watching from her fire, laughing as her granddaughter stumbled through the puppies.

Frankie was pleased that the littlest girl-pup was on her way to her new home; thinking it was the perfect time—the little blond wolfhound-cross would help both Ida and Everett through their heavy loneliness for the Cheyenne families. Seeing Everett without his Hóh-keeheso and his wild prairie boys, was a sad thing; seeing Ida without Dandelion tagging along after her, was a sad thing. The pup would add some life and laughter to their homestead.

PART IV

WINTER SOJOURN

Two days later, low-hanging clouds began moving across the land of the Sand Hills, coming in from the northwest horizon—thick and dark and foreboding. The entire western half of Frankie's world turned a deep, dark blue-gray. The temperature was dropping while she brought the horses and cattle to the two front pastures. She put Blossom and Primrose inside the barn. She moved Fanny, Rock, and Boone into stalls, wanting to have them near at hand.

She visited Wild Bird in her lodge, asking her to come and stay in the house until the storm moved on. The old woman chuckled and waved her away, so Frankie gave up her argument and moved extra wood next to the lodge door for the lodge's small center fire. She carried armload after armload of wood inside her own home. She forked piles of grass hay into the dog-stall for Laughing Girl and her two pups—Ghost Dog and Too Shy.

Three times during the afternoon, Frankie rode Fanny up to her Lookout Hill, and Matilda, sensing the coming storm, stayed close to her on each trip. From the crest of the hill, Frankie studied the sky and the expanse of the horizon, watching the movement of the clouds. Studying the hills and the expanse of land, watching the movement of the wild creatures. Trying to learn the changes and patterns.

The day before had been warm—warmer than even the hottest of the Indian summer days. By late afternoon, the air had taken on the heaviness of a hot summer day. 'Oppressive', her father would have called it. But there had been a subtle difference, Frankie thought. The air had definitely been oppressive, but there had also been something ominous. When she talked to Wild Bird about it, the old woman nodded and said the warning was there; it was 'floating in the air'. She told her exactly what would happen and told her to go out onto the land and watch.

"You'll see everything I tell you, Granddaughter, if you look. They are things you should see."

And so far, it was happening just as Wild Bird had said. The rabbits and the striped gophers—and all the small creatures—had been busy filling their bellies with grasses and seeds, and then they began gathering mouthfuls of dried grass and disappearing down their burrows.

The deer and antelope were out in the meadows, heads down and grazing with an intensity, with an urgent purpose today. And by late afternoon, Frankie saw as they began to cluster together; then they started drifting toward the tree line, seeking shelter from the coming storm—well aware that it would be a heavy storm. Far to the east, she watched a massive herd of elk moving toward the North Loup, toward the protection of the trees, heads held low, moving quickly.

Above her, no eagles were drifting in their easy circles of flight. There were no faraway cries of hawks. The birds everywhere had gone silent—the birdsongs that usually filled the air during the mornings and afternoons were gone, even though whole flights of birds were gathering in the riverside trees. Listening, Frankie realized there were no birdsongs anywhere. No coyotes called. There were no sounds anywhere. The Sand Hills had gone silent.

She spent the time on her Lookout Hill, tucking all the information away into a corner of her mind. This, she knew, she should remember for the rest of her life; this was knowledge she needed to retain. This was all a truth about life out here among the Sand Hills; it was a truth that needed to become part of her. It was more than just knowledge; applied properly, it would become wisdom.

Wild Bird had told her the day would sit hot and warm and then, she said, the air would cool suddenly, and the clouds would come down and ride low against the land. As Frankie turned Fanny down the hillside and headed to her meadow, she knew that was exactly what had been happening.

The old Cheyenne woman had told her that once the clouds started lowering, she was to go to her house, or come into the lodge, and not leave again. She told her the winds would race across the sky above the valley; they would scream their anger as they passed above the meadow. She said the prairie land above and beyond her home would feel the greatest pain of the wind and snow. Here in this valley, Wild Bird said, it would be quieter. She said the storm would be here on the land for three days and all the animals of the Sand Hills would sleep. After three days, everything would wake again and begin to move again.

Frankie looked to the windmills, making sure she had set the levers so they would ride out the storm. The troughs were full; there was an axe just inside the barn door for breaking ice in the troughs. The chickens were settled into the henhouse with enough feed for three days. She put Fanny into a barn stall to ride out the storm with Rock and Boone. She had buckets of water inside the house—plenty of buckets—and the oak barrel in the stone-room was full of water too.

She walked around the porch of the house, closing the wood shutters and fastening them in place, and then she did the same to the Barracks. As she headed back to the house, the wind started racing across the sky above the valley, sweeping and raking its way through the tops of the trees. She saw Laughing Girl head into the barn with her two pups, knowing they would burrow deep into the mass of hay in the puppy-pen, making a warm hay-cave—she grinned, thinking back to the hay-cave she had made in the stable-loft at Fort Kearny.

The winds were just beginning to whistle as she slipped into the kitchen doorway; she held the door as Matilda crowded in after her, feeling a new and sudden deep-chill in the winds. Knowing it was the sudden drop in temperature that Wild Bird had spoken about. Then she closed the door to the coming storm.

This was her first winter storm and Frankie was sure it was going to be the kind of blizzard the people of the Middle Loup settlement feared. She stood in the kitchen for a few minutes, thinking through everything she had done. Thinking through all the steps she had taken to prepare for the coming storm. Assessing everything. Hoping she had remembered everything she had been told.

She had water. And firewood. And even more water than she knew she would need. And more firewood than she needed. She had food; plenty of food for the house and plenty of food for Wild Bird. She had put extra feed in the pens for the livestock in the barn, and then she had put in even more. The calf was in the pen with the cow. She had the three horses in the barn-stalls, just in case she needed a horse quickly. The chickens were shut inside in the henhouse with extra food—twice as much food as they would need. Laughing Girl and the pups would be warm in their hay-cave.

Frankie went through everything in her mind, glancing out the kitchen window, wishing she had spent more time with the Hyatt brothers. Realizing she should have asked more questions when she had last seen them. Because William and Tipp understood the land and the weather so well; maybe better than anyone in the region. They understood how to handle a homestead through the year, and through all the weather the Sand Hills could offer.

She stoked up the fire in the cookstove and built up the fire in the center fireplace. Later, if the storm dragged on, she could close the copper mantel-doors in the sitting-room and the back bedroom. Like William Hyatt had said, by closing off the fireplace openings and closing the connecting doors, the heat would stay in the kitchen and her bedroom. William had told her to heat the whole house before the storms hit, so the walls would hold the heat.

'Start with the house warm and keep the heat steady. Let the walls do most of the work,' he'd said. 'It's wasted time and wood to try to bring a house up to heat from a cold start.'

The brothers had brought coils of rope with them on the day they had talked to her about the storms. Tipp had strung the ropes between the buildings, fastening them high on the building walls— higher than a horse's head, higher than a rider's head. One line stretched from the house to the barn; one to the chicken-house. The brothers tightened the clothesline rope running from her bedroom porch to the outhouse.

Then, they added lengths of rope that hung down from each of the lines next to the buildings, loops that would slide along the tethered lines, loops that she was to tie around her wrist whenever she went out. If she went out. But they said, she was not to go beyond her house during winter storms.

'Not once the clouds are here and the wind is up.' William had made her repeat his words. 'And don't you *ever* step off this porch without being attached to a rope. Not ever. Not even if you're sure you'll be fine. Not even for a few steps.'

Tipp warned her there would *never* be a safe time to wander outside during a blizzard, no matter what the reason. But if she decided to go out anyway—and everybody eventually did—she was to walk with the rope attached to her wrist. Even if there was a lull in the storm, she was still supposed to use the wrist loop. Tipp squatted down in front of her; he pointed his finger right at her face and made her watch him while he talked to her.

'Frankie. Don't you forget what I'm telling you now. People see a break in the storm and decide to run out to the barn and check on the livestock. The storm hits again, sometimes in minutes, and the person decides to hurry back to the house rather than be snowed-in out in the barn,' he said. '*Those* are the people who die. They get caught in the swirling snow and they lose their sense of direction. They freeze to death, sometimes just a few steps from their door.'

He had watched her carefully and William had stood by, watching her as intensely as his brother. Making sure she was hearing his brother's message.

'Frankie,' Tipp had her chin in his hand at that point. 'You don't *beat* a winter storm out here. You don't fight it. You wait it out. That's *all* you do. Prepare as best you can, then you *wait*. Do you hear what I'm telling you?'

She had nodded. He then said it again, talking once more about using the rope. And about getting stuck out in the barn. And about tying the rope tight around her wrist.

'And don't just hold onto it. You tie it around your wrist.' And then Tipp made her repeat what he told her again.

'Listen to me, Frankie,' William spoke up then. 'We've told grown men and women what we just told you, and they still didn't listen. I can tell you the names of three of them who didn't pay attention. Two men and one woman who froze to death are buried out in the Reverend's churchyard. One of 'em was a smart man who spent several winters out here. He *knew* better, and *still* he decided to run out for a quick check on the animals during a break in the storm. He froze to death on his way back to the house. Not ten steps from his door. Don't you take a chance. *Ever*. Do you hear me?'

Frankie knew the two brothers had a reputation for being tough and a little wild. There had always been questions about some odd business they had with horses—questions about their activities and their travels. But the Hyatt brothers had always been good to her.

She remembered their first visit to her meadow; they had tested her that day, and that day, they seemed to have made a decision about her. Because from that day forward, they had kept a close eye on her. A protective eye.

They had made a special trip to visit her before winter set in, before the Indian summer had come. They had visited with her and they had eaten dinner with her. Then they had gone about, setting ropes in place—ropes they had brought with them. And the last thing they did was to put a special hook in the wall in the barn. Then they had given her the talking-to.

'Those ropes *stay* tied in place until you start planting your garden. Then you take them down and hang them right here,' William had indicated the new hook they had placed in the barn. 'The ropes go on that hook in the barn for the summer and you don't use those ropes for *anything* else. Ever. They stay on that hook until the fall. The day you come back from the Harvest Picnic, make *that* be the day you put them up. Make it a habit. Just like that, every year.' They made her promise and they said they would remind her in the spring, and again on the day of the Harvest Picnic in the fall.

'First time I visit you after the Harvest Picnic and I don't see those ropes in place, I swear I'll put you across my knee, and by God, I'll make you squall like a baby.' Tipp had said that, and given the look in his eyes, Frankie was pretty sure he wasn't kidding—she was sure he would do what he promised.

So now, Frankie was adding up all the different things they told her, adding up all the advice everyone had given her. She finally nodded, sure she had thought of everything. Sure that she was settled in and safe.

An hour later, the storm hit. Frankie could hear the winds roaring and howling as they came across the far hills, beyond the walls of the valley. Gray-black clouds came in, ripping through the sky, scudding low and dark above her meadow. The wind swirled and swooped high along the hillsides of her valley, screaming through the treetops and screeching like a hoard of furious banshees racing beyond her valley.

Twice she looked out from the kitchen door, peering into the darkened world, watching the low-lying gray-black clouds whipping across the sky above her valley. She shuddered at the thought of the full fury of the storm sweeping across the open land of the Sand Hills. Knowing that mostly, she was only seeing and hearing the storm; knowing any humans or any creatures out on the land beyond her protected valley, would be feeling the full force of the storm.

Her thoughts went downriver to the Dunbars; Everett and Ida had no protecting valley walls; they would be hit hard. The Reverend and the others down at the Middle Loup settlement were mostly on the river-flats of the Middle Loup—they too would be feeling the storm in a far different way than she was. Her home was down below the level prairie; the real noise and fury of the storm was above her, rather than down in the meadow and beating against the walls of her house. She thought about the wisdom and the foresight of Daniel Kinison; he had known and he had planned. *And I'm reaping the reward of that.*

But still, she worried. She stared across the darkened meadow, looking toward Wild Bird's lodge, seeing the dull glow of her center fire inside the tipi. Knowing the old woman was there, alone, with just the buffalo-hide walls between her and the wicked storm. Twice Frankie was ready to venture out and head across the meadow to her lodge. *Maybe now, with the storm howling so loud and the temperature dropping so fast, maybe now, she'll decide to come over here.*

Twice, she almost went to talk to the old woman; twice she stopped herself, remembering that Wild Bird had lived many winters out here on these lands, reminding herself the old Cheyenne woman knew far more than she did. Wild Bird had known exactly what would happen and when it would happen; she had told her to go into her house and stay there. There was nothing the old woman, with her wrinkled old face and her wise old eyes, didn't know about the coming storm.

She thought about the two Hyatt brothers and what they told her. She remembered their eyes and their faces as they talked, and the way they made her promise to stay inside. To not go outside while the storm was on. Not even if there was a break in the storm.

'Don't you leave this house, not even for a minute. Not to check on the chickens or to run out to the barn.' They made her listen to their warning; they made her repeat what they said. Several times.

So Frankie stayed in the house. She put aside her worries about Wild Bird, deciding to follow the advice of the old Cheyenne woman and heed the warnings of William and Tipp. She pulled a handful of books from the shelves, stretched out on the buffalo-robe in front of the fire and lost herself in the stories of Alexandre Dumas and Daniel Defoe and James Fenimore Cooper. Matilda joined her on the robe in front of the fire, so Frankie read to her, reading the flowing lines of Alfred Tennyson's "Charge of the Light Brigade" and Walt Whitman's "Leaves of Grass".

And later in the night, when the world outside had gone from the deep, dark-gray of the day-storm, to the deep, dark-black of the night-storm, Matilda followed Frankie into her bedroom and curled up on the bed; she listened politely as Frankie read "Self-Reliance" from Ralph Waldo Emerson's book of essays.

Frankie read to the tawny little collie-dog late into the night, the bedroom warm and safe, heated by the center fireplace. Several times she stopped to watch the fire crackling and snapping, sending its heat throughout the house. Outside the temperature fell and the blizzard shrieked and howled above the valley, but the square house with its cleverly-built fireplace and its stout log walls and shuttered windows held the heat. Frankie smiled, reveling in the warmth that radiated there within her perfectly square house. *It's exactly the way Daniel Kinison and the Swede brothers knew it would be.*

On the first morning—after a night of ripping across the Sand Hills and leaving the bulk of its snow outside the valley—the blizzard had left only scatterings of snow and finger-drifts around the edges of the meadow and streaming out from the buildings. It continued roaring through the skies and across the land, but it was just as Wild Bird said and just as the Hyatt brothers had said—the worst of the storm stayed above her valley walls and went beyond her meadow.

In the afternoon, the storm slowed. Then it stopped. The winds quieted, and the snow from the storm—what little was left—drifted down and settled quietly on the winter grass of the meadow. The clouds were still dark, and still looked a little menacing—but they seemed to have lifted and slowed. There was even a hint of light beyond the clouds, from where the sun would be sitting high above the clouds. Frankie thought about Blossom, wondering if she should milk her, in case Primrose wasn't nursing enough. She wondered if she should check to see if any of the hens were still laying. She started wondering why the storm had blown itself out quicker than everyone expected.

She thought about bundling up in the big coat her Uncle James used to wear and pulling on her marten-fur mittens, to take a crock of stew to Wild Bird. Thinking that she could check on the chickens on her way back. And then, she recalled the Hyatt brothers and their words. She stopped her thoughts about going out in the meadow, because this was the very thing William and Tipp told her about. Plus, there was no high-line running to the tipi.

Again and again, Frankie stepped out the porch doors, watching the skies, wondering if the storm had really finished its rampage, or if was just in one of the 'lulls' that had William described. Thinking that maybe she was just being overly cautious. Once again, she made the decision to stay inside. Because there was nothing outside that needed tending to. Because she had set everything in place before the storm. And because, the clouds were still there—they looked like they were higher and they looked lighter—but they were still there.

Eight minutes later, just like the Hyatt brothers had warned her, the storm came on again. It hit again—darker and harder and louder than ever—sending sheets of snow swirling and twisting down and around and through her little valley.

Three more times there were the quiet lulls that suggested the worst of the storm was over—and three more times, the blinding snow and screaming winds came again. For Frankie, any and all thoughts of making quick trips outside were gone. She understood the lulls and the distortions of the storms now; she understood now, that she wasn't being 'overly cautious'; she understood that the Hyatt brothers hadn't been exaggerating. *Winter storms out here can be sneaky. Downright treacherous.*

By the second morning, the blizzard was still howling and the clouds were still dark and low; the light scatterings of snow had become an eight-inch layer of snow across the meadow and the valley hillsides. The finger-drifts had grown higher and longer; the temperatures had dipped even lower.

The house stayed warm, but by noon, Frankie decided to close off the fireplace to the back bedroom and close its two doors—partly to conserve heat and save on wood, but mostly, just to learn about the effects of doing so. Because there would be other years and other storms and other times when it would be a good thing to know about her house.

She spent some of her time in the sitting-room, curled up in the rocker and reading, and some of the time in the kitchen. She kept a pot of stew simmering on the back burner; she baked cornbread; she set bread-dough to rising; she baked two apple pies, a sweet potato pie; she started a batch of applesauce cooking. The sweet potato pie, and the applesauce, she decided, she would take to Wild Bird after the storm passed, because the old woman favored them—she loved the flavors and she said it was easy on her mouth. And with all her chipped and cracked teeth, Frankie thought it probably was.

Late in the afternoon of the third day, the howling and screeching winds died down; the storm moved off, traveling off to the southeast to wreak its havoc onto other lands. Frankie watched the back edge of the storm move beyond her homestead, watching as it took its clouds and its driving snow along with it. Watching as it gathered itself up, and left.

She stood on the kitchen porch, studying the prairie sky as it cleared to a sharp and shimmering silvery-blue. Around her, the meadow and the valley slopes were cloaked in wind-swept snow, glimmering in the fresh sunlight. The layer of snow that had blanketed the meadow and hillsides had been swept up and piled onto the finger-drifts, laying bare great patches of the meadow floor.

Frankie figured the highest drifts to be four and five feet long, and maybe two and three feet high. Probably nothing compared to the drifts out on the open land. The best thing about the drifts around her little valley was that they were scattered, with plenty of space and gaps between them. Which meant they would offer no great problems. *And that means, no need to dig anything out.*

She grinned, suddenly realizing it was over—she had made it through her first real blizzard. Across the meadow, Wild Bird emerged from her lodge and started her trek to the barn, stepping over the tail-ends of the lower finger-drifts, weaving her way around the deep-drifts. It was milking time for the white-man's buffalo.

Frankie reached for her boots and the heavy coat; she pulled on her marten-fur mittens and dashed through the kitchen door. Bounded off the porch with Matilda bouncing out after her. Both of them happy to be free again, happy to be out in the sharp, fresh winter air. Excited to be out of the house. Excited she had weathered her first winter blizzard in the Nebraska Territory.

Racing across the meadow and leaping from one wind-swept patch to the next, she tripped over Matilda twice and sprawled into waist-high snow-drifts. She laughed and brushed herself off each time, and went running again, pulling the fresh and crisp air into her lungs. Calling to her grandmother as she waded and wrestled her way through the wildly ecstatic greeting by Laughing Girl and the two pups racing out of the barn.

Wild Bird called to her from inside the barn, saying something about the cow and calf. Wild Bird, Frankie knew, would be down the alleyway in the milking-pen. *Probably already milking Blossom.* Frankie grinned, realizing everything was returning to normal.

The next day, Frankie headed out of the valley, riding Fox and leading Rock. Wild Bird had insisted—demanded—that she take both horses; she also insisted she take her rifle, a poke of food, a buffalo-robe and the rawhide rope. And the makings for a fire.

Frankie was planning only to go for a *short* ride. That's what she explained to Wild Bird—she explained that she wasn't going to stay out more than an hour or so. She told her she didn't need to pack a lot of things, because she just wanted to see the prairie. She wanted to see what the storm had done outside of the valley, up on the land beyond the shelter of the meadow.

"Taking a pack is just extra work, Grandmother," she said. "I just want to see the snowfall patterns and the way the drifts formed. I want to learn about the sizes and the areas of the drifts."

But even with her patient explanation, the Cheyenne woman was still immoveable; she stamped her foot and wagged her crooked old finger at Frankie. Frankie listened to her demand that 'little Fire Heart Child needs to behave like a good Cheyenne girl and do what is expected'.

"Listen to your elders and stop behaving like a little-white-girl," she said.

Finally, Frankie relented. She took both horses and the buffalo-robe and the food and the rifle and the rope. And the makings for a fire. She rode out fully packed and loaded.

Once she topped out on the prairie, she had a shock. There were huge patches of land that had been laid bare by the winds. But there were drifts too, all kinds of drifts. There were finger-drifts looking to be four and five times the size of those in her valley. There were broad and sweeping drifts, and drifts that were long and tall and massive. And there were some drifts stretched out across the land and created an odd illusion, making the surface of the land appear smooth and level, even in places where Frankie knew there were dips and low draws in the land.

She grinned, proud and pleased because she knew the land of her homestead. She had studied the land. *Lucky for me, I know the land.* Because, after all, she had ridden all over this part of the countryside; she knew the lay of the land and where the valleys and hillsides were; she knew where the slopes and dips and low meadows were. It made her wonder for a moment, why she had agreed to Wild Bird's demand that she take the extra horse and the supplies. *Because it's not like I'll get lost out here, or stuck in a drift or something.*

She reined Fox, turning him upriver, traveling beside the apple trees before turning to the north, planning to ride in a broad sweep to the east and head back toward her Lookout Hill. Thinking it would be wise to survey the Sand Hills from high on the crest. Figuring the land would look very different today.

Fox, though, wasn't relishing the idea of walking in the direction she chose. When he resisted and swung to the side, she hauled on the rein; she pulled him back around, insisting. And Fox insisted more. He tossed his head and gave a few rears of protest. It puzzled Frankie a bit; she was trying to understand his irritation.

He was fighting the idea of crossing the river-flats where the Indian village had been—the low grassland covered with a blanket of snow that Frankie knew would only be half-shin deep. She decided to take a slightly different course; she turned his head, swinging out to allow a broader sweep across the flat grasslands. After a short distance, she turned him to the flats, turning once again toward the slope of the Lookout Hill in the distance. Once again, Fox fought the rein and the direction.

So Frankie forced the situation; she yanked his head in the direction she wanted and smacked her heels into his sides. Surprised, he leaped forward, landing a good six feet ahead.

He sank deep into the snow—snow more than halfway up his barrel. He twisted around, rearing, floundering in the snow, fighting to gain solid ground again. Frankie dropped Rock's lead and grabbed for Fox's mane while he thrashed backwards and sideways.

In that moment, it occurred to Frankie that she might have to use the rope and Rock's strength to get Fox out of the deep snow. It also occurred to her she wasn't exactly sure how she was going to get back to Rock because it looked as though the snow might be neck high to her. The rope, the extra horse, the warnings—now she understood why Wild Bird had stomped her foot.

Finally, Fox managed to break his way through the deep snow and plow his way back to Rock's side. It had been no more than a minute or two—Frankie knew that—but it felt as if it had taken an hour for Fox to extricate them from the deep snow. She wasn't sure what Fox thought about the timespan, but it was clear he wasn't happy with her behavior. Because once he was back on solid ground, he shook his hide free of the snow, and when he swung his head around to look at her, Frankie was pretty sure he was glaring at her.

There seemed to be a lot of irritation in the Indian pony's eyes as he stared at her, and Rock wasn't looking any happier with her. He looked every bit as put-out with her as the Indian pony, and right then and there, Frankie realized the two battle-wise horses were forming an alliance. From that point on, they were joined by a common purpose—they decided it was their duty to make their person learn to follow their lead.

Within a few minutes, Frankie realized the two warhorses weren't playing around. They were agreeable enough as the ride continued, but they both made it clear they had no intention of engaging in any of her nonsense. For her part, Frankie decided she'd better take heed and learn what they were trying to teach her. And it didn't take long before she changed her thinking and quit fighting the reality—the blizzard had changed the prairie.

She decided to continue upriver for a while, staying close to the wind-swept regions, until she had a better sense about the winter-land around her. Because the truth was, she had no idea what she was doing in the aftermath of the three-day blizzard. The storm had blanketed the Sand Hills with snow that had been whipped into a wild frenzy by the winds. The snow had stayed wherever it had been laid, and it had created a very different world. Today, Frankie realized, she was in a world she knew nothing about.

Fox and Rock had set their rules in place; they would let her choose her direction and set the general course, but they would dictate the actual path. Fox simply stopped in his tracks whenever he sensed danger—refusing her choice and ignoring her urging. Rock had taken his own stand—he had yanked the lead-rope out of her hand and he was following his companions at a distance of his own choosing. His plan, to Frankie's thinking, was to stay back from any developing problems and remain ready to come to their rescue if necessary.

They traveled on and Frankie surveyed the changed lands around her. Thinking. Observing. Assessing. And as the three of them moved through the snow-covered valleys and along the windswept slopes, Frankie found herself smiling, seeing the true wisdom of Wild Bird's demands regarding the two horses and the supplies. The value was clear—it was about life and death—because trouble and death could happen anywhere out here. It could happen five miles upriver, or less than a mile away. In fact, she'd gotten herself in a mess less than a hundred yards from her meadow's entrance.

The old Cheyenne woman knew the land and she knew the dangers of taking 'a nice little ride' on the prairie during the winter months. And she knew her little-white-granddaughter well; she knew exactly what kind of trouble a little-white-girl could conjure up.

And now, Frankie understood the difference—thinking that 'a short outing' was somehow less dangerous than 'a long ride', was nonsense. There was no such thing as a pleasure ride during the winter days. Not while there were drifts on the ground. And not, while storms could crop up within hours.

The Sand Hills of the winter was a different world than the Sand Hills of the summer. A different level of respect was required in the winter; a different understanding and a deeper wisdom was required of any traveler who moved through a snow-covered Nebraska

Territory. And that same wisdom and understanding would be required of anyone who chose to settle and survive in the Sand Hills.

Frankie and her two horses continued traveling, slowly now, on a more cautious journey, moving through a land she had thought she knew so well. But the truth was, now, she was passing through a strange land—a snow-cloaked winter-land—a land she didn't recognize or understand. Sometimes Rock stayed beside them and sometimes, he stayed back, keeping himself at a distance. But he was always alert.

It was while she watched the two horses working together, and separately, that she gained a new understanding of the protective instinct in the hearts of her two warhorses. The two warhorses—the Cheyenne-trained pinto and the Cavalry-trained liver-chestnut—had been bred, raised and trained in vastly different worlds. And yet, their instincts and their hearts were the same. Because no matter what the situation, these horses knew how to take care of their rider. Any horse could be taken into battle, but there was a certain depth of instinct and wisdom that coursed through a *true* warhorse, something in the breeding and the blood and the bones. Something that couldn't be taught.

For two hours, she stayed on Fox's back, showing him her desired direction, and then allowing him to choose the safest course through the hillsides and valleys. She watched Fox making his choices and movements; she watched Rock making his choices. And finally, she felt the relief that came with accepting the lead the two warhorses offered.

A mile upriver, figuring she had learned her lessons, Frankie turned Fox out onto the open land; she began to swing him in a wide circle toward the Lookout Hill. This time though, she let him find his own path. Rock followed, diligently alert, still doing his duty.

Once the high hill was in sight, she directed the pinto toward its north slope, and as soon as Fox understood her destination, she relaxed the rein and let him choose the course. The pinto put his head down and picked his way across the land, winding around the vast and spreading drifts, finding his path and keeping them safe.

When they reached the base of the Lookout Hill, Fox and Rock trotted up the windswept slope, side-by-side, snorting and sucking in the scents on the high breeze drifting along the hillsides. New scents that they understood—scents that told them a story about the creatures and their movement on the land.

Once they topped out on the crest, Frankie stared out across the snow-swept world, surveying a landscape that was unrecognizable. To the north and west, the blizzard had cloaked the leeward slopes and lowlands with a massive white blanket, To the east and south, the wind-blown land looked more like a quilted blanket with broad patches of brown and yellow winter-grasses scattered across the rolling hills, stitched in place among fields of snow. In every direction, whether blanketed in white or patched together like a crazy quilt, there was only desolate stillness and stunned silence—as if nothing dared to move across the winter-land. *Nothing except a little-white-girl and two wise warhorses.*

Wild Bird's words came to Frankie's mind.

'Watch,' she had said. 'Watch and you'll see the animals come out from their holes and their homes. They'll come out when the land is safe from the storm. Look around you, Granddaughter. Watch the creatures and see what they will teach you.'

So Frankie stayed on the Lookout Hill, sitting on Fox's back with Rock beside them. Watching and waiting like her grandmother had said. And just like the old woman said, the world of the Sand Hills began to come alive. The animals knew it was safe; they knew it was time. They were waking from their rest; waking to this new world.

Frankie sat on the hilltop, watching as the creatures of the land emerged. She saw a red fox trotting across the snow; she saw as it stopped, cocked its head, turned and took a few steps. Halted. Leaped vertically, arched and pounced straight down into the snow. When it lifted its head from the snow, there was a mouse dangling from its jaw. It trotted off, head held high.

A pack of coyotes, six of them, drifted across the low valley to the north, traveling in their coyote-way—glancing back over their shoulders every ten or fifteen paces. Far to the east, she saw a wolf gliding along across the white landscape. She studied it for a while, watching as it trotted along, moving smooth and steady in the way of wolves; she watched for a mate, saw none, and decided it was traveling alone. *Lone wolf. Traveling north. Moving fast. Going somewhere fast, for some reason of its own.*

On a windswept patch across the valley below her, a badger trundled about, snuffling among clumps of yucca plants at the base of the hillside. Rabbits were out, and they seemed to be everywhere, busy eating for a while, then busying themselves with carrying mouthfuls of grass back to their burrows. Antelope and deer showed themselves, clustering together on the wind-swept patches of grass, intent on grazing; they had their noses down, working their way through the exposed grasses.

Frankie watched them grabbing a mouthful, then raising their heads. Eyes watching, ears flicking, noses lifted high. Then noses down again, grazing again, then heads up. Busy with their business. Hurrying. Like they knew something.

Above her, birds were flying. No cheerful songs today. Just fast-flying flights. Moving through the sky in huge flocks. Hurrying. Going wherever they needed to be going. Two flights of geese passed overhead, traveling in their tight v-formations, flying fast, moving farther to the south, honking their way through the heavens.

None of these animals had gone out during the storm; none of them had fought against the storm. They all laid low; they rode it out, resting and waiting. Now they were outside; they were busy filling their bellies or busy getting to wherever they wanted to go. As she watched them, Frankie could see a sense of urgency in them. There was haste and hurry about their actions—as if they knew something was coming and they were preparing. *I see it, now. Another storm is on its way. No doubt.*

Frankie slipped down from Fox's back, settled herself on one of the big rocks. Snuggled down within her oversized coat and scanned the sky. Watching and waiting, pretty sure about what she'd see before long. Pretty sure she had understood the message from the creatures of the land.

She stayed there on the rock, eyeing the far hills to the west. Studying the horizon to the northwest. It was another half-hour of waiting and watching while her horses grazed near the cluster of rocks. She stayed where she was, watching the skies, bundled in her coat, feeling the warmth from the glaring winter sun.

Finally, it showed—a cloudbank was forming along the western horizon. It stayed low for a long time, as if it was purposely staying close to the ground, sneaking along while it was building and growing and darkening. Like a predator crouching and gathering strength. Stalking slowly. Carefully; patiently. Preparing for the pounce.

She watched until the storm began to rise, lifting itself above the land, showing itself for the storm it would be. It spread itself out, stretching across the far hills, staying low and riding the horizon for a long time. But it was building fast. Coming fast. *This is what the animals sense. This is what they already know. This is the message of their movements.*

Frankie took the hint. She stood up, whistled for her horses. Glanced again to the horizon and the looming storm. She shivered, partly because of the cooling wind, partly because she was considering the lessons of the day. She grinned and nodded. *A lot of lessons. Lessons learned.*

She turned to Fox, boosted herself to his back from the top of the rock and turned him toward home. She gave him his head again, trusting him to find the safest path down the hill and back to the track. Rock followed in his footsteps. They headed toward the river, and as they wound their way along the riverbank and circled around the rows of apple trees, Frankie spent the time studying how the storm had treated the river bottoms. Because there were more things to learn. *Because there will always be more storms on their way. Always more winters to come.*

Once back in the meadow and back at the barn, Frankie settled the horses into the stalls, added forks of hay and broke ice in the water troughs. At the chickencoop, she filled the feeders and added water to the troughs.

Back in her kitchen, she filled a mixing bowl with stew and tucked it into a dishpan, along with a pot of applesauce and a crock of butter; she tucked biscuits and pieces of cornbread wherever there was space, then balanced the sweet potato pie on top. She headed across the meadow, toting the dishpan, heading to Wild Bird's lodge.

She sat in the lodge by the fire, smiling and waiting politely like a good-Cheyenne-girl while her grandmother took her time, enjoying a couple of biscuits slathered with butter. Once the old woman was satisfied and settled back on her pile of furs and buffalo-robes, Frankie talked about her horses protecting her, explaining how they carried her safely across the snow-covered land. She said she understood how quickly everything could change around out on the open land. And how death could have found her if she hadn't been traveling with horses wiser than her.

"The robe, the rifle, the supplies, the fire-makings—it was wise for me to have those things," she said. "Because nothing is the same after such a storm. I know that now. Thank you, Grandmother."

Old Wild Bird nodded at her. Smiled and patted her arm. Told her she was a wise little girl. Told her she had done well. And when Frankie told Wild Bird of the coming storm, the old woman smiled and nodded again; she gave her a sly smile and Frankie knew the truth of the matter.

Wild Bird didn't need to ride out of the valley to understand what the storm had left behind. Neither did she need to go to the top of the Lookout Hill to study the horizon. Nor did she need to study the clouds. Because she had lived on this land and she already had within her all the wisdom that the earth and sky had given to her. She already knew about the coming storm; she knew everything about it.

So this morning, she had sent her little-white-granddaughter out—sending her with the protection she might need—so she could learn for herself. Wild Bird had given her little-white-granddaughter protection for the future, for the winters and the storms yet to come. It had been a gift. A gift of life.

When Frankie asked the old woman to come to her house during this next storm, she shook her head. No, Wild Bird said, she would be warm and safe in her lodge. She had been warm and safe in her lodge for many, many snows. Many thousands. *Haesto no'ka-måhtóhtoa-måhtóhtó-nó'e.*

She patted Frankie's knee and said again, that this meadow was a good place to winter. She had no needs that had not been met, and she had no fears about another storm. There had been many storms and many winters; she had no reason to go into the great dark lodge, into the spider-people's lodge—the *vé'ho'é-måheo'o.*

Frankie heard her use the Cheyenne word for white people again and cringed inside herself. She had never liked the word; it was not a pretty word. Or a pretty thought.

She stayed a while longer, and then left her grandmother comfortable and content in her lodge; she ducked through the door-flap, smiling, because the old woman was already busy buttering another biscuit. She spent some time carrying a few more armloads of firewood to the stack beside the lodge door, then she walked out to each of the pastures, wading through the low ends of the finger-drifts to check on her animals.

They had all weathered the first storm just fine, and now, like the wild creatures of the land, they had their heads down, grazing on the open patches of grass. Wild Bird's bony old buckskin and her two pinto packhorses were busy filling their bellies, wise in the ways of the weather, knowing what they would need for the coming storm. The four Shires stopped their grazing long enough to greet her. Sunny Jim and Little Bub nuzzled and nudged her; Black Mack blew his warm breath down her neck; High Boy nipped at her braids and snuffled at her ears. The four oxen, Bo and Benjamin, Buck and Billy, stood and swayed as she rubbed their faces and their shoulders. The herd of roan cows had already settled themselves down into a tree-sheltered corner of the pasture; the oxen, Frankie knew, would soon join them to weather the coming storm.

Trumpeter and the mares were galloping and bucking around their pasture, tossing their heads, whipping their tails, warming themselves up. Getting their blood flowing. They too, had the scent of the coming storm.

In the barn, she tossed a few forks of hay into Blossom's pen. Laughing Girl came racing into the barn, bounding down the alley-

573

way with a rabbit hanging from her jaws. She handed it off to Frankie with a sly-eyed look and a goofy grin.

"So. You've been preparing for the storm too?" Frankie took the proffered rabbit, ruffled her ears. "Running your muscles and grabbing some food, eh?"

The hound dropped her chest to the ground, stuck her bottom up in the air, wagged her long skinny tail for a moment. She flashed her big wolfhound grin again before turning and trotting back to the dog-stall; she leaped over the low barrier and burrowed into the pile of straw with her pups.

Frankie headed out of the barn and felt the sudden cooling in the air—a fresh and shocking cool. Above her, clouds were already arriving, already sliding through the sky, the soft roll-clouds of the early-front were showing themselves over the western rim of the valley, changing the bright prairie blue sky to a muddied gun-barrel gray. She walked to Wild Bird's lodge; she scratched at the door-flap and slipped inside to hand her the rabbit.

"For your fire, Grandmother. The storm is here now. Stay warm."

"Stay warm, Granddaughter."

Frankie backed out of the lodge and saw Matilda already heading toward the house. She grinned; the tawny little collie-dog knew what was coming too. She was ready to curl up in front of the kitchen fireplace.

A blast of icy air hit the back of Frankie's neck as she followed Matilda across the meadow. She turned to look at the sky beyond the barn's ridgeline; the hard-front of the storm had arrived; it was there above the west rim of her valley. The high limbs of the trees began dipping and bending as the wind raced across the slopes.

Frankie broke into a trot, feeling the winds tugging at her coat and pushing at her back as she headed to the house. Ahead of her, the winds were surging up the eastern slope behind the house, whipping through the stands of trees, twisting between the trunks and swirling among the high branches.

On the porch, she stopped to take a final look at the sky, shivered again, held the door as Matilda slipped through. Sure enough, the collie-dog bee-lined for her spot in front of the kitchen fireplace. Frankie grinned and headed for the big Majestic stove, thinking about getting a pot of coffee brewing. And thinking about which books she wanted to read. Outside, the winds above the valley began their howling.

Two days later, the second storm wore itself out; it passed beyond the meadow, leaving the homestead blanketed with another layer of snow. The bright rays of the winter sun began heating the winter-scape; the sun-warmed air pressed down across the snow-blanketed hills and valleys.

In the afternoons, the snow began receding. Some of it melted and disappeared silently into the soil, and some evaporated into the prairie sky, twisting into rising vapors that swayed and curled and swirled above the surface of the land in spellbinding waves.

Frankie spent the days wandering, watching the land come alive again as the creatures of the Sand Hills emerged from their hidden places in the wake of the storm. The surface of the snow softened under the bright heat of the winter sun, vapors lifted and curled into the air, and the drifts began shrinking, the edges of the snow melting and soaking into the soil.

The winter-birds of the Sand Hills announced their presence again, launching their songs into the sun-warming air, as if working to make up for their days of silence. They sent out their cries and trills and whistles and warbles, releasing their musical riffs and rolling melodies into the prairie-blue sky, singing and calling from the snow-barren hillside grasses and from the trees of the riverbanks. Small herds of deer and antelope grazed in the patches of grass beside the snow banks. Rabbits and gophers and mice emerged from their tunnels and went to work on the grasses in the bare, wind-blown areas. And weasels and foxes went to work on the rabbits, the gophers and mice.

At night, the land froze again, and in the mornings, the surface of the snow was crusted over, crisp and hard. Hard enough, Frankie discovered, to bear the weight of small and medium-sized animals, as well as eleven-year-old girls. By early afternoon, the rays of the winter sun softened the world of the Sand Hills once again—the hard crust on the snow was gone and the exposed soils turned soggy and soft.

So Frankie and Laughing Girl learned to do most of their exploring and hunting in the early part of the day, when they could stay on top of the hard crust. Because they both discovered that the hard crust offered a number of advantages for the hunter.

The great brindle wolfhound-greyhound learned the ease of taking rabbits from the surface of the snow. For the lurcher, hunting from the surface of the snow, where she could race at top speed and where her vision was unobstructed, was a joy. At first, when the hound came running up with a furry mouthful of prey to lay at her feet, Frankie gave her brief scoldings for abusing the unfair advantage of the crust. The scoldings, though, were half-hearted, because Frankie wasn't at all saddened by the thought of the extra meat hanging on the pantry hooks.

For herself, it wasn't long before she discovered her own ease in hunting on the crusted-snow. It was a simple thing to shoot grouse and prairie chickens as they trundled about in plain sight on the snow's surface. And hunting deer became an uncomplicated process, because as their sharp hooves broke through the crusted surface, their fleet flights became clumsy flounderings. The shot was easy. And dragging the carcass across the thick icy crust was an easy endeavor. Pulling the rock-sled loaded with her kill across the crusted snow was much less of a chore than handling the dead weight on the ground.

With a little clever thought and a few calculations as to the lay of the snow-covered land, Frankie found she didn't even need the rock-sled; she and a horse could slide a deer all the way into the meadow and right up to the barn as easy as skating on ice. In the end, it seemed wiser to drop the idea of the 'unfair advantage' of the crusted snow, and apply the term of 'clever tactics' instead.

It wasn't long before the pups began following their mother on the morning hunts, joining in her pursuits. At first, they seemed to see it as all part of another 'wild-chasing-game'. Halfway through the first morning, their minds shifted focus and suddenly, their puppy-brains understood—it was a 'wild-hunting-game'. And it was a very serious pursuit.

By the second morning, both Ghost Dog and Too Shy were learning the necessary skills. Despite a few tumbles and tangles due to their over-sized puppy-feet—they quickly managed the sight-hound art of coursing-snatching-and-flipping rabbits. In their initial pursuits, they took plenty of wide and wild slides across the icy surface, slipping and swerving off-course, time after time. But somewhere in all the slipping and sliding and scrambling, they finally learned the reason for the sharp claws on their over-sized paws.

On their third morning, as they hunted beside their mother, Frankie could see the two pups had not only acquired the necessary hunting skills, but those skills had become an art. They were working as a pack with their mother and suddenly, the hunt took on new dimensions. For the three hounds, *that* was when the real fun began. Fun in *their* minds, but *not* necessarily in the minds of the foxes and coyotes. Because, as the wolfhound-deerhound-greyhounds became perfect predators, the foxes and coyotes suddenly became their perfect prey—the instinct and breeding of the coursing-hounds made it so.

The foxes, both the red foxes and the little gray swift-foxes, received much the same treatment as the rabbits; when Frankie examined them she saw they had succumbed to the same neck-snaps as the rabbits had. It was a fast and effective kill. No blood. The hunted creatures put up no fight, because they had no opportunity.

The end of the hunt for the coyotes, though, tended to be more of a grisly affair, because at some point in the chase, when the coyotes realized they had three wolfhounds angling toward them—converging upon them from different directions—they chose to turn and fight. It was always their last fight. It was always a fight to the death.

Ghost Dog and Too Shy had become hunters like their mother, and like their mother, they didn't play around when they hunted. And since Laughing Girl was already in her self-designed habit of bringing her prey to her person, Ghost Dog and Too Shy followed her lead; they brought their kills to their person, and like their mother's kills, most of their prey were un-bloodied and the hides unmolested.

Frankie never returned to her meadow from her morning forays without three or four rabbits and a few cleanly-killed fox-skins. And coyote-hides, if they weren't badly mauled. She shared the rabbit meat with Wild Bird who loved adding it to her stew-pot. To Frankie's surprise, the old woman laid claim to the rabbit-hides, along with any other hides she brought in. Frankie cheerfully handed them over to the old woman. *Let Wild Bird put them to use. Better yet, let the old woman do the cleaning and scraping.*

Wild Bird was ecstatic over the fox-hides and any of the unmolested coyote-hides, and Frankie was happy enough to hand them over. There was a beauty to the hides, especially the glossy and bright golden-red fox-hides—far too beautiful to leave behind after the hunt. And while Frankie didn't mind stripping the hides from the carcasses, it was the after-work she dreaded—she had no love for the time-consuming job of cleaning, scraping and stretching the hides.

So at Wild Bird's urging, Frankie kept bringing in hides. Always, there were the rabbit and fox and coyote-hides; sometimes she returned to the meadow with the hides of badgers and racoons. And if they hadn't released their spray, Frankie brought in skunks. To her surprise, the skunks pleased Wild Bird immensely. And once the hounds started finding and chasing down the fierce and wily ferrets and equally fierce weasels, she brought those in too.

"Xáa'e," Wild Bird gave her the name for the weasels and Frankie recognized the connection to the Cheyenne word for urinating. 'E-xáa'e'. Which, she decided was probably a reference to the rank musk-odor.

And once, Frankie thought she was bringing in a large weasel—almost two feet in length and twice as big as the other weasels she had found—but Wild Bird named it differently.

"Náehe," she said. She spread the toes to show hidden webbing. It took a moment for Frankie to realize she had brought in a mink, not a weasel. Weasels, according to Wild Bird, lived on and within the dry land, in burrows among the roots and rocks. The minks were creatures of the wetter lands, living in mud-bank tunnels or stealing the burrows and waterways of muskrats—thus, the webbing.

Once the hounds discovered a pair of porcupines lumbering across a drifted hillside. All her yelling and scolding and ordering did no good—by the time she managed to pull all three dogs away, they had muzzles and front legs full of quills. She finished the kill herself, but unsure about how to handle the skinning of those particular creatures, she brought the two porcupines home, whole and intact. Lugging them along, holding them by hooking their front claws over her fingers. Making frequent stops either to rest her hands, or to yell at the hounds, making them stay back, in an effort to avoid any further muzzle-and-quill encounters.

As far as Wild Bird was concerned, it was a particularly auspicious event. While Frankie spent the rest of the day pulling quills from the hounds' muzzles and paws, she watched her grandmother applying her expert skills in skinning the porcupines and harvesting the quills.

"Heškóveto." The 'thorny-one'. Wild Bird spoke the name for the animal and Frankie watched her gnarly old fingers, plucking and sorting the quills by size.

"Heškóvetsée'e," Wild Bird explained, holding up a handful of the quills. Frankie had first heard the word from Blue Feather and grinned again at the sensibility of the word. 'Porcupine-feathers'. A very literal description.

Frankie continued her mornings, prowling with her rifle and her hounds; and Wild Bird spent any bright, sunny days outside her lodge, scraping and tanning her array of hides in the warm winter sun. She stretched the hides, lacing them onto frames she made from branches, and then hung them to dry on the walls and posts inside the barn.

During the cold evenings, Frankie sat in the lodge, listening to Wild Bird talking softly about life and lessons, watching while she threaded sinew into bone needles and stitched fox-hide to fox-hide, and rabbit-hide to rabbit-hide—making blankets and robes. Watching as her grandmother sewed the hides of the mink and weasels, the racoons and the badgers, into mittens and high-topped winter-moccasins and winter leggings.

Frankie sat by this wonderful grandmother of hers, listening to her stories about Cheyenne life and Cheyenne lessons while her mind traced back to other evenings. Because there had been other evenings like this—other December evenings by a warm fire—evenings back in Indiana, in the great white house, when she sat listening to her Aunt Sarah speaking of life and lessons as she stitched her crazy quilts.

By the time most the snow from the blizzard melted away, there was a great selection of hides from a great variety of animals of the Sand Hills, hanging in the barn. Within the Cheyenne lodge, there were long leather cords stretched between the tall lodgepoles, each hanging heavy with fox-tails and coyote-tails, all waiting to be used for other things. To Frankie's eyes, it was both an interesting and appealing effect, one she decided would look awfully nice in her own house.

When she asked Wild Bird about having a string or two of the tails, Wild Bird nodded, gestured at the long strings of tails—tails of coyotes, of red foxes and of the little gray swift-foxes—and waved her away as she kept working with her needle. And Frankie selected strings of tails, of both the swift-fox and the red fox, and headed to her house, figuring they'd look fine hanging high across the top of the wall in the sitting-room.

There was one morning, when Frankie woke to a new sound drifting across the meadow—a musical clicking, an almost mystical ticking; she followed the sound to Wild Bird's tipi. There, dangling from the lodge's highest pole—the slender smoke-flap pole—was a long strand of deer-hooves. The hooves were flipping and twirling in the breeze and sending out a rhythmic little tap-dance of clicks and clacks.

She stared at the dancing hooves, wondering exactly how the frail old woman had managed to fasten the strand at the top of the highest lodgepole, when Wild Bird emerged from the door-flap.

Wild Bird's craggy face broke into a wide smile when she saw Fire Heart Child's fascination with the deer-hooves; she ducked back into her lodge and re-appeared a moment later with another string of deer-hooves in hand. She waggled the strand, sending them into their own dance of clattering clicks; she grinned her gap-toothed grin and laughed as she handed them to her granddaughter. The old Cheyenne woman laughed harder as her white-granddaughter danced and bounced around, twirling with the hooves and sending them into a fresh frenzy of clicks and clacks.

Wild Bird beckoned to Frankie and pulled another clicking strand from behind her back. This one, Frankie saw looked like a miniature version of the deer-hoof strand. She gasped when her grandmother lifted the small strand over her head and settled it around her neck; she stared at it, marveling at the shining black beads. *No. Not beads. Dew-claws!* A necklace of the tiny dew-claws of deer hung around her neck, lying black and shiny against her skin. Glistening in the sunlight.

The old woman smiled, watching her granddaughter, excited and filled with all the joy of the gift. Wild Bird nodded; her smile softened. It was just as she intended. A gift for her little-white-grand-daughter, to make her happy, to make her dance. She watched as Fire Heart Child danced across the meadow to her house, doing a dance with steps that looked to be a bit of the Round Dance and a bit of a War Dance. *Yes. Only this little-white-girl of mine could do a dance like that. Only Fire Heart Child could find a way to do a happy war-dance.*

Frankie was in the root-cellar, gathering up what she needed for the coming visit from the Dunbars; she was pretty sure they would come tomorrow, even though it was Saturday, and not Sunday. Because the roads would be dry and the weather clear. Her plan today was to start cooking the filling for a couple of meat-pies. Already, she had dried buffalo meat soaking, readying for the stewed filling; in the morning, it would only be a matter of putting everything in the crusts and slipping the pies in the oven. And today, she would bake several pumpkin pies—one for the afternoon dinner tomorrow, one to send home with the Dunbars, and one whole pie to take over to Wild Bird. *One pie just for her.*

Her very next thought was that she should make yet another pumpkin pie. Just in case the Reverend Austin and Betsy showed up too. Because it was a strong possibility. Because they hadn't been here for a while. *If they're true to form, they might just drive down the track midway through the morning.*

There were two reasons for the Austins' visits and Frankie knew what they were. One had to do with a lingering need to provide something akin to parental guidance, now that their own sons were grown and living their own lives. The other reason had to do with what her father would have called 'a sense of churchly obligation'. Both were strong pulls for the Austins and it was obvious to Frankie that a child living alone within the community, filled that particular cup. Simeon Austin and his wife had decided to keep a close eye on her because they believed it was the right thing to do.

So probably, they would turn up in the next day or so. As soon as the Austins thought the weather would hold, the nice little red molly-mule would come down the track, pulling the nice little wagon. And just about the time the Reverend would pull the mule to a stop, Betsy would say something about stopping in because they were 'just wanting to see the goings-on in Frankie's meadow'. She'd offer that politely stated reason for their visit so Frankie wouldn't suspect they were checking on her.

And Frankie knew that as soon as the Reverend Austin knew Betsy wouldn't notice, he'd give her a sly wink. Because he knew she understood the real reason, and he knew she didn't mind. So they had an unspoken pact between them—they'd let Betsy believe what she needed to believe.

And even with all that, the Austins were playing an important part in her life and Frankie was finding great affection for them. Betsy had raised two sons to adulthood, and Frankie figured she was probably missing 'the mothering part' of her life now. So if she needed to do a little 'mothering' during their visits, Frankie accepted it.

The Reverend Simeon Austin, Frankie knew, had his own needs; he had put himself into the role of gentle-advisor, and his methods were not unlike her father's had been. Like Justus Harding, Simeon Austin shared his insight and wisdom when she needed it; he gave her guidance when she asked; he always offered encouragement. He listened; he asked questions; he offered advice. He was watching over her in the way he felt he could, always gentle and respectful. And Frankie accepted it for the gift that it was.

Realizing the possibility of having more than just Ida and Everett at the table, Frankie grabbed up more carrots and parsnips, more potatoes and onions and tucked them into the basket she was filling. She reached to the bundles of herbs hanging from the ceiling hooks and broke off sprigs of sage, basil and dill. She had just turned to the bin of pumpkins, when she heard scratching and snuffling beside the wall-bins.

Matilda had followed her into the cellar, and now, her nose was pressed against the corner where the front vegetable bins met the wall, sniffing and scratching at a crack near the floor. Calling her back from the corner, Frankie stood for a moment, looking at what seemed to be an awfully large gap. A strange thing to see—because gaps and cracks weren't a common thing in anything Daniel Kinison built.

Looking closer, Frankie thought it was a very odd thing. Because certainly, of all the construction Daniel Kinison had done in the meadow, he would have been most cautious about the root-cellar's construction. Cracks and gaps in cellar walls were an open invitation to mice and rats and other creatures; it was a sure way to have a winter's food supply destroyed.

Frankie settled the basket on the top of the long sorting table and walked over to the corner of the bin-wall, eyeing the gap—a gap she had never noticed before. She was thinking she should mention it to Everett tomorrow; thinking he'd help her mend it before some critter found its way into the cellar and the bins.

She squatted down and poked her fingers into the crack, exploring the gap, surprised she could wiggle her fingers in the space. Surprised she could feel air filtering through, from beyond the crack. Surprised because her fingers didn't encounter either dirt or wood. Just space. She sniffed at the air, feeling a bit like a collie-dog. The air smelled clean—no musty smell, or dirt smell, or hillside smell.

Standing up again, Frankie studied the wall of bins. She pushed against it; she tried yanking on it. And finally, when she put her shoulder to it and shoved, a portion of the bin-wall moved. It shifted. Just a bit. She stepped back and looked at it. The gap had widened.

She applied her shoulder again and shoved harder. The end portion of the bin-wall shifted again. She shoved again, and it moved again. Easier, now. Another push and the bins shifted to expose an opening—an opening that Frankie thought looked a lot like a doorway. She pushed against the bins once more and the opening showed as a narrow doorway.

A framed doorway—a purpose-built doorway that, she realized, must lead somewhere. Her mind whisked back to rainy days in Indiana when she and her cousins read aloud to each other, reading stories about castles with secret passageways and cabinets with secret doorways leading into hidden rooms.

Frankie breathed in the cool air coming through the doorway and gasped a little. Grinned a little. Feeling the excitement and mystery in the air. A shiver shimmied up her spine. She took the kerosene lamp from the sorting table, lit it, and turned back to the doorway. Holding the lamp high, she peered through the door. *Not a secret passageway. A secret doorway to a secret room. A neat little room.*

Frankie stepped through the doorway, letting the lamp-light reveal the room. She gave another gasp as something brushed against her leg—Matilda crowded past her into the space, eager to lay claim to the marvelous little room she had discovered. The collie-dog headed to a long low bench along the wall opposite the doorway; she jumped onto it and settled her backside down, looking at Frankie with her toothy dog-grin, clearly pleased with what she'd found.

Matilda's find was a small room tucked behind the side wall of the root-cellar. Looking around the little room, Frankie saw that it was a smaller version of the Dwelling Place, built and supported and framed-in, sitting under the hillside, snug and comfortable. She'd never known it was here. In five months, she had never found it. *It's been right here all along.*

Frankie could see it was furnished with basic items, necessary items. Along with the bench where Matilda sat, there was a large oak-barrel standing in one corner. Lifting the lid, she discovered it was filled to the brim with water. There were two smaller oak kegs— inside of them she found canvas bags holding jerky and dried fruit, parched corn and pilot bread. There were matches and candles in a crock; there was a kerosene lamp hanging from the ceiling. There was a chamber-pot on the floor beside the bench.

The bench, Frankie discovered, was actually a long box which apparently became a bed, because when she lifted the lid, she discovered a rolled-up corn-shuck mattress and several blankets, all kept safe and clean in the box. There was a hunting knife, a Henry rifle, and a box of ammunition.

Frankie turned around in the room, smiling, realizing what she had—a hideout built deep into the hillside. Tucked away just like a wolf's den. Built as protection from danger; all you had to do was step inside, pull the wall back in place with the heavy wooden handle on the inside of the wall, and stay put until the danger was gone. Here, there was food and water, shelter and protection.

Maybe Daniel Kinison had been thinking about a safe place from the tornadoes that came with the summer storms. Or maybe, when he first came and was still unsure of the land and the people roaming around on it, he thought it wise to have a place to hide—a hiding place from unfriendly Indians. Certainly he knew it would be a safe place for his wife and children. Because no one would discover the room. Because she, herself, had been in the cellar once or twice a week since late July and she never even suspected it was here.

Frankie smiled. This was a clever kind of protection. This was another treasure, another gift, from Daniel Kinison. This, she decided, needed to stay a secret from the rest of the world. At least, for now.

She called to Matilda and shoved the bin-wall back into its rightful place. The gap was gone. There was no sign that a room was behind the bins. After all the months of loading the bins and moving produce around, the bin-wall must have shifted a bit.

"This is a fine secret we have, Matilda. A very fine secret." Frankie grinned at Matilda, and Matilda grinned her toothy-grin right back at her. She decided she was going to do some more thinking after the day's discovery, because she was already wondering about other hidden places. She picked out a pumpkin and grabbed the basket and started up the cellar steps. And all the while, she was trying to figure out exactly what had been in Daniel Kinison's mind.

By the time she reached the house, she was pretty certain the hidden room wasn't about protection from tornadoes. Because the Hyatt brothers had told her that the low-lying valley itself would likely be enough protection; tornadoes, like the wind, would, for the most part, sail over the valley. And in her mind, the Dwelling Place and the root-cellar, just as they were, would offer additional protection from the weather if necessary.

She was still turning things over in her mind as she began cutting the pumpkins apart, setting the seeds aside, planning to clean and dry them for planting in the spring. Her mind stayed on the snug little room that was so cleverly disguised. She decided the hidden doorway must have to do with dangers that would come from people—people with dangerous intent.

The more Frankie thought about it, the more she doubted it was the only hideout on the homestead. Because if Daniel saw the need for a hiding place in the cellar, then as clever as he was, he would have realized a need for hideaways in other places. Given enough time, when a dangerous situation was imminent, a person might be able to dash to the cellar and hide. But if danger came into the valley suddenly, when a person was in the barn or in the house, there might not be the option of running to the cellar. *No. Surely, Daniel Kinison put a hideout somewhere in the house. And he would have a hiding place in the barn too. Maybe in the Barracks.*

Frankie decided she'd spend tomorrow with her company. She'd say nothing to anyone about her discovery. But after they left, she was going to do some treasure hunting. *Because there must be other hideouts.*

She looked at Matilda, curled up in her spot in front of the fireplace.

"And don't you say a word to anyone. This is *our* secret."

Frankie put her attention back on the pots of pumpkin pieces, setting them to the burners. Matilda gave a yawn and put her attention toward taking a nap.

Early the next morning the Dunbars rolled up in their light wagon and sitting right between them on the wagon-seat, was their very own pup. Frankie laughed at the sight—the little blond runty-pup had found her place in her new family. As soon as Everett pulled his team to a stop, the blond wolfhound bounded down from the wagon to greet her sisters and mother. In less than a minute, all four took off like a pack of crazy-dogs, careening around the meadow in a wild and exuberant lurcher race, with wide, wolfish grins and laughing eyes.

"So is that runty little hound working out for you or do you want to be rid of her? Because I can take her back if you want." Frankie knew Ida would give her a glare for suggesting such a thing. Which she did. She wagged her finger at Frankie with a serious warning in her eyes.

"Don't you start in, you naughty little thing. You leave off thinking you'll be getting our sweet little girl away from us." Ida held her stern look while Everett helped her to the ground.

Frankie grinned at her and Ida broke out in laughter as she pulled her into a hug, rocking her from side to side. As quick as Ida released her, Everett had his arms around her, hugging her.

As the three of them stepped back to the bed of the wagon, Frankie pointed at the dog-pile of rolling and twisting wolfhounds, growling and yelping, sounding as if they were tearing each other into pieces and eating each other alive. She said as much, and mentioned that their hound certainly didn't sound much like a 'sweet little girl'.

"*Don't* you say a bad word about my Blond Bessie." Ida was reaching for a basket under the seat. Everett lifted a burlap sack from the wagon-bed, a sack that seemed to be doing a lot of moving on its own.

"What have you got in that sack, Mr. Dunbar? Or do I even want to know?" Frankie was eyeing the sack and stepping back warily.

"Frankie, we brought you a little gift as a thank you for adding Blond Bessie into our lives. We decided it was time we added a little life to your place." Everett was smiling, and Ida stood beside him, her eyes shining; both clearly happy about whatever was squirming around in the sack.

Frankie watched with serious trepidation as they held it out to her, lifting it high enough to keep it out of Matilda's reach. The little collie was already interested in the squirming bag; she was sniffing at it, standing on her hind legs, ears perked up. No doubt, she was hearing the same mewling that Frankie was hearing.

"You remember that old calico cat of ours? The one that came back about a month ago?" Ida was flashing a pleased smile. "Well, a few weeks ago, Everett found where she had a litter hidden. Six kittens."

So now, Frankie realized, the Dunbars wanted to share their bounty. Ida reached into the sack as Everett opened it and started bringing out the kittens. Three of them—an orange-and-white spotted one, an orange-striped one, and a calico. Before anyone could stop her, Matilda reached up to Ida's hands and helped herself to the striped one. They all watched, laughing, as Matilda trotted off toward the barn, carrying the kitten gently in her mouth.

"She's back to mothering again." Ida was delighted. "She's got herself another adopted baby.

Frankie, though, wasn't quite so delighted. She didn't particularly care for cats. There had been plenty of cats back in Indiana, but other than spotting them as they were slinking around the horse-barns and dairy-barns and gardens, she'd never had much to do with them. She eyed the two wriggling kittens still in Ida's arms, trying not to grimace as Ida announced the three kittens were 'early Christmas presents for you, Honey'.

"Now. They're a bit young yet, so you may want to keep them in the house for a spell. Because they won't have their momma to keep them warm on the cold nights."

Ida was smiling and cooing to the kittens and Frankie, not wanting to hurt Ida's feelings, concentrated on holding her tongue. Because the last thing she wanted was a passel of cats scurrying and scrambling around in her house during the night. And she knew that cats had a knack for seeking out comfort. Once those kittens experienced life inside a house, they'd never be content outside.

But Ida and Everett were standing right in front of her—one holding the sack and one holding the cats—with their eyes shining as bright as sunlight on a church window. They clearly believed the sack of cats was a marvelous surprise.

So Frankie smiled and 'thanked them so much'; she told them it was a wonderful Christmas surprise and it would be 'so nice to have some cats around the place'. And just about when she could think of nothing else to say, Matilda saved the day. Having settled her first new baby somewhere in the barn, the little collie-dog returned for a second kitten. She stood on her hind legs, expecting Ida to hand over another one; Ida complied, relinquishing the calico to the collie. Matilda spun around and trotted off toward the barn.

The three of them burst into laughter and followed the tawny collie, with Ida still cuddling the orange-and-white kitten. By the time they reached the barn, Matilda was already on her way back to collect the third kitten. Ida handed it to her and they followed her through the doorway and watched as she leaped over the plank into the former puppy-stall. The little collie-dog curled up in the hay, gathered her new brood around her and began tongue-washing her new-found family.

Ida and Frankie broke out in laughter, realizing that Matilda had found a cure for her broken little collie-heart; she still ached for her rooster-puppy who had finally answered the call of his true nature—his interest was in the hens now and not the collie-dog that had raised him.

They stood for a moment, watching Matilda curled up in a nest of hay in the stall's corner with the kittens tucked in against her.

Ida was delighted. Everett shook his head, grinning. And Frankie breathed a little easier, knowing she was off the hook as far as kittens in the house—Matilda had solved that problem.

It was an hour later, as Frankie and Ida were pulling pumpkin pies and dinner rolls out of the ovens and spooning the meat and vegetable filling into pie shells, that the hounds sent up their warning barks. Within a couple of minutes, a wagon pulled by a team of snappy sorrels rolled into the valley. Frankie grinned. The Hyatt brothers had decided to come for a visit.

Tipp turned the sorrels—nice-stepping sorrels that Frankie had never seen before—toward the barn-lot as Everett came out of the barn. Everett walked toward them, greeted them, and by the time the three men started unbuckling the hames and harnesses, Frankie knew they'd be discussing the weather—because that's what men out here in the Territory always talked about. They talked about the weather of the previous days, about the weather of the current day, and about the weather for the coming days. They'd talk about what the spring weather might be like. And then whether the summer would be hot and dry. Which would lead into a conversation about what the harvest weather might be. And once the word 'harvest' was uttered, there'd be talk about crops and fields and planting and how the weather might affect those things. Because that's how it always was with the men who were settling the Sand Hills.

Frankie and Ida looked at each other. Smiling and nodding, both knowing the same thing about men and their weather-talk. Ida headed into the pantry.

"We'll need more flour for more pie crusts," she called over her shoulder. "Two meat pies won't be enough. Because I still expect the Reverend and Betsy will be driving in before long."

Frankie grinned and agreed; they had already been planning for a visit by the Austins, but now, the Hyatt brothers would be sitting down at the table too. Ida started mixing the dough and Frankie grabbed the rolling pin.

As soon as they had four meat pies baking in the ovens, they went across the meadow to greet Tipp and William. Before they reached the three men, though, the four hounds set up another warning bark. The sound of hooves and wagon wheels came from beyond the entrance and a moment later, sure enough, a nice red molly-mule came down the track, pulling the nice little farm wagon. Betsy and the Reverend Austin were smiling and waving, and there on the seat between, them Frankie could see a dishpan with a flour-sack dishtowel tucked around it.

Frankie shouted out a welcome, grinning at the sight of the dishpan, because if Betsy Austin was carrying a covered dishpan, it was a sure bet she had been baking. Betsy Austin was known for her baking every Monday. And once she got her oven going in the morning, she kept it going until she had a week's worth of baked goods filling up the shelves of the high baker's cupboard in her kitchen. And no matter what else she might pull out of the oven, or off the stovetop, there would *always* be doughnuts.

It was Frankie's bet there were sugary spiced-doughnuts in the dishpan on the wagon-seat. Because Betsy knew they were her favorites.

The first part of the afternoon was centered around food and conversation. Tipp and William had been surprised to see a Cheyenne lodge standing by the windmill pond. Wild Bird had left early in the morning to forage along the river, a task that she'd be at for most of the day, so the brothers had missed meeting her. Nonetheless, they expected to hear the whole story of her presence in the valley.

And as soon as mention was made about the Cheyenne and Oglála visits to the meadow, the brothers wanted to know every detail about those visits too. As it turned out, even though Frankie began the story and started replying to their questions, it was the Dunbars and the Austins who ended up telling the Hyatt brothers most of the story.

By the time the desserts reached the table, the brothers started telling their own stories. Frankie thought she had heard most of their stories, because she had heard a lot. But as it turned out, the two brothers had far more tales than she had heard. And even though they were true stories, the way the brothers told them, their adventures sounded a lot more like tall-tales.

Each brother had his own way of telling a story and Frankie was having a hard time deciding who had the best style; it sent her thoughts back to Fort Kearny and memories of the two soldiers—Crazy Eddie McClure and Thomas Braddock—who always managed to keep everyone doubled-up, laughing at their stories.

By the time the last of the pie was eaten and the doughnuts were gone, William and Tipp had everyone wiping tears from their eyes and holding their jaws. But the real fun started after the food and the stories and the laughter. As he popped the last bite of the last doughnut in his mouth, William excused himself from the table and went outside. When he came back into the kitchen, he was carrying two violin cases.

"Me an' Tipp just happened to bring these fiddles along," he said it casually, but Frankie saw the wink he directed to Reverend Austin. "And since we have 'em here, I was thinking maybe we'd see if this little Prairie-Girl knows anything about playin' those violins of hers. We've been wonderin' ever since we seen 'em in her sitting-room the last time she fed us."

Frankie hadn't expected it, but it didn't really surprise her. With the Hyatt brothers around, almost anything could happen.

"Get some rosin on your bow, Pretty Girl, and let's see what you kin do." Tipp nodded to her.

Frankie hesitated, and then she slipped into the sitting-room; she selected her father's violin, lifted it from the shelf and started working the rosin on the bow, grinning as she did. Because she was betting that the Hyatt boys could rip into a tune. They had told her stories about the barn dances they had played at back in Iowa; there had been four Hyatt brothers who played together back then—and Frankie knew what that meant—four boys in one family who all played the fiddle, would mean a lot of good-natured competition.

And that meant they could probably get a lot of music out of a violin, music that could probably move good and fast and wild.

She was also thinking about songs commonly played at barn dances and fairs and weddings. There might be a few songs that were unique—certain songs that certain players were known for—but mostly, there would be songs the dancers would know. She had gone with her father and uncle and her cousin Samuel whenever they played at dances and fairs; they had lifted her to the stage to play with them plenty of times, so she figured there was a good chance she'd know a lot of the songs the Hyatt brothers knew.

The three of them tuned their fiddles together in a corner of the sitting-room, working the tuning-pegs until the tones matched up the way they wanted. On the other side of the room, Frankie could see the members of their little audience getting themselves and some chairs arranged; Everett was moving a couple of chairs from the kitchen and Betsy was pointing out where they should be. The Reverend Austin was standing out of the way, smiling, letting Betsy manage the seating. And to Frankie's surprise, Ida's hands were shaking as she dabbed her hankie at tears in her eyes.

Once Tipp was satisfied with the sound of the fiddles, he stepped back, lifted his violin to his chin and looked to Frankie.

"William and me, we'll start out and you just step in whenever you feel like moving them little-bitty fingers of yours."

The Hyatt boys began with some fairly easy songs, simple tunes that were easy on the fingers and the bow—waiting to see when she would step in, and pretending that they weren't. She stayed back, letting them play the first two songs together, watching their styles and their timing.

William's style, she recognized; it was quite a bit like her father's. But Tipp's was different than any style she had ever seen or heard; it was rollicking and free and it didn't seem to follow any of the rules or methods she knew. Which, Frankie realized, probably had a lot to do with Tipp's personality. But somehow, his style seemed to work just fine with William's.

When they started playing the third song, "Goodbye Liza Jane", she stepped in beside them, grinning at them. Because she

saw the looks they exchanged—a little surprised and more than a little pleased. She was used to playing that particular song a bit faster
and hardier than they were playing it, but she knew very well that
they were keeping all the tunes at a slower tempo. Partly, because
they were testing her—in a polite way—to spot her level of skills.
And partly, because they wanted time to warm up together as a trio.
Doing what her father used to refer to as 'finding out where each
other's fingers were at'.

Tipp and William, she realized, were used to playing with four
fiddlers together, so they knew how to bring another player into their
songs; they knew exactly how to help her slide into a comfortable
spot with their styles. Frankie took William's cues, and by the fourth
song, the music was coming out strong and smooth. It wasn't long
before the brothers grinned at each other, declaring that 'she has the
same style as John Quincy'.

From what William had told her, all the Hyatt brothers were
named after American presidents or famous statesmen. There was a
brother named Benjamin Franklin Hyatt and another named Samuel
Adams Hyatt—and apparently, John Quincy Adams Hyatt was one
of the other brothers who carried the name of a president, as well as
the two playing with her—William Henry Harrison Hyatt and George
Washington Hyatt.

After Tipp and William each called another song, Tipp nodded to Frankie. She gave him one of her crooked grins and called
for "Drowsy Maggie", figuring that their faces would light up at the
selection. And they did.

"Well, let's git on with it then!" Tipp shouted the words. He gave
her a wide grin and a wicked wink, no doubt knowing exactly why
she chose that song. He knew she was telling them to put aside the
kid-stuff; he bowed to her and took a step back, giving her the lead.
She started the tune and they joined in, and the three of them made
Drowsy Maggie move.

Frankie knew the song well; it wasn't a particularly difficult
tune, but there was a trick to it—because if it was played right—the
tempo picked up, moving faster and faster the further you went into
the song. Three times past the chorus, she and William and Tipp had

their fingers flying and their bows racing across the strings; they were laughing their way through the tune just like their audience was. And the faster Drowsy Maggie moved, the wilder the laughter became.

To Frankie it seemed as if they had played together a thousand times, and she was pretty sure the music must be setting the last of the unfallen leaves in the trees to quivering, because they were sending the songs and the notes flying fast and high. By the time they quit the song, both the fiddlers and their audience were working to catch their breath.

They rested for a few minutes, drank a little water, and then worked their way through half a dozen more songs. And in the middle of one of the songs, when she looked through the sitting-room window, Frankie could see Wild Bird across the meadow. She was standing in front of her lodge, listening to the music coming from the little-white-girl's lodge.

And that had Frankie wondering if the old Cheyenne woman had ever heard fiddles before. She realized in the same moment, that it was unlikely—this, she decided was probably a first for Wild Bird.

She was also watching Ida and Everett and she was seeing a lot of delight in their faces. A lot more than she would have guessed. And that was when she realized that even though Simeon Austin and Betsy had heard her play before, Ida and Everett had not. But they were hearing now. And they were loving what was happening there in the sitting-room—they were both laughing and smiling and tapping their feet. Ida, though, was still doing a lot of eye-dabbing with her hankie. There was, no doubt, a reason for the tears, and Frankie suspected she'd hear about it later.

The Reverend Austin was smiling and tapping his foot to the music, and Frankie noticed that he was also spending a lot of time fingering the little brown tuft of the beard that sat right on the very end of his chin. She suspected there was some thinking and planning going on deep inside that busy preacher's-mind of his.

The next time they took a rest, William caught Frankie's eye—he gave a slight nod toward where the Reverend and Betsy were sitting. She understood and returned his nod, knowing it was time for the direction of their music to shift. Now, the sound of the fiddles would become the sound of violins; now, they would be asking for sweeter and gentler sounds from their strings. Because they couldn't keep playing in front of the Reverend and his wife, and not honor them with some selections that would befit the work of the man of God.

William asked the Reverend Austin to choose their next song and Frankie wasn't surprised by his choice—she'd played it for him and Betsy before—but she was pleased because it was a sweet soul-filled song. She started playing "Softly Now the Light of Day" and when Tipp and William came into the song with her, the beauty of the notes filled the room.

Betsy called for the next song and they played "Abide with Me". But it was William who called the third song and when he did, he flashed a wink at her. And his wink was enough to tell Frankie something different was going to happen. They started into "Stand Up and Bless the Lord" and sure enough, something happened—the Right Reverend Simeon Austin stood right up and sang the words, his beautiful bass-baritone filling the room.

When they played the next song, "Sun of My Soul", it didn't surprise Frankie to see their whole audience of four, rising to sing the words. With a bass-baritone, an alto, a tenor and a soprano, they formed a fine quartet. And when they sang the line that spoke of singing 'with heart and soul and voice', Frankie decided the Reverend, Betsy, Everett and Ida were doing exactly that.

Frankie had been expecting a request for a Christmas song—given that they were in December and Christmas was coming—but she was surprised that it was Everett who asked for it; she was even more surprised that it was "The Brightest and Best". A moment later, she understood why, because as they started into the song, Ida stood up; she sang solo, her soprano soft, pure, and sweet. She never bothered to wipe at the tears that began trailing down her cheeks while she sang, but everyone else was busy wiping away at theirs.

Three more times they sent Christmas hymns heavenward for the audience and Frankie pictured the notes traveling out of the valley and rippling across the winter-grasses before rising high into the cool blue sky of the prairie. The notes rang with the clarity of peace and truth, and when she and Tipp and William lowered their violins for the day, there were tears in Simeon Austins eyes. Ida had her hands to her face. And Everett sat motionless, his eyes soft and gentle. The smile on Betsy's face was soft and warm.

After the Austins pulled out of the meadow, with the Hyatt brothers driving the team of snappy sorrels along behind them, Ida and Everett walked back to the house with Frankie. It was only after they were in the kitchen, that they turned to Frankie, asking the question she had been expecting.

"How did we not know of this, Young Lady?" Ida was trying to sound stern again, trying to be serious, but mostly she sounded like a giddy school-girl.

"I think it never came up because we always have so many other things to talk about. I never really thought about violins when we were talking." Frankie gave the answer, knowing they had all realized it already. She turned to Ida, ready to ask her own question. Because there was something more to be said; because there had been such a strong reaction from her. But Everett enlightened her before she could ask.

"Honey, music is one of the things Ida loves the most in life. She plays the organ and the piano, but she hasn't heard music in a long time. Neither of us have. Not for more than three years now. Not since we started out from Iowa."

Frankie remembered the look in Ida's eyes, picturing how she had been pressing her hands against her cheeks as they began playing. *Of course. I should have known. We never asked Ida for any songs she wanted to hear.*

"Ida, tell me what you want to hear." She motioned for Ida and Everett to sit down again, to be an audience again. "If I don't know it, just keep asking until we find one I know."

Ida asked for several songs that Frankie didn't know, and then with a wistful look in her eyes, she asked for one of Johann Sebastian Bach's creations. "Sleepers Awake".

Frankie nodded; grinning. Pleased with the selection. She knew it alright. She knew it by its German name. "Wachet Auf". It had been her grandfather's favorite—one which he considered to be the most beautiful of all Bach's compositions. And Frankie thought so too.

She lifted the violin to her shoulder, settled it softly under her chin. *This* song, Frankie knew, was her grandfather's legacy to her. Now, she could gift it to Ida. To Ida, who was way out here on the prairie, living in the Sand Hills of the Nebraska Territory. To Ida, who hadn't heard this song—this most beautiful music of all—in more than three years.

Her mind drifted back; she pictured her grandfather playing "Wachet Auf". She recalled the three weeks he had dedicated to her, teaching his granddaughter the notes, the tune, and the beauty. She could see the stern look on his face as he guided her fingers along the violin's neck. She could picture his frown, as he sought out perfection. His voice serious and crisp; his manner serious and crisp. And yet, always gentle and calm and patient. Encouraging; inspiring. Nodding his head slowly when she achieved what he wanted. Expectant; demanding. But *always*—gentle, calm, patient. That was always his way when he taught. And it was the way he played too.

Morgan Harding had never played the 'fiddle'; he had only ever played the 'violin'. *Nothing* but the violin. Because Morgan Harding had played as a concert violinist, and in his mind and heart, he considered fiddling to be a crass and coarse use of 'such a fine instrument of such radiant sound'.

So now, out in the Sand Hills, out here in her meadow on her homestead, Frankie played for her grandfather; she played for the man who had passed the music down to his sons and on down to her, just as he had passed down the violin she was holding—from his hands, to his son's, to his granddaughter's.

She played for Ida, passing along the gift of that same music to her friend, to Ida Dunbar—to ease her heart, to fill the empty place, and to give answer to her yearning for the sound of music.

Frankie drew the notes of Bach's masterpiece out from the depths of the violin; she sent the notes and the song, silky and strong, circling around Ida. The song traveled out of the house, floating out

598

into the meadow, reaching the old Cheyenne woman standing beside her lodge, listening once again.

For the first time in Wild Bird's long life, Frankie realized, the old Cheyenne woman was hearing the sounds of Johann Sebastian Bach—something she had never heard. Something the grasses of the Sand Hills had never heard.

Frankie smiled, knowing this would please her grandfather, because today, his granddaughter was doing something with his gift of song that he could have never imagined—she was giving the song to a Cheyenne woman and to the prairie grasslands. She was sharing the gift with her homeland.

For the next three days Frankie spent a good amount of time searching for hidden spaces in the other buildings of the meadow. She found no hideout in the Dwelling Place or the chicken-house or in the Barracks. She checked them just to be sure, and she wasn't surprised when she found nothing. It was the house and barn that she believed to be the most likely places.

She started searching the house by checking the ceiling, using a long pole to push up against the wood planks. She went from room to room, and finally, in the back bedroom, just when her arms and shoulders were about worn out, a ceiling-board lifted—actually, several boards shifted as she pushed with her pole. *A trapdoor!*

Frankie studied it for a moment, because it was an odd-shaped trapdoor. It sat flush into the ceiling, nestled into a hidden framework near the wall between the bedrooms. A clever trapdoor made of several different lengths of boards, all fastened together and settled into the room's ceiling. It was the different board-lengths that created the odd shape and displayed the cleverness. Because, once it was in place, there was no way to see anything other than ceiling.

Frankie shoved at it again, shifting it farther to one side. She stared at the open space—a framed opening big enough for an adult to crawl through. Plenty big enough for her. She thought about getting one of the ladders from the barn. Rethought it. *There has to be a quick way. Because you can't be running for a ladder every time you need to get up there to hide from danger.*

On a hunch, she opened the door of the wardrobe sitting against the wall, right below the trapdoor. Sure enough, its shelves would work like a ladder. She grinned and climbed up the makeshift ladder, scrambling upwards like a tree-squirrel. Boosted herself up through the ceiling and found herself in the attic. And even with just the light from below filtering into the attic, she could see it was one big open room, with the chimney standing straight up in the center where the four angles of the roof came together. *The attic of my perfectly square house.*

Frankie stood there grinning. This was a *big* room, echoing with its emptiness. Even in the limited light, she could see Daniel Kinison had put down a solid plank floor. This room had been here all along and it was surprising her a bit that it had never occurred to her to explore it. She stood in the massive room, breathing slowly, looking around her, wondering if maybe something was wrong with the curiosity part of her brain. *Because this is a marvelous place. Just sitting here. And I never even wondered about it.*

Looking around the dimly-lit space she saw a cluster of objects beside the chimney. A long and narrow box-bench just like in the wolf-den room in the root-cellar. Two crates; a small barrel; a kerosene lamp, a small box with matches and candles. She had no doubt there would be a mattress or two, blankets, maybe a rifle and knife in the long box. There would be water in the barrel, food in the crates.

There was no sign the attic had actually been used, but there was safety and protection here. It had its own disguised entry door and a ladder of sorts. *So Daniel Kinison had set this up as a possible hideout too.* And given it already had a floor of planks in place, it was also likely he'd planned on opening it up into real rooms someday.

Frankie climbed down the wardrobe shelves, eyeing the trapdoor as she shifted it back into its resting place. She stood staring up at the ceiling, chewing on her lip, thinking that if Daniel Kinison wanted to create safe places that were fully disguised, then he had achieved it.

Her thoughts then trailed over to the Wolf Den in the cellar, thinking about the hidden doorway. Grinning, because she was understanding more about Daniel Kinison all the time. He was a master at making concealed spaces; he had decided to keep himself and his family safe. She'd found two places so far, and thinking about it, it made sense to assume there were more hidden places. And maybe, not just for people.

Her mind flicked over to the Conestoga in the barn, then back to the cold and rainy morning, two days before her family left Indiana for the journey out West. Her Uncle James had taken her and her cousins into the big blue-green wagon to show them a hidden space in the wall of the wagon—a clever little compartment he made for the family's valuables—money and the land titles.

And thinking about that, Frankie decided it would be a very odd thing if Daniel Kinison hadn't done something similar. *Surely, he would have some hidden compartment somewhere. Some cubby-hole of sorts where things smaller than humans could be hidden. There has to be someplace where he hid the family's valuables.*

Now, Frankie realized, that along with big spaces, she needed to be looking for small spaces, too—hiding places for humans and hiding places for valuables. Because whether for humans or valuables, any hidden spaces would be handy things to know about.

So far, given what she had already found, she knew Daniel Kinison had either blocked the openings or masked them. That, Frankie decided, was a valuable clue. Looking around her, she ruled out the walls of the house. They were solid logs, so she was sure there was no way to make a hidden compartment in them. But there were the floors. She tapped her toe on the floor. *The floors. There might be something there. The floors might be the most likely place.* She glanced up, considering the attic space. *If not the main floor, then maybe somewhere up in that floor.*

After an hour of searching, she found what she was looking for. In the floor of her bedroom, she found a little knothole in a floorboard. She poked her finger in, hoping she didn't end up getting bitten by some little creature that lived beneath the hole. She crooked her finger and tugged; the board lifted and Frankie grinned. The floor-plank came up from the floor—three planks actually, all lifting as one unit.

No bug-bite. Just another trapdoor. One looking a bit like the one in the ceiling—boards of different lengths, all fastened together as a lid to conceal a framed opening. And there, underneath the clever lid, she found a wood-lined space sitting between the floor supports. Two feet wide, two feet deep and about five feet long. To her surprise though, it wasn't empty. Not at all.

There, nestled into the hidden niche, resting in a Hudson Bay blanket, was a rifle, a shotgun and a pistol. She lifted each one out, checking them—each one loaded and ready. Along with the guns, there were wooden boxes of ammunition, two hunting knives, and a metal box.

This, then, was Daniel's hidden cache for weapons. A safe place to ensure protection. *So. Daniel Kinison even thought of that. So he'd never be without weapons, even if someone ransacked his home. Even if someone took the other guns in the house and the Dwelling Place. Or in the Barracks and the tack-room, Daniel would still have weapons.*

Frankie stared at the cache for a moment, realizing she had never considered such a thing. She had all the weapons Daniel placed in the different buildings, and she had her own rifles and pistols in the house and barn. And she had put a pistol in the root-cellar. It made sense to have a weapon at hand wherever she was. Just in case. But those guns weren't hidden, and if they had ever been stolen, she would have found herself without protection. And that, would have been a significant problem. But now, she had an answer to a problem that she hadn't even considered.

The metal box puzzled her a bit. She assumed it was more ammunition, but when she lifted it from its place in the hidden niche, the box's weight surprised her. *Too heavy for bullets; way too heavy.*

She shifted the box into her arms and toted it to the kitchen table. She flipped the latches and tilted the lid back. Envelopes and canvas drawstring bags. Several of each. She picked up one of the envelopes, lifted its flap. *Greenbacks. Lots of greenbacks.* She lowered the flap and checked the other two envelopes. More of the same; greenbacks. She tucked them back where they had been. She reached for one of the canvas bags, hefted it, feeling solid weight and hearing telltale clinks. She opened it to be sure. *Yes. Coins. Large coins. Lots of coins.*

Frankie leaned back in the chair. Eyeing the metal box. Eyeing the envelopes and the canvas bags. Suddenly feeling a sense of guilt sweep over her. Because this wasn't about weapons or ammunition. This was something different. Something that felt private. It was a personal thing—someone else's very private and very personal thing.

She decided then and there to leave it as it was, to leave everything in the metal box, safe and secure. Knowing it was far more than what her aunt and uncle had secreted away in the Conestoga—there had been envelopes of money hidden both in the bottom of the tooled-leather box and in the secret compartment of the wagon's wall. But the amount of money stashed in this metal box, she knew, was a lot more.

None of this was what she had expected when she started her hunt for hiding places. And at the moment, she had no idea what she should do. So she did what her father advised her to do on more than one occasion. She decided to 'not decide'. Because, he had taught her that sometimes, the decision 'not to decide' was a viable decision. And at the moment, Frankie decided not to decide—at least, not yet—because there was no hurry. There was no rush. No other decision needed to be made.

She stoked up the firebox in the stove, set some potatoes and onions and bacon to frying. When the frying was done, she cut a wedge of cornbread and sat down to her meal. She sat at the table, sipping at a cup of milky sweet-coffee, and eyed the open box. Thinking. Because she had two things to think about.

First, she realized she had been foolish to keep her money and documents in the tooled-leather box on the mantle. Having them hidden under the false bottom of the leather box was better than in its main compartment, but she needed to do better. This metal box, along with the hiding place in the floor, was a much better option. At least for now. *Surely, Daniel Kinison won't mind sharing some space in the box.*

Second, was her concern over the money that had belonged to Daniel Kinison. And to Lillian Kinison. Frankie understood that legally the money had become part of the property. Because the papers signed that night in the big house in Indiana said that anything and everything on the property—any and all items remaining on the property—became the possessions of the new owners. She remembered the exact words.

But she was thinking about what her father would say. Justus Harding would have said there was a moral element to this. 'That,' he'd say, 'was the crux of the matter.' The moral point, according to Justus Harding, was the only thing that really mattered. 'It is the pivotal point,' he'd say.

And he'd expect her to see it as such. She could picture his face as he said the words; she could even picture his right eyebrow lifting, just a bit. She knew she couldn't argue with him on such matters. Not then, not now. This wasn't about words on legal documents. This was about the morality and the spirit of the situation. 'Decisions of the soul should never be argued. They should just be known.' *That's what he would have said.*

As soon as Frankie finished her meal, she went for the tooled-leather box; she stood tip-toe to reach it, eased it down from its place on the mantle and carried it to the kitchen. Set it carefully on the table and shifted everything out of the top compartment. She unfastened the pins with the Captain's pearl-handled penknife and tipped the box to remove the false-bottom.

Her mind went back to the Captain's quarters at Fort Kearny, remembering how gently Captain Connell had handled everything in the box. Now, just as gently, she transferred all the documents and the envelopes with her family's money into the metal box. She settled everything in the box and lowered the lid. *Right now, this metal box is the best protection. I don't believe Daniel Kinison would mind at all.*

She would need advice on this situation—she knew that much for sure. And until she could figure out who to ask, she would follow her father's advice.

"No decision has to be made right now. Except the decision 'not to decide. Yet'." She said the words out loud. She looked at Matilda lying on the rug in front of the fireplace. Matilda who had been following her during the entire hiding-place hunt. She grinned at Matilda; Matilda grinned back at her, looking as if she was in full agreement and happy about it.

Frankie clipped the lid's latches in place and toted the metal box back to her bedroom. She tucked the box into its niche in the floor, replaced the floorboard-lid and laid the buffalo-hide back in place, covering the floor's little secret. Leaving her valuables, and Daniel's, where they were safe and secure.

An hour later, Frankie discovered another hideaway; it was in the barn-loft above the tack-room. Flush into the knee-wall, she found another trapdoor between two stacks of lumber. Like the others, it was disguised with differing board-lengths, and it was two knotholes that caught Frankie's eye. She hesitated for a moment before inserting her fingers—thinking once again about some resident bug chomping down on her finger—but she took the risk.

When she poked her fingers in the holes and gave the board a tug, she ended up with a three-foot trapdoor in her lap. Before her was another of Daniel Kinison's hidden rooms. A clever little room, Frankie decided, tucked under the barn's eaves. With the barn's sloped roof for a back wall, it was a sort of lean-to room, four feet at its highest and running along the length of the loft. A long and low hideout, clever and cozy under the eaves.

A kerosene lamp and a box of matches placed just inside the doorway made Frankie grin. *Sensible and accessible. And awfully handy for the moment.* She lit the lamp, let the light flood through the low room; her grin grew bigger as she inspected the room and its supplies. *Fully stocked. Just like the others. Enough for a couple of days, just in case there's some kind of danger in the meadow that sticks around for a while.*

There were crockery jugs with water, lidded crocks with jerky and dried fruit and parched corn. A low wooden box held blankets, candles, a couple of knives, a handgun, a rifle and boxes of bullets. And to Frankie's delight, there was something she hadn't seen in the other spaces—there were peepholes.

Two openings had been cut into the outer walls—three inches high and eight inches long—each with clever little lengths of wood that slipped in and out of place. Looking through them, Frankie could see the meadow from two different directions. One gave a view of the house and front pastures; the other gave a view of the front of the meadow and the entrance track. A third peephole at the far end of the hideaway looked down onto the ground floor of the barn.

Frankie lay back and laughed, and when Matilda and Laughing Girl came running up the loft stairs, wanting to see what was going on, Frankie invited them in and laughed some more. This, like the Wolf Den, would give her protection; protection she never had and probably should have. *This* kind of protection offered safety and a clear view. She could see outside without being seen. It was a bird's-eye view of everything, just like the hay-cave in the stable-loft at Fort Kearny. This, she decided was her Crow's Nest. And since it was her space now, she decided to add a few things.

She spent some time lugging one of the buffalo-hides over from the house, just like she had hauled one into the Dwelling Place. She spread it out on the floor of her new hideout and settled a wooden crate with an assortment of canned goods in a corner.

And somewhere in the process of outfitting her Crow's Nest, she decided to spend the night there. She nestled into the Crow's Nest in the corner of the loft and woke up grinning. Knowing a different level of safety was here in her meadow.

The catfish grays clipped along in their silky-smooth road-trot, heading along the track toward home. Their dark manes flashing in the moonlight; their hooves drumming a steady beat on the track. Frankie was wrapped up in her buffalo-robe on the seat of the buckboard, her hands warm in her marten-fur mittens, watching the winter sky with its winter stars, while the grays trotted through the night.

She was smiling as her mind traveled back across the miles, back to Indiana. Back to this same day a year ago—the day before Christmas Eve. She and her Aunt Sarah had christened the day as Christmas Eve Eve—literally, the Eve of Christmas Eve. They had laughed when they made up the name, wondering why—after all their Christmases together and always spending the day before Christmas Eve doing all the baking for the holiday—they had never thought of the name before.

So that had been the first time they had declared the 'Eve of Christmas Eve' as a day with an official name. And that very day, they had promised to always celebrate the Eve of Christmas Eve together. Now, Frankie realized, it had been their first official Christmas Eve Eve together. And it had also been their last.

She pictured the kitchen in the big white house that day. She could almost smell the cinnamon rolls and spice cake. She could picture her aunt sliding the tea cakes into the oven. Then they had started making the Scottish shortbread. She could see her Aunt Sarah's smile and hear her laughter, as they christened 'Christmas Eve Eve', declaring it to be 'a new and official Harding tradition'.

'We'll honor it for being the perfect day for getting all of the special things done,' she had declared. 'This way, Christmas Eve and Christmas Day won't ever get lost in the hurry and flurry of all the preparations.'

Frankie slowed the grays, easing the lines back, watching as Ada and Adeline bowed their necks. They complied with the request in the lines, though not especially happy about it.

"We've got another five miles, Ladies. Take it easy on your legs." She laughed as Adeline tipped an ear back to listen, and then swiveled it forward again and snorted. Tossed her head and snorted again. Frankie kept the pull on the lines, waiting until both mares adjusted and finally, settled into the slower trot.

Tonight, she decided, would become another favorite memory—because it was her second Christmas Eve Eve. It had been an evening that would have made her Aunt Sarah smile. And really, Frankie realized, it would have made her father smile too. Because this year on Christmas Eve Eve, she had 'worn the cloak of a servant'. That had been her father's term. Because Justus Harding had always had a high reverence for the accepting the role of a true servant.

'Immersing oneself into a task of full-servitude, for nothing more than the sweet sense of offering heart and spirit.' He had said that to her many times and he had always applied that concept to his life as a professor—as a teacher of teachers.

Her father understood the power of taking on the role of a servant for a good and worthy cause. And thinking about this particular evening, and everything that had led up to it, Frankie thought he would be pleased with her choice today. *And maybe Aunt Sarah would be pleased too. She would probably like to see a new tradition added to our own declared holiday.*

Frankie hadn't been surprised when Simeon Austin had approached her and the Hyatt brothers with an idea—and a request. She had suspected the Reverend had some idea forming in his preacher-brain for quite some time. And William Hyatt had suspected as much too. Because, on the day that she and the Hyatt brothers had played their violins for the Reverend and Betsy and Everett and Ida in her sitting-room, William had leaned down as they were closing their violin cases. He had whispered in her ear.

'You'd best be expectin' to hear about some up-and-coming scheme, Little Prairie-Girl. That there preacher of ours has been mulling over some things while we were playing.'

Frankie had suspected as much because she had seen the preacher fingering his wispy little sprig of a beard while he listened to the violins. Apparently, William had seen it, too, and he knew as well as she did that, when the Reverend Simeon Austin started pulling and twisting on his beard, it usually meant that he had some idea forming inside that nimble preacher-mind of his.

She had figured that at some point he'd probably have a request for her and the Hyatt brothers play at some Sunday church service.

But when his actual request came, she'd been a bit surprised. Because, he didn't want them to play at 'some Sunday church service'.

Before he climbed up in his wagon that day, the Reverend Simeon Austin asked if she and William and Tipp would consider offering a night of Christmas music and worship to the congregation.

'It would be a wonderful gift for the people of the Middle Loup settlement,' he had said. 'A night of music inside our humble little church. Perhaps, on the evening before Christmas Eve.'

Frankie had been more than surprised when she heard he had chosen the evening before Christmas Eve. Because that day already had a special place in her heart. And she liked the idea of sharing Christmas Eve Eve with everyone around her.

As it turned out the Reverend had his own reasons for that particular night. Because, he had explained, that for three of the last four years, weather had prohibited a Christmas morning service. Storms had moved in and made travel either dangerous, or impossible. This year, his idea was to have three possible days at his congregation's disposal.

If weather allowed it, he and his wife would host a night of Christmas music on the evening before Christmas Eve—which meant that even if a storm blew in over Christmas Eve or Christmas morning, the members of the congregation would at least have that night together. And if weather on the eve of Christmas Eve was bad, the music event could be moved to either of the next days.

The Reverend Austin explained his concept to his chosen musicians and when Frankie spoke about her family's tradition of Christmas Eve Eve, the Reverend adopted the idea and sent word out through the community. There would be 'a Christmas Eve Eve service, a night of beautiful music' for all the people of the Middle Loup settlement. 'Hot coffee and hot chocolate and a pot-luck dinner,' the announcement said; it proclaimed that 'the woodstove and the earthen walls of our fine chapel will keep our congregation warm and comfortable'. It would be the beginning of 'a new tradition of music and worship for our wide-spread community'.

To Frankie's eyes, it had truly been a fine Christmas Eve Eve. The wagons filled with homestead families had started rolling into the churchyard by late afternoon. Men unhitched and unharnessed; women and children carried baskets and dishpans and crates of food to rows of plank-tables set along the outer walls of the sod-church. Neighbors greeted neighbors; people talked and laughed and ate their fill as they caught up on news about families and farming.

Men discussed weather and planting; women discussed Christmas cooking and dressmaking; children ran about the church-yard laughing and shouting and shrieking their excitement. It all took on an atmosphere much like the Harvest Picnic, except now, everyone was wrapped in coats and blankets, mufflers and mittens and scarves.

No one seemed to mind the cold because it was, after all, the Eve of Christmas Eve, and it would be a night of music. 'It's a new idea,' they acknowledged, 'something the Reverend Austin and his wife thought up.' And from the talk and chatter that went on all through the late afternoon and into the evening, to Frankie, it seemed as though everyone was excited.

As twilight came on, the people of the community began moving inside, lighting the sod-church with candles and with the lanterns they had brought to light their way home. Looking around her, looking at the glimmer and glow from the lanterns and candles, Frankie thought the sod-church was a beautiful sight. With the heat from the potbellied stove and the lanterns—and with the earth-en-walls of the sod-church holding the heat—it was toasty-warm inside. Warm enough that the double-doors of the church were left standing wide-open.

The women found places on the earthen pews, holding their youngest children in their laps, while the men stood around the perimeter. Shawls and blankets had been lowered; coats and gloves and mittens had been shed; voices had quieted and conversations hushed. The Reverend Simeon Austin stood at the front of the church and spoke of the Christmas Child and of the many loving gifts from God. He led the congregation in prayer, praying about human grati-tude and about heaven's grace. And then, he offered the people of his parish the gift of music.

The Hyatt brothers and Frankie stepped to the front of the little sod-church, tucked their violins under their chins, and when William Hyatt started the notes of "The Brightest and Best", Frankie and Tipp joined in. The night of music on the Eve of Christmas Eve had begun.

They had given the music of their violins to the people in that earthen chapel; they let it circle among the congregation and sent it coursing out through the double-doors that were open wide to the world. They sent the notes across the prairie night, up to the velvet darkness of the sky and to the bright shimmer of the stars. The sound of the violins and the songs of the congregation reached out to the far hills and up to the high heavens.

They played longer into the night than the Reverend Austin had asked, and to Frankie's mind, they played better than he expected. And maybe, better than anyone had expected. They played mostly Christmas music and hymns, and they surprised the Reverend with his favorite, "What Child is This?" But before the night ended, they diverged from the Christmas songs, playing Bach's "Sleepers Awake" for Ida, and "Amazing Grace" for Betsy Austin.

Frankie spent a good amount of her time while she was playing, watching tears in the eyes of Simeon and Betsy Austin. She didn't know if the Reverend Austin had ever before planned for a night of music such as this, but she suspected something of the sort had been in his mind and heart and prayers for a long time.

He had taken a simple idea and turned it into a beautiful night of beautiful music for the people of his congregation. Frankie had seen the joy and the rapture on the faces of those good and decent people in that plain and humble little sod-church. That alone, she decided, had been a rich reward for her and William and Tipp.

The last offering from the three violins were the soft strains of "Silent Night". And it had been fitting. The weather stayed clear and the winds stayed still. The devoted people who traveled safely through the chill of the day to reach the humble sod-church, would travel safely through the soft and silent hush of the prairie night to return home. Many of those hard-working and kind-hearted home-steaders hadn't heard music for years. But on the night of the Eve of Christmas Eve, they heard music that glorified God and his grace and his gifts. On the still and silent night, the sound of music would carry them home.

So while Frankie drove her catfish grays up the north track, she thought about the promises the Dunbars made as she left the church-yard—their promises to see her tomorrow. 'We'll be there early!' Ida had called out; Everett had waved. They would spend Christmas Eve and Christmas Day at her home. Another new tradition—her new family coming to spend Christmas with her.

Frankie was also thinking about her grandfather and her father, her Uncle James and her cousin Samuel. The gift of music they had given her had served her well. And tonight, it had served the congre-gation of the Reverend Simeon Austin.

And she was thinking about William and Tipp. Because once the Reverend had secured their agreement to play for his congrega-tion, the brothers had driven to her homestead twice to practice with her—arriving each time, of course, with Tipp driving a different team of horses. And in spite of the careful practice sessions, Frankie knew they had still carried her through portions of several songs there in the sod-church. Yet after the service, as they helped her hitch Ada and Adeline, and as they settled her onto the buckboard-seat and tucked the buffalo-robe around her, they never said a word about it.

They had put a lot of effort into making the night and the music come together; they had shown a level of dedication and devotion she hadn't expected. And that had surprised her a bit, because usu-ally, the Hyatt brothers pretty much subscribed to their own ideas about life—they tended to follow rules of their own making.

But here tonight, and in the days leading up to it, they had gone well beyond what had been asked of them; they had gone the extra mile and they had taken on the cloak of a servant as well as any men she had ever known. And Frankie decided she was proud to have them as neighbors.

The catfish-grays traveled swift and sure through the clear night, and Frankie pretended not to notice that they had picked up their pace and were back in their fleet-footed and far-reaching road-trot. It was the pace they liked best—the trot was natural to them. They knew the track and they knew the way home, so she gave them their heads and let them glide along the track toward the home meadow.

She tucked her hands and arms under the buffalo-robe and studied the horizon. Off to the west, the stars had disappeared behind a cloudbank—a cloudbank that would be moving eastward. It was lying flat and riding low on the land. *Storm coming in. Nothing's boiling up; nothing's rising and building. Probably, just a light snow.*

Still, it would be nice to be home. Nice to stoke up the fireplace and slip into a warm bed. She snuggled down further into the curly hair of the buffalo-robe and watched the rolling rhythm of the backs of the grays. She watched the moonlight shining on their silvery winter-coats and listened to the steady staccato-beat of their hooves on the frozen track. A steady beat, as steady as the drumming of the Tattoo at Fort Kearny every night.

She watched the track ahead that led toward her home, but her mind was on her Lieutenant and Isabelle. Frank and Isabelle Halliday. Wondering if they had heard the night-drumming tonight. Wondering if they thought about her anymore. Wondering if Captain Connell or Septimus Travers or Will Trask ever thought of her. Wondering if they even wondered.

Christmas Eve morning, the sun was shining sharp and bright across two inches of fresh snow. Frankie spent the early morning visiting with Wild Bird, and then she went to fulfill another Christmas tradition—another Christmas tradition of the Harding family. The gifting to the animals. This was the first Christmas of her life that she would not have her aunt and her cousins with her to visit the animals. So in her mind, the best she could do, would be to continue the tradition.

She started at the chicken house and put out a pan of warm oat-mash for the roosters and hens. She gave boiled eggs to the dogs, and cream to the kittens. She took an ear of corn to each of the horses, the mules, and the cows. She spread millet and barley for the wild birds.

And all the while, she was thinking about how different every-thing would be if the fever hadn't taken her family away from her. Thinking about how different this very morning would be if they had all finished the journey and were living on the homestead together.

She knew her Uncle James would be proud to have this for his home, proud to be building the future for his family here. She started wondering if maybe, it was possible that they were able to see the homestead from up in heaven. Wondering if maybe, they could see the home they had been traveling to. If maybe, they could see her. Maybe, she thought, they could even see that she was missing them so desperately right now.

Once done with her chores and the gifting, Frankie headed to the house with her thoughts drifting down to Fort Kearny—think-ing about her family there—down beyond the Platte River. She was thinking about her Lieutenant and Isabelle again. Wondering what they were doing today. Worried about whether they were missing her; worried about whether their hearts were hurting. Because she was missing *them*, and *her* heart was hurting again. Breaking again.

In the middle of the morning, the dogs signaled the approach of visitors. Frankie stepped out from the kitchen, shivering in the cool air as she waited on the porch. Watching the entrance to her meadow. Within a few minutes, she saw the team of fat and happy seal-browns pulling the spring-wagon, trotting around and down the track into the valley. Everett was handling the reins and grinning; Ida was smiling, half-standing in the jockey-box, already waving.

The sadness of the past faded and Frankie felt the joy of today rising. She hopped off the porch and bounced and danced up to the horses when Everett pulled them to a stop in front of the kitchen porch. Blond Bessie leaped down from the wagon to greet her mother and her siblings; they danced and pranced around each other for a moment before they spun around and went racing around the meadow, their long bodies stretching and their long legs reaching.

Ida and Everett grabbed Frankie up in wild and excited hugs, holding each other and laughing like it had been years since they had seen each other, and not just a matter of hours. Then they started unloading the wagon—they toted baskets and boxes and bags into the house with Ida warning Frankie to leave certain bundles alone—bundles that had flour-sacks and cloth wrapped tightly around them with ribbons tied in bright bows. And Frankie just giggled and acted as if she didn't know why.

Once the wagon was emptied of the baskets and crates and bundles, Frankie helped Ida unpack the goods in the kitchen, chattering about their winter picnic plans—firewood and food—all part of what Frankie wanted to be a new tradition for the afternoon of Christmas Eve.

Everett and Ida were excited for the day, too; Everett wanted another load of firewood to make sure he had enough to get them through until spring. And as Ida packed the dishpan-dinner, she agreed it would be a wonderful tradition.

"The firewood days are always days for laughing and making memories." Ida waved Frankie toward the door. "You go on out and help Everett with the oxen. I'll finish up in here. Go help him span and yoke. He'll like that."

Ida watched as Frankie bundled up and dashed out the door, laughing at how the poised young lady who had been playing hymns for the congregation the night before, had transformed once again into a wild, excited and giggling girl. She stood in the doorway for a moment, watching Frankie racing across the meadow. Matilda and the bounding hounds joined in her run, racing silly circles around her, coming close enough a few times to send Frankie into a series

615

of stumbles and one serious tumble. One moment, she was running, and in the next instant, she had disappeared into a swirling mass of long-legged dogs.

Ida broke into laughter as Frankie rose from the midst of leaping and laughing hounds, yelling at them, scolding them as she scrambled back to her feet. The hounds only dashed about, their wolfish grins getting wider as she yelled, her scoldings making less than a little difference to them.

From the kitchen doorway, Ida could see the moment when Frankie realized that her admonishments were having no impact on the dogs—they kept prancing and grinning as they danced around her, leaping close enough to slap a sloppy tongue across her cheeks a few times, amusing themselves with their own antics. In the next moment, Frankie burst into laughter, brushed off the dusting of snow, and resumed her run to the barn.

Ida could hear Frankie shouting to Everett as he emerged from the barn after turning Jenny and Jake into a stall, calling out something about the oxen. Everett was calling back to her, laughing, nodding and waving.

Turning back to the trestle table, Ida poured hot sweet-coffee into a jug and started humming the tune of "Sleepers Awake", remembering the sweet sounds of the violins within the sod-walls of the chapel. Picturing the people gathered together in the lantern-light. Thinking about the gift of music. And thinking that Frankie was right, because celebrating Christmas with these *new* traditions—Christmas Eve Eve and the Christmas Eve woodcutting picnic—was indeed such a nice thing.

'It's all such a nice thing for us, isn't it?' Frankie had asked while they were emptying the crates and pans at the table. 'We can have these as some wonderful Christmas traditions, can't we? The night of music *and* the woodcutting picnic.'

Her crooked little grin had been flashing and there had been such a wonder-filled shine in her eyes. Ida had nodded, seeing the excited plea in those dark, dark eyes of hers—a sweet plea for assent.

'Yes, Honey. They'll be our very own traditions.' Ida had leaned down, kissed her on the cheek.

Yes, maybe it's a good thing to have new traditions. Something bright and new. Because all the other holidays are past. The families and all those traditions are gone now. Maybe it's a very good thing for Frankie, with all she's lost, to have new and bright Christmas traditions.

Ida tucked a few more biscuits into the edges of the dish-pans, even though they were already full of food for their woodcutting picnic. *And maybe it's something that'll be good for me and Everett too. After all we've lost. Something new and bright for us too.*

They spent the afternoon at the deep cove with its great pile of wood, cutting firewood, eating their noon picnic beside a campfire and talking about what Frankie deemed to be their 'good old days of woodcutting'—days that were actually only back in August and September. They laughed and teased each other, and spent some of the time watching the four lurchers racing around the prairie and the river-bottoms.

The hounds brought in five rabbits throughout the day, and Frankie and Ida decided on a late Christmas Eve supper of cottage pies made with rabbit meat; they decided their Christmas Eve suppers would always consist of rabbit pies, and would 'forever-after be known as bunny-potpies'. It would be yet another new and wonderful holiday tradition.

Blond Bessie learned the skill of coursing rabbits by watching the actions of her mother and siblings; it wasn't long before she snatched-and-snapped her first prey. She stood with her first kill at her feet, looking both astonished and proud. Not knowing what else she should do, she picked up the furry prize and carried it to the woman she adored. She approached Ida, walking slowly, the limp rabbit hanging from her wolfhound-greyhound jaws and offered it to her favorite person.

When Ida sweet-talked to her, thanking her and praising her, Bessie decided the whole idea to be a marvelous thing; an excellent trade for a loving exchange. The blond hound spun away with clear intent—it was a wondrous way to please her person. She raced off into the river-bottoms and in less than ten minutes, she returned with another rabbit, expecting and receiving the same attention and affection as before.

Frankie and Everett were laughing at the hound's expressions of bliss over the two rewards. First, the hurried and happy hunt, and then the cuddling caresses. The blond hound stood still, accepting the adoration, and grinning like a giddy idiot.

Frankie told Everett he had better learn to like rabbit meat, because they'd likely have one for the pot every day.

"Exactly how many different ways can you cook a rabbit for the dinner-table? So a man might not get tired of eating rabbit every single day?" Everett asked, winking at Frankie, knowing Ida would have something to say.

"You two hush up and stop making fun of my sweet little hound," Ida was busy fussing over Bessie, declaring it was a wonderful way for her blond baby to earn her keep.

They poured cups of hot coffee from the heavy jug and ate slices of cold ham on buttered rolls. They had beans and rice, still warm in a crock. Cold buttermilk and spice-cake for dessert. And then, after a final cup of coffee and some more talk and laughter, they went back to cutting firewood.

Buck and Billy had spent most of the morning grazing on the short winter-grass; in the early afternoon they lowered their heavy bodies down onto a sun-warmed patch of grass—they smiled their contented bovine smiles and worked their cuds with their side-to-side chew. And then, they dozed, dreaming their oxen-dreams in the winter sun.

Done with their hunting, the hounds napped the afternoon away under the wagon, their legs and paws jerking and twitching as they chased after the rabbits of their dreams. Frankie and Ida and Everett talked and laughed their way through the afternoon of fire-wood-cutting and wagon-loading. The sun was settling down to the far horizon as they tossed the last of the wood onto the wagon. They spanned and yoked the oxen and headed back to Frankie's meadow.

The next part of the new traditions took form. Frankie and Ida worked on the Christmas Eve supper while Everett took care of the oxen and did the evening chores. When he came into the kitchen after the chores and carrying the pail of Blossom's milk that Wild Bird had handed to him, the house was warm, the bunny-potpies were hot and bread was fresh out of the oven. The supper was simple, the meal was filling, the conversation was thoughtful, as they worked their way through sweet potato pie for their dessert and cups of milky sweet-coffee.

The Dunbars reminisced about Christmases past, talking about the traditions they had when their children were young. Traditions that had run their time, Ida said.

"They're traditions that maybe need to be packed away. Now, out here in *this* part of our life, we deserve to have new traditions." She reached to pat Frankie's arm and smiled at Everett. "We all have a chance to start fresh now, don't we?"

There wasn't much to be said beyond what Ida had gently declared. Frankie and Everett nodded. Agreeing. Settling themselves into the truth of the statement. This was, indeed, a fresh start with new and bright traditions—traditions that matched their life here among the homesteads in the Sand Hills.

A bit to Frankie's surprise, Ida and Everett then started talking about their boys, not just about their family traditions, but about their early family years. Maybe, Frankie thought, to bring out the memories and freshen them a bit; maybe to reassure themselves that they were holding onto the old memories, even as they were releasing the old traditions.

Ida talked about the mischief and the delight their sons had brought into their lives. The love and the light and the laughter. Her tears were flowing as she spoke about her three sons—a mother's tears borne of a mother's love.

Everett picked up the story, staring out the window, looking far beyond the meadow. Looking back to a farm in Iowa. His eyes took on a far-away dreamy-look as he talked about his boys, talking about how they loved following him around in the fields there on their old homeplace.

"They loved the idea of working the land. They loved it when I would dig my fingers down into the dirt and show them the seeds coming to life. Emmett would squat there in the dirt beside me, staring for the longest time at the tiny roots coming from the seeds." Everett gave a soft smile. Sad and soft. "Benjamin was the one who watched the fields every day. He was the one who got his heart broken if he found I had gone out in the fields without him."

"Oh, Lord. He would set up such a wail." Ida spoke up. "When he was too young to run and find his daddy on his own, I'd make him stay at the house until Everett returned. That poor sad little boy would sit on the back step sobbing the whole time."

"I think they would have loved working this land out here." Tears were welling in Everett's eyes. "They all wanted to farm as a family. They couldn't imagine anything else. We had talked about moving out West together as soon as the War was over. The boys had their hearts set on it." Everett's voice broke then and Ida took up the conversation.

She started describing their three boys, recalling their personalities. Emmett, she said, had a way of keeping them laughing no matter how hard the work or how long the days. Benjamin, their middle son, had a habit of slipping up behind her and lifting her, swinging her around to make her laugh.

"He would stand me back on the floor and make me dance with him. He would have me laughing till I ran out of breath," Ida paused with a soft smile on her face. Tears in her eyes again. She wiped them away and went on.

"Our youngest, Caleb, was our 'solution-son'," she said. "He was forever figuring out different ways to make things easier. *Always* tinkering with things to make them work better."

But everything had changed with the War in the South. Because Emmett and Benjamin had been lost in the War.

"It was early on in the War," Ida said. "And suddenly, on one single day, we got two letters from the government. Our boys were gone. Just gone." Ida's tears were flowing as she went on, talking quickly, hurrying to say it to get beyond the words and the pain. "It was shortly after that when Caleb's heart gave out. He had a long bout with pneumonia. But he had licked that. He had come out of it and we were sure he'd be fine. The doctor was sure too. And then, one night, he was just gone—gone like my other boys." Ida was sobbing, and Everett was holding her. Frankie waited.

Ida shook her head and took a deep breath. She started talking about the Cheyenne boys—the wild little prairie boys—and how the sight of them tagging along after Everett reminded her of their own boys.

The conversation turned again and they were talking about Little Mouse and Dandelion. And the scurvy-sickness. And Whirlwind. And Ida and Everett were asking if Wild Bird had said anything about when the Cheyenne families might return.

Frankie moved into the new subject with them, understanding the reason for the shift in topics. Healing had been going on there in the kitchen, and it had been enough for Ida and Everett. At least, for now.

"At first, I didn't think they'd come back until springtime. But Wild Bird says they'll come during the hohtsté-eše'he. That means the hard-faced moon, which is sort of during January, but He's Proud says it's not exactly the same as white people think of it. So I think she means her family will come for her in a few weeks. She wants to go with them for a while, but she says she'll come back again before the heše'e-venéhe-eše'he comes. That's the time of the muddy-faced moon, and I think that's mostly during March."

When Everett asked her about who all would come to get Wild Bird in January, Frankie could hear the hope in his voice.

"Maybe just Whirlwind and a few others in the band. I don't think the whole slew of them will come with all the lodges and families. I think the biggest number of the families will be traveling somewhere else. For a gathering of a lot of bands. Wild Bird wants to go meet up with them."

Frankie didn't think Ida or Everett regarded the Cheyenne as family exactly, but certainly they considered them to be wonderful friends. Now, all the talk about their own children had brought out their loneliness for the laughter and love of the Cheyenne children. They were missing Little Mouse and all the little boys. Which strengthened Frankie's suspicion there had been healing going on around the trestle table through the evening—healing that had probably never happened while they had been following Rebecca and her husband around.

Because through the whole evening—through all memories and recollections, through all the laughter and the tears—there had been no mention of their daughter. There was no great sadness because there had been no great love. And Frankie understood how that gap could exist in one's emotions. Her own mother, not unlike the Dunbars' daughter, had never offered love to anyone.

Her mother had achieved the ability to appear to offer love to some people, but she could only maintain that pretense for a short period of time. From what Frankie could figure, she had managed to maintain it long enough to get herself married to Justus Harding, but love wasn't an emotion that was natural to her.

Her mother had an assortment of ways, both obvious and sublime, to punish people who enjoyed life and lived according to love. In the end, that relentless resentment had been her undoing—she had made her whole life crumble, and finally, she had crumbled along with it. There was no doubt in Frankie's mind that Ida and Everett's daughter Rebecca was much the same—there was no love lost, or missed, because it had never existed.

Later in the night, seeing that the fire in Wild Bird's lodge was still glowing, Frankie and Ida took one of the bunny-potpies and a sweet potato pie to Wild Bird. The old woman was busying herself with quill-work when they slipped through the hide-door. She gave them a wide grin, and when she saw the pies, her grin grew even wider.

The three of them talked into the night, talking about the food and the winter, about the meadow and about the Cheyenne. And when they left the lodge, Ida looked up at the string of pretty deer-hooves dangling from the high smoke-flap pole, rapping and tapping out a soft beat in the night breeze. She smiled, talking about the musical sound.

"It sounds just like the wood-chimes I had beside the door back home in Iowa."

Frankie just smiled as they walked toward the house.

Ida fixed their Christmas breakfast while Frankie and Everett did the morning chores. And after they had returned to the kitchen and eaten their fill of the porridge and hot-cakes and sorghum syrup, fried eggs and sweet potato hash—the gifts came out.

Everett gave Frankie wind-chimes he made from triangles of metal cut from a tire iron; Frankie squealed with delight and decided they would hang from the porch outside her bedroom door. Grinning, she handed Everett his gift—a string of deer-hoof chimes Wild Bird had showed her how to make. The three of them laughed, talking about how perfect the exchange was—the very same gift, but made so very different.

The string of deer-hooves, Everett decided, would hang by the front door of their sod-house. Ida flashed a smile at Frankie, and Frankie grinned at her. Ida would have chimes at her door, again.

When Frankie gave Ida mittens of mink-fur and Everett a muffler made of red fox-hides—gifts she had sewn under the watchful eye of Wild Bird—there was more laughter. Because Ida had knitted mittens and a muffler for Frankie.

After the laughter died down over the same-but-different gifts, Ida handed Frankie another package. Frankie opened it, smiling as she held up a dress made of rose-brown cotton. Ida made the dress from cloth Everett selected at Fort Cottonwood, a color he thought would be perfect with Frankie's eyes and hair. Ida had added a crocheted collar and cuffs to match the ivory buttons.

Frankie ran to her room to try it on, and then danced her way back into the kitchen, swirling to make the skirt flair. She and Ida decided that since Everett had chosen so well, he should be the one to pick out her dress-goods from that day forward. Everett blushed and stood to hug Frankie. When he released her from the hug, he gave a low and formal bow.

"Young Lady, I'd be proud enough to take on that duty."

Frankie hugged Ida and danced herself around and through the house, taking the long way around to her own room, calling out that E-Hahpeno'e had done a beautiful thing. Hearing her Cheyenne name 'She Sews', set Ida to blushing and laughing.

During the afternoon hours, and right up to the evening meal, Frankie and Everett took turns reading aloud from a novel about Christmas. Ida listened as she crocheted in the rocker by the sitting-room fire with Matilda and Blond Bessie dozing on the braided rug beside her. And Frankie suggested they should have another tradition—reading out loud to each other while venison roasted in the oven for Christmas dinner.

Everett nodded and Ida smiled. She kept rocking and crocheting and listening to the story of Tiny Tim and his family and the miserly old man. A story that, Frankie told them, had been written ten years before she was born. It was, she said, the story her father had read aloud every Christmas. *So yes,* Ida thought, *this will be one of our traditions every year. Because we should keep this tradition alive for Frankie. And for her father.*

Part V

Travels and Travails

Frankie's mind had been on springtime for the last week; she'd been thinking a lot about the green grasses of spring coming up from the earth, and about the green leaves sprouting on the twigs and branches. She was looking forward to the days of lasting warmth, days when she wouldn't have to watch for snowstorms and blizzards.

Christmas and its new traditions had gone. The year of 1863 was gone. The new year of 1864 had arrived. And now, even January was gone. And Wild Bird had gone with it.

Whirlwind and her daughter, Mourning Dove, had returned with Charging Crow and two other men; they had come during the time of hohtsté-eše'he, the hard-faced moon. They spent two nights in Wild Bird's lodge and Frankie spent the nights with them.

During the cold mornings and the cool evenings, they stayed near the cookfire in the lodge, talking and laughing together; they drank cups of milky sweet-coffee; they ate cornbread and biscuits slathered with butter and honey. They had plates of roasted root vegetables and bowls of steaming venison stew, and dishes of apple pie and peach cobbler and bread pudding.

The women brought gifts for Ho-esta Hesta Ka-ėškóne—a pair of moccasins with a thick sole of buffalo-hump leather, an antelope-shirt beaded in yellows and greens and whites. They gave her a sash-belt decorated with porcupine-quills stitched in flowing zigzag patterns.

Frankie learned that once the coldest and the longest snows had passed, Strong Hand's band had left the black-rocky place, the Mo'óhta-vo'honáaeva; the families were on the move again, heading east to a new place. Traveling to meet up with their relatives along the spreading-water river to visit with them. Which was, Frankie knew, the Niobrara River that showed on her colored map. After that, they would hunt for the buffalo herds together. Wild Bird said she would come back when the new plants were rising and the grasses were turning green. But now, she said, she would travel with her family.

Early on the third day, in less than ten minutes, the three women took down Wild Bird's lodge, packed it on one travois, stowed all her belonging on the other. Frankie tucked a crock of butter and a flour-sack full of biscuits in with her belongings, and stood back as Wild Bird grabbed a handful of her bony old buckskin's mane and swung up on his back, as easily as any young warrior.

The old woman grinned and patted her on the shoulder. Nodded. She said Fire Heart Child was a good Cheyenne girl. A good granddaughter. Then the women left, trailing out of the valley single-file, leading the ponies that pulled the travois and following the three warriors.

Frankie had watched as they left her little valley, following the track up and around until they were out of sight. She stood there in her meadow, listening until they were beyond her hearing. She looked over her shoulder at the empty place beside the windmill pool, the place where the old Cheyenne woman's lodge had stood. Empty. As empty as her heart. Because her grandmother was gone.

For now. She'll come back when spring is coming on. The others will come too. Whirlwind and Little Mouse. And Strong Hand and Knife and He's Proud. Dandelion and Wood Flute might come too. Maybe. Probably.

Except for a few blizzards and a handful of heavy snows, the winter had been mild. Most of the storms had come through gently, leaving a few inches of snow at a time—snow that would stay for a few days and then politely melt away within a week.

The sun was still playing a major role in the Sand Hills this winter, still heating up the ground in the afternoons for weeks at a time. When the storms moved in, the winter-sun would bow out and disappear for a time, and then it would return, bringing the bright blue prairie sky with it.

The Hyatt brothers drove into her valley one morning, about halfway through the morning, and the time of day didn't surprise Frankie one bit. Because it was their preferred time for a visit. Because they knew they could count on her inviting them to sit down to the midday dinner.

This time they drove a team of red roans, and from the size of the roans, Frankie figured them to be half-Belgian. And trotting along behind the wagon, tied to the back of the buckboard, was a solid little sorrel gelding. Frankie eyed it for a minute, wondering exactly what the brothers had in mind. Because typically, the Hyatts concentrated on teams, and not individual saddle horses. So she had a hunch Tipp might be planning to try a little trading.

Frankie complimented the roans while the brothers unhitched, pulled the bridles, and turned the roans into the barn-lot.

"Yup. They're a nice pair. Plenty stout for hauling. Got them from an acquaintance of ours who lives by the Missouri. Figuring on selling 'em down to Fort Cottonwood."

Tipp spoke a bit more about the roans, talking about how 'they'd work fine hitched to wagon or to plow', but Frankie noticed he hadn't said a word about the sorrel. Not even when he released the gelding into the barn-lot to join the team. She figured he was biding his time, choosing to let her wonder for a while before offering some kind of trade for him.

While she and Tipp talked about the roans, Frankie noticed William eyeing the blizzard-line that ran from the barn to the house; then his eyes roamed the rest of the meadow, surveying the other blizzard-lines stretching to various buildings in various directions. William grinned that wide grin of his when he realized she noticed.

"I suppose you saw me looking to your high-lines. We can't have you forgettin' what we put into that wild little brain of yours." William chucked her chin. "To tell you the truth Prairie Girl, we had two things in mind on our way up here. For one, we wanted to check up on you and see how you weathered the storms. Did you fasten yourself up to those lines like we told you?"

"No, Sir. I never did. Because I never went out at any time during the storms. Which was exactly what you told me." Frankie gave him a triumphant smile.

"By damn, you just gave me the right answer. Any other answer and I was gonna smack your scrawny little bottom a few times." William broke into a broad smile, picked her up and swung her around. "You just made me proud, Little Girl."

"So, William Hyatt, what's the second thing you had on your mind?"

"Well hell, you little Prairie Brat," Tipp spoke up before William could reply; he reached to hug her against his side. "We had it in our minds that you might just invite us inside and give us a good feed. And William and I were laying bets as to whether you'd have one of them fine peach cobblers of yours a-baking in your oven."

"Well hell, yourself, Tipp Hyatt. I don't have one of 'them fine peach cobblers' in the oven right now. But I do have one that I baked last night."

That little twist on the cobbler situation sent the brothers into an argument over who had won the bet and who had lost it—since there *was* a peach cobbler for them, but it wasn't actually *in* the oven. They were still arguing over the terms of the bet, glaring and snorting at each other, as they each grabbed one of her hands and walked with her to the house.

So Frankie fed them. They visited while they ate, feasting on a platter of roasted grouse, sweet potatoes and onions Frankie had sitting in the warming shelf. They talked about the violins and the Christmas Eve Eve service and how Simeon Austin was still smiling and bragging about the night of music. They caught Frankie up on the news from down around the Middle Loup settlement. They asked about the old Cheyenne woman and wondered 'where she had got-

628

ten to'. And of course, they talked about the weather; because men always got around to discussing the weather. Always.

Frankie spent most of the time listening as they talked on, letting them have their weather conversation, knowing they'd probably already talked about it on the drive to her place, and knowing they'd probably end up discussing it again on the way back to their homesteads. And while they talked, she watched the whole platter of biscuits disappear under ample slatherings of butter. After they finished the biscuits and their coffee, Frankie filled their cups again and set out the pan of cobbler and a pitcher of thickened-cream. It wasn't long before the whole cobbler had disappeared too.

An hour after they had arrived, the brothers were readying their team to leave.

"We got business to attend to, little Apple Dumpling," Tipp was setting the traces. Got some traveling to do down by way of Fort Cottonwood. But we wanted to check on our favorite little homestead girl afore we left."

William, Frankie noticed, was lifting something from behind the buckboard's seat and when he turned to her he had a wooden crate in his hands—a crate packed with a ham, two large slabs of bacon and a pile of cased sausage.

"We've been taking more than a few meals off of you, Frankie Harding. We just butchered down to our place and thought we'd do a little payback." He reached under the seat and pulled out a large crock. "And we'll add this crock of honey to sweeten the deal. Does this square things up a bit?"

She grinned and nodded and thanked him; he reached to tousle her hair. While Tipp finished with the team, William followed her into the stone-room pantry, toting the crate while she carried the honey.

Once they returned to the buckboard, she saw Tipp squinting at her in a funny way; he said he needed her to pronounce the exchange to be a square deal. Frankie laughed at him, pronounced it as such, saying it was more than enough to square things. He kept up with his funny squint, looking at her like he wasn't fully agreeing.

"No, Ma'am, I'm not so sure things *are* even yet. With all that fiddlin' you did with us, an' with all the practicing, and then all the playing at the church, we damn near wore your little arm down to a nub." He kept talking while he was walking around to the back of the buckboard. He untied the sorrel gelding and brought him around to where she stood. He winked at her as he handed her the lead-rope.

"Here. See if you can take care of this feller. We ain't got a match for him to make a team, so he ain't of much use to us. Why don't you do us a favor and take him off our hands? *Then* we can call things even. For all the times you fed us and for all the fiddlin'."

Tipp said everything casually, making it sound like the idea was a light and simple thing, but when Frankie glanced at his face and looked into his eyes, she saw he was dead serious. Off to the side, she could see William standing still, watching his brother and watching her. Waiting. And maybe, looking a bit hopeful.

"Well, Tipp, I believe that'd put me beholding to you. Because I'm not sure you owe me anything for the fiddling." Frankie hesitated, not completely sure she understood what was going on. Because no one was ever completely sure about what might be going on when dealing with Tipp Hyatt.

Tipp glanced toward the horse and when he looked back at her, his eyes had a serious glint. Frankie realized suddenly that he *really* wanted her to take the sorrel gelding. And in that instant, she also understood that this had nothing to do with the food or the fiddling. Tipp Hyatt, for whatever reason, needed to get this tough little sorrel out of his own hands.

"I'll tell you true, Little Prairie Girl, it'd be a big help to me if you'd go ahead and take this here horse. I'd be lookin' at it as me and William bein' beholden to *you*."

"Then, we'll let it be how you need it, Tipp. I'm happy to do it for you."

Those boys grinned, hopped up in the buckboard and as Tipp turned the team of roans toward the valley entrance, he called over his shoulder.

"Might be a good idea if you maybe didn't take to riding that little sorrel very far from your place here. Maybe just for a while, anyway."

He sent the roans trotting out of her meadow, up and around and over on the track, heading out toward the river. Frankie stood watching them. Stood a little longer, listening until she heard the sound of hooves and wagon wheels in the water, crossing the ford. She was grinning a little. And grimacing a little.

She knew it was William who would have decided to check on her to see how the winter was treating her. And it would have been William who decided to bring along the crate of ham, bacon and sausages. And the honey too. Because that was William—just as wild and tough as his brother, but as thoughtful and true as a person could be.

And it was in Tipp's nature, too, to want to check on her, and he would have been more than happy to bring the crate of pork to her. But along with all that, Tipp Hyatt—being the way Tipp Hyatt was—would almost certainly have had another motive for the drive to her place, something even beyond the meal and the peach cobbler. And apparently, the tough little sorrel, was the other motive. Because for whatever reason, Tipp needed to get the little sorrel off his hands.

The Hyatt boys did what most of the settlers in the area called 'a lot of wild roaming'. And in spite of that reputation, they considered William Henry Harrison Hyatt to be a straight and decent man. But according to most folks, George Washington Hyatt—called 'GW' by some and Tipp by others—had 'a slight *bend* to his character'.

Frankie had heard comments about how 'Tipp Hyatt certainly knows good horses and he always drives a fine team'. And those comments were always followed with a remark about how 'of course, no one's ever seen Tipp Hyatt driving the same team twice'. There was always a lot of speculation as to how he actually came by all those different teams, and more speculation as to exactly where all those different teams actually went.

Tipp and William had lived in both Iowa and Missouri, and after their time fighting in the War, they had come out to the Territory. Everyone knew they had some sort of connection with the outlaws Jesse and Frank James back in Missouri. And with the Younger brothers too. And apparently, two of the other two Hyatt brothers—John Quincy Adams Hyatt and Samuel Adams Hyatt—were both lawmen near Council Bluffs, Iowa. 'Elected sheriffs,' William had told her. And whenever they talked about their 'brothers the lawmen', both William and Tipp always seemed a little amused.

There was a lot of speculation around the Middle Loup settlement about the two brothers, and plenty of folks chuckled over the fact that 'an awful lot of horses seem to pass through Tipp Hyatt's hands'. But curiously enough, while Tipp always did a lot of *talking* about horse trading, he never seemed to do very much horse-trading around the settlement.

Frankie was grinning as she looked the gelding over. No brand; no markings. She walked him toward her barn. She had a hunch Tipp had a reason for getting this particular horse away from his place—and for wanting to do it fast. And apparently, there was a reason that the brothers had no interest in taking the gelding on down to Fort Cottonwood where they could certainly sell or trade him.

She had seen the glint in Tipp's eyes; a glint that said he really *did* need a favor. And thinking about it a bit more, Frankie was willing to bet that neither Tipp nor William would ever say another word about this particular horse.

After settling the gelding in a stall, Frankie spent some time chatting with him while she gave him a good brushing. Studying him, watching his behavior. Deciding he was a fine horse. He was put together well and he was sensible. But there was definitely a mystery surrounding him. She knew, without a doubt, he hadn't come from anywhere around the Middle Loup settlement, because there had never been any horse-theft in the region.

The sorrel had come from somewhere, though. And thinking about it, Frankie decided it might be a wise thing to just let the mystery stand. The truth was, that for now, she was stuck with a nice, tough little sorrel that she probably shouldn't be riding around for anyone to see.

Late in the night, a little more than a week later, Frankie stood on the porch outside her bedroom, watching snowflakes drifting down from light-gray clouds. This storm, she knew, would be light, no more than a dusting of snow. Because *this* was the 'lead storm'; there would be more storms following it in the next few days.

She had seen the signs earlier in the day from the crest of her Lookout Hill. A long and wide system of clouds had been sitting high off the ground, white and roiling, but distinct and separate from any other clouds. Those were the clouds coursing across the Sand Hills tonight, dropping snow on her meadow. The way they had been shaped, looking like a long bedroll, meant there was probably another storm behind them—pushing and rolling them forward. Tomorrow night, she figured, the second storm would move in, probably a little heavier than this one. And then, given the feel in the air right now—given how compressed the air was feeling—there would be a much heavier snowstorm behind that one. That storm, the third storm, would come in as a blizzard.

She started thinking about everything she had to do to prepare for that one. She picked up an armload of firewood from the stack beside the door and headed inside. She dumped her armload into the wood-box beside the fireplace, tossed a few pieces onto the fire and slipped into her bed. Ducked under the covers and tucked the top quilt against her sides. She lay there, watching the flickering patterns of firelight playing on the ceiling as she thought through the next few days. Thinking through everything; making her plans.

There'd be a light cover of snow in the morning which would probably melt by mid-morning. So it'd be a matter of doing the typical morning chores, but adding a little more to the process—like bringing all the water troughs up to full and forking extra hay inside the barn stalls. Then she'd bring all the geldings into the first pasture. She planned to put Rock and Fox and Samson in barn stalls and shut Blossom and Primrose in the milking pen. All that, she could complete by late morning.

When Frankie woke in the morning, the whole valley was blanketed with a couple inches of fluffy snow, just as she had expected. The morning chores went the way she figured, and it didn't surprise her to see that most of the snow had melted before noon. Once she finished her noon meal, she started a pot of chicken stew simmering on the back-burner, planning to add dumplings later, thinking it'd be a comforting thing to have a big pot sitting warm on the back burners when the big storm hit. When she had the stew simmering, she decided to head back to the barn to add more hay to the stalls. Just in case.

It was as she stepped out the kitchen door, with Matilda squeezing out behind her, that the three hounds began barking. It was their warning bark, but it wasn't their typical warning; this was more of a chorus of startled woofs and halting, throaty growls. They were standing close together, looking toward the meadow's entrance, barking and woofing. Sounding a little hesitant and maybe, a little confused.

Looking across the snow-covered winter-grass, Frankie saw the reason for their hesitancy and confusion. Something was out there in her meadow, out toward the entrance—something was standing there. Standing quiet and motionless. She had to blink a few times as she tried to sort out exactly what the something was. Because she wasn't at all sure. Because it was something she'd never seen before.

Mostly, it looked like a buffalo—four legs and a big hump of curly buffalo hair. It was standing in the grass beside the track, halfway between the chicken-house and the windmill pond. Frankie stared at it. Squinted. Stared some more. It looked like a buffalo. *Sort of. But I don't think it's a buffalo.*

She squinted again, not at all sure why a single buffalo would be standing all by itself in her meadow. Still squinting, she wondered if maybe the glare of the sunlight across the remaining snow was playing tricks on her. She stepped back toward the door—slowly and cautiously—wanting her Henry rifle, but wanting to keep her eyes on the strange creature at the same time. She threw a few quick glances toward the hounds who were doing their own fair share of staring and squinting at the creature. They were still doing their cautious woofing and growling, and they were shooting a few glances her way, looking for a cue, wondering what she had in mind.

When she was close enough to reach inside the door-frame, she grabbed the Henry and moved back to the edge of the porch, bringing the rifle's stock to her shoulder. Her eyes were still on the strange creature standing quietly in the grass; she was still trying to see clearly; still trying to get the idea of a buffalo out of her head. Because she was pretty sure it wasn't a buffalo.

She stayed on the porch a moment longer, thinking and watching. Telling herself that there wasn't any need to rush into anything. *At least, not yet.* Because whatever it was, it was just standing right where it had been. Perfectly still.

Finally, the hounds began walking toward it—stalking forward, stiff-legged. Growling; hackles up. Hesitant and unsure. Frankie watched them for a clue about what they thought they were stalking, but they didn't seem to have any idea of what was in front of them. Laughing Girl was watching the strange apparition and the younger dogs were watching their mother. She was moving slowly, then stopping, then moving forward again. And the pups were doing the same thing.

Matilda slipped through the screen-door, brushing against the back of Frankie's leg, her eyes on the creature across the meadow. She was growling, too, but *her* growl didn't sound normal either. Not at all. Which Frankie found more than a little unnerving. Four dogs and one person, all living right there in the meadow, and none of them had any idea what was going on.

Plus, every one of her horses were watching the scene at the entrance track. They were there in the barn pens and the pasture, standing alert, heads up, ears perked—but not one had called out a greeting. Not even Sunny Jim. And to Frankie's mind, none of that boded well.

She whistled to the three hounds, calling them back, deciding it'd be wiser to know exactly what was out there before letting them go at it. Her mind was drifting to thoughts about Dante's Inferno and she started wondering if this was some sort of heinous monster or diabolical beast that had been released from one of the divisions of hell.

And then, as she stood on the porch watching the strange hellish-apparition, she saw an odd thing happen—the apparition changed shape. The hump of the beast shifted its shape. In the next instant, the beast took a step forward. Laughing Girl uttered a surprised woof and almost fell backward; the pups followed suit, scrambling backwards, bumping into each other and falling all over themselves on their over-sized puppy-feet.

Another minute of watching and Frankie decided she was tired of the wondering and the not-knowing—it was time to do something. Because now, she was pretty sure it wasn't a buffalo. She was also pretty sure that it wasn't actually a creature from Dante's imaginings. But whatever the beast was, she decided that, since it was there on her homestead and in her meadow, she had a right to know what exactly was going on.

Frankie shook her head to rid herself of the crazy thoughts bouncing around inside her mind; she took a breath and stepped down from the porch. Curiosity winning out over fear. She began walking toward it, knowing there had to be much simpler explanation than what she was imagining.

Then the beast, which still had the appearance of a full-fledged apparition, moved again. It huffed and it snorted and it stomped. The curly-haired buffalo-hump shifted a bit and suddenly, Frankie could see ears and part of a head. *Not a buffalo's head. Not a buffalo's ears or eyes or nose.* Frankie stopped in her tracks. Staring again. Thinking about how it sounded when it snorted and huffed. *It sounded like a horse.*

Frankie squinted at it again, and suddenly, she could see that it absolutely *was* a horse. But something else was going on, because something was hunched up on the horse's neck and back. Something that looked like a buffalo. She walked a few steps closer, realizing it looked a little as if maybe a buffalo was riding a horse. *Sort of.*

She was halfway across the meadow, when it moved again—both the horse-part and the hump-part. Frankie jumped back, watching as the horse-part took another step and the hump-part collapsed.

She stared as a human slid out from underneath the hump and hit the ground. An Indian human.

Suddenly, it all became clear. A buffalo-robe had been on top of the Indian, and the Indian had been on top of the horse. *Not an apparition. Not one of Dante's beasts.*

Part of the mystery was solved—and while she felt a certain level of relief, she still had a couple of immediate concerns. Because part of the buffalo-hump was still there and something else was still under the robe. That was one of her concerns. The other concern had to do with the horse.

Frankie could see its head now and she could see the whites of its eyes—it was looking toward her, looking pretty spooked, looking like it was ready to bolt out of the meadow. And she didn't really want that. Because someone was in trouble.

The growls from the dogs that were staying close behind her had been getting louder and the two pups were letting out occasional woofs. Now that her interest was in keeping everything calm, Frankie figured none of that was helping. She ordered them back, ordered them to be quiet, and as soon as the dogs hushed, the horse settled. Its eyes softened, its head lowered just a bit.

Frankie moved closer, taking slow steps, talking softly. Speaking in both English and in Cheyenne, not sure which language the horse might know. Not at all sure that it made a difference. And all the while, she was trying to watch both the horse and the human, watching both for any sudden movement—any movement that could mean a potential problem.

When she finally reached the horse's side, she rubbed its face and cheek. Gently, carefully; she stroked its neck slowly. Lifted the rein trailing on the ground. She kept talking to the horse, rubbing behind its ears, while she studied the Indian on the ground. *A warrior. Not Cheyenne. Oglála. Probably.*

Looking closer, she decided he was definitely Oglála. She was also very sure he hadn't moved since he hit the ground—and very unsure, as to whether he was dead, or just unconscious. For a brief moment, she considered the idea that maybe, he was fully conscious and trying to trick her—just wanting to make her believe he was dead or unconscious so he could attack her. *No. An Oglála warrior isn't just going to come riding into my homestead hunched up under a buffalo-hide, just to fall off and play dead.*

Frankie realized she needed to do one of two things—she either needed to check on the man on the ground, or she needed to look under the robe to see what else was there. But she had no idea of which to do first. It was exactly what her cousin Thomas would have called 'a bit of a peculiar dilemma'. She had no experience in life that compared to this, and right now, she suspected that was exactly why she had no clear idea of what to do.

She stood there for what seemed like a year when suddenly, the buffalo-robe on the horse's back started moving. It shifted a bit, and then it slid down and landed in a crumpled heap on the ground between the horse and the fallen warrior. And there on the horse's back was another Indian; he was tipped forward against the horse's withers, badly stained with blood and looking a lot like a dead man. Frankie saw his ribs rise as he sucked in a breath. *Definitely not dead. Maybe conscious. Maybe not. But definitely alive.*

Frankie tried to gather her thoughts, trying to add things up. She had two Indians in her meadow; one slumped forward on the horse's back and the other one face-down on the ground. Both, she could see, had a fair amount of blood on them—some dried blood and some fresh blood.

Once she was sure the Indian pony had put aside any thoughts of bolting out of the meadow, she laid her rifle on the ground. She crouched down beside the man in the grass; she tried a Cheyenne greeting, and then a Lakotah greeting.

"Haáhe! Han!"

There was no response from him, but she did see his chest move. *Breathing. He's alive. That's a start.* She eyed his left leg, wincing a bit as she saw the amount of blood he had lost—blood had soaked through most of the legging on his left leg, all the way down to his moccasin. *Bad wound. Really, really bad.*

She stood then and turned her attention to the warrior on the horse. She spoke to him. Touched his knee. Watched and waited. There was no response. *Alive. Bleeding wound on his right arm.*

Right shoulder bloody. Plenty of fresh blood. And a lot of dried blood.

Suddenly, it occurred to her that the warriors might not be alone; she glanced around, realizing that they might have friends with them. Or—given the wounds and the blood—they might have enemies nearby. She glanced toward the meadow's entrance and scanned the valley's slopes. No movement; no motion. She listened. No strange sounds; no noise.

She looked to the hounds and Matilda—still behind her, staying where she had told them to stay. They were watching her and the Indians and the horse. Waiting for a clue as to what she wanted them to do. But they weren't looking anywhere else; they weren't seeing or smelling anything else. Over in the barn pens, Rock and Fox and Boone were watching the activity in the meadow, but they weren't looking anywhere else. In the pasture, the horses standing at the front fence were watching the meadow, too—none were watching the hillsides.

The Indian on the horse moved; he shifted his shoulders and lifted his head. His leg moved slightly and Frankie touched his thigh. The warrior pushed himself up from the withers, just slightly, just enough for his eyes to meet hers.

"Ho-esta Hesta Ka-éškóne." He said her name. And then, he spoke to her, saying a few Cheyenne words. Telling her they needed to hide.

Frankie stared at him, reached to grip his arm. She knew this warrior; it was Šungíla Hóta. Gray Fox. Wood Flute's father. He had come to her meadow with Knife; he had taken his father's buffalo-horse home.

The Oglála chief reached to touch her shoulder; he offered a weak smile. He spoke again, speaking in Cheyenne, speaking slowly.

"Soldiers follow us."

Frankie stared at him for a moment, grasping his meaning. Understanding the coming danger. *A troop of horse-soldiers. Crap! Dammit!*

Her mind started racing. Her first thoughts were about protecting this Oglála warrior and his friend. She needed a safe hiding place— she needed to get them hidden and it needed to be fast, because there was no telling when the soldiers might show up. And she would need to see to their wounds. *The hidden room in the root-cellar. The Wolf Den! If I can get them there...*

Her next thoughts were about soldiers. Soldiers who might be riding into her valley any moment. *Crap! A troop of some sort. Surely, not a whole company. Probably just a small troop. Maybe just a squad.* Whatever it was, she realized there was a possibility the soldiers had lost the warriors' trail. *Maybe, they won't actually follow them here.*

And at the same time, she was offering a quick prayer to the heavens-above, because her thoughts were suddenly racing south to Fort Kearny. She gave a groan—a groan that came from deep inside her. *Please God... please don't let them be soldiers from Fort Kearny. Please, God. If soldiers come here, then please don't let them be from there. Please, God! Please!*

Her thoughts returned to the moment. Gray Fox began to move; he was shifting his weight to the left side of the horse, attempting to slide off the horse. Frankie stepped to his side and let him brace his hand on her shoulder. He slid down the horse's side and to her surprise, once he reached the ground, he managed to stay on his feet. But only barely.

And in that moment, Frankie saw why he had chosen to dismount from the left side of the horse instead of the right, like the Cheyenne and Oglála usually did. Most of his right side was covered in blood; it was worse than she thought—his legging from the knee down was saturated with blood, his whole right sleeve, the shoulder and back of his buckskin shirt were all stained with blood. Some fresh blood; a lot of dried blood.

Both warriors had lost a lot of blood and they needed doctoring. They also needed to be hidden. And it all had to happen fast. The Wolf Den in the root-cellar was the answer.

Frankie already had her mind made up about that; all she needed to do was to get them to the door, down the steps and into the room. At the moment, she wasn't at all sure how she was going to manage it. The cellar door wasn't far, but she doubted Gray Fox could walk the distance. And she had no idea how she was going to get the unconscious man there. But somehow, she needed to. And she needed to do it before the Cavalry came.

She took a breath and gathered herself. She told Gray Fox she could hide them, that she had a good place. That the soldiers would not find them if she could get them there. She pointed to the door of the cellar and asked him if he could walk there, if she helped. He nodded.

It was in that moment, that the other warrior moved; he rolled slowly onto his side, his body trembled as he propped himself on his elbow. He said something to Gray Fox in Lakotah; then he spoke to Frankie, and to her surprise, he spoke in English. He motioned to his companion.

"Hide my friend," he said. "I will come behind you."

Frankie nodded, feeling relief sweep over her; she nodded, taking him at his word. She tucked herself tight against Gray Fox, under his left arm; she made her way toward the root-cellar, walking the horse along with her and keeping Gray Fox propped up between them—keeping him wedged between her and the Indian pony.

It was a slow process and several times she was sure Gray Fox was going to pass out. Once they made it to the doorway, he surprised her with more strength and balance than she expected. He made his way through the doorway and eased himself down the steps leaning against the wall with his good shoulder, supporting himself.

Frankie squeezed past him to open the hidden door; she shoved at the wall of bins, pushing and yanking until she had the doorway open. She lit the lantern, pulled the mattress from inside the bench and settled it in place. She went back to Gray Fox's side as he reached the bottom step. He leaned against her and they staggered their way into the room.

She let him collapse on the buffalo-robe that was lying across the mattress on top of the wooden bench, then dashed back up the steps and found her second Indian almost to the door. He was dragging himself through the winter-grass, using his arms and elbows and one leg to pull and push himself along. The other leg, bloody and useless, was dragging behind. She ran to retrieve the buffalo-robe from where it had fallen from the horse; she dragged it to the cellar steps and spread it out, draping it down the steps.

The warrior smiled at her, understanding what she was doing. He eased himself onto it and slid down the robe like an otter on a riverbank. When he reached the cellar floor, he dragged himself to the doorway of the Wolf Den. He paused there, waiting while she dragged the hide past him and settled it on the floor of the little room. When she stepped back, he pulled himself forward and rolled onto the hide. He lay there for a moment, eyes closed quietly, breathing hard. And then, he looked at her, talking quietly. Still breathing hard.

"Hide the horse. The soldiers," he said, "they will know it."

Frankie nodded, knowing he was right. She dimmed the lantern and put it on one of the crates; she stepped out of the room, started shifting the wall, telling the men she would close them in.

"Just for a while. While I hide the horse. But I'll be back."

Neither man gave her a response and she figured they had both passed out. She dimmed the lantern to a low glow and stepped through the doorway, shoving the bin-wall into place across the opening.

Now, it was a race against time. Because if soldiers were following closely, Frankie knew they could ride into the valley at any moment. As far as her warriors were concerned, they were safe behind the wall; if soldiers rode in and saw the blood-covered horse, all she'd have to do is explain is that the horse had wandered into her meadow. But it would be far better all the way around if she could keep them from seeing a bloodied-up bay Indian pony.

She headed to the horse, wondering whether it was wounded or if the patches and streaks of blood along its shoulders and sides were human blood. She did a quick check, running her hands along its hide. She found no wounds, but both forelegs showed considerable swelling. Both knees were hot and feverish; the fetlocks were swollen and tender.

The lameness, she wasn't worried about—that would heal with remedies, poultices and rest. Her big concern was where to hide a full-grown horse; she didn't have anything like a wolf-den for horses. The best option, she decided, was to hide it in plain sight. Get the blood off it, put it in with the geldings, and hope that it blended in as one of her herd.

She took the bay horse to the windmill pool, gasping as she led him into the icy water; she started working at the streaks and patches of blood, scrubbing his sides and legs. By the time she had his hide cleared of all the blood, both she and the horse were shivering. She led him to the back pasture and turned him in with the geldings. She watched her own horses and mules prance and snort and paw around him, acting the way horses always did when they greeted a newcomer.

Gray Fox's horse greeted them back, snuffling with them, pawing the ground and working his mouth the way a horse does when he wants to assure others of his kind that he'll be polite. As soon as introductions were over, the bay dropped his nose to the ground and started pulling at the grass, looking as if he was desperate to get food in his belly.

Frankie watched him for a minute or two, wondering how long it had been since he had a chance to just stop and graze and fill his belly. Wondering how many days he had been traveling with two warriors on his back.

She stayed by the pasture fence for a couple of minutes, watching the herd, wanting to be sure they accepted him; but all the while, she was flinging glances toward the meadow entrance and eyeing the back valleys and the hillsides. Watching for any movement, watching for any sign of soldiers.

Her horses moved around the Indian pony for a few more minutes, and then they put their heads down and went to grazing beside him. Accepting him into their herd, acting as if they had been together all along. With things settled in the herd, she headed to the house, watching her surroundings on the way. Glancing to the dogs, to the valley hillsides, to the meadow's entrance. No signs; no sightings; no movement.

Once in the house, she ladled broth from the chicken soup into a crock, gathered a few blankets from the back bedroom, snatched up her remedy-chest and a good number of dishtowels and flour-sacks. She headed back to the cellar, eyeing her surroundings once again. Watching to see if the dogs were looking in any particular direction. *Nope. Nothing.*

She had already made the decision to close herself into the cellar with the men while she did the doctoring on them. Deciding she would stay hidden with her warriors if the soldiers arrived while she was working on her Indians. The Cavalry could search all they wanted, but they'd never find the Wolf Den. She didn't know how long it'd take for them to do a search, but eventually, they would have to leave to continue their hunt.

Before she tucked herself away with the two warriors, she settled her armloads inside the cellar door, and went to remove any sign of their presence. She splashed a few buckets of water on the grass to wash the blood away. She took the broom from the cellar and swept at the dirt in front of the root-cellar door, sweeping away the drag-marks and moccasin tracks. She closed the dogs in the dog-pen in the barn so they wouldn't be waiting at the cellar door if a troop of soldiers *did* ride into the meadow.

She scuffed around in the dirt by the windmill pond hoping it was enough to remove any sign of an Indian lodge—because that kind of thing would certainly bring some questions to the minds of any soldiers who spotted the tipi-ring.

Finally, she toted several buckets of water into the cellar and pulled the upper door closed. She stepped into the Wolf Den, tugged the wall into place behind her.

Frankie went to work on the wounds, clearing the blood away so she could see what she had. And what she had, was four bullet wounds. Three in Gray Fox, and one in the man named Čhankhá Iyáphe, Flint Striker. Two of Gray Fox's wounds were flesh wounds, and given the heavy loss of blood from those wounds, Frankie understood at least some of the reason for Gray Fox's weakness. His third wound was in the back of his shoulder, after pressing the skin and tissue around it, she knew a bullet was sitting deep in the muscles that encased the shoulder blade.

Her mind whisked back to the textbooks in Dr. Gannon's office, remembering the medical books with their detailed line-drawings that showed the muscles and the bones. Remembering all the captions and little arrows and paragraphs that named the muscles and the bones and all the little features on the bones. *The joints and the tubercles and the fossae.* Remembering the drawings that showed how the muscles were positioned, that showed where they began and where they ended. She could picture the drawings of the shoulder blade. *The scapula. The spine of the scapula.* Remembering the wording of the captions. *The subscapularis muscle originates in the subscapular fossa. The infraspinatus muscle originates in the infraspinous fossa.*

The pictures swirled in her mind; she could see the drawings with the curving lines showing the muscle fibers and the blood vessels—the hand-colored arteries and the veins. She was hoping the visual memories would help. Praying they would help. *Because pretty soon I'm going to be digging in between all those fibers and veins and arteries. Because the bullet has to come out.*

Her mind skipped back to Indiana. Memories there too. Watching her Aunt Sarah working by lantern-light. In someone's house late at night. Some man with a bullet in his chest—the bullet lodged deep in the muscle. Her aunt had talked to her, showing her what she was doing. Explaining. Instructing her to daub at the blood. Showing her where to press so the blood-flow was staunched.

Frankie took in a breath, held it. Then released it slowly as she uttered another quiet prayer. *Please God. Please help me here. Please help me to remember.* She gave Gray Fox's shoulder wound a last glance before she turned to her other warrior. Her other patient. Wondering suddenly what Dr. Gannon would think of her working on these patients.

The wound in Flint Striker's left leg was by far the worst of all the wounds; he had lost a lot of blood. Plus, Frankie could tell the bullet had torn up a lot of tissue. The biggest problem, she knew, was that the bullet was still buried deep in his thigh muscles. *The quadricep muscles. Four of them. The muscles on the front of the thigh. Muscles that run from the hip to the knee. The muscles that lift the leg and bend the hip.*

Images of the pictures that adorned the pages of the medical texts were spinning around inside her mind, racing like the hounds when they careened around the meadow. She took a breath, slowed her thoughts, gathered her memories. Calmed her concerns. *One step at a time. Do the simple things first and the rest will come.* Because this was, after all, a journey. *Different than traveling West alone. But the same rule holds—one step at a time.*

Frankie took in another breath. The trembling in her hands slowed and quieted. She released the breath. Slowly. Steadily. *Start with cleaning the blood; clean the area around the wounds, then clean the wounds. Step by step.*

By the time she had all the dried blood cleared away and the new bleeding staunched, Frankie knew what she would have to do. She knew the process and the next step. She talked to the Oglála men about what she needed to do, speaking mostly in Cheyenne. And because Flint Striker spoke a fair amount of English, she resorted to using English words when she needed.

She told them about the bullets and explained that she had seen bullets taken out of wounds. And she told them that she had the right tools to remove bullets. But, she explained, she had never done it by herself. The men nodded, seeming to have no concerns about her lack of skills. They smiled at her. Nodded. Told her to take them out.

So Frankie went to work, laying out what she needed. Just like her aunt used to do. Just like Dr. Gannon and Thomas Braddock used to do. The forceps, the scalpel, the bandages. The remedies and powders. She mixed the poultices so they'd be ready to apply. She had the stack of towels and flour-sacks close by.

She thought about her Aunt Sarah, trying to picture her working on the bullet wounds. Twice, Frankie recalled, there had been patients with bullet wounds. Both times she had been beside her aunt, watching, handing her the instruments, cleaning them. And always, dabbing at the blood oozing from the wounds.

And there had been Dr. Gannon down at Fort Kearny. Teaching her, showing her the medical texts, talking about patients he had worked on. She tried to remember his words, trying to think about what he would do in this situation. Trying to think about what he would say; what he would tell her.

She began with Gray Fox, choosing to start with his shoulder wound, knowing Flint Striker's wound would require a steadier hand and a more intense focus. Gray Fox's wounds, she decided, would allow her a little time to practice, and learn, and settle into the work—before she even attempted to work on Flint Striker's ragged thigh wound.

She slipped the forceps into the opening of the wound at the back of his shoulder, nosing the tips of the forceps slowly into the muscle fibers. The words of the texts swirled through her mind. *The infraspinatus muscle, running from the bottom of the scapula to the humeral head.* She eased the beaks of the forceps deeper, spreading the muscle fibers apart as she went. Little by little. *Careful, now. Gently. Gently. Don't tear at it. Gently.*

The beaks tapped against a hard surface. *Bone? Did I miss the bullet? No. It is the bullet. That's the tap.* It was the bullet lodged against the smooth bone. She eased the forceps handles apart, opening the beaks. Slowly; carefully. Turning, twisting. *Gentle. Easy, now. There!*

Once she felt the beaks gripping the bullet, she reversed the process sliding the forceps back, easing bullet out through the muscle. And the whole time, Gray Fox stayed as still as a stone. His muscles quivered and went into rippling spasms, which she expected. But Gray Fox, himself, never flinched; he never made a sound.

Finally, with sweat dripping down her temples, Frankie leaned back, looking at the bullet in the grip of the forceps. Gray Fox turned his head, looked into her eyes; he smiled at her, his face soft. Still, showing no sign of pain. Frankie felt the tears welling up in her eyes; she nodded back, looking into her warrior's eyes. Suddenly realizing she was seeing a new and different level of strength and bravery.

She cleaned the wound a final time. Decided not to suture it. *It's small enough. It'll heal on its own.* She bandaged a poultice in place. Then she turned her attention to his other wounds.

First, the bullet holes in his forearm—both the entrance and exit wounds. Then she worked on the wound in his calf. She dusted all the bullet holes—both the entrance and exit wounds—with healing powders, packed them with poultices, wrapped them with the rolled-cloth bandages. And all the while, she was thinking about Flint Striker's wound—the ugly wound awaiting her attention.

Flint Striker, himself, was waiting quietly, patiently; fully aware of what she would have to do. Likely, he would handle the process much like Gray Fox had. Because he had the same kind of strength and courage. Because these men were of the Oglála people; these men were Oglála warriors.

When she left Gray Fox's side and turned to Flint Striker, she was feeling more certain, and a little more confident. She took in a slow, deep breath. Steeled herself. Daubed at the fresh blood that had been draining from his wound while she had been working on Gray Fox.

The wound in Flint Striker's thigh was deep and ragged; the tissue was hot and swollen. *Infection. Deep in the wound. And in the muscles around it. Days old.*

She took another breath. Stalled for a moment, thinking and wishing she had the courage of these two warriors. Then, she reminded herself that she didn't have a lot of time. She couldn't keep stalling. Because somewhere out there beyond her meadow, there was a squad, or a troop, or maybe a whole company of horse-soldiers. They were out there, somewhere beyond her valley. Hunting for her two wounded warriors.

It took a long time to find exactly where the bullet had lodged— it was deep in the swollen and damaged tissue. It took longer than Frankie expected to tease it from among the taut muscle fibers—fibers that had drawn together, fibers that were hard and tight after the days of continuing trauma. Because there had been constant movement. Because there had been a constant pulling and tearing within the muscles. And the whole time, the infection had been growing.

Now, Frankie could see that there was a vast amount of swollen tissue—some of the tissue was hard, some was still oozing. There were pockets and patches of infection—some ugly and dark, some stinking and yellow. And there were small pockets of blood—some bright and fresh; some dark and stale.

The wound continued to bleed steadily while she worked and she told herself it was probably a good thing. *At least some of it.* Because bleeding was a cleansing process that flushed the infection and washed the region. 'The body's own blood can clean wounds better than water, or any agent.' That's what her Aunt Sarah had said. Many times.

But Frankie was beginning to fret about the sheer amount of blood. Because she didn't know how much blood he had already lost. And because she was hard-pressed to know how much of the current bleeding was necessary, and how much was excessive. It was a narrow line to walk and she knew her lack of knowledge was the greatest danger to Flint Striker right now. It was something she really needed to *know*, and all she could do was guess.

Plus, she faced another problem. Because once she extracted the bullet and was ready to staunch blood-flow, she was suddenly doubting whether she would actually be able to stop it. She pressed, and held, and pressed some more. Repositioned, and pressed and held. And pressed still more. Waited. Pressed some more. When she did manage to slow and then finally stop the blood-flow, Flint Striker was unconscious.

For a tense moment, Frankie listened for his heartbeat and felt for his pulse, scared and uncertain. *Nothing. Nothing...*

She kept searching for a pulse and kept failing to find one. The carotid pulse. The femoral pulse in his good leg. The pulses at each wrist. She pressed her ear to his chest.

Nothing...

The tears rose, welling up in her eyes; she struggled to hold them back. Felt for a pulse again, checking all the pulses again. Already pretty sure he had died.

No, God. Please, God, please let him be okay.

She kept checking.

Nothing...nothing. Still nothing.

She listened for his heart.

Nothing. Ohh, God. Please.

She pressed her fingers to the femoral artery again, feeling for its pulse.

Ohh! There! The pulse. It's there...

She leaned, her ear pressed to his chest.

There it is! Yes! The heartbeat! It's there. Shallow. Low. Slow. But it's there. Oh, thank you, God!

She gasped, sucking in a ragged breath. Felt her own heart pounding. Gasped again. Said another prayer. A prayer of gratitude. Realizing suddenly, that she seemed to be doing an awful lot of praying on this particular day; she hoped that God and the angels-on-high didn't mind all the repeated petitions for assistance. *They must not. Because they keep helping me out.*

Frankie stayed at Flint Striker's side, her focus on the bleeding. Daubing at the blood. Pressing gently at the tissue around the wound's edge, watching for the effect she wanted. Waiting for the blood to get thick and sticky. Remembering Dr. Gannon's term for it.

'Coagulation', he had called it. 'A cascade-effect,' he had said, 'where all the necessary chemicals within the body begin to fall in place. It all happens exactly the same way. Every time. In every human. In every animal.' The medical texts had called it the 'natural physiological response necessary to effect the healing process'. She could picture the words on the textbook page. The right-hand page; second to the last paragraph.

When the bleeding had finally slowed enough for her to see the muscle tissue, she began stitching the inside muscles like Dr. Gannon had done on Boone's wound, using cat-gut for the inside muscles. She was trying to concentrate on the suturing, but she kept finding that her mind was wandering. She was thinking about how odd it was that the suture-thread was made of the same thing as violin strings. *Cat-gut for stitches. Cat-gut for violin strings. Not really 'cat' gut though. Which is probably a lucky thing for the three cats in the barn. Cow or pig guts, usually. Any old type of animal gut, actually.*

The bleeding slowed a little more as she finished with the inside muscle stitches; she relaxed a little as she began working on the outer skin stitches—gently easing the tissue edges together, piercing his skin again and again. Watching for any sign of Flint Striker waking, expecting him to start flinching at the stitches. He didn't wake; he didn't flinch.

She finally finished with the sutures. She stayed beside him, though, dabbing at the drops of blood oozing through the stitches, hoping that the heaviest bleeding was done. After a while, she moved over to Gray Fox, studied his bandages, saw some fresh blood stains on the bandages. *Just some of the last blood from the wounds. Not much. Just some. Just the last of it.*

She wiped the back of her hand across her forehead. Sweating. Or perspiring. Or 'glowing', like Isabelle called it. Because, apparently, Isabelle's mother had declared that ladies didn't sweat *or* perspire. That, according to her mother, was only for horses and men, respectively. With ladies, it was only 'a little glow'. Isabelle had told her all that while they had been weeding in her little garden behind the cottage at Fort Kearny. They had both burst out laughing. Because, they decided, that out there under the hot July sun in the Nebraska Territory, it didn't feel like a little 'glow' on their brows; it felt a lot like sweat. Frankie could feel her grin growing, thinking back to that day; thinking back to Isabelle. *Isabelle with the tender smile. Isabelle with the tender touch.*

Done with the cleaning and the doctoring, the daubing and the stitching and the bandaging, Frankie stayed in the Wolf Den for a while. She sat on one of the crates, watching her patients sleep. She realized that a troop of horse-soldiers could ride into her meadow at any moment; she knew that it'd be better if she was outside in the open when they did arrive. But she was worried about leaving the men. Afraid for Flint Striker, especially—deeply concerned that he had lost too much blood to recover.

The warriors, though, slept on. *Maybe just healing. Maybe just recovering. From the wounds. And from their long ride. And from the doctoring.*

She continued to watch. Gray Fox was drifting in and out of sleep. Flint Striker though, was sleeping deeply. His pulse and heartbeat were slow, but steady. *And his breathing is steady. Steady pulse, steady heartbeat, steady breathing. That's good. That's really good.*

Finally, Frankie left them; she closed them in the room and spent more time setting things right in the meadow, looking for anything that might reveal that two wounded Indians had ridden into her valley. She brought Blossom and Primrose to the tipi-site and staked them out, hoping their hooves would stir up the ground and conceal the truth about the Cheyenne tipi.

Then, she worked in her house, stowing away as many of her 'Indian things' as she could—some in the attic, some in the cubby-hole in the floor. So if the horse-soldiers did come, if they did search her house, they would see nothing that might bring up additional questions and suspicions.

Through the rest of the day, Frankie returned to the cellar periodically to check on her warriors. Flint Striker slept on, never stirring. Gray Fox was awake and asleep by turns, drinking water and the broth she offered him, but refusing any food. They spoke together, speaking softly in Cheyenne, the language they both knew, and that's when Frankie learned the story of their ordeal.

Gray Fox told her that he and Flint Striker and another Oglála warrior, had been fording the Platte at the Sioux Path when the soldiers attacked. They had both been wounded and one horse killed; the three of them traveled north, followed by the horse-soldiers. They gained distance from the soldiers during the nights, and they tried different tricks to elude them. Riding in streambeds. Backtracking. Covering their tracks. But still the soldiers followed. Finally, because of their wounds, their friend split off, hoping to lead the soldiers away from them. But the soldiers stayed on their trail instead.

The scout for the soldiers was good, Gray Fox said. Even when they kept their horse in the river to hide their trail, the Army scout still tracked them. From the description, Frankie figured they had reached the Middle Loup at some point; they had stayed within the banks, traveling downstream for a long time, going in the opposite direction the soldiers would expect. Then they had ridden north to the North Loup River and reversed direction, moving upriver.

Wounded like they were and with only one horse, Gray Fox had known by then that they couldn't outlast or outrun the soldiers. So they came to the home of Ho-esta Hesta Ka-éškóne. He thought the soldiers were still following them; he thought they were traveling a day behind them.

When she asked if he thought the soldiers might give up the hunt and turn back to their fort, he shook his head.

"No, Fire Heart Child. They will keep coming."

Frankie showed Gray Fox the water-barrel and the food and how to use the matches and candles if they needed to. She showed him the chamber-pot, told him what it was for. He shook his head, showing some surprise, and Frankie thought he must think that white people had strange customs. But he nodded, apparently understanding the sense of it—at least, under the present circumstances.

She told him she had to make it safer outside, to keep the soldiers from finding them when they showed up. And she told him when the soldiers *did* come, they would probably search her buildings. But the soldiers wouldn't find where they were hidden. She also told him she was worried the soldiers might decide to stay for a while. She would try to get them to leave, she explained, but if she couldn't, she would find ways to let him and Flint Striker know what was happening. If the soldiers were watching her, though, she'd have to stay away from their hiding place. He understood. He nodded.

When she left the root-cellar for the last time that day, she dragged and shoved the bin-wall back into place, closing the Wolf Den for the night. When she emerged from the cellar, she breathed in the evening air. Twilight air. Fresh air. Clean and cold. Cooling-air with moisture in it. *A storm's coming, for sure. The second storm. It'll be right in the front of the third storm—leading the big storm in.*

Halfway to the house, she paused, feeling the cool of the evening air flowing into her lungs again. She listened for a few minutes to the sounds of the twilight, listening to the sounds of the birds of the Sand Hills, singing their evening songs. Their last songs of the day. Singing to their mates of love and loyalty; singing to their neighbors about their territories. *Maybe singing about their love of the land and the skies.*

Frankie looked over toward the valley's entrance, staring at the track, chewing on her lip. Because Gray Fox was sure that the soldiers would come. She scanned the meadow and surveyed the hillsides, seeing nothing out of the ordinary. Everything was normal. Birds were singing in the trees on the valley slopes and that meant that nothing was disturbing them; no one was lurking there among the trees. *Not yet, anyway. But maybe by morning. Probably. Sometime tomorrow. Probably.*

She walked to the windmill pond and led Blossom and Primrose to the barn, pleased with the way they had stirred up the ground where Wild Bird's tipi had stood. She milked Blossom, penned her and Primrose for the night. Threw extra hay into the milking pen. Walked down the alley and released the dogs from their pen.

And then, she headed back to the house carrying a full pail of milk. Enjoying the quiet of the evening. Enjoying the last of the evening songs of the birds in the hillside trees. Well aware that everything could change tomorrow. Because tomorrow, the birds might stop their singing. Because tomorrow, someone *might* be among the trees. Tomorrow, someone might be watching from the hillsides. It would be the birds, and the dogs, and probably Sunny Jim, that would alert her if a stranger was near. *Or maybe, a whole troop of strangers. Maybe a whole troop of horse-soldiers. Oh, please God. Don't let them be from Fort Kearny.*

She went into the house. Ate a bit. Went back out to check on her warriors, talking to them through the wall. Unwilling to open the den again, just in case someone was near. Unwilling to take any chances now. Flint Striker was awake and he spoke to her in English, answering her questions about his wound. They told her they would wait; they told her that she should be careful.

"Be watchful, Fire Heart Child. Be like the prairie-wolf."

When she returned to the house, she was carrying vegetables in a basket, just in case someone was watching her. Just in case, the soldiers had come in the evening. She ate again and slept again. Waiting.

The next morning, Frankie tromped around the meadow in five inches of fresh snow, going in and out of the buildings, trying to look like a busy-little-homestead-girl. Feeding chickens; milking the cow. Clomping around in her work-boots and her uncle's coat. Getting the morning chores done. Doing normal homestead things. Because she knew that, *now*, there were watchers among the trees—they were there—high on the slopes above the meadow.

She had known it before she saw any real sign or heard any movement. Because the dogs told her so. They sensed a presence; she had seen their quick glances to the hillsides. She saw Laughing Girl's telltale walk—stiff and halting—with her head up, her eyes watching, her nostrils quivering as she sought out a scent.

Frankie had no doubt that the horse-soldiers were out there somewhere, and that someone was high on the valley slopes—not only because of the dogs—but because she had felt eyes on her earlier in the morning. First, when she was breaking ice in the outside troughs. And again, as she carried the milk-pail to the house after milking Blossom.

She had felt someone watching her as she walked to the henhouse, too, and once inside the henhouse, she had peeked through the window, studying the hillside above the barn. She had seen a movement then, a movement that didn't belong to a bird or animal. It was the movement of a human.

So at least one person was high on the slope; the rest of the Cavalry, she figured, would be somewhere outside the valley. Waiting for word and making plans. The soldiers must have settled in close to her homestead in the evening, or maybe, in the early hours of the night. At first light, someone—probably the scout—had moved in among the trees on the slope.

Thinking it would be wiser if the watcher believed she was unaware, Frankie pretended she hadn't noticed the behavior of the dogs. She kept Laughing Girl and her pups and Matilda close to her, talking to them, roughhousing with them, tossing sticks into the air for them to catch. Working to keep their attention on her, rather than on the hillside.

And after she played with the dogs for a few minutes, she went into the house, grabbed a basket and headed to the root-cellar. She spoke to Gray Fox and Flint Striker through the wall, letting them know the soldiers had found her meadow. Then she filled a basket with potatoes and apples, took in a slow breath, and headed back to the house—just an ordinary morning on a homestead, with a little-homestead-girl carrying a basket of vegetables to the house.

Back in the house, she waited. She stoked the fireplace. Poured herself a cup of coffee. Pulled pans of cornbread from the oven. She put together two pots of stew—deciding to make enough stew for several days—for herself and for her two Indians. She made her bed. She poured the ready-coffee into a pitcher and put another pot of coffee to brewing. Thinking it might be handy to have extra coffee made, because it might be a long wait. Thinking that sitting and waiting for the big event was a nerve-racking way to spend a morning. And all the time, she was listening for any sounds that meant the Cavalry was coming.

She spent plenty of time adding up everything she had been doing over the past day, thinking through everything she had done to clear away any sign that Indians had been in her meadow—not just her wounded warriors, but all her Indians. Because there was no sense in arousing suspicions.

She wasn't wearing the buckskin shirt and her trousers; today, she was wearing her blue-green dress and her linsey-woolsey apron— just like a good little-homestead-girl would wear. *No antelope shirt today. No trousers. No moccasins. No wolf-tooth necklace.*

No buckskin laces to secure her braids this morning; this morning it was the blue-green ribbons on her braids. She had her work boots on and was wearing the heavy winter coat. Work-gloves. *Homestead clothes. No sense in letting soldiers find anything that'll bring up questions.*

She had gathered up all her buckskin shirts and moccasins and dresses—all of the gifts from the Cheyenne and the Oglála—along with her whole collection of arrows and shoved them up in though the attic trapdoor. She had hidden everything connected to Indians except the huge buffalo-hides on the floor—too heavy to move and too bulky to hide.

She had spent time removing any sign that a tipi had been in her meadow; along with picketing Blossom and Primrose where the tipi had been, she had moved the stones from the tipi-circle and added them to the fire-ring. And luckily, the fresh morning snow would help cover any remaining sign.

Thinking about Wild Bird, Frankie was thanking the heavens and her lucky stars that the old woman wasn't here, thankful she had left with Whirlwind and Mourning Dove several weeks ago. And in the moment, she was praying softly that she wouldn't return any time soon. *Not until the soldiers are gone. Long gone.*

After sipping at another cup of coffee and pacing for almost an hour, she decided to make another trip to the root-cellar. The little-homestead-girl would carry a couple of pumpkins back to the house; anyone watching would assume the busy little girl was planning to make pumpkin pies. The trip to the root-cellar would allow one more chance to make everything seem normal and one more chance to talk to her warriors.

Frankie pulled on her coat and trudged out into the morning again; she threw a couple of snowballs high into the sky, entertaining the dogs with the tosses, laughing as they jumped to catch them. Playing at being innocent and unaware, and all the while, she was throwing a few glances up along the hillsides—watching for the watchers.

And it was in the midst of the snowball-play that she realized the dogs were no longer showing any interest in the hillsides—Laughing Girl wasn't walking stiff-legged and Matilda wasn't sniffing at the air. *Probably, the watcher's gone. Probably, he's taking word back to the officers. Please God, don't let them be soldiers from Fort Kearny. Please don't do that to me. Please!*

She stood staring out across the valley at the fresh-fallen snow, thinking it was a bit odd she hadn't paid any attention to the new snowfall. The second storm had come in the night, just like she had expected, and this one had dropped more snow than the first. There were five or six inches of fresh snow blanketing the winter-grass and resting on the roof-tops and fence-rails. The morning sunlight had the snow sparkling like millions of tiny diamonds. Her homestead world was sitting in sweet silence—the silence that always settled on the land after a night-storm's passing.

Any other time, Frankie knew she'd be taking great delight in the beauty of the snowfall. But today, things were different. Because today, the Cavalry was coming. And probably, they'd be arriving soon.

She called to Matilda and tromped through the snow, heading toward the root-cellar again. Kicking her boot-toes into the snow and sending swaths of the powdery snow into the air, watching as the sparkling flakes fluttered back to the ground in glistening arches. Doing anything that might make the little-homestead-girl seem innocent and unaware; just in case someone was still somewhere on the slopes and watching from the trees.

Frankie stayed where she was, standing just inside the root-cellar door, hidden behind it. Listening and waiting. Peering through the hinge-gap of the half-open door and eyeing the meadow's entrance. Because out in the meadow, Laughing Girl's growl was announcing the approach of riders. The time had come. She gave a wry smile, remembering one of her father's favorite phrases. 'The time is nigh, Sweet Child.'

Behind her, she could hear Matilda coming up the steps; Frankie motioned for her to lie down.

"Down. Wait." Her words came out in a hissed whisper and she heard the soft rustle as Matilda flattened herself down on a step.

Beyond the door, out in the meadow, Laughing Girl still uttering her deep-throated growl and it was growing louder and uglier. Too Shy and Ghost Dog were out there, too, standing near their mother and taking their cues from her. Their growls were getting louder because their mother's were getting louder; their hackles were raised because their mother's were raised.

Frankie stayed as she was, quiet and still. Listening. And then, finally, the sounds came—the sounds she had been expecting, sounds that were traveling sharp and clear in the crisp morning air. Horsehooves pounding on frozen soil; bits and bit-rings jingling; saddle-leather creaking. Sounds from just beyond the valley's entrance. Sounds that were growing louder.

Sunny Jim called out with a loud neigh, his voice echoing off the valley walls. A moment later, mounted soldiers appeared at the top of the entrance, moving at a fast clip. And quite suddenly, they were following the track down into the meadow. The Cavalry had arrived.

The hounds erupted, bawling out their warnings; from the far end of the meadow, Trumpeter's voice rang out—a stallion's call—challenging the strange horses entering his domain. Sunny Jim called out again. One of the mules gave a huffing bray.

659

At the bottom of the track, the lieutenant pulled his mount to a hard halt and raised his hand; the sergeant pulled up beside him. Behind him, the column-by-twos halted. The soldiers stayed as they were, sitting silently on their mounts, scanning the valley before them. Every man on the alert.

Through the hinge-gap, Frankie watched the horse-soldiers, leaning forward and twisting awkwardly to gain a better view. Trying to figure out exactly what she had out there in her meadow. She spotted the lead officer as a lieutenant; a sergeant rode close behind him. A short column of soldiers followed. Another man, not in uniform, was next to the lieutenant—a man mounted on a mule. *Not a whole company. Just a small troop. Just two officers and eleven troopers. Probably a scout.*

Frankie studied the soldiers, trying to gain what clues she could. Looking at the riders, she recognized no one. Not the lieutenant; not the sergeant. Not the troopers. Not the scout. So wherever this Cavalry troop had come from, it wasn't Fort Kearny. She gave a slow and heart-felt sigh. *Thank you, God.*

Her mind went to Gray Fox's words; he had said the chase began at the ford across the Platte River, far west of Fort Kearny. So it was likely these soldiers were from Plum Creek Garrison, or maybe, Fort Cottonwood. Frankie breathed another sigh of relief. *Thank you, thank you, God.*

She saw the sergeant's mount duck its head, tugging at the reins; the sergeant gave a sharp tug on the reins and the horse snapped its head up, jingling the bit-rings; it pawed the ground, irritated, and the sergeant snapped the reins again. The horse stood still.

Looking at the man on the mule, the man not in uniform. *Probably, the scout.* Frankie breathed another sigh of relief. *A white scout and not a Pawnee scout.* And that, Frankie decided was a very lucky thing. Because the Pawnee scouts who worked for the Army could see things and smell things that soldiers and white scouts would miss. She studied the scout, knowing that no matter how good he was, he wouldn't be as good as a Pawnee scout.

Frankie knew she had to make a move soon, because while the soldiers were sitting their mounts and studying her meadow, the tension was rising. There was a growing concern among them about the hounds and their ugly growls and barks. The sergeant already had his pistol out of his holster—he wasn't pointing it at the hounds yet, but he was ready.

The scout pointed toward the root-cellar, apparently concerned about the half-open door. The sergeant and lieutenant both glanced toward the door. The lieutenant said something to the scout, and then spoke to the sergeant. Frankie couldn't hear the lieutenant's words, but when he started pointing to the other buildings—indicating the Barracks and the house, the barn and the corncrib—she knew he was about to order his men to start a search.

She took a deep breath. Knowing it was best to make her move while every man was there in front of her. So she would know where everyone was; so she could watch everything and understand what was happening.

Putting on her best little-girl-homesteader face, she picked up the two pumpkins she had carried up the steps, figuring they would serve as a distraction—and right now, she needed a distraction. She needed something that none of the soldiers were expecting. An innocent little-homestead-girl carrying two pumpkins in her arms, stepping out from the cellar doorway, would likely get every soldier's attention, at least for a moment. Then, she knew, the action would start; then she would see how things went and what the lieutenant might have in mind.

Frankie pushed through the doorway; she stepped out the cellar door, holding her pumpkins. Bumping against the door and tripping on the door-sill. Stumbling out. All part of her plan—to startle and distract. And it worked. She saw the surprised looks on the soldiers' faces; she returned the look, trying to give them her best surprised-and-astonished-homestead-girl expression.

She shouted to the dogs, calling them back, ordering them down; she took another step away from the door, still staring at the soldiers, the pumpkins still clutched in her arms. She stumbled again, and as she grabbed at the door-frame for balance, one of the pumpkins slipped from her arms. It smacked against the ground with a dull splatting-thud. Just like she wanted. And in that instant, an order rang out.

Frankie didn't know if it was the lieutenant or the sergeant who gave the order, but the order was in the air and the troopers were moving. And they were moving fast. She lost track of the exact sequence of events in the jumble of shouts and churning hooves and blue Cavalry uniforms, but somehow during the process, the sergeant and two of the troopers had dismounted and were rushing toward her.

She dropped the second pumpkin as the sergeant grabbed her by her arms. Pistols were drawn from holsters; there were more orders and more shouts. She was being dragged away from the cellar-door by the sergeant; the two troopers headed into the cellar, their boots pounding on the steps. And as quick as the troopers went in the door-way, Matilda darted out, yelping from what Frankie assumed was a solid kick.

The collie-dog ran to her, still yelping and adding in a few growls and yips—angry and frightened and confused—her eyes flitting between her person in the grip of a stranger and the men who were stomping around in the cellar. Matilda, Frankie could see, was clearly unsure about what she should be protecting.

She ordered her down and Matilda crouched in the grass—still angry, still frightened. Still unsure. Frankie's eyes were on Matilda, but from the side, she caught a glimpse of another soldier approaching her and the sergeant. The next thing she knew, she was being jerked sideways; the second soldier was behind her then, holding her, keeping her arms pinned to her sides. New hands; a harsher grip. She twisted against the grip and shot a look upward. Saw the soldier's face; she saw a gold bar on his shoulder. *Not a trooper. An officer. The lieutenant.*

He was calling out more orders; the sergeant was repeating the orders and directing the troopers. The mounted riders had already split into pairs and they were reining their mounts hard as they sent their horses across the meadow, each pair heading to a different building.

Frankie watched it all—waiting and watching and worrying—and all the while, trying to listen to the movement in the cellar. Boots on the floor. Rustlings and bangs and thumps. But no sounds that told of the wall of bins being dragged open.

The lieutenant spoke to her, low and harsh, telling her to call off the dogs or he'd have them shot. She complied; she called to Laughing Girl once again, ordering her back, knowing the two pups would follow her lead.

In the next moment, she heard boots on the cellar steps and the two troopers emerged from the cellar shouting that it was clear. Frankie stifled a sigh of relief, watching as the sergeant motioned to them and led them toward the Dwelling Place at a run. Pistols still in-hand, they darted into the dugout; there was the sound of boots on the floorboards, and then they were out again. Shouting.

"All clear!"

Next, they headed to the chicken-house at a run, with the sergeant in the lead; Frankie played at being the little-homestead-girl again.

"*Don't* you let those hens out!" She shouted at them.

"Quiet down!" The lieutenant gave her a hard shake and yanked her back against him. She leaned back against him, trying to show him that she wasn't fighting, hoping he'd take her meaning. He did. He relaxed his grip slightly while he watched his troopers and the activity around the various buildings.

The next thing she knew, the lieutenant was striding forward, holding one of her arms, pulling her along beside him. He stopped at the outhouse, tightened his grip on her arm as he pulled his pistol and yanked the door open. He scanned the inside and kicked the door shut. Frankie tried not to grin, wondering if he really expected to find two Indians and a horse hiding in there.

Two troopers emerged from her house. One came toward the lieutenant, declaring that the house was clear; the other trooper joined the sergeant and the two troopers emerging from the Barracks—they all headed to the barn to join the search there. Shouts were coming from inside the barn; the troopers were calling out 'all-clear' and 'nothing-found', again and again.

Frankie felt the lieutenant's grip tighten again as he headed toward the house, pulling her along and ordering the trooper to follow. She was half-trotting and half-stumbling beside him; he slowed his pace a little; his grip softened a little. He began asking questions as he pulled her up the porch steps and pushed her ahead of him through the door and into the kitchen.

"What's your name?"

"Frances Dunbar." She gave the name that the Dunbars, the Austins, and William and Tipp had decided she should use if she was in doubt of her circumstances. The name, they had decided would connect her to 'relatives' if she needed. And like Everett had said, it would cover her identity as Frankie Harding.

"Where are your folks?"

"Gone."

"Where?"

"For supplies."

The lieutenant nodded and stepped back outside the kitchen door, dragging her beside him. He looked toward the barn, watching the activity. Waiting. When he saw the sergeant, he called out, pointing toward the corncrib and sweeping his arm out toward the fenced pastures. Then, apparently satisfied, he posted the trooper at the door with instructions to watch the progression of the search.

Then, to Frankie's surprise, the lieutenant pulled her back into the kitchen again, and began his own walk through the house; his grip was still tight on her arm and he was still half-dragging her along.

"Stop yanking me around! You're hurting my arm." She tried to make it a whining complaint, doing her best to sound like an innocent little-homestead-girl, and once again, the lieutenant relaxed his grip. He shortened his stride as he continued his walk through the house, stalking through the same rooms his troopers would have searched. He finished his prowl with a quick scan of the pantry and went to the kitchen door again. He stood watching the activity in the meadow.

While he watched outside, Frankie was watching him, trying to size him up, trying to figure out exactly what she could expect of him. He was a six-footer to her thinking, but she suspected he would probably pass for being taller because he carried himself straight, with his shoulders squared. His hair was light blond, his eyes were brown and he had a strong lantern-jaw. And at the moment, his jaw was set hard. Which, to Frankie, was a little worrisome.

He turned around, stepped to the table. He yanked one of the chairs out and sat down. He pulled her around in front of him, standing her to face him.

"Okay, Frances, let's you and I have a little talk. Tell me where your parents are."

"Why are you here? What are all the soldiers doing out there?" Frankie ignored his question, acting confused and worried. She looked toward the door, twisting to see outside. Acting as if she had never been around soldiers before. *Scared little-homestead-girl.*

He pulled her toward him by her shoulders. Making her face him again.

"First, you *answer* me and you answer quick. Now. Where are the adults? Who's here on the homestead with you?" His grip tightened again.

"I *told* you. They went for supplies. There's no one here but me. I'm taking care of things while they're gone." She gave him what she hoped was a confused look; then she glared at him. "But I want to know who you are and why you're here. And why are you doing this?" *Snippy little-homestead-girl.*

He ignored her question and stood up, switched his grip to her wrist and pulled her toward the doorway again. He scanned the meadow, watching his men. Listening for a moment. Nodded, apparently satisfied. He pulled her back toward the table.

"Stop pulling me around! *Why* are you doing this?" She pulled back, struggling just enough to show she was scared and confused.

"Stop fighting with me. You start cooperating, or things are going to get rough." His voice was louder. He gave her a solid shake and sat down in the chair again; he pulled her and stood her in front of him again. Holding her in a hard grip, telling her—ordering her—to settle down.

Frankie stopped her struggle and waited, doing what he demanded of her. She was trying hard to find the balance she needed in the circumstance. A little bit of fight would look right to him. But she was finding it difficult not to react to the man-handling and send a few Cheyenne kicks and elbows into him. She held back, reminding herself that there were two Oglála warriors in the Wolf Den who were more important than her pride.

He told her then that he was Lieutenant Leland Pierce from Fort Cottonwood. He was leading a troop and they were in the region 'hunting for some Indians'.

"Why are you way up *here* hunting for Indians? And why are you hunting in *my* meadow? Don't you have enough Indians to hunt down by your fort?" Frankie was playing it for all she was worth. *Innocent little-homestead-girl. Half-scared and not very knowledgeable about such things.*

Lieutenant Pierce gave a half-smile, paused to compose himself, and then showed what seemed to be a semblance of patience. He explained that they were looking for *certain* Indians. Three Indians, he said, who had been up to some mischief and got into a fight with the Cavalry. The Indians, at least two of them, were wounded. Maybe, he said, all three were hurt. He and his troop were hunting them, intending to take them back to the fort. He explained that his soldiers needed to look everywhere. And when they were sure the Indians weren't anywhere on her homestead, they'd head out and keep looking.

"How long are you going to be here, then? Because I have work to get done." Frankie was trying to get an idea about how long they would be staying. More than that, she wanted to get an idea of what this lieutenant was thinking.

"We'll be here until I say differently. And *you* will be cooperating with me."

His voice had gone harsh again; acting the way he apparently thought a lieutenant should act. Probably, Frankie figured, because she had heard the footsteps on the porch like she had—some of his troopers had come back from their search and were outside the door and within earshot.

He stood up, swung her around and sat her down in the chair. He scooted the chair against the table, stood behind her; he put her hands on the table and pressed them down on the surface. He leaned down and spoke close to her ear.

"You sit right here and answer my questions. *Now.* I want to know if you've seen any Indians around here."

Frankie didn't look toward the door but she had heard more soldiers arriving at the porch. They were listening, and likely, Lieutenant Pierce knew it. So, Frankie figured, he probably wanted his men to see him handling things like an officer.

Her concern, suddenly, wasn't with him; her concern was with the man who rode the mule. The scout. Because from the corner of her eye, she could see he was there on the porch with the others; he was just outside the screen-door and *that* had her worried.

Because if he was the scout, as she had him pegged, then he'd probably be a lot like Corporal Buchanan down at Fort Kearny. And that meant he'd be able to read people well. Because along with knowing the land and having the skills to follow tracks, scouts were also translators. As such, they had to do more than just interpret words; a good scout had to read people well, so he knew if someone was being truthful or not. And if this scout was only half as good as Corporal Buchanan, then she had to be very careful.

"I've seen a lot of Indians around here." Frankie answered the question carefully, knowing the scout was listening. Knowing he would be able to tell if she was lying.

"I'm talking about in the last couple of days, you damn little brat. Now, *have* you seen any Indians around here? Did you see any Indians going by here? Down by the river, maybe?"

"I haven't seen any Indians going by here in the last couple of *weeks.*" She was staying truthful. No Indians had gone *by* her meadow; nor, had she seen any Indians down by the river. "I've been working here in the meadow, trying to get things done before the big storm comes in. I haven't even *been* out by the river, so I haven't seen *anyone* there."

667

She spoke the words loudly, partly to sound scared, and partly to make sure the scout heard. Hoping he'd be convinced the Indians weren't here. Then she tried adding in another tactic. Distraction.

"And I need to know how long you're gonna be here. Because I have work to do. And I'm gonna get thrashed good and hard, if I don't have it done by the time everyone gets back." She gave a quivering little sniff and made her lower lip tremble a bit. *Worried little-homestead-girl.*

Frankie heard a few chuckles from out on the porch. *Worked!* The lieutenant, however, didn't seem to think there was anything to laugh about. *Didn't work. Crap!*

"You better listen to me, little girl. We *know* those Indians were headed in this direction. And there's no sign they went beyond here. So if they're here, you better believe it's only matter of time till we find them."

"Well, just because some Indians were headed in this direction, doesn't mean I *saw* them go by. If you really believe there *are* Indians around here, then hurry up and catch them. And get them out of here. Because I've got enough things to deal with." She tried the lip-trembling tactic again. It didn't faze him—his mind was on what she had just said.

"How old are you, Frances?" He leaned down closer, his hands on the table on each side of her. She knew that mostly he was trying to scare her, but he also knew that his men were still out on the porch. He was well aware that they were watching and listening, and a lieutenant wouldn't want to look soft in front of his men; he wouldn't want his men to think a little-homestead-girl had bested him.

"Eleven."

"Then you're old enough to know I'm an officer in the United States Cavalry and eleven-year-old little girls don't tell me where I go, or what I do." His voice was raw and angry; there was a sharp and mean edge to it.

Frankie knew he was mostly angry about the unfound Indians and the long, drawn-out chase; she also knew he wasn't far from giving her a slap or two if he decided to direct some of that anger toward her.

"Yes, Sir."

"You stay here at this table. Don't you move. Not one damn inch."

He turned and strode out of the kitchen and down the porch steps, motioning to his soldiers; they all walked away from the house, believing that once they were out in the middle of the meadow, they'd be out of her earshot.

Frankie grinned, knowing the air was still sharp and clean after the storm last night, knowing the layer of snow on the ground would make their voices carry through the air. She laid her head on the table and listened to the voices across the snow-covered grass. Because she needed some information. Because even though things had gone well so far, she needed to know what the lieutenant had in mind. Because right now, she could see four options the soldiers had.

They might leave right away. Or they might stay and search for a few more hours and *then* leave. Or they might decide to stay overnight, or maybe, even longer. The fourth option was of the greatest concern to her, because if the lieutenant believed the Indians were being hidden somewhere on her homestead, the troop might actually leave her meadow itself—and then stay close by and secretly watch her place.

And *that,* Frankie knew, was the most dangerous option, because she would have no way of knowing how long they'd stay and watch. If Lieutenant Pierce—and the scout—believed the Indians were hiding somewhere on her place, they might decide to dig in for a long stretch. And being watched by the soldiers for any length of time—and never knowing when they were actually gone—could be a big problem for her and her two warriors. *Please God. Please have your angels help me out. Please, keep my Indians safe.*

So Frankie kept her head down on the table; she kept her breathing slow and quiet, and she kept listening to the voices drifting in through the screen-door, listening to their words floating on the crisp air. Hoping to hear something that might guide her.

It was the scout's voice that came to her first; she knew it was him because he wasn't talking like a soldier would speak to a ranking officer. He spoke with an earthy, relaxed twang; his voice steady and sensible as he laid out the facts.

"Lieutenant, like I tole you afore, I ain't convinced they even come this far. I ain't seen no sign in the last two days."

Another man spoke up, his voice serious, his words calm; Frankie recognized the tone and the demeanor. She grinned. It was the same tone Sergeant McCallister down at Fort Kearny was prone to using. This sergeant was agreeing with the scout, and it sounded as though he was trying to convince the lieutenant to trust what the scout was telling him. The sergeant, Frankie had seen, was a lot older than the lieutenant, and just by years alone, he'd have a better understanding about the value of a scout's perspective.

They kept talking and Frankie kept listening, trying to decide whether the lieutenant was stubborn or just stupid—because usually, officers relied heavily on advice and guidance from their scouts. This young Lieutenant Pierce, though, didn't seem willing to take advice from two men who clearly knew a lot more than he did.

The discussion continued and Frankie stayed at the table, shivering as the crisp air found its way into the kitchen. The cold air reminded her of another problem. There was a new storm moving in tonight—the one following behind the two lead-storms. Given that, the soldiers were going to have a whole new problem. A big problem.

She shivered again, suddenly not so interested in the argument in the meadow. Because with everything else going on, she hadn't been out on the Lookout Hill this morning; she hadn't had a chance to watch the cloudbank that was probably already forming on the western horizon.

But even without actually seeing the horizon, she could tell there was change in the air—the temperature was beginning to drop. If another blizzard was coming—another one like the one a couple of weeks ago—Lieutenant Pierce and his troop would be in serious danger if they left.

So now, Frankie realized, she had more than just the two Indians to worry about. Now, she had a whole Cavalry troop that might be in danger. And no matter what she thought of their lieutenant, none of those soldier-boys deserved to leave here cold and hungry. No matter when they were leaving, she could, at the very least, feed them.

Frankie stood up from the table. Unconcerned with the lieutenant's orders now. She figured he'd probably yell at her when he came back inside; maybe he'd yank her back to the table and remind her of his orders. *Maybe.* But she was betting that once he saw what she was doing—once he saw the coffeepot and smelled the coffee— he'd probably settle down.

She tossed a few pieces of wood into the corner fireplace, squatted down to pet Matilda on the rug in her usual place, trying to reassure her after all the rough-and-tumble activity. Thanking her for listening. Because it had been a hard thing for a loyal little collie-dog to understand.

Then, she went to the cookstove and stoked up the fire under the brewing coffee. She shifted the pitcher of ready-coffee over the front burner to get it heating again. She was ready to pull the two Dutch-ovens full of stew from the oven and lift them to the stovetop when she heard boots on the porch. The screen-door creaked open and slapped itself shut.

"I thought I made it clear you were to sit at the table where I put you." Lieutenant Pierce was behind her. His voice harsh again. Frankie kept her face turned away so he wouldn't see her rolling her eyes. *Because rolling your eyes in front of an officer is a sure way to get yourself smacked.*

"I thought maybe everyone could use a cup of hot coffee." She went for a tone halfway between innocent and annoyed. "And I thought it might make sense to get this stew up to a quicker cook, so your men would have a warm meal in their bellies before you head out on this stupid Indian hunt of yours."

She was lifting one of the heavy Dutch-ovens to a backburner just as the sergeant was coming in from the porch. He glanced at her, then at his lieutenant. He sized up the situation quickly and stepped in.

"Here, let me help with that, Miss. It must weigh as much as you." The sergeant was suddenly beside her, reaching for the pot. He set it on the burner she pointed to, then pulled the other pot out of the oven and settled in on another burner. He glanced to her as he did so, giving her a soft and quick wink, making sure his lieutenant couldn't see.

"Thank you, Sergeant." Frankie gave him a careful nod, understanding suddenly that the sergeant had the whole situation figured out. "If you could have one of your men go and get the pumpkins I dropped by the root-cellar door, I'll get some pies going." Frankie saw him nod to one of the soldiers by the doorway.

Frankie stepped around the lieutenant and headed into the pantry-room; he followed her, still angry she had ignored his orders.

"Where are you going?" His voice was harsh.

She saw him glance toward the outside pantry door, as if he expected her to attempt an escape. She gave him a wry smile, letting him see she was annoyed with him and his question.

"Sir. If I was planning to run away, where *exactly* would I go? I'm already home where I want to be." She stopped herself from rolling her eyes, just in time. She reached for the jar of heavy cream on the counter. "Here. Take this and put one of your soldier-boys to work."

Frankie watched as he took the jar and stood looking at it. Clearly stumped. *Not a country-raised boy, then.*

She took it from him and stepped around him, back into the kitchen; she turned her head toward the sergeant and rolled her eyes. She stifled a laugh when she saw him grin and duck his head. She walked past the table—where she was supposed to be sitting—and went to the doorway. She looked at the group of soldiers standing on the porch.

"Which one of you is country-boy enough to know how to get the butter to come up in this jar?"

Three of them reached for the jar, grinning at her. She left them to it, beckoned to another trooper and went back past the lieutenant.

Ignoring him again. She turned to the trooper, pointed to the pitcher of coffee on the stove and the cups on the shelf.

"You get to work pouring coffee for everybody." She didn't wait to see whether or not the lieutenant was going to mind that she was giving orders; the soldier didn't wait either. He reached around the sergeant, lifted the pitcher and gathered up a handful of cups; he started filling cups and called another trooper in from the porch, telling him to start passing cups around.

The sergeant shifted the coffeepot to the burner where the pitcher had been and pulled a second coffeepot from its high shelf and started filling it with water. He poured coffee beans into the grinder and called for another trooper to 'get to grinding'. Frankie grinned, delighted to see the sergeant taking charge. He grinned back at her and winked again.

A few minutes later, the trooper with the pumpkins appeared at the screen-door. Frankie handed him a few knives and put him and some others to peeling and cutting up the pumpkins at the porch table. She turned to the lieutenant, sitting at the table—done now with his huffy moment—and sipping at a cup of coffee.

"Sir, if you'd send someone with me, I want to ride up on the hill and get a look at the horizon. There's a storm coming in and I need an idea of what to expect. And so do you, for that matter."

Before Lieutenant Pierce had a chance to agree or refuse, the scout was suddenly in the kitchen.

"I'll take this young lady, Sir. We'll go take us a gander at the western sky."

Frankie wasn't sure exactly how the scout had made his way into the kitchen as fast as he did, but he was there—reaching for her big winter coat on its wall-peg before the lieutenant had a chance to answer. And before she could object, he had her by the arm and was guiding her out of the kitchen and across the porch.

His grip was gentle but he was moving her along. Clearly, in a hurry. Frankie didn't resist, but she was calling over her shoulder as they went down the porch steps, calling to the sergeant.

"Someone needs to add water to the stew and stir it good. And there's two pans of corn bread in the warming oven."

673

And then, she found herself trotting toward the barn with the scout's hand on her collar. Still hurrying her along. Gently; firmly. No slowing down; no nonsense. Just moving swift and sure, all the way to the barn.

"It's best we get a move on, Honey, afore that lieutenant goes an' gets hisself an idea to the contrary." He winked at her when he said it, as if there was some sly secret between them.

While she slipped the bridle on Rock, he told her that Jim Key was his name, and explained that he was 'scoutin' for the Army outta Fort Cottonwood'. He watched her swing up on Rock's back, and then mounted his mule. He nodded to her, expecting her to take the lead.

She turned Rock through the door on the backside of the barn and sent him up the high slope; Jim Key's quick-stepping mule surged up the narrow track behind her. They broke out of the trees on the hillside and burst onto the open grassland beyond the valley.

Once they were beyond the meadow, Frankie led the way to the Lookout Hill; they rode side-by-side up the hill's eastern slope and when they reached the crest, Jim Key reined his mule, putting him right next to Fox. He sent a stream of tobacco juice into the grass, and then looked at her, grinning.

"Don't let the lieutenant git to you."

"He's not getting to me. I just can't figure out whether he's stubborn or just plain stupid." She grinned at him and saw his grin grow a little bigger.

She looked at him for a moment, studying him. Liking him. But not really sure if that was a safe thing. This man named Jim Key was a smaller man than most. Wiry and tough. He had brown eyes that were warm and kind at the moment, but Frankie figured they could probably get cold and harsh pretty fast. He had a long mustache that drooped down to each side of his mouth, down to his chin. It showed some gray hairs mixing in with the brown—the same as the hair on his head. And as long and droopy as his moustache was, it was still carefully trimmed. And Frankie thought it looked awfully neat and pretty.

"Oh, he's mebbe a little bit o' both. Stubborn, fer sure. Not so much stupid, though. Has more to do with him still bein' fresh at what he's doin'."

Frankie watched the scout out of the corner of her eye; he had his eyes on the cloudbank to the northwest, but she knew he was well aware of everything she was doing—he had been studying her as much as she had been studying him. He was just more discreet in the way he went about it. He was sitting next to her on his flop-eared mule there on the hilltop, looking out to the northwest, looking as if all his thoughts and attention were focused on the coming storm.

But Frankie knew better; she knew it was only a matter of time before Jim Key would start talking—and it probably wouldn't be a conversation about the storm. Because the scout clearly had things on his mind. He had things he wanted to say to her and he had things he wanted to hear from her. She had no doubts about that. Because he had been awfully determined to get her away from the meadow. Away from the soldiers and off by herself. So she did her best to ready herself for whatever might happen next.

She heard the scout draw in a long breath. She watched him work his mouth for a moment, before sending another stream of tobacco juice flying. And then, he turned to look at her, his eyes steady and still.

"Now. Lissen up and lissen well. I *know* yer not jest some innocent little homestead kid. I'm figgurin' you've got a purty good handle on what's goin' on here, no matter how yer actin'. So. Tell me what yer thinkin'."

Frankie looked at him, trying to sort out what he knew, and exactly how *much* he knew. She took in a slow breath, trying to steady herself, hoping he hadn't figured out about the Indians being on her place. She gathered herself, and then waded into the conversation, deciding to stay away from any talk about the Indians or the search itself.

"Well, I'm thinking I'd like to get this troop of soldiers out of my home and off of my homestead. But we both know from the look of those clouds there's a big storm heading here. And we both know it'll hit well before dark." She turned her eyes to the scout and took in a slow breath. "Look. I don't really care where the lieutenant wants to spend the night. He can sleep in a snowbank for all I care. But neither you nor those soldier-boys need to be out on some crazy hunt tonight. Freezing-cold and soaking-wet in a roaring blizzard. Getting frost-bit and worse. They're already exhausted and they're riding worn-down horses. And if they come up against a band of fifty or sixty trouble-minded Pawnee, it'll end up being an ugly thing." She paused; Jim Key stayed silent. After a moment, she went on.

"So I'm trying to think of the best way to get your lieutenant to hunker those troopers down at the house. And right now, I'm thinking the best way to get him to stay put, is to act like I don't want him to."

"Well, Honey, you *do* have the lieutenant figgured right." Jim Key tipped his head back and laughed. Then he sent another line of tobacco-juice arcing downwind behind their mounts. "But if yer really willin' to put up with the whole passel of us, I kin tell you ever' one o' them boys would appreciate it. They're purty well all wore out. An' when it comes to convincin' the lieutenant, I kin handle him jest fine. But how're you fixed to feed us? I'm not wantin' to be cuttin' into yore stores."

"Thank you for that Mr. Key, but there's plenty. You likely know there's a buck hanging in the barn right now. There's plenty of food in the cellar. And I have plenty of staples in the pantry."

"Okay then, Darlin'. You an' me, we'll sort out the lieutenant. But they's another reason I brung you out here. What I'm really wonderin' about, is what yer thinkin' 'bout them Indians we're a-huntin'?" He was eyeing her. Watching her hard and steady.

Frankie did some fast thinking. Because even though he seemed pretty honest and genuine, there was a chance that this Army scout already *knew* she had the Indians hidden somewhere. He might just be working her around to get the information he wanted. She took a wild shot, trying to take the conversation in a completely different direction.

"Well, I guess I'd have to know more. Are we talking about Pawnee?"

"Nope." He shook his head. "Sioux. Oglála."

"What are *they* doing this far east? At *this* time of year?" She acted a little astounded at the thought.

"Well. They was west o' here a good piece. An' a fair piece to the south. We were down yonder to the Platte when this all got started. I ain't fer sure they was really up to nything' more'n jest travelin', but the lieutenant got it in his head to stir things up once we spotted 'em. One's an Oglála chief I recognized. A feller called Gray Fox. An' they was a couple others a-travelin' with 'im. I'm figgurin' you might know 'im."

Frankie stayed still, sitting on Fox, fiddling with the mane at his withers, her eyes once again on the horizon to the northwest. Breathing slowly, not sure what to say. Thinking that this man was going to be difficult to fool. But then Jim Key went on.

"See, I know a few things about what's goin' on here, Frankie Harding." He spat another arc of tobacco-juice. "Jest like I know that red-and-white pinto in yer barn is one that the Cheyenne chief, Strong Hand, rides."

"Yes, Sir. It is." Frankie sat still on Rock's back. Very still. Looking down at Rock's mane. Stunned that this man knew her name. Shocked that he knew *exactly* who she was. She stayed quiet, unwilling to launch into a conversation about her name. Or about Strong Hand. Or Fox. Not until she knew what he was planning to do with these 'few things' he knew.

"So then? You know Gray Fox, or not?" Jim Key leaned toward her, just a bit. Not unkindly, but as a way of letting her know he wasn't messing around.

Frankie took in a breath and let it out in a sigh. He *definitely* knew some things. Too many things. Things that spelled danger for her. But suddenly, in that moment, she realized something else. He definitely didn't know *where* the Indians were. And he didn't know *for sure* that they were on her place. If he actually thought they were nearby, he wouldn't be up here on a hilltop talking with her. He and the troopers would still be searching. *So my warriors are safe. At least, for now.*

She decided the best course was to answer what questions she could, and answer them honestly. But push-come-to-shove, she would refuse to answer any questions about her hidden Indians. Whatever happened to her as a result, was just what she'd have to deal with. But she was not going to turn Gray Fox and Flint Striker over to Lieutenant Pierce. Or to the Army. She looked at Jim Key, looked right into his eyes.

"I have *met* Gray Fox, Mr. Key. I met him through Knife. Knife's a brother to Strong Hand. I met them once down near the Little Blue." In her mind, she meant 'them' as Strong Hand and Knife—and she *had* met them near the Little Blue. But Gray Fox hadn't been with them. But she had, actually, met Gray Fox through Knife when they rode into her meadow. It was a bit evasive, but it was all true enough so she wasn't lying to the Army scout.

Jim Key would have seen the lie if she had denied knowing Gray Fox—Frankie was sure of that much. But she didn't have to say exactly *where* she met him. And it wasn't the Army's business if he had been in her meadow before. Jim Key could assume whatever he wanted from her words, and beyond that, she'd have to hope for the best.

She saw him nod and Frankie figured that meant that he knew Knife, or at least, he knew *of* him. She went on, carrying the conversation forward, seeing if she could redirect it.

"Mr. Key, I don't think Gray Fox, or any sensible Oglála, would want to travel very far east into Pawnee country. Not in the winter. And, especially not if they were wounded. They would be more apt to try to get north. It'd make more sense for them to head to the Black Hills. To their own people." She turned her attention back to the western horizon. "Honestly, coming this far east could put them in a peck of trouble. If I was a wounded Oglála warrior and I had to choose between fighting a dozen soldiers, or two hundred Pawnee on their own lands, I think I'd rather fight the soldiers." She looked at the scout sitting next to her on his mule; he grinned at her and nodded.

"I'll tell you Frankie Harding, I'm a-lookin' at it the same way. Tell me though, on account of this ain't country that I know well, how far east do you figgur the Pawnee would be? How far you reckon a feller'd have to go afore he'd be runnin' across 'em?"

"What I *know* is that a few Pawnee bands roam through this area once in a while. I haven't seen any, but I've found a few Pawnee arrows at different times. Mostly, they stay more than a day's ride east of here. I've heard they roam further west up above the Niobrara River, but that's only what I've heard. Don't go counting on it."

Jim Key sat on his mule, stroked his moustache and nodded. Frankie watched him, feeling her caution fading. She figured him to be a fair man and a sensible man. And probably, a lot like Corporal Buchanan in that way. She thought about asking how he knew her, but she decided to wait. Because she wanted to stay on *this* subject a little longer; she was giving him information he asked for and she was pretty sure he'd return the favor.

She stayed quiet for the next few minutes, waiting for him to take the lead. Finally, after sending another stream of tobacco-juice sailing through the air, he turned to look at her.

"I spend a big share o' my time down 'round Camp Rankin and Camp Wardwell in the Colorado Territory. An' mostly, I deal with the 'Rapaho an' some of the Cheyenne in those parts. Some Kiowa, too. So, I don't know the Oglála as well. And mebbe you know 'em better than me. Honestly, Darlin', I ain't heard too much 'bout this Gray Fox bein' a big trouble-maker down along the Platte. You holdin' any ideas on that?"

"I don't know much about what's going on down along the Platte. All I know, really, is that I've heard soldiers at Fort Kearny talking about how things with Indians are heating up along the Overland. I think Gray Fox and his people probably do some traveling down to where Lame Horse's people are. Down south of Fort Cottonwood somewhere," Frankie hesitated, trying to acting as if she was thinking over the past. Then, after a pause, she went on.

"And I don't remember exactly what I heard to make me think it, but I have it in my mind there might be a family connection there somehow. Among Gray Fox's people and Lame Horse's people.

679

Maybe like a marriage or something. But I believe Gray Fox's people stay pretty far up north most of the time. I don't think he'd be traveling down to the Platte just to stir up a hornet's nest. I'd figure he'd be more interested in keeping his own people away from all that."

"Kin I ask how it come to be that you have Strong Hand's warhorse here on yer place? Just on account of I'm a-wonderin' fer myself. An' not fer anyone else." He leaned back on his mule, swung his leg over his mule's withers and hooked his knee across the pommel.

And suddenly, Frankie understood him. Jim Key wasn't trying to trick her; he was just being who he was. This was just pure Jim Key. He'd protect her, not hurt her.

"I helped his family once. His mother and his little girl were sick. Strong Hand and Knife showed up with them here on my homestead and I did some doctoring on them. When they were better, they moved on. And I found this pony tied to my porch post."

They sat there on the hilltop for a while longer, feeling the wind picking up and the temperature dropping down. Frankie knew the scout had something else to say, and she knew it wouldn't be about the Indian hunt. Because, Frankie realized, he had just found out what he needed to know about *that* situation—and, he had already decided what he was going to do. And he already knew how he was going to handle Lieutenant Pierce.

Now, she realized, the time had come. Now, he would talk about how he knew who she was. She was surprised with herself, because she knew she ought to be worried about it. And yet, she wasn't feeling any great amount of fear. Probably, she decided, because this man wasn't Cavalry—even though he worked for the Army. He wasn't a soldier. He was his own man and Frankie figured he was a lot like Bill Wheaton down on Fort Farm Island. She had a strong hunch that just like Wheaton, Jim Key would keep her secrets.

"We got us a mutual friend, you an' me." He sent another line of tobacco juice in a high arch behind his mule. "When I seen that big Conestoga a' yourn in the barn an' spotted them four black Shires,

I come to thinkin' you might be the Frankie Harding that I'd heard tell of."

"From Corporal Buchanan?"

"No, Ma'am. Though, I do know 'im. And if you don't already know, he's put out word to all us scouts to keep an eye peeled fer you. But no, it ain't him. Like I said, I scout fer the Army—sometimes outta Fort Cottonwood—but mostly outta Camp Wardwell down on the Denver Road." Jim Key worked his lip for a moment, repositioning his chew, before he continued. "It's the commander at Wardwell, that's the mutual acquaintance I was referrin' to. Colonel Maxwell." He winked at her, grinned a bit bigger under his droopy moustache.

"I'm thinkin' you'd mebbe know 'im as *Major* Maxwell. From when he was posted at Fort Kearny. But him an' me, we've known each other fer a good many years. An' we've spent some time a-talkin' and drinkin' of an evenin' now an' then. I've heard a-plenty about you from him. My *Lord*, he has some stories to tell."

Frankie broke into a smile, thinking about Major James Madison Maxwell. *Her* Major. She looked at Jim Key, right into his eyes.

"I only ever had one grandfather that I knew. My father's parents were the only grandparents I was around, but if I'd had the choice of another grandfather, I'd want it to be Major Maxwell. Can you tell me if he's doing all right, Mr. Key? If he's happy?"

"I kin tell you that he *is*. On *both* counts. He landed hisself in a nice situation. He was sent there to the camp as a major, to help with the plannin' fer the camp. Army's looking to establish it as a fort. He was ranked up to colonel and posted there permanently. And I believe he's happy being there." Jim Key spit a stream of tobacco juice to the far side of his horse, then looked off to the western horizon for a moment. When he spoke again, his voice was soft. "I'd like to be able to tell 'im what you jest said to me, if you'd give me the right to do so. I'm thinkin' that'd make 'im happiest of all. Him not knowin' if yer safe, I believe, is the only thing what keeps 'im from being content."

"Mr. Key, if you can tell him that, without telling him *where* I'm at, then I'd be fine with it. My biggest fear, Sir, is having the Army find out where I am. There's a lot of danger in that for me."

"I kin tell you Frankie Harding, no one'll hear 'bout you from me. Not that big Buck Buchanan, as much as I like an' trust 'im. Not them soldiers over there in yer home right now. An' no one in the Army. An' as fer yore major, he'd know better'n to ask it of me. I'm not *in* the Army. I just get paid to scout an' track an' translate. Ain't the Army's business 'bout nothin' else I know. I don't answer to the Army no more'n you do."

"Then tell him this too. Tell him I managed to sneak his blood-bay Kentucky Charger away from the colonel who confiscated him. You tell Major Maxwell, or *Colonel* Maxwell, that Trumpeter is here with me. And as soon as it's safe, I'll send his warhorse back to him."

"By dab, he's talked about that stallion. 'Bout how he wanted to start a bloodline by him. It tore him up somethin' terrible when he heard he'd been sold off by the commander down to Kearny."

"Well, you tell him that six foals sired by Trumpeter will drop this spring. Three of the dams are five-point bay mares. Clean lines. Strong and elegant. One's my Morgan mare and two are catfish grays. We'll see what we get out of them. You tell him that." Frankie took one last look at the skyline, shivered in the cold wind that had come up, and reined Rock to head down the hillside.

"That the stud with them mares out in the pasture, then?"

"Yes, Sir. You take a good look at him and the mares too. And then, you take word to my Major. You tell him I think it'd be a wonderful thing if the Cavalry had a line of horses known as the Maxwell Bays. And tell him I plan to come to visit him some time, so we can talk about all that."

Jim Key was smiling awfully big behind that big droopy moustache of his. He reached over and gripped her arm; squeezed it gently. Smiling at her with his eyes all crinkly.

"I *will* tell him that, Honey. Jest as soon as I kin git back there.

The troopers were waiting in the sitting-room, standing in the warmth of the fireplace, finally indoors, and out of the cold wind that had begun to rip across the meadow. They were waiting for word about the remainder of the day; they were looking out the windows at the darkening sky and they weren't looking very happy.

They had been standing outside, near the porch, shivering in the icy wind, looking pretty miserable when Frankie and Jim Key rode into the meadow. She had pointed them toward the sitting-room's porch door and ordered them into the house, and they hadn't argued with her. She and Jim Key walked into the kitchen and she had flashed a warning glare at the young Lieutenant Pierce, daring him to countermand her.

Now, as she was stirring another batch of cornbread, the lieutenant, the sergeant—Sergeant Tibbs, Frankie had learned—and Jim Key were sitting at the kitchen table, discussing the Indian hunt. The lieutenant had it in his mind to head out in an hour and continue traveling east, continuing the hunt for the Indians.

Frankie kept mixing the batter, listening to the conversation behind her. Jim Key described the clouds moving in from the west and was talking about the likelihood of a blizzard. He was assuring the lieutenant that any chance of picking up a trail after the snow would be impossible. The sergeant added his own concerns, talking about the condition of the troopers and the horses, explaining they had already been pushed too far. Jim Key stepped in again.

"Lieutenant, they's another problem waitin' fer us if we keep headin' east. That'll put us on Pawnee land. We run into a band of Pawnee and we'll have our hands full. Yore boys ain't up to fightin' a full-on battle with a band o' them bastards. And we sure as hell don't have enough ammunition to launch into a full battle." Jim Key was bringing new information into the conversation, information the lieutenant hadn't expected.

Frankie ducked her head, intent on the batter, trying to hide her grin, because she could hear some of her words sprinkled into the scout's arguments. He had told her he could handle the young lieutenant, and from the sound of things, he was doing just that. It sounded as if Lieutenant Pierce was beginning to listen to sense;

he was finally hearing what his sergeant and scout were saying. He didn't exactly give in, but he did say that he had some thinking to do. He decided to take a walk outside.

"I want to think things through for a bit," he said. "I don't see the sense of stopping the hunt after coming this far. I don't like the idea of heading back to Fort Cottonwood when we have a mission to complete."

"You go on your walk then, Lieutenant. But think on this. If those troopers freeze to death, or if they die fightin' the Pawnee, you'll be ridin' back to Fort Cottonwood alone. An' all of it fer no damn good reason."

Frankie winced when Jim Key said those words. Because he was saying what no one else in the whole house would dare say to the lieutenant. But then again, Jim Key wasn't Army; he was a scout. And he said what needed to be said. Because the way Frankie had him figured, Jim Key didn't knuckle-under to anyone.

The lieutenant left to do his walk and Frankie watched him through the window. She thought Lieutenant Leland Pierce probably wasn't particularly interested in catching the two Indians anymore. Instead, he was worried about losing face by admitting defeat. But no matter what, given the way the temperature had been dropping, she figured it'd take less than ten minutes outside in the icy wind for the lieutenant to change his mind. When she suggested that to Jim Key and the sergeant, they both smiled. Nodding.

As it was, the lieutenant returned in less than five minutes, shaking from the cold. He looked at Frankie, asked to speak to her and led the way into the pantry. He motioned for the sergeant to join them. Looking at him once they were in the pantry, she could see something had changed in the lieutenant. His voice had softened; the strain in his face was gone. The pressure he had been putting on himself was gone.

He asked her for permission to have his soldiers stay on her place. He and his men could bed down in the barn, he said, *if* she would allow it. He asked if her parents would mind. He said that as an officer in the Nebraska Territory, he could require it, but he'd rather have her permission—and her invitation, if he could ask it of her. He told her that if she didn't want them to stay, then he and his men would head out. The sergeant caught Frankie's eye, gave her a soft wink.

"Lieutenant, with the storm that's coming in, it's your *horses* that need to be in the barn tonight. Not you and your men. There are two beds in the backroom. You and Sergeant Tibbs use that room. I'll sleep in this bedroom here by the kitchen." She motioned to her own room, wanting him to think it was her parents' room, wanting him to assume the backroom was probably where she and any other kids slept. "The other house over there has ten bunks and a fireplace that'll keep your troopers plenty warm. And there's floor space here in the sitting-room, if they need it. As long as everyone has a bedroll, they can decide among themselves where they want to sleep."

Lieutenant Leland Pierce smiled at her. Gently now. For the first time. He offered an apology for his behavior to her. He suddenly became the officer and the gentleman he was supposed to be. Frankie smiled back at him.

"Sir, if you think it's a good idea, I'd like those horses unsaddled and settled in the barn. Have your men close the doors across the back entrance. Let your mounts have the center row as shelter. If the men leave the front door open a bit, the horses can water-up at the trough in the front barn-lot. Have your troopers toss them hay from the loft."

While she was talking, the sergeant motioned to the troopers in the sitting-room. Once they stepped into the kitchen, Frankie turned to them, asking if any of them knew about butchering, because she needed someone to cut up the buck hanging in the barn.

Two troopers stepped up, grinning, asking what cuts she wanted; she told them to bring her two or three roasts and a couple of dozen steaks for breakfast.

"Everything else can be pieced for stew-meat."

"You want them ribs cut short?"

"Cut them any way you want them roasted in the oven."

"There a hand-saw somewheres in the barn?"

685

"In the front workshop. Help yourselves to any tools you need. You're butchering for your own dinner and breakfast, so bring the meat you want into the kitchen."

Those two soldier boys broke into wide grins, realizing suddenly that it was official—they would be staying put for the coming storm. They'd be sleeping in a warm house in front of a roaring fire.

They clambered out of the house, racing off toward the barn, cutting loose with more than a few loud yips and whoops. She and Jim Key grinned at each other, listening to them whooping and hollering clear across the meadow.

At a nod from the sergeant, the rest of the troopers started pulling on their coats, knowing their sergeant, understanding from his nod that they were tasked with bedding the Cavalry mounts down in the barn. Frankie called after them as they headed out the door, telling them to make sure all the troughs were full and the ice broken.

"And for God's sake, get *every one* of those poor, worn-down Cavalry horses a bait of corn from the corncrib. I want extra firewood in the house, and someone should get the fireplace going in the small house. And both houses need to be shuttered.

An hour later, Frankie was stirring and mashing the cooked pumpkin pieces in a big cookpot on the stove, while the soldiers were busy wolfing down mashed potatoes and hot stew; they were sopping up gravy with cornbread and burning their throats with steaming-hot coffee.

They had spread themselves out in the sitting-room, eating and laughing and talking—acting like soldiers who had just been given a reprieve—because they knew full-well the storm was moving in fast and cold. They could see the clouds hanging low and heavy with snow. They understood exactly how close they had come to spending the night camping in the damp and freezing air beside a cold river—out in the middle of nowhere—half-buried by a blizzard. At the moment, every soldier-boy in the house knew he'd be sleeping in a warm room with a roaring fireplace. And that seemed like a fine change in fortune to them.

In the kitchen, Sergeant Tibbs worked side-by-side with Frankie, talking about his past while they were preparing food for the evening meal. His mother, he said, had been a baker and a cook for a hotel back East; he had grown up working beside her in the kitchens. Which, for Frankie, explained how easily he had stepped in to work beside her. He was busy mixing and kneading bread dough, and she went to work on the pie dough.

She knew it was going to be a full-time job to keep coffee made, so she put the lieutenant to work brewing pots of coffee and pouring them into the copper-boiler on the back-burners. For a moment after she assigned him the task, he looked like he was going to get all huffy again; then, quite suddenly, he grinned and stepped up to it. He brewed the coffee and made more than a few trips with pitchers and pots of hot coffee to refill cups for his troopers.

His whole demeanor had shifted—the harsh tone, the anger and bravado were gone. And when Frankie pulled on her coat, readying for a trip out to the root-cellar, he offered to go and bring back what she needed.

"No, Sir. With what I want to get, I need to pick out everything myself. But grab another basket and come with me."

She wanted to go by herself so she could talk to her Indians through the wall and tell them all that was happening, but this would work as well. With the English that Flint Striker understood, he'd hear what was going on. He and Gray Fox would know the soldiers were still around. They would stay hidden. They were safe and warm in the den; the dressings on their wounds would hold for now; for warmth, they had their own buffalo-robe as well as the robe that had been on the mattress on the bench. And they had plenty of food and water.

"Do you stay alone like this a lot, Frances?"

"Sometimes, Sir. It's just kinda how it has to be. But I love it here, so, it doesn't matter whether anyone else is here or not." Frankie was sorting through the bins of apples, working to fill the two baskets, surprised with the change in the lieutenant's disposition. He had been a changed man from the moment he returned from his five-minute walk in the icy air. He was pleasant and soft-spoken. Attentive and gentle-minded.

"I was wondering why your family would be going for supplies. It seems like you have plenty of food stored here in the cellar and plenty of staples in the house. Why would your parents go now? Risking travel in this weather?"

"Seed, Sir. Seed for planting. You have to have it ready as soon as the ground can be worked. We're working more land for spring than we originally planned on."

Frankie was trying to keep her answers honest by talking in general terms, knowing she had to be careful. Because now that he was past the rush and hurry of the hunt, this lieutenant was starting to consider things differently. *Now that things have slowed down, he'll start to notice anything that's inconsistent.*

He actually wasn't a stupid man at all, Frankie realized. He had just gotten caught up in a string of bad decisions. Because bad decisions always follow tunnel-vision—and the Indian hunt had narrowed his vision and his thinking. She could picture her father, standing in front of his classroom at the teaching academy, explaining the dangers of tunnel-vision to his students. *'Tunnel-vision is always followed by distortion. It's a cascade of foolhardiness because the mind shuts down to knowledge, experience, and sensibilities.*

When she moved to the apple bins closest to the end of the wall, she started choosing her words carefully, because those bins were right in front of the hidden doorway. Gray Fox and Flint Striker would hear her voice, so she tried to say things in a way that would let them know what was happening.

"And as far as the weather and traveling, Lieutenant Pierce, we *know* how to watch the weather out here. With a streak of bad weather coming, no one's gonna travel anywhere. Everyone will hunker down and wait it out. Your scout and me, we both saw the clouds building in the west. There's a nasty storm coming in and it's carrying a lot of snow. *Nobody* out here in these hills will be traveling tonight. If the storm's still going on tomorrow, you'll be here for another day. Any Indians around here are gonna hole up somewhere and wait out the storm, just like you and your soldiers are doing. When the storm's passed, you can go back to your hunt."

"To tell you the truth, Frances, I plan to give up the hunt. We're not going to find those Indians. They're long gone by now. What really made me change my mind, though, were my troopers. I saw how they acted when you sent them out to prepare for the storm. I saw how relieved they were. And I can see how tired they are." The lieutenant looked down to the floor, shook his head. "They're exhausted. We're all exhausted. We all need some rest. God's truth, Frances, I don't relish the journey back along that cold river-bottom. And I don't relish putting the men through it."

"Well, you're resting here tonight, Lieutenant Pierce. And maybe you should figure on staying tomorrow too. Your horses need the rest more than your soldiers. And as far as returning to Fort Cottonwood, there's an easier way than following the rivers. It'll save you a good three days. I can draw a map for Jim Key."

To Frankie's surprise, the lieutenant suddenly sat down on a crate near the bottom of the stairs. She picked out two apples and went over to sit on the crate next to him, knowing his own exhaustion had just hit him. They stayed there for what seemed like a long time. Saying nothing. Just sitting together, eating their apples side-by-side, quiet and still in the dim light of the root-cellar. And all the while, Frankie was hoping her two warriors on the other side of the wall would stay quiet too. They were almost done with their apples when Frankie spoke.

"Lieutenant Pierce. Most folks figure it takes a good six months just to get a *feel* for this land. And that still doesn't mean you *know* it. It's not the same as back East. This land is big and broad and it takes years to understand it. And just because you know one area, doesn't mean you know anything about another area. These Sand Hills are different from any other place. Jim Key has traveled the prairie for years and years; he knows a lot of different areas, but he'd be the first to tell you he doesn't know *this* region. Life gets a lot easier out here in the Nebraska Territory as soon as a person admits he doesn't know much about the prairie at all. About the time a person admits *that*, the prairie will start showing him things."

Frankie stood up, reached for one of the baskets of apples. She decided to say something else that'd be a big favor to Jim Key; she figured she owed the scout a favor or two.

"The lucky thing for you as an officer in the Cavalry, is that you get a *scout* assigned to you. I wish I had a scout like that. My life would be a lot easier. I wouldn't have to figure everything out for myself. I'd just ask him what I needed to know."

Lieutenant Pierce smiled at her, a relaxed and easy smile, a smile that was almost happy. He picked up the second basket of apples, took her elbow and guided her up the steps. Gentle; gentlemanly. He held the door for her, then closed it tight, making sure it was latched against the coming storm.

"Allow me, Miss Frances." He smiled at her and took her basket. He glanced at the contents of the basket as they walked to the house. "It looks as though you picked out some rotten apples, Frances."

He was smiling at her, teasing her, and Frankie was thinking that this was all very different than their first trip from the cellar to the house.

"It's all a matter of cutting out the part that's rotten, Lieutenant. Cut away the part that's of no use and save the parts that are good. Then you got yourself a pie everyone enjoys. It's no different than with people and how they should carve out what doesn't work in their character." She gave him a smile as he opened the kitchen door and guided her in ahead of him.

The storm hit in the late afternoon as Frankie and Sergeant Tibbs were putting apple pies into the oven. The first heavy swirl of freezing wind and snow smacked against the side of the house just as three of the troopers slipped in the door. They sniffed the kitchen air, grinned and started talking about the 'good smell of good cooking'.

Two of the troopers stepped over to the fire in the corner of the kitchen to warm themselves; the third trooper—the one named Styles—took the pail of milk into the stone-room. A moment later, when they heard the rattling of pails and separating pans back in the pantry, Frankie and the sergeant gave each other a knowing look. Apparently, young Private Styles knew exactly what he was doing.

When he came back to the kitchen a few minutes later, Styles had the separated cream from the last batch in the churning jar; he sat himself down in the rocking chair by the fireplace and started bringing up the butter as if he'd been doing it most of his life.

Once the butter came, he tipped the butter out onto a butter dish and pressed the butter into the wooden mold. He divided the butter-milk into two glasses and sat the glasses in front of his lieutenant and Jim Key sitting at the table peeling apples. He gave Frankie a quick kiss on her cheek as he passed behind her and headed into the sitting-room to join the rest of the troopers.

The sergeant started chuckling.

"I'd say it's been a few years since he did simple things like that. Milking a cow. Feeding chickens. Making butter. Kissing a pretty girl by the stove." Sergeant Tibbs leaned over and kissed her cheek, himself. "I haven't seen that boy looking so content in three years. Same for the others. You're doing a fine thing here, Miss Frances."

"I think it's working out for everyone. I sure don't mind having someone else doing the evening chores on a cold day like this."

She smiled at him, and then suddenly, she cocked her head toward the sitting-room doorway. Listening. She gave the sergeant a puzzled look and looked at Lieutenant Pierce and Jim Key at the table. They stopped their conversation and listened, too; they heard it. Silence. There was *no* noise coming from the sitting-room. Not a sound.

It had been a rollicking and boisterous couple of hours while the troopers had their fill of stew and cornbread and pumpkin pie out in the sitting-room; there had been even more laughter and noise coming through the doorway once they moved on to playing cards and telling their tales.

The hoots and howls of laughter at their own stories had been getting louder and wilder as the afternoon wore on. And there in the kitchen, Frankie and Jim Key, Sergeant Tibbs and the lieutenant had been listening to the troopers, chuckling at the stories and yarns the soldiers had been spinning.

Now, the four of them were looking at each other, wondering about the sudden and complete silence. They walked to the doorway and stared at the scene in the sitting-room—every trooper in the room was sound asleep, all eleven of them. Dead to the world. Stretched out in chairs, sprawled on the rugs and the buffalo-hides, curled up with their heads pillowed on their arms and their bedrolls.

"A warm fire and a full belly *will* do that." Jim Key said it, speaking the quiet truth. Saying aloud what they were all thinking.

"It will." Sergeant Tibbs shook his head, scanning the room of sleeping troopers. "It finally hit 'em. They're too tired to even snore."

Frankie glanced toward Lieutenant Leland Pierce, watching as he tipped back to lean against the doorframe, suddenly looking weak and pale. Looking a little sickened. He stayed there with his back against the doorframe, shaking his head and looking as if he was in agony.

Sergeant Tibbs motioned to Jim Key as he took a step toward his lieutenant. The next thing Frankie knew, Jim Key had his hands on her shoulders and was guiding her over to the big stove. They left the sergeant and the lieutenant standing together, talking softly there in the doorway.

"The lieutenant's understandin' that he took too much outta them boys. He'll be a little shook up over it. But the Sarge, he'll bring him through it. That's why a good commander will pair them older, wiser sergeants with the young officers." Key was whispering as he helped her slide the pans of venison roasts and root vegetables into the oven.

"The good thing about this, is the lieutenant's learning this lesson *early* in his career. And no one had to get hurt or killt fer him to figgur it out. Some officers never learn to take notice o' their men. Or the mounts neither, fer that matter. The lieutenant was lissening when you tole them boys to get corn into them horses. It got him to

692

thinkin'. This was a hard journey, an' now, I'm thinkin' mebbe none of this was ever about them Indians. We jest thought it was. Mebbe it was jest the good Lord's way of teachin' what needed learnin'."

Frankie nodded, thinking that she and Jim Key seemed to see a lot of things the same way. She stood for a moment, looking at the oven door, realizing that the roasting meat and vegetables would probably end up just being for the two officers, Jim Key and herself. The troopers would probably sleep on. Their stomachs were full; they were warm. Left undisturbed, they'd probably sleep until morning.

The storm raged, ripping across the skies above the valley through the night; by morning, it had worn itself out. The clouds had moved eastward; the sky had cleared. In the first light of dawn, when Frankie looked into the sitting-room, she saw all the troopers still sprawled around the room. They had stayed where they lay; they had slept through the night, few of them moving from where they had been in the late afternoon. At some point during the night, a couple who had fallen asleep in chairs, had stirred enough to spread their bedrolls on the floor and crawl into them. But now, as dawn was coming on, every one of the troopers was still sleeping deeply.

Lieutenant Pierce and Sergeant Tibbs had bedded down in the backroom, and Frankie could hear no sounds that suggested either was awake or moving around; they were every bit as exhausted as the troopers. And given what Jim Key had told her about their journey, it wasn't surprising everyone in the troop was exhausted.

Jim Key had sat with her at the kitchen table late into the night, long after the officers finished their supper and headed for the back bedroom. He had told her the whole story. The troop, he said, had been returning from a ten-day winter patrol, still a day out from Fort Cottonwood, when they sighted the three Indians.

The lieutenant, Jim Key told her, 'had it figgered they must be up to trouble, so he decided to give chase'. Believing it would be a quick mission, Pierce had sent the supply wagon on to Fort Cottonwood with his corporal and most of his troop. He had kept a small troop with him—this troop—for the chase.

The 'quick chase', though, had become a long hunt; it stretched out over seven days, tracking and back-tracking through the Sand Hills and the river-bottoms, with the lieutenant unwilling to give up his self-assigned mission. Long days of riding and short nights of sleep. Freezing temperatures and no provisions except jerky and hard-tack. 'Jest whatever food the men had in their kits. And there weren't much o' that,' Jim Key had said.

Now, in the soft-silvery light of the early dawn, Frankie stood staring at the sleeping soldiers. *Young. Not much more than boys. Not much different than my troopers at Fort Kearny.*

She built up the fire in the center fireplace, adding the wood from the kitchen side, wanting to take the chill from the rooms. Deciding it'd be a fine thing if they woke up in a warm house. Given what Jim Key had described about the week they'd just lived through, she figured it'd be a nice change for them. After stoking the cook-stove and starting coffee brewing in two pots, she bundled up and went outside.

Out on the front porch, Frankie eyed the meadow and hillsides. Finger-drifts mostly, pretty much the same as after the last blizzard. The windblown bare patches in the meadow grass looked about the same. Outside the valley, she figured the land would be blanketed much the same as before, but probably not as deep. Travel today wouldn't be a wise choice, but she didn't know if the lieutenant would understand that. *But Jim Key will. He'll handle the lieutenant.*

Frankie took a last look around the valley and headed toward the chicken-house. She gave the entrance of the root-cellar a quick glance, thinking about Gray Fox and Flint Striker, knowing there was no safe way to check on them—not without a serious risk of giving away the secret. Knowing that one wrong move, or one wrong word, could ruin everything. Knowing that even with everything on friend-lier terms with the soldiers, there was still a strong likelihood she was being watched. And she had no doubt Lieutenant Pierce would be more than happy to take prisoners.

She crossed a bare patch, then waded through a long fin-ger-drift. Before she ducked into the henhouse, she glanced toward the root-cellar door once again, wondering if she could just go closer to listen, to make sure things were quiet, that no one was groaning in pain or calling for help. *No. Not even that.*

Because, even though the soldiers and officers were still sleep-ing, there was the possibility that Jim Key might have his eyes on her. Because he hadn't been in the sitting-room with the troopers, and she doubted he had slept with the officers. She hadn't seen him since she had gone to her room last night, but the clever old scout with the droopy moustache was somewhere in the meadow. *Probably in the Barracks. And he might be watching right now.*

Because Jim Key wasn't anybody's fool. If he had any suspi-cion that she was hiding the Indians, he would keep an eye peeled. He wouldn't miss anything. And even though he was proving to be a trusted friend who would keep *some* of her secrets, Frankie wasn't sure he would be willing to keep a secret about the wounded warriors in the Wolf Den.

Frankie fed the hens and broke the ice on their trough, then walked across the meadow, skirting some drifts and jumping others on her way to the barn. The inside of the barn was a wonderful kind of warmth, filled with the body-heat of thirteen Cavalry horses and one mule. And three of her horses in their stalls. And one Jersey cow and calf in the milking-pen.

She walked down the wide alleyway, weaving her way quietly among the snoozing Cavalry mounts, listening to their horse-grunts and horse-snores. Their snuffles as they woke. She smiled when she heard the soft lowing from the far corner of the barn—Blossom was calling to her from the milking-pen. Waiting to be milked.

She spoke to Fox and Rock and Samson in their stalls and stopped to rub their noses; she decided to leave the feeding and ice-breaking for the soldiers, knowing they would see to her horses when they took care of their own mounts. She slipped between the rails of the milking-pen and scratched Primrose's back while she waited for Blossom to step into place and slip her head into the stanchion.

Halfway through milking, her forehead pressed against Blossom's warm flank, Frankie heard footsteps coming along the alleyway—human footsteps among the slow-shuffling hooves of the Cavalry mounts. Someone was speaking softly to the horses and a moment later, when she heard the mule give a soft huffing mule-call, she grinned. Jim Key was coming.

She heard the gravelly twang of his voice, soft and low, in quiet conversation with his mule. Then he was coming down the alleyway again. Without looking over her shoulder, Frankie knew when he stopped at the milking-pen fence.

"Well, good mornin', Miss Frankie. What you doin' chores fer, with all them able-bodied soldiers right over yonder in yore house?"

"Good morning yourself, Mr. Key. I decided to let those soldier-boys sleep for a while. I only intended to feed the chickens and milk Blossom. The troopers can do the rest of the chores," Frankie looked over her shoulder at him. "And hey, where exactly did *you* sleep?"

"Hellfire, Honey. I took myself over to that other little house o' yore's. Had that fine place all to myself. All heated up, warm and quiet. Mighty nice sleepin' up off the ground on a real mattress fer a change. After all them nights sleepin' on rocks and dirt and listenin' to snorin' soldiers, it was a mighty fine thing."

Frankie heard the soft splat of tobacco juice hitting hardpacked dirt and she knew Jim Key was already working on a chew. There was a pause before he went on and she knew he was repositioning the wad in his lip.

"Now, Honey. What kin I do to help you out this mornin'?"

"I'm almost done here. But I was thinking we need an idea of what the prairie looks like beyond this valley. It'll be a lot worse than what we have here in the meadow. Could you cross the ford and follow the track downriver for a piece? Just to get a feel for things? And maybe look to the clouds and get an idea about today and tomorrow?"

"I was already a-plannin' on it, Honey. So we're thinkin' alike, you and me. I'm thinkin' it's a day too soon fer any kind of trek across this land. And I'm more'n a little concerned our young lieutenant might have it in his mind to head out anyway."

Another pause and another splat in the dirt. Frankie grinned. The scout went on.

"But when we do set out, you got any ideas as to how we might make that trip back to the fort?"

"Well, Sir, I think you ought to head downriver for about nine miles. There's a main track that'll take you up out of the river-flats and south for another ten miles where you'll cross the Middle Loup. About ten miles south of that, you'll see a tall standing-stake marking the trail's turn-off to the southwest. It'll lead down to the Platte and your fort. Three-and-a-half days. Maybe four, depending on drifts and such."

They talked about the trail for a few more minutes. Jim Key hadn't traveled it, but he knew about the trail running to the north from Fort Cottonwood. He nodded, pleased with the idea—the new route would be faster and easier than backtracking the way they had come.

"If the weather doesn't settle till tomorrow, are you fixed fer puttin' us up fer another night?"

"I can put you up for as long as you need. And I don't think the weather's gonna be stable until tomorrow. Maybe not until the day after." Frankie turned on her stool, looked at the scout, watching him leaning against the top rail of the fence. "I wouldn't chance it myself, Mr. Key. But I'm not in the Cavalry. You take a look at the skies for yourself. You know them better than me."

"I 'spect you know the skies amongst these hills better'n I do. But I'll head out across the river an' see how the snow's layin'. Then mebbe I'll have an idea of how to counsel young Pierce."

"Mr. Key, let your mule rest for the day. Take that chestnut-sorrel." Frankie pointed him towards Samson. "Your mule's saddle won't fit him, so use that McClellan beside the stall-gate. You'll have to let the stirrups down, though. And maybe you could watch for a doe or buck along the river-bottom. There'll be a herd weathering the storm at a bend in the river, three-quarters of a mile downstream. More venison would be a fine thing. We've got soldiers to outfit for their trip south."

"I'll see what I kin do, Darlin'." He nodded and started for Samson's pen.

"And halter up that liver-chestnut in that other stall for packing anything you might hunt up. Grab a few lengths of rope in the shop."

Jim Key nodded and reached for Samson's stall gate.

Frankie left him to ready the horses and walked across the meadow, heading for the stone-room door, thinking it'd be quieter to enter that way. Thinking the soldiers could use all the sleep they could get.

After she poured out the milk in the different pans in the pantry, she looked into the sitting-room. With the windows still shuttered against the storm, the room was dark and the soldiers slept on. Except for the snoring, it was quiet. They were safe and sound. Resting and recovering.

She watched the troopers for a moment, thinking about Travers and Trask. Thinking about Crazy Eddie and Thomas Bates, the music master. And Thomas Denning who was so much like her cousin Samuel. Thinking that she wanted to keep these boys warm and safe for as long as she could, because they were a whole lot like her own troopers back at Fort Kearny.

Turning back to the kitchen, she got busy, knowing they'd all be hungry as soon as they woke. She poured the brewed coffee from both pots into the copper-boiler and set new coffee to brewing. White beans that had soaked through the night went into one pot to simmer. She shifted the copper-boiler over to one back burner and started two pots of oatmeal and raisins cooking on the other two back-burners. She mixed up three batches of biscuits and slid them in the largest oven, and set a pan of apples baking in the smaller oven. She diced the meat from the venison roasts from the evening meal—the meal that the troopers had slept through—and made a hash with the left-over root vegetables.

She had the hash frying and was ready to start frying eggs when she heard sounds from the sitting-room. The troopers were waking. Grunts and groans. Hushed voices. Hushed laughter. Coughs. Joking. She heard the thuds of a few logs landing in the fireplace, tossed in from the sitting-room side. She heard the scuffing and scraping that told her boots were being pulled on; she heard the shuffling sounds of blankets and bedrolls being rolled and stowed.

Frankie ducked her head, smiling as doors started creaking and banging, knowing the troopers were heading out through the sitting-room porch doors, going to do what men always needed to do first thing in the morning. Some, she knew, would head to the outhouse; some, she knew, wouldn't. And she knew that, if at some point, she happened to look at the snow on the far side of the house, there would be yellow streaks cutting across the white drifts. *Because men are men. Because in some ways, men have it so easy compared to women.*

Within a few minutes, she heard voices out in the meadow; through the kitchen windows, she could see a handful of troopers heading out to the barn. They'd see to the livestock. Three other troopers came into the kitchen, poured themselves cups of coffee and asked for 'the morning's Mess Hall chores'.

"We'll need more of those before the day's over." Frankie pointed to baskets of onions and potatoes and squash.

They went to work peeling and chopping, and they amused themselves by snatching hot biscuits from the baking pans while Frankie had her eyes on the hash and eggs in the frying pans. More than a few times, she slapped at their hands when they tried snatch-ing pieces of bacon from the frying pans.

She really didn't mind them grabbing biscuits or pieces of bacon—it was the same thing her cousins used to do while she and her aunt cooked breakfast in the kitchen in Indiana. Mostly, she slapped at them because they wanted her to. They were playing with her—pestering her and teasing her—because, as Frankie figured it, they just needed to be boys for a little while. Instead of being soldiers.

As soon as the private named Styles came into the kitchen after morning chores, he stepped in beside her, working with her at the stove. And as soon as Sergeant Tibbs came into the kitchen, he and Private Styles sat her in the rocker by the fireplace.

"You just keep outta the way, Young Miss, and let us soldier-ing-men take care of things. We know how to serve up food for these troopers." Sergeant Tibbs said it kindly, but there was no doubt that he meant it.

He and Styles took over at the stove; they started working the pots and pans like they'd done it a thousand times before. Frankie stayed in the rocker, petting Matilda, and watching the action at the cookstove. Lieutenant Pierce showed up in the kitchen, poured him-self a cup of coffee and sat down at the table. He sat there, watching his two men; he was grinning and enjoying the show.

By the time breakfast was over, the decision had been made; the soldiers would stay in Frankie's meadow for another night. Because once Jim Key returned from surveying the countryside, he sat down at the trestle table, drinking coffee with the officers, talking about the winter landscape beyond the valley. He described the snowfall and the drifts; he spoke of storm clouds building to the northwest and said they needed watching.

"They might swing north o' here. Or they might build into another blizzard that'll sweep through here again." His advice was calm and confident and Lieutenant Pierce was listening. "I'd advise we wait an' watch till mornin'. If things look right, we set out early. Miss Frances told me 'bout a trail that runs south o' here. From what I seen this mornin', I believe it to be our best route. I'd figgur to make Fort Cottonwood in three days. Mebbe, four."

What Frankie heard was a discussion, rather than an argument. The three men were talking, drinking coffee, and working their way through the last of the baked apples and cream. They spoke of other options and possibilities, but in the end, Jim Key's advice carried. They would hunker down for the day, the lieutenant decided, and leave in the morning.

"If," Lieutenant Pierce said, "Jim Key thinks it wise."

The lieutenant called his men together in the sitting-room and spoke to them while Frankie and Sergeant Tibbs began making cottage-pies for the midday meal. Once they had them in the ovens, along with more cornbread and apple pies, they began planning meals for the troop's journey to the fort. They figured on three days of meals, and then, just to be safe, they decided on four.

Pilot bread and jerky, parched-corn, dried apples and raisins, and coffee would go into the saddle bags. Potatoes, bacon, onions, and dried peas would go into a flour-sack for each trooper. Cans of beans, peaches, and sardines would be packed into the sacks along with biscuits and hard rolls. Boiled eggs and cooked venison steaks would be wrapped in squares of canvas and tucked in with the other food.

While they began frying steaks and boiling eggs for the troop's journey, the soldiers disappeared outside with Jim Key and Lieutenant Pierce. A few minutes later, Jim Key stepped into the kitchen.

"Miss Frances? You okay with us borrowin' that heavy farm-wagon and a hitch o' mules?"

"Mule harnesses and collars are on the tailgate of the Conestoga." Frankie nodded and gave the information. She asked no questions, knowing enough to let them keep their Army business to themselves. It wasn't long before she and the sergeant saw the farm-wagon pulling out of the meadow with Aloysius and Artemis in harness. A handful of mounted soldiers, bundled up against the cold, rode beside it. Two troopers, though, had been left behind; they were busy near the front entrance of the barn, wielding hand-saws and knives, with Jim Key working beside them. They were butchering the buck he had brought in.

She and Sergeant Tibbs kept to their own work in the kitchen, keeping pots and pans and baking dishes moving in and out of the oven throughout the morning. The two troopers butchering the buck

701

kept making trips back and forth to the house, bringing whatever cuts of meat Frankie and the sergeant asked for. Then heading back with fresh instructions for more cuts.

Four hours later, right about noon, Lieutenant Pierce and the troopers returned with the wagon loaded double-high with firewood. Frankie saw the sergeant watching the scene out the window, nodding and smiling to himself. Clearly pleased with what he saw. The lieutenant was working side-by-side with his troopers; there had been a change in the man who led this troop and the sergeant knew it boded well for the future.

For the midday meal, the lieutenant, the sergeant and the soldiers took their plates and spread themselves around the sitting-room. They dug into the meat-pies and cornbread; they oohed and aahed over the apple pie and thickened cream. And when Frankie handed out some of the twists of tobacco and the rolling-papers that had come up the Cheyenne Trail with her, all the way from Fort Kearny in the late summer, the troopers declared she was 'an-angel-straight-from-God-hisself'. They went to work rolling their smokes before Frankie had even gotten to the kitchen doorway.

Stories and laughter and cigarette-smoke swirled around the sitting-room; Lieutenant Pierce stayed in the room with his men, making himself part of the fun. From the kitchen, Frankie could only hear bits and pieces of the stories he was telling about his time at West Point. But he had the troopers laughing and snorting and choking as they smoked the cigarettes and started in on second and third helpings of the dinner. When she went to fill coffee cups, the troopers were holding their sides and tipping back on the floor, howling with laughter.

Jim Key sat in the kitchen with her, helping her pile venison short-ribs into roasting pans. They quartered onions and sliced carrots and chopped squash and turnips to tuck into the pans with the ribs, planning to bank the fire for the night and let the ribs slow-cook until morning.

Then, they went to work peeling sweet potatoes—some to bake for the evening meal, some to make into pies—and talking about the bay mares and Trumpeter. Pausing occasionally when they were interrupted by especially loud fits of laughter coming from the sitting-room. At one point, Jim Key gestured in the direction of the noisy sitting-room, smiling and nodding.

"The lieutenant's learnin' how to build a position with them boys of his. He's findin' a way to know 'em, and to let 'em know him. Them boys'll decide to fight for him now in a way they never did a-fore." Jim Key rose and stepped outside to send a stream of tobacco juice arching beyond the porch. He came back in and settled himself at the table again. "The lieutenant stayin' here with his troop has been a good thing. An' to tell you the truth, I don't know fer sure it woulda ever happened iffen we hadn't come ridin' into yore meadow. More'n that, darlin', I'm thinkin' things woulda got real bad fer us iffen we hadn't found yore place."

"You want to know something, Mr. Jim Key?" Frankie smiled at this new friend of hers with the big droopy moustache. "I think I'm really going to miss you. You better know that you're *always* welcome here."

"Well, you better know I'll be back, jest as often as I kin be." His eyes were bright and crinkly above his drooping moustache.

They worked together cutting up one of the hams William and Tipp brought, adding the pieces to the big pots already filled with the white beans and carrots, onions and sweet potatoes, turnips and dried corn. Jim Key started telling stories of his mother and the way she made ham soup.

"It's been a good twenty-some years since I've set down to a bowl of ham and bean soup."

"Well then, I guess it's about time, Mr. Key."

"It's my hunch yer gonna make some of them soldiers mighty happy when they're eatin' bowls of steaming-hot ham soup, cornbread, and sweet-potato pie. I'm bettin' they ain't had such a meal in a good long time." He leaned in and spoke low. "I'm bettin' Colonel James Madison Maxwell will be a bit perturbed when he hears he missed all these wonderful feasts you've been settin' in front of us."

"Just as long as you don't tell him exactly where the feasts were, Mr. Key."

703

She saw him nod, and she saw a mischievous little grin under the big droopy moustache. His eyes crinkled up and he nodded.

"Oh, I reckon I kin find a way to tell 'im without givin' up any secrets." His grin grew bigger under the moustache and his eyes stayed crinkled-up above it.

The next morning, the troopers were out of the Barracks at first light; once they had their mounts fed and saddled and ready for the day's ride, they came tromping into the house, stomping their boots and slapping their arms. Private Styles stepped in to help at the stove. He got busy stirring potatoes in the frying pans, pouring coffee into cups, and lifting the heavy pans out of the oven. Twice, he gave Frankie a quick peck on her cheek, grinning at her like a school-boy.

All the soldiers were in a high and happy mood. Rested and ready now, they were excited about the trek back to Fort Cottonwood. They were looking for another adventure, acting the way boys-be-coming-men tend to act. And it was all making Frankie laugh.

These soldier-boys weren't worried and they weren't dreading the journey. Not now; not at all. They were a lot different from the exhausted, pale, stone-faced horse-soldiers that rode into her valley two days before. They were cutting up and joshing with each other, reminding Frankie of her boy-cousins back in the big white house in Indiana; it was just exactly how they acted up in the kitchen on the cold mornings after chores. *Boys-becoming-men.*

Frankie started loading plates with biscuits and gravy, eggs and bacon, fried potatoes and fried squash. To that she added short-ribs; then she slathered fried onions on top of everything. It wasn't long until the teasing began—the troopers started fretting, studying their breakfast plates, claiming the cook was 'being a mite stingy with the goods' and worrying they 'might be near to starvation by noontime'.

She groaned and called them on their silliness, rolling her eyes as she slid extra fried eggs on the top of the mountain of food and pointed to the platters of biscuits and corn bread on the counter. They laughed and broke into loud guffaws. They didn't go out to the sitting-room to eat like they had the day before; they stayed in the kitchen, sitting at the table and standing around the room, wolfing down the food on their plates and discussing among themselves how 'grouchy and stingy certain cooks could be'.

When Sergeant Tibbs stepped in and gave some smacks to the backs of a few heads, along with a warning about manners, it made no difference; their laughter and teasing only increased. They moved beyond pretend-fretting about their breakfast and started pretend-whining about their 'deplorable sleeping accommodations last night'.

They had moved their bedrolls out of the sitting-room and settled into the small house for the night, and now, they began complaining that it had been 'a night that was purely hellish'. 'Because we damn-near roasted to death.' They decided that 'in the future, maybe Miss Frances needed to calm that fireplace down a bit'. 'On account of someone could actually die of heat-stroke in there.'

Frankie tried telling them that they were the cause of their own discomfort because of all the firewood they loaded into the fireplace. Her argument did her no good; it only fed their complaints and the teasing. When she glanced at the lieutenant and saw him smiling into his coffee cup, she ducked her head, realizing that this morning, their silliness was going to override any sensibility in them. They were just feeling their oats, like her aunt used to say about her boys. Frankie decided to let them have their jokes.

As the breakfast was winding down, Private Styles helped her fill all the canteens with hot venison-broth. When she advised the troopers to tuck the warm canteens into their coats until they nooned, they changed their tune, declaring that she was 'just maybe the smartest and prettiest girl west of the wide-Missouri'. She had them put hard-rolls and canvas-wrapped fried venison steaks into their coat-pockets, telling them they'd have good hot broth for noon with the steaks and rolls. And after their meal, she told them, they could fill their canteens with water from the clear creek beside the trail.

Those troopers decided that the idea of the broth-warmed canteen in their coats was 'about the best *damn* idea' they'd ever heard. 'Damned if it won't keep us warm and the soup warm at the same time. Hell and damn! Everyone's gonna be in a fine state for this ride.'

Frankie asked Jim Key to put a saddle on Rock, and when the lieutenant called for the column-by-twos, she rode out of the valley with the troop. Lieutenant Pierce beckoned to her, motioning her to move up beside his mount.

When she glanced back over the column, she saw that every trooper had a grin on his face. Partly, she figured, because they were heading home. And partly, because they knew they were well-set for the journey. Their canteens were warm against their chests, their saddle-bags were packed with food, and they each had a poke-full of meal-fixings.

Private Styles had predicted it in the kitchen as the troopers were picking up their bags and sacks. 'Having saddlebags and pokes full of food like this—that's enough to put a smile on the face of any soldier.'

Jim Key rode out in front of the column, a quarter of a mile ahead. Riding where a scout should be riding, leading the troop southeast along the river. When they reached the main track, he turned them south, heading toward the cut up the high ridge.

Frankie stayed with the troop for another mile after they rode through the steep cut, and then she pulled up. She told Lieutenant Pierce she was turning back. He nodded, agreeing that she had gone far enough.

"We're set up fine, Frances. You've done a wonderful service for me and my men." He looked at her then, his eyes soft and calm, and Frankie decided he looked a little sad. To her surprise, she realized she was feeling the same way.

Behind her and the lieutenant, she heard Sergeant Tibbs call out a command. The troop formed into a single line and as the troopers filed between her and the lieutenant, she garnered a kiss on the cheek from each one of them. There were a few flirting comments, and even a few teasingly-sweet marriage proposals.

She said goodbye to these new troopers of hers, feeling more than a little surprised that she was sorry to see them go—given what she had back in her meadow, down in the Wolf Den.

Lieutenant Leland Pierce waited at the side of the track while his troopers thanked her, wished her well, and promised 'to come a-courtin' someday'. Once they passed by, Pierce reined his horse beside Rock, reached into his cloak and handed her a folded piece of paper. He had asked for paper and a pen in the evening, and now, Frankie knew why. He had written out a requisition order 'for any wagon belonging to Frances Dunbar, her family or agents', to be loaded with any and all provisions of choice, to be supplied by Fort Cottonwood.

"We posed a serious imposition for you, Frances Dunbar, and you handled us far better than we had a right to expect." Lieutenant Pierce touched her cheek. "Young Lady, I truly don't know how to offer an apology that would equal what you are due. But I hope a wagon-load of provisions next time you're at Fort Cottonwood helps to balance out at least some of what you gave to us." Tears started to well up in his eyes and Frankie felt some rising in her own.

"We'll return safely to Fort Cottonwood because of you and don't think I don't know that. As an officer, I am in your debt. And *personally*, I am in your debt. I hope you'll consider me a friend. I'd be honored if you'd ask for me whenever you're at Fort Cottonwood."

Frankie couldn't keep the tears back; the lieutenant wiped at his own and teased her about the dangers of tears freezing up on her cheeks. He leaned close to her, wiped them with his handkerchief. He gave her a gentle kiss on her cheek. Like a true gentleman. And then, he told her to head back home where it was warm.

"If we meet up with your folks somewhere between the fort and here, I'll explain everything to them." He gave her another kiss and signaled the sergeant. He looked her in the eyes for a moment, and then he nodded. "We'll be fine now. *My boys* and I will make the journey in fine shape."

The troop moved out and Frankie sat for a moment before turning Rock for home, watching them heading south on the trail. Off to the west, high on a hillside, she saw Jim Key sitting on his floppy-eared mule. *Eyeing the trail ahead, no doubt. Being the Army scout he is.*

She saw him raise his arm, waving to her. Saying his goodbye. Frankie waved back to him; she was pretty sure she could see his eyes crinkling above his moustache.

Frankie stayed where she was, shivering in the cold wind, watching the troop, waiting for them to disappear from her view. They were going south at a steady road-trot—the men were fed and fresh; the horses were fed and fresh. She figured they'd make the trek to the fort in three days, even with the prairie covered in snow.

She was pleased as she watched the troop riding away. For one thing, she had liked being in the company of soldiers again. And the other thing she had liked, was how everything had played out in the end—everything would be fine now, because now, she knew *for sure* that no one would be watching her place. Her warriors would be safe.

Once the lieutenant and his troop were beyond her sight, Frankie turned Rock and sent him back down the cut. Once they were on level land, she put her heels to his ribs and sent him running for home. She gave him his head and within a few strides, she felt him settle into the pace he wanted for the journey back to the valley—he knew exactly where they were going and he knew the pace that would last him. He flew across the snow-covered land, moving his butt and carrying hers.

Rock had her in the home meadow well before noon, and as soon as she had him settled in his stall, she headed back down the alleyway, grinning. Thinking about how confusing and shaky it had all started out. But by the time they left, the soldiers had made her life easier—the center-aisle and all the pens were swept clean as a whistle. Fresh hay was in the stalls and milking pen. Fresh water was in the troughs. The remainder of the deer that Jim Key had brought in was hanging near the entrance. The soldiers had added to her stacks of firewood. Plus, she had a requisition order for a wagon-full of supplies. In the end, the lieutenant had handled things well.

And now, with the dogs bounding along beside her, Frankie raced to the root-cellar. She slipped through the door and down the steps; she called softly to Gray Fox and Flint Striker, telling them that the soldiers were gone. That they had left; that it was safe now. She shoved the bin-wall to the side, surprised it moved as easily as it did.

Gray Fox was there on the other side of the wall, standing up; the wall had shifted easily because he had helped move it. She grinned, liking what she was seeing—he was doing fine. He smiled and patted her shoulder, looking toward the open door beyond her. Blinking at the sunlight cascading down the stairway. The fresh air was flooding into the cellar and into the Wolf Den. Flint Striker smiled at her from where he was sitting on the buffalo-robe.

Frankie changed the dressings every other day on the warriors. The muscles in Flint Striker's leg had cooled—the heat of the fever was gone. Which told Frankie that the infection was gone. The stitches had held. He would have a large scar, and probably a permanent depression in his thigh muscle, but he was healing. And Gray Fox was healing too. His right shoulder and arm were healing rapidly; the wound to his calf, for whatever reason, was taking longer.

They stayed in the meadow, sleeping in the Wolf Den and spending their days in the fresh air and winter sun. Frankie doctored their wounds. She worked on the bay Indian pony, using remedies to heal his knee joints from the inside, and applying poultices to reduce the swelling on the outside.

The first meals for Gray Fox and Flint Striker had been weak broths, but once the soldiers had gone, she started bringing them full meals. It didn't take long for her to sort out what the two warriors liked best. Rabbit stew seemed to please them the most, roasted grouse ran a close second. They loved cornbread slathered with butter and any pie or cobbler made them smile. But nothing made them happier than the cups of sweet-coffee she made for them.

Laughing Girl and the pups took to dozing in the sun and walking beside them when they limped their way around the meadow, strengthening their legs. The three kittens that Ida brought to the meadow were half-grown cats now and they were just beginning their most reckless and obnoxious stage of life.

They insisted on entertaining themselves in and around the root-cellar—they pestered the warriors endlessly, romping and rolling and hissing themselves into a frazzle, climbing and clawing their way up the walls and into the bins of the cellar. They screeched like furry little banshees in the midst of their silly half-grown cat-fights, and they twisted and turned themselves around the men's legs, purring and mewing when they wanted attention.

It surprised Frankie that the warriors didn't smack them down with one of their tomahawks, because there were a lot of times she felt like doing it. She found it more than perplexing that the men didn't seem to mind the arrogant little beasts; they actually seemed amused by their antics.

The afternoons with the men were what Frankie liked best about their stay. After she finished her chores, she would sit with Flint Striker and Gray Fox, listening to the Oglála language while they talked. It was her chance to learn the Lakotah words and as soon as Flint Striker understood her hunger for the language, he taught her as much as he could—teaching her, not only the words, but about the complexities of the language itself.

Like the Cheyenne language, Lakotah had a flow and rhythm, but that's where the similarities ended. Cheyenne, which she had learned so easily, had a very different and solid foundation—a simple sensibility. In the Lakotah language, though, there was no simplicity. It was a complex language, full of tiny little changes in sounds that could alter the entire meaning of almost any given word. It was not an easy language to learn and it wasn't long before Frankie realized that the more words she learned, and the more she understood, the more confused she became.

Flint Striker smiled when she told him that; he told her it meant she was truly learning more than she thought. After that, he spent more time teaching her about the differences between the Lakotah and Cheyenne languages and between the Oglála and the Cheyenne tribes, helping her to bridge the languages and the cultures. Helping her to understand the reasons for the brotherhood between the two tribes.

Twice during their stay, when the three hounds and Matilda warned of visitors coming up the track, the two warriors disappeared into the Wolf Den. They stayed hidden when the Hyatt brothers drove a team of light buckskins into the meadow and stayed for dinner and peach cobbler, and then left her with a ham and more bacon. The warriors disappeared into the den again when Ida and Everett showed up for their regular Sunday visit.

Even though Frankie was sure that neither the Dunbars nor the Hyatts would present any problems for them, the Oglála men chose to stay hidden away; it was how they wanted it, and Frankie figured that it was just as well that no one had any idea that two Indians were hidden away in the cellar.

But Frankie did tell the Dunbars about the visit of the Cavalry troop—and their prolonged stay. Once they understood the soldiers presented no future problems for her, they asked to hear the entire story. She supplied all the details they asked for—except for the part about hiding the two warriors.

Of everything she told them, Everett was most pleased about the soldiers replacing the venison and increasing her store of firewood. Ida though, was most pleased with the requisition order. And since they all knew there was still too much danger for Frankie to be seen near the Overland Road, Ida was almost ecstatic with the idea that, according to the lieutenant's requisition letter, she and Everett could act as 'agents for young Frances Dunbar' the next time they traveled to Fort Cottonwood.

They would see to the wagon-load of supplies, and Ida, with a spark of devilish delight in her eyes, decided that Frankie could make out whatever list she wanted. But once at the fort, Ida declared, she and Everett would be free to add whatever they wanted to the load. 'Frankie,' she said, 'would just have to wait and see what all came home in the wagon'. When Frankie suggested Ida had a bit of a wicked streak in her, Ida just nodded and gave a wicked little smile.

In the late evening on the sixth day after the Cavalry left, Gray Fox told Frankie they were ready to leave. They were both ready to ride, he told her.

The following morning before the sun was up, Frankie led two horses to her two warriors at the root-cellar. Along with the bay Indian pony, now sound and strong, she brought the sorrel gelding—the mystery horse Tipp had left with her. She was sending the sorrel for their journey, she told them, because they each needed a horse. Because meeting up with enemies with only one horse between them, would mean certain danger.

She gave them each a flour-sack of food, enough to get them several days along their trail toward home. She gave them the buffalo-robe from the Wolf Den so they'd each have one for warmth. And she handed Flint Striker the rifle and a canvas pouch of bullets from the bench in the Wolf Den.

"You need the rifle to hunt, to keep your bellies full. So you can keep healing," she told him. "And to keep you safe." She turned to Gray Fox, holding up one of the pearl-handled penknives she had taken from the Sutlers Store the night she escaped from the fort. "This is for my sister, Wood Flute." She put the knife in his hand. Smiled at him when he touched her cheek.

She rode out of the meadow with them in the pre-dawn hour. Riding on Fox, staying beside her two warriors as they rode to the northwest. After a couple of miles, she pulled Fox to a halt and turned him back toward her homestead.

When she reached the Lookout Hill, she rode to the crest and sat in the slanting light of the rising sun. Watching until the two Oglála warriors disappeared into the Sand Hills. Watching them going deep into the hills, deep into the winter grasses until she could see them no more. Watching until the two Oglála warriors, the bay pony, and the mysterious sorrel were gone.

Part VI

Rites of Spring

More than a month had gone by since her Oglála warriors had left, and now, Frankie was spending a lot of time on the Lookout Hill watching for buffalo herds, hoping to see the dark patchwork of some great herd out among the distant hills. So far, she had only seen two great herds of elk, several smaller herds of deer, and dozens of small herds of the antelope. Each day she had been on the crest of the hill, watching the prairie-scape. Waiting for the Sand Hills to show her its secrets.

She was also watching for her Cheyenne people, hoping they would come soon. Hoping they would be bringing Wild Bird back; hoping the families would come to do their hunting; hoping they would stay again. Hoping they would bring word that Gray Fox and Flint Striker made their way home safely.

When Wild Bird and Whirlwind left in late winter, they had talked of returning in the time of the *heše'e-venéhe-eše'he*, the muddy-faced moon, when the early plants would begin to come up on the land. The old Cheyenne woman said she wanted to show Frankie the plants used for healing, plants that were best if found in the early weeks after snow left. *So maybe Wild Bird will be coming soon. Because we're in the muddy-faced moon. We're almost in April.*

And finally, near the end of one day, deep into twilight, she saw them. Her Cheyenne. She stood up on Sunny Jim's broad back, her spyglass trained on the procession of riders; she watched and managed to do a little jigging-dance on the Shire's broad back.

They were coming from the northwest, angling toward the river and still a good twelve miles out, looking a little like a long, winding snake—twisting around and through, behind and between the hills of the prairie. Traveling slow and steady through the land of the Sand Hills that stretched beyond her vision.

Frankie grinned at the sight in the lens of the spyglass. She could pick out men and women and children. There were horses of every color and size—some carrying people, some carrying packs, some dragging the loaded travois. Behind the long line of riders, she could see the herd of loose horses—more of the Indian ponies, more of the horses of every color—being pushed along by the band's herd-boys.

The procession slowed and seemed to bunch up in a gap among the hills; then the movement stopped entirely. After a moment of watching, Frankie knew what it meant—the band was setting up camp for the night. There were trees in that gap and Frankie was pretty sure that meant there was either a lasting slew or a rising spring. So they would stay where they were, camping by the water. They'd come the rest of the way in the morning.

A wave of disappointment swept over her—she stared at the sight, watching the shadowy little specks of movement as the people began setting up their campsite. *So close.*

She thought about riding out to meet them, but decided against it, telling herself to be patient. Telling herself to allow them their choices and the time they wanted. Because it was *their* journey and it was their decision. It wasn't for little-white-girls to go about deciding things for them.

As the twilight deepened into dusk, she continued watching through the spyglass. She could see little shadowy movements and she knew the mounts and packhorses were being released into the herd for the night. She saw the dim glow of the faraway campfires. Her people were settling in for the night. Her Cheyenne.

If the families started out at dawn, Frankie knew they would be at her homestead by noon. She felt a grin forming. *Strong Hand and Knife will probably ride ahead of the procession. They'll come earlier. And maybe Dandelion too.*

She tried watching the campsite for a while longer, trying to see through the deepening gloom of dusk, but finally, she could see nothing except the dim-glowing specks of their campfires.

Her thoughts turned to her meadow and her own campsite by the windmill pond. She remembered that she'd need to reset the campfire ring and replace the standing-forks and the long spit; she would cut up the last of the meat from the venison quarter hanging in the pantry. She'd set the meat to simmering in the cookpot over the fire first thing in the morning.

Frankie turned Sunny Jim in a slow circle on the hilltop; she surveyed the land as he turned, wishing for a herd of buffalo to suddenly appear. Knowing it was unlikely; knowing it was already too dark to see anything. She felt a deep disappointment that this time, she had no buffalo herd to show to her friends; she had seen no buffalo herd in the last weeks. Just herds of elk and deer and antelope. This time, her Cheyenne people would come to visit and she would have no buffalo herd for them.

She circled Sunny Jim again, slower this time, still scanning the distant hills through the telescope, hoping to see *some* sign of buffalo. She saw no buffalo, but she *did* see something.

There were tiny spots of light—a cluster of faintly glowing specks of light out among the grassy hills far to the northeast. She trained the spyglass on the glowing spots, watching the little cluster of faint lights. Playing with the focus as she tried to bring the vision to clarity, she suddenly understood what she was seeing—campfires.

Out there, way to the north, there was another campsite. She worked with the lens, trying to bring the image closer, but the tiny glowing specks remained faint. Blurry in the lens of the spyglass. She knew there was a river up there, a river which ran a course between the North Loup and the Niobrara. The map showed it as the Calamus River and she figured the campsite to be somewhere between her place and that river.

She watched the distant specks of light, knowing it was unlikely any white-men would be traveling out there, deep in the wildness of the Sand Hills. And her own Cheyenne were to the northwest. The fires to the northeast must then belong to other Indians. Maybe another Cheyenne band coming to meet them, maybe with plans to join up with them to hunt. Or it might be people of the Oglála. Or another tribe of the Sioux people.

There was also a chance that it was a Pawnee camp. Or maybe, a band of Crow who had traveled from their lands that lay far, far to northwest. Maybe people of the Arikaree tribe, the Cree people, who lived far north of the great Missouri River had come farther south. The trouble was, the Pawnee and Crow and Arikaree were all enemies of the Cheyenne and their Sioux brothers.

Frankie took in a slow breath. Thinking about the situation. Deciding that whoever was there to the north—friends or enemies—they were settling down for the night. They wouldn't move until dawn. Come morning, when her Cheyenne came to her meadow, she'd tell Strong Hand and Knife. They would know what to do.

Turning the spyglass back to the northwest toward the camp of her Cheyenne, she took a last look at the campfires, eyeing the faint glowing specks of the campfires for a moment. Then she turned Sunny Jim and sent him down the hill; she whistled to Laughing Girl and the two pups, and headed to her meadow.

She had her mind set on getting a fire going, so she could set a stew simmering in the coals of the fire-ring through the night. She was thinking it'd be a good idea to get some cornbread and butter ready too. Because it was likely that she'd have visitors arriving around sunrise.

The morning sky was just beginning to show pale and silvery-pink in the east as Frankie poured milk into the separating pans in the pantry. She was watching the meadow's entrance through the window, watching for her Cheyenne to arrive, when suddenly, she realized it was Sunday. Which meant she'd have more company than just the Cheyenne—the Dunbars would be rolling into her homestead today.

Frankie poured the last of the milk into the pans, grinning at the thought. Because Everett and Ida would have no reason to expect the Cheyenne would be in the meadow. So it'd be a reunion of sorts. And once everyone was here, Ida would likely have Dandelion beside her most of the day. And Happy Man would have Little Mouse holding onto him.

She was laughing to herself, thinking that Happy Man would definitely be happy, and that was when she saw Matilda and the hounds rising to their feet. They had been dozing on the pantry porch, but they were awake now—awake and alert. Their eyes on the track; their hackles raised. Laughing Girl was uttering her low, rumbling growl. Frankie stepped out the stone-room door, pretty sure of what she'd be seeing in a matter of minutes.

Sure enough, a few minutes later, she watched a bony buckskin pony coming down the track. Old Wild Bird was there on the buckskin's back and Frankie could see the wonderful, wrinkled old Cheyenne woman smiling her wonderful, wrinkly old smile. Coming along behind her were her two packhorses—the bay pinto and the gray pinto—each with a travois fastened to its back.

Whirlwind was following close behind, riding her brown pinto, with Little Mouse sitting in front of her, already waving her hands in the air. Already calling out a greeting to Fire Heart Child. Already chattering up a storm. She was calling for Happy Man and hollering about wanting to see the amó-eneo'o, the 'rolling thing'. And the kokóhéaxas. The 'chickens'.

A whole passel of other women then came down the track; their laughter and calls and greetings filled the meadow and echoed around the valley as they halted the line of horses carrying packs and dragging the long-poled travois. A moment later, Frankie saw a flea-bitten gray trotting down the track, skirting around the women and horses, coming straight to her. It was Dandelion. *Dandelion's here!*

Frankie started waving and hollering to her sister and Dandelion kicked her horse into a quick lope, waving and calling out. Sliding off her gray horse as she pulled it to a stop. They barely had time to greet each other before Frankie heard calls coming from beside the windmill pond.

Willow was lowering her bulk down from her horse, smiling her wide and wonderful smile and Whirlwind was calling out for her white-daughter as she slid off her brown pinto. And Old Wild Bird was beckoning to her, calling for her granddaughter to hurry.

"Ne-náestse! Ne-náestse!" 'Come here! Come here!'

Little Mouse was dancing and running in excited circles around the bony buckskin and the other horses, swept up in the excitement, hollering 'ne-náestse, ne-náestse, ne-náestse', same as her great grandmother, but to no one in particular—she was just running and waving her arms and hollering.

When Frankie reached the women, she was engulfed in hugs. Wild Bird and Whirlwind were patting her face and cooing her name; Willow was stroking her shoulder. And suddenly, Frankie found herself surrounded by all the Cheyenne women. They were saying her name. Ho-esta Hesta Ka-èškóne. Calling her 'daughter' and telling her she was beautiful. Nǎ-htona. Na-mo'onaha. She was being held and squeezed and patted by the women, and it seemed to Frankie as though it took an awfully long time for the excitement to die down.

Somewhere in the midst of all the greetings, she learned that the other families—the rest of the band—were still making their way downriver from the night's campsite.

"But now, your grandmother is ready to put her lodge up," Whirlwind motioned to the place beside the pond.

And about then, Frankie realized Whirlwind was done with her greeting and the explanations—because she was already calling to the other women. They were making their way to the ponies with the travois and releasing the lashings and pulling the poles; lifting the packs from the ponies.

Frankie tried to turn her attention to Dandelion, wanting to talk to her sister, but Willow was calling to her.

"Ne-náestse," she was beckoning, holding out a fringed shirt.

And before Frankie knew what was happening, her own linen shirt was being pulled off and a new deerskin shirt was being slipped over her head—a shirt decorated with rows and rows of black, red, and white beads that circled around the neck, stretched across both shoulders and trailed in strips down both arms. She was studying the beadwork, fingering the pretty patterns when Willow and Dandelion started yanking her britches down and pulling her moccasins off;

they tossed them to the side and began fastening a new breechcloth to her waist. A moment later, Dandelion was helping her pull on a new pair of moccasins decorated with yellow and white beads sewn in lightning-strike patterns.

Frankie spun around in a circle, examining her new clothes, shouting her excitement; Willow reached for her and wrapped her big arms around her, hugging her until she had squeezed most of the breath out of her. Then Willow let her go and stood back, smiling her pretty smile as she looked her white-daughter up and down. Nodding her approval.

"Today, my little-white-daughter is Cheyenne again." She laughed at her own comment, pleased with her own words. Then she turned and rushed off, shuffling her big body over to help unload the horses.

The work had started; Wild Bird's tipi was taking shape; and this time around, Frankie knew enough to stay back. She and Dandelion watched as the women began laying out the three main lodgepoles— the south-pole, the north-pole and the door-pole—on the ground. They tied them together near the tops with one end of a long buffalo-hide rope; they stood them up as a tripod, and then began standing the rest of the poles upright and tipping them inward, leaning them against the tripod, building the framework of the lodge.

Once all the lodgepoles were in place, it was Wild Bird who did the final tie-off, working with the long tail of the rope; she walked three circles around the outside of the cone of lodgepoles with the long rope in her hands, flicking it occasionally to keep it high among the poles. Tugging at it, tightening it as she walked. And finally, securing the tail of the rope by spiraling it down one of the poles.

Then came the most glorious part—the lifting of the massive skirt of hides. The women tied the center of the great half-circle skirt of hides to the lift-pole; they stood the pole up, settled it in place among the other lodgepoles, opposite from the door-pole. They took turns standing on each other's shoulders, easing the rest of the massive hide up the poles, smoothing it and tightening it against the framework.

About then, Frankie saw the three half-grown barn-cats charge into the action—they had invited themselves to the lodge-raising party, apparently deciding the hides that were being lifted up the poles presented a new and wonderful challenge for climbing.

Frankie and Dandelion sat in the grass with Little Mouse, hooting with laughter as the cats leaped into the fray, scrambling in a desperate bid to climb and conquer the rising lodge-cover. For the cats, in spite of all their scrambling and clawing up the hides, it wasn't just about climbing the poles and hides; they seemed to be taking a peculiar and perverse delight in disrupting the efficient rhythm of the Cheyenne women's work.

Frankie watched the action, holding out hope that a few of the women might decide to grab them up, skin them out, and toss them into the stew-pot. But they never did. The women only laughed at the fearsome growls and hissing-fits, and at most, they only resorted to sweeping the cats aside with moccasined-feet whenever necessary. They just kept on with their work, occasionally breaking into paroxysms of laughter at the persistence of the hellish little creatures.

Not only did the women tolerate the cats and their antics, but to Frankie's chagrin, there was a point when Wild Bird decided the three cats actually *remembered* her. After that, the old woman gave in to their demands for affection—she laughed at their twisting-turns as they rubbed against her ankles; she bent to give them affectionate little pokes to their ribs and scratches to their heads. She gave them gentle nudges with her feet, along with a few less-than-harsh kicks when they kept pouncing on her moccasins and tangling themselves up in the fringes of her dress.

Frankie kept watching Wild Bird, thinking she might tire of the nuisance and aim a couple of well-timed Cheyenne heel-kicks to send the half-grown cats somersaulting across the winter-grass. But it never happened.

In what Frankie figured was less than eight minutes, the final work was being done to the lodge. Whirlwind was standing on

Willow's shoulders, pulling the free-edges of the hide together above the doorway and sliding the lacing-pins into the front seam.

The smoke-flap poles were settled in place. The bottom of the lodge was staked down. The door-flap was fastened.

The women then carried Wild Bird's belongings into her home—buffalo-robes and elk-hides and bundles of furs were carried in, along with painted rawhide-boxes, leather pouches, and fringed-bags decorated with quilled-patterns and bright beads.

With the show over, Frankie and Dandelion leaped to their feet and did a running tour of the valley. Dandelion wanted to see everything she remembered—all the usual sights—including the ho-haa mo'éhė-no'ha, the 'very-much-horses', and the vé'ho'é-otóva'a, the 'white-man's buffalo' that gave them the heóve-amėške, the 'yellow-grease'. They stopped to see all the animals in the pastures and ended their run at the henhouse to see the kokóhéaxas.

When Frankie told Dandelion that Happy Man and She Sews would be coming to see them, they decided to ride downriver toward the Dunbars' place to meet them on their way to the meadow.

Frankie swung up on Fox, and Dandelion swung up on her gray; they snatched up Little Mouse and headed out of the meadow, giggling with the excitement of the surprise, knowing She Sews and Happy Man had no idea the Cheyenne families had returned.

And for Frankie, after Whirlwind told her Strong Hand and Knife, He's Proud and Blue Feather had ridden downriver, hunting for meat for the meadow, there was also the excitement of seeing her brothers. Plus, she had business with them; they needed to know about the campfires she had seen out to the northeast. Because the people there would be either friend or foe.

They found Everett and Ida about three miles downriver, and from fifty yards away, Frankie could see Everett's face light up. Once they met on the track, he almost fell out of the wagon reaching for Little Mouse. Little Mouse was calling for Happy Man, hollering for him to 'come here, come here, come here' and waving and paddling her way through the air as Frankie handed her across to the wagon-seat.

On the other side of the wagon-seat, Ida was busy wiping tears from her eyes as Dandelion stepped across the gap between her horse and the wagon. She grabbed for Ida's arms, her eyes sparkling and her smile flashing. Ida let the tears roll down her cheeks as she hugged Dandelion, calling her 'my dear little Cheyenne-girl'. Frankie watched the reunion, happy that their plan had worked, but thinking all the scrambling and crying was a bit much.

A moment later, her perspective on the scrambling and crying changed when she saw movement among the trees beside the river. Horses were moving through the low brush, and then hooves sounded in the river-water. Four Indian ponies—a red roan, a black-and-white pinto, a buckskin, and a palomino pinto—were winding their way through the undergrowth.

She turned Fox, kicking him toward the red roan coming up the riverbank. Then she was scrambling, launching herself off her pinto's back, reaching for Strong Hand on his roan. He caught her in mid-air, a broad grin across his face, every bit as wide as Everett's had been.

Behind her, Frankie could hear Little Mouse jabbering to Everett and Ida, telling them how happy she was. She was calling out her happiness to the horses hitched to the 'rolling thing'. Then she was hollering to her father and his companions telling them she had found Happy Man. She then hollered the news to a bird flying above her. She was telling all of them how happy she was.

He's Proud rode beside the wagon, talking to Ida and Everett and doing what translating was needed. And somewhere in the mix of all the people and the horses, and all the noisy greetings, Frankie ended up riding in front of Knife on Magpie, his arms were wrapped around her waist. Blue Feather's hand was gripping her arm, and Strong Hand had his roan close against Magpie's side with his hand resting on her knee.

They were all following the track toward the meadow with the Dunbars and Dandelion and Little Mouse all riding in the wagon. Everyone was talking and laughing and smiling. And Little Mouse was calling out to everyone, explaining how she was making the horses pull the rolling-thing. She kept jabbering and giggling, and when Frankie glanced back to the wagon, she could see Everett doing his best to keep Jenny calm while Little Mouse's little hands were flopping the reins around.

Everyone with the wagon, Frankie decided, could travel to the meadow at their own pace. Because she and her brothers had other business to handle. She took the reins from Knife's hand, motioned to Strong Hand and Blue Feather. She whistled for Fox and turned Magpie toward the river, following a narrow game-trail down the bank, explaining about the encampment to the north as they were crossing the North Loup. They all lifted their ponies into a lope, heading toward the Lookout Hill.

Once they reached the crest of the high hill, Frankie pointed to the north, showing them where the campfires had been the night before. Knife stood on Magpie's back and lifted Frankie to her feet in front of him; Strong Hand and Blue Feather stood on their horses. The four of them scanned the hills, looking for any movement out in the grasses. They saw an elk herd moving to the east and herds of deer. But no humans; no horses.

They stayed as they were, standing on their ponies. Watching. Waiting. Patiently eyeing the hills, watching the land to the north-east, knowing the rolling hills could hide movement for a long time. Strong Hand believed the fires had been Gray Fox's people. The two bands had been traveling together after they left the camp deep in the Mo'óthá-vo'honáaeva, deep in the black-rocky place. Then Gray Fox and his people left to travel to the east, scouting for buffalo; he planned to circle back to meet the Cheyenne at Fire Heart Child's home. After that, the Cheyenne and the Oglála would leave and hunt together.

Gray Fox and Flint Striker, Strong Hand told her, had returned to the winter camps of their people in the black-rocky place. They had ridden for many days, traveling with the food and weapons Fire

Heart Child had given them. The two warriors told the story of the soldiers and the long chase and how Fire Heart Child hid them from the soldiers and healed their wounds.

Both the Cheyenne and the Oglála had heard the story many times, Strong Hand said. And then, he talked about his pride in his little sister. Frankie reached to him, and he lifted her across to his horse, standing her on his roan's withers with his arms wrapped around her shoulders. They stood together, saying nothing else—looking to the north, still watching for any movement that would betray the presence of humans.

Frankie understood there would be nothing more said about the time Gray Fox and Flint Striker stayed at her home; Strong Hand had said everything that was important—he was her brother and he was proud of her, and that was enough.

Another five or six minutes passed before they saw what they were watching for. It was Blue Feather who first saw the riders, pointing to them as they rode from around a high slope. Frankie squinted, seeing nothing more than little dark specks far to the north, seeming to be barely moving, barely shifting position out across the far hills—a cluster of tiny little dots trailing across a long slope. At that distance, to her eyes, they could just as easily be deer or elk or a handful of buffalo. But her warriors knew exactly what they were looking at—the little dark specks were people on horses.

"Watch the movement," Knife told her. "Not the individuals. Herds run, or they graze."

She watched the faraway procession moving across the land, suddenly understanding what he meant. It was not how herds of animals moved. The distant specks were neither running in fright, nor grazing in the grasses. She tucked the knowledge away in her mind, knowing it was crucial information. She looked at Knife and nodded, understanding what he was teaching her. Understanding it might someday save her life. He gave her a slow smile, a slight smile. Pleased she understood.

But the other things her warriors knew from watching the tiny dark dots, perplexed her—they were seeing horses and riders, while she only saw only dark specks. They also knew the riders were Indian and not white-men. And they knew the riders were Oglála, and not Cheyenne. Nor Pawnee. Nor Crow, or Arikaree.

Strong Hand chuckled when she asked how he could be sure the tiny dark specks were Oglála. Blue Feather smiled at her and assured her they were people of the Sioux Nation. And they were a band of Oglála. More perplexing to Frankie, all three men seemed to know exactly who the distant specks were.

"Those are Gray Fox's people." Knife told her. "We know it is his band."

"How?" Frankie looked up at her brother. "How can you see all that?" She was wishing she had her spyglass with her but then decided it would be cheating. Because there might be times when she would need to recognize things in the distance when she wouldn't have her spyglass with her.

"It is knowing and understanding, Sister. It is more than seeing with the eyes." Strong Hand looked down at her, saw her confusion and the frustration. "You are still new to this land, but you are learning. You must learn to walk before you can run."

He tickled her neck, teasing her, distracting her from her frustration. He turned his attention back to the Oglála out to the northeast, talking to Blue Feather. Estimating the distance and the travel.

Frankie listened to their conversation, learning that Gray Fox's band would arrive in the evening. Before dark. She knew her three brothers standing on their ponies there on the hilltop were right about everything they said. It was not Cheyenne nor Pawnee out among the rolling hills. It was an Oglála band. It was Gray Fox's people and they would arrive before dark, just like they said.

She was still frustrated and her brothers knew it—but they only smiled. They stayed as they were, keeping their eyes on the line of little dark specks far to the north.

Frankie knew there was food cooking at the fire as they all rode into the meadow; she knew the women had been adding food to the stewpot, adding to what she had started cooking early that morning.

They had the heat high now, and the aroma was wafting across the meadow. Knife reached to pull her down from Fox as he slipped off Magpie; he flopped her over his shoulder, tickling her as he carried her to the fire.

She went along with him, lying belly-down across his shoulder and laughing all the way, fully aware of why he was doing it. He was letting everyone know that for a while, she belonged exclusively to him. For a little while, he would be unwilling to let go of her, unwilling to turn her over to anyone else. Because it was Knife's way—the way he showed his love for her.

He settled down by the cookfire and sat her in his lap, holding her tight against his belly. He leaned forward, reaching to the stewpot. He selected a few pieces of food from the pot and just like always, he held the pieces for her until they cooled, teasing her about her tender little-white-girl fingers.

Ida was already seated on one of the logs by the fire and Frankie figured she had probably been swept along in the midst of her ladyfriends as soon as she climbed down from the wagon. She was sitting between Whirlwind and Willow, chatting with all the women and keeping Whirlwind busy translating. Dandelion was there, too, nestled in against Ida's knees, looking happy and dreamy-eyed, tracing her fingers on the gingham cloth of Ida's dress.

From deep inside the barn, Frankie could hear bits and pieces of a conversation Wild Bird was having with Blossom. The old woman was already back into her regular routine, milking the Jersey cow so there would be yellow-grease to make later.

And out in the meadow, Everett was being pulled along by Little Mouse—going first toward the henhouse because Little Mouse decided the chickens must have a talking-to. Moments later, the two of them were proceeding to the barn.

And all the while, Little Mouse was having a hurried conversation with Happy Man, chattering in Cheyenne with a smattering of English words thrown in here and there. From what Frankie could hear there wasn't any real sensibility to her words, but Little Mouse seemed to think it was all very important. The chatter kept up while she and Happy Man walked through the barn, with her husky little

726

voice and Everett's steady responses echoing from inside the alley-way. After a few minutes, they emerged from the back end of the barn and continued their jaunt toward the windmill in the center of the back valley.

It wasn't long until everyone at the fire was roaring with laughter, because once the two of them arrived back in the front meadow, Little Mouse kept going, still pulling at Happy Man's hand, her mind set on leading him on yet another tour around the meadow.

And soon after that, the sound of drums came throbbing through the air, followed by the steady rhythm of haunting songs. Frankie leaped to her feet and Blue Feather rose, walking toward his pinto mare. She dashed ahead of him, yipping her excitement, whistling for Fox. The Grass Dancers had arrived. And her brother was going to take her out to watch them lay the grass down. And then, the rest of her Cheyenne family would come.

By early afternoon, the rest of Strong Hand's band arrived and began setting up the encampment on the grassy flats near the apple trees, setting up their lodges in the circles the Grass Dancers had created. It wasn't long until the women came to the meadow, calling for Ho-esta Hesta Ka-éškóne, laughing and waving; they greeted her, giving her their sweet touches—pats to her shoulders and arms, pats to her cheeks. They talked about the warm sun and the green grass and the new plants coming out of the warming soil. And Fire Heart Child, they said, must come with them to find plants and roots for the cookpots.

Cheyenne kids on horse-back circled their ponies in the meadow's grass, calling for her to come with them. They were ready for a game; they were shouting and beckoning and leaning down from the backs of their swirling ponies, grabbing at her sleeves. Imploring her to come and ride with them.

It seemed as though everyone had ideas and plans for her, and Frankie was laughing, not sure what she should do first. But after a few moments of indecision, it was two men sitting horseback in the middle of the meadow that caught her eye—two men and three ponies.

Knife and Strong Hand were on their ponies, with Fox standing beside them, a surcingle strapped around his barrel; the two men were just sitting there, watching her. Waiting for her to see them. She grinned, knowing they had some kind of adventure in mind; they grinned back at her, knowing she wouldn't be able to resist. She left the cluster of women and children at a run, ready for whatever her brothers had in mind.

When she reached them, Strong Hand told her to get her rifle; she dashed to the house, grabbed the Henry from its pegs inside the kitchen door and snatched three breakfast biscuits from the pan on the stove. By the time she darted back out the door, the warriors had their ponies beside the porch. She tossed a biscuit to each of them and bounded across the porch. Strong Hand reached for her rifle and slipped it into a loop on the surcingle. Frankie leaped toward Fox, grabbing at his mane and swinging onto his back.

Strong Hand gave her a wild grin; he and Knife reined their ponies, backed them away and spun them in a couple of circles. They gave a few yips and yells, laughing and shouting, questioning whether 'a little-white-girl could keep up with two such fine warriors'. They sent their ponies into a headlong gallop, around and behind the house and up the steep winding track. Frankie sent Fox after them, leaning low along Fox's neck, a few strides behind, racing to catch up. Yipping like her brothers.

They topped the slope and to Frankie's surprise, He's Proud and Blue Feather were already there, waiting for them on their ponies. Bows and quivers in-hand and holding the leads to three more ponies. They were throwing out their own yips and calls, laughing while their ponies were spinning, dancing and jigging with the excitement.

Looking at the men around her, Frankie suddenly understood what the adventure would be. Three of the men had bows and quivers of arrows; Knife had his rifle; the extra ponies would be used as packhorses. This adventure, she realized, was to be a hunt; her brothers were taking her with them to bring meat for the families at the encampment.

She let out her own series of excited yips, and then she let loose with a loud and long shriek of happiness, sending her call high into the sky. Surprising herself a little with its force. The men joined with her, sending out their own answering shrieks and yells. Laughing with her; pleased she was excited.

Frankie let Fox rear and spin, allowing him to do the excited quick-step dancing she would do if her feet were on the ground. This, she knew, was an honor—there were no other children going on this hunt; this was *just* for her. Just *her* and *her* brothers.

Below them, down in the meadow, Frankie could hear the shouts and laughter. All the people already knew about the hunt; they knew exactly what was going on. The women were singing out their long strings of 'li-li-li-li's', shouting out their encouragement, and calling for e-peva'e-émóhne. 'A good hunt'.

Strong Hand turned his roan and the band of hunters followed him at a fast lope around the slope and down to the river. They rode through the lines of nut trees, splashed into the water and crossed to the south bank and then Strong Hand motioned to Frankie. He said nothing; he just nodded to her. She looked at him, locked eyes with him. She understood—the play and excitement were over; the horses were warmed up and ready. The hunt was on.

Strong Hand was the leader of the hunting party, but Frankie suddenly understood he wanted her to guide them. *Her* role was to lead them to where there would be game—because this was land she knew. This was another honor, because she was being trusted with the outcome of the hunt.

Frankie sucked in a breath, feeling the weight of her role. Because, if she didn't find any game, then the people would have no fresh meat tonight. She would be failing both them, and the men who were placing their trust in her. She held back a groan as she pictured returning to the valley in the evening with the packhorses carrying nothing. No one would say anything, no one would ridicule or crit- icize—because it wasn't the Cheyenne way. But she would live with her own shame.

She realized she was still locked on Strong Hand's eyes and she wasn't sure exactly how long it had been. It felt like something between three seconds and three-thousand years. She let out the breath she'd been holding. Nodded at him. Made her decision.

Frankie led her warriors to the west, angling away from the river and going across the grassy-flats. Riding toward the bordering ridges. She thought there might be a deer herd, or maybe a herd of antelope, out in the deep valley beyond the first ridge—the high, long ridge she had named Hunter's Ridge. Usually, there was *some* kind of herd—deer or antelope, or sometimes elk—grazing in the deep hard-grasses of the long valley on the far side of the ridge. *Usually.*

She suppressed another groan. Wondering if there would be a herd there today. Given the time of day, she figured any herd grazing in the long valley would still be a mile or so to the south, gradually grazing northward to the river to water-up for the night.

She spoke to Strong Hand riding to her left, telling him what she wanted to do. She told him about the long valley and what she hoped to see there. They would have to swing to the south, she told him, and then work their way up the slope to the crest of the long ridge. He nodded. Grinned like he had been expecting her to have a plan. They swung their horses to the southwest, angling toward the long rise beyond the river-flats.

They covered the distance at an easy lope. Blue Feather brought his pinto up to ride beside her; he looked at her, his eyes soft and clear, giving her a look that said he knew about her fears. He grinned and she relaxed, knowing he understood. She pointed ahead and he looked to the next ridge, a half mile in the distance. When he looked back at her, he nodded.

The band of hunters slowed their horses, dropping down to a walk as they approached the long hill. At the base of the slope, Frankie slid off Fox when the men slipped off their horses; they were all watching Strong Hand, because now, he would make the decisions; because he was the leader now. Because her job was done.

They left their horses standing and started up the slope, walking carefully, slinking along, and to Frankie's eyes, looking a little like cats; they were choosing their steps, bending low. Crouching lower as they climbed higher up the hillside.

Frankie followed their lead—bending, then crouching, then knee-crawling, then slithering into a slow belly-crawl as they reached the crest. She moved with the warriors, sliding snake-like beside Knife, pretending that the poking and prickling and tickling of all the grasses and burrs and tiny thorns and stickers weren't bothering her. Trying to ignore the jabs and scrapes, trying to concentrate on the hunt like the warriors seemed to be doing. When they topped-out on the crest, they all stayed belly-down, scanning the swale below.

Frankie breathed a sigh of relief. Because there, grazing right below them, there in the hard-grass that was just starting to come green, was a herd of antelope. *There! Forty; maybe forty-five.*

Knife touched her arm; he looked at her, smiling. From his look, she realized that he too, had known about her fears. They all watched the herd, staying belly-down on the warm soil, lying motionless. Watching; assessing. So Frankie did as her brothers did—she stayed motionless. Waiting. Wondering though, about the length of time they remained there. Glancing to each side, unsure about the delay. Thinking they should move quickly. Thinking they should have brought their rifles and bows. The shooting could be well under way. But still, the men stayed as they were. Motionless; watching.

A few minutes later, as she grew tired of waiting and began thinking about scooting backwards and going back down the hill-side for her rifle, she felt Knife's hand move to her arm. Gripping it; pressing down. Somehow, once again, knowing exactly what she was thinking. His hand was a signal, telling her to stay still.

She threw away any thought she had of scooting backwards; she tried to make herself sink lower into the ground—embarrassed by her thoughts, ashamed her brother needed to correct her. She didn't know how long they stayed pressed low and hidden there on the hill-top; she had no idea what the men were seeing or thinking. But she didn't care anymore—all she cared about was staying still.

Because *this* was the hunt and this was the way it was done. These Cheyenne men knew the best ways, because it was their life.

Because it was how they fed their families. It was about life and death in their villages.

Suddenly, lying there on the hill beside Knife, Frankie knew they hadn't brought her along just to lead them to a herd—these men had hunted their whole lives. They didn't actually need some little-white-girl to find game for them to hunt. They brought her along to teach her. This was all a lesson, so her life would be better; it was all for her benefit, so she could learn and understand. None of the men told her they were going to be teaching her—they had waited, trusting that she'd realize it on her own.

When the men finally began moving back from the edge, they did everything in reverse. Frankie moved with them, slithering backwards through the tickling and prickling grasses, through the nasty thorns. Then knee-crawling, then crouching, then bending and walking low.

Twice, on the way down the slope, Knife stopped her in her steps, pointed to thick stems of winter-dead weeds that would snap under her moccasins and alert the antelope. Twice, she followed his direction, stepping to a different place, moving to where he pointed. Knowing it was just another part of the lesson.

At the base of the slope, they all went to their horses. Frankie stayed at Knife's side, staying within arm's reach—staying where she knew Knife wanted her, even though he had said nothing about it. The other men swung onto their horses; no words had been spoken, no plans had been made, no strategy had been agreed upon, but they all knew exactly what would happen. Because they all knew each other and they knew the skills and the weapons and the goal. They had all seen the same thing up on the crest of the hill and they all knew the plan.

Strong Hand and Blue Feather reined their ponies to the south and rode away slowly and quietly along the backside of the slope. He's Proud slipped up on his horse and rode to the north along the hillside. Frankie stayed with Knife, staying silent, watching him. Waiting for his guidance. Waiting for the next part of the lesson.

They stayed by Fox and Magpie and the three packhorses and Frankie started wondering if it was possible to get three kills. It was a big herd offering a lot of opportunity, but antelope were quirky animals that didn't always do what a person expected. Deer tended to be mostly predictable, but the goofy prong-horned creatures could skitter off in the most unlikely directions for their own crazy-minded reasons.

To Frankie's thinking, no matter how the warriors had things planned, the antelope, in the midst of their fleeing frenzy, could twist things around fast. And as things stood, there were only five hunters—four Cheyenne warriors and one little-white-girl. Three bows and two rifles among them. And one of the rifles, rather than being in the hands of a seasoned hunter, would be in the hands of the little-white-girl.

Frankie felt her doubts rising, wondering if she should have offered her rifle to Strong Hand. Now, she realized, it was too late. Realizing she might have ruined the hunt just because she didn't think of it sooner. *He didn't ask me for it, but maybe that's why he told me to bring it. Maybe he was hoping I'd let him borrow it.*

Knife squatted down and Frankie did the same, her mind still on her rifle and Strong Hand. She felt Knife's hand on her shoulder, squeezing it; he rocked her gently from side-to-side. When she looked to him, his eyebrows drew together; he gave a slight shake of his head. She nodded, understanding he was telling her not to worry. She shifted her position, moving closer to him; he laid his arm across her shoulders.

They stayed where they were and it dawned on Frankie that they were already full into the hunt and Knife wasn't just waiting with her. He was timing the stages of the hunt. He knew full-well what the other men were doing, where they were going, and how long it would take them. No words had been spoken, but Knife knew. And Strong Hand, Blue Feather and He's Proud all knew they would have the time they needed.

When Knife stood, Frankie stood. When he moved to Magpie and slipped his rifle from its loop in the surcingle, Frankie went to Fox and slipped her Henry out of its loop. Knife checked his rifle and load and waited while Frankie did the same. She looked at him when she was done, waiting for his cues, worrying she would miss something because no words were passing between them.

She saw Knife sniff at the breeze that drifted past them, sifting its way down the hillside; she sniffed the air too, not exactly sure what she should be smelling. But she sniffed anyway. Knife grinned, gave a slight nod, then turned his eyes up the slope, looking into the wind.

Ohh. Frankie suddenly understood what he was showing her. The herd of antelope was out there in the valley, just beyond the hill. Upwind. There would be certain scents floating along on the breeze. She nodded to him; lesson learned.

She sniffed the air again, paying attention now, open to the messages in the wind. The smell of soil, dusty soil. *From the sandy soil of the hillsides.* The smell of rich soil. *From the dark, rich soil of the valley.* The dusty scent of the dry winter-grasses; the sweet scent of the new coming-grasses. *The fragrance of the Sand Hills grasses.* She smiled, glancing to Knife. He smiled, just slightly. Giving her the time she needed. Patient. Waiting.

Frankie sniffed again. *There!* The smell of the animals. *The antelopes! Maybe.* The scent drifted away then. It came again. Went away again, floating off in the afternoon breeze. Once again. *There it is!* Then it was gone again. *There! Back again!*

The scent of dung. Fresh dung. She had the scent moving into her nostrils, into her memory. Animal smell; herd smell. Faint and soft, almost like a whispered sound. *A whispered scent.* Almost like the smell of the barn in the stillness of early morning. *But so very, very faint.*

Then, she heard a sound. A sound traveling with the breeze—a slight sound mixed in among the slight smells. A soft and distant snort; and then another. *Very faint. Very far-away. So faint it was almost not there.* She cocked her head. Listening, letting the soft flowing afternoon air bring the sounds along with the smells. *There!* Another far-away snort. *Or a sneeze, maybe.*

She saw Knife out of the corner of her eye, ducking his head just slightly. Smiling. Just slightly. A little pleased; a little amused. She ignored him for a moment, still listening. Still sniffing. Still learning.

His smile grew. He knew. She was learning her lessons, and he was pleased.

Frankie realized suddenly that her hunting companions had likely been sniffing the air and listening to the sounds in the wind before they even reached the base of the hill. They knew that antelope were grazing down in that valley before they had even started the climb. Knife already knew what was in the air and the breeze—he was just taking the time to teach her now.

When she finally turned to look at him, he nodded and started up the slope, his rifle in-hand. Frankie followed, rifle in-hand. Watching for twigs and weed-stems at her feet. Sniffing the air. Listening.

Frankie stayed beside Knife, lying belly-down on the crest of the ridge; she slowed her breathing and her heartbeat, matching it to the pace of the prairie and the rhythm of the grasses, finding the natural movement and flow within her. She was waiting for Knife's messages to her, messages she knew would come from his hand resting on her forearm. There would be no words; his fingers would speak to her.

She felt the tap. Strong. Clear in its intent. His finger pressed down, then it shifted ever so slightly. He was telling her to stay low and telling her to look for what he wanted her to see. All from the tap of his finger and its direction. She shifted her gaze, looking to her left, down to the south in the valley.

Two soft taps. He was showing her where Strong Hand and Blue Feather were. Down there somewhere among the tall grasses.

Another soft tap and another shift. Showing her that He's Proud was somewhere to the north, somewhere in those grasses.

Frankie remained still, but her eyes were scanning the grasses. Seeing no movement, seeing no sign of warriors to the south. Nor to the north. Nothing.

Below her, the herd moved among the grasses, meandering slowly, intent on their grazing. The watchers in the herd, the biggest bucks, were scanning the valley, eyeing the hillsides. Alert to any danger. But apparently, Frankie decided, *they* weren't seeing any Cheyenne warriors moving through the grasses, either.

But they were somewhere among the grasses. Strong Hand and Blue Feather *were* there; He's Proud *was* there. They were right where Knife knew they would be. She understood it all now. This was the Cheyenne way. Here, there was no need to hurry. Here, there was a need to be wise.

Frankie felt Knife's grip change, felt the angle change, felt a nudge from his thumb. She knew what he wanted. She moved to her left, easing away from Knife, moving inch-by-inch. Moving slow; staying low. Staying on her belly; staying deep among the grass-stems. Knowing in her gut what Knife wanted from her, knowing how it would all happen.

The first kills would be from the south—from Strong Hand and Blue Feather. The antelope would spook and begin their mad dash up the valley, going to the north because it was the easiest and fastest escape route. She and Knife would fire together from the hilltop as the herd passed below them. He's Proud would make his kill as the herd raced toward him. Five hunters; so there should be five kills. And Frankie knew she was expected to make one of them.

She felt Knife's eyes on her; she stopped where she was, know-ing it was what he wanted. She was barely eight feet from where she had been. She looked to him; locked on his eyes and nodded, just slightly. Letting him know she understood; letting him know she was ready.

Now, they would wait for Strong Hand. Because he was the hunt leader. He had commanded the entire hunt without saying a word. He knew exactly where everyone was and what everyone would do. He would choose the timing—he would know the exact and best moment. Because this, Frankie knew, was the Cheyenne way; this was the way of the Indian, not of white men.

From the corner of her eye, she saw Knife shifting his rifle into position, slowly, carefully. Frankie shifted hers, slowly, carefully. She eyed the antelope—heads still down in the grasses, minds still on the new rising-green grass that was tight against the soil. She studied the main body of the herd, noting the stragglers and wanderers. She kept her body still but her mind was racing; she was trying to think through everything—her load was good, her view was unobstructed, her aim had to be adjusted for the downhill shot.

Off to her right, she saw the barrel of Knife's rifle—it lifted ever so slightly. She saw him set his stock deeper to his shoulder. She did the same, shifting ever so slightly and setting her stock. *It's time. It's coming.* She had her eyes on the herd; she widened her vision to take in more of the meadow. *Hold steady. Because it's coming.*

The moment came—there was not a single sound, but suddenly, there was movement down in the meadow. *There! Right behind the herd.*

Strong Hand and Blue Feather had risen from the grasses and taken their shots in the same instant. In a single instant. Their arrows hit their marks. Two antelope fell. And in that moment, the herd was running—turning and running as a single body—racing away from the movement in the grass, charging through the long meadow to the north.

Frankie lined her sights, aiming for a buck at the edge of the herd. She shifted, adjusting her aim for her hilltop position. Holding her aim, leading her target. Listening for Knife's shot. When he fired, she fired. Two antelope crumpled in the meadow grass an instant apart. To her surprise, Knife fired again and another antelope collapsed, tumbling and rolling in the grass. She reacted—she shifted her barrel, sighted on another buck, found her mark, led and fired.

She saw the puff of dust on the hillside beyond her target, knowing it was the dirt kicked up by her bullet. She had missed the shot; the antelope kept running. She had forgotten to correct for her uphill position. She groaned, shook her head, watched the herd in its headlong flight.

Seconds later, as the herd approached the north end of the valley, she saw an antelope tumbling forward, crumbling. And then another collapsed in its run. *He's Proud!* He had been there in the grass, waiting. Carrying out his part of the hunt. *Two arrows. Two antelope.*

Frankie stared as He's Proud rose from the grass, walking toward the two fallen antelope as the rest of the herd swerved, racing away. They disappeared beyond a far slope. Back to her left, she saw Strong Hand and Blue Feather walking toward their kills.

Knife stood. Reached and lifted her to her feet in one simple, effortless motion. He turned and started down the back slope; Frankie trotted after him. No belly-crawling or crouching or bending this time. He grinned at her as they swung onto their horses and gathered up the leads to the three extra horses.

"Nésohto vo'kaa'e. Pave ho'ame Ka-éškóne." 'Seven antelope. Good-Shooting Child.' It was his pet name for her; she hadn't heard it since the day when he and Strong Hand and He's Proud had ridden into Fort Kearny.

"Pave ho'ame Notaxe." 'Good-Shooting Warrior'." She grinned at him.

They rode back home with two antelope lashed to each packhorse and one lashed onto Fox behind Frankie. They teased her about being so light that Fox didn't know he had anything other than an antelope on his back. But none of them said anything about the shot she had missed.

When they reached the ford at her meadow's track, Blue Feather and He's Proud led the three packhorses with six antelope toward the village. Food for the people. Frankie stayed with Strong Hand and Knife, heading to her meadow with the antelope still tied behind her.

The sound of drums and singers came to Frankie's ears while she worked beside the cookfire, piercing and sliding strips of antelope meat onto sharpened sticks. She stopped her work, tilting her head to listen to the haunting sounds.

"The Oglála Grass Dancers have come. Gray Fox's band will be coming soon." Whirlwind handed Frankie several more strips of meat she had sliced from the haunch of the antelope.

Frankie was hurrying to finish with the strips of meat, wanting to ride over to watch as the dancers laid down the grass for the Oglála lodges. Curious about the Oglála dancers, wanting to see if their dances were different than the Cheyenne. The beat of the drums was similar to the Cheyenne drums, but the songs were different. The words were different and the timing was different.

She finished with the last strips that Whirlwind had handed to her and she turned away from the fire, deciding to bridle Fox and go to see the dancers. Or since she had heard the calls of some of the Cheyenne kids—calls and shouts that told her they were riding out to greet Gray Fox's people—maybe she'd ride out with them. But Wild Bird and Whirlwind called her back.

"No. Stay here with us." Whirlwind brushed away her idea. "There will be time later."

"Let the Oglála women raise their lodges and make their fires." Wild Bird smacked her shoulder lightly with her stick. "You hunted this meat with your brothers. Now you stay here. Help put it on the fire."

Frankie was a little surprised that they refused her ideas, but she complied; she stayed in the meadow, taking the pieces of meat that Whirlwind handed her, helping Wild Bird and Ida slide and twist the strips of meat onto the spit-sticks and prop them across the fire. She tried to hide her disappointment, listening all the while to the sounds that came from beyond her home valley.

She heard when the Grass Dance ended, and a little while later she heard the shouts and laughter and calls that told her Gray Fox's band had arrived. It wasn't long before she could hear the sounds of the Oglála people settling into the camp. Twice more she was ready to go out to the encampment, but each time Whirlwind and Wild Bird found other things for her to do beside the cookfire.

So Frankie stayed with them, knowing that the Oglála women would already be arranging the lodgepoles on the ground and laying out the huge lodge covers—the great half-circles of sewn-hides with all the glorious paintings telling of battles and exploits and honors. *Pretty soon, the lodgepoles will be going up. Then the tripods for the warriors' war-shields will be put up. And I'll miss all of it.*

She didn't protest, because that wasn't something a little Cheyenne girl should do, but she did give a sigh that she knew was loud enough for the women around her to hear. She saw Whirlwind and Wild Bird exchange odd little smiles.

Within a few minutes, there were more sounds. Sounds that were closer; sounds that drifted up from the river. Shouts and shrieks of laughter—children's laughter. Frankie knew her Cheyenne and Oglála friends were out there, swimming and bathing in the icy water. She stifled another sigh and ducked her head to hide her disappointment at being relegated to doing campfire work. No one had stopped Dandelion from going. She was out there somewhere; she had abandoned the meadow earlier when she rode out to greet the Oglála band. *Now, she's probably down in the river, splashing and playing around the island. Probably with Wood Flute. And all the others.*

She wanted to see Wood Flute, her Oglála sister. She wanted to go play with her and Dandelion. But she didn't really want to take the chance of getting another rap from Wild Bird's stick. So she stayed by the fire, skewering more antelope meat onto the long sticks, doing all the little tasks that Wild Bird kept giving her. She made a trip to the cellar to gather handfuls of onions and turnips, carrots and parsnips to add to the big stewpot. The whole time, she could hear the shrieks and laughter coming from the river. And the whole time, she was feeling more annoyed that she had to help cook the meat she had hunted.

"I don't see the men helping cook the meat *they* shot." Frankie gave Whirlwind a hard stare. "Shouldn't He's Proud be helping with the strips of meat? He shot more antelope than I did."

She saw Strong Hand smirk and she saw Everett duck his head and chuckle as He's Proud translated for him. She pointed to Blue Feather and Knife. "They all shot antelope too. And they're just leaning against the log, watching me do all the work."

Her grousing got her nowhere. The warriors just kept talking among themselves, relaxing and leaning back against the logs—acting as if they hadn't heard her comments and pretending they weren't amused. And Frankie was thinking about all the times Wild Bird had talked about Cheyenne men being lazy. She decided the old woman was probably right.

Later in the evening, as the light in the valley dimmed and the sky began showing the russets and bronzes and deep purples of dusk, a group of Oglála came down the track, riding slowly into the meadow. The conversations around the fire halted. Everyone stood up, their eyes on the riders.

Frankie stood up, too, thinking it was a strange arrival. No greetings. No laughter and shouts. No smiles or calls. Just a small group of Oglála—two warriors, three women and four children—riding quietly. Further back, more riders followed, with a string of pack-horses trailing behind them.

She stared at the procession arriving in the gathering dark, a little confused and a little unnerved. Because this was not a normal thing. There were no wild and ecstatic greetings; no racing horses; no excited calls. No yips and yells. Instead, everyone riding down the track was moving quietly. Somber and serious.

Whirlwind walked toward the group of Oglála beckoning for Frankie to follow. Wild Bird poked her ribs with her stick, motioned for her to go with Whirlwind. And suddenly, Strong Hand was walking beside her, his hand gripping her arm, guiding her toward the riders.

As they approached the visitors, close enough to see them in the half-light of dusk, Frankie broke into a grin and gave a quick yip of excitement. She could see the two men at the front of the band of riders. Šungíla Hóta and Čhankhá Iyáphe! Gray Fox and Flint Striker!

Her mind whisked back to the last time they had ridden into her meadow, riding double under a buffalo-robe and weakened from their wounds. This time their arrival was very different; this time they were sitting straight and tall, watching her steadily as they pulled their ponies to a stop—stopping almost exactly where they had halted on that other day.

She was ready to run to greet them, but Strong Hand tightened his grip, holding her back. She looked up, frowning at him. Confused. She pulled against his hold, but he shook his head, murmured softly to her. Told her to stay by him.

Frankie checked herself, realizing that even though these men were her friends, they *were* Oglála, after all. Not Cheyenne. And maybe their customs were different. She stepped back, moving closer to Strong Hand. Watching as Gray Fox and Flint Striker slipped down from their mounts and walked toward her. Everything in the meadow had become serious and solemn as the two Oglála warriors approached.

Glancing beyond them, she saw Čik'ala Thawinyela, Young Doe, on her horse with Čhán Šiyóthanka, Wood Flute, riding double behind her, peeking around her mother. Behind them, there were other riders along the rise of the track—ten or fifteen warriors were sitting quietly on their ponies, with the ponies on lead-ropes behind them. They sat motionless, only their feathers and buckskin fringes and the edges of their horse-blankets were moving, lifting and flitting silently in the evening breeze.

"We've come to visit you, Daughter." Flint Striker spoke the words in English, and then he spoke in Lakotah, his people's language. "You kept us at your home, Fire Heart Child, and you sent us back to our families. Our families and our people have brought you gifts."

Frankie heard He's Proud's voice; he squatted down behind her, speaking close to her ear, translating the Lakotah words. Telling her what Flint Striker and Gray Fox wanted her to know. Beside her, she heard Strong Hand speaking to her in Cheyenne, telling her that this was a gift-giving. A novaheséve-stótse, he said, giving her the Cheyenne word. It was to honor her, he said. It was a serious and important thing among the Oglála and Cheyenne people.

"It is a Giveaway Ceremony of the Oglála. The Wóotuh'an'otúh'aṅpi," He's Proud gave her the Lakotah word and explained, "to honor your bravery. And a gift-giving for a healer. The Wóheyaka."

Frankie understood suddenly that this was not just an exciting reunion for her. Her Cheyenne family was guiding her in this, because it was a very serious thing. A very important ceremony.

"The Oglála warriors have things to say," He's Proud told her, "things that rise from their hearts. And from the hearts of their families. This is about honor, Fire Heart Child."

He's Proud stood up and moved his hand to her shoulder. With Strong Hand standing to her other side, Frankie suddenly understood. For now, she needed to stay quiet between these two warriors. They were standing silent and solemn, acting, she realized like sponsors at a baptism or wedding. This, then, was the time for her to be silent and solemn, too—to be what her Aunt Sarah would have called 'gracious'.

Now, she realized, she needed to act with the humble grace that a true woman should show, whether white or Cheyenne or Oglála. She looked to Whirlwind standing straight and tall beside her son. So Frankie did the same—she stood straight and tall just like Whirlwind. Standing just like her Aunt Sarah would have done. Just like Isabelle would have done.

Frankie stood between He's Proud and Strong Hand, listening to the Oglála men. When she felt Strong Hand touch the base of her neck, she knew she should drop her eyes. To be humble. To give others their moment. Because this was not a quick mention of some incident; this was about pride and respect.

Flint Striker spoke his peace, then Gray Fox began talking. Frankie listened to his words, staring at the ground in front of her, hearing his words and listening as He's Proud translated. They were words for her to hear—words for all the people around them, to hear.

There was a moment when Frankie glanced up at Gray Fox and she could feel her tears welling up in her eyes; he stepped closer to her and squatted down in front of her, speaking to her as a father would speak to his daughter. Speaking to her like her own father would have.

Gray Fox spoke of his gratitude and the gratitude of his family, telling her they understood the sacrifice she made; they understood the danger she faced. He was telling her that her choice had been one of bravery. That her choice spoke of strength from deep in her heart. She had put her life between them and the soldiers, he said, and her name from Strong Hand, Fire Heart Child, was a true name.

She was of their lives now, he said, and they were of her life. She was family with the Oglála now. His people were her people.

Frankie stood before him, watching his eyes, feeling the pride and the love in his hand as he put it to the back of her head and rested it there. Tears were flowing down her cheeks and she knew it was because the words from this man were the same kind of words that would have come from her father and her uncle. From her Lieutenant. From the Captain and Dr. Gannon, and from Major Maxwell. Strong Hand would have said these same words to her.

They were words that *true* men spoke. Men who chose to be worthy of the role they played in the lives of others and in the lives of their children. He was thanking her—but he was also praising and guiding her. He was teaching her about her character, exactly the way her father would have.

And then they were done speaking. Gray Fox and Flint Striker walked to their companion riders. When they came back to her, they were leading six horses. Each horse carried a pack.

The two men handed the six lead-ropes to Frankie, and without another word, they walked back to their horses and swung up on their ponies. The band of Oglála turned and rode out of the meadow, following the track up and around and over. Leaving the valley as quietly and as solemnly as they had arrived.

Strong Hand squatted down beside Frankie, his arm wrapped around her shoulders, speaking softly into her ear—explaining that her Oglála family would come back later. Tomorrow, they would visit. Tomorrow, there would be laughter and games, he said. Now, he said, she should spend time caring for the gifts they had brought for her.

It was full dark as Frankie led the horses across her meadow to her kitchen porch, with Whirlwind and Willow and Wild Bird walking beside her. Blue Feather and Strong Hand, He's Proud and Knife walked behind them. When they reached the porch, the men shifted the packs from the horses and settled them at the porch steps, backing each horse away after it was unloaded.

744

The three women motioned to Frankie; they helped her unpack her gifts and lay them out along the edge of the porch. It was the Oglála tradition, He's Proud told her, to place the gifts at the door of her lodge. From that moment on, Frankie became lost in the process, a process that was gentle and reverent.

Each horse carried a buffalo-robe atop its pack and those soft robes were the first gifts laid out. Then there were dresses and leggings made by the Oglála women—all decorated in the beautiful beading and quilling and painting of their people. All just as beautiful as the designs of the Cheyenne.

There were Oglála shirts and moccasins, dyed and beaded. A quilled and painted belt. A blanket of soft bobcat-hides. A shawl of white ermine-fur. There was a cougar-hide. A blanket of dark and rich beaver-fur. A fan made of turkey-feathers with beads and fringe.

There was a reason for everything the Oglála people had brought to her, Wild Bird told her. Each gift offered to the girl who had protected their loved ones, had a special meaning, she said. The necklace of elk-teeth would give her endurance. Another necklace of badger-claws would give her a fierce strength. A necklace of the claws of a black bear—was a gift for a healer—because bear-medicine was the medicine of a healer, Wild Bird explained.

There were bundles of sage and cedar in painted leather cases—the smoke from those plants would cleanse and protect her lodge and her meadow. There were parfleches of dried meat and fish, of pemmican and corn, dried berries and plums—all foods to sustain her, all to honor the gifts of food and sustenance she gave to their warriors.

Frankie was stunned by the gifts, astonished by the number and the variety. She stood back, staring while the three women showed her the items, gently and carefully. They explained that the gifts were not just from Flint Striker and Gray Fox; they were not just from the wives and families of the two warriors. These gifts were from all the people of their village, from every person who wanted to acknowledge her courage in protecting and caring for their loved ones. These were gifts to thank her for her bravery.

Ida and Everett stood close to the porch, watching quietly, with Dandelion and Little Mouse beside them. And even though the

Dunbars might not understand exactly why this ceremony was taking place, Frankie could tell that they understood the gravity of it.

Wild Bird, Whirlwind and Willow were guiding her as they continued to lay out the gifts, explaining as they went. When a wolf-hide blanket was laid out on the porch floor—a square of tawny-gray wolf-hides with the blanket edge trimmed in white wolf-fur—Wild Bird explained the importance of the gift. These wolves, she said, had shown themselves to the Oglála—the ancestors of Gray Fox and Flint Striker had sent the wolves to the people—so they could gift them to the Fire Heart Child. The wolf-blanket held great medicine for Fire Heart Child, Whirlwind told her, and it must always stay in her own hands. Willow spoke of the power and the medicine of the gift, her voice soft and reverent. It was powerful medicine, she said, and was only for her, in this life.

There was a bow with a quiver made from a complete bob-cat-hide and filled with arrows; these, she was told, were to honor her courage, because she had the courage of a warrior. A warrior-woman, Whirlwind said.

"Winoxtca." She said the Oglála word. There was a society of warrior-women, she said—women who were brave and strong, and chose to fight in battle when the battle was in their hearts. "They are honored for their strength and courage. The Oglála believe you live with that strength and courage."

There was a beaded bridle and quirt. A knife-sheath made from the tail of a buffalo calf. These were gifts made and offered by the warriors of Gray Fox's band. These gifts from the warriors were offered to one with the courage of a warrior.

Of the six buffalo-hides, one was massive—bigger by far, than the other five. *This one,* Wild Bird told her, was from Gray Fox himself. *This* was from the hunt last fall. Whirlwind nodded, saying she had watched Young Doe and her daughter, Wood Flute, work on it during the winter.

It was a full-hide, with the head-skin intact; the whole hide was tanned buttery-soft. It was the one that Gray Fox had promised to bring her; it was the hide of a lead bull from the hunt. Whirlwind, though, had more to say about it. The gift of *this* hide, she said, was a great honor. The bull had separated from the herd and shown itself to Gray Fox; it had stood watching and waiting for Gray Fox. It was the bull Gray Fox knew was meant for Fire Heart Child, the girl who had called the buffalo to his people.

Frankie squatted down, reaching out, running her hands over the gifts lying in front of her home—in front of her lodge. Knowing there was much honor here in front of her. Her eyes began filling with tears; spilling over with tears.

Strong Hand was behind her then, his hands on her shoulder; he stood her up and turned her to face the six horses. Frankie stared at Knife and Blue Feather holding the leads of the six horses, suddenly realizing they were gifts, too—the horses that had carried the packs, were also gifts from the Oglála.

Frankie let her eyes move over the horses. There were two tri-colored pinto mares—fine calicos, straight of limb with pretty-faces, pretty-ears and pretty-eyes; both looking to be sensible and kind. There was a bay filly with an alert look to her—a two-year-old alert-look that showed her to be maybe a bit *too* wise, and maybe, just a bit *too* clever—which meant she might prove to be a handful of trouble. There was another pinto, a sleek and shiny mare, all white except for a buckskin-brown patch over her ears and the top of her head, and a buckskin-brown circle on her bottom—a perfect circle right in the middle of her pretty round backside, with her pretty white tail smack-dab in the middle of the circle. She had a startlingly pretty face, with a pink muzzle and blue eyes.

"She is a gift from Flint Striker." Strong Hand spoke to her. "She is a war-bonnet horse. She has special medicine and powers. Flint Striker gives her to you because her powers will protect you and bring you good magic."

Beside the pretty pinto, stood a solid and tough, mouse-colored dun horse, looking smart and wise and sensible. Frankie stared at the pony; now with it standing in the light from the kitchen windows, she could see it clearly—it was the buffalo-horse that had belonged to Gray Fox's father.

"He is called Čhánčhega, 'Drum'," Strong Hand told her. "He is Gray Fox's most prized horse. Gray Fox gives him to you."

Then, as Frankie looked at the sixth horse, she grinned and ducked her head. That horse was one she recognized, too—it was the tough sorrel gelding she had sent with the two warriors. She shook her head, suppressed a groan. It was back again. Like a bad penny.

Frankie looked at the six horses lined up before her. Gifts. Precious gifts from the Oglála people. This precious ceremony that the Oglála called the Wóotuh'an'otúh'aṅpi. She leaned against Strong Hand, suddenly understanding the honor of this gift-giving; suddenly afraid that she would crumble to her knees and start sobbing. He held her tight against him, his arm warm and strong around her shoulders. He waited for her. And when she was ready, he stood her up straight. She took a breath and did what she knew would calm her inside—she walked over to the horses.

One by one, Frankie talked to each horse, letting each horse know who she was. And one by one, she learned about each of the Indian ponies. She stroked their cheeks, touched their faces, tickled their lips. She blew softly into their nostrils; she whispered to them, rubbed behind their ears, slid her hands along their necks. Soft voice, slow touch. Letting them smell her, hear her, feel her. She stroked their necks and shoulders, scratched their withers, slid her hands along their ribs and backbones. Talking, listening, touching. Until she knew each pony; until each pony knew her.

The tri-colored mares, Frankie decided, were probably sisters. They thought alike; they moved alike. They were proud; they were definitely pretty and they definitely knew it.

The bay filly was, indeed, a two-year-old. She was strong and sturdy, just beginning to gain the size and weight of an adult. She was clearly smart, but more than that, she was a quick-thinker—and, she had a little knowing-glint in her deep brown eyes that seemed to say that she thought being a two-year-old was a pretty good thing. Frankie knew what her Uncle James would have said about the filly— he would have said that she was *too* clever. 'Train her right,' he would have said, 'and she'd be a fine mount. But no matter how well she's trained, she'll go find trouble the minute she's ignored.' In her own way, the bay filly was a bit like Sunny Jim. In that moment, Frankie named her Trouble.

Next to Trouble, the mostly-white pinto mare, the war-bonnet horse, stood watching everything around her. Her blue eyes were magical, piercing and soft at the same time. She was alert and watchful, and yet, remarkably calm. Frankie thought she showed a lot of wisdom and sensibility in her sky-blue eyes. She stood square and balanced; she was deep in the chest and narrow in the withers; she seemed perfect in every way. And with the perfectly round circle on her backside, Frankie named her Perfect Circle. And she had already fallen in love with her by the time she stepped to the next horse.

The dark-faced dun, with the dark stripe down his spine and the zebra-stripes on his legs, clearly remembered his little-white-girl; he welcomed himself back into her life, blowing his soft warm breath on her hair, and nibbling along her neck and shoulders. He tickled her arms and ribs with his lips. Nudged her gently. He belonged to her now, and he was showing that he knew it.

Frankie stepped over to the tough little sorrel—the horse Tipp Hyatt had left in her hands, the same horse she had put in the hands of the wounded warriors. The horse she had named Mystery. She stroked his face and neck; she laughed, accused him of being a bad penny for turning up again. She stroked his back, talking softly to him. But he had his own things to say. He was the same gentle-minded horse she had known, but he was pawing the ground and pushing his nose into her chest. Suddenly, Frankie understood; the mysterious little sorrel wasn't happy—and he would never be happy until he had a person of his own. Because he was the kind of horse that needed a person that belonged only to him.

A few months ago, through whatever means, he had lost his person; Tipp Hyatt had acquired him from God-knows-where. And in the sorrel's mind, he was still lost. He was a good and reliable horse; he was compliant; he was always agreeable. But he had been taken away from what he knew, taken away from his person, and now, he desperately needed to be *one* person's horse again. Frankie whispered to him; she assured him that she had an answer.

Once she had spent the time she needed with her gift-horses, Frankie turned and looked at the people around her, looking at her family—all of them smiling, all of them patient. All of them giving her the time she needed, giving her the time to honor the gift of the horses. Word would get back to Gray Fox and Flint Striker; they would be told of her love for the Indian ponies.

Then, while Blue Feather, Strong Hand and Frankie walked the gift-horses over to the gate of the front-pasture to release them for the night, the rest of her family walked toward the cookfire.

Standing at the pasture gate with her brothers, watching her six fine new horses trot off to greet their pasture-mates, Frankie leaned against Strong Hand for a moment, tucked herself against his chest; he wrapped his arms around her, pulled her in against him. He rocked her side to side, reminding Frankie of the way Septimus Travers used to do the same thing. She was remembering her soldier-boy and his warm gray-brown eyes; she was seeing him once again, and for just an instant, she could see his quick wink and his slow grin.

Strong Hand turned her around, draped his arm around her shoulders, and the three of them headed to the fire. Frankie was suddenly realizing how hungry she was, and when she said so, Strong Hand told her he was feeling that way too.

Frankie fell asleep in Strong Hand's lap by the cookfire; she woke up next to him, toasty-warm, tucked into his arms within his buffalo-robe. She stirred and felt the deep chill of the early dawn sifting into the robe, cool against her face and shoulders.

Through the opening at the top of the robe, Frankie could see that Whirlwind was already busy stirring the cookfire to life. Beside her Strong Hand eased out from the robe, and when Frankie started to follow him, he pushed her head back into the warmth of the robe, telling her to wait there until the fire warmed the air.

She stayed buried within the soft curls of buffalo hair, wriggling deeper into the warmth and away from the cold pre-dawn air, thinking about the evening and the arrival of the Oglála band. Remembering the solemn talk and the wonderful gifts. Remembering the six horses. Remembering how she sat in Strong Hand's lap by the fire while he shared his meal with her. The talk had gone on late into the night; there had been talk about the encampment and about the antelope hunt and about everything through the day. But there had been no talk about the Give-Away. Because it was not theirs to discuss.

Her mind turned to Dandelion, confused for a moment because she wasn't beside her within the robe. She thought for a few minutes, wondering why that was. Wondering where her sister was. Finally, remembering.

Dandelion and Little Mouse had piled onto the wagon with Everett and Ida when the full moon had shown itself. They traveled to the Dunbar homestead so they could sleep at the lodge of She Sews and Happy Man. And Blue Feather and He's Proud had ridden along.

The girls had been excited at the prospect of staying at the lodge of She Sews; they had been ecstatic they would be helping Happy Man with the kokóhéaxa, 'chickens' and the vé'ho'é-otóva'a, 'the white-man's buffalo' in the morning. And they would bring the heóve-ameške, 'the yellow-grease', and the ve'kea-hanoo'o, 'the sweet baked-things' to Fire Heart Child's home when they came back in the morning in the amó-ene'o, 'the rolling thing'.

"Ne-náestse, Nå-htona," 'Come here, my Daughter.' Whirlwind was calling to her, knowing she was awake. Telling her she must hurry. "We ride to the camp this morning. The women want to hunt the plants soon. There's much work to do today, because we leave tomorrow."

Frankie was shocked when she heard the last part. Stunned that the people would leave so soon. Wild Bird, though, must have anticipated her surprise and the disappointment that would follow.

"I will stay with you, Granddaughter." She patted Frankie on the head as Frankie emerged from under the robe. "Those who want to follow the hunt will leave, but you and I will stay here. We will hunt plants and roots instead of the buffalo. We will be happy here."

The old woman smiled at Frankie; she pointed her stick at her and then swung it, pointing to the front of her house.

"Go move your gifts into your lodge where they will be safe. Then come back and eat."

Frankie was up and darting away from the waving stick, dashing toward her house. She understood the admonitions to hurry, but the warning in the waving stick was enough to make her feet fly.

She heard Knife and Strong Hand laughing at the way she had run from the reach of the waving stick, accusing her of 'not being very brave this morning'. Frankie fired back a comment, saying she had learned to run from their grandmother's stick by watching them. They busted up laughing and Frankie ignored them as she reached the porch and grabbed up an armful of her sweet bounty and headed inside.

She kept making trips back and forth to the porch, loading her arms each time with the precious gifts, transferring them to her bedroom. Deciding to sort and arrange everything later. Finally, she only had the hides left; she dragged them along the floor, trying to decide where they should go, finally giving up on any immediate decisions, and deciding 'not to decide', as her father had counseled. She left them on the floor of the sitting-room.

Before she headed back to the fire with her belly rumbling from hunger, she changed into one of the new Oglála shirts; she fastened the beaded belt with the knife and its calf-tail sheath at her waist; she pulled on a pair of the new moccasins. Today, she decided, she would dress as an Oglála girl. And she would ride her Oglála buffalo-horse.

Strong Hand nodded when he saw her, pleased with her decision, understanding why she had chosen the Oglála clothes. He pulled her onto his lap and started stirring the long spoon in the pot, selecting bits of food for them. While they shared breakfast, he talked to her quietly about the Give-Away of the night before. He told her she was being wise in her choice to wear some of the gifts. And he said, that riding Drum to show her pleasure, was a good thing too.

But, he warned her, she should not speak of the gifts. Everything had been said last night. Any talk about the gifts would be boastful today. She would be calling attention to herself and it wouldn't be humble in the eyes of the Cheyenne. Or in the eyes of the Oglála.

Frankie ate the pieces of antelope and onion and sweet potato he handed her and watched him eating his own share, understanding two things. First, she knew he was being a big brother to her—helping her along by teaching her what she didn't know about the gift-giving—trying to spare her any shame and embarrassment. And second, she knew that out of everything in the stewpot, he liked the same foods she did—they both liked the meat and the onions and the sweet potatoes best.

The sun had just cleared the eastern horizon and was blanketing the Sand Hills with its warm rays when Frankie started out to the encampment with Whirlwind and Wild Bird. The Cheyenne and Oglála lodges with their crowns of lodgepoles stood just beyond the rows of apple trees; some nestled in among the trees of the riverside and some standing out in the open grasses.

All of them stood proud and tall, rising like conical sculptures with the buffalo-hide walls showing off their painted patterns to the morning sun. The poles of the smoke-flaps angled backward, letting smoke from the lodge fires rise and drift up into the morning sky. Pots were hanging over the cookfires outside, already simmering, their aromas swirling around and between the lodges, and out across the land.

To Frankie's eyes, there seemed to be a lot of lodges, more than she had ever seen before and when she said as much to Whirlwind, her Cheyenne mother laughed.

"There are more here in this camp than before," she said. "But there are many, many more in the encampment to the north where more of our people wait for us. Many more Cheyenne tipis and many more Oglála tipis. They camp beside the Niobrara—the spreading-water river. They will wait there for our bands to join them."

Frankie listened as she rode beside Whirlwind, balancing her two biggest dishpans across her lap and against Drum's withers; it made her smile, figuring it was probably the first time this wise and wonderful buffalo-horse of hers had ever carried such a thing. The dishpan was filled with cornbread and biscuits and two large crocks of butter and she had to keep shuffling and resetting her load to keep it steady.

When Mourning Dove came out from among the lodges and saw the dishpans full of sweet breads and butter, she called to the other women—telling them to hurry, because 'the sweet baked-things and the yellow-grease are here'. The women seemed to come from every-where at once. They started reaching for biscuits and squares of cornbread from the pans, and in less than a minute, Frankie gave up any thought of an orderly distribution. She passed both dishpans to the women, deciding to let them sort everything out for themselves.

There were both Oglála women and Cheyenne women standing around her and most of them had never tasted the sweet breads or the yellow-grease. Frankie watched as their smiles grew and their eyes widened with their surprise and delight. She laughed at them, teasing them and widening her own eyes to look like theirs. They laughed harder than she did, patting her hands and arms while they kept passing around the breads covered with great smears of the butter.

Off to one side, Frankie could see Gray Fox standing among a group of men, deep in some kind of discussion. But he had seen her—he was watching her sitting on Drum. She smiled at him and reminded herself to drop her eyes. She kept her eyes down as he walked toward her; he patted her knee as he passed her and turned his attention to the delicacies in the dishpans. Frankie grinned, remembering his love for cornbread and butter.

A moment later, she saw Flint Striker standing close to one of the dishpans, a square of corn bread in his hands. He caught her eye and grinned broadly as he took a sizeable bite from the chunk of cornbread. Then he gave her a nod, slight and slow. She saw it and gave back as good as she got, knowing they were both thinking back to the cornbread and butter from their days sitting in the sun, in front of the Wolf Den.

And then, Frankie saw a small form weaving through the crowd of Indian bodies and buckskin clothes. She saw the bright, flashing eyes—Wood Flute was working her way to Drum's side. Wood Flute reached up and Frankie reached down and her Oglála sister slipped up behind her on Drum's back.

She turned Drum and they trotted away from the noise and chattering of the crowd. They had their own talking and chattering to do. Frankie saw the little pearl-handled penknife hanging from a braided and beaded piece of rawhide around Wood Flute's neck. She smiled. Gray Fox had delivered the gift.

The midday sun was warming the land of the Sand Hills and it had been beating down on Frankie's back for the last two hours. Ida looked at Frankie and smiled, and Frankie smiled back. Even though the bending and kneeling was taking a toll on both of them, they were still pleased—because there was a lot of teaching and learning going on. The Cheyenne and Oglála women were showing them all the early spring plants, medicine-plants that could be used to cleanse the body from the heavy foods of the winter.

Frankie could remember her Aunt Sarah talking about using some of the early plants to purify the blood; there were other early spring plants that would clear and disinfect the liver and the kidneys. And now, here within the land of the Sand Hills, there were familiar fragrances from the same plants. Fragrances that took her mind back to the white house in Indiana. The same smells; the same plants. What grew there, grew here. And there were also new and different plants that grew out here in the Sand Hills—new and different plants that would work much the same way.

The women were pointing out the plants and showing her and Ida how to harvest them—teaching them to always leave some of the plants in the soil so they could continue growing. They talked about drying them and pounding them into powders. Much the same, Frankie thought, as her Aunt Sarah had done. And just exactly what she, herself, could do. These were plants that could be added

755

to the remedy-chest. More remedies; more powders for tonics and poultices.

There was a growing period for the different plants, too, and Frankie was intrigued when the women talked about how the plants grew and matured across the prairie. Moving east to west. These same plants—the ones they were picking now—would be done growing here and die back in a matter of weeks. But in another month, they would begin to emerge from the soil in the lands out to the west.

And that had Frankie thinking about making a short trip out to the west of the Middle and North Loup Rivers. Because these were plants she wanted in her remedy-box—it would be worth a journey to get more of these for drying in the root-cellar and pounding into powders. *Maybe, I'll just go on a little jaunt in a few weeks. Maybe a two-or-three-day ride. Or four days. Just to see what I find. Because I want more of these.*

After two hours or so, and with most of the women from the encampment gathering plants—along with Dandelion and Wood Flute and Ida and herself—Frankie could see the containers on the dog-travois were getting full. And that had her wondering about the Indian dog dragging the travois harnessed to its back. He had been with the foraging women all morning, with leather bags and rawhide boxes riding on the travois, dragging the ever-increasing load of roots and harvested leaves.

Looking at his perpetual grin, Frankie thought he didn't really seem to mind spending the morning hauling the dog-sized travois around. The *oeškésé-améstó'ee-seo'o*. The 'dog-tie-across-thing'. The big brown dog seemed to have a lot of patience in his character and didn't seem to mind that Matilda and Laughing Girl and the pups were running about free and unencumbered by the long-poled contraption like he was. She decided he handled the assigned duty a lot like the troopers at Fort Kearny did.

Septimus Travers had said once that 'orders don't change just because you go into a stomping fit'. The dog seemed to understand that concept because he looked like he was taking his lot as it came to him. He wasn't fighting the orders that had been handed to him—he just kept dragging his travois and grinning about it with his tongue lolling out one side of his mouth. Frankie decided that he was probably a pretty philosophical dog.

She glanced to her side and saw Dandelion and Wood Flute working right along with her; she gave Dandelion a second glance, still finding herself surprised to see her wearing the blue gingham blouse—the blue cloth looking sharp and bright against her dark skin.

Beyond the group of women bent over their tasks, Frankie could see a flash of bright rosy-calico as Little Mouse dashed through the grass, leaving the gathering party behind and running toward the lodges. Frankie smiled, knowing Little Mouse was abandoning the foraging women; no doubt, she was off on a search, her mind set on finding Happy Man.

It was an odd sight, seeing the bright blue cloth and the rosy-flowered cloth on the Cheyenne girls. It was Ida's doing—she had sewn the two blouses while the two girls were at the sod-house, working through the evening and probably late into the night. The pretty blue gingham blouse for Dandelion, was sewn to the same size and pattern as her buckskin shirt, with a fringe of white ribbons sewn along the neckline. Ida had made a similar one in a rosy calico, sized down for Little Mouse.

Dandelion was incredibly proud of the cotton shirt and Frankie decided it looked prettier on Dandelion than anyone else in the world—white *or* Indian. When the girls had returned to Frankie's meadow with Ida and Everett early in the morning, the Cheyenne and Oglála women coo-ed themselves crazy over the pretty shirts. And Frankie couldn't decide who was blushing and smiling more—the two girls, or Ida.

Frankie had teased Dandelion about becoming a little-white-girl, telling her she was going to have to learn English, and Dandelion surprised her with a handful of English words. And then she had chattered on in Cheyenne with a whole slew of stories to tell about their trip to the lodge of She Sews.

Dandelion told all the women about the lodge of She Sews and Happy Man, and how they had a white-man's buffalo, just like Fire Heart Child had, but it was spotted like an Indian pony. He's Proud and Blue Feather slept by a fire outside the lodge with Happy Man, she told them, but she and Little Mouse slept on a great 'white-cloud-thing' in the 'ground-lodge' with She Sews.

When Frankie asked her why she and Little Mouse were brave enough to go into She Sews' lodge but not into her own lodge right across the meadow, Dandelion collapsed into giggles and had no way of explaining why.

It was late in the morning when Frankie saw two riders coming toward the group of gatherers; Strong Hand and Knife were heading right toward her, leading her dun horse. She grinned, realizing her brothers were rescuing her from all the bending and cutting; they had some sort of adventure on their minds and she was to be a part of it.

She straightened up and leaned backward, stretching out her belly and relaxing her back muscles. She brushed off her hands as she waited for them. She told the women and her sisters goodbye as her brothers stopped beside her. She grabbed Drum's mane and swung up on his back; she put her heels to his ribs and turned his head to follow the two warriors into the grassy hills to the north.

They rode at an easy lope, riding through the winding valleys, staying in the lowlands between the hillsides. The two men talked back and forth as they rode along, and mostly, Frankie stayed quiet. Waiting to see what was in store; knowing they wouldn't tell her if she asked.

She figured they had traveled two or three miles when the men pulled their ponies to a stop in a narrow valley. They slipped off their horses and Frankie slid off Drum's back. When she turned to look at her brothers and saw the looks on their faces—sly grins and odd smirks—she suddenly started wishing she was back with the women, bending to pluck leaves and crawling on her knees to dig up the roots. Because the expressions on the faces of Strong Hand and Knife said *something* was in the works and it might not be a lot of fun for her. Their knowing glances were fair warning.

Frankie saw Knife take a step closer to her and she knew what was coming. She ducked as soon as she spotted his weight shifting and his foot lifting. An instant later, she yelped and dodged in the opposite direction as he sent a second kick her way, and then she managed to jump beyond the reach of his third kick coming hard and fast at her face.

To her side and almost beyond her view, Frankie saw another movement, Strong Hand was sending a kick toward her—she leaped sideways, ducking, then dropped into a crouch. Then, as Knife grabbed at her, she threw herself backward, rolling away from his reach.

As she came to her feet, Strong Hand reached for her; she ducked from his hand and flashed an ugly look at him. Snarled at him. In that moment, she decided to do what Knife had taught her—to stop reacting and start attacking.

She stepped forward, driving her left heel toward Strong Hand's knee. He dodged that kick and she stepped in again, moving fast as he twisted to the side—she sent her right heel toward the middle of his breechcloth, aiming for his crotch. He dodged again. Bursting into laughter.

Frankie leveled another kick at him and suddenly, she felt the air knocked out from her lungs and found herself sailing through the air. She smacked down on the ground, realizing it had been Knife's shin that made contact—he had come in behind her. *Dammit!*

She rolled and righted herself into a crouch. She stayed in the crouch, keeping low to the ground, gasping to get air back into her lungs. Spitting sandy-soil from her mouth. Spitting mad. Angry because they were laughing. She paused, wiping the dust from her eyes and found herself sailing through the air again, sent flying by a kick from Strong Hand. She rolled again, scrambled to her feet and caught a kick from Knife before she had a chance to regain her balance. *Dammit! Dammit!*

"Wake up, Little Sister! See your enemies, not the dirt in your eyes. The dirt will not hurt you."

Frankie knew what was going on—this was another lesson. There were things to be learned here. Life-lessons; life-and-death lessons. And they were teaching her.

"It takes two Cheyenne warriors to fight this little-white-girl? That's not fair, Brothers." Frankie leaped to avoid one of Knife's heels. Dropped down, ducking from a forearm blow—a forearm she assumed belonged to Strong Hand.

"That's war, Little-White-Girl. You don't always get to choose the enemies who attack you." Strong Hand twisted and dodged as she sent a heel-kick his way. He laughed and swung his leg, knocking her grounded foot out from under her.

Frankie smacked down in the dirt, twisted away from a hand snatching at her shoulder; she squirmed and turned and rolled to her feet. She took a step back, and then another. Swiped at the dirt on her lips. She glared at Strong Hand and spit dirt from her mouth. She called him a bastard, spitting out the word in English and hoping he understood its meaning by the ugly tone she attached to it.

The two warriors busted up laughing and Knife told Strong Hand that if Fire Heart Child put that kind of ugliness into her kicks, she'd be a better fighter. Frankie launched at Strong Hand, deciding to catch him off-guard while he was laughing. It didn't work. She ended up taking an elbow in her side and found herself gulping for another breath of air. Once again. *Dammit to hell!*

"I thought you taught this little-white-girl to fight, Brother. Did she not learn? Or did you not teach her well?"

The fighting had stopped; at least, for the time being. Frankie wasn't sure how much time she'd have before they started up again, so she bent forward, hands on her knees, pulling air into her lungs. Eyeing the two warriors. Wary. Not at all sure they'd give her fair warning about whatever else they had in mind. *Bastards!*

She glanced around the meadow. The horses were grazing, ignoring the battle of the Cheyenne-warriors and the little-white-girl. The grass was rippling in the wind; hawks were circling above in the prairie sky. The Cheyenne warriors were standing side-by-side. Grinning. Talking softly. *Planning something.*

Frankie stayed as she was, letting them think she wasn't paying attention. Hoping it might give her an advantage. At least, a little one. In case they tried something else. She looked at them standing in front of her, beyond her reach.

They both shed their buckskin shirts and stood there in the shining sunlight, their skin glossy from the bear-grease. The breeze moving through the meadow grasses was sifting through the loose strands of Knife's hair and the fringes on his leggings; his necklace with the buck-killing bullet rested on his chest, the sunlight glinting on the beads threaded onto the rawhide beside the lead bullet. The feathers hanging from Strong Hand's braids lifted and flitted in the breeze, rippling. Flowing like the grasses on the hillsides.

She started to pull her antelope shirt over her shoulders, then hesitated, eyeing the distance between her and her brothers. Cautious suddenly. Realizing that she would be vulnerable the instant she started pulling her shirt over her head. Knowing they might have planned for the moment. Suspecting that they might just be setting her up for another lesson about letting her guard down.

They both saw her pause and they both knew why. They burst into laughter again.

"No, Little Sister. We have more for you to learn, but take your shirt off. You'll need the free movement." Strong Hand was grinning at her.

"Do I need grease on me, too? Because you two have it."

"No. You'll be plenty slippery from your sweat by the time we're done."

She watched Strong Hand's eyes, seeing the tease and the love. Seeing how much he cared. This part of lesson, she realized, had been just to get her ready. She had taken their hits and kicks and she had ended up on the ground more times than a few. The fighting had been rough, but none of it had been harsh or hard. Not once had they caused a real injury.

But they had made her work hard; they had made her move swiftly; they had made her think fast. And that had been their intent. Now, though, they had more things to teach her—more ways to keep her safe.

761

And a moment later, the rest of the lesson began. They went at it again and both men started putting her through every move she knew, working her once again, teaching her more about the use of the elbows and the knees and the kicks. They schooled her in more of the ways of Cheyenne fighting. They had her swinging and swirling and kicking, striking at them as they called to her. Yelling to distract her. Whistling and shrieking to confuse her. Working her mind, as much as her body and limbs—teaching her to stay focused, to keep her concentration and attention on her target. They worked her long, and they worked her hard.

Frankie learned that the swift twists and turns, the crouching and weaving was Knife's style. His was medicine from the weasel. Strong Hand, though, had badger medicine and his moves were hard and surging with fierce power and a ferocious response.

They taught her both kinds of fighting and both kinds of power; then they had her blend both together and choose what she needed to find her own response. The combination of the two, added to her wolf-medicine, they said, would allow her to be at her strongest.

Because the prairie-wolf knew, Strong Hand said, the prairie-wolf always knew when to move away and when to move in. A prairie-wolf knew how to observe and assess; it knew how to stay out of sight and out of reach, and it knew when to launch an attack and move forward into danger. A wolf knew how to read its enemy and how to time its own response. And it knew when to wait, when to den-up, and when to slip away.

For hours on that early spring afternoon, the warriors taught her; they trained her; they laughed and teased, grunted and growled. They pushed her and led her. They took her ability to observe and assess, and they showed her how it allowed the wolf to survive. They talked to her about instinct from the gut and the heart, and how those instincts gave the wolf the wisdom it needed to survive. And the power it needed to win.

Understanding the wolf's power seemed to give her kicks more strength; it made the moves cleaner and meaner. More confident. More accurate. Frankie didn't understand how it happened that way; Strong Hand and Knife just laughed when she asked about

762

it. They said she shouldn't try to understand it. She should trust her wolf-medicine, and use the weasel and the badger to make the wolf-medicine stronger.

When they were content with what she had learned, they let her stop. They all rested in the grasses, leaning back against the slope of a hill, letting the breeze cool them. Frankie lay there, relaxing in the sunlight, feeling the air drying the sweat on her face and neck, on her arms and her chest. On her legs. *Strong Hand was right. I got plenty slippery.*

They stayed where they were, resting and recovering, and then Knife brought water, jerky, and parched corn from a leather pouch on Magpie's surcingle. They shared the food and spent the time laughing about the fighting, laughing at each other. Then they lay back against the hill and rested some more.

Frankie woke to Knife's fingers tickling her side. The sun had moved, time had passed and she realized she had been napping there against the hillside.

"We all slept, Sister. We all needed to rest." Knife explained to her. "You made us work too hard." He rolled on top of her and tickled her until she was out of breath from giggling and squirming.

When Knife finally rolled off her and stood up, Strong Hand reached down and pulled her to her feet; he tossed her belly-down across his shoulder, carrying her as they walked to the horses, talking the whole way about how Fire Heart Child was learning to fight. He called out to the skies, telling the world how brave and fierce and wild she was. Laughing and teasing and tickling her thighs while she was flopped across his shoulder.

Frankie laughed the whole way, accepting the teasing, hearing the praise hidden in the teasing. Because that's how her brothers were. That's how they were letting her know she had done well. Because it was the Cheyenne way.

When they reached the horses, Strong Hand tossed her on her buffalo-horse and handed her her buckskin shirt. He and Knife swung up on their own horses as she pulled her shirt over her head.

Frankie rode back to her valley with her brothers riding to each side of her, feeling the heat of the late afternoon sun on her face. They were all silent now—the lesson and the talk and the teasing was over. Now, they let their ponies pick the path back to the encampment.

Part of the time, Frankie rode with her eyes closed against the bright rays of the sun, and part of the time, she watched Strong Hand and Knife riding beside her. Watching them on their horses—Strong Hand on his red roan and Knife on his pinto—she realized that she rode the same way. Her thighs moved with her horse's sides, following the sway of her horse's back, the same as theirs did.

And when she saw the sun against their dark skin, she looked to her own arms and her belly and thighs. She smiled, because the sun would do its own work on her skin; it was already starting to darken her skin again; it was starting to give her the brown skin-color again, the color she had lost during the winter months. She grinned because she was becoming Cheyenne again.

Strong Hand touched her shoulder, taking her away from her thoughts.

"Fire Heart Child. Where will the buffalo be waiting for us?" Strong Hand was looking straight ahead.

"North and to the east. Five or six sleeps beyond the Niobrara. They'll be there." Frankie gasped and pulled hard on Drum's rein, stopping him suddenly. She stared at Strong Hand, shocked at how she had answered his question, surprised she had spoken about buffalo that way. She had seen no buffalo herds; she had no idea where the buffalo were, or where they would be waiting. These people needed buffalo to live; to hunt. They didn't need a little-white-girl blurting out some silly nonsense.

She stared at Strong Hand; she shook her head and tried to explain that she was wrong. She had said that about the buffalo, she told him, but she didn't really know.

"I don't know why I said that. Because I don't know, Brother." She reached to grab his arm. "Please, Strong Hand, don't go there because I said that. The buffalo might be somewhere else. I just said it without thinking."

He leaned toward her and put his hand to the back of her head, kept his hand there for a moment. He told her not to worry. Because, he said, she *did* know.

"The ancestors know. You know because you were listening to them. Do not worry, Little Sister." He grinned at Knife and Knife was grinning at him.

Knife reached across and lifted her from Drum and pulled her over to Magpie; he sat her in front of him, nuzzled her low on her neck while he laughed. He told her not to worry.

"We know how to listen, too, Fire Heart Child. We heard the message that came with your words. There will be buffalo to the north, and then to the east. Five or six sleeps beyond the Spreading-Water River."

The next morning, by the time the sun rose above the faraway hills, the village had been taken down. The entire encampment had disappeared from the land faster than it had appeared—the cook-fires, the lodges, the tripod-racks for the warriors' shields and weapons were all gone. Everything was packed away. Packs with the life-goods of the Indian families were already strapped onto packhorses or loaded onto the travois.

Frankie watched in stunned silence; it had happened so fast. She thought she would have more time, but now as she rode through what had been the encampment, the last ponies were being loaded. The herd boys were already moving the loose herd northward. The women and children were already mounting their horses; the Cheyenne and Oglála were leaving. Her whole family was heading north to hunt.

Already, far out to the north, she could see a group of riders— the men who would ride ahead of the main band. She knew who they were and why they rode ahead—some were scouts who would search for buffalo. Some were watchers, who would look for any danger to their people as they traveled. And somewhere among the lead riders, there would be a few old men.

They were men who knew the secrets of the land, the men who would know how to find the best water and grazing for the next camp. And some of them would be carrying drums that they would play for the group of boys who were following them—older boys who were not quite men—the boys known as the Grass Dancers. And once the old men chose the campsite, the Grass Dancers would prepare the site; they would begin their dances, dancing to the drums and the songs to lay the grass down. Dancing for their people, dancing to honor the grass of the earth, dancing to protect the grass so it would rise again after the people moved on.

Now, as the sun cleared the eastern horizon and the morning sky brightened, Frankie sat on Fox's back, holding the lead-rope of the mystery-sorrel, watching the Cheyenne and Oglála leave her homestead. The last signs of the camp had disappeared; the people who had filled her life with stories and laughter and lessons were leaving. The last of the riders moved away from what had been the river encampment, heading into the Sand Hills. Riding slowly and steadily to the north, riding in search of some great buffalo herd that roamed the land beyond the spreading-water river.

Frankie could see Knife and Strong Hand, sitting on their ponies halfway up the slope of a hill, watching as the families began their journey into the hills. She saw the two men rein their ponies, sending them down the slope to join Whirlwind and Willow and Mourning Dove at the rear of the band. She saw Knife motion to her, beckoning. Grinning at her. Inviting her to join them, to ride with the people. For a while.

She turned Fox's head and lifted him into a lope to catch up with them, tugging on the mystery-sorrel's lead-rope. Ahead of them, Frankie saw He's Proud and Dandelion halt their ponies, letting the line of packhorses and travois move ahead. They were waiting for her too. She caught up with Knife and Strong Hand. And in another fifty yards, the three of them caught up with He's Proud and Dandelion. Frankie moved Fox up to walk next to the flea-bitten gray and smiled when Dandelion reached over to pat her arm.

"Na-semahe." 'My Sister.'

"Héehe-e. Na-semahe." 'Yes. My Sister.' Frankie nodded, meeting the eyes of the girl who was the only sister she had ever known. *Well, her and Wood Flute.*

Her mind flicked back to the bank of the Little Blue River, thinking about her Aunt Sarah and her Uncle James. Wondering, suddenly, what they would think about her sisters. Wondering if they would love them the way she did. Wondering how it would be, if that family—her aunt and uncle and her four cousins—had lived and had all traveled here to the meadow together. Wondering if she would have even met Strong Hand and Knife and Blue Feather out on the prairie if her aunt and uncle and cousins had been alive. She wondered if her white family was living here, would the Cheyenne and Oglála families still come and visit.

"What do you look for, Sister?" Dandelion's dark eyes were on her, watching her; Frankie realized she had been scanning the band of people while her mind had been wandering.

"For Wood Flute. I see Young Doe ahead, but not our sister."

She had been scanning the line of riders, looking among the Oglála women, unable to see the girl among them. Feeling worried suddenly, feeling a little desperate. Because she needed to find her; because there was something she had to do.

And then Dandelion tapped her arm.

"Šungíla Hóta." 'Gray Fox.' Dandelion pointed to a rider on a hilltop far ahead, near the front of the traveling band.

He was there on the crest of the hill, sitting on his bay—the horse she knew so well, the one she had hidden in place sight from the troopers—watching the parade of Cheyenne and Oglála people pass below him. And there, sitting behind him on the bay, was her other sister. Čhán Šiyóthanka. 'Wood Flute'.

"Go see your sister, Fire Heart Child. Go and show her what you have for her." It was Strong Hand speaking to her, his hand pressing on her thigh. "Then, you should go back to Wild Bird. She'll be watching for you."

Frankie looked at her brother, looking into his dark eyes, realizing that he knew what she planned to do. She had said nothing to anyone, but he knew. *Probably, Knife knows too.* She looked at Knife riding on Magpie on the far side of Strong Hand; he wasn't looking at her—he was looking straight ahead. But he had a slight smile on his face. *He does know.* She wondered about her two brothers, wondering how they knew. Then she saw He's Proud riding beside Knife, leaning forward so he could see her, grinning at her. He knew too. *They all know why I brought the mystery-horse.*

Dandelion tapped her arm, and suddenly, the flea-bit gray was whirling away, half-rearing, before dashing off, its hooves churning up the sandy soil. Frankie leaned forward and Fox launched after the gray horse with the mystery-sorrel racing right beside him.

The three horses charged through the hard-grass of the valley in a wild race to the hill. As they surged up the hill in a headlong run, Frankie could see the amusement on Gray Fox's face. She could see the excitement on Wood Flute's face; Frankie could see her wide smile and she could hear her laughter.

They topped the hill and pulled up beside Gray Fox's bay; Frankie beckoned to Wood Flute; she reached out to her Oglála sister, holding the bridle reins of the mystery-sorrel. Handing them to her.

"He needs to go with you, Sister. He wants to go back to live with your people and to be your horse. Keep him with you so he can be happy."

Wood Flute squealed her delight; she was on the sorrel's back in a single move, stroking his shoulders and speaking to him. She leaned forward, wrapping her arms around his neck. When she sat up again, she ran her fingers through his mane. Then she turned to look at Frankie; she gave her widest smile and Frankie knew that it was a smile of freedom. Because out here on the open lands, a horse meant freedom.

Wood Flute turned the sorrel's head, locked eyes with Dandelion, her Cheyenne sister. Dandelion said something to her, something about a race, but Frankie didn't hear all her words. The two girls spun their ponies and sent them down the hillside.

Frankie, though, stayed where she was; she stayed by Gray Fox. He sidestepped the bay horse, moving closer to her. She looked at him as he smiled at her, listening to his words as he spoke softly to her. He touched his hand to her cheek.

"Wakhánheža," he said. 'My child.' His eyes stayed on her. "We are your people, Fire Heart Child. Someday," he said, "you will come to visit your Oglála family."

He laid his hand on her shoulder and they stayed as they were, sitting side-by-side, watching Dandelion and Wood Flute in a hard gallop, racing up the long valley. Passing the long line of Cheyenne and Oglála at a dead-run. Their ponies were still churning up the sandy soil with their hooves as they passed the herd-boys with the great herd of loose ponies—ponies of every color.

Frankie stayed beside Gray Fox, watching as the long line of people passed below. She could see the people looking up; she could hear as a few shouted out her name. They laughed; they waved to her. And they rode on. Going north. Notama, the Cheyenne called it. Wazíyata, according to the Oglála. Going to the buffalo. Hótóa'e in Cheyenne. Tatanka, in Lakota.

At the back of the traveling band, she saw the red roan and the black-and-white pinto. Strong Hand and Knife. He's Proud on his buckskin. Whirlwind on her bay pinto and Willow on her stout palomino. Mourning Dove was there too. And her husband, Charging Crow, the Oglála man who made the blend for the long pipe was there too, riding beside Strong Hand.

Frankie gave Gray Fox a last look and he nodded. Knowing what she knew—the time had come for her to go back. She reined her red-and-white pinto war-horse, turning away from Gray Fox, turning away from the long valley the Cheyenne and Oglála were following.

She rode away, going down the slope on the far side of the hill. Away from the people she loved; putting the hill between her and them. Because she didn't want to watch them leaving. Not anymore. She had said her good-byes. For now, they were traveling to the north. Notama. She would see them again when they returned. And now, she would go home. Home to her meadow.

She gave Fox his head, relying on him to find the way back to the meadow because she could only see a blur of the colors of the Sand Hills now. Tears were flooding her eyes and the watery-film was making all the different browns and yellows and greens of the grasses of the prairie float together in a soppy-swirly mess. The tears were rising. And her heart was breaking. She knew her heart was breaking again, because she recognized the feeling.

A moment later, a yellow-breasted bird burst up from the grasses in front of Fox; Frankie spotted the black V-shaped breast-mark as it whirled away, in a hurried flurry of feathers and flight. *Honóxeaso! Meadowlark!* Frankie grinned, knowing what that meant. *The meadowlarks are back. Winter's over. Well, except for one more snowstorm. Because there's always one more snow after the first meadowlarks return. Because Wild Bird said so.*

But even with another snowstorm coming to the Sand Hills, the bright greens and the silvery greens, the blue greens and the yellow greens of the grasses would keep rising from the soil as the days passed. The new plants, the leafy-plants and the root-plants and the medicine-plants that the Cheyenne and Oglála women had shown her would keep sprouting up. Seeking the light, reaching to the sun.

Frankie's mind went back to what the women had shown her about the different medicine plants. The healing plants. Plants that she needed for her remedy-chest. So for the next week or so, she would keep searching for them here along the river. But the women had said something else, and Frankie could hear their words again— those plants, they said, would be growing to the west of here in another month. And further west after that. They would grow as the sun warmed the land; the plants would move west, pushed by the sun. So she could follow them to the west. Following them and harvesting them. It was a nice thought, and maybe, she thought, it could become a plan.

It might just be a fine adventure for a few days. To ride out on the prairie again. Alone again. Spending some time following the plants as they grow. And then, they can hang and dry in the root-cellar. Maybe it'd be nice to see some of the hills to the west. Maybe.

Frankie mulled over the idea, turning it around in her mind, trying to keep her thoughts off her Cheyenne and Oglála families riding away into the hills. She laid the rein across Fox's withers, letting him continue to the meadow. And with the thought of her meadow, suddenly, Frankie was smiling again; she started wiping at the tears that had been trailing down her cheeks. Happy again, because she knew who would be waiting there in the meadow for her. Wild Bird would be there. *Waiting for her little-white-granddaughter. Probably waving her Cheyenne stick. Calling for her to come and fill her belly.*

Frankie pictured the old Cheyenne woman stirring the coals in the cookfire. She would probably have antelope meat roasting on the spit. And probably, she'd have a skinned-out rabbit from Laughing Girl's pre-dawn hunt, stretched out on the spit beside it. Everything would be fine again; because Wild Bird would make it all be fine.

And later, she and Wild Bird would go hunting for plants together. And just maybe, Wild Bird would help her fasten a dog-sized travois to Laughing Girl's back. And later in the day, Frankie decided, she would put a bridle on her marvelous blue-eyed war-bonnet horse and go for a ride. Just to feel what it was like to ride a magical war-bonnet horse. A magical horse with a perfect circle on its bottom.

And maybe tomorrow, Ida and Everett would come visiting. Their sleek brown mare and their sleek brown gelding would come trotting into the meadow, pulling the light spring-wagon; Ida would be waving her hankie and Everett would be smiling. They'd come to visit because they'd be feeling a little lonely too. Because they'd be missing the Cheyenne and Oglála families too.

Frankie's mind drifted out across the Sand Hills, picturing Dandelion and Wood Flute on their horses. They would be riding together now. Side-by-side. *One on a flea-bitten gray and one on a bright, coppery-sorrel. Probably, racing through the prairie grasses together. Probably, laughing. And come summer, or maybe in the fall, they'll be back. We'll all ride together when they come through here again.*

But at least, the mysterious sorrel was gone again—he had gone to live with his new person. And Frankie thought that was probably a good thing all the way around. Wood Flute would be happy with the sorrel; the sorrel would be happy with Wood Flute. And Frankie was happy enough that the mysterious sorrel was gone from her place once again. *Maybe for good this time.*

And for whatever reason, Tipp Hyatt had been plenty happy that the sorrel was out of his hands. Because with the Hyatt brothers, there was no way of telling exactly where that mystery-horse had actually come from. Frankie grinned and shook her head, thinking about the Hyatt brothers—George Washington Hyatt and William Henry Harrison Hyatt. *They're always driving a fine-looking team. You just never see them driving the same team twice.*

Frankie rode through the grassy-flats where the encampment had been; she eyed the circles of flattened grass where the lodges had stood, smiling, because she knew that within a few days, the grasses would begin to rise up again. She rode on, passing beside the rows of apple trees, and then she turned Fox onto the track and rode up and over, around and down into her meadow. Matilda and Laughing Girl, Too Shy and Ghost Dog met her at the bottom of the entrance. Laughing Girl was grinning her wolfish-grin, the pups had their tongues hanging out the sides of their mouths. Matilda was wiggling and waggling herself in a circle, showing her toothy-grin. Happy with the world.

And off to her left, over at the lodge by the windmill pool, Frankie saw old Wild Bird standing by the cookpot, waving her Cheyenne stick in the air. Calling to her.

"Ne-náestse." 'Come here.'

Sure enough, there was meat on the spit—a long strip of dark meat. And the skinned carcass of a rabbit on the spit right next to it. Frankie grinned and slid down from her red-and-white pinto's back. Released him to graze. She walked over to Wild Bird's lodge. Smiling, realizing that everything was fine on her homestead. Everything was back to normal in the meadow. A new normal.

ILLUSTRATIONS

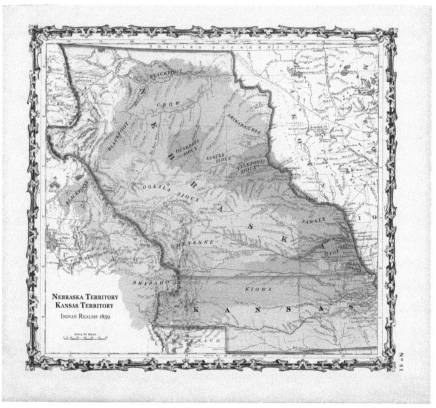

If you suspect this (seen in actual color on the book-cover) is the 'pretty-colored map' that Frankie carried with her to her homestead—the one that showed the historic Cheyenne Trail that led her home—then you're on the mark. While historically accurate, for the sake of this novel, this map is actually an artist's compilation of four such maps that were in circulation from 1859-1863. (All included within the author's private collection.)

It's worthwhile to note that from the early 1850s to the 1880s, and beyond, *numerous and differing* maps of the state boundaries, the territorial regions and the tribal realms were being designed, produced and distributed every year. The state and territorial maps changed often enough; the maps related to Native American Tribes changed even more often.

The constantly changing maps were being issued by the constantly changing governmental departments, for each department's own reasons and purposes. The boundaries of the states, territories, and Indian lands were being altered often—some by legal prescription, some by political perception. The resulting depictions were always dependent upon which governmental department issued the maps, in which part of which year, and also, according to which contractor was retained to provide the advice, guidance and land-surveys to the given department.

Typically, the maps designating Indian *'territories or reservations'*—due to treaties and negotiations—usually showed harsher divisional lines, often showing blocked regions with squared boundaries established by proposed government surveys. Whereas, the maps which depicted Indian *'realms'* tended to be more free-form with relaxed borders that often corresponded to rivers and other geographical features.

This 'pretty-colored map' that Frankie Harding treasured, depicts the 'realms' of indicated tribes showing the more free-form boundaries. While *slightly* more realistic in regard to general tribal realms—from approximately 1858 to 1863—the maps had still been developed and designed by a government that had no true understanding of the life and culture of the indigenous peoples. In reality, none of the Native American tribes during that period would have agreed with, nor even been slightly concerned by, the perceptions, or designations by the government in Washington. But, it still made for a 'pretty-colored map'. And, it did serve to get Frankie home.

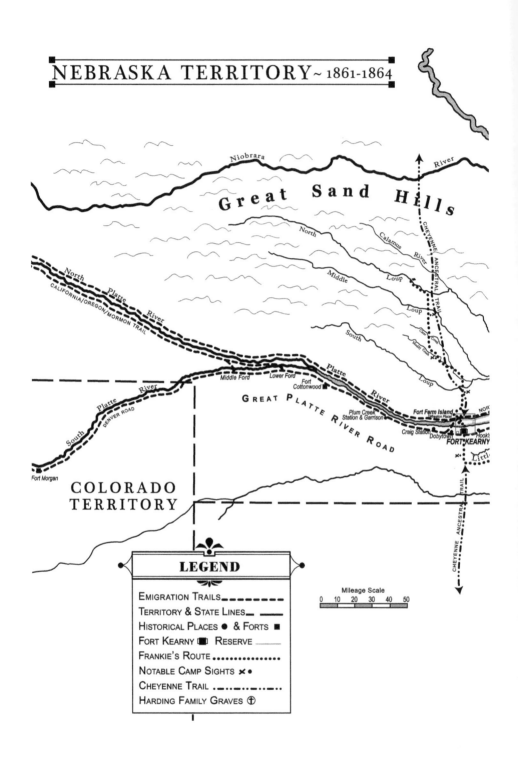

NEBRASKA TERRITORY ~ 1861-1864

Niobrara   River

Great Sand Hills

North   Calamus   River
Middle
Loup
North
Platte
CALIFORNIA/OREGON/MORMON TRAIL   River
South   Loup
Loup

CHEYENNE ANCESTRAL TRAIL

South   Platte   River   Middle Ford   Lower Ford   Fort
DENVER ROAD   Cottonwood

GREAT PLATTE RIVER ROAD

Plum Creek
Station & Garrison   Fort Farm Island
                          (Wheaton Place)   NOR

South   Platte   River   Craig Station   Dobytown   Hook
Fort Morgan   FORT KEARNY

COLORADO
TERRITORY   Littl

CHEYENNE ANCESTRAL TRAIL

LEGEND

Emigration Trails ___ ___ ___
Territory & State Lines ___ ____
Historical Places ● & Forts ■
Fort Kearny ▦ Reserve _____
Frankie's Route ....
Notable Camp Sights ✕ ●
Cheyenne Trail ._.._.._..
Harding Family Graves ✟

Mileage Scale
0   10   20   30   40   50

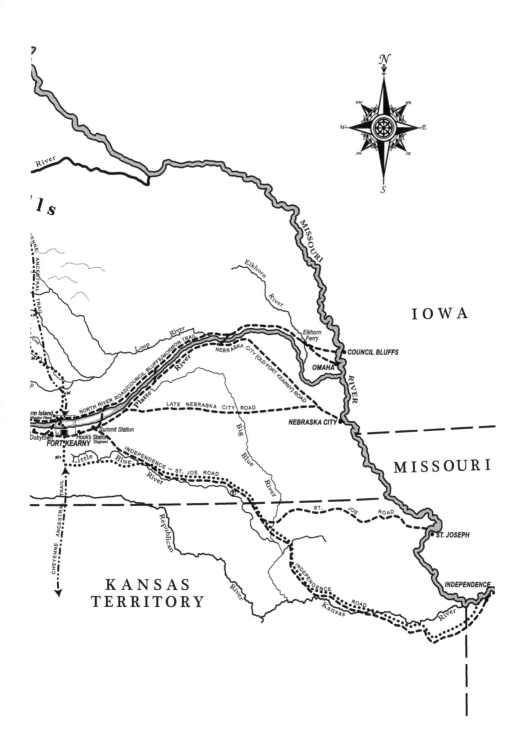

MISSOURI RIVER

Niobrara River

Great Sand Hills

North Loup

Middle Loup

Calamus River

CHEYENNE ANCESTRAL TRAIL

NEBRASKA
TERRITORY
~ 1861-1864 ~

SETTLERS' TRAIL

South Loup

Clear Creek

Muddy Creek

Loup River

Platte River

Fort Cottonwood

Plum Creek Station & Garrison

Fort Farm Island (Wheaton Place)

Craig Station

Dobytown

FORT KEARNY

Hook's Station (Dogtown)

Summit Station

NORTH RIVER ROAD/COUNCIL BLUFFS/MORMON TRAIL

Platte River

Big Blue River

LATE NEBRASKA CITY ROAD

INDEPENDENCE – ST. JOE ROAD

Little Blue River

Republican River

CHEYENNE ANCESTRAL TRAIL

LEGEND

CHEYENNE ANCESTRAL TRAIL ·-··-··
FRANKIE'S ROUTE ●●●●●●●●●●
SETTLERS' TRAIL ·—··—
HARDING FAMILY GRAVES ✝
WHEATON PLACE ✪
A) CAMPSITE WITH SOLDIERS
B) HIDDEN VALLEY CAMP
C) MUDDY CREEK CAMP
D) CONICAL HILL CAMP
E) MIDDLE LOUP SETTLEMENT
F) DUNBAR HOMESTEAD
G) FRANKIE'S HOMESTEAD

Mileage Scale
0   10   20   30   40

KANSAS
TERRITORY

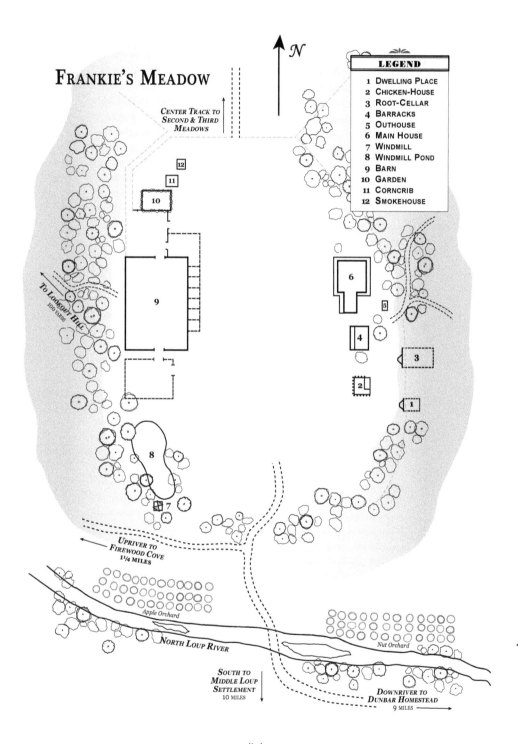

FRANKIE'S MEADOW

CENTER TRACK TO
SECOND & THIRD
MEADOWS

LEGEND

1 DWELLING PLACE
2 CHICKEN-HOUSE
3 ROOT-CELLAR
4 BARRACKS
5 OUTHOUSE
6 MAIN HOUSE
7 WINDMILL
8 WINDMILL POND
9 BARN
10 GARDEN
11 CORNCRIB
12 SMOKEHOUSE

TO LOOKOUT HILL
100 YARDS

UPRIVER TO
FIREWOOD COVE
1¼ MILES

Apple Orchard

NORTH LOUP RIVER

Nut Orchard

SOUTH TO
MIDDLE LOUP
SETTLEMENT
10 MILES

DOWNRIVER TO
DUNBAR HOMESTEAD
9 MILES

(iv)

 Afterword

The Homesteads
   The Laws
   The Loopholes
   The Reality

The Homesteaders

The Descendants

AFTERWORD

THE HOMESTEADS

At various times in my childhood and early adulthood, while visiting with farming and ranching families in the Nebraska Sand Hills, I heard the family stories about homesteading in the 1800s; I listened to remembered tales and re-told stories—some sweet and endearing, some sad and troubling, some wild and hilarious.

And always, I heard those tellers-of-tales using terms such as 'quarter-sections' and 'tree-claims' and the 'Kincaid Act'. Likewise, terms like 'turkey-foot markers', 'pulling up stakes', 'claim-jumping', and 'proving-up' were thrown about as the memories rose and the stories were told. Those somewhat random terms and fleeting references to homesteading history became familiar enough to me, but they all had rather vague meanings in my mind.

Over time, I came to have a general understanding of the 'homestead acts' and their historical significance. I knew that the homestead laws were created to encourage and allow for the settlement of the western territories which took place mainly during the late 1800s. I gained a general knowledge of the existence of at least some of the various legislated homesteading acts. I also knew that additional and amended homestead laws had been implemented over a span of several decades; they were created in a continuing effort to address the legislative oversights, the administrative ignorance, the rising problems, and the changing circumstances that reared their heads during the decades involved with 'the homesteading of the West'.

Years later, as I was well into writing *Homestead*, I realized that my general understanding of the history and legislation involved with the homesteading of the West was woefully inadequate. And as

I followed Frankie into her life on her homestead—as she allowed me to tramp along with her through the Nebraska Sand Hills—it finally dawned on me that I would need to delve deep into the intricate the history of homesteading.

I chalk up that rather slow awakening to the fact that, while I tend to be a quick study in a lot of ways in my life, sometimes, I can be a bit slow on the uptake. It gradually became apparent to me that I had an obligation—to both the novel and the readers—to provide some historical clarity regarding, not just the homestead legislation, but all the rules and regulations involved with it.

When I realized that, I surrendered to the idea and decided to spend the necessary time digging into all the specific laws that governed the process of homesteading. I admit here that I was, initially, a bit annoyed with the idea of having to seek out all the details of the implementation and administration of the homesteading legislation.

But as I went deeper into the story behind the legislative and political aspects of the homestead acts, the subject began to grow on me. I became intrigued. Intensely intrigued. And in a lovely little twist, my search for the truth ended up leading me back to some of my former haunts in Washington, DC, and offered me the opportunity to revive a few friendships and to reconnect with a handful of former contacts.

True to their characters, those individuals extended themselves for the sake of this novel and began guiding me on this journey of discovery. They encouraged me; they shared their knowledge; they searched the hidden halls where records are stacked ceiling-high. Together, we delved into the records of the National Archives. We located files and records in the back offices of the Senate Historian in the US Capitol. We also did a deep dive into the vast resources in the backrooms of the Library of Congress. And ultimately, I learned what I needed to learn—both for *Homestead* and for you, the reader.

Predictably, with all the information and history regarding the homesteading legislation, there was plenty of 'dry and boring stuff' to wade through. And lucky for you, I'm not going to pass on the great bulk of it to you in these pages. I'll give you enough information to provide what I hope to be a solid foundation, but I won't go much beyond that.

I will mention here, that settling the West was a political process from the beginning, which meant there was a lot of political wrangling, a lot of legal arguments, and a *whole* lot of political treachery involved. Suffice to say, with every piece of homesteading legislation (or attempted legislation)—as with anything involved with the congressional and administrative processes that swirl around 'law-making'—there was some good stuff happening. And there was some ugly stuff.

But to get back on track here, the purpose of the homesteading acts—as you likely remember from your grade-school and high-school history lessons—was to inspire the settlement of the western territories of the United States. The whole point was to 'grow a nation'. That in itself may not have been a bad concept—at least, in terms of the purposes the United States government had in mind.

But while the reasoning might have had a sound foundation, the application had many flaws—not untypical of other government programs, both past and present. That's especially true when the application and implementation are under the direction of individuals with little or no knowledge of that which they are attempting to govern. That's where reasoning can go awry, implementation can be twisted, and administration can be inept and, often, corrupt.

Regarding the legislation for the 'settling of the West', there were six Homestead Acts and amendments, all of which were passed and instituted during the late 1800s and early 1900s—all in the effort to settle the vast lands of the plains and mountainous regions of the West. Sometimes, the acts and amendments were a sensible response to the natural changes and expansion during the homesteading process. More often than not, they were enacted because, in hindsight, there was a need to adjust and correct the actual shortcomings and failures of the homestead acts already in place.

That was because, in reality, there were very few individuals involved in the homestead legislation who showed any level of responsible foresight for the actual enactment of the programs. Few had any clear understanding, experience, or concern for the lands that were being opened for settlement. Nor was there any advisory avenue in place to ensure a true understanding of the soils and lands, the climates, or the variability in the geography and topography of the regions to be settled and governed.

Few legislators or administrators seemed to have any understanding of the crucial importance of those factors. Even fewer seemed to have any level of compassion or concern for the needs, the lives, or the futures of the people who would actually be settling on those lands.

As I immersed myself into studying the legislative leadership, the legal foundations, and the practical applications of the various homesteading acts, I learned about all that. And I learned far more than I expected—I learned about the good and the bad, the ugly and the amusing. I learned about the reality and the distortions, the truth and the lies. And I came to understand about the dreams realized and the dreams destroyed.

THE LAWS

There were a series of federal legislative bills introduced in Congress between 1841 and 1916, most originating in the House of Representatives, which sought to grant varying portions of public land for the purpose of 'homesteading by private citizens, or aspiring citizens'. Some of those legislative bills were defeated or delayed; some were passed and enacted.

For your perusal, I'm listing the facts of the matter below:

The Preemption Act 1841: Settlers could claim up to 160 acres of federal land for themselves at a cost of $1.25 per acre. To qualify, claimants had to reside on their claim, thus homesteading it, for 14 months. To receive permanent title, the claimant had to agree 'to continue to reside on it and improve upon it for a period of five years, neither leaving nor abandoning the quarter-section claim for more than six months at any time'. Legislatively, there was a dual intent to the Preemptive Act: *first*, it was to encourage the settlement of the western territories; *second*, it was to ensure that federal lands would not end up exclusively in the possession of large landowners and corporations—which was, in fact, a developing situation.

1852, 1854, 1859: Numerous and various 'homestead acts' were introduced and passed in the House of Representatives; all were defeated in the Senate.

1860: Both the House of Representatives and the Senate passed a homestead bill providing federal land-grants to settlers. The comprehensive bill was vetoed by President James Buchanan in his effort to protect the interests of pro-slavery factions in the South, as well as a number of large eastern industrialists who feared losing employees to the westward movement. Buchanan also showed select favor to a number of eastern corporations that were interested in securing vast portions federal land for their own use.

The Homestead Act of 1862: Passed both Houses of Congress and was signed into law by President Abraham Lincoln. It provided that any adult citizen, including freed slaves or intended citizens, twenty-one years of age or as head of a household, who had never borne arms against the US Government, could claim 160 acres (a quarter-section) of surveyed government land.

The Timber Culture Act 1873: Granted a quarter-section of land to a claimant. The 160-acre tract could be added to an existing claim and had no residency requirements. The claimant was required to plant at least forty acres of trees over a period of several years. Commonly known as the 'Timber Act', it was later revised, requiring only ten acres of planted trees.

The Kincaid Act / Amendment 1904: Granted a full section (640 acres) to new homesteaders settling in western Nebraska. This act was a result of governmental acknowledgement that a homestead in the Sand Hills region of Nebraska required more than 160 acres for a claimant to support and sustain a family.

The Enlarged Homestead Act 1909: An amendment to the Homestead Act, which doubled the allotment of 160 acres to 320 acres, in certain regions of the West.

The Stock-Raising Homestead Act, 1916: An amendment that granted 640 acres 'for ranching purposes'.

The Homestead Act of 1862 was the most significant of all the homestead acts—it's the one most often referred to and is generally considered to be the 'original Homestead Act'. It is also the homestead act that is the most lauded and the most hated—depending on your political stance and your personal take on history. There was a great amount of excitement and praise for the legislation, from both public and private sectors. And as I mentioned above, there *were* several political factions that didn't favor the idea of public land being conveyed into private hands. Also worthy of noting: in the view of the ruling government, 'the West' was considered empty land; to the Native Americans, it was where they lived and roamed. Therein, was yet another rub. Suffice to say here, it was all arguable then; it is still arguable today.

The original 'Homestead Act' itself, is a fairly simple document—you can view it and read it, if you wish, at the National Archives in Washington, DC, where it resides behind glass-faced cabinets. I freely admit here that the National Archives on Pennsylvania Avenue in Washington, DC, is one of my most favored haunts; I never visit Washington without spending time there. *You*, however, can always honor your ease and simply google a copy.

It is not a complicated document, but the implementation of it, along with its immediate and lasting ramifications on America—and in fact, on the entire world—were vastly complicated. It was actually a revolutionary concept for the distribution of public land by turning over vast amounts of public domain to private citizens.

As an historical point... 'upon receiving An Act to Secure Homesteads to Settlers on the Public Domain which was created and passed by the 37th Congress Session, on May 20, 1862, to the office of the President, and which President Abraham Lincoln did sign into reality'. I'm quoting here a newspaper article contemporary to the event—with capitalizations, punctuation and wording intact—

just to provide you with the actual name of the bill and the specifics. Because I think it's a cool little example of the lexicon of the time.

As a simple point... the Homestead Act of 1862 provided that any adult citizen, intended citizens or freed slaves, twenty-one years of age, who had never borne arms against the US government, could claim 160 acres of surveyed government land.

A filing fee of $18 was required. The act stipulated that the claimant must agree to live on the land, build a home, and 'prove-up' their claim by cultivating the land and making other specified improvements over an established period of time—most commonly, five years. In some regions, the time-period could be mitigated by paying a small up-front fee per acre, thus shortening the prove-up period.

A few interesting points...

~ The first claim under the Homestead Act of 1862, was filed in the Nebraska Territory by Daniel Freeman, near present-day Beatrice, Nebraska. Records showed he filed on January 1, 1863, the first day one could legally file for a claim under the Homestead Act. A total of 417 other claims were filed that same day, all paying the filing fee and signing claim-documents in which they agreed to live on their claim and meet the required improvements.

I personally think that's an interesting little tidbit and thought you might like it also. But keep in mind that Daniel Freeman was not the first settler in the territories. Tens of thousands of families and individuals had already been settling the western lands for decades, typically under the Preemption Act of 1841. Daniel Freeman was just the first to file under the new Homestead Act.

There is, by the way, a monument—the Homestead National Monument—established by the Department of the Interior, which commemorates the changes brought about by the Homestead Act of 1862. It stands on Daniel Freeman's original homestead. Just so you know, and just in case you ever find yourself near Beatrice, Nebraska and in a curious and adventurous state of mind.

~   Ultimately, some 260–270 million acres (depending on which government agency and archives you search) were 'claimed and settled'. Which amounted to roughly 10 percent of the area of the United States. Those numbers, though, say nothing about the 'success rates' of the homesteading.

In actuality, the success of homesteaded claims was relatively low compared to the number of families who actually took up those claims. By most accounts, less than 40 percent of people taking up claims, remained on them for two years. And of those who did remain into the third year, approximately 47–52 percent of those (depending, again, upon the agency and archival records) left their claims before proving-up at the end of their fifth year.

~   The basic guidelines and regulations of the Homestead Act remained in effect across the US until 1976; the Federal Land Policy and Management Act of 1976 repealed the Homestead Act in the forty-eight contiguous states. In Alaska, the Homestead Act was in effect until 1986, although with some new provisions. I assume this is all common knowledge to plenty of people; it's just one of the things that I never knew—admitting here once again that sometimes I can be a little slow on the uptake.

THE LOOPHOLES

In a matter of months, and for all the years following the implementation of the Homestead Act and its rules, there proved to be more exceptions to the rules of the Act, than there were actual rules. If I wanted to write non-fiction, I could write an entire book on just some of the more famous twists and turns and loopholes that arose in an effort to sidestep the intent of the original Homestead Act. And if I included examples of all the creative twists that were instigated and applied by individuals and corporations after each of the subsequent homestead acts and amendments were enacted, I would be writing volumes.

Interestingly, of all the descendants of the original homesteading families with whom I've had the occasion to speak, most have stories of the various loopholes and legal-sidesteps that their grandparents, or great-grandparents, or great-great grandparents had known about—loopholes and sidesteps that they, or neighboring homesteaders, had used in an effort to secure or grow their homesteads. Not illegal maneuvers necessarily; usually, just some infinitely clever ones.

I've included a couple of the loopholes most often used, just because I find them amusing and entertaining.

For your perusal...

~ The 1862 Act declared an 'adult' to be either twenty-one years of age, or the head of a household. Declaring oneself as head of a household in those years legally amounted to owning a house. It wasn't a rare thing for sons and daughters of homesteading families to each be designated as head of a household on separate 160-acre claims—as long as there was a house—thus, a household—on that claim. So a husband and wife could each claim 160 acres, as could their seventeen-year-old daughter or fifteen-year-old son. A reasonably intelligent settler could build four structures at the adjacent corners of four claims and term them all as house-holds—even if they were in actuality, a house, a barn, a shed, or a chicken-house.

~ Requirements for the house were clearly stipulated as having to be 'a dwelling of a size measuring eleven by fourteen, with a fixed-roof'. Not so *clearly*, actually, because the size was never stipulated as having to be measured in 'feet'. Thus, it *could* be legally interpreted to be in 'inches'. So an eleven-by-fourteen-*inch* model of a house sitting on the claim and presented to an assessing official as meeting the stipulated size, proved to be legally viable. And because a cave or a dugout, a tent or a lean-to could be assessed as having a fixed roof, claimholders could make the choice to live in any of those, or any variation of those—if he, or she, preferred to put their earliest efforts into working fields and planting crops—rather than building a more permanent structure.

~ The twists and turns weren't necessarily unscrupulous—many were simply common-sense application of the rules. A huge percentage of married couples settled on two adjoining quarter-section claims (thus procuring a half-section, 320 acres); they joined two eleven-by-fourteen-foot houses—either sod or lumber, or a combination of the two—to straddle the property line between both claims. Thus, they fulfilled the dwelling requirement for both quarter-sections, but only one family home. And fenced pens and farmed land to each side would meet the prove-up requirements for both claims.

THE REALITY

The name of the game with the 'Homestead Acts', as far as the government was concerned, was to populate the western territories. Gradual settlement of the western lands had been taking place since 1841 under the Preemption Act, but that all changed radically with the enactment of the Homestead Act in 1862. It was no longer a gradual process.

Government information, pamphlets and fliers, newspaper articles and advertisements flooded the markets and the minds of the public. Some of it was officially sanctioned information, coming straight out of the government agencies; some was released via corporate and private endorsement. Some of the information was born of schemes and scams. In 1866, even *New York Tribune* author and publisher Horace Greeley, in full support of the concept of 'Manifest Destiny', was shouting "Go West, Young Man, Go West", from the front pages of his newspapers.

Looking through the government information provided to prospective settlers, along with the newspaper stories and the advertisement pamphlets, it's easy to see the focus of most of the information was to lure individuals and families into 'taking up the free land' in the western territories. Most of the information was written by men who may have had some understanding of the land east of the Missouri and Mississippi, but it's easy to discern that relatively few had any true understanding of the land to the west.

Most of the information available was written by men without foresight, compassion, or concern for the people they were urging to relocate out to the territories. The truth was, the lives and futures of the people who actually settled the land were not their concern.

One of the very real truths about the Homestead Act of 1862 was that by the end of 1864, there were reports of a significant percentage of failing homesteads. That failure rate not only continued, but the percentages increased with each year. And while there were many reasons that the homesteaders left the land—both prior to proving-up and shortly thereafter—in retrospect, it appears that all the reasons fell into two classes—poor information and poor timing.

First, people were misinformed. Quite often, the necessary information, the crucial and accurate information, that they needed, was withheld. There had been the promise of free land and five years to prove-up, but there had been deception—to an astounding extent—by those who made the promises. Sometimes the deception was borne of ignorance; sometimes, it was intentional.

Those who filed for claims and traveled to what they believed was a bright new life and livelihood, simply did not understand what they were getting into with regard to the land and the lifestyle. The essential elements of the land itself could not be reconciled. Soils, geography, climate and seasons were vastly different than what the majority of the new homesteaders were led to expect. Relatively few families who attempted homesteading understood that vast difference. Even fewer could cope with it.

Second, the implementation of the Homestead Act was ill-timed. In 1862, the greatest share of Washington's focus, energy, and finances were directed toward the War in the South, and not toward the land out West. Settling a new land required more than just a team and a plow to turn the soil. For success and survival, there had to be communities, viable markets, and transportation that were already in place or that at least had the capacity to develop rapidly.

The original plans for the homesteading of the western regions had involved the development of railroad systems to provide transportation to markets for all the new communities that would inevitably develop to serve surrounding homesteads. The Civil War brought the plans for those western railroads to a halt.

Regarding the railroads, it's probably best that I speak here about Abraham Lincoln. Being a man of vision, he had a profound clarity about the true meaning of the Homestead Act. He saw the reality of settling the western lands; he saw what he believed to be the true value of populating the land. He understood that the new populations of homesteaders would need communities and markets within reasonable distances; he also understood that those smaller communities and markets had to have viable connections and transportation to access larger communities and larger markets. That was what he envisioned. And that vision, inspired yet another vision.

There is a newspaper article that tells of President Lincoln standing beside the Missouri River in the town of Council Bluffs, Iowa, where he spoke of his desire to build a railroad across the continent. The article described what Lincoln envisioned as 'the intertwining and coordinated timing required' to ensure the success of the homesteads and communities, the transportation and markets. He saw the need for railroads across the West as part of 'the intricate web required to unite all the elements necessary to connect life in the territories'. And that, he said, required timing—a crucial timing.

And *that* is the timing to which I am referring. Lincoln had a passion for the idea of a trans-continental railroad—an idea that had first been fronted by a man named Asa Whitney. Asa Whitney had the idea for a railroad that would traverse the whole continent; his idea meant that a person traveling from the east coast by train could reach the west coast in days, instead of months. Lincoln knew he was right, and he knew that the westward expansion of the railroad network would be essential to the success of the Homestead Act.

But the Civil War had erupted and the active planning and construction of a cross-continental railroad came to a halt. Whitney's idea had been put aside and nearly forgotten—except for Lincoln's continued interest in developing the idea, even during the war.

Lincoln's plan—once the War in the South was over—was for the construction of the railroad to move forward immediately. But the timing of that passionate plan died with Abraham Lincoln. The building of the railroad would still happen, but it would happen years later.

During and immediately after the end of the war, the politicians, as well as the articles in the newspapers, described the years it would take to develop the full operation of just the mainline railroads. The network of branch-lines that would be needed to reach deep into the lands of the territories, they admitted, would take even longer. The settlements and communities in those regions could, conceivably, be waiting ten, fifteen, or even, twenty years.

That was a long wait; too long for homesteaders and small settlements to survive without access to the markets where the great populations were—in the eastern states. The crucial timing for the homesteaders and the communities, the markets and the necessary transportation—all of which had to happen in a perfect order and in a perfect timing—had been lost.

Within a couple of years after the Homestead Act of 1862 had passed through Congress and was signed by President Lincoln, the majority of the homesteaders were already failing. They were already 'pulling up stakes'. They were moving back East, or moving further West, looking for, and hoping for, something better. Looking for some place, or some life, that was more viable.

The crucial need for accurate information had been ignored and the intricate timing had been interrupted. And of course, it was the homesteaders who paid the dearest price. That's what happened to so many of the settlers spread out in the lonely and far-flung pockets of homesteads.

THE HOMESTEADERS

No matter what reasons were in the minds of the people who chose emigrate to the western territories—necessity, hope, a new start, new land, free land, adventure, wanderlust—the decision to leave a known life and build a new life on unknown lands came with far more challenges than most expected. In reality, the land in the western territories wasn't actually 'free land'. It came with a price far above-and-beyond the initial $18 filing fee required to lay claim to 160 acres.

There were initial costs to staking a claim. Along with everything required for setting up a household in a new land, there was a need for healthy livestock, farming equipment, seed for planting, and a sizeable reserve of supplies. It was all necessary, not just for the journey, but for the early months of start-up. Typically, anyone taking up a claim needed enough resources and reserves to support themselves and their families until the harvest and sale of their first crop. And typically, that meant at least twelve to eighteen months. If, all went well.

There were also the legal requirements set in place by the homestead acts, stipulating specific developments to the claim—a dwelling, fencing and enclosures, and specified amounts acreage to be tilled and planted. All those requirements needed to be met for the claimant to receive legal title to their land.

Meeting all those obligations within the five-year period was referred to as 'proving-up'. Basically, it meant that a homesteader was required to prove that he, or she, was worthy of being a steward over the quarter-section claim and was fully capable of living a productive life on that land.

In actuality, the term 'proving-up' was more than just a legal reference. The truth was, *everything* about surviving the homesteading process revolved around proving-up. Every choice and every action, on every day—from the initial decision to file for a claim, to the final day of the five-year period—was about proving-up. Proving one's character and mettle. Proving one's courage and strength of commitment.

Truthfully, just the choice to 'seek out' new land and a new home was an initial test of character. A second testing came during the actual journey west to take up a claim—and there are, literally, tens of thousands of history books and emigrant journals detailing those trials and travails of the westward journey. The third testing happened in the early months of homesteading; the initial 'settling-in' after arrival on the new lands was perhaps the most difficult time, both emotionally and physically, for everyone on the homestead—men, women and children.

The fourth testing came over a longer period of time. That 'long-term test' required both working the land and learning the lessons of the land. The newly arriving homesteaders had to establish a viable homestead with the required structures, the fields, and the crops; at the same time, they also had to learn everything about the soil, the weather, the seasons, and the inherent dangers. And all of it had to happen in a relatively brief amount of time.

Finding the ways and means of enduring, surviving, and hopefully, thriving, through the months and years was, in reality, the final prove-up. It was a very personal prove-up, and it counted for far more than the legal prove-up ever did. Quite literally, it was the living proof of whether the claimant had the character and mettle necessary to make and maintain the commitment to build a new life and a solid future.

A surprisingly small number of the individuals who filed for a claim and took on the challenge of homesteading in the western territories, actually became 'settlers' in the true sense of the word. The greatest percentage of people who filed for claims through the Homestead Act of 1862, left their claims and either 'went back East' or 'moved on West'. They gave up their homestead claims and their dreams for whatever reasons they had. They 'pulled up their stakes'—referring to the 'turkey-foot corner-stakes' that designated the borders of their claim—and left.

My personal fascination, obviously, is for those who *did* remain—those first-generations of homesteaders who proved-up their claims, settled the land, and forged their futures. I confess to having an enduring fascination and admiration for their descendants—the second, third, fourth, and fifth generations—many of whom still farm and ranch on land that usually encompasses and includes the original homesteads. Those people, those families, hold a special place in my heart.

I also admit that I have a special fascination for the history and the stories of the settlers of the Nebraska Territory, because Nebraska soil—and most especially, the soil of the Nebraska Sand Hills—is the soil that held and still holds my family's roots.

Interestingly enough—but perhaps, not surprisingly—Frankie Harding had a special perspective about the settlers of that region. And honestly, she says it best because she saw it and she experienced it. So I'll include an excerpt of Frankie's perceptions about the settlers of the Sand Hills—from a book yet to come—because, she says it better than I can:

Frankie looked around the crowd, watching the people gathered there in the churchyard on that warm September morning. She was studying those people, her neighbors who lived here on the land in the Nebraska Territory, raising their families and their crops and their livestock. She realized that none of them were boasting or bragging. Given what they had done over the past few days, they certainly had reason to boast. Yet there wasn't a prideful or self-serving word from any of them.

The truth was, they were making light of what they had done. Because, in their minds, coming together and taking care of their neighbor—making things right for that family—was a natural response for them. No one spoke about the reason they had stepped up to help a neighbor because deep in their hearts, they all knew the reason. There was no need to speak of it.

So while Frankie watched the people around her and listened to their conversations, she knew she was learning about the character of the settlers of this land. There was a difference to these people, there was something different about these people who had chosen to settle here on this land.

She already knew about all the other emigrants who had traveled across and through the Nebraska Territory; there had been hundreds of thousands of emigrants over the last twenty years. Some had traveled to the gold fields in California, some to the mining towns in Colorado, some to Oregon in search of the 'land of plenty'. The bulk of those people had been looking for some kind of quick gain, for gold-fields and fast money; many were looking for 'easy land', for greener pastures, for an easier way of living.

But most of *these* people around her today at the sod-church were families who would stay here. These people had no intention of leaving this land. It was not fleeting thoughts of gold or the promise of fast gain that had brought these people to this land. These people around her had come to the Nebraska Territory to build something permanent. They had come to build their homes and grow their families, to create communities and forge new futures. They were willing to learn and live in the land of the Sand Hills. They had come to stay.

They were right here in this churchyard, here by the quiet, unassuming sod-church made of God's earth that served as a gathering place to worship the God who had created this land and blessed their lives. Right here was a gathering of people of like-minds and like-loves—love of God, love of land, and love of family.

These people who chose to settle in this land of sandy soils and sweeping grasses had shown that they knew when it was time to step in quickly and extend a hand when a neighbor needed it. They did it because they believed it was the right thing to do and the right way to live. And they expected nothing in return. Because in their hearts and minds, this life in the midst of the Sand Hills was about community and neighbors. And this was what they were teaching their children and their grandchildren. This was the legacy they were building.

Frankie could remember her father and her uncle and aunt talking about such things. Her family had made the decision to come here. They had chosen to start a new life and to build a legacy that would continue beyond them. They had died on the trail as they traveled to this life, but this was exactly what they had envisioned for their children—and eventually, for their children's children. This was the life that her family had been seeking.

And as she walked among the people in the churchyard, Frankie knew that it was what she herself had been seeking when she had decided to continue her family's journey. It was what she had fought for and longed for; this was what she had yearned for. This land, this life, and these people here in the Sand Hills had been calling to her months ago, back when she was still on the prairie camping near the trail that ran beside the Little Blue River.

Frankie looked around her, watching. Suddenly, she felt an understanding and a different pride than she had ever felt before. A pride of place. Because these people were the future, and that future was revealing itself to her. It was unfolding right in front of her. These people, without even realizing it, were already part of their futures—and in time, their futures would build a state that would stand as part of the United States.

So that speaks of the homesteaders. To my mind, it speaks to the people who began settling in the Nebraska Territory in the 1860s, people who lived their dreams and planned their futures there. And it also speaks to the people who still choose to live their lives within the lands of Nebraska in these current times. And for my entire life, I've been fortunate enough to be privy to their stories and tales.

As to the qualities that Frankie described in the excerpt above, I see those same qualities in the people who live in the Sand Hills to this day. So even though Frankie was speaking about the homesteaders around her that day in the Reverend Simeon Austin's churchyard, she was actually speaking about the families of the Sand Hills today too. At least, that's my experience.

THE DESCENDANTS

It is my own history—specifically my family history—that instilled in me a deep personal interest in the Nebraska Territory. That personal interest led me into a realm of intrigue that began back on the first day of April in 1979; it was the day my family buried my grandmother in a mostly-remote cemetery, deep in the land of the Sand Hills, out in the center of what was originally the Nebraska Territory.

My interest was piqued on that day and as a result, some unexpected pathways opened up for me. Pathways which not only took me deep into my own history, but also into the history of the people of that land within the Nebraska Territory. It is the land of the Sand Hills, specifically, that has a strong allure for me. It is a land that pulls deep at my heart.

The novel *Prairie* was the beginning of the journey for me, much as it was for the main character, Frankie Harding. If you haven't read *Prairie*, then you might want to consider taking the time to delve into it, because it is the true beginning of the story that is being told in *Homestead*.

The specific reason I refer to both novels here is to acknowledge that, as historical novels, they present factual history blended into a fictional story. The points of history presented in both *Prairie* and *Homestead* are solid; the research was deep. For me, the small historical items matter every bit as much as the larger picture and major events. And I believe that if done right and done well, blending actual history into a fictional story is an art. In my life, it has also become an adventure. And on occasion, it is a fine line to walk. Because while both poetic license and fictional leeway are at my disposal, there is, in my mind and heart, no justification for arrogant and lazy misrepresentation.

There's more actual history than meets the eye in both *Prairie* and *Homestead*. A surprising number of the characters in Frankie's stories were true, living figures—people who lived portions of their lives in the Nebraska Territory—many of whom actually home-steaded in the Sand Hills. Those settlers left their homesteading leg-acy behind; many have descendants still farming and ranching in the land of the Sand Hills to this day.

If I was of a mind to, I could show you exactly where most of those referenced individuals were laid to rest. I know where the mostly-hidden, mostly-forgotten country-cemeteries are; I know how the headstones of those pioneers read; I know the dates and years of their births and deaths. I know where most of their home-steads were; I know of the families, past and present.

The Cheyenne Trail—that ancient passage into and through the Sand Hills Frankie followed in *Prairie* and about which she speaks in *Homestead*—is actually still used as a passage into and through the land of the Sand Hills. Now though, it's a two-lane highway. The 'north-south track' that traversed the land between the North Loup River and the Middle Loup settlement—which passed beside Reverend Simeon Austin's sod-church—is a still in use. But now it's mainly used by local farmers and ranchers. And many of the other tracks and trails that the homesteaders in the 1860s used, and which I acknowledged in *Prairie* and *Homestead*, are current-day country roads—most of them sandy-soiled dirt-roads winding among the Sand Hills.

I could show you exactly where Simeon Austin's sod-church was, if I wanted to—which I don't. (The land is currently owned by a rancher who has a remarkable aim with a Remington .30-.30; she has been known to shoot at trespassers more than a few times. And I can attest to that, I kid you not. I'll tell you that story someday.)

Nowadays, all that remains of the sod-church are slight linear mounds that show faintly in the grasses—long and low mounds not much higher than your ankle bones—that indicate where the walls of that humble sod-church once stood. Looking carefully, the slight rises where the rows of the sod pews stood can still be discerned, especially in the angled light of the setting sun.

A century after the sod-chapel was left to fade back into the earth from whence it came, I found a broken piece of the potbellied stove that once stood at the front of the chapel; the piece, half the size of my palm, was lying partially buried next to one of the time-faded walls, near one of the low-mounds that show the position of the time-faded sod bench-pews. That broken piece of Simeon Austin's pot-bellied stove—the stove that warmed the congregation in that sod-church during the cold winter months—now sits in a place of honor on my bookshelf, just behind my chair while I write about it. I also have a spent bullet from a Remington rifle sitting on the shelf beside it. (Like I said, I'll tell you the story someday.)

I can also tell you that Frankie's meadow still exists. I have spent time there—a few warm summer afternoons beside the windmill and its pond which are still used to this day. I've spent summer evenings listening to the vespers of the mourning doves; I've heard the lengthy repertoire of a mockingbird that nests in the trees beside the wind-mill pond. Beyond the slopes of that low-lying valley, meadowlarks still sing about their territories and coyotes still do their yip-yipping into the twilight skies. But now the buildings are gone, and it's just a valley used for cattle grazing. The buildings were mostly disassem-bled, moved and repurposed.

And I suppose I should mention here that Frankie's actual meadow is in a different location than depicted in the novel and illustrations—writer's license allows me such leeway, and I thought it wise to protect the privacy of the current owners of the property.

But interestingly enough, while Frankie's actual house is gone, there *is* still a house, a perfectly square house, that stands to this day. It's in another meadow on what was a neighboring homestead to Frankie's, but it was built in exactly the same manner—the same dimensions and the same floor-plan as her house. The neighboring homesteader apparently understood the sensibility of the layout, and some thirty years after Frankie's was built, he modeled his own house after hers. His though, was built as a wood-frame house, rather than square-cut logs. (Thirteen children were born and raised in that house in just the first generation of that homestead, by the way.)

That house, when I last saw it, was sitting mostly hidden in the midst of a grove of overgrown trees and brush on what was once a thriving homestead—and is currently a thriving ranch. The square house sits empty now—it's clearly seen its better days. Now it's mostly forgotten and definitely ignored, but it's still sturdy and strong. And the center fireplace still works. Around the same period, two other homesteading families in that region followed suit and built houses with the same floor-plan—but both of those houses are long gone.

I was there on the ranch some years back—the ranch where the perfectly-square house still stands in the grove of overgrown trees—and I watched as a man named Earl Dunbar, ninety-seven years-old, bent-over and 'stove-up with age and time' (as he put it), led his neat-footed sorrel mare into the barn. He flipped the end of the lead-rope over the horse's neck, slipped a saddle-blanket onto the horse's back, and then he walked over to a rope that was hooked around a peg on the barn wall. The horse, left to its own sensibilities, calmly walked over to a spot in the center of the barn's alleyway and stopped. Waiting. Knowing.

A saddle descended slowly from the rafters of the barn and settled on the sorrel's back as Earl worked the rope and pulley. A moment later, the horse lowered its head as Earl walked back to him to switch the halter for a bridle. After he cinched the saddle, that clever little cow-horse sidestepped himself over to a wooden block. Earl Dunbar stepped onto the block, stepped into the saddle, and rode out to check his cattle. Five hours later, ninety-seven-year-old Earl returned from his day's work under the hot Nebraska sun. Once in the barn alleyway, Earl stepped out of his saddle onto the wooden block, and the entire process was reversed.

Then Earl and I went into his house to eat the dinner that his wife had waiting on the table. Beef stew and homemade bread. Fresh milk and jar-churned butter. Spice-cake and peach cobbler for dessert.

I wanted to tell you about Earl Dunbar and what I saw that day, because he was the epitome of the men who settled and remained in the Sand Hills. He was a fourth-generation rancher. He knew his land; he knew his work; he knew his horse. And he knew how to get things done. He was pretty typical of the people of that land—both past and present. He was one of my heroes, and I never made the time to tell him that. So I guess I'm saying it here. He inspired me in a lot of ways, and I'm betting you'll recognize some of them.

So as you read about these people of the Nebraska Territory and of the Sand Hills, keep in mind that there is truth and history here. The land is real, and the people were real. And the stories of Frankie Harding's adventures are far from over...

Milton Keynes UK
Ingram Content Group UK Ltd.
UKHW012251231123
433173UK00010B/186/J